Praise for the Moon Fall series and James Rollins

"An action-filled fantasy quest that is gripping and thought-provoking. The high stakes and smooth writing made it a page-turner. . . . As in his thrillers, [Rollins] includes science, historical secrets, and suspense."

—*Mystery & Suspense*

"An interesting blend of science and magic, flying ships and prophetic gods, propels this fantasy into epic territories." —*Library Journal*

"Fun . . . The fantastical creatures and landscapes are imaginative. . . . Readers looking for plot-driven fantasy will enjoy the action."

—*Publishers Weekly*

"Adventurous and enormously engrossing." —NPR on *The Eye of God*

"After Crichton passed away in 2008, he clearly passed the baton to James Rollins who, like Crichton, is a Renaissance man." —*HuffPost*

TOR BOOKS BY JAMES ROLLINS

THE MOON FALL SERIES

The Starless Crown
The Cradle of Ice

THE
STARLESS
CROWN

JAMES ROLLINS

TOR

TOR PUBLISHING GROUP

NEW YORK

THE STARLESS CROWN

Copyright © 2021 by James Czajkowski

Map provided and drawn by Soraya Corcoran

Creature drawings provided and drawn by Danea Fidler

All rights reserved.

A Tor Book
Published by Tom Doherty Associates/Tor Publishing Group
120 Broadway
New York, NY 10271

www.tor-forge.com

Tor® is a registered trademark of Macmillan Publishing Group, LLC.

The Library of Congress has cataloged the hardcover edition as follows:

Names: Rollins, James, 1961– author.
Title: The starless crown / James Rollins.
Description: First edition. | New York : Tor, 2022. | Series: Moon fall ; 1
| "A Tom Doherty Associates book." | Identifiers: LCCN 2021033044 (print)
| LCCN 2021033045 (ebook) | ISBN 9781250816771 (hardcover) |
| ISBN 9781250851406 (signed edition) | ISBN 9781250852632 (International, sold
outside the U.S., subject to rights availability) | ISBN 9781250842510 (ebook)
Subjects: GSAFD: Suspense fiction.
Classification: LCC PS3568.O5398 S73 2022 (print)
| LCC PS3568.O5398 (ebook) | DDC 813/.54—dc23
LC record available at https://lccn.loc.gov/2021033044
LC ebook record available at https://lccn.loc.gov/2021033045

ISBN 978-1-250-76671-7 (trade paperback)

Our books may be purchased in bulk for promotional, educational, or business use.
Please contact your local bookseller or the Macmillan Corporate and Premium
Sales Department at 1-800-221-7945, extension 5442, or by email at
MacmillanSpecialMarkets@macmillan.com.

First Tor Paperback Edition: 2023

Printed in the United States of America

0 9 8 7 6 5 4 3 2 1

FOR TERRY BROOKS,
*whose creativity inspired me
and whose generosity of spirit is the only reason
you are reading this book.*

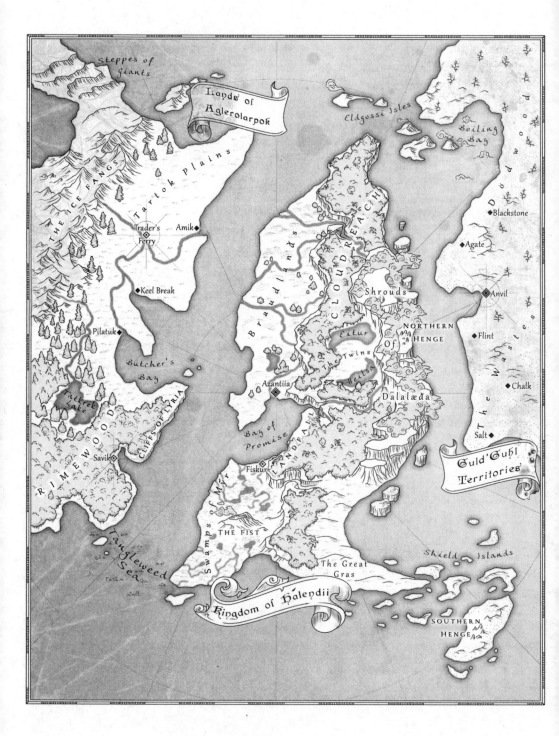

Steppes of Giants

Islands of Aglerolarpok

Eldgossi Isles

Döddwood

Boiling Bay

THE ICE FANGS

Tartok Plains

Trader's Ferry

Amik

Keel Break

Blackstone

Agate

Anvil

Braudlands

CLOUDREACH

Shrouds

NORTHERN HENGE

Flint

Pilatuk

Eilur

The Twins

OF

Butcher's Bay

Azantiia

Meilsa

Dalalæda

Chalk

Tibbet Lake

CLIFFS OF LYRIA

Bay of Promise

LANDFALL

The Wastes

Savik

RIMEWOOD

Fiskur

Salt

Guld'Guhl Territories

Tangleweed Sea

Swamps of Myr

THE FIST

The Great Gras

Shield Islands

Kingdom of Halendii

SOUTHERN HENGE

Life is full of holes.

Even in the best of times, the span of one's years is never a perfect tapestry, laid out in a sprawl of days, months, and years, all woven in flawless detail, each color as bright as when its thread was plaited into the whole. Instead, over time, bits of this tapestry get worn away by age. Other sections stretch out of shape as one worries over them, returning again and again to pull and tug at certain threads. Worst of all, large pieces go threadbare, to the point of indecipherability. Still, memory proves to be a devious trickster—filling in gaps, darning rips, patching gaps—often with stories that are not true, only necessary. They are the yarn needed to create a whole that one can live with.

At this old age, I am not in the best of my times. My own tapestry is far more motheaten. I am nearing my hundredth year. So, if I don't remember you, it does not mean I do not hold you dearly. If I don't recall every detail of this long story, it does not make it any less true. Here in my attic croft where I write, I have my sketches and drawings that anchor my past, that do not let me forget, that remind me of the man I once was.

As I begin this story, I leave the last of my many journals propped open, near to its last page. Her image in ink stares back at me, judging me, daring me. I had used ashes to capture the sweep of her hair, a crush of azure shell mixed with oil for her bright eyes, my own blood for her lips. Her smile is sad, as if disappointed in me. Her gaze is hard and unforgiving. Her cheeks are blushed with barely restrained fury.

Long ago, I drew this image from memory—as it was the last time I ever saw her.

She who was prophesied to destroy the world.

And did.

BEFORE

SHE GIVES BIRTH in mud and mire.

She squats and strains under the fog-shrouded bower of a gnarled cottongum. Vines choke the massive tree, dragging its limbs to the mossy hillocks and draping leaves into the boggy waters of a slow-moving stream. To her side, a trunk as wide as a horse twists around and around, as if the tree were seeking to escape these drowned lands.

She sweats and pants, her legs wide under her. Overhead, her hands remain clamped to a vine. As she hangs there, thorns pierce her palms, but the pain is naught compared to the final contraction that rips her wider and pushes the babe from her womb. She stifles her scream, lest the hunters should hear her cries.

Still, a moan escapes her, wordless from her lack of a tongue. As a pleasure serf of Azantiia, she was never allowed the luxury of speech.

With one last push, she feels the release. The child spills from her and drops to the wet mud underfoot. She slips off the vine. Impaled thorns rip her palms open. She slumps to the mud with the babe between her thighs. The child is still tied to her by a twisted bloody cord.

She sobs with wracking heaves and picks up the skinning knife near the base of the cottongum. The hunting blade is not her own, neither is the blood that already stains it. The knife was thrust into her hands by her savior, by a man who broke a vow to help her escape the castle keep. After sailing across the Bay of Promise, under the glowering eye of a winter's sun, pursued by the king's legion, they had made landfall along the treacherous coast of Mýr. Its shoreline was less land and more a blurring where the blue sea met the brackish waters lined by a drowned mangrove forest. Once the skiff could traverse no farther into the swamps, her rescuer had sent her off on foot, while he poled the skiff away, intending to lead her pursuers elsewhere.

Alone now, she slices his blade through the thick cord, freeing the babe from her body and from her past. She had thought herself emptied, but her belly convulses again. She gasps as blood and tissue flow out, washing over the babe. Fearing the child would drown with its first breath, she wipes the baby's face clean. Its eyes remain closed to this harsh world. Her torn palms smear more blood. Still, she reveals little pursed lips—too blue, nearly black in the shadows.

Breathe now, little one . . .

She rubs and prays.

One prayer is answered when the child sucks in its first breath, stirring, only slightly, but enough. Her other prayer is ignored when she discovers her child is a girl.

No . . .

She picks up the knife again. She lowers the blade to the baby's throat.

Better this . . .

Her hand trembles. She leans down and kisses a brow furrowing toward a first cry at this harsh world. She prays, both as apology and explanation. *Be free from me. From my past. From my shame. From those who would take you.*

Before she can act, the Mother Below punishes her for daring to forsake the gift granted to her womb. Her stomach clenches again. Hot blood pours out between her thighs. The pain is at first fiery—then turns to a dreadful cold. And still the flow continues, pouring her life into the mud.

She reads the truth in the spreading stain.

Having been raised among the pleasure serfs, she had assisted midwives with other girls who had found themselves with child, despite the teas of Bastard's Herb. Over the passing two decades, she had witnessed births in all their myriad forms: some joyous, others fearful, most with resignation. All had involved tears. There had been blood, shite, torn flesh, babes born backward, others deformed by the teas, or bodies broken by their own mothers in attempts to end the child's life before it was born. When she was very young, she had reviled the latter. She had not known then what it meant to be a child born under the whip, to be eventually broken under the heaving throes of a master.

She eventually learned the hard and necessary lessons.

She stares down at the knife at her daughter's throat.

By now, blood pools heavily under the babe. The scent draws flies and suckers. As she stares down into eyes just now peeking open, the forest grows hushed, as if awed. Birdsong falls silent, leaving only the hum and whine of insects. A new noise intrudes. A heavy splash to her right.

She stirs her cooling flesh enough to turn her head. Even this small movement closes the darkness tighter around her. From the sluggish current of the swamp, a reptilian beast thrashes onto shore. Claws gouge the muck, dragging its massive length, led by a snout edged by sharp teeth. Though eyeless, it aims unerringly through the reeds and moss, drawn by her blood as surely as the biting flies.

No . . .

Her instinct to protect overwhelms the bitter lessons of her past. She lifts the blade from her daughter's neck and threatens the approaching beast. But she knows she can inflict no more than a pinprick—if even that. The reptilian hunter is twice her length, ten times her weight. She senses its age, reads the centuries in the thick growth of emerald moss fringing its black scales.

Despite its age, it barrels faster toward her, blind to the knife and all its uselessness. It carries with it the reek of carrion and brackish waters. The moss across its back and flanks glows faintly in the forest shadows.

Still, she kneels over her child. She is too weak even to stand. Her arm quakes to hold up the dagger. Darkness continues to pinch her world smaller and smaller.

She girds herself for the heavy strike to come, as she did many nights in the perfumed beds of her masters. Her body was never her own.

Anger flares through her. Even this fire had been forbidden to her in the past. In this last moment, she takes hold of that flame and screams the last of her strength away. She closes her eyes and cries to the heavens, at the beast, at herself, at a child that would never get to live.

For the first time in her life, she is truly heard.

A piercing cry rings forth from the skies. The screech is less heard with her ears than with her entire body. The scream cuts through her skin, sharp enough to reach bone. The force lifts the hairs over her body. She opens her eyes and sees the reptilian beast slide to a stop in the mud, coming to rest no more than an arm's length from her. Panicked, the beast twists and writhes to turn its massive bulk, to return to the safety and succor of black water.

Before it can, branches shatter overhead. A shadow dives through the canopy and crashes into the beast. Sickle-shaped claws cleave through hard scale. Bones break under the impact of a creature as large as a hay cart. Leathery wings snap outward, striking her broadside, knocking her from her child.

She is flung far and crashes into the twisted trunk of a tree. She collapses amidst the tangle of its roots. From her side, she watches those heavy wings beat once, lifting the creature back into the air. The reptilian beast is carried aloft. Impaled claws rip it into halves and fling its centuries-old body back into the dark waters.

Then the winged creature lands in the mud.

It swings toward her, revealing its malignant splendor. It holds high its leathery wings, thin enough at the edges to see the sparkle of patchy sunlight through them. It keeps its head low, close to the ground. Large tufted ears swivel toward her. Its long slitted nostrils fan open wider, rippling, testing the air. It hisses at her and raises a furred ridge along its short neck and arched back.

She knows this beast, all of Azantiia knows them, the terror of the swamps, the dreaded Mýr bats, the poisonous denizens of the shrouded volcanic mountain—The Fist—at the heart of these drowned lands. Stories abound of these creatures—though few had ever lived to tell a tale of such an encounter. No hunter had ever returned with such elusive, dangerous prey. Not even their bones had ever made it into one of the castle's bestiaries.

With her heart choked in her throat, she studies the monster before her.

Merciless eyes, as cold as black diamonds, stare back at her. A continual hiss flows from its throat. Her hairs shiver to a sound beyond hearing. She feels it in her teeth, in her skull, playing across the surface of her brain, like an oil fire on water. She knows she is being studied more deeply than any eye could discern.

Its lips wrinkle back in threat, exposing long fangs, glinting with a sheen of poison. It stalks closer to her, knuckling on its wings.

No, not closer to *her*—but toward the baby in the mud.

Tiny limbs paddle at the air, as if beckoning the beast.

She tries to move to her daughter's defense, but she has lost her knife. Not that it mattered. She has no strength left to even crawl. Her body is as cold as the mud under her. All that is warm are the tears coursing her cheeks. Knowing there is nothing more she can do, she accepts the inevitable and sags into the tree's roots.

Darkness embraces her.

Before it consumes her, she stares one final time upon her child. While she failed to give the girl a life, she had given her a gift almost as precious.

Her freedom—as brief as it might be.

She takes solace in this as the shadows erase the world.

But another was not so easily satisfied.

As she fades away, she hears her babe's first cry, lustful and angry. She can do nothing to comfort that wail at a life cut before it has begun. Instead, she offers her final counsel, a lesson hard learned.

Better to die free, my daughter.

ONE

THE
BECLOUDED GIRL

A curse allesweis growes from a wyssh.
—Proverb from *The Book of El*

1

Nyx sought to understand the stars with her fingertips.

Near blind, she had to lean far over the low table to reach to the heart of the orrery, to the warmth of the bronze sun at the center of the complicated astronomical mechanism. She knew the kettle-sized sphere had been filled with hot coals prior to the morning's lesson, to mimic the life-giving heat of the Father Above, who made His home there. She held her palm toward that warmth, then took great care to count outward along the slowly turning rings that marked the paths of inner planets around the Father. Her fingers stopped at the third. She rested a tip there and felt the vibrations of the gears that turned this ring, heard the *tick-tick-tick*ing as their teacher spun the wheel on the far side of the orrery to drive their world to Nyx's waiting hand.

"Take care, child," she was warned.

The device was four centuries old, one of the school's most precious artifacts. It was said to have been stolen from the courts of Azantiia by the founding high prioress and brought to the Cloistery of Brayk. Others claimed it wasn't stolen, but crafted by the prioress herself, using skills long lost to those who lived and taught here now.

Either way—

"Better not break it, Dumblefoot," Byrd blurted out. His comment stirred snickers from the other students who sat in a circle around the domed chamber of the astronicum.

Their teacher—Sister Reed, a young novitiate of the Cloistery—growled them all to silence.

Nyx's cheeks heated. While her fellow students could easily observe the intricate dance of spheres around the bronze sun, she could not. To her, the world was perpetually lost in a foggy haze, where movement could be detected in shifts of shadows and objects discerned in gradations of shimmering outlines in the brightest sunlight. Even colors were muted and watery to her afflicted eyes. Worst of all, when she was inside, like now, her sight was smothered to darkness.

She needed to touch to understand.

She took a deep breath and steadied her fingers as the small sphere that marked their world rotated into her hand. The bronze ring to which it was pinned continued to turn with the spin of the wheeled gears. To keep her fingertips in place atop the fist-sized sphere of their world, she had to scoot around the table. By now, the bronze sun had heated one surface of the sphere to a subtle warmth, while the opposite was cold metal, forever turned from the Father.

"Can you now better appreciate how the Mother always keeps one face perpetually gazing at the Father Above?" Sister Reed asked. "A side that eternally burns under His stern-but-loving attention."

Nyx nodded, still circling the table to match the sphere's path around the sun.

Sister Reed addressed both her and the other students. "And at the same time, the other side of our world is forever denied the Father's fierce gaze and remains frozen in eternal darkness, where it is said the very air is ice."

Nyx did not bother to acknowledge the obvious, her attention fixed as the Urth completed its circuit around the sun.

"It is why we live in the Crown," the sister continued, "the circlet of the world that lies between the scorched lands on one side of the Urth and those forever frozen on the other."

Nyx ran her fingertip around this circumference of the sphere, passing from north to south and back again. The Crown of the Urth marked the only hospitable lands where its peoples, flora, and fauna could flourish. Not that there weren't stories of what lay beyond the Crown, terrifying tales— many blasphemous—whispered about those dreaded lands, those frozen on one side, scorched on the other.

Sister Reed stopped turning the wheel, bringing the dance of planets to a rest. "Now that Nyx has had her turn to study the orrery, can anyone tell me *why* the Mother Below eternally matches her gaze with the Father Above, without ever turning her face away?"

Nyx kept her post, her fingers still on the half-warmed sphere.

Kindjal answered the teacher's question. She quoted from the text they had been assigned to study this past week. "She and our world are forever trapped in the hardened amber of the void, unable to ever turn away."

"Very good," Sister Reed said warmly.

Nyx could almost feel the beam of satisfaction from Kindjal, twin sister to Byrd, both children of the highmayor of Fiskur, the largest town along the northern coast of Mýr. Though the town lay a full day's boat ride away, the two lorded their status among the students here, proffering gifts on those who fawned over them, while ridiculing all others, often resorting to physical affronts to reinforce their humiliations.

It was perhaps for that reason more than any other that Nyx spoke up, contradicting Kindjal. "But the Urth is not trapped in amber," she mumbled to the orrery, her fingers still on the half-heated sphere. She hated to draw attention to herself, longing to return to the obscurity of her seat near the back of the class, but she refused to deny what her fingers discovered. "It still turns in the void."

Byrd came to his twin's defense, scoffing loudly. "Even blindfolded, any fool could tell the Mother *always* faces the Father. The Urth never turns away."

"This is indeed immutable and unchangeable," Sister Reed concurred. "As the Father burns forever in our skies, the Mother always stares with love and gratefulness toward the majesty of Him."

"But the Urth *does* turn," Nyx insisted, her mumble firming with frustration.

Though already nearly blind, she closed her eyes and viewed the orrery from above in her mind. She pictured the path of the sphere as it rotated around the bronze sun. She remembered the tiniest ticking under her fingertips as she had followed its course. She had felt it turn in her grip as it made a full passage around the sun.

She tried to explain. "It must turn. To keep the Mother forever facing the Father, the Urth turns once fully around as it makes a complete circuit through the seasons. One slow turn every year. It's the only way for one side of the Urth to be continually burning under the sun's gaze."

Kindjal scoffed. "No wonder her mother tossed her away. She's too stupid to understand the simplest truths."

"But she's right," a voice said behind them, rising from the open door to the astronicum dome.

Nyx froze, only shifting her clouded gaze toward the patch of brightness that marked the open door. A shadow darkened the threshold. She did not need sight to know who stood there, recognizing the hard tones, presently undercut with a hint of amusement.

"Prioress Ghyle," Sister Reed said. "What an honor. Please join us."

The shadow moved away from the brightness as the head of the cloistered school entered. "It seems the youngest among you has proven that insight does not necessarily equate with the ability to see."

"But surely—" Sister Reed started.

"Yes, surely," Prioress Ghyle interrupted. "It is a subtlety of astronomical knowledge that is usually reserved for those in their first years of alchymical studies. Not for a seventhyear underclass. Even then, many alchymical students have difficulty seeing what is plain before their eyes."

A shuffle of leather on stone marked the prioress's approach to the orrery.

Finally releasing her grip on the world, Nyx straightened and bowed her head.

"Let us test what else this young woman of only fourteen winters can discern from today's lesson." The prioress's finger lifted Nyx's chin. "Can you tell us why those in the northern Crown experience seasons—from the icy bite of winter to the warmth of summer—even when one side of the Urth forever faces the sun?"

Nyx had to swallow twice to free her tongue. "It . . . It is to remind us of the gift of the Father to the Mother, so we better appreciate His kindness at being allowed to live in the Crown, in the safe lands between scorching heat and icy death. He gives us a taste of hot and cold with the passage of each year."

The prioress sighed. "Yes, very good. Just as Hieromonk Plakk has droned into you." The finger lifted her chin higher as if to study Nyx more intently. "But what does the orrery tell *you*?"

Nyx stepped back. Even with her hazy sight, she was unable to withstand the weight of Ghyle's attention any longer. She returned to the orrery and again pictured the path of the Urth around the coal-heated sun. She had felt the waxing and waning of the warmth as the sphere rotated fully around.

"The Urth's path is not a perfect circle around the sun," Nyx noted aloud. "More like an oval."

"An ellipse, it is called."

Nyx nodded and cast a quizzical look at the prioress. "Maybe when the Urth's path is farthest from the sun, farthest from the heat, could that be our wintertime?"

"It is not a bad guess. Even some of the most esteemed alchymists might tell you the same. But they are no more correct than Hieromonk Plakk."

"Then why?" Nyx asked, curiosity getting the better of her.

"What if I told you that when we have our *dark* winters here in the northern half of the Crown, that the lands to the far south enjoy a *bright* summer?"

"Truly?" Nyx asked. "At the same time?"

"Indeed."

Nyx scrunched her brow at what sounded like absurdity. Still, she sensed the prioress was hinting at something with the words she had emphasized. *Dark* and *bright*.

"Have you never wondered," Ghyle pressed, "how in winter the Father sits lower in the sky, then higher again in the summer? Though the sun never vanishes, it makes a tiny circle in the sky over one year's passing?"

Nyx gave a tiny shake of her head and a wave toward her eyes. There was no way she could appreciate such subtlety.

A hand touched her shoulder. "Of course, I'm sorry. But let me assure you this is true. And as such, can you guess from your study of the orrery why this might be?"

Nyx turned back to the convoluted rings of bronze on the table. She sensed she was being tested. She could almost feel the prioress's intensity burning next to her. She took a deep breath, determined not to disappoint the head of the school. She reached out a hand to the orrery. "May I?"

"Of course."

Nyx again took her time to center herself on the warm sun and fumble to the third ring. Once she found the sphere affixed there, she examined its shape more closely, taking care of the tiny bead of the moon that spun on its own ring around the Urth. She particularly noted how the sphere of the Urth was pinned to the ring beneath it.

Ghyle offered a suggestion. "Sister Reed, it might help our young student if you set everything in motion again."

After a rustling of skirts, the mechanism's complicated gears resumed their *tick-ticking* and the rings started to turn again. Nyx concentrated on how the Urth slowly spun in place as it made a full pass around the sun. She struggled to understand how the southern half could be brighter, while the northern side was darker. Then understanding traveled up her fingertips. The pin around which the Urth spun was not perfectly up and down. Instead, it was set at a slight angle from the sun.

Could that be the answer?

Certainty grew.

She spoke as she continued her own path around the sun. "As the Urth turns, its axis spins at a slight *angle,* rather than straight up and down. Because of that, for a time, the top half of the world leans toward the sun."

"Creating our bright northern summer," the prioress confirmed.

"And when that happens, the bottom half is left leaning away from the sun."

"Marking the southern Crown's gloomy winter."

Nyx turned to the prioress, shocked. "So, seasons are due to the Urth spinning crookedly in place, leaning one side more fully toward the sun, then away again."

Murmurs spread among the students. Some sounded distraught; others incredulous. But at least Byrd offered no overt ridicule, not in the presence of the prioress.

Still, Nyx felt her face heating up again.

Then a hand patted her shoulder, ending with a squeeze of reassurance.

Startled by the contact, she flinched away. She hated any unexpected touch. Many a boy—even some girls—had come of late to grab at her, often cruelly, pinching what was most tender and private. She could not even accuse and point a finger. Not that she often didn't know who it was. Especially Byrd, who always reeked of rank sweat and a sour-yeasty breath. It was a cloud that he carried about him from the stores of ale secretly sent to him by his father in Fiskur.

"I'm sorry—" the prioress said softly, plainly noting Nyx's reaction and unease.

Nyx tried to retreat, but one of her fingers had hooked through the Urth's ring when she had flinched. Embarrassment turned to panic. She tried to extract her hand but twisted her finger wrong. A metallic pop sounded, which earned a gasp from Sister Reed. Free now, Nyx withdrew her hand from the orrery and clutched a fist to her chest.

Something *tinged* and *tanged* across the stone floor near her toes.

"She broke it!" Byrd blurted out, but there was no scorn, only shock.

Another hand grasped her elbow and yanked her back. Caught off guard, Nyx stumbled and tripped to her knees on the floor.

"What have you done, you clumsy girl?" Sister Reed still clutched her. "I'll have you switched to your core for this."

"No, you won't," Prioress Ghyle said. "It was an accident. One for which I'm equally at fault for startling the child. Would you have me tied to the rod and beaten, Sister Reed?"

"I would never . . ."

"Then neither will the child suffer. Leave her be."

Nyx's elbow was freed, but not before those same fingers squeezed hard, digging down to the bone. The message was clear. This matter was not over. It was a bruising promise. Sister Reed intended to exact payment for being humiliated in front of the students, in front of the prioress.

Ghyle's robes swished as her voice lowered toward the floor. "See. It is just the Urth's moon that has broken free." Nyx pictured the prioress collecting the bronze marble from the floor. "It can easily be returned to its proper place and repaired."

Nyx gained her feet, her face as hot as the sun, tears threatening.

"Sister Reed, mayhap it's best that you end today's lesson. I think your seventhyears have had more than enough celestial excitement for one morning."

Nyx was already moving before Sister Reed dismissed the class to break for their midday meal. She raced her tears toward the brightness of the door.

No one blocked her flight, perhaps fearing to catch her humiliation and shame. In her haste to escape, she left behind her cane—a sturdy length of polished elm—which she used to help guide her steps. Still, she refused to go back and fled out into the sunlight and shadows of a summer day.

2

As OTHERS HEADED to their dormitory hall, where a cold midday repast awaited the students, Nyx hurried in the other direction. She had no appetite. Instead, she reached one of the four staircases that led down from the seventh tier to the one below, where the sixthyears were likely already eating in their own hall.

Though the world around her was only shadows against that brightness, she did not slow. Even without her cane, she moved swiftly. She had lived half of her life in the walled Cloistery. By now, she knew every nook and crook of its tiers. The number of steps, turns, and stairs had been ingrained into her, allowing her to traverse the school with relative ease. At the edge of her full awareness, a silent count ran in the back of her skull. She instinctively reached out a hand every now and then—to a carved lintel, to a wooden post of a stall, to a stone flogging pillar—continually confirming her location and position.

As she descended through the tiers, she pictured the breadth of the Cloistery of Brayk. It rose like a stepped hill from the swamps of Mýr. At its base, the school stretched over a mile across, built atop a foundation of volcanic stone, one of the rare solid places among these watery marshlands and drowned forests. The school was the second oldest in the Kingdom of Hálendii—the oldest being on the outskirts of its capital, Azantiia—but the Cloistery was still considered the harshest and most esteemed due to its isolation. Students spent their entire nine years in Brayk, beginning at the lowermost tier where the young firstyears were instructed. From there, classes were winnowed smaller and smaller to match the ever-shrinking tiers of the school. Those that failed to rise were sent back to their families in shame, but that did not stop students from arriving here by boats and ships from all around the Crown. For those who succeeded in reaching the ninth tier at the school's pinnacle, they were destined for honor and prominence, advancing either to the handful of alchymical academies where they'd be instructed into the deeper mysteries of the world or into one of the religious orders to be ordained into the highest devotions.

When Nyx reached the third tier, she glanced back to the summit of the school. Twin fires glowed amidst the shadows at the top, bright enough for even her clouded eyes to discern. One pyre smoked with alchymical mysteries; the other burned with clouds of sacred incense. It was said the shape and fires of the Cloistery mimicked the volcanic peak at the heart of Mýr, the steam-shrouded mountain of The Fist. In addition, the infused smoke rising from the top of the school served to keep the denizens of those cave-pocked slopes—the winged bats—from approaching too close. Still, in the gloom of winter, dark wings occasionally shredded through the low clouds. Screeches would send first- and secondyears cowering and crying for reassurance from the sisters and brothers who taught them—until eventually one grew to ignore the threat.

Nyx could not say the same was true for her. Even at her age, the hunting cries would set her heart to pounding, her head to burning. And when she was younger—a firstyear new to the school—terror would overwhelm her, sending her into a dead faint. But she had nothing to fear now. It was the middle of summer, and whether from the brightness or the heat, the massive bats kept away from the swamp's edges, sticking close to their dark dens in The Fist.

By the time she finally reached the lowermost tier of the Cloistery, her shame and embarrassment had waned to a dull ache in her chest. She rubbed her bruised elbow, a reminder that there would still be repercussions to come.

Until then, she wanted reassurance and aimed for the only place she could find it. She headed out through the school gates and into the trading post of Brayk. The ramshackle village hugged the walls of the Cloistery. Brayk fed, supplied, and maintained the school. Goods were carted upward every morning, accompanied by lines of men and women who served as chambermaids, servitors, sculleries, and cooks. Nyx had thought this to be her own fate, having started at the school as a housegirl at the age of six.

Once out into the village, she moved just as surefooted. She not only counted her footsteps through the crooked streets, but her ears pricked to the rhythmic hammering of Smithy's Row to her left. The steady ringing helped guide her path. Her nose also lifted to the pungent smoke and heady spices of markets, where fishes and eels were already frying under the midday sun. Even her skin noted the thickening air and growing dampness as she reached Brayk's outskirts. Here the stone-and-plaster palacios closer to the school's walls declined to more modest homes and storehouses with wooden walls and thatched roofs.

Still, she continued onward until a new smell filled her world. It was a heavy brume of sodden hair, sweet shite, trampled mud, and sulfurous belch. She felt her fears shedding from her shoulders as she drew nearer, enveloping herself in the rich odors.

It meant home.

Her arrival did not go unnoticed. A rumbling bellow greeted her, followed by another, and another. Splashing headed her way.

She crossed forward until her hands found the stacked stone fence that marked off the bullock pens at the swamp's edge. A heavy shuffle aimed toward her, accompanied by a softer grunting and a few plaintive bleats, as if the great lumbering beasts thought themselves to blame for her long absence. She lifted a hand until a wet nose, covered in cold phlegm, settled into her palm. Her fingers were nosed up and gently nuzzled. From its size and the shape, she knew this snout as readily as she did the village and school.

"It's good to see you, too, Gramblebuck."

She freed her hand and reached up. She dug her fingers through the thick matted fur between the stubby horns until her nails found skin. She scratched him hard where he always liked it, earning a contented huff of hot air against her chest. Gramblebuck was the eldest of the herd, nearly a century old. He rarely pulled the sledges through the rushes and marshes any longer, but he remained lord of the bullocks. Most of the shaggy herd here could trace their blood to this one beast.

She reached up both arms and gripped his horns. Even with his head bowed low, she had to lift to her toes to get hold. She pulled his head to hers, his crown as wide as her chest. She inhaled his wet musk, leaned into the warm hearth of his bulk.

"I missed you, too," she whispered.

He grunted back and tried to haul her up by arching his short neck.

She laughed and let go of his horns before she was carried aloft. "I don't have time to go for a ride with you. Maybe on my midsummer break."

Though Gramblebuck no longer pulled the sledges, he still loved to trek the swamps. All her life, she had spent many a long day on his wide back, traversing the marshes. His long legs and splayed hooves made easy passage through its bogs and streams, while his size and curled tusks discouraged any predators from daring to approach.

She patted his cheek. "Soon. I promise you."

As she headed down the fencerow, running her fingertips along the posts, she hoped it was a promise she could keep. Other bullocks shuffled and sidled up, wanting attention, too. She knew most of them by touch and smell. But her time was limited. The bells would soon be summoning her back to her studies.

She hurried toward the corner of the hundred-acre bullock pen, where a homestead stood. Its foundation was anchored to the stone shore but also stretched out atop a massive dock, which extended a quarter league into the swamps. The home's walls were stacked stones matching the fence, its roof thatched like the homes nearby. Higher up, a rock chimney pointed at the skies, where the shadows of low clouds scudded across the brightness, rolling ever eastward, carrying the freezing cold of the dark toward the searing scorch on the other side of the world.

She crossed to the stout door, lifted the iron latch, and shoved inside without a knock or a shout. As she stepped into the deeper shadows, her world shrank, but not in a disconcerting way. It was like being wrapped in a warm, familiar blanket. She was immediately struck by a mélange of odors that meant home: the smell of old wool, the oily polish of wood, the smoke of dying coals, the melting beeswax from the tiny candles in the home's corner altar. Even the waft of composting silage from the twin stone silos that flanked the docks pervaded everything.

Her ears piqued to a shuffle of limbs and creak of wood near the ruddy glow of the hearth. A voice, wry with amusement, rose from there. "Trouble again, is it?" her dah asked. "Is there any other reason you tumble back home nowadays, lass? And without your cane?"

She hung her head, staring down at her empty hands. She wanted to dismiss his words but could not.

A gentle laugh softened his judgement. "Come sit and tell me about it."

WITH HER BACK to the fire, Nyx finished her litany of the morning's humiliations and fears. It lightened her spirit simply to unburden them.

All the while, her dah sat silently, puffing on a pipe smoldering with snakeroot. The tincture in the smoke helped with the crick and rasp of his joints. But she suspected his silence was less about tempering any pain than it was to allow her the time to fill the quiet with her complaints.

She let out a sigh to announce the ending.

Her dah sucked on his pipe and exhaled one long bitter breath of smoke. "Let me ken it better for you. You certainly tweaked the nose of the nonne who taught you this last quarter."

Nyx rubbed the bruise from Sister Reed's bony fingers and nodded.

"But you also impressed yourself upon the prioress of the entire school. Not a small feat, I imagine."

"She was being kindly at best. And I don't think my clumsiness helped the situation. Especially breaking the school's treasured orrery."

"No matter. What is broken can always be set aright. On the balance of it, I'd say you fared well for one morning. You'll finish your seventhyear in another turn of the moon. Leaving only the eighthyear to go until the final culling to the ninth and highest tier. It seems, under such circumstances, earning the good graces of the prioress herself versus irking a single nonne—a sister who you'll soon leave behind anyway—is not a bad trade."

His words helped further temper her misgivings. *Maybe he was right.* She had certainly endured far harsher obstacles to reach the seventh tier. *And now I'm so close to the top.* She shoved that hope down deep, fearing even wishing it might dash her chances.

As if reading her thoughts, her dah underscored her luck. "Look where you started. A babe of six moons mewling atop a floating raft of fenweed. If not for your bellyaching, we wouldn't aheard ya. Gramblebuck would have dragged my sledge right past ya."

She attempted to smile. The story of her being found abandoned in the bog was a point of joy to her dah. He had two strong sons—both in their third decade now, who managed the paddocks and ran the sledges—but the man's wife had died giving birth to his only daughter, losing both at the same time. He took Nyx's discovery in the swamps as some gift from the Mother, especially as there was no evidence of who had left the infant naked and crying in the bog. The spread of fenweed, a fragile and temperamental plant, exhibited no evidence of any treadfall around her body. Even the tender blooms that covered the floating mat's surface showed no bruise to their petals. It was as if she had been dropped from the skies as a reward for the devout and hardworking swamper.

Still, while this oft told story was a point of pride for her dah, for her it was laced with an uncomfortable mix of shame and anger. Her mother—maybe both her parents—had abandoned her in the swamps, surely left to die, perhaps because she had been born afflicted, the surfaces of her eyes glazed to a bluish white.

"How I loved ya," her dah said, admitting another truth. "Even if you hadn't been picked to join the firstyears at the Cloistery. Though my heart just about burst when I heard you passed the test."

"It was an accident," she muttered.

He coughed out a gout of smoke. "Don't say that. Nothing in life is simple chance. It was a sign the Mother still smiles on you."

Nyx didn't believe as devoutly as him, but she knew better than to contradict him.

At the time, she had been a housegirl at the school, assigned to washing and scrubbing. She had been mopping one of the testing wards when she tripped over a tumble of small blocks—some stone, others wooden—on the floor. Fearing they might be important, she gathered them up and set them atop a nearby table. But curiosity got the better of her. While neatly stacking them, she felt how different shapes fit against one another. It was how she experienced much of the world around her—then and now—through the sensitivity of her fingers. With no one around, she began fiddling with the blocks and lost track of the time, but eventually the ninescore of shapes built themselves into an intricate structure with crenellated towers and jagged walls that formed a six-pointed star around the castle in the center.

Lost in her labors and concentrating fully on her work, she had failed to notice the gathering around her. Only when done did she straighten, earning gasps from her hidden audience.

She remembered one nonne asking another, "How long has she been in here?"

The answer: "I left when she came in with the mop and pail. That was less than one ring ago."

"She built the Highmount of Azantiia in such a short time. We give the aspirants an entire day to do the same. And most fail."

"I swear."

Someone had then grabbed her chin and turned her face. "And look at the blue cast to her eyes. She's all but blind."

Afterward, she had been granted a spot among the firstyears, entering the Cloistery a year younger than anyone else. Only a handful of children from the village of Brayk had ever been granted entrance to the school, and none had climbed higher than the third tier. She secretly took pride in this accomplishment, but it was hard to maintain that satisfaction. As she climbed the tiers with the same shrinking class, the others never let her forget her lowly beginnings. They shamed her for the stink of the silage about her. They teased her for her lack of fine clothes and manners. And then there was her clouded vision, a wall of shadows that continually separated her from the others.

Still, she found solace in her dah's joy. To stoke that happiness, she kept steadfast in her studies. She also found pleasure in learning more about the world. It was like climbing out of the darkness of a root cellar and into a bright summer day. Shadows remained, mysteries yet to be revealed, but each year more of the darkness about the world lifted. The same curiosity with which she handled those blocks in the testing ward remained and grew with each tier gained.

"You will make it to your ninthyear," her dah said. "I know it in my bones."

She gathered his confidence into her heart and held it there. She would devote everything to make that happen.

If nothing else, for him.

Off in the distance, a ringing echoed from the heights of the Cloistery. It was the Summoning Bell. She had to be in her latterday studies before they rang again. She did not have much time.

Her dah heard it, too. "Best you get going, lass."

She gained her feet by the hearth and reached to his hand, feeling the wiry muscles under thin skin, all wrapped around strong bones. She leaned and kissed him, finding his whiskered cheek as surely as a bee to a honeyclott.

"I'll see you again when I can," she promised him, remembering she had sworn the same earlier to Gramblebuck. She intended to keep that promise to both.

"Be good," her dah said. "And remember the Mother is always looking out for you."

As she headed toward the door, she smiled at her dah's undying faith in both her and the Mother Below. She prayed it was not misplaced—not with either of them.

3

SENSING THE PRESS of time, Nyx returned along the same path that brought her home. Only now she wielded her spare cane ahead of her, a worn staff from when she was years younger. Its length was nicked and pitted from long use. It was also slightly shorter in length than the newer one she had abandoned in the classroom. Still, it felt like a comfortable old friend in her hand. She swept it along ahead of her. Though she knew the path well, the cane's assurance and weight helped steady her.

She quickened her pace. It would not be good to be late, not after this morning's travails. Once past the school gates, she dashed up along the six tiers. She was breathless upon reaching the seventh, but she made it before the second Summoning Bell.

Relieved, she hurried to the left, away from the shame of the astronicum dome. She intended to collect her other cane later, when no one was looking. Each morning, their studies were devoted to the matters of the world: the riddles of arithomatica, the dissections of biologica, the applications of balances and measures. The latterdays were spent in the scholarship of histories, the orders of religions, and the literata of the ancients.

She preferred the mornings, mostly due to the amount of reading involved later in the day. Though her fingertips were deft, they were not sensitive enough to read the ink impressed into the sacred tomes. To help her with her studies, a young acolyte had been assigned to her as an aide. Jace had failed in his fifthyear, but rather than being sent home, he had been offered a place at the school in the scriptorium, mostly copying texts, but also serving as her eyes. During the day, he softly recited what she needed to understand, sometimes continuing in her dormitory cell at night.

She rushed to where he usually waited. While Jace could have made her life even more difficult, he was kind and patient with her. She also suspected he might be fond of her in ways more than tutorial. Jace was four years older, but he was far more boyish than even her fellow seventhyears. To help compensate, he grew a scruff of beard to roughen his round face. His sedentary life contributed to a wide belly and a slight wheeze when he hurried to keep up with her. But he, more than anyone, could make her laugh. In many ways, he was the reason she could tolerate her latterday studies.

She headed to the archway outside the scriptorium. As she rounded a corner, she heard her friend's telltale huff, heavier and pained, as if he had run all the way here. She smelled the odor of lime on his clothes, indicating he had spent the morning preparing fresh vellum for his work.

"Jace, I'm sorry I'm late. We should—"

Then a new note struck her nose. Bitter and rich in iron. It wafted off of him with each exhale. *Blood.* Startled, she tripped over something on the ground. Even her cane had missed it. She fell and realized quickly it was one of her friend's legs. Why was Jace sitting under the archway? Her hand patted up his body.

"Jace, what's wrong?"

Her fingers found his face, earning a gasp from him. She felt the hot blood under his nose, all swollen and crooked. He winced from her touch and pulled her hands down.

"Nyx . . . they mean to hurt you."

"Who—?"

But even she could guess the answer. A scuffle of leather on stone sounded from all around her. She heard a hard snicker behind her.

"Run," Jace urged, and pushed her up.

She hesitated in a crouch, frozen by fear.

"Don't let her get away!" Kindjal shouted.

The words broke her panic. Nyx searched for a way to escape. She extended all her senses, reflexively filling the world around her with each rasp, whisper, and scuff. She shied from a shift of shadows to her right and fled the pall of sweat and breath swelling behind her. As she headed away, she sought succor from the school, from any sister or brother who might be nearby.

With her heart hammering in her throat, the reach of her ears stretched. They piqued and fixed to the familiar tones of Sister Reed around the next corner.

". . . proper place. She'll wish she was merely switched."

Another responded, his voice a high-pitched grate. It was Hieromonk Plakk, who led the latterday studies. "And the prioress?"

"What happens between bells, especially between vexed students, cannot be laid at my feet. I shall claim—"

The second Summoning Bell clanged across the tiers, cutting off her words.

Gasping, heart pounding, Nyx felt herself near to fainting with terror, almost lifting out of her body. For a moment, a strange new sense overwhelmed her. The echoing of the bells shredded through the shadows, pushing them back, revealing with greater clarity the walls, stairs, and paths around her. She could even make out shapes closing upon her.

One neared, and she spun away from it. Fingers snatched at her sleeve, but she kept free.

A curse blurted out behind her.

Byrd.

She followed the path revealed by the ringing echoes, leaning upon this newfound sense to make her escape. Still, as she fled, she confirmed this new sense with her cane as best she could. The hunters quickly fell behind her, but they did not give up their pursuit, gathering like a storm at her back.

She reached the stairway that led up to the eighth tier. As a seventhyear, she did not know that level all that well. Still, she swept up the steps, leading with her cane. Her awareness strangely split as she climbed. Her chest burned, her heart pounded, but she also felt as if a part of her were floating above, looking down at herself. But she had no time to dwell on the strangeness.

At the top of the steps, she dashed across the tier. With the bells fading, the world closed around her again. She sank back into her body.

"There she is!" Kindjal shouted behind her.

Nyx fled in terror from the approaching slap of sandals on stone. With the eighthyears already ensconced in their classes, there was no one else about. Panicked, she tried to go faster. Her shoulder struck a corner and spun her a full circle. Still, fear kept her upright and moving.

But where could she go?

Having lost that momentary new sense of the world, she headed along the only path she knew well. Every student eventually crept up to this level and made a secret pilgrimage. The journey ended where their hopes were either dashed to the ground or lifted high.

Nyx was no exception. She had crossed the eighth tier several times each year to reach this spot. She sped toward that goal. It was the only route she had memorized.

The hunters followed, laughing darkly, chasing her with threats.

She finally reached another set of steps. These were no steeper or longer than the ones she had climbed to reach this height, but she skidded to a stop at their base. This set of stairs led up to the ninth and final tier. Only those deemed worthy of Ascension were allowed to traipse these steps. It was a path forbidden to all others. Its mysteries were for those chosen few. To trespass meant immediate expulsion from the school.

She trembled at the bottom. She had spent her first seven years in Brayk, the next seven here at the Cloistery. At this moment, her life teetered between a bright future and a shameful fall. Though she could not know her final fate, she had always strived for her best and hoped for the same.

But now . . .

Behind her, the others closed in. Byrd noted her hesitation. He guffawed, but there was no amusement, only threat. He punctuated it with his next words. "She's trapped. Just you watch. I'm gonna take her cane and whip her arse good. Till she can't sit down for a fortnight."

Laughter burst out as the others closed off any escape.

Her cane was suddenly ripped from her grip. She tried to snatch it back but was shoved away.

Another voice, maybe Rymal, urged Byrd to greater harm. "Crack it across her hands instead. Good'n hard. Shatter 'em both. Like she broke the orrery. Only fitting, I tell ya."

Nyx clenched her fists, her heart pounding in her ears. Over the years, she had broken a bone or two from the occasional misstep and bad fall. Pain did not scare her, but her hands contributed as much to her vision as her clouded eyes. Her palms knew every vibration in her cane. Her fingertips revealed details that her eyes could not. What was threatened here wasn't just the snap of a few bones, but a crippling that would leave her all the more blind.

Still, there were even worse fates.

Kindjal found her brother's ear. "You should go ahead and *ruin* her instead," she said with menacing glee. "Make sure she's cast out of the school forever."

This earned more laughter, only now veined with nervousness. They all knew the menace behind this new threat. For a girl to reach Ascension, she had to be a virgin, untouched and pure. For some reason, this did not seem to apply to the boys. Not that there weren't fervent trysts in the dormitories, involving everything but the final act. To cross that last line meant exile— not just from the school, but from Brayk itself. Such was the shame.

"I think a beating is good enough," Byrd said, his voice struggling to sound firm. "That'll put this swamper in her proper place."

His sister scoffed. "She deserves worse. She doesn't belong here. We all know it. You're just scared."

Nyx heard the acid in Kindjal's voice. The highmayor's daughter had always struggled in her lessons. It was whispered that her father paid for her climb up the tiers with chests of silver eyries and gold marches. No one dared say such in her presence. For some reason, Nyx had always drawn her ire, perhaps because of the high marks Nyx had earned in their classes.

Byrd sputtered against his sister's aspersions of cowardice. His voice strained with fury and embarrassment. "Ansel, Merkle, grab her. Lackwiddle, help them, too."

He intended to involve as many as possible to ensure no one spoke. Afterward they could easily blame her violation on some random tryst in the village.

Nyx backed away, her heels striking the first step behind her. With that touch, anger erupted inside her, driving back her terror. A coldness snuffed the heat from her body.

If I'm to be cast out, let it be by my own action.

She lifted her leg and backed onto the first stair. This small act drew shocked gasps. She ignored them and took another step, then another. She refused to give Byrd or Kindjal the satisfaction of ruining her.

Byrd must have recognized the same and growled his fury.

She did not flee from his anger, but instead she used it like a wind to fill her sails and push her upward. Behind her, the heat of the twin pyres grew with each step. The smoky incense washed away the reek of the threat below.

Byrd cursed. "Don't think you can escape that easy."

Though she couldn't see him, she heard him rush the stairs. Startled at his boldness, she froze.

Kindjal called to her brother, panic in her voice, perhaps only now realizing she had pushed him too hard. "Byrd, no! You can't."

He stopped long enough to growl back and reassure his twin, "Don't worry. Father will clear my debt if it comes to that."

The exchange cut through Nyx's shock. She turned and fled up the steps, running toward her doom.

ALREADY ADDLED, NYX fought to keep her footing as she reached the school's summit. With only rumors and stories to guide her, she was lost.

According to Jace, the ninth tier was nothing like the others. It supported a circle of towers, each holding various levels of study. The western half—its towers built of dark volcanic stone mined from the foundations under the school—held the classes in alchymy. On the other side spread an arc of blazing white turrets constructed of limestone hauled in from the cliffs of Landfall to the east. Among those white towers, the mysteries of godly orders and ancient histories were revealed to the ninthyears.

Knowing such knowledge would be forever forbidden to her, Nyx ignored both sides and fled toward the twin pools of brightness at the summit's center. The two pyres glowed like the very eyes of the Father Above. For centuries, the pair had stared down at the students below, daring them to come closer, to gaze deep into the wonders and terrors contained therein.

Above the pyres, darker shadows roiled into the sky, stirring with bitter alchymies and sacred incenses. As she drew nearer, the scents overwhelmed Nyx, erasing all detail around her. The roaring fires deafened her. Even the flames cast aside all discerning shadows into one continuous blaze.

It was as if the world had vanished, leaving her floating in a brightness of stinging smoke and grumbling flames. *So be it.* Knowing she could go no farther, she stopped between those pyres, ending her frantic flight.

She put her back to the fires. She refused to cower.

Steps away, a harsh panting cut through the roaring.

Byrd.

"I'll drag you back by your hair if I must," he threatened.

He punctuated his threat with a hard smack of her cane against the stones. She heard the wood crack with the impact, sounding like the break of a bone. It felt as if he had shattered an old friend.

Both despairing and angry, Nyx considered tossing herself into the flames, to thwart him even now. But she had been raised by a dah who tamed bullocks, alongside brothers who never relented. She lifted her arms, prepared to do as much damage as possible before it was over.

As she readied herself, her dah's last words returned to her: *Remember the Mother is always looking out for you.* She wished that were true, most of all now. But she held out little hope. Still, she prayed with all the strength inside her.

And an answer came.

Only it wasn't the Mother Below.

As Byrd rushed at her, the tiny hairs along Nyx's arms and neck shivered. Then she heard it. A screech split the sky. The cry crashed into her, washed through her, shook her bones and teeth. Then her body ignited into a torch. She felt her skin blister, her eyes boil. She imagined the flames of the pyres had struck her, buffeted into her by the sweep of large wings overhead.

Despite the pain, she ducked low.

Ahead, a scream—not a beast, but a boy—carried toward her.

It cut off in mid-cry.

Then a body struck her, knocking her onto her back between the two pyres. The fire inside her instantly died, as if snuffed out by the bulk atop her. Knowing it was Byrd, she fought to free herself.

As she did so, a gush of hot blood washed over her neck and chest. Her fingers tried to stanch the flow—only to discover torn flesh, the stump of a neck. She gasped and struggled in terror. Byrd's head was gone, ripped from his body.

Tears burst along with a sob.

No . . .

She struggled to get free of his weight—then it was ripped off of her and tossed into the alchemical pyre. On her back, she elbowed and kicked her way deeper between the fires. Flesh and blood sizzled and smoked to her left.

No . . .

Through the brightness of the twin blazes, a dark shadow grew before her. Her left leg was grabbed, pinned to the stone. The shape crested over her. A bony knuckle crushed into her belly, another into her right shoulder. She had once been trampled by a panicked hundred-stone bullock heifer. What held her trapped now was far heavier, its purpose more deliberate.

No . . .

The shadow covered her fully, ensconcing her in the darkness of wing and body. A hot breath, reeking of meat and iron, blew across her face. Wet nostrils snuffled her from her crown to her neck and settled there.

No . . .

She felt bristled lips part—then the icy press of daggers into the tender flesh of her throat.

No . . .

Fangs stabbed deep, bringing a flash of sharp pain, followed by a cold numbness. The press of muzzle choked her. She could not breathe. The icy chill spread outward, pumped into her body, tracing through her blood.

Then shouts cut across the roaring fires.

The ninth tier had finally woken to the assault.

The mass atop her burst away, crushing her worse, then carrying her aloft for a breath, before finally letting her go. She crashed to the stones. On her back, she felt the heavy beat of wings, the roil of heat from whipped flames. Smoke swirled, bringing the smell of sweet incense and burning flesh.

For a moment upon the stones, she again had the strange sensation of both staring up at the sky and down at her body at the same time.

Then it was gone.

As she lay there, the coldness continued to spread. It numbed her limbs until she could not move, barely breathe. She felt the ice, like poisonous claws, dig into her heart and clench. The world immediately went dark, far blacker than any blindness. All sound dissolved to silence as if she were diving into the deepest pond.

All that was left was her heartbeat.

She bore witness to each slowing spasm.

No . . .

She fought to hold, to will another beat.

As she did so, a new noise rose from the dark depths. It distracted her focus. Screams and shouts filled her head—hundreds, then thousands, then more. The ground trembled under her, then bucked wildly. It all ended with a thunderous cracking that left her hollow and barren. In the aftermath, all that remained was an awful silence, far emptier than anything she had experienced.

If she could have, she would have wept.

Only then did she realize the truth.

In that empty silence.

Her heart had stopped.

Arkival limne of
M'jr Bat
(native to The Fist)

TWO

THE ROOTLESS STATUE

Smash the hamer
An' crack the anvelt,
Karve the brimstan
An' empti the vein.
Onli then can a hard heart be brok'n,
Brok'n enough to mende.

—Old miner's canticle

4

RHAIF WOULD HAVE died if his bladder hadn't been so full.

The only warning came from the cloud of dust shivering into the air from the chalky floor of the tunnel. Rhaif would've liked to attribute this unusual phenomenon to the strength and fury of his stream splashing against the nearby wall. But he knew better. Fear crimped off his flow and drove him to his knees. He propped a hand against the large boulder behind which he had sought privacy. The surface vibrated under his palm.

He glanced to the lantern hanging from his leather waistbelt. The oil flame jiggered and snapped behind the pebbled glass.

His chest tightened to a hard knot.

Down the tunnel, the other prisoners hollered and screamed, accompanied by a rattle of chains as they tried to flee. But it was too late. Stone groaned with an ominous intensity—followed by a thunderous clap. The ground jolted up, throwing Rhaif into the air. The boulder next to him bounced high, rebounded off the roof, and crashed to a floor now riven with cracks.

Rhaif landed hard on his rear and scuttled backward as the tunnel continued its collapse. His lantern, mercifully still intact, bobbled atop his knee breeches. Before him, a massive slab of the roof broke free and smashed to rubble and dust. More fissures chased him down the tunnel, coursing across roof, walls, and floor.

A choking black cloud rolled over him, heavy with sand and chalk.

He coughed to keep from drowning in that silt. He hurriedly rolled to his feet and rushed away. The flickering flame at his thigh looked like a lone fireflit lost and bouncing through a dark bower. Its light was too feeble to pierce the thick veil of dust. Still, he kept running, both arms out. His ankle chains rang with each step, giving strident voice to his distress.

In his haste to escape, his hip struck an outcropping. He spun, and glass shattered at his hip. A few pieces pierced his roughspun breeches and sliced his leg. He winced and slowed, taking great care not to lose his lamp's flame. Only the overseer had a flint to relight it if it should go out.

That must not happen.

He had witnessed other prisoners punished with darkness. Poor souls lowered into pits without lanterns, sealed down there for days on end. They often came out frail, maddened creatures. It was Rhaif's greatest fear: an eternal darkness without end. How could it not? He had lived all his three decades up in the Guld'guhl territories on the eastern edge of the Crown, at the fringe of the sun-blasted world, where night never fell and the lands were a sandy ruin, where heinous creatures made their home, alongside tribes of savages who eked out a meager, violent existence. Having lived all his life under a Guld'guhl sun, he held night to be no more than a rumor, a darkness to be feared.

As he hobbled free of the worst of the dust cloud, he finally stopped. He unhooked his lantern and lifted it high. He took care doing so, fearing too much jostling might knock the flame from its oiled taper.

"Just stay where you are," he warned the pale flicker.

As the dust thinned, he listened to the settling of rock behind him. The pounding of his heart grew quieter, too. He checked the passageway. The cave-in had stopped a hundred steps away, completely collapsing the tunnel. A few stray rocks fell from the roof. A timber support shattered with a loud pop, enough to make him jump back.

Still, it looked like the worst was over.

But what now?

He sneezed loudly, startling himself, then turned and searched around him. He did not know this level of the mine, not that he hadn't heard stories. Earlier, roused from their piles of hay in the mine gaol, he and a dozen others had been kicked and threatened with cudgels to this remote area of the chalk mine. There, they had been lowered on hempen ropes tied to an empty ore cart, winched down by the ox-driven windlass somewhere outside the pit mouth. It was said this section of the mine had been long abandoned. Some said its shafts and tunnels had dried out centuries ago, but most believed it was accursed, haunted by spirits, plagued by malicious ilklins.

Rhaif hadn't placed much stock in such tales. He knew some miners who snuck crusts of bread into crevices in the rocks; overseers who did the same with coins, mostly brass pinches, once even a silver eyrie. All to appease such spirits.

Not him.

He had learned in the back alleys of Anvil to trust only that which he could touch with his hands or see with his own eyes. He took no account of gods, of stories of ghostlies and spookens. Living in Anvil, he'd learned there was plenty enough to be afraid of. What went bump in the night in Anvil was not some haunting, but someone trying to steal what was yours.

Then again, he was often the one doing the bumping.

Anvil was the territory's main port. It hunkered along the sea, a squalid pisshole, if ever there was a place. It was a city of cutthroats and rogues of every ilk. It shat and sweated like a living creature, ripe with corruption, pestilence, and decay. By season, by storm, by fair weather, it never changed. Its bay was constantly festooned with the sails of a hundred ships, its dockside a continual brawl.

The saying went that no one *lived* in Anvil, they only *survived* it.

Rhaif sighed.

How I miss it . . .

Not that he held out any expectation of ever seeing it again. Betrayed by his own guild, he ended up being buried a hundred leagues to the south, sentenced to spend the rest of his life in the mines. His offense: crossing the wrong thief, the master of their guild, Llyra hy March. He thought it illfitting a punishment for simply stealing from the woman's former lover, the archsheriff of Anvil. The man was too tempting a mark, and Llyra was not someone prone to pining, let alone loyalty. In fact, Rhaif himself had shared the warmth of her bed many a time.

He shook his head.

Even now, he remained stymied. To be so harshly punished, he suspected there had been more afoot than he had been privy to.

No matter, here I am.

But where was *here*?

As the dust settled to a haze, he reached a free hand to the secret pouch sewn into his breeches. He removed the wayglass, an item he had pilfered from an overseer of another crew and quickly hidden away. The loss was blamed on those other prisoners, who each lost a finger until someone confessed to stop the torture and claimed he got scared and threw it down a privy shaft. No one bothered to search the filth.

Rhaif lifted the wayglass to the flicker of flame. The sliver of lodestone shivered back and forth. It refused to settle. *Strange.* He had stolen it in the vague hope of one day making his escape. Though truth be told, he had noted the opportunity to nab it—and could not resist. After he had been buried down here for nearly two years, the thought of freedom was always on his mind. And a wayglass *could* prove useful. He figured if he ever had the opportunity to escape the overseer's eye and take flight through some deserted section of mine, such a tool might point him in the right direction.

Like now.

He turned in a circle. He had come to a stop at a crossroad of tunnels. He tried to fathom the best path. He dreamed of his freedom, but he also valued his own hide. If it meant living, he would happily return to the whip and cudgel. Death was an escape he would rather avoid.

He decided on one tunnel, choosing it only because the lodestone shivered a little less in that direction.

"Good enough."

AFTER SEVERAL HUNDRED paces, Rhaif was thoroughly lost.

By now, he sensed he was going in circles, slowly traversing downward, as if marching into his own grave. As to the wayglass, it only confounded him. The lodestone now spun round and round the glass, as if as baffled as him.

Maybe this place is accursed.

He turned at another tunnel, growing frantic. His heart pounded in his throat. He had at best a half-day of lamp oil left. His ears strained for any telltale sign of the mine proper: shouted orders, the ring of hammers, the cries of the whipped. But all he heard was his panted breath and his occasional mumbled curses.

He had to duck his head from the low roof—which itself was disconcerting. Like all Guld'guhlians, he was bowlegged and hard-headed in all manners of that term. It was as if the sun had beaten all of them into squat shapes, maybe all the better to work the thousands of mines that spread the breadth of the territory's coast, from the stone forest of Dödwood to the north to the endless southern Wastes.

He ran a hand along the wall, feeling the cracks in the chalk. Here the timbered supports had long turned to stone, hardened by the centuries in the mineral-rich air. As he continued, those fissures widened and grew in number.

He craned his neck, noting the fractures along the roof.

Distracted, he tripped over a pile of loose stone and fell. He came close to smashing his wayglass, but he caught himself with his other hand. His lantern swung wildly from his waistbelt. He held his breath, fearing the flame would snuff out.

It flickered wildly but held true.

He checked the stones on the floor. Their edges were too sharp and a gap in the roof suggested they had recently broken from up there. If he had any doubt about circling toward his doom, he had proof in hand.

"Gods be," he muttered. "I'm straight back under the section that caved in."

He shook his head, pushed up, and dusted himself off. He glanced down to the wayglass. The lodestone had stopped spinning round and now pointed down the tunnel. He sighed and placed his hopes that it meant something.

"So be it."

He headed along the narrowing passageway, only to discover in another hundred steps that the tunnel had shattered into a slide of broken rocks and sand that cut even deeper. He checked his wayglass. The lodestone still pointed straight ahead, down the precarious ramp of scree and sharp boulders.

His fingers gripped the wayglass with frustration.

"My arse if I'm traipsing down there."

Exasperated more than scared, he swung angrily away. As he did so, the feeble flame at his hip blew out. Darkness collapsed onto him.

No, no, no . . .

The blackness drove him to his knees, then to his palms. He gasped and quaked. He squeezed his eyes closed, then open again, struggling to see, refusing to accept his fate.

"Not like this," he mumbled.

He rolled onto his backside and hugged his knees.

Though godless, he prayed to the entire pantheon. To the Mother Below and the Father Above, to the silvery Son and the dark Daughter, to the shrouded Modron and the bright Bel, to the giant Pywll who held up the skies and the lowly Nethyn who hid deep in the Urth. He continued, leaving no one out, begging everyone in the Litany. He stuttered this way across every prayer taught to him on his mum's knee.

Then, as if someone heard him, a faint glow rose ahead. He rubbed a knuckle against his straining eyes. At first, he thought it was some figment dredged up by his fear. But it did not go away. Maybe it had always been there.

He shifted to his knees and crawled forward. As he reached the edge of the chasm, his hands knocked loose a rock and sent it tumbling down the slope. The shine—a faint pearlescent blue—rose from the bottom. He did not know what created that glow. All that mattered was that it was a haven from the darkness, a bright port in a dark storm.

With a jangle of his ankle chains, he swung his legs forward into the chasm, gritted his teeth, and set off down the steep slope. The way was treacherous, the descent precarious.

Still . . .

Anything is better than this infernal darkness.

5

BLOODY AND BONE-BRUISED, Rhaif slid down the last of the rockfall. He dug in his sliced heels and drew himself to a stop at a towering fresh-cracked slab of black brimstan. Ten times his height, it rose from the white chalk floor like the fin of a monstrous Fell shark.

The glow rose from its other side.

As he gulped down his fear, he swiped away strands of sweat-plastered auburn hair and tucked them under the felt hat that protected his head. He rose into a wary crouch. He did his best to pull up his breeches, the bottom all but ripped away, and tightened the short leather vest over his roughspun shirt.

He did not know what awaited him ahead, but he did his best to ready himself.

An acrid odor filled the lower reaches of the chasm, like burnt chalk and oil. He took short whiffs, fearing it might be poisonous. He had witnessed miners being lowered into a deep shaft—a pit that was safe the day before—only to fall into a stupor or die from air gone bad.

After several breaths, all seemed well, so he continued ahead.

He edged around the brimstan outcropping and peeked at what lay beyond its shoulder. It took him several blinks to make sense of it. The raw chalk wall ahead looked like a shattered mirror, the cracks all radiating out from a crumpled copper egg near its base. The egg appeared to have been cracked open long ago, its edges blackened and torn.

The shine rose from inside it.

He squinted but could make out no details from this distance.

"Just go look," he told himself.

"Maybe I'd better not," he argued just as forcefully.

He chewed his lip, then nodded and set out toward the mystery. With each step, the bitter burnt odor grew. He gaped at the wall ahead of him. His gaze followed the cracks into the darkness overhead. A worry grew.

Could this be the source of the earlier quake?

If so, he feared any misstep could bring it all crashing down atop him. His pace slowed but didn't stop. Curiosity drove him forward. He could not resist knowing the truth. It was that or retreating into eternal darkness.

So, he kept going.

As he neared the shattered opening, the walls of copper looked polished and seamless and over two hands' breadths thick. Cringing, he noted something at the edge of the egg. A skeleton lay sprawled just outside, half buried in chalk, as if drowning in the rock. The hue of the bone was not white or a hoary yellow, but a dull greenish blue. He knew the color was not a trick of the glow, but some alchymy of pyrites and minerals that had infused into the bone over untold centuries.

He skirted the dead, touching fingertips from forehead to lips to heart in solemn respect, lest he wake the spirit trapped here. He reached the blasted opening of the egg, wanting—no, *needing*—to know what cast such a sheen in the dark.

He bowed his way under the copper lintel, all twisted and scorched, and pushed into the glow. What he saw froze him in place.

Gods below . . .

The inside of the egg was the same seamless copper, like a glass bubble blown by the subterranean goddess Nethyn. Its inner surface shone from a complicated web of glass piping and copper joinery. A golden fluid bubbled through those tubes. But the true source of the glow was on the far side, where it seemed all that contrivance led. A shape stood within a glowing glass alcove, like a shining bronze spider in a web.

What manner of god or daemon is this?

Despite the cold terror, he could not look away.

The figure was a woman, sculpted of bronze, as seamless as the copper shell. Her face was a handsome oval, her hair a smooth plait of the same bronze. Her limbs were long and shapely, with hands clasped at the belly, hiding her privacy. Her breasts, though mere suggestions, added a subtle beauty.

It was a masterwork of a skilled artisan.

But it was the expression that captured his attention. Her closed eyes hinted at a hidden grace, while the shape and fullness of her lips suggested a profound sadness, as if somehow Rhaif had already disappointed her.

"Who are you?" he whispered.

With his soft words, eyelids parted, revealing—

A shout rose behind him.

He ducked and searched around. As a thief, his first instinct was to hide when exposed. He followed that instinct, hurried out of the egg, and dove behind a nest of chalk boulders to the immediate left. The rocks were unusually warm, hot to the touch. Still, he tucked himself in tight. A glance to the side revealed that the chalk that rimmed the egg was blackened and scorched. He lifted a hand toward the surface. His refuge was close enough to the side of the egg that he could touch the curve of copper on this side. With his palm raised, he felt no heat wafting from the metal. He tested a fingertip, then the rest of his hand against the cool copper, confirming the same.

Strangeness upon strangeness.

Under his palm, he felt a faint vibration. More shouts drew his attention back up the slope, where a score of lamps and torches now lit the upper tunnel. Orders were barked. The lights began to descend down the rockfall. As Rhaif waited, the vibration of the egg faded to his touch. Even the faint glow ebbed into darkness.

His hiding spot did not allow him to see inside any longer.

Still, he pictured the bronze statue in its glass alcove. He would've sworn it had responded to his voice, its eyelids opening. He gave a small shake of his head at such nonsense.

Just a trick of the light.

In short order, the searchers descended to the bottom of the slope. After so long in the gloom, Rhaif had to blink away the glare of their bright lamps and flaming torches. He kept low, tight to the shadows. But all focus appeared to be on the egg. No one seemed to be looking for him, an escaped prisoner, as he had initially feared. In their haste, they must have missed the telltale signs of his trespass.

At their forefront strode a pair of thick-muscled overseers, dressed in their hooded blue cloaks with short-whips at their belts. They carried lanterns high. Behind them came a clutch of enslaved miners. A few held torches aloft, but they all had pickaxes and hammers strapped to their backs.

But it was the last member of the party that nearly drew a gasp from Rhaif. The figure shoved to the front. The man was far taller and thinner than the others. His long silver-white hair had been braided and tied in a noose around his neck. He wore a long gray robe with its hood tossed back. His exposed eyes were banded by the stripe of a black tattoo. It was said to imitate a blindfold, representing such men's ability to see what all others were blind to. Across his chest, he wore a thick leather bandolier, studded with iron, and lined by square pouches, each etched with symbols.

Rhaif hunkered lower.

None of the chained miners even dared look in the man's direction.

How could they?

Here stood a holy Shrive.

It cannot be.

Rhaif had only heard rumors of such a secretive sect. They were rarely seen. It was claimed most of the Shriven were hundreds of years old, though this figure looked no more than a decade or two older than Rhaif.

"Stay here," the Shrive ordered, and went alone into the now dark egg.

The overseers flanked the opening, while the miners in tow nervously shuffled their ankle chains.

The Shrive entered with no lamp, lantern, or torch. Still, from inside the egg, strange lights flared. A soft chanting echoed out—then an eerie high-pitched cry set Rhaif's teeth to aching. Everyone outside cringed and covered their ears as best they could.

With Rhaif's palm still resting on the copper shell, he felt the metal momentarily vibrate—then go quiet again.

A white smoke billowed out of the egg, reeking of bitter alchymies. It drove the others away from the opening. From that cloud, the Shrive reappeared. His features were dispassionate, but sweat pebbled his brow.

He stepped to one of the overseers, a man Rhaif now recognized as the head maestrum of the mines. "Have your team remove the statue and come with me." Those tattooed eyes hardened. "And take great care."

"Your will is ours," the man promised.

Before the Shrive swept past, he leaned closer to the maestrum. His next words were meant only for the man's ears, though Rhaif eavesdropped from his hiding place. "Afterward, none must know."

The Shrive's gaze swept over the chained men.

The maestrum bowed his head, a hand coming to rest on the hilt of the curved dagger sheathed at his waist. "It will be done."

Rhaif sank deeper into hiding, confused but knowing one certainty.

I should not be here.

BY THE TIME the bronze goddess was hauled out of the shell and up the treacherous slope, Rhaif's knees ached from crouching for so long. It took all six prisoners, three to a side, to carry her to the mouth of the tunnel. The Shrive kept alongside them, while the maestrum trailed, whip in hand.

A second overseer remained behind to guard the copper egg and its secrets. Rhaif sneered. He knew Overseer Muskin all too well. In Rhaif's pocket, he carried the man's wayglass. The overseer had taken clear pleasure in removing the fingers of his crew as punishment for the theft, searing their stumps with a smoldering brand. The prisoner who finally confessed—false though it was—had his throat slit.

Rhaif felt the press of the wayglass in his pocket. While his thievery might be partly to blame for the others' suffering, he carried no guilt for the torture and death. Such harsh punishment was ill-fitting for a petty crime. *Even down here.* Rhaif had thought Muskin would've simply believed he'd misplaced the wayglass or lost it. Rhaif had not accounted for Muskin's pleasure at inflicting pain, of burning his mark on those beneath him.

From his hiding place, Rhaif watched the lights vanish into the tunnel above, one after the other, until the world shrank again down to the single pool of light from Muskin's lantern on the floor. The overseer stalked back and forth before the egg, clearly not happy to be left behind, even less so about the press of shadows. From the man's nervous glances and how he jumped with every rasp of sifting sand or tumble of loose rock, Muskin was similarly afflicted as Rhaif by the threat of darkness.

Rhaif waited for his chance.

It was not long in coming.

The man's tenseness worked its way down to his bladder. The warning signs were evident enough from the growing agitation to his pacing, the occasional clutch at his privates. Finally, Muskin swore and headed to the far side of the egg. He grumbled as he unhooked his breeches to free himself.

Rhaif waited for the splashing and relieved groan. He then slipped from his boulders, and with all the stealth gained from his many years as a thief, he crept up behind Muskin. Without even a single clink of his chains, he stopped in the man's shadow.

He eyed the hilt of Muskin's sheathed dagger.

Quick now, he urged himself.

Still, Rhaif hesitated. He had never killed a man before. Yet, he knew only death would free him from here. He could not risk a shout drawing the others back.

He gulped and reached out a hand.

As he did, a rumble sounded behind him. A trickling avalanche skidded down the slope. Muskin flinched and swung around. His stream splashed wildly, even more so when he spotted Rhaif standing there.

The overseer snatched for his whip, and Rhaif lunged for the man's dagger. They both gained their weapons. Muskin's face purpled with anger, his chest swelling toward a bellow. Rhaif could not wait. Nimble and fast, he sprang at the man. Muskin, still addled, tried to block him and failed. Rhaif drove the blade through the overseer's throat. The point burst out the other side of his neck.

The damage done, Rhaif jumped back.

Muskin dropped his whip and pawed at the impaled knife—then he fell to his knees with a gurgle that turned bloody. His eyes went huge, both surprised yet knowing the truth.

Rhaif backed away, horrified and shaking all over.

"I'm sor . . . sorry," he mumbled.

While the overseer deserved a harsh end, Rhaif had not wanted to be the one to deliver it. He had witnessed countless deaths, but none by his own hand.

Rhaif took another step away.

Muskin's end took far longer than Rhaif would have wished. Long after the man toppled on his side, blood continued to pool and spread. His chest rose and fell. Rhaif stared unblinking until all movement stopped with a last rattled sigh.

Rhaif took another three breaths of his own before finally approaching the body. To the side, the bluish skull on the floor stared its empty sockets at him. He touched his fingertips from forehead, to lips, to heart. It was less this time to ward off spirits than it was to settle himself to the task at hand.

With this death, Rhaif had committed himself to one course.

Escape or suffer a worse fate than Muskin.

"Get on with it," he whispered.

Working swiftly, he searched Muskin's body and found the keys to his ankle irons. As miners were commonly shifted from one crew to another, the locks were typically the same. Still, he huffed with relief when the chains fell from his legs. He felt a hundred stone lighter.

Encouraged, he stripped Muskin of his blue overseer cloak and used the man's waterskin to rinse away the worst of the blood. Once satisfied, he set about trading clothes with the dead man, including the short boots to hide his scarred ankles.

Lastly, he hauled on the overseer's wide belt and secured the whip and dagger. He inspected himself one final time and pulled up the cloak's hood to shadow his features.

He started to collect the lantern from the floor, then remembered.

He returned to his pile of clothes and fished out the wayglass. He was about to return it to the same pocket from which he had pinched it when he noted the lodestone no longer pointed toward the egg. Instead, it pointed in the opposite direction, toward the tunnel where the bronze woman had been hauled away.

Strange.

Rhaif set back along the same course, climbing the slope with care.

He reached the tunnel and followed the scuff of bare feet and boots. It was an easy trail to follow. He knew this path would eventually lead him to the mine proper. Still, he did not hurry. He had no intention of catching up with the others. He knew—once he got his bearings—he would split along another course. Using his disguise and keeping his face hidden, he would do his best to escape the mine and flee.

If he failed, it would mean his death—and an end far worse than the one Muskin had suffered. Like all prisoners, Rhaif knew the punishment for a prisoner who tried to escape. When he had first been dragged into the mines of Chalk, he had noted the rows of decaying, bird-plucked bodies, all impaled from arse to mouth, that lined the entrance.

His pace increased with the memory. He had to force himself to slow. Overseers—the lords of the mines—did not rush about. And now was certainly not the time to be hasty. Even when disguised, it would take stealth and artifice to safely make his escape.

As he hiked the tunnels, he pictured his freedom and all that it entailed—but the serene face of the bronze goddess kept intruding.

"It's not my concern," he intoned.

But deep down, he suspected he was wrong.

6

RHAIF HAD NEVER been happier to hear the crack of a whip.

The pained cry that followed echoed down the dark tunnel to him. He took heed of the warning. It meant he was nearing the mine proper. He re-checked his stolen clothes and pulled his cloak's hood farther over his head.

At last . . .

He had been following the trail of the others for at least two bells. He wagered it must be close to last meal. The fare was usually a maggoty gruel, crusts of bread, and maybe a sliver of hard cheese or sometimes the rind of a melon left over from feeding the oxen. Still, his empty stomach growled in complaint at missing out.

"Hush," he whispered. "I'll feed you later."

Taking an extra bit of caution, he trimmed the lamp's oil taper and squeezed the flame to a flicker. Shadows drew more tightly around him. He knew he had to hurry.

If it was indeed close to last meal, that meant the hundreds of overseers would be corralling their charges into the various gaols and afterward heading topside, leaving only a bare few to watch over the mines.

Rhaif intended to leave with them.

He continued to follow the trail that skirted along the edge of the busy core of the mine. Clearly the Shrive did not want to be spotted, let alone draw attention to the mystery hauled forth from the copper egg.

For now, that worked for Rhaif, too.

The rumble and grind of the mine grew ever louder. Soon a constant hammering echoed from all directions, discordant and arrhythmic, interrupted by barked orders and harsh laughter. It was all undercut by a cacophony of squealing wheels on iron tracks and the strident whistles from the mine's many shafts, where tubs full of chalk and kohl were hauled upward or lowered empty.

Rhaif had long grown accustomed to it, barely heard it any longer, like the beat of his own heart. But not now. His ears strained for every note of this dark chorale of misery and hardship, listening both for any hint of discovery and to orient himself to his location.

He was fairly certain he had his bearings. His nose picked out the scent of the burning brimstan from the smelting fires topside, which only could be smelled near the main shaft.

I must be close.

He tightened his jaw. Muskin's body could be discovered at any moment. When that happened, the mine would ring with gongs and every shaft would be sealed or guarded. Then the hissing thylassaurs would be set loose on the trail, following the blood scent with their flared nostrils and running down their prey.

Namely me.

Rhaif checked the damp side of his cloak. The bloodstain had mostly dried, making it almost indistinguishable from the blue of the cloth. But it would not fool the sharp nose of a thylassaur. Knowing that, he dared wait no longer.

Now or never.

He tightened a fist and abandoned the trail. He took the next tunnel that aimed for the heart of the mine. As he rounded the corner, focused still on his stolen cloak, he ran square into a pair of hulking overseers coming his way.

Startled, he stumbled backward—only to have his shoulder grabbed, his cloak bunched in a scarred fist. Rhaif was sure his ruse had been exposed. Still, he kept his head down.

"You're with us," the overseer said, and marched past him, dragging Rhaif along.

He dared not resist but tried his best. "I . . . dumped my crew and was headed topside."

"That can wait," the man's partner said. "Work's not done yet."

Rhaif was released and was plainly expected to follow. He obeyed but he trailed by a few steps. In another few breaths, he found himself back in the tunnel he had abandoned a moment ago.

It seems I'm destined to walk this path.

The overseers grumbled to each other, looking no more pleased than Rhaif about this extra duty.

"What's all this tumult about anyway, you think, Hrahl?"

A heavy shrug. "Best not to be too curious, Berryl."

Rhaif wished he himself had heeded that wisdom earlier.

Berryl leaned closer. "Word is that there are Shriven about?"

The other scowled. "What did I just a'say?"

The pair looked to be brothers, both black-haired with thick noses, fleshy lips, and pinched eyes from years of squinting at the endless sun glaring off sand and rock. Only the crisscrossing of scars mapped their faces differently.

Rhaif's mother was from across the seas, from the highland forests of the Cloudreach. He only had vague memories of her. She had been svelte, with fiery hair and pale skin. She was nothing like the folks in the territories with their dark sun-burnished complexions and beefy frames. From such a commingling, Rhaif ended up slightly taller and thinner of limb than most. His hair was a ruddy auburn, his features less rocky. Best of all, he had been born with his mother's natural gift of agility, speed, and balance. It was why he had been so readily recruited into the guild at a young age. *Slippery as a fresh-oiled eel,* Llyra had once described him, encompassing both his body and his skills.

"Be's quiet now," Hrahl warned, nudging and pointing ahead.

Their two bulky forms blocked Rhaif's view. He heard voices carry back to him from the tunnel. He recognized the low tones of the Shrive, accompanied by the cowed acquiescence of the mine's maestrum.

Rhaif inwardly winced.

Can't rid myself of these pevvy swinks.

The maestrum called over to them. "You two, take this lot to the privy gaol uppaways. Wait for me there with them."

A clank and rattle of chains announced the presence of the doomed miners. Rhaif remembered the whispered words of the Shrive, the maestrum's palm resting atop his dagger. Rhaif wanted to shout a warning, but what would that accomplish?

Only get me killed, too.

Hrahl and Berryl grunted their assent. They hurried forward, exposing Rhaif to the attention of both the maestrum and the Shrive. He kept his face low, which was not unusual in the rare presence of such a holy man, someone who had achieved the status of Highcryst in both alchymy and the religious orders.

Even the two brothers hurried past with hardly a glance.

The maestrum turned away with a command for Rhaif: "And you help me with this."

The Shrive stood bent over the figure of the bronze statue. It had been laid atop a wheeled flatcart. The man's hands hovered over the gilded shape, not touching, as if he were warming his palms over a fire.

He finally straightened and turned enough to reveal the black tattoo across his eyes. "Follow me," he ordered, and led the way into a side passageway. "And be alert, Maestrum Keel."

Keel waved Rhaif to his side. "Get your arse over here."

Knowing he could not refuse without drawing attention, Rhaif hurried over. The flatcart had a front and rear handgrip. Keel took hold of the one at the back. Without being told, Rhaif edged around the cart to reach the other.

Together they set off along the tunnel, Rhaif pulling and Keel pushing.

AFTER A TIME, as they rolled after the Shrive, Rhaif found his gaze returning to the bronze figure. He studied her unblemished form, free of any tarnish. He was awed by the curve and smooth suppleness of her shape. He kept returning to her face. He remembered the serenity captured there, only now from this angle, it looked slightly less peaceful. The perfect brow bore no crease but looked close to pinching with concern. And the full lips appeared drawn thinner. He cocked his head back and forth, squinting at those eyelids. He remembered thinking they had started to open, but now they were plainly sealed, fused even, showing no gaps.

He noted tinier details. Fine wires, a darker bronze, represented delicate lashes. Even her hair—which he had thought was a solid plait—was made of an intricate twining of bronze filaments.

It made no sense to him.

Why go to such detail?

The cart bumped over a ridge in the floor, interrupting his reverie.

"Watch yourself!" Keel warned. "I'll stripe your hide if any harm is done."

Rhaif grumbled an apology and focused on the path behind the robed Shrive. He guided the cart to as smooth of a course as possible. Only now did he realize he was lost again. The Shrive was leading them into a maze of ever-narrowing passageways. It was a section of the mine that Rhaif hadn't known existed.

The walls here had drifted from white chalk to a dark glassy stone. There were no ax or chisel marks. The tunnel looked less like it had been dug out as melted through.

Where are we?

He risked a glance toward Keel. Even the maestrum looked disconcerted, his gaze nervously sweeping the tunnel, as if he had never been here either.

Finally, the Shrive led them to where the tunnel ended at a bronze door. Black diamonds had been imbedded in its surface, forming a curled asp crowned in thorns. All knew that foul mark: the *horn'd snaken,* the sigil of the dark god Ðreyk.

Rhaif gave the Shrive a harder look as the man hauled open the thick door. While the Shriven were a reclusive bunch, there were rumors of a cabal within the order, called the Iflelen, who pursued forbidden arts, ancient magicks and spylls of the darkest nature, and alchymies even blacker still. It was said the Iflelen worshipped Ðreyk, marking their efforts with the *horn'd snaken*. Whispers spoke of blood rites, burnt sacrifices, and the summoning of daemons.

Rhaif wanted to run and keep running. But he caught a firm scowl from Keel. The maestrum's expression was easy to read.

Move and you die.

With the door open, the Shrive stepped through and waved for them to follow. "Bring the statue to the center."

Rhaif balked, but Keel pushed the cart, ramming it into him. With no other choice, Rhaif guided the statue across the threshold. The next room was a circular chamber with a domed roof. All the glassy surfaces had been polished into a thousand-faceted mirror, reflecting everything, which dazzled the eye and confused the gaze. It was like walking into the eye of an oxfly.

The view was further confounded by the clutch of figures that swept down upon their group, circling the cart. Their movements, reflected all around, churned his stomach.

Rhaif had to look away. He focused on the cart and statue. But from the corner of his eye, he spotted a shuffle of robes and faces banded in black.

More Shriven.

The one who led them here met three others. They spoke rapidly in a tongue Rhaif did not know. The others were all far older, wrinkled and pocked. One's features looked more skull than flesh.

Then another figure jostled forward.

Rhaif's fingers tightened on the cart's iron handle.

The gods have surely cursed me.

The last of the group was a black-haired man. He was tall with a pointed face, his chin and cheeks shadowed by a trimmed and oiled beard. He wore silken trousers, polished boots, and an embroidered leather vest. He also carried a sheathed sword at his hip, the pommel topped by a priceless diadem of sky-iron.

Two years ago, Rhaif had tried to steal that blade.

He lowered his face and shook the edges of his hood lower. He did not know if the archsheriff of Anvil would remember him, but Rhaif dared not risk being recognized.

Not here, not now.

What is Laach doing in Chalk, a hundred leagues south of Anvil?

A clue came from the man's next words as he stepped up to the cart with the Shriven. "I don't understand. How could this accursed object turn the tides of the coming war?"

Rhaif frowned within his hood. Before he was sentenced to Chalk, there had been rumblings of a conflict between the northern Kingdom of Hálendii and the lands of the Southern Klashe. Apparently, over the past couple years, tensions had worsened.

One of the Shriven attempted to answer Laach's query. "We will need further study, but what we have fathomed—"

He was cut off by the Shrive who had led Rhaif here. "Best to let our conjectures and speculations rest, Skerren," he intoned. "Until we know more."

The other's eyes narrowed to slits, but his head bowed. "Yes, until we know more," Skerren repeated. "You are indeed correct, Wryth."

Clearly the leader among them, Wryth turned to another of his brethren. "Now that we have confirmation, go prepare what we need."

A nod answered him. "We've already consecrated a bloodbaerne." He motioned to the Shrive next to him. "We'll fetch it here."

"Very good."

The two set off toward a small door on the far side of the room.

As they waited, Wryth turned to Archsheriff Laach, but his gaze fixed to the statue. "We registered its stirrings seven days ago. It's what drew us all here."

"Why was I not alerted at that time?"

"We wished to be certain first. And as you've witnessed, you arrived at a fortuitous time. What with the quake erupting as you entered the mine. Maybe your presence even played a fateful role. If so, it would suggest the Lord Đreyk deems you one of great importance and worth."

Laach stood straighter. All of Anvil knew that the archsheriff held himself in the highest esteem and absorbed praise like a watered weed. Still, the sick set of his lips revealed a measure of his uneasiness at this particular honor.

All knew, it was seldom good to draw the gaze of the dark god.

Laach swallowed hard and pointed to the statue. "What do you propose to do with it now?"

"A simple test. To ensure the ancient texts prove true."

"And after that?"

"I suspect we'll need at least another moon's time—maybe twice that— before we will know if there is any value in this artifact beyond academic."

The door at the back opened again, and the two Shriven returned, leading a huge Gyn. Rhaif gaped at the hulking servant who had to bow through the doorway. Bald-headed and craggy-faced, he looked more like a boulder that had sprouted rocky arms and legs. He was naked, except for a loincloth. His muscles rolled under the hairy mat of his chest and legs. Rhaif had rarely seen such tribesmen. They hailed from the steppes of northern Aglerolarpok, a land far to the west. The Gyn were considered dull-witted, often used for the hardest of labors. But this man bore a hundred brands scarred into his flesh, ancient alchymies of submission and control.

The figure pushed a rolling cart, twice the size of those used to haul ore. Atop it rose a complicated stack of steel, bronze, and copper structures, like a tiny version of a shining city. Each was connected and intertwined to its neighbor by a baffling labyrinth of copper tubes. Throughout, toothed gears turned in some arcane spectacle, perhaps driven by magick or alchymy.

At the back rose a glass cylinder bubbling with a golden elixir. It reminded Rhaif of the fluid coursing across the inside of that infernal copper egg. Only here, there was no glow or sheen.

The Gyn and two Shriven drew abreast of their group. Only then did Rhaif spot what lay at the heart of the contrivance. A young woman, barely older than a girl, lay on her back, imbedded within the monstrous contrivance, as if she were the foundations of this dread city. But that was not the worst horror.

Rhaif gasped and backed away. He couldn't help it. But his reaction was ignored, especially as Keel did the same. Even the archsheriff paled and lifted a hand to his throat.

The Gyn pushed the cart alongside the bronze figure.

Rhaif wanted to look away, but dismay gripped him. The girl had a window cut into her chest, exposing a beating heart and a pair of lungs billowing in and out. A tube ran into her mouth, connected to a set of moving bellows, not unlike those found at a smith's forge.

The only bit of mercy found here was that the girl looked gone from this world, alive but not here. Her glassy eyes stared blankly at the domed roof. Her entrapped limbs did not fight the steel and bronze that bound her in place.

"What . . . What is this?" Laach asked, stepping forward and lowering his hand from his throat as his horror faded.

"A bloodbaerne," Shrive Wryth explained. "You need not understand. Few do beyond our circle. But it will serve as the test I mentioned."

Wryth circled to the tall cylinder and manipulated something back there. As he did so, a darkness flowed into the golden fluid. It spiraled and spread. The exposed heart of the girl began to beat faster, as if in panic.

Rhaif returned his attention to the darkening cylinder and recognized what contaminated the golden fluid.

Blood.

Pumped into the chamber by the girl's own heart.

As they waited, the Shriven whispered in their arcane tongue, occasionally pointing or peering closer. It did not take long before the beating heart slowed and finally diminished to a shivering quiver—then stopped. The lungs lost their air and sank into the chest.

Wryth nodded, clearly satisfied. He stepped around, drawing forth a tube that draped back to the dark cylinder. He crossed to the statue, and with the help of the Shrive Skerren, the two connected the tube to the figure's navel.

Wryth then nodded to another, who pulled a lever.

With an ominous moan, the cylinder drained, emptying its elixir through the tube and into the hollows of the statue's belly. Once it was finished, Wryth unhooked the tube and tossed it back to the cart. The Shrive's attention remained on the statue.

"What's supposed to happen?" Laach asked.

"Patience," Wryth whispered. "We shall see."

Rhaif held his breath—then a soft sheen brightened the bronze, so subtle only Rhaif seemed to note it. None of the others reacted. He gulped and wanted to back away, but feared drawing attention.

The sheen seemed to warm the coppery bronze. While the metal remained unmoving and hard, the reflection of the room's lanterns off its surface shimmered and flowed, refracting the light into brighter hues of crimson, azure, and emerald, like oil spreading over water.

Gasps rose from the others now. Some drew nearer, others retreated.

Rhaif kept his spot.

As he watched, one of the folded hands lifted, drawing up an arm.

Stunned, they all withdrew, except for Rhaif. He remained transfixed at the wonder of it all. He remembered those eyes opening earlier. As if stirred by the memory, those lids parted again, shining forth with a golden light.

I hadn't imagined it.

The bronze head turned, swiveling slightly to one side.

The archsheriff shifted away, as if to avoid that gaze. He kissed his fingertips and touched each ear in a warding against evil.

Rhaif simply stared, suddenly wanting to see what was behind that golden glow. But it was not to be. The brightness dimmed in those eyes and the lids sank back closed. The arm fell back to its side. All the magick seemed to fade from its form. Even the shimmer of radiant oil returned to a dull bronze.

No one moved. No one spoke for several stunned breaths.

"What was that?" Laach asked, his voice pitched high. "What manner of daemon did you summon into this shell?"

"Not summoned," Wryth said. *"Woken."*

"What is your intent with it?" Laach pressed.

Wryth's answer was full of dark hunger. "It may take another moon or two before we can answer that. Countless more bloodbaerne sacrifices."

Rhaif glanced to the dead woman and shivered under his cloak.

Laach scowled, looking dissatisfied, but also pale with terror. "I cannot wait in the depths of Chalk for such a long span. I've matters to attend in Anvil."

"As you should. Return to your duties and leave us to our own work. I will dispatch a skrycrow, keep you abreast of our progress. We have much to study."

"I will leave you to it then." The archsheriff turned on a heel and headed stiffly toward the back door. He looked anxious to be rid of this place.

Rhaif narrowed his gaze as Laach departed.

Does that door lead to another way out of the mines, one kept secret from most?

Before he could ponder it further, the Shrive Skerren addressed Wryth. "I would like to assess where the artifact was preserved. It might give us some guidance on how best to proceed from here."

The others also mumbled their consent.

Even Wryth nodded. "It's a trip well worth taking, I assure you. I had to hurry earlier. And haste is the scourge to knowledge."

Rhaif kept his face passive, but his chest squeezed tighter. He pictured the copper egg—and the body sprawled in a pool of blood at its entrance. He prayed the Shriven would put this off for another day.

Wryth ruined this hope with his next words. "I'll take you now. I'm anxious myself to study it more."

He headed toward the main door, drawing the others with him, even the hulking form of the Gyn. He stopped long enough to point to Maestrum Keel. "See to the prisoners from earlier. They must not share what we discovered."

Keel bowed and prepared to follow. "It will be done."

Rhaif took a step after them, but instead he drew Wryth's attention.

"You remain here," the Shrive instructed. "Guard the chamber. None must enter."

Following the maestrum's example, Rhaif bowed. "It . . . It will be done."

With that, the others reached the entrance, filed out, and slammed the bronze door behind them.

Alone now, Rhaif turned to the statue on the flatcart and the cooling body of the poor sacrifice. His lantern, still hanging at his hip, reflected a thousand times in the mirrored facets.

He crossed over to the bronze woman.

"I can't seem to escape you," he whispered.

He remembered how the wayglass's lodestone had directed him toward her, then continued to point after her, as if fixed to her, drawn to her. He could not dismiss a similar pull in his own chest. Whether it was simple curiosity or something more profound, he felt a connection, as if massive gears had turned the skies and the Urth to bring them together.

He shook his head at such delusions, especially for a lowly thief from Anvil. He pushed down such thoughts. He did not intend to stay a moment longer. With time running short, his best course was to seek another way out of the mines of Chalk—hopefully through that back door that Laach had used.

Still, Rhaif stepped next to the flatcart.

He reached and touched the hand that had lifted earlier, its movement fueled by forbidden alchymies. He found the bronze weirdly warm, but still hard and stiff—which made his heart sink.

What were you expecting, you daft swink?

He lifted his palm and turned toward the back door, knowing he must hurry.

Before he could move away, he felt a touch—then warm fingers closed over his hand.

7

AGHAST AT THE sight of bronze fingers latched on to his, Rhaif yanked his arm back—only to have the grip tighten and trap him. He tried again, but the more he pulled, the more those fingers squeezed. Fearing he might end up with a crushed hand, he relented.

"What do you want?" he gasped at the figure.

The bronze grip grew warmer, the metal going strangely softer.

He gulped and searched around. He stared at the door through which he had hoped to escape. It looked an impossible distance away, especially anchored down by a bronze statue. Still, he knew it wouldn't be long before the gongs of discovery would be ringing. He had to be gone before they let loose the pack of thylassaurs.

"Let go," he pleaded. "I have to escape."

With a wince, he tugged again, expecting a crush of bone. But the grip remained the same—only the response was much worse.

The bronze figure stirred on the cart. The waist bent, lifting her upright, though it took two attempts, requiring her to prop her other arm under her. The head rolled atop its shoulder, as if stretching a kink, and the drape of filamentous hairs shivered, falling loose like any woman's coif.

Then eyes, framed by long delicate lashes, opened.

He cringed back, expecting to see into the fires of damnation. But instead he found eyes not unlike his own staring back at him, only glassier, with pupils of azure blue that seemed to glow faintly—though the last could be his panicked imagination. That gaze found him, flicking from his trapped hand to his face.

Her head cocked in plain curiosity. Her lips parted, showing a glimpse of bone-white teeth. Her other hand rose and touched those lips, her bronze brow wrinkling, as if sculpted of tanned flesh.

Rhaif noted the fingers clasped to him felt soft and warm.

What manner of daemon has animated this statue?

As much as he should be horrified, he could not look away as she continued to wake. Had she been feigning earlier, perhaps sensing the ill intent of those gathered around her? He knew of many beasts that would pretend to be dead to ward off predators. Or had she simply been building her strength, stoking the alchymies into a mightier fire to rouse her fully?

He could not know—but down deep, he suspected her stirring was meant for him alone. Her eyes continued to stare at him, as if appraising him.

As she did, her hand shifted from her lips and gently combed fingers through her bronze locks, which had taken on a darker sheen as if tarnished. Then with an arch of her back, which lifted her small breasts higher, she swung her legs from the cart to the floor.

He backed to the length of their two joined arms.

She stood, shakily at first. He stared down at her toes, inscribed with fine nails. She began to lose her balance, teetering and leaning toward him.

He tried to steady her, but her weight came close to dropping him to his knees. Despite her animated appearance, she remained as heavy as a statue. Still, he caught her arm with his free hand and helped keep her upright. It took all the strength in his legs and back.

"I got you," he whispered.

She finally straightened, finding her ease.

He studied her countenance. Ages ago, he had visited the Holy Kath'dral in Anvil. Adorning its main nave, a towering stained-glass window displayed the pantheon of the gods. While the Mother Below had been depicted with a loving expression, the Daughter's face was as hard as the glass, resolute and unforgiving. She carried a bow in hand and a quiver of arrows across her back. She was sometimes also called the Huntress.

Rhaif stared at the bronze figure, naked and unashamed. From visage to shape, it was as if the Daughter herself had been given form on Urth.

As wondrous as this all was, Rhaif recognized the press of time. He swallowed and tried again. "I must go."

He headed toward the smaller door at the rear of the chamber, while trying to free his hand. She refused to let go. Instead, she followed his steps, keeping abreast of him.

Rhaif exhaled in relief.

Good enough for now.

He continued across the chamber, fearing she might stop at any moment and anchor him in place again. He sensed he needed to keep her moving, like a boulder rolling down a hill. Still, he did not hurry, lest she lose her balance. As he led her, her gaze swept the room, her face hard and unreadable.

He reached the door and found it unlocked. He hauled it open and got them both through into a small anteroom. The reek of blood and bowel struck his nose. Even the bronze woman recoiled.

To the left was a stone table with shackles. Blood pooled around it. On the floor, as if tossed aside, was a square of bone, flesh, and skin. Rhaif pictured the poor girl, the bloodbaerne sacrifice.

The bronze woman stepped toward the bloody remains, but Rhaif restrained her—or, considering how much she weighed, at least discouraged her. "No, there's nothing we can do."

A glance to the other side revealed a pile of discarded clothes: worn leather sandals, a shapeless beige shift, and an overcloak that looked more patches than cloth.

Must've belonged to the sacrificed girl.

Rhaif urged the bronze woman over to the pile. "You need to dress. Can't have you traipsing around bare-assed to the world."

He certainly couldn't sneak off with a walking bronze statue next to him. She cocked her head, her expression quizzical.

Gods, woman, must I do everything?

He pantomimed with one hand, and with some guidance, he got the shift over her head. Slowly, she grew to understand his intent. She let go of his hand long enough to drape the dress to her knees. She then bent down to the cloak and frowned a moment. Before he could tell her anything, she began to don it.

"Sandals, too," he warned.

No one went barefooted in the territories, not across the ember-hot sands that could blister a sole in two steps. It was one of the reasons the overseers kept the prisoners shoeless, all the better to keep them from running. He stared over at the woman. While he didn't know if such bronze could be damaged by the heat, the oddity of a woman strolling without protection across the scorch would draw unwanted attention.

Then Rhaif finally realized the truth. He looked down at his empty hands.

I'm free.

He glanced to the tunnel that exited the antechamber. He stepped in that direction as the woman struggled with the overcloak. If he ran now, he might get away. Escaping unseen would be far easier without such a mystery in tow.

Still, he closed his eyes with an exasperated sigh, knowing he must stay.

You are such a swink.

He opened his eyes and turned to her as she managed to secure the overcloak. He crossed over and pulled the cloak's hood over her head, doing his best to hide her unnaturalness. He stared into her eyes, which in the shadows of the hood did indeed glow faintly. Her expression—like her bronze form—softened.

An arm rose. He expected her to grip him again, but she only passed the back of her hand across his cheek. The warmth melted into him. Then she lowered her arm and bent down to the discarded sandals.

He helped her don them, then gave her a final inspection. He eyed her up and down as she stood. "As long as no one looks too closely . . ." he muttered, then silently added, *What am I thinking?*

He shrugged and headed toward the tunnel.

He reached it just as a distant ringing echoed. With each breath, it grew louder, spreading throughout the mine.

The gongs.

He glanced back to the bronze countenance.

We're too late.

RHAIF GAVE NO heed to caution. He had no time for a studious assessment of his route. He simply ran, only checking every now and again to see if the woman followed him. She kept pace. Her eyes glowed back at him from the shadow of her cloak's hood. He read no panic in that gaze, which greatly irritated him.

Gods be, I should already be gone.

The clanging gongs chased him down the tunnel. He stuck to what appeared to be the main passageway. Side tunnels cut away, but they appeared smaller, more likely to winnow away to dead ends. Other chambers stood open or were barred shut. He ignored them all—though he was thief enough to wonder what treasures might be buried down in these Shriven halls.

The only promising sign was that the glassy black rock returned to white chalk veined through with dark brimstan. He also felt the tunnel steadily rising. The pressure in his ears eased with every hundred steps. The air turned drier with each panted breath.

Finally, the passageway leveled out and ran for some straight distance. Hoping for the best, he fled faster. He found the end of the tunnel sealed with a door. He ran up to it, his heart choking him with its hammering.

He feared the overseers had already locked this way down, as they would all the exits from the mine once the gongs sounded. Still, he prayed he was in time. He reached the door and tried the latch. It would not give. He fought it some more, but to no avail.

Already barred . . .

He leaned his head against the studded wood, accepting his cursed fate.

Then a hand shoved him aside. The bronze woman placed both palms against the door and pinioned her legs behind her. She braced her limbs, put her shoulder against the frame, and strained harder. Her feet ripped clean out of the leather sandals and dug into the chalk, gouging deep.

Rhaif backed away.

Gods be . . .

Metal groaned—whether door or woman, he could not say. Then came a booming splintering, and the door crashed open. Sunlight blasted into the dark tunnel.

Rhaif lifted a forearm against it but was still blinded. He stumbled out of the tunnel. "Hurry," he urged the woman who had freed him.

They were far from safe.

As he hobbled into the open, he blinked away the glare, needing to get his bearings. Shouts rang out all around. The braying of oxen rose to the right. The pounding of raw ore under hammers was everywhere. Not far off, sifters and washers sang brightly at their slurries and cribles.

Within a few steps, Rhaif's sight returned to reveal the chaos of topside. Past the mine's many pit mouths, a whole village spread. A mix of tents, wooden stables, smithies, foundries, and whorehouses were all set amidst towering hills of mine tailings and waste gob. Ox-driven wagons worked their way through a maze of roads, the paths long ago rutted into the stone by the passing centuries. All about men and women labored: pumpmen, smelters, sorters, carpenters. Others straddled horses or rode hardy Aglero-larpok ponies—a rare sight so far east and said to be worth their weight in silver.

Rhaif glanced behind him to the open door and shattered wood. The entrance was well to the side of the village, far from the nearest pit mouth. No one seemed to have noted their arrival or heard the splintering blast.

Clearly this entrance was meant to be far from prying eyes.

All the better.

"This way," he urged his companion.

He set off on a path to skirt around the village of Chalk. He wanted to keep those hills of barren ore between him and any eyes looking this way. He hurried but did his best not to look rushed or suspicious. He had a goal in mind and intended to reach it.

To his side, the woman slowed. Her face craned to the cloud-scudded sky and the blaze of the sun. She finally stopped, lifting her palms to the same.

He stepped back to her and scolded her, "No time for gaping about."

She ignored him, standing still, seemingly returned to a statue. He was ready to abandon her, but she had broken him out of the mine. He also noticed that the shade of her bronze face had lightened under the sun, same with her palms, as if the sunlight were polishing her brighter. Or maybe it was the Father blessing her, imbuing her with His vital essence.

Then in the distance he heard a familiar howl.

He stiffened and ducked.

Thylassaurs.

He searched back toward the village, squinting at the main pit mouth. He saw a pair of overseers each lead out a trio of leashed thylassaurs. Anyone near fled backward, opening the sight farther. The overseers unshackled two of their oil-furred charges, keeping hold of the third.

The released pair shot out into the village. Each was a quarter the height of a horse and twice as long. Their sinuous, striped bodies snaked through the tents and structures. Their long tails swept the path behind them, casting a musk that wiped away all other scents except one.

Blood.

One—then another—arched onto their hindlimbs. Nostrils were shoved high, flaring with a pink star of fleshy, sensitive feelers. They waggled the air, testing scents. A howl followed. Then another. And another.

Rhaif knew what that meant.

The beasts had caught a whiff of their prey.

He reached over and grabbed a fistful of the bronze woman's cloak. He tugged hard. "Enough! We must go!"

Her face turned from the skies. Her gaze found him, and she gave the barest nod. Together, the two set off across the sand and rock. Rhaif led the way around a hillock of waste ore, pounded and sifted of anything of value ages ago.

The howls of the thylassaurs pursued them, sounding to his ear as if they were drawing ever closer. He searched ahead as they rounded the mountain of broken rock. His ears strained, listening for any warning.

Please, don't have left already.

As he continued, a faint singing wafted over to him from ahead, easily carried across the desert plains that stretched to all the horizons. Then he heard a heavy grind of iron wheels.

No, no, no, no . . .

He increased his pace, though it was likely already futile. He finally rounded the hill and a wide sandy stretch opened. Ahead, some quarter reach away, stretched a chained caravan. A dozen iron-strapped wooden wagons—each filled to the top with brimstan, chalk, and other metalliferous rock—sat atop huge iron wheels fixed to steel rails. The tracks started in the salt mines far to the south and stretched a hundred leagues north, all the way to Anvil. With the day ended, the caravan would make the long sojourn to the trading port, returning the next morning to be filled again.

Rhaif watched the caravan roll along the outskirts of Chalk.

At the front, a pair of giant sandcrabs flanked the tracks, tethered by chains to the lead of the caravan. The black armored beasts were twice the size of the wagons they pulled. The creatures' eight jointed legs ended in spikes that dug into sand and rock. The front pair normally bore scythe-like claws, but those pincers had been clipped long ago when the crabs had been captured in the broken wastes of the deep desert. The two beasts dragged the dozen wains of the caravan behind them. When truly moving, they could outrun the fastest horse across the desert. But for now, the pair started slow, fighting the stubborn wagons from their standstill. It would not take long before that changed.

Seated on the front wagon, the pair's driver—who had been bonded to them long ago—sang them into motion, encouraging them, coaxing them. Unlike the imprisoned miners, they required no whips or cudgels to get them moving. Instead, the lilting strands of the driver's song penetrated their armor and played across their brains. Rhaif did not understand, and he wagered few did. Such a talent was rare and growing even rarer. Such drivers could command a steep price for their service.

Despite the futility, Rhaif chased after the moving caravan. Maybe it might stop, maybe a load needed to be shifted and balanced better. But more than anything he ran as more howls rose along the trail behind him.

He dared not even look over his shoulder as he cleared the hillock and raced across the open sand.

Instead of slowing, the line of the caravan was gaining speed.

Still, he ran—then movement drew his eyes to the right. A lone thylassaur rounded the far side of the rock mound and raced to ambush him. Its sinuous form ran low, arrowing straight at him. From its frothing muzzle, a glint of fangs showed. It would not kill him—that would be too kind an end. Instead, the thylassaurs had been trained to bring down an escaped prisoner, often ripping the back tendons of their legs.

From there, it was straight to the spikes for such a crime, where death would come much more slowly. Many died not from the impalement, but from the flocks of carrion birds and blister-ants scavenging on them, picking them apart with razor-sharp beaks and fiery jaws, while the sufferer screamed and writhed in agony.

Despite the threat, Rhaif found his legs slowing, too exhausted and weak after so much time in the mines. Even terror-stoked fires eventually sputtered and died out.

Then a hard blow struck him across his back and knocked him forward.

Thylassaur . . .

He sprawled headfirst toward the sand, expecting to feel teeth rip into flesh. Instead, an arm hooked around his waist and kept him upright. It hadn't been the thylassaur attacking him. He turned to the bronze woman. She hiked him up, until only his toes still touched, dragging across the sand.

"What're you—"

Then she sped faster, her legs pounding, her toes digging deep. She fled across the sand like a storm-blown dustwhip across the desert. He found his legs trying to match her pace, his feet scrabbling uselessly as the ground flew underfoot.

She sped past the lone thylassaur, who tried to give chase but was swiftly left in the breath of her dust. It howled its frustration after them, echoed by the others.

Ahead, the last wagon of the caravan grew before them.

She chased after it, but even her considerable pace was not enough. With the last wagon only a few dozen steps away, the caravan gained more speed. The wain began to pull away.

So close . . .

Then Rhaif's stomach lurched as she leaped high, bounding like a desert hare from the poisonous strike of an adder. She sailed across the last of the distance and hit the wagon's rear with a jolting impact. He would've been knocked loose, if not for her kidney-bruising grip. Her other hand latched on to the wagon's top frame.

She did her best to push him upward, almost dropping him, but he caught hold and scurried into the wagon. Once on top of the ore pile, he sprawled on his back, spent and exhausted, oblivious to the shards poking and cutting. He didn't care. Right now, it was the most comfortable bed in the world.

She climbed up and settled next to him on her knees. She cast her gaze back toward Chalk.

"It's all right, lass," he gasped. "They can't catch us now."

He didn't even bother looking for any sign of pursuit. He felt the trundling wheels of the caravan roll ever faster. Few creatures were faster than a sandcrab. They could even outrace a skrycrow. At such speeds, the caravan would reach Anvil long before any message could be sent. And once there, he could quickly lose himself in the tumult and chaos of the port. Maybe even take a ship abroad if need be.

"We're safe," he sighed out, assuring the woman and himself.

He patted her thigh, again noting the strange pliancy of her bronze, as if it were merely tanned flesh.

She ignored him. Her gaze aimed skyward, but not toward the sun. She stared toward the low horizon, where a half-moon sat. He remembered his earlier assessment of her, how her countenance reminded him of the Huntress. Both the dark Daughter and silvery Son made their home in the moon. It was said the two continually chased one another, round and round, leading to the moon's waxing and waning. But such a chase remained a great phylosophical argument. Did the Daughter pursue the Son? Or was it the other way around? Wars had been fought over such a religious quandary.

But at this moment, he couldn't care less.

I'm free . . .

He laughed up at the sky.

It seemed impossible. Joy swelled through him, calming his hammering heart and breathless panting. He finally sat up. He stared as the caravan crossed over a sea of black glass, where the sands had been fused by some fiery cataclysm. The reflection of the sun off its surface was blinding.

At the same time, the day's heat grew steadily. He searched around him. They needed to get out of the direct sun—or at least, he did. He considered how best to dig a shelter in the broken rock.

Seems my mining duties are not yet over.

Despite the burn of the sun, he returned his attention to the mystery kneeling beside him. What exactly had he stolen from the Shriven? What manner of spirit was trapped in that bronze? He recalled the archsheriff mentioning a coming war, how such a creature could turn the tide. Rhaif now understood. Any army led by such a miracle—or, for that matter, a legion of the same—would be unstoppable.

Still, he sensed such an abuse of her would be wrong.

It was not her nature.

He tried to read her face as she stared at the moon. Her features were now sculpted in an expression of sorrow, as if mourning a great loss. He reached again to her, then lowered his arm. He owed her, this spirit who had bought him his freedom, who saved his life. He wanted to ask her how he could repay such a debt, but he feared she could not speak. Or maybe she simply needed more time to fully settle her spirit into the bronze. Either way, there was nothing he could say.

In their shared silence, she continued to look at the moon. As the caravan continued its course north, Rhaif settled back. A lethargy spread through him after the day's many terrors. He listened to the driver's song trailing back to them, to the steady rumble of wheels. He knew he should get started on that shelter, but his eyelids grew heavy and drooped closed.

After a time, a low moan rose from beside him, stirring him back awake.

Arkival limne of
Thylassaur
(native to
Guld'ghul)

THREE

POISONED DREAMS

What are portents but dremes of the morrow.
What are dremes but the dai's hopes cloth'd in dark
* shadows.*

—From the poem "Allegory of a Scryer,"
by Damon hy Torranc

8

THE SUDDEN PLUMMET startled Nyx awake. She flailed, scrabbling for any handhold to keep herself from falling. As her heart leaped to her throat, a part of her recognized this feeling. Many times in the past, half-asleep and adrift, she had felt the world shatter under her. In such moments, she would jerk in panic as she fell—only to wake a moment later and find herself safely back in her own bed.

Not now.

As she continued to plummet, she thrashed at the blackness around her—not to beat it back, but to hold it closer. Darkness was as familiar to her as her own skin. Below, a strange brightness grew. Kicking, gasping, she tried to stay in the comfort of the shadows. But there was no halting her fall into that light.

She attempted to cast an arm across her eyes, to ward against the brilliance, but something gripped her wrist and would not let go.

Words reached her, sounding both distant and at her ear.

Is she having another convulsion?

The answer calmed her panic with its familiarity. *No, I don't believe so.* Nyx recognized Prioress Ghyle's calm but certain voice. *This is different. It's as if she fights against waking back into herself.*

With those words, memory flooded into Nyx, like a dam bursting, letting loose a roiling whitewater of terror.

—*a flight up steps.*
—*a threat of violation and banishment.*
—*the wash of hot blood through her dread-cold fingers.*
—*a headless body.*
—*the mountainous shadow looming through the smoke.*
—*bone-crushing weight.*
—*fangs and poison.*
—*a violation unimaginable.*
—*then darkness.*

One final memory swelled through her, pushing all else aside. Thousands of screams and cries filled her head, her body—until it was too much and finally burst out her throat. The world quaked inside her again, growing ever more violent. Still, beyond it all, she sensed the cresting of a silence without end. She cowered from its immensity and inevitability.

Then a cool hand rested atop her feverish brow. Words whispered in her ear. "My child, calm yourself. You're safe."

Nyx fought back into her body, not so much heeding the words of the prioress, but to argue against them. "No . . ." she croaked out.

Even that pained protest exhausted her. She breathed heavily, drawing in a scent of acrid tinctures, of steeped teas, of dusty sprigs of drying herbs. Still, the agonizing brightness refused to wane.

She tried to lift an arm—then the other—but her wrists remained gripped. She squeezed her eyelids shut and turned her head away, but the blaze was everywhere. It was inescapable.

"Unbind her," Ghyle ordered.

A man responded, "But if she convulses again, she could hurt—"

"We must help her wake now, Physik Oeric, or she may never do so. I fear she is too weak. She has slept near onto a full turn of the moon. If she sinks again into her poisonous slumber, she will never escape it."

With a tug, then another, Nyx's wrists were freed. She lifted her trembling arms against the brightness. The prioress's words settled to her chest. *A full turn of the moon.* How could that be? Nyx could still feel the crush of monstrous knuckles, the fangs piercing her flesh. She was certain no more than a bell had passed since the attack. Instead, if Ghyle spoke the truth, most of the summer was already gone.

Nyx's hands reached her face and discovered a wrap already in place, bound over her eyes, around her head. She fingered its edges. Another tried to pull her hands away.

"Leave it be, child," the school's physik warned.

Nyx had no strength to resist him. Not that she truly tried. By now, darkness ate at the edge of the brilliance. She welcomed its return, its familiarity amidst all the confusion. She let her arms fall back to the bed. She was suddenly so tired, a stony torpor that weighted down her bones.

"No," Ghyle snapped sharply. "Raise her head. Quickly now."

Nyx felt a palm cradle the back of her neck and lift her head off of the pillow. Fingers unraveled the wraps around her eyes. Though it was done gently, her head lolled listlessly with each unwinding of the cloth. She grew dizzy from the motion. With it, the darkness coiled ever closer toward the brightness at the center.

"I thought you warned us to leave her eyes wrapped," Physik Oeric mumbled. "To make it easier on her."

"A precaution born of hope," Ghyle said. "Now such caution presents too great a risk. She swoons even now back toward oblivion. We must do what we can to stop that from happening."

With one final tug, the wrap fell from her face. The end brushed her cheek before being lifted away. She found the strength to shift an arm higher, to ward against the blinding light. She squeezed her eyes even tighter. Still, the radiance stabbed into her skull, driving the darkness back, burning it away.

Then fingers gripped her chin, and a damp cloth smelling of almskald softened the sandy crusts sealing her eyelids.

"Don't fight it, child," Ghyle urged. "Open your eyes."

Nyx tried to pull her head away, to refuse, but those fingers tightened on her chin.

"Do as I say," the prioress demanded in tones that underscored her lofty position at the Cloistery. "Or be lost forever."

Nyx wanted to balk, but her dah had taught her too well, to always respect her betters. She peeked her lids open and gasped in agony. The light—as blinding as the darkness she had known all her life—stung with a nettle's burn.

Hot tears burst and flowed, flushing away more grime and crusts from her eyes. The tears also melted the hard brilliance into a watery brightness. Shapes swam through the haze, not unlike shadows on a bright summer day. Only with each painful blink, the shapes grew sharper; colors she had only imagined bloomed into brilliance.

Her heart fluttered in her chest like a panicked flutetail in a cage. She scrabbled backward on the bed—away from the impossibility of the pair of faces staring back at her. Physik Oeric squinted at her, his countenance wrinkled like a marsh plum left too long in the sun. Her gaze traced his every line. With her vision always clouded in the past, any colors—the little she could see even on the brightest days—were always muted and muddy.

But now . . .

She stared, mesmerized by the shining blue hue of the man's eyes, far brighter than any clear sky she had ever experienced.

As the physik turned to his neighbor, his bald pate reflected the sunlight through the room's lone window. "It seems you were correct, Prioress Ghyle," he said.

Ghyle kept her focus on Nyx. "You can see us. Is that not true, child?"

Dumbfounded, Nyx simply gaped. The prioress was darkly complexioned, her skin far darker than Nyx had imagined. She knew the prioress had been born to the south, in the lands of the Klashe. The woman's hair, though, was white as chalk and bound up in a nest of braids atop her head. Her eyes were far greener than any sunlit pond.

The prioress must have noted Nyx's attention. A smile played about the corners of her lips. Relief softened the prioress's eyes. Though, in truth, Nyx could not be sure of any of this. Having never witnessed the subtlety of expressions, she could not know for certain if she was interpreting them correctly.

Still, Nyx finally answered the prioress's question with a nod.

I can see.

While Nyx should have been joyous at such an impossibility, she now only felt dread. Somewhere in the darkness she had left behind, she could still hear screams rising from those shadows.

As if the prioress sensed her inner terror, the smile faded on the woman's face. She patted Nyx's hand. "You should mend well from here. I believe you've finally found your path out of the poison's oblivion."

Ever obedient and not wanting to appear ungrateful, Nyx nodded again.

But it was not how she felt.

Though she could miraculously see, she felt more lost than ever.

THE NEXT DAY, Nyx sipped at a thin porridge, cradling the bowl between her palms. Still weak, she needed both hands to hold the bowl steady.

Her dah sat on a stool beside her cot, leaning his chin atop his cane. He gazed at her with an encouraging grin, but his eyes and brow remained pinched. "It's a broth of hen bones mixed with oat grindings." He glanced to the door and back again, then leaned closer. "With a few splashes of wine cider. Should square you off right quick, I just knows it will."

Hope rang in his last words.

"I'm sure it will." To reassure him, she drew in another long sip before turning to set the bowl on a nearby table.

As she straightened around, she took in the small cell in the physik's ward, with its lichen-crusted stone walls, its high narrow window, and rafters hung with drying herbs. A lone flame danced wanly atop a tarnished oil lamp. She still felt overwhelmed by the very sight and details of the room: the wavering strands of spider silk in the corner, the dust motes floating in the sunlight, the whorled grain of the wooden rafters. It was too much. How did one cope with such an overload of details all the time? She found it dizzying and wrong.

Instead, she turned and concentrated on her dah's eyes. She tried to soothe the worry shining there. "They're taking good care of me here. Nearly the entire horde of the school's physiks, alchymists, and hieromonks have traipsed through here."

In fact, they had barely let her sleep.

Perhaps they fear I will never wake again and dared not lose this opportunity.

They hadn't even let her dah visit until this morning. Once allowed, he had spared not a moment. With the day's first bell, he had hobbled his way up to the fourth tier—where the Cloistery's wards were housed—accompanied by Nyx's brother. Bastan had carried a huge pot of porridge, resting in a bucket of coals to keep it all warm.

Her brother had already returned home to join their older brother in taking care of their duties at the paddocks. Apparently even someone returning from the dead did not slow the pace of the busy trading post. Still, before leaving, Bastan had hugged her in his beefy arms, grabbed her cheeks in his palms, and stared deeply at her.

"Don't go a-scaring us again," he had warned her. "Next time you go about tangling with a Mýr bat, you fetch your brothers first."

She had promised to do so, trying to smile, but his reminder of the attack had stoked the terror inside her. At least, the constant attention by the parade of physiks through her small cell had kept her distracted. The curious visitors had poked and pinched her all over, often leaving her blushing. Others had spent time examining the healing punctures in her throat, measuring the scabs, picking the edges, taking pieces with them. One pair—bent-backed with age—had placed leeches on her wrists and ankles, then whisked off excitedly with their blood-bloated slugs.

Prioress Ghyle sometimes appeared with the others, but she rebuffed any attempt by Nyx to get answers, to fill in the holes since that dreaded day. Still, Nyx knew word had spread throughout the Cloistery. Occasional faces would appear at her room's high window, requiring a leap to the sill to get a quick peek at the miracle inside.

She knew the reason for all the attention—both in the room and beyond.

No one had ever survived the poison of a Mýr bat.

It was a mystery that the alchymists sought to solve, and a miracle that the hieromonks wished to attribute to the correct god. To distract herself, she had eavesdropped on the conversations of those who trotted through here. She listened to their speculations and fascinations. They spoke as if she weren't even in the room.

She could not have been properly poisoned. I wager it was the slightest envenomation at best.

Or likely some trickery, some feigned debilitation.

Or perchance the Daughter smiles darkly upon the child.

Or it could have been the Son's bright blessing. Didn't I hear that in the depth of her slumber, she cried out to the moon and—

This last conversation had been cut off by the arrival of Prioress Ghyle, who sent the pair of monks out with an exasperated roll of her eyes and a stern frown at Nyx—as if she had done something wrong.

But Nyx's survival was not the *only* miracle hidden away in this room.

She rubbed her tender eyes, knowing her lids were bruised from the constant attention paid to her returned sight. Every time her eyelids drooped in exhaustion, someone would pry them back open.

Nyx had paid extra attention to any attempts to explain this particular miracle, a wonder that had still left her unmoored. It was as if she had come out of the darkest cave into the brightest day. While she should have been grateful, a part of her still wished to return to the comfort and familiarity of that cave. Even her first attempt at walking this morning, supported on the prioress's arm, was as if she were a babe new to this world. She wanted to attribute it all to the weakness from being bedbound for so long, but she knew part of it was her adjusting to her eyesight. After so many years, her shadow-riven blindness was writ deep upon her spirit, on her bones, on how she moved through life. Now her mind struggled to balance who she was in the past with this newly sighted person today.

Ghyle seemed to innately understand. "You will find your equilibrium," she had promised.

Nyx stared at the cane in the corner, the length of elm wood she had abandoned in the astronicum a lifetime ago. She still needed it, even with her sight miraculously returned to her.

With a sigh, Nyx placed a palm over both eyes.

Darkness still felt more like home to her.

"Awf, I've gone and overstayed myself," her dah said. "Look at you rubbing your eyes and all. You must be tired. I should leave you to your rest."

She lowered her hands, a smile on her lips and an ache in her heart. "Never, Dah. You could never overstay."

She stared at the man who had rescued her from the swamps and offered up his home and all his love. In just one day's time, her newfound sight had revealed details both subtle and profound in the world around her, but it had offered nothing new here.

Her father's face was as she had always known it to be. Over the years, she had traced his every line, his every bump and scar of his past. Her fingers had combed through his hair as it had thinned. Her palms had felt the skull under his skin. More so, by now, his every smile and frown were as familiar to her as her own. Even his eyes were the color she had always imagined: a muddy green, like the quaggy bottom of a bright pond.

She didn't need sight to know this man.

In this moment, she recognized how mistaken she had been a moment ago. She stared deeply at the man who mirrored back all of her love.

This is my truest home.

Her dah stirred, plainly readying himself to stand. "I should go."

An objection came from the doorway. "Mayhap not yet, Trademan Polder."

Both their gazes turned to the doorway. Prioress Ghyle stepped inside, leading Physik Oeric behind her.

"I would like to ask you about the day you found Nyx in the swamps, a babe abandoned in the fen." Ghyle waved Nyx's dah to settle back on his stool. "It could prove fruitful to understanding what has happened. Mayhap even in her care from here."

Her dah yanked off his cap and nodded vigorously. One hand smoothed his bog-stained summer vest, as if ashamed to be found in such a state. "Most certainly, your prioress. Anything to help you or the lass."

Irritation flashed through Nyx at her dah's humbleness. He had no reason to bow or scrape before anyone at the Cloistery.

Ghyle crossed and sat on the edge of the bed with a tired sigh. The prioress nodded to Nyx's dah, the two of them now eye to eye with one another. "Thank you, Trademan Polder."

Her dah's shoulders relaxed. Nyx realized she had never seen the prioress in any other posture but one of straight-backed authority. Her manner now was warmer, one of invitation versus command.

Physik Oeric joined them, but he remained standing with his arms crossed over his thin chest.

"What do you all wish to know?" her dah asked.

"As I understand, Nyx was a babe of six moons when you found her."

"Aye, that's right." Her dah smiled, relaxing even more, happy to recount his story, one he gladly shared with anyone willing to hear it. He told again of hearing Nyx's cries in the swamp. "'Course ol' Gramblebuck heard her first. All but dragged our sledge straight to her."

"And you saw no one else about?" Ghyle asked. "No sign of who left her?"

He shook his head. "Not a footfall or broken reed. 'Twas as if she fell straight out of the sky and into a floating bed of fenweed."

Ghyle glanced at Oeric, who shared a silent pinched look, then spoke up. "And young Nyx was blind even then?"

Her dah's smile faded. "Truth. Poor thing. The surfaces of her eyes were already clouded and blued over. Not clear as polished crystal like now. Maybe that was why the baby was abandoned to the swamp. It is hard enough to eke a living in the deep fen. But their loss was my gain."

Nyx again wondered about her true parents. An old bitterness sharpened inside her. She was not as forgiving as her dah. She cleared her throat, wanting to turn the conversation from such a prickly subject.

"What does any of this have to do with what's happened to me?" Nyx asked.

All gazes swung to her, but the prioress answered. "Physik Oeric and I believe you were not born sightless."

Nyx flinched at such a claim. "I have no memory of ever—"

"You might not remember it," Oeric said. "But plainly you always had the ability to see. It was the bluish haze across the surface of your eyes that hid the world from you."

"And now it's cleared," her dah said. "A miracle. A true blessing of the Mother."

Nyx kept her focus on the prioress. "What do you think happened to me, what blinded me all those years ago?"

Ghyle looked to Oeric, then back again. "We believe something in the swamps tainted you. A poison, perhaps. Maybe a pall of noxious air."

Her dah nodded. "There be all manner of nasties out there."

Oeric stepped closer, his voice sharpening with interest. "It could also be an ill reaction to something you encountered. I've read treatises about how the dust in ancient rooms can bring about a phlegmonous catarrh. It's often ascribed to hauntings or to the presence of trapped daemons. But others believe it might be related to a similar affliction that strikes many in the springtime, due to the casting forth of a flower's must during the blooming season, what those in the Southern Klashe call Rose Fever."

Her dah's confused expression matched her own. "But what does that have to do with Nyx's blindness?"

Oeric answered, "Usually, if not proven deadly, such reactions fade on their own. But sometimes they can leave lasting debilitation." He waved thin fingers at Nyx's face. "Like blindness."

"But why am I cured now?" Nyx asked.

The prioress turned to Nyx. "In fighting off the poison, we believe your body shook off this old taint, too."

"If true, it has made us wonder," Oeric added. "If perhaps the present might offer insight into the past."

She furrowed her brow. "What do you mean?"

Ghyle patted her blanketed leg. "As you might suspect, I am not one to put much stock on fen-witches who read the future in a toss of bones. Instead, I look for patterns hidden in plain view. If the venom of a Mýr bat cured you, it perhaps portends that what afflicted you as a babe was also somehow connected to that same denizen of the swamps."

"Another bat?" Nyx frowned. She wanted to dismiss such a claim, but she also remembered the abject terror she had felt—far worse than her fellow students—whenever such a creature screeched past overhead.

Could it be true?

Ghyle wondered the same. "Do you have any recollection of such an encounter? If you had sight back then, perhaps you might have seen such a creature."

Nyx glanced down. She pictured her dah's discovery of her as a babe and his words a moment ago: *'Twas as if she fell straight out of the sky.* She closed her eyes, imagining herself lying on her back in a bed of fenweed, staring up through the moss-shrouded branches. She was again blind, abandoned, angry, scared, squalling, searching those skies through clouded eyes. A brighter patch marked the sun—then a dark sickle-shaped shadow cut across the glow and vanished into the shadows.

She stiffened.

Ghyle noted this. "What is it?"

Nyx opened her eyes and shook her head. She did not know if what she saw was a true memory or one born of the prioress's speculation. "Nothing," she mumbled.

Ghyle continued to stare at her, her gaze as piercing as any fang.

Nyx kept her face lowered. She didn't know what to make of that flash of memory—if it was memory. But she could also not dismiss it, especially with the feeling that had accompanied the recollection. As she imagined herself as a baby, Nyx hadn't felt even a flicker of terror at the sight of that sickle shape passing over the sun. Instead, in the darkest recesses of her heart, she knew what she had felt at that moment. It made no sense.

She glanced to her dah.

It had felt like home.

9

"FOR NOW, LET'S leave this matter for another time," Ghyle said. "When you're better rested and further recovered, you might remember more. Instead, I'm sure you have many questions about your current circumstances. I'm not oblivious to the concerns and fears you've attempted to voice over the past day. Mayhap we should also put those to rest as best we can."

Nyx was more than ready to set aside her past and address her present—but she was also frightened to do so. There *were* questions she needed to ask, but she remained fearful of the answers.

She licked her lips. She knew she needed to address the aftermath of the attack atop the ninth tier of the school, to face the condemnation that was sure to come. To start with, she voiced her foremost fear. It was a boy's name, a fellow seventhyear.

She closed her eyes to speak it, finding strength in the darkness.

"Byrd . . ." she whispered.

Ghyle's answer was blunt. "Dead. But I suspect you already know this."

She did not deny this. "And what of the others?"

"Your fellow seventhyears?"

She opened her eyes and nodded, remembering the throng chasing her heels.

"They attempted to hide the truth of that day, but Jace spoke up on your behalf and broke their impasse."

Nyx sighed in relief, silently thanking Jace. The young man—ever her eyes when she was blind—proved yet again to be her most stalwart friend here at the Cloistery. And he had suffered for that friendship. She remembered his bloody nose.

"Journeyman Jace fares well," Ghyle answered, as if reading her concern. "He's been anxious to see you, but we've encouraged his patience."

Nyx swallowed. "And how does Kindjal fare, Byrd's twin sister?"

Ghyle sat back slightly. A deep line formed between her brows. "She returned to Fiskur with her brother's remains, or at least the little of his body that the pyre had not consumed. But she will be back once the midsummer break ends in a fortnight. I tried to discourage her return."

Ghyle stared at Nyx, silently adding what remained unspoken. Kindjal would not suffer the death of her twin brother without consequences. Neither would their father, the highmayor of Fiskur.

"What's to become of me?" Nyx asked, shying over to a more immediate fear. "I trespassed onto the ninth tier."

It was an inviolate rule of the Cloistery. To tread that tier before being accepted to the ninthyear was punished by immediate banishment. There were no exceptions—not even if one's life was threatened.

Ghyle pointed a finger at Nyx's chest. "That was not *you* who trespassed."

She scrunched her face in confusion. "But it was. I can hardly attest otherwise. Many bore witness."

Oeric spoke up. "And as many bore witness that you *died*. Both alchymists and hieromonks. Your heart had truly stopped. For half a bell, maybe longer. None thought you'd survive."

"Yet, you came back from the dead," Ghyle added. "You were reborn anew, purified of your past. All have come to believe that the Mother doubly blessed you. First with your life, then with your sight."

Oeric chuckled under his breath. "A conceit well seeded by the prioress."

Ghyle shrugged. "And who is to say I'm wrong?"

"I'd love to see someone try," he mumbled.

"But it surely *was* the Mother's hand," her dah pressed. "I have no doubt. She has always smiled on my daughter."

Hope rose in Nyx's breast. "Does that mean I can stay at the school? Finish my seventhyear studies and continue on to the eighth?"

"I'm afraid not," Ghyle said dourly. "It was put to the Council of Eight, and they cast their stones against such a plan."

Her dah stood up. "That's not fair, I tell you!"

Nyx reached over and grabbed his hand, which trembled in her grip. She squeezed him quiet, ready to accept her fate but no less despairing. "It's all right, Dah. What's done is done."

"You both misunderstand me." Ghyle's gaze focused on Nyx. "It's been decided that you should *not* proceed to the eighthyear with your fellow students. As you were clearly blessed atop the ninth tier, none would dare cast a stone against the expressed wishes of the Mother."

"I don't understand," Nyx said.

Ghyle explained. "In a fortnight, you'll ascend straight to the ninthyear."

It took three full breaths for Nyx to even comprehend what the prioress was saying. She tried to blink away her shock.

Ninthyear . . .

Her dah was quicker to respond. He whooped loud enough to make them all jump. "What didda tell ya! I knew it all along." He let go of Nyx's fingers and dropped to his knees at her bedside. He clasped his palms together and raised his thumbs to his forehead. "Thank the Mother Below for her glory and blessings upon us."

But even his faithfulness could not hold back his joy and excitement for long. He was soon back on his feet—not even needing his own cane. He grabbed Nyx's cheeks and planted a kiss on her forehead. Only then did he calm himself enough to stare fully at Nyx. Tears wet his eyes and cheeks.

"Can ya just believe it?" he mumbled around a smile. "My Nyx. A ninth-year. I can hardly wait to tell Bastan and Ablen. The boys will be burstin' with pride."

Ghyle stood up next to him. "Mayhap you should share those good tidings now. There is another matter I wish to discuss with your daughter. Words that require privacy."

"Aye, aye, of course." Her dah turned to collect his cane. "I know you and the physik must be busy, and I won't keep ya from it."

"Most obliged, Trademan Polder."

Her dah turned once more toward Nyx. His face glowed with such pride. It made him look a full score younger. He gave a small shake of his head that failed to loosen his smile. "Can ya believe it?" he repeated.

No, I can't.

Nyx tried to accept the unfathomable. After so many miracles, she mistrusted this last one. Still, she did her best to return her dah's smile. If nothing else, it warmed her to see him so happy. It was worth almost dying to see his faith in her fulfilled, his generosity of spirit rewarded.

"I'll bring your supper before the first bell of Eventoll," he promised. "I'll drag up Bastan and Ablen. We'll celebrate with sweetcake and honey."

She found a truer smile. "That sounds wonderful."

He bowed to both the prioress and the physik, muttered his thanks, and left her cell. Nyx listened to the tap of his cane as it faded through the wards.

Ghyle did, too. She waited until it was gone, then waved for Oeric to close the door. Once obeyed, the prioress turned back to Nyx. Her countenance had turned far sterner.

"What we speak of next must not be shared."

Nyx shifted taller in the bed and waited as the prioress and the physik whispered by the door. She only caught snatches of their furtive conversation.

. . . get word to Azantiia . . .

. . . rumors of the Iflelen . . .

. . . the king will not abide . . .
. . . calumny and blasphemy . . .
. . . must know for certain.

The last was spoken by Physik Oeric, who glanced over at Nyx. The prioress sighed heavily and nodded. She turned and crossed back to the bed and sat on its edge again.

Nyx shivered, sensing the stirring of forces far larger than herself. Ghyle studied her face intently for too long a time. Whatever the prioress was looking for, she eventually seemed satisfied and spoke.

"Nyx, while you were lost in that poisonous oblivion, you thrashed and fought, as if trapped in a nightmare. Do you remember any of that?"

She shook her head, denying it. Though it was a lie. She certainly remembered the chorus of screams in the dark, of the quaking world, and then a crushing, unending silence. She didn't mean to lie, but she was too fearful to speak aloud of it, as if doing so would make it inescapable. She wanted to forget it, to dismiss it all as a fevered dream, a phantasm born of her fear of death.

Only now the prioress sought to add flesh and bone to that dream.

Ghyle clearly read her fear. "We must know, Nyx. What you speak now will remain among us three. That I swear to you."

Nyx took another two breaths. How could she refuse the woman who had so championed her? If only to honor that debt, Nyx knew she could not remain silent.

"I . . . I remember just pieces," she finally admitted. "It was as if a great calamity had befallen the Urth. Every voice in all the lands raised in terror. The world shaking and being torn apart. And then . . . and then . . ."

Her mouth went dry as she relived it.

Shrieks echoed in her skull, setting all her fine hairs on end.

"What came next?" Ghyle pressed gently, reaching to Nyx's hand.

She cringed for a long moment, wishing to hold it inside her. Instead, she stared up at the prioress, so the woman could see both her sincerity and fear. "A silence absolute. Stretching out into the void. To the cold stars themselves."

Nyx's throat tightened around her next words, as if trying to strangle them from being spoken, such was her certainty. "I . . . I know it will happen. I don't understand how, but it *will* come to be."

Ghyle looked over to Oeric.

The physik moved closer. "You said the silence reached the stars. What about the moon?"

She frowned. "The moon? I don't understand."

Ghyle's fingers tightened on Nyx's hand. "During your thrashing, you mumbled and cried out. Often about the moon. You kept repeating the word *moonfall*."

Nyx shook her head again, denying any knowledge of this—and this time it was the truth.

As the prioress studied Nyx, the woman's eyes slowly widened in dismay. "You are certain you have no memory of the moon?"

"Perhaps you saw it in your dream?" Oeric pressed.

Nyx looked between the pair. "I *saw* nothing. I swear upon the Son and Daughter who make the moon their home." She lifted her free hand and touched one eye, then the other. "I heard the screams. Felt the quakes. But in that nightmare, I was as blind as I ever was."

Ghyle sagged. "Of course."

"I'm sorry," Nyx said, knowing she had disappointed the woman. "That's all I remember. Truly."

"I believe you."

Oeric closed his eyes with a tired groan. "It seems the gods picked a broken vessel to fill with their wisdom."

Nyx rankled at his description. While she might have wished for her sight when she was very young, she had never considered herself *broken*. Certainly, her rise through the tiers at the school was proof enough of that.

"It may not have been the gods who chose her . . ." Ghyle mumbled cryptically, and stood. "No matter, while we can't confirm what is considered blasphemous, we will share what we know. I'll send a skrycrow to Highmount."

"But if the king should—"

"Fear not, my high-spirited former student will keep our counsel. We both know the surreptitious work he performs atop Kepenhill."

Nyx still felt ill, sensing she had somehow failed the prioress and physik. But her ears pricked at the mention of Kepenhill. It was the oldest of the land's schools, positioned on the tallest hill at the outskirts of Highmount. It was also home to the ancient Shrivenkeep, where it was said those who achieved the emblem of Highcryst in both alchymy and religious scholarship delved into the most arcane of studies.

In her grandest of dreams, Nyx imagined herself joining such ranks. Though, in truth, she had never given it more than half a hope. Then again, she had never thought she'd ever reach the ninth tier of the Cloistery.

Ghyle finally returned her attention to Nyx. "You must speak to no one about any of this. Not about our conversation, certainly not about your nightmares. Not even to your family."

Nyx nodded. She had no intention of doing any of that. She was happy to dismiss it all. She intended to shove it down deep—until she could no longer hear those screams. She also recognized the warning behind the prioress's command, that Nyx's life depended on her keeping quiet.

But will my silence be enough?

She again sensed a swirling of forces far larger than herself, of machinations and plots beyond her understanding, of a storm building. She pictured the copper orrery in the astronicum, its gears turning, spinning planets around a coal-heated sun. But in this particular case, whose hand was turning those massive gears around her?

And how long until I'm crushed within them?

10

As the last bell of Eventoll echoed down from on high, Nyx crossed toward the cot in her cell. Cane in hand, she moved unsteadily across the room, partly from her residual weakness but more from the generous amount of rum in the sweetcake. Bone-tired and stuffed near to bursting, she had no doubt sleep would come quickly.

Her ears still rang with the laughter and songs of her dah and two brothers, celebrating her coming Ascension to the ninth tier. She smiled at the pride in the lot of them. The fears and trepidations from this morning's furtive talk with the prioress and the physik had been chased away by the merriment of family, by her own hope for her future.

Best let it all fall behind me, she had decided. She would cast aside her frightful dreams and let them be forgotten. Whether portentous or not, matters of such import and intrigue were best left to those who knew what they were doing—or at least, those who had the power and influence to make a difference.

That's certainly not me.

As she rounded the foot of the bed, the oil lamp's flame flickered, dancing shadows over the stone walls. The movement dizzied her. Before she lost her balance, she dropped heavily to a seat atop her bed with a groan.

She breathed deeply to clear her head. Bog brine salted the warm summer breeze through the high open window. The steady hum of gnats and meskers competed with the croak of frogs and scissor-song of crickets. In the distance, the haunting lilt of a marsh loon stirred a sad longing.

She sighed and glanced up to the window. The Father Above still shone outside—but His face remained hidden from view. Though the sun never vanished, Eventoll was marked by a slight dimming of His brilliance and a thickening of shadows. Such a change had been more evident before, when her clouded eyes were more sensitive to the vagaries of light and shadow. The shift was barely perceptible now, which saddened her, as if she had lost a part of herself with her returned sight.

Sobered by this thought, she stood up and crossed to the window. She drew the shutters against the sunlight, darkening the room. But she could not bring herself to close them completely. She had lived in shadows for too long.

Standing there, she gazed out at the full moon sharing the Eventoll sky. She studied its countenance, shining with the bright face of the Son. She noted vague dark eyes, maybe a nose, definitely a mouth. Before this past day, she'd never had the sharpness of vision to observe such details before.

It does look like a face up there.

She smiled back at the Son, knowing over the coming days that the dark Daughter would chase that face away. Such had been their dance since the beginning of time.

"And when I see your face come around again, O silvery Son," she whispered to the moon, "I'll be in my ninthyear."

She could hardly fathom it. In a fortnight, the wish that had been clamped tightly in her heart was about to come true. The joy inside her shone as brightly as the Son in the sky. Yet, she could also not discount the gloom there, like her own dark Daughter waiting to eclipse her bright joy.

She knew the source of that glumness, remembering the prioress's inquiry. She searched the moon's face for any sense of enmity or danger. But she discovered nothing, felt nothing.

She dredged up the word used by the prioress, testing it on her lips. "Moonfall."

What did that even mean?

With no answer forthcoming, she shrugged and returned to her bed. She climbed onto her cot and nestled into her blankets and pillow. She lay on her back and stared up at the drape of drying herbs in the rafters overhead. The flickering flame of the oil lamp made them look as if they were jerking and clawing toward her.

She shivered.

It seemed sight brought about its own unique terrors.

With a huff, she snuffed out the oil lamp, rolled on her side, and clutched her blankets tighter. She closed her eyes, but she doubted sleep would come as quickly as she had earlier surmised.

She was wrong.

SHE FLEES UP the shadowy mountain slope, through the fringes of a leafless forest made of stone. Screams of man and beast chase her the last of the way. The clash of steel rings all around, punctuated by the thunder of war machines.

Panting and breathless, she skids to a stop at the summit. She takes in everything, recognizing she is older, taller, scarred, missing a finger on her left hand. But she has no time for such mysteries.

Ahead, a cluster of figures with tattooed faces and blood-soaked robes circle an altar where a huge shadow-creature thrashes and bucks, its wings nailed to the stone with iron.

"No . . ." she screams with a raw throat, fire stoking inside her skull.

Dark faces turn toward her, curved daggers flashing into view.

She swings her arms high and claps her palms together as words, foreign to her, burst from her lips, ending in a name. "Bashaliia!"

With that last word, her skull releases the fiery storm held inside. It blasts outward with enough force to shatter the altar stone. Iron stakes break from black granite, and the shadow-beast leaps high. Its blood blesses the dark gathering, sending them scattering.

One figure runs toward her, a blade held high, a curse on his lips.

Wasted and empty, she can only fall to her knees. She cannot even raise an arm in her defense. She simply lifts her face to the smoke-shrouded skies, to the full face of the moon. The sickle form of the winged creature passes over its surface and disappears into the smoke and darkness.

As she watches, time both slows and stretches. The moon grows ever larger. The war machines fall silent all around her. Screams and cries of agony malform into a chorus of terror. The ground quakes under her knees, ever more violent with each breath.

And still the moon fills more and more of the sky, its edges on fire now, darkening all the world around it.

She finds the strength to name this doom.

"Moonfall . . ."

Then a dagger plunges into her chest—piercing her heart with the truth.

I've failed . . . I've failed us all.

WITH A GASP, Nyx sat upright in her bed.

Tears blurred her newfound vision. Her heart hammered against her ribs. She fought a hand free of her tangled blankets and wiped at her eyes. Her other hand rubbed the fiery pain between her breasts, expecting her fingers to come back bloody.

Just a dream, she assured herself.

She swallowed to free her tongue in her fear-dried mouth.

"Just a dream," she repeated, this time aloud to further reinforce her conviction.

She glanced to the window, to the moon still shining there, hanging as it had before, no larger, no smaller. She forced her breathing to calm. She lifted her left hand, opening and closing a fist.

All five fingers.

She lowered her arm, lifting her face in relief.

"I'm being daft, that's all," she argued with herself. "Dah was always heavy-handed with the rum in his sweetcake. And all that talk . . ."

Moonfall . . .

She was sure her rum-fueled imagination had churned up all of her misgivings and doubts into a nightmare. That's all it was.

With her face still raised, she watched the drying branches and sprigs of herbs wave down at her from the rafters. The dream was no more real than the shift of shadows from a flickering flame.

She stiffened in her bed.

Her gaze flicked to the bedside stand, to the dark oil lamp. She remembered snuffing out its flame. And the window shutters were wider than how she'd left them. She craned her neck and searched the nest of shadows above the rafters.

Something's up there.

With this thought, her world upended. Suddenly she was seeing herself staring up, seated atop the bed. She let out a cry, watched herself cry out. Then the world righted itself, and she was back in her bed, gaping up at the rafters.

A row of dried addleberry branches shivered, drawing her gaze.

From the rafters, a pair of red eyes glowed back at her.

A scream built in her chest, but before it let loose, a keening reached her from above. It was soundless but felt all over. Her skin prickled in response. It reverberated off the stone wall, filling the breadth of the ward. It knifed past her ears and echoed inside her skull, setting fire to the surfaces of her brain.

She palmed her ears, but it made no difference.

The fires stoked into a blaze, bringing with it strange sensations. Her nose filled with a gingery musk, redolent with oil and sweat. Her tongue tasted a milky cream, rich and sweet. Shadowy images fluttered as her head lolled back, as if buffeted by the keening winds from above.

The world dimmed around her, while another grew sharper.

—her tiny fingers scrabble through fur.

—pursed lips find a dark nipple, where a single drop of milk hangs.

—she suckles and kicks chubby legs to push herself greedily forward.

—soft leather scoops her tighter, keeping her warm and safe.

Nyx shook her head, trying to dispel these thoughts, to deny what she began to suspect. But she could not escape it.

Other glimpses cascaded through her. Sometimes it was her looking outward; other times, it was as if she was viewed from afar.

—she crawls through rushes.

—she struggles to suckle her own toe.

—smoking brimstan stings her nose.

—a hot tongue cleans her all over.

—she is clutched and swept high, winds brushing her limbs.

As the images flashed faster and faster, her vision of them grew strangely cloudier.

—the milk she suckles still tastes rich and sweet. It fills her belly, makes her stronger, deepens her slumbers, but it also slowly darkens her world.

—the warm tongue wipes at her eyes, not as gently, more fervently with concern.

—the high-pitched squeaks and whistles that have always filled her world and skull, which etched her very being, now sound mournful, grieving. As if the entire world wept around her.

—then aloft again, carried through shadows.

—her tiny ears hear the lowing of a great beast below, along with the bony rattle of reeds as the creature moves through the swamp.

—she is gently lowered to a spot near the beast. Her new bed is damp and perfumed by blooms all around.

—by this time, she can barely see.

—a shadow looms over her. Huge eyes gaze down. A whiskered cheek presses to her own. A tongue tastes her one last time. Nostrils huff and sniff, drawing her into memory.

—then with a final buffeting of huge wings, she is abandoned.

—she bawls her grief, her loss, echoing the keening that still bathes her from above, but which grows fainter and fainter.

—she watches a shadow crest the moon and vanish.

Finally, the world returned fully to her. She was back on her cot. Tiny eyes still glowed from above, but the terror of them had dimmed to a dull glow. She wanted to deny what she had been shown—lost memories inflamed back to life by the keening—but she could not. She knew them to be true. Still, it was too much to take in, upending all she understood about herself.

Before she could even attempt such an impossible task, the piercing cries from the rafters sharpened. Once again, she was staring down at herself from above. She knew she was peering through the eyes of the creature hiding up there. Then another image overlapped this one, shimmering like a reflection on a still pond.

She was a naked babe again, snuggled to a nipple, nestled in the fur and wing of a massive shape that protected her. She stared across to the other nipple, where a dark shape, naked and downy, suckled. Its thin wings were held awkwardly to the side. Small claws dug for purchase in the furry pelt—while tiny red eyes stared back at her. This other had always been there beside her, sheltered and protected under the same wings.

The shimmering view finally faded. The room went quiet again.

She gulped several breaths, dizzy with knowledge. Her gaze narrowed on the rafters, to the pair of red eyes. She now knew what hid in the rafters.

As if acknowledging this, a dark shape—barely larger than a winter goose—cartwheeled into view. Its wings snapped wide, then with a single beat, it dove sideways out the narrow window. Her gaze followed after the young Mýr bat as it turned on a wingtip and vanished away.

She held her breath, testing how she felt about this trespass.

Such creatures were the scourge of these harsh lands, predators like no other. But no fear iced through her. Instead, her earlier terror had hardened to a cold certainty.

She knew who had come to visit her this Eventoll.

She continued to stare at the window, picturing that other nipple, the small shape—only now velvety furred and grown larger.

My lost brother.

FOUR

THE PRINCE IN THE CUPBOARD

All the beauty of the worlde can be found in the lands of Hálendii. From east to west, it falls in colossal stepes, as if meant to be tredan upon by the gods themselves. From the steaming highlands of the Shrouds, down to the misti forests of Cloudreach, & at last to spread its bounty out into the fruit'd & fertile plains of Brauðlands. Yet, no wonder is greater than the city upon which these lands & most the worlde turns, the triumphant magnyficence of Azantiia.

—Annotated from the eighty-volume treatise,
Lyrrasta's *Geographica Comprehendinge*

11

WITH A GROAN, the son of the highking woke amidst lice and the foul of his own heave. Off in the distance, the dawn bell clanged down from the heights of Azantiia. Its ringing passed from one tower bell to another, six in all, positioned at each point of Highmount's star-shaped ramparts.

He tried to stuff the thin pillow in his ears as the new day sounded. But the noise still rattled his skull and made his teeth ache. His stomach lurched, and bile threatened to rise. He swallowed it back into submission, but not before a loud burp escaped.

Finally, the last of the morning's tolling echoed across the Bay of Promise, and the bells fell mercifully silent.

"Aye, that's better," Prince Kanthe sighed out to a room shuttered and dark.

He closed his eyes and tried to remember where he was. He smelled sweat, piss, and the soured ale of his own mess. Fat sizzled on a grill and smoked through floorboards under him. From that cookery came the clanking of pots, interrupted by bellows of an irate innkeep.

Ah, yes . . .

He foggily remembered a painted wooden sign depicting an armored knight with a sword raised to his lips. *The Point'd Blade.* Long ago, someone had crudely altered the sword into a jutting manhood. No one had ever bothered to change it back. Amused by such artistry, he could not leave the tavern unvisited. If he recalled, it had been the third such establishment that he had graced with his illustrious presence. Not that he had given his truest name. As usual, he had arrived in roughspun and a simple cloak, hiding his princely nature.

He sat up, thought better of it, but persevered. He swung his naked legs over to the floor, wondering where his pants had gone. He scratched his privates, attempting to dig out a couple of biting nits. It was a futile battle. Only a steamy lyeleaf bath would win this war.

With a groan, he stood up and shoved open a shutter above the privy to let in fresh air. The brightness stung, but he suffered it as punishment. It was already hot. The skies were blue, with a few fingers of rosy fire-clouds smearing in from the east. Contrarily, lower down to the west, dark storm clouds stacked at the horizon. They had blown off the seas and towered over the grain fields on the far side of the Tallak River, inevitably heading toward the city.

He pictured the twin sky-rivers that Alchymist Frell had tried to describe to him. The scholar claimed that a hot river coursed over the sky, carrying the fiery heat from Urth's sun-blasted side over to its frigid half—then returned again in a colder stream that hugged closer to the lands and seas, flowing in the opposite direction, west to east. It was said those twin rivers—forever flowing in two different directions—blessed the lands of the Crown with a livable clime. Hieromonks believed it was due to the twin gods, the fiery Hadyss and the icy giant Madyss, who blew those rivers across the skies, while Frell and his order insisted it was due to some natural bellows of fire and ice. The debates continued across the divide of the ninth tier of Kepenhill.

Kanthe sighed. He could not care less—even when he should. He himself was due to climb to the ninth level in less than a fortnight. Not that he had earned such a lofty position. But he was the king's son. The Council of Eight could hardly deny him his Ascension.

Until then, he intended to use the last of his midsummer break to enjoy his freedom. Of course, he hardly needed any excuse for such carousing. By now, all knew his reputation. Kanthe had earned his many nicknames, often snickered across a scarred bar while he hunkered in disguise over a tankard: the Sodden Prince, the Tallywag, the Dark Trifle. But the most apt slur was simply the Prince in the Cupboard. He was a prince whose only use in life was to be a spare in case his older twin should die. His lot was to sit on a shelf in case he was ever needed.

He turned and searched for his pants. He found them crumpled in a corner and quickly donned them. He felt no shame in those slanders, having well earned them. In truth, he had purposefully done so. As the younger of the king's two sons, he would never sit on the throne. So, he played his role well. The more he lowered himself, the higher his twin shone.

It's the least I can do for you, dear brother Mikaen.

He scowled as he finished dressing, hopping on one foot while he tugged a boot onto the other. *Maybe I shouldn't have tarried so long in our mother's womb.* Instead, Mikaen had shouldered his way out first, squalling his lofty place with his first breath. Destined for the throne, Mikaen had been doted upon and cherished. At seven years, his brother had been sent to the Legionary on the castle grounds. Over the past eight years, Mikaen had been trained in all manner of strategy and weaponry, polishing himself for his role as future king of Azantiia.

On the other hand, Kanthe had been shoved out of Highmount and into the school of Kepenhill. It was not unexpected. The royal families of Azantiia had a long history of twin births, some born with the same face, others with different appearances. Mikaen looked as if he had been sculpted out of pale chalkstone, sharing their father's countenance, including his curled blond locks and sea-blue eyes. Girls—and many a woman—swooned as he passed, especially as Mikaen's years at the Legionary had layered his body with hard muscles. Not that any of it went to waste. Many nights, Mikaen practiced a different type of swordsmanship at Highmount's palacio of pleasure serfs.

Nothing could be further from Kanthe's life. As a second-born son, he was forbidden to touch a sword. In addition, with the exception of one rushed, embarrassing, flustered attempt, he was all but a virgin. It didn't help matters that Kepenhill prohibited such pleasures—and Kanthe certainly didn't stir the desires of women as soundly as his older twin did.

While Mikaen was all brightness and boldness, Kanthe took after their dead mother. His skin was burnished ebonwood, his hair as black as coal, his eyes a stormy gray. His manner was quieter like hers, too. He certainly preferred his own company.

To that end, while he was forbidden to wield a sword, he took up a hunter's bow instead. His father had even encouraged this pursuit. Over the many centuries of his family's rule, the Kingdom of Hálendii had carved a foothold across the breadth of the northern Crown. The expansion of their lands had been achieved less with swords and warships and more with plows, wood axes, and scythes. Taming the wilds was as important to securing their territory as fortifying its walls or building castles. Nature was as much an enemy to be conquered as any foreign army.

So, whenever freedom permitted, Kanthe took off into the rolling hills and patchwork forests of the Brauðlands to hunt and hone his skills, both sharpening his aim and heightening his ability to track and stalk. He entertained dreams of one day climbing the cliffs of Landfall to reach the misty forests of Cloudreach—and maybe even up to the jungled highlands of the Shrouds of Dalalæða, where few dared tread and even fewer returned.

But that's likely never to be.

In fact, of late, such escapes had become harder and harder, especially the higher he climbed up Kepenhill's tiers. His studies consumed more of his freedom. Because of that, he had grown to resent the school for keeping him trapped in Azantiia. To compensate, he discovered a new distraction. He learned that *escape* could be readily found at the bottom of a tankard.

It was how he found himself here, beset by lice and his head pounding.

Once dressed, he pulled a threadbare traveling cloak over his thin shoulders and ducked his head under its peaked hood. He headed out the door, down a crooked stair with several loose steps, and into the inn's common room. A handful of fisherfolk occupied a table closest to the kitchen, ensuring they got the hottest meal.

The innkeep swiped a greasy rag across an oaken bar. "What about a bit of tucker?" he called over to Kanthe. "Got porridge with boiled oxfoot and griddled oatcake."

Kanthe groaned. "As tempting as that sounds, I think I'll beg off." He jangled free his coin purse, pinched loose a silver ha'eyrie, and flipped it through the air. The coin bounced once and landed near the innkeep, who made it vanish with his rag. "For the night, with my thanks."

"This be more'n enough, lad. Too much even," the innkeep said with rare honesty.

"Ah." Kanthe placed a palm on his belly. "But you've yet to see the state of the room you lent me."

This earned a few knowing chuckles from the table of fisherfolk.

"Best imbibe what you can, laddie," one of them called over, while gnawing on an oxfoot. It appeared more porridge had made it into his beard than down his gullet. "With the lordling's fancy carousal coming up, Highmount'll be draining us dry down here in the Nethers."

Another nodded sagely. "You wait and see. They'll be rolling all our bestest casks up into their castle."

"Leaving us swill and dregs," a third concurred.

The stout man with the porridge beard spit the bones of his oxfoot onto the table. "'Course, you know who'll drink most of their stock." He elbowed his neighbor. "The Tallywag!"

Laughter spread.

"The Trifle can't be too happy," another concurred.

"That's certainly true," Kanthe admitted dourly.

"Not with his bonny brother one step closer toward the throne." Porridge Beard elbowed his other neighbor. "Especially if that Carcassa wench truly has pudding warming in her pot."

More laughter followed.

With a half-hearted wave, Kanthe left them to their merriment and headed out of the inn. He grimaced at the sun, silently cursing the Father Above. To the west, thunder rumbled, as if scolding his blasphemy.

He growled under his breath.

It seemed no one was happy with the Tallywag.

Least of all me.

With a self-pitying groan, he shaded his eyes and stared up from the city's Nethers toward the shining Crown of Highmount. He still had a long trek back to his dormitories at Kepenhill.

He lowered his face and tugged his hood higher, hiding his countenance from the Father Above. Unfortunately, it wasn't the sun that should have concerned him. As he climbed the crooked streets, his head pounded with each step. The bright morning reflection in the windows stabbed at his bleary eyes.

He staggered onward, leaning on a wall every now and then, trying to hold his stomach in place. He nearly lost his footing as he crossed the mouth of a narrow alley. A hand caught him, steadying him.

"Good thanks to you," Kanthe mumbled.

Only the same grip suddenly yanked him off the street and into the dark alleyway. More hands grabbed him, revealing a trio of brigands in shadowy cloaks. Panic iced through him at the threat. He cursed himself for letting his guard down—always a mistake in the Nethers, even in the brightness of the morning.

The point of a dagger in his side punctuated his lack of caution.

"Scream and die," a voice warned in his ear as he was forced deeper into the alley.

Kanthe remembered the heft of his purse, the generosity of a silvery ha'ey-rie tossed through the air to the barkeep. He should've known better than to be so careless with his coins. Generosity was seldom rewarded in the Nethers.

Once deep in the shadows, the thief hissed in his ear, "Looks like we caught ourselves a prince out of his cupboard."

Kanthe stiffened. He had been reaching for his coin purse, ready to relinquish it. He now recognized that its weight of brass pinches and silver eyries would not buy him his freedom this morning. Even the Sodden Prince was worth more than a fistful of eyries.

As his head spun, Kanthe barked a half-laugh. He staggered as he tried to crane back at the thief with the dagger. "You . . . You think . . . just because I'm so handsomely dark that I'm a prince?" He guffawed his contempt.

The thief's companion leaned closer, coming nose to nose with Kanthe. His breath reeked of stale beer and rotted teeth. "You sure it's him, Fent?"

Taking this opportunity, Kanthe employed his only weapon. He unclenched the tenuous hold on his gut and heaved forth a thick stream of bile. The acidy spew struck the brigand square in the face.

The man fell back with a bellow, pawing at his burning eyes.

Kanthe used the momentary shock to slam his bootheel atop the instep of his captor. As the thief cried out, Kanthe spun out of the man's grip. The dagger sliced through the fabric of his cloak, but the knife found no flesh. He kicked out with his other leg, catching the third man in the chest and slamming him into the far wall.

Kanthe did not wait and leaped away, driving for the street. He silently thanked the Cloudreach scout who taught him how to hunt, how to wield a bow, and more importantly, how to deal with the danger when a hunter became the prey. *Sometimes flight is one's greatest weapon,* Bre'bran had instilled in him.

He took that lesson to heart and burst back into the brightness of the street. He jammed into the clutch of pedestrians, knocking a wrapped bundle from a woman's arms.

"Sorry," he gasped without stopping.

He reached the first cross street and took it. As he fled, he made a silent promise to himself.

To be more cautious in the future—and far less generous.

KANTHE PANTED HEAVILY and covered his ears against the next bell's ringing. It felt like the bronze clappers were clanging against the insides of his skull.

While he outwaited the noise, he cowered in the shadows of the tunnel that passed through the Stormwall. Searching behind him for any sign of pursuit, he leaned his shoulder against its massive bricks.

The furlong-thick fortification had once marked the outermost boundary of Azantiia, protecting the city for thousands of years from the fierce storms that would sweep off the sea and into the Bay of Promise. It had also shielded Azantiia from more than foul weather. Its colossal mass had been burrowed through long ago with armories and barracks, its outer face peppered with arrowslits. Untold numbers of armies had shattered against its ramparts—not that any had dared try to for centuries.

Though if rumors of war proved true, its battlements might soon be tested again. Skirmishes were growing along the southern borders. Attacks on the kingdom's trading ships occurred with greater frequency.

As the ringing ended, Kanthe continued down the tunnel and out the opposite end, leaving the Nethers behind him—and hopefully a certain trio of thieves. Still, he kept a wary watch all around him.

Over the passing centuries, Azantiia could no longer be constrained by the Stormwall. It had spread in all directions, even out into the bay itself, building atop packed siltfields, requiring the dockworks to be extended farther and farther out.

Unfortunately, the storms still came.

Thunder rumbled behind him as a reminder.

The Nethers outside the walls were subject to sudden floods, with large swaths often drowned or blown away. But such areas were quickly rebuilt. It was said the Nethers were as variable as the weather. Maps of the place were drawn more with hope than on any measure of wayglass or sexton—and certainly never with the permanency of ink.

Beyond the Stormwall, Kanthe continued into the city proper, known as the Midlins. Under the protection of that massive fortification, homes here grew taller, some towering half the height of the wall's battlements. Many of the buildings' foundations had been built upon older foundations, one regency burying another, stacking up like the pages of a book, a history writ in stone.

The Midlins was also where most of the city's wealth settled, flowing from all directions: from the bountiful farms of the surrounding Braudlands, from the mines of Guld'guhl to the east, from the western ranches of Aglerolarpok. Everything flowed through the Nethers and into the Midlins, ending at last at the heights of Highmount, the castle-city at the center of Azantiia.

As Kanthe continued, the fly-plagued butcheries closer to Stormwall became quaint hostelries, dressmakers, cobblers—and the farther he climbed, silversmiths and jewelers appeared, along with banks and financiers. Homes became adorned with flowering window boxes. Small perfumed gardens dotted the way, often walled and behind spiked gates. At these heights, the air was salted from a near continuous blow off the bay, washing away the reek and filth of the Nethers.

With a final look around, he allowed his heart to stop pounding, feeling certain he had escaped the thieves. As he continued, he dodged his way upward through the growing throngs. Wagons and carts—the ever-flowing blood of the city—plied streets and alleyways, pulled by ponies or dehorned oxen.

A shout burst behind him, accompanied by the snap of a whip. "Aye! Out the way with ya!"

Kanthe ducked aside as a huge wagon laden with wine casks, doubly stacked, headed toward the glare of Silvergate, the towering ornate doors into Highmount. He watched the horses rush past him and remembered the fisherfolk's words at the Point'd Blade.

Seems those men had been right to be concerned about their future drinks.

Kanthe also noted how these upper streets were festooned with hundreds of flags, adorned with the sigil of the House of Massif: a dark crown set against the six points of a golden sun. In fact, the walls of Highmount had been patterned after that sun on the sigil, constructed when his family's house had assumed the throne four hundred and sixteen years ago.

Long may we rule, he thought sourly. *Not that I ever will—or even want to.*

Still, a twinge of loss pained him. When he was much younger, he would often return heartsick to his rooms at Highmount. It was the only home he had ever known. He and Mikaen had once been inseparable, the best of friends as only twins can be. But even such bonds could not withstand the destinies that pulled them in opposite directions.

Over time, Kanthe's visits grew less and less.

Which certainly suited their father.

As the king's pride in his bright son grew, his tolerance for his darker son lessened. Cold-shouldered rebuffs became fiery affronts or accusations. And maybe that was part of the reason Kanthe had found himself at the Point'd Blade, with his head aching and his stomach churning. Maybe it was to validate his father's disdain of him.

To spare them both, Kanthe had learned to avoid Highmount. But in eight days, he would have to pass through Silvergate once more.

A fierce gust blew through the streets, pushed by the approaching storm. Flags snapped overhead. A few were now emblazoned with the horned head of an ox, marking the House of Carcassa, who secured their wealth from a hundred ranchholds throughout the Brauðlands and the Aglerolarpok territories. While wagons might be the blood of the city, Carcassa put the meat on the bones of all these lands.

He scowled at the bright flags of the two houses. With each snap of cloth, they signaled that Kanthe's days as the Prince in the Cupboard were coming to an end.

A week ago, his brother had made the surprising announcement of his betrothal to Lady Myella of the noble House of Carcassa. They were due to marry in eight days. Supposedly the quick date had been picked to match when Mikaen had been born, marking the prince's seventeenth birthyear. Though whispers—like those in the tavern—wondered if such a hasty marriage might have another explanation, that perhaps Lady Myella was already with child. Of course, to speak such a rumor aloud risked getting one's tongue cut out.

Either way, it seemed Mikaen's march to the throne—with maybe a new heir apparent on his way—was assured. From here on out, Kanthe's role in life was at best counsel to the king. It was why he had been sent to Kepenhill, to be properly schooled for his future position on the king's council. And he should be grateful for the opportunity. From his historical studies at school, he knew many royal twins were not granted such a boon. Often cupboard-born princes found themselves shoved off their shelf, with a dagger in their side as a parting gift, lest there be any question of lineage that could bolster a future insurrection.

Though no one seemed to place such ambitions upon Kanthe.

Just as well.

He turned off Silverstreet and headed south, where a tall mound had been carved and sculpted into the ancient school of Kepenhill. Its nine tiers climbed to the height of Highmount's walls, with the ninth peering over its top. Twin pyres burned at the school's summit, ever smoking with incense and alchymies, beckoning him back to his home in exile.

Resigned to his role, he headed back to school. Upon reaching Kepenhill, he hurried through the school gate and began the long climb to the eighth tier. He kept rooms at that level—or, at least, for another twelve days—then he would advance to the ninth and last tier of the school.

But what after that?

He shook his head, deciding to leave such mysteries to another day— when hopefully his skull did not feel like it was about to break at the seams.

By the time he reached the eighth tier, he had sweated away the worst of his carousing. Even his sour stomach growled demandingly. He considered skipping past his rooms and going to the commons to see if he might grab a bit of cold larder, but he thought better of it, remembering the state of the room at the inn.

Best not risk fouling another bed.

He ducked out of the sun and into the eighthyear dormitory hall. His rooms dwarfed most of his fellow students' austere cells. His bedchamber's window faced Highmount, as if taunting him in his exile. Upon arriving at this level, he had shuttered that window and never opened it again.

Finally, he reached his door and found a sealed scroll tacked to its frame.

He sighed, wondering what trouble plagued him now. He snatched the parchment from the door, ripping it slightly. Out of habit, he made sure the blood-red wax seal was intact. In the hall's torchlight, he recognized the sigil—a book bound in chains—hinting at the forbidden knowledge locked in the ancient tome.

The symbol of Kepenhill.

The knot of tension between his shoulders relaxed. *Better this than the sigil of a dark crown against a golden sun.* Any word from Highmount was bound to be bad for him.

He broke the seal and unrolled the scroll. He recognized the tidy hand of Alchymist Frell. The man had been his tutor and mentor since he had first entered Kepenhill. For such an esteemed scholar, it had to be a frustrating and—more often than not—fruitless task. Still, Frell persevered with a bottomless well of patience.

Or maybe it was pity.

Holding the scroll closer to a torch, he read what was written there.

> *Prince Kanthe ry Massif,*
> *There be a matter of some import that I wish to address in confidence.*
> *If you would be so kind to join me in my private scholarium at your ear-*
> *liest convenience. It is a subject of some urgency and requiring an equal*
> *measure of discretion. Alas, I believe the resolution thereof will require*
> *a man of your status and circumspection.*

Kanthe groaned, picturing the soothing lyeleaf bath he had been dream-ing of during the long climb here. It would have to be put off. While the note's wording was genteel and one of invitation, he had no trouble gleaning the order written therein. As one of the school's Council of Eight, Frell was not to be ignored. Even worse, the summons had been posted yesterday— well after Kanthe had already started his slow slide down to a lice-ridden bed in the Nethers.

He crumpled up the parchment and turned his back on the door. He wondered what this summons could possibly be about. But from experience, he could guess the answer.

Nothing but trouble for me.

12

KANTHE STOOD AT an ironwood door branded with the sigil of Kepenhill. The only additional adornment to the mark was a silver mortar and pestle, representing the alchymists. Across the eighth tier was another locked door with a similar symbol, only its book bore a gold star, representing the hieromonks.

Kanthe had never passed through that other door.

From under his longshirt, he pulled free a heavy iron key that hung from a loop of braided leather. Though he had unlocked this particular door a thousand times during his eight years at Kepenhill, he still felt a twinge of trepidation. He turned the key and swung the door open. Past the threshold, a narrow stair spiraled upward and downward. These steps were only allowed to be used by those who had achieved the Highcryst of alchymy.

Or in Kanthe's case, a prince who had been assigned a tutor of that order.

With a steadying breath, he ascended the steps. The staircase ran from the first tier at the base of Kepenhill all the way up to the ninth tier. It allowed the alchymists to traverse the levels of the school and not be disturbed by the scrabble who ran up and down the outer steps. Overhead, the spiral ended within the confines of the half circle of towers reserved for alchymical studies on the ninth tier.

A similar stair, reserved for the hieromonks, ran from bottom to top on the other side of Kepenhill, ending in the towers committed to religious studies and devotions. Not that Kanthe had ever traversed that path—or had any interest in ever doing so.

He reached the top of the stairs where an archway—carved with all manner of arcane alchymical symbols—led out into a cavernous main hall. He kept his head down and slunk across the stone floor. Above, a massive iron candelabrum glowed with strange flames that flickered in different hues. The centermost and largest bore a black flame that expelled a stream of white smoke.

He hurried under it, holding his breath.

The very air of the hall smacked of arcane mysteries, thick with the scent of bitter chymistries and hair-tingling energies of a thunderstorm. This sense was likely heightened by his own unease. He knew well the condemnation of anyone who trespassed onto the ninth tier without proper invitation. It was certainly forbidden to students.

Kanthe had special dispensation—not so much because he was a prince of the realm, but due to the esteem of the man who tutored him. No one expected Frell to traipse up and down the school to deal with the Prince in the Cupboard. Instead, it was Kanthe who made this climb—shorter now that he had reached his eighthyear—nearly every other day.

After so many years, the other alchymists had worn past their initial shock at the sight of him. With the exception of a few annoyed glares, he was mostly ignored now—which was not much different than how his fellow students treated him. Some continued to avoid him out of jealousy, spite, or resentment at this privilege. Others had tried to curry favor initially, but after years of failure, they eventually gave up and joined the others in their disdain.

A loud boom made Kanthe jump nearly out of his boots. It came from somewhere above him. He ducked his head, picturing some experiment gone awry. Muffled shouting from the same direction reinforced this assumption. Each alchymist here had his or her own private scholarium in which to conduct studies.

Kanthe rushed to the far side of the main hall and down a curved hall lined by torches and age-blackened oils of the school's most famous scholars. He reached the doorway into the westernmost tower and climbed yet another set of steps that wound to the very top of this spire. It was where Alchymist Frell secured his own scholarium.

He reached a simple oaken door and rapped his knuckles against it. He had no idea if Frell was still here, especially as the summons was a day old.

"Hold!" a voice shouted back at him.

As Kanthe waited, a nervous shiver shook through him.

Finally, a bolt scraped on the door's far side, which surprised Kanthe. Frell seldom barred his private rooms. If anything, the man was more than happy to drone on and on about his work or get into heated discussions with other brothers or sisters of his order. He even welcomed input from the hieromonks on his work. It was this cooperative nature that likely granted him a seat on the Council of Eight, the youngest person to have ever achieved such an honor.

The door cracked open enough for Frell to peer out into the hall. The man let out an exasperated sigh and hauled the door the rest of the way open.

"Remind me to tutor you on the definition of *urgency* again," Frell scolded. "Now get yourself in here."

Kanthe stumbled inside and waited while Frell secured the door behind him. He gaped at the state of the scholarium—not to mention the scholar himself.

What is going on?

Normally Frell's spaces were orderly to the point of fussiness: books neatly aligned on shelves, scrolls ordered in their numbered cubbies, worktables free of even a speck of dust. Kanthe had understood the need for such tidiness. The space was packed from floor to vault. It was part ancient librarie, part scholarly study, and part hall of curiosities. Arcane apparatus—some glass, others bronze—rested on shelves or had been set up on tables, sometimes bubbling with elixirs and strange chymistries. And while windows looked out in every direction, they were usually—like now—shuttered tight to preserve the integrity of the precious texts kept here. Still, the room glowed with a scatter of oil lamps, their flames kept behind glass amidst all the parchment and vellum in the room.

But no longer.

"What happened here?" Kanthe asked.

Frell ignored him and hurried past with a swish of his black robe, belted at the waist with a crimson sash. The alchymist was twice Kanthe's age and a head taller in height. His dark ruddy hair had been tied to a tail in the back. Normally his features were shaven and bare, but his cheeks were shadowed with stubble. His eyes—which had always been wrinkled at the corners from his constant squinting at faded ink—were lined deeper and shadowed below. It looked as if the man hadn't slept in days and had aged a decade because of it.

Frell waved to Kanthe. "Come with me."

Kanthe followed his mentor toward the room's center. The place looked as if a gale had blustered through it. Books were stacked everywhere. Scrolls had been knocked and forgotten on the floor. Most of the oil lamps dotted one long table that had been dragged from a wall and positioned alongside the scholarium's chief apparatus—a device that also appeared to be the eye of this particular storm.

Kanthe joined Frell at the long bronze scope in the room's center. Its base was bolted atop a wheeled gear, while the far end poked through a sealed gap in the tower roof. The shaft of the huge scope was twice the size of his own thigh and lined by polished crystals and mirrors in some arcane design.

Frell leaned over a sheaf of parchment strewn atop the nearby table. He rubbed his chin, while his other hand hovered over a row of crystal inkwells—each a different color—with quills resting in them. "Let me mark this before I forget my calculations. With the moon no longer at its fullness, I must record what I can."

He selected a quill from an azure inkwell and shifted one of the parchments closer. He quickly and neatly jotted down a series of numbers next to a detailed depiction of the moon's face.

Kanthe used the time to furtively glance around. He spotted a spiral ribbon of black oilskin, recognizing a missive carried by a skrycrow. What was written there could not be discerned, but he noted a prominent sigil on one side. It was similar to Kepenhill's own mark, only the tiny book inscribed on the missive was not bound in chains but tangled in a vine of thorny nettles. He knew that sigil.

The Cloistery.

It was the school where Frell had originally been taught.

Kanthe returned his attention to the alchymist, who had finished his notation and frowned up the length of the bronze scope, as if trying to peer through the roof. Frell's studies concentrated on the mysteries of the skies, what the hieromonks ascribed to be the lofty sphere of the gods. Kanthe knew that Frell sought to understand what was written in the movement and pattern of stars—though most of his studies had to be reserved to the winter, when the sun sat at its lowest and the barest peek of stars became visible across their section of the Crown.

Kanthe could guess the reason for Frell's interest in the skies. The man had grown up at the Crown's westernmost edge, in the shadow of the Ice Fangs, marking the boundary between the Crown and the frozen wastes beyond the mountains. In those territories, the Father Above shone pale, if at all. Frell had once described the spill of stars visible from there, but Kanthe could hardly imagine it.

Here in the starless Crown, Frell had focused his study on what was most readily visible in these skies. Kanthe glanced down to the sheaf of papers, noting the detailed drawing of the moon, freshly inked and swathed in cabalistic notations, lines, measurements, all in different colors. It was quite beautiful in a cold and frightening way.

The other papers sharing the table appeared far older, yellowed by age, the ink faded to near obscurity, but all appeared to delve into the same mystery.

The moon . . .

Frell finally sighed and gave a shake of his head. "Maybe I'm addled, or moonstruck by the Son and Daughter into delusions."

"Why do you say that?" Kanthe asked. He had never heard Frell doubt himself, which disturbed him far more than he would expect. In many ways, the alchymist had been his rock throughout his turbulent youth. "What has so suddenly vexed you?"

"It's not that I'm so *suddenly* vexed. It's just that I can no longer deny a hard truth. I can no longer perch in my scholarium, read ancient texts, and continue my idle measurements. Studies can only carry one so far. Eventually speculation becomes inevitability."

"I don't understand. What's inevitable?"

Frell reached over and gripped Kanthe's arm. "That the world will come to an end, that the gods intend to destroy us."

KANTHE STRUGGLED TO understand what followed. Shock continued to deafen him to Frell's words. Kanthe couldn't believe the blasphemy being spoken aloud by his mentor.

". . . wanted to dismiss it," Frell tried to explain. "Then two days ago, word from the Cloistery arrived, and I knew all my measurements and calculations could no longer be ignored or pushed aside."

Kanthe glanced at the black missive, then over to the spread of drawings of the moon. He finally found his voice again. "What measurements? What calculations?"

"Let me show you, so you'll better understand what I fear will come to pass."

Frell shifted the older parchments and reordered them in a row. He tapped the parchment on the farthest left. "This limne was inscribed seven centuries ago, near the time when Kepenhill was first founded. Look how detailed the moon's features were drawn, truly remarkable considering how crude the viewscopes were back then. It must have been painstaking work, especially gauging the breadth of the moon's face."

"What of it?" Kanthe pressed.

Frell shifted three more pages closer. "These are from two hundred, one hundred, and fifty years ago." He glanced to Kanthe. "The last was mapped by the cartographer Lyrrasta, after she turned from her study of geographica to chart the skies."

"Wasn't she the one burned at the stake?" Kanthe asked, scrunching up his face as he dredged up an old history lesson. He could easily be wrong. There was a long litany of many who had suffered such a fate—or worse— for questioning matters best left to the gods.

"She was," Frell admitted. "She made the mistake of doubting the existence of the Son and Daughter, attributing much of their dance to invisible forces. But that's not the point here. Her map of the moon's face and its calculations add to a pattern going back centuries, if not farther."

"What pattern?"

Frell tapped a number inscribed on each page, corresponding to the width of the moon's face. Even Kanthe could see the numbers had steadily grown larger over the centuries.

Kanthe squinted at the pages. "I don't understand. Does this mean the moon has been getting bigger?"

"Or more likely it draws closer to the Urth. Still, I could not be certain from historical accounts alone. There could be vagaries in the method of measurement, or the seasons they were recorded, or even the positions along the Crown where they were mapped. I tried to account for those changes, while searching for additional validation."

"Like what?"

Frell gave a small shake of his head. "Changes in the tides over the centuries. Or the frequency of a woman's bleed, which we know is tied to the Daughter. I even researched the behavior of nocturnal creatures, which abide to the waxing and waning of the Son's face."

"And did these studies reveal anything?"

"Nothing that I could use to definitively corroborate my growing fears. So, I've been doing my own measurements of the moon's face, every time it reaches its fullness. For over a decade now. Yet, I still could not be sure. The changes were so minuscule over such a short time. I feared it would take my entire life to confirm or rule out my worries."

"Then what's got you so lathered up now?"

Frell pulled more pages forward. "Over the past year, the changes have become more prominent. With each turn of the moon. And I certainly cannot discount these results."

"Because it's all your own work. Right here at Kepenhill."

He nodded. "The moon's face grows with each turn. It cannot be denied. Faster and faster."

Kanthe craned his neck, trying to peer at the moon through the roof. "But what does that mean? You mentioned the end of the world."

"I fear, before long—certainly within the next few years—the Daughter above will return to her Mother, crashing to the Urth and ending all life."

Kanthe pictured the moon striking the world, like a hammer against an anvil.

"The king should be warned," Frell said. "And soon. To that end, you can be of great assistance. I need to gain an audience with your father and his council. Action is required—though I can't imagine what that might be."

Kanthe turned sharply toward his tutor. There were some things princes knew far better than alchymists. "You mustn't do that," he squeaked out. "My father—like every hieromonk here—believes the gods to be immutable. To even whisper elsewise would get you condemned."

He pictured Lyrrasta burning at a stake.

"And even if your warning isn't judged blasphemous," Kanthe said, "my father is ruled by portents. He has scores of soothers and bone-readers who whisper in his ear. He hardly takes a morning shite without first consulting them. And you wish to tell the king—a man preparing for war with the Klashe—that the gods will soon punish us. To whisper of doom when he rallies for war—he'll deem it not just blasphemous but traitorous. If he kills you on the spot, you'll be lucky."

Despite his best effort, Frell looked far from dissuaded. The man rubbed a finger along the stubbled crease of his chin. He clearly accepted Kanthe's words but sought a path around them.

Kanthe huffed his exasperation and tried a different tack before Frell outmaneuvered him. "You know the tale of the Forsworn Knight."

Frell stiffened, likely baffled by the change in topics, though he did glance at the curled missive from the Cloistery.

Ah, at least he knows where this particular tale ends.

Frell turned back to Kanthe with a frown. "What does that sad story have to do with—"

"So you can understand my father better," Kanthe explained. "Everyone knows Graylin sy Moor—whose name was stricken from the legion and who would be damned forevermore as the Forsworn Knight. He who broke his oath of fidelity and fealty, by bedding one of my father's most cherished pleasure serfs, a beauty unlike any other."

Frell nodded. "And when she grew with child, the knight absconded with her, fleeing into the swamps of Mýr."

"Where she died. Her body gutted, torn to pieces, and coated black with flies. The babe ripped from her womb." Kanthe closed his eyes, recognizing there were worse fates than being born a Prince in the Cupboard. "Graylin was eventually captured, broken on a wheel, and exiled from the kingdom, forbidden to ever wield a weapon or even raise a fist. But it's also said he refused to deny his love for the woman, even under torture. He ultimately died in exile—not from his injuries, but from heartache."

Frell crossed his arms, looking away. "Indeed. It is a hard lesson, both of broken oaths and broken hearts."

"But that is not the entire story," he said, drawing back Frell's attention. "Did you know what my father believed? Why he so pursued knight and serf, sending most of his legion after them?"

Frell answered with silence.

"In truth, my father cared nothing about that serf. The woman is not even named in those tales. In fact, the king was generous in opening his palacio of pleasure serfs to other men, both those in his legion and members of his inner council."

And to a certain beloved first son.

Kanthe continued, "And my father certainly did not care if the babe in the womb was of his own loins or the knight's. For centuries, the matrons of the serfs knew how to deal with royal bastards, those that slipped past their thwarting teas."

Frell swallowed. "Then why did your father pursue the knight and serf with such fervor?"

"Because of the word of a bone-reader, one he holds in great esteem. And not just any soother but one who binds his brows in black and wears a gray robe."

Frell's eyes widened. "One of the Shriven."

"Only this holy man kisses the symbol of the *horn'd snaken,* and according to my father, communes directly with the dark god Đreyk."

"So, an Iflelen . . ." Frell looked aghast, like he wanted to spit.

"Back then, the Shrive hissed in my father's ear, warning that the child carried by the serf—whether a royal bastard or the knight's—would end the world. Upon that whisper, my father hunted Graylin, a man he had long considered one of his most loyal knights, whose friendship he had once cherished. All to kill a poor child shadowed by a portent of doom."

In the narrowing of Frell's eyes, Kanthe read the understanding there. Still, he pressed harder. "And you want to bend a knee before my father and stoke that old fear. You think he will welcome such counsel in a time of pending war?"

"I don't intend to bring him portents found in a toss of bones or the entrails of the sacrificed, but in proper alchymies that cannot be denied."

The pounding in Kanthe's head had started again. He rubbed at his temples to try to drive it away. "I have no more faith in soothers' prophecies than you. I think that cursed Shrive just whispered what my father wanted to hear so he could justify ridding the world of a potential bastard. Or maybe the Shrive's portent was self-serving, telling this tale to drive a stake into the heart of a beloved knight who had the king's ear, thus eliminating a competitor. But since that time, my father has fallen further and further into the sway of such whispers, especially from that Shrive."

Kanthe stared hard at Frell. "Your voice will not be heard above those whispers. And even if you are believed, your words will be turned against you. I know this to be true. And what will you gain from it? By your own admission, you offer no solution, no action that can stop the doom you wish to lay at my father's feet."

Frell slowly nodded. "You've persuaded me."

Kanthe should have been relieved, but he noted a hardening resolve in the other's eyes.

"To truly convince the king," Frell said, "it will take an even greater blasphemy."

"No, that's not what—"

Frell patted Kanthe's arm. "No reason to go to battle with my sword half-drawn." He shrugged. "I can only be put to death once, right?"

Kanthe groaned. "What do you intend to do?"

"You were correct a moment ago. I can't only bring a *problem* to the king, but I must also offer a *solution*." He turned to study the spread of parchments on the table. "To accomplish that, I must delve into the *cause* of it all. And I suspect I know where to start."

"Where's that?"

"There's a forbidden text, rumored to have been written by Lyrrasta herself. It is said to address the relationship between the moon and the Urth, between the Son and Daughter and their Mother Below. It speaks of those invisible forces that bind all together in a dance. But the tome is said to also attend to the greatest blasphemy of all."

"Which is what?"

"That long ago, before our histories were written, Lyrrasta believed the Mother Below did not always face the Father Above—that she once turned on her own, spinning all the Urth's surfaces toward the sun."

Kanthe scoffed loudly. Such an idea was not only blasphemous, but a ridiculous impossibility. He tried to picture the world twirling round and round, the sun baking one side, then the other. The world going cold, then hot again. He felt his own head spinning at just the thought. How could anyone survive such madness?

"I must secure that text," Frell insisted. "I know answers can be found there."

"But where do you hope to find such a book?"

"In the Black Librarie of the Anathema."

Kanthe felt the ground open up under him. He even stared at his feet, knowing where that cursed librarie was buried. It lay down in the darkest depths of the Shrivenkeep.

Frell stepped toward the door. "I must go there. Before it's too late."

13

What am I doing?

Kanthe followed Frell down the winding stairs, passing one tier after another. Throughout most of the descent, he had tried to dissuade Frell from this course, from bringing his dark fears to the bright thronehall of Azantiia—and certainly from traipsing into the Shrivenkeep.

He finally gave up and went silent.

Every student of Kepenhill knew what lay beneath the roots of their school, the shadowy halls of the holy Shriven. It was said the Shrivenkeep delved as deep as Kepenhill climbed high.

Of course, rumors abounded of the place: of arcane rituals, of chained monsters, of witchcraft and warlockry. Kepenhill's teachers sought to allay such stories. They insisted the keep beneath the school was merely a monastic hermitage of deep study and scholarly pursuits. The Shriven—those rarified few who achieved the Highcryst in both alchymy and religion—continued loftier arcane studies down there. They pursued dangerous inquiries, involving deep meditations and herbal-induced trances. They delved into cabalistic experiments and sought paths beyond all boundaries of horizon and history. To ensure secrecy, their labors had to be buried away from the common eye, even from the oversight of Kepenhill's alchymists and hieromonks.

It also didn't help with the gossip-mongering when the Shriven themselves were rarely seen. No one quite knew how they came and went from their keep. Whispers of secret passages and hidden doors kept students wary to be alone, lest they be whisked to some bloody sacrifice. Compounding this, students *had* disappeared, vanishing without a trace—though, Kanthe suspected those missing few were merely malcontents who sought the freedom beyond the school's walls.

I certainly appreciate that desire.

Whether any of the stories of the Shrivenkeep were true, Kanthe did not have any particular desire to find out. Still, he continued after Frell down the steps.

The alchymist slowed as they reached the first tier of the school. The staircase spiraled even deeper. Frell paused before leading Kanthe down into the dark roots under the school. He glanced back over a shoulder.

"Prince Kanthe," he warned, "perhaps you should return to your rooms. I will do my best to argue my way into the keep's librarie. Though permission is rare, it's not unheard of. In addition, I know several Shriven who will at least consider my plea."

Kanthe waved for Frell to continue their descent. "When it comes to prying open the Shrivenkeep's doors, you may need more help than a couple of friends on the inside. If you truly wish to gain entrance, a prince at your side is far better than a wind out your arse."

Frell sighed and continued down. "Perhaps you're correct."

Kanthe followed. He was certainly not above using his station to help Frell in his cause—but such generosity was also self-serving. Hopefully his mentor would spend many days in the librarie, or at least long enough for Kanthe to devise another way to keep Frell from bringing portents of doom to the king.

With things settled, they passed under the first tier and descended even deeper. The stairs wound another five turns before they ended at an ebonwood door strapped and studded in iron. The sight of it sent a shiver down Kanthe's back, especially the emblem carved into its lintel. It was a book yet again, bound not in chains or nettles, but in the grip of a fanged viper. Such a symbol warned of the poisonous knowledge found beyond this threshold.

Frell stepped forward, removed a key from his pocket, and undid the lock. As he pulled the door ajar, Kanthe stopped him with a palm against the ebonwood. Frell scowled in consternation, but Kanthe shook his head.

Don't.

Voices reached them both—faint at first, then clearer with the door peeked open.

Kanthe had no trouble recognizing the gruff authority of his father. He also knew from long experience that it was best not to catch the king by surprise. He also feared Frell might use this sudden opportunity to blurt out his fears right here and now.

I can't let that happen.

Keeping his palm on the door, Kanthe motioned Frell to the side so they could spy upon the proceedings in the next room. Four figures clustered in the center of a cavernous space that had been carved out of glassy black stone. The walls and roof had been cut into large facets, each mirroring the movement in the room. A score of ebonwood doors, identical to the one they hid behind, lined the walls, each with a different symbol carved into its lintel.

Where do all those lead to?

Kanthe remembered the rumors of the Shrivenkeep's secret passages. Certainly, *one* must lead to Highmount, especially as the king was here without his usual retinue of guards.

He studied his father, who had come dressed in polished kneeboots, silk leggings, and an embroidered velvet doublet. A thick dark blue cloak draped from shoulder to ankle, as if any garment could truly hide the grandeur of Highking Toranth ry Massif, the Crown'd Lord of Hálendii, rightful ruler of all the kingdom and its territories.

His father's pale and stony countenance was reflected a hundredfold in the polished facets of the walls. His features were all sharp-edged but softened by a halo of white-blond hair, the curls of which had been oiled nearly flat. A scowl of disappointment—an expression well familiar to Kanthe—currently marred his lips.

"You lost the bronze relic?" Toranth boomed. "An artifact that could assure our victory in the war to come. Is that why you flew all the way back here, to lay your failure at my feet?"

"A setback, I assure you, Your Majesty. One that will be duly corrected once we find the escaped prisoner who stole it. All of Anvil is being tossed and turned over. The thief cannot keep such strangeness out of sight for long."

Kanthe knew the man down on one knee, recognizing the gray robe, the black tattoo banded across his eyes, and the silver hair braided around his neck. It was the Shrive who was always whispering darkly in his father's ear. The man kept his head bowed, trying his best to soothe the fury before him with determined obeisance.

Frell hissed under his breath, "Wryth."

The single word held enough disgust to fill a thousand-page tome.

So, I'm not the only one who knows this bastard.

"I will return on the morrow's wyndship back to Guld'guhl," the Shrive promised. "I will personally see to the artifact's return. My entire life has been devoted to the search for ancient magicks born of lost alchymies. I will not let this godling in bronze slip our nets."

"It must not," the king ordered. "Liege General Haddan fears your thief may try to ransom this great weapon to the Klashe to buy his freedom. He believes it's the cur's only recourse."

"Indeed. We have already taken such a possibility into our accounting. Klashe spies—those known to us—have been rounded up and questioned under torture. In addition, the docks of Anvil are watched through every bell. There is no escape. The godling will be ours again."

The king's shoulders shifted away from his ears. "Make it happen," he finished with less fire. "In the meantime, I have another problem to address. A plea from a second cousin across the bay. Trouble out in Mýr."

Wryth's eyes narrowed at this last.

But Kanthe's father dismissed the man with a wave of his hand. "Attend to your search in Anvil. Haddan and I will address this other matter. If we're successful, we might not even need ancient magicks and godlings to ensure our victory."

The interest in Wryth's face sharpened, but he simply stood and backed a step, offering a humble bow that from the Shrive came off as mocking.

The king missed this as he turned to the tall youth standing in light armor at his side, another figure all too familiar to Kanthe. "Mikaen, it seems in short order we'll find a use for your younger brother yet."

Kanthe stiffened.

What's this?

The king turned to the fourth member of the group. The figure was as round as he was short, dressed in the white of the hieromonks, but he was no simple teacher. He was the speaker of the Council of Eight, the head of all of Kepenhill.

"Abbot Naff, summon my son and have him brought to my council chamber by the first bell of Eventoll."

"It will be done," the man said with a bow of his head.

Kanthe shifted back as the group began to disperse. Frell silently closed the door and keyed the lock. He then herded Kanthe up the steps.

Neither of them spoke until they'd reached the third tier of the school.

"What was that all about?" Kanthe stammered. "Ancient magicks? A great weapon? A godling in bronze?"

"I don't know," Frell admitted. "But if that damnable Wryth is involved, it can't be good. Of late, the Iflelen have grown stronger in the darkness of Shrivenkeep. A turn not unexpected. Too often, words of wisdom are drowned out by the drumbeats of war. Fear stokes direr ambitions, sometimes even in the best of us. And in the worst of us . . ."

Frell's words died off.

Kanthe pictured Shrive Wryth. "What are we going to do?"

Frell increased his pace. "First, we're going to make sure I join you in that council chamber."

Kanthe stopped. "You're not planning to bring up—"

"No, we'll leave the moon to the Son and Daughter for now. Something is amiss in the swamps of Mýr. I don't quite fathom how this all hangs together, but I put little stock on chance and happenstance. Something is stirring. Here, off in Guld'guhl, and now in Mýr."

Kanthe remembered the black missive on the alchymist's table, wondering again what message had been sent to Frell. He rubbed his throat as he climbed the steps. Like Frell, he also sensed forces just out of sight.

Only for him, they felt like a noose tightening around his neck.

AS THE FIRST bell of Eventoll died away, Kanthe stood straight-backed before the long council table, as stiff as the finery he had dusted off and the formal boots he had donned after his lyeleaf bath. He'd even curried his dark velvet half-cloak until it shone.

Best play the prince while I can.

He kept his hands clasped behind him, his shoulders back. Before him, the table was sparsely seated. It was as if the gathering in the Shrivenkeep had simply shifted to this stone chamber behind the thronehall. Only Kanthe was relieved to discover that Shrive Wryth had been replaced by Liege General Haddan sy Marc.

The head of Hálendii's legions sat to the right of the king. Even seated, he towered over Kanthe's father. The man kept his head shaved, all the easier to don his helm, though Kanthe suspected it was more about baring his scars for all to see, especially the jagged line that cut from crown to jaw on his left side. He was likely prouder of those hard-earned wounds than any ribbon, badge, or medal. The man's black eyes were always polished flints. It was doubtful his lips had ever formed a smile—at least, not that Kanthe had ever seen.

The only stranger here was a reed-thin man with straw-colored locks who sat a few seats down from the others, as if not allowed any closer to the king. The man's gaze darted all about, when it was not directed at his lap. His brow shone damply. His raiment was neat and clean, but far from the regalia on display here and looked several years behind in fashion, like the silly ruffles of his shirt.

Kanthe's father must have noted the direction of his attention. "Vice-Mayor Harlac hy Charmane, from Fiskur across the bay," King Toranth introduced. "A second cousin to you and your brother."

The man stiffened, near to leaping out of his seat. He looked from king to prince to yet another prince.

So, a poor relation, one clearly out of place here.

Kanthe noted a small smile of derision on Mikaen's face. His twin lounged to their father's left, leaning on the arm of his chair. He had trimmed his gold-blond hair to a skullcap of tight curls, again likely for ease of suiting into armor. He looked far harder than when last the two of them had faced one another. His sea-blue eyes had an ice to them now. He seemed far more a man than Kanthe, no longer the boon companion who chased his younger brother through these halls, shouting and laughing.

In even this way, they had grown apart.

Dressed in his best finery, Kanthe still felt like a coarse chunk of coal before a hard, polished diamond.

Their father spoke again. "Your cousin Harlac has come to us with a tale both strange and tragic. A difficulty that his brother, the highmayor of Fiskur, seeks our help to amend."

Kanthe heard Frell stir behind his left shoulder. The alchymist had accompanied him here after the summons from Abbot Naff, offering his assistance. Naff had tried to discourage his attendance, but the abbot had no more luck than Kanthe in turning aside the stubborn alchymist.

"What tale did our cousin tell?" Kanthe asked, finally speaking up.

The king leaned forward. "The mayor's son—who was in his seventhyear at the Cloistery—was slain most brutally. His head ripped from his shoulders by a monstrous Mýr bat."

Kanthe inwardly flinched, knowing any outward reaction would be judged.

"The mayor asks for a force to accompany his daughter back to school, and once there, to rid the swamps of such a savage monster."

Kanthe frowned. He knew such beasts numbered in the thousands, hunting throughout the swamps and marshes. "How can we possibly know which beast slew our cousin's son?" he asked, stymied how any just vengeance could be achieved.

"Ah." The king motioned to the liege general. "I'll let Haddan elaborate."

The huge man cleared his throat of what sounded like a blockage of rocks. "We'll proceed into the swamps with a full century of our forces."

Kanthe choked back a gasp.

A hundred knights? For a hunt?

But Haddan wasn't done. "And they'll be led by a score of Vyrllian Guard."

Now Kanthe did gasp, which earned a humorless smile from his older twin. The Vyrllian Guard contained the legion's most elite fighters, battle-hardened with faces entirely tattooed in crimson, both to mark their blooded status and to strike fear into their enemies.

"We will not be hunting for a lone killer," Haddan continued. "For too long, such monsters have plagued the swamps. We will commence a great hunt, to eliminate as many of the foul beasts as we can over the turn of a moon. If we can't rid them all, we'll at least knock them back and give them good caution to ever return to the haunts of men."

Kanthe felt sick, trying to imagine such a slaughter. As a hunter, he had learned to take only what one needed from a forest or meadow. Wanton killing for no other reason than bloodshed struck him as cruel and heartless. He could not even stomach the steel traps he sometimes encountered. When he did, he would spring them with a branch or stick, lest those sharp teeth imprison and needlessly torture a beast.

Frell stepped forward into Kanthe's stunned silence. "Excuse me, sire, but if I might make an inquiry, as I spent nine years in Mýr."

Toranth waved permission.

Frell bowed his thanks, then spoke. "If I'm not overstepping myself, I imagine that such a culling of these creatures goes beyond mere vengeance."

The king lifted one brow. "It seems there is a reason you're the youngest of Kepenhill's Council of Eight."

"I'm honored, sire."

"But you are correct. There is another purpose behind this hunt. For the past year, Haddan and Abbot Naff have strategized ways to strengthen our weaponry. From novel designs of war machines to new chymistries of quick-lime and pitch."

Kanthe remembered the loud boom that had shaken through Kepenhill.

His father continued, "But the Shriven have suggested another way to add potency and malignancy to our arrows, blades, and spears."

Frell nodded. "Poison."

The king's other brow rose to join the first. "Exactly. It is well known that the venom of these winged beasts is inordinately deadly. No man has survived it. The Shriven believe that if that poison could be properly distilled from the glands of those monsters that the lethality of our weaponry could be increased a hundredfold."

Kanthe swallowed hard, both impressed and horrified.

"Which brings us to a last detail," Toranth said. "I said no *man* has ever survived this venom—but a *woman* has. A blind girl who was involved in the attack atop the Cloistery. Not only did she survive the poison, but her sight was returned to her. Surely such a miracle is a sign from the gods."

Frell's shoulders tightened.

"I want her brought back to Highmount," Toranth said. "Here where the Shriven and our physiks can properly study her in full. Blood, bile, flesh, whatever is necessary. Knowledge of her uniqueness might prove valuable. And whether it does or not, such a blessing from the gods should not languish in the swamps."

The king's gaze finally fixed upon his dark son. "And as these matters are of utmost importance to the realm, Prince Kanthe will join the hunt."

Kanthe fell back a step, shocked.

The king continued, "Word has reached me of his considerable skill in such pursuits. It is high time for my second son to come out of the shadows and prove his worth."

Kanthe tried to balk, imagining himself slogging through a bog. He sought words to argue against his involvement, but he found none. How could he refuse the king, deny his father?

Mikaen looked no happier. He sat straighter and leaned over to whisper in the king's ear, but he was scolded away. All Mikaen could do was cast an aghast look at both king and liege general.

Heat built in Kanthe's breast. Was his brother so enamored with himself that he couldn't let his brother be polished a little brighter?

Frell stood taller. "My liege, if I may, I would like to accompany Prince Kanthe. If he's to be gone a full moon, I can continue his studies, using lessons found in the swamp or at the Cloistery. And mayhap my knowledge of the winged denizens could prove useful in the distillation of the beasts' poison."

The king waved flippantly. "Whatever you think best."

Frell bowed and backed to join Kanthe. The alchymist cast him a worried sidelong look. Kanthe remembered the black missive on his mentor's table and felt the noose around his neck snug even tighter. But now was not the time to discuss such concerns, especially as all eyes were now upon the king's dark son.

"Wh . . . When do we depart?" Kanthe stammered out.

"Your ship sets sail in two short days," his father replied. "So you best ready yourself."

Kanthe nodded. He understood the haste. The king wanted his youngest son—ever the embarrassment to the family—gone from the city before the coming marriage of Mikaen to Lady Myella.

So be it.

With everything settled, the king pushed his chair back with a loud squeak and stood.

Mikaen quickly followed suit. So did all the others. As Haddan shoved up, he stared over at Kanthe, his face stoic and cold. A hand rested on the pommel of a sheathed dagger as he sized up the younger of the two princes. From the deepening scowl before he turned away, the liege general did not like what he saw.

I can't disagree with you, Kanthe thought. *But maybe that could change.*

And he knew the first step toward that goal.

KANTHE IGNORED THE glances cast his way as he climbed the stone stairs that wound through the barracks of the Legionary. He had never set foot inside here before. He had expected to hear the clash of steel, the raucous calls of hard men, the ribaldry of comrades-in-arms.

Instead, the training halls of the king's legions seemed as studious as any found at Kepenhill. The only exception was the bawling and barking from the kennels at the base of the barracks, where the legion's war dogs were housed and trained alongside the boys and young men.

As Kanthe climbed, he was eyed by those he crossed on the stairs. Even if he wasn't still dressed in his formal finery, everyone knew the Tallywag, the Sodden Prince of Highmount. Whispers and smatters of laughter followed in his wake, but he kept his back straight.

He reached the eighth tier of the barracks, searched for the proper door, and rapped his knuckles on it.

A muffled curse answered him, accompanied by a shuffling. The door was yanked open. "What do you want—"

Mikaen's words died as he recognized the visitor standing at his threshold. The storm building atop his brother's brow blew out and was replaced with a narrow-eyed wariness. "Kanthe, what're you doing here? Did you get lost on your way back to Kepenhill?"

Kanthe ignored the jibe and shoved past his brother. As he entered Mikaen's room, he was surprised to discover the domicile of the king's bright son was even smaller than Kanthe's place at Kepenhill. There was a mussed bed, a small scarred desk, and a large wardrobe, which stood open, revealing the silvery glint of armor. Mikaen had stripped out of his own finery and wore only a longshirt, exposing his bare legs. He looked far younger, less the polished knight-in-training.

Kanthe raised the small ebonwood box that he had carried here. "A gift. For your wedding. Since I won't be attending your nuptials."

Mikaen frowned. "You could've sent a courier."

"I wanted to deliver it in person."

Mikaen sighed and accepted the box. He undid the clasp and opened it. He stared inside for a long breath. When he lifted his face again, a small smile graced his handsome lips. The expression was both winsome and amused.

"You kept it," he said.

Kanthe shrugged. "How could I not?"

Mikaen lifted out the small sculpture that was cradled inside the case. It was a rough bit of pottery, formed of molded clay, rolled and prodded into the crude shape of two boys. The figures faced each other, clasping arms. One had been glazed in crackles of white, the other in dark gray.

Kanthe nodded to it. "You made that for me when I was laid up in bed with a bout of Firepester, when no one was allowed in my sick room."

Mikaen's voice cracked a bit. "I remember . . . I wanted to be beside you, even when I couldn't." He glanced over. "Why do you return this to me now?"

"For the same reason you gave it to me long ago. I leave in two days. You will soon be married. I wanted you to know that as much as we've grown apart—" He pointed to the kiln-fused arms of the tiny figures. "I'll always be with you in spirit."

Still, there was another reason Kanthe had snuck back to their old rooms in Highmount and removed the box hidden under the floorboards. He had wanted to remind Mikaen of the boy he once was, someone kind to a feverish younger brother. While they had spent the past eight years growing apart, maybe now was a chance to reverse that, to find their way back to one another.

Mikaen gently lowered the piece of pottery into its case, returning both princes to their tiny cupboard. He placed the box on his desk and rested his palm atop the lid. "Thank you, brother."

"Know this," Kanthe said. "To the best of my abilities, I will always be at your side. This I swear."

"I'm going to hold you to that promise." Mikaen faced around; a boyish grin played about his lips. "That is, if you don't get yourself killed in those swamps. I tried to dissuade Father from sending you, but his mind is set. You know how stubborn he can be."

All too well.

Still, Kanthe inwardly cringed. He remembered Mikaen whispering in the king's ear at the council table, only to be scolded away. Kanthe had thought that particular exchange had been motivated out of jealousy, not concern.

Kanthe stepped forward and hugged his twin brother. Mikaen stiffened for a breath, then relaxed, finally encircling Kanthe in a hard embrace. The years fell away between them.

"I can try again," Mikaen offered in his ear. "To convince the king that you should remain here."

Kanthe broke their hold. They were left grasping each other's forearms, as if the brittle pottery had come to life.

"No, dear brother," he said, "it's high time for this prince to get out of the cupboard."

Once and for all.

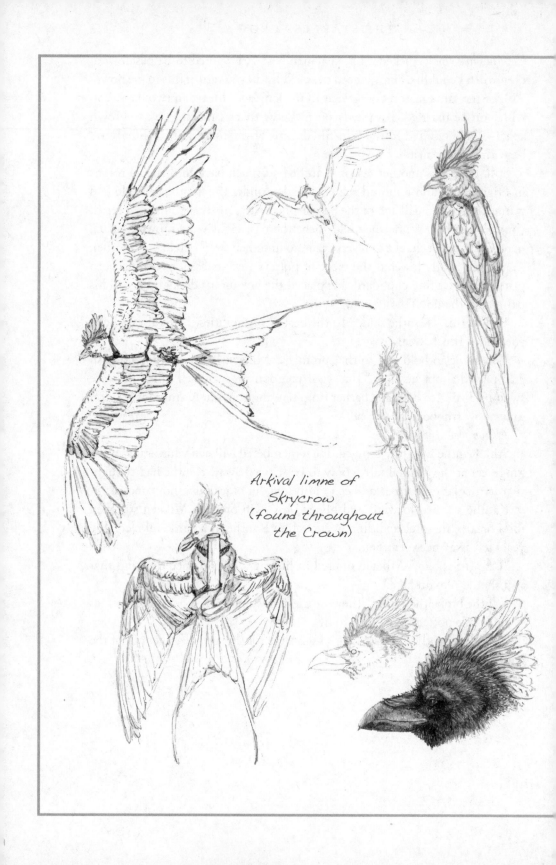

Arkival limne of
Skrycrow
(found throughout
the Crown)

FIVE

RUMORS OF RUIN

Those who ascend the heyest
Risk suffering the grettest fall.
Those who turn their back in fear
Will næffre knou what awaits
Biyonde the far horizon.

—Words etched on the ninth step of the ninth tier
of every school across the Crown; tradition holds
it be kissed by each Ascendant

14

NYX STARED IN the silver mirror at the miracle before her.

"It suits you," Jace said. "Like you were always meant to wear it."

Nyx smiled shyly, smoothing a palm down the ceremonial robe. One side was starkly white, so bleached that it ached the eye in bright sunlight. The other was as black as burnt coal, so dark it seemed to draw shadows to it with every swish. She had never imagined she would ever wear such finery, certainly not a robe of Ascension.

In three days, she and the other aspiring ninthyears would climb the steps to the summit. Starting down at the first tier, their ascent would begin with the dawn bell and take until the final ring of Eventoll. They would traverse the course on their hands and knees, contemplating where they had started and where they were headed. Only once they kissed the ninth step leading up to the top could they stand and take their place at the summit of the Cloistery.

For seven years, she had watched the procession from the side, both envious and proud of those crawling skyward.

And soon I will be among them.

"I can hardly believe it," she mumbled to the mirror.

"I never doubted it," Jace said, grinning broadly.

She smiled back at him in the reflection, but her expression was strained by guilt. Jace had failed his fifthyear. He would never wear this robe. Yet, over the past span of days, he had never once showed a flicker of jealousy or spite. Even now, she read the pride shining in his bright round eyes, in the genuineness of his smile. He also showed no resentment for the crick in his healing nose. The break was surely still sore after the pummeling he had suffered because of her.

The wound tempered her jubilation, reminding her that she had enemies.

With the midsummer break ending in three days, many of the students who had left for home or escaped the hottest part of the year for more pleasant climes were already returning. The stairs between levels had grown more crowded. The noise and bustle of the school increased each day.

During this time, Nyx had kept wary watch for any of her former classmates, especially those who had hunted her, one in particular. So far, there had been no sign of Kindjal, the sister of Byrd. She glanced down to her palms, expecting to see blood there.

Jace must have sensed the darkening of her mood. He shifted and rubbed his ink-stained hands. He had come straight from the scriptorium to review her final fitting. He still wore a leather apron from liming fresh hides this morning.

"Now that we know your robe is properly hemmed," he said, "you had best return it to its chest until the ceremony. I'll step outside. Once you're done, we should start on that last volume of Hálendii histories and review those geometrical theorems that you were struggling with."

"Of course," she said, but it came out like a groan. She apologized with a warmer smile at Jace. "I'll be right out."

Jace met her gaze for a breath, then turned away, his cheeks blushing nearly as bright as the red locks that poked from beneath his leather cap. He hurried out of the dressing chamber. Once alone, she faced the mirror again. She chewed her lower lip, reluctant to take the robe off. She had worked so hard to obtain it. She feared if she slipped it off that it would vanish away, like in some taunting dream.

She pinched the rich linen, testing its thickness and solidity.

"This is mine," she whispered, staring at her face, watching her lips move. "I've earned it."

She tried to force those words into her heart, as she had every day. But again, she failed. She knew the only reason she was wearing this robe was because Prioress Ghyle had convinced the others that her survival was some portentous blessing of the Mother, marking Nyx as worthy of Ascension.

Unfortunately, Nyx could not convince herself of the same.

Especially considering how far I'm behind in my studies.

She glanced back to the door.

Jace had spent most of the past fortnight instructing her here, in a set of rooms near the fourth tier's healing wards. The space—abandoned by a physik who had left for the jungles of the Shrouds in search of new herbal medicums—had been granted to her by the prioress. Nyx had no other place to go. She was no longer a seventhyear, and as she was skipping the eighth, she had no room on that level. Even the ninth was forbidden to her until after the formal ceremony.

She could have gone home to her dah and brothers, but the prioress had wanted her close to Physik Oeric in case her health worsened. Plus, she had a slew of studies she needed to complete, to fill the gaps in her knowledge from skipping her eighthyear and to do her best to catch up to the ninthyears.

Ghyle had given Nyx and Jace a long list of assignments, the essentials of the eighthyear lessons. The prioress had also sent over a bevy of novitiates and alchymical students to help with this task. Still, most of the work had fallen on Jace's considerable shoulders.

Up until now, Nyx had been proud of her accomplishments, confident that she could tackle any thorny problem if given enough time. No longer. She felt like a firstyear again, unsure, lost, struggling. Jace even had to teach her to read. He had always been her eyes in the past. Now that she could see, she needed to learn to read on her own, and she still fared poorly at it.

It was all too much, too daunting.

She covered her eyes with her palms, letting the darkness calm her.

I can do this.

Her only hope of making that come true was Jace. Even after she ascended, he would continue to aid her. The prioress recognized that Nyx would need his ongoing support—both in her studies and as a friend. All the other aspiring ninthyears had climbed through the tiers together as a class. She would be joining them as a stranger, an interloper, and likely viewed as someone unworthy to be among them.

She took a deep breath and lowered her hands. As much as she might wish to return to the comforting familiarity of her clouded vision, she had to learn to live in this new world.

She opened her eyes and searched her face in the mirror. Her reflection still struck her as strange. It was the face she had always pictured in her mind's eye, but then again not. When her vision had been clouded, she thought she had a good notion of herself, between what she could read with her fingers and how others described her. But her returned vision added details she hadn't imagined.

She ran fingers through her brown hair, so dark it could be misconstrued as black, but within its shadows were golden strands, as if a sun lay hidden somewhere within. Her complexion was a richer color of polished amber, her lips rosier, and her eyes bluer, speckled with flecks of silver.

In many ways it was a stranger in that mirror, but maybe therein lay another measure of hope. Maybe she could set aside the girl she was, the meek and beclouded girl. And become the woman in the reflection, the one stranded in gold and flecked in silver.

"I can do this," she tried again.

She almost believed it.

Almost.

She firmed her resolve to redouble her efforts on her lessons. If nothing else, the hard work had pushed the fear nestled inside her deeper and deeper. Collapsing into bed each night, exhausted and mind-numbed from studying, she slept soundly. No more screams or visions of arcane rituals under a swelling moon plagued her slumbers. She refused to even utter the word *moonfall*. She certainly hadn't shared any of this with the prioress, especially as that strange bat had never returned to haunt her rafters. How could she try to explain her inflamed memories, of the sweet taste of milk on her tongue, the spicy warmth of pelt and wing, the red eyes glowing across to her from another nipple?

She wanted to dismiss it all as a fevered dream from her poisoning, to put that darkness behind her. Instead, she concentrated all of her efforts and energies on the immediate task ahead of her.

She ran her hands down the robe one last time. The contrast of black and white represented the choice facing her over the next year. Once she completed her ninthyear, she must pick a path forward. To take the *black* of alchymy, or the *white* of religious studies. Once she had chosen, she hoped one day to achieve the status of Highcryst in one order or the other.

Or maybe both.

She pictured the two halves of her robes merging to the gray holiness of a Shrive—then shook her head at such foolishness.

Let me just complete my ninthyear.

Determined and knowing Jace was waiting for her in the next room with a stack of books, she wiggled the robe over her head. Standing in a simple shift, she neatly folded the garment and gently returned it to its lacquered scentwood box. She closed and clasped it, securing all her hopes inside.

She placed her palm atop it.

I can do this.

NYX ROLLED THE nub of sharpened charcoal between her thumb and forefinger, both of which were grimed black as she struggled through the last of the morning. She squinted at the triangular shape that Jace had jotted down, along with the numbers written on two of its sides. She had been instructed to divine the length of the third and the space held within all.

"Remember the dictum of squaring the triangle," Jace offered.

She huffed out her frustration. "I know, but what damnable use is any of this?"

He reached over and forced her hand down and drew her attention toward him. His green eyes sparked with sympathy and amusement. "Knowledge can often be its own reward, but more often it reveals the inner truths of the outer world. It can raise a lamp and lift the shadows around us to show us the beauty within."

She had to look away from his intensity, sensing a more personal meaning behind his words. She noted the warmth of the hand still clasping hers, the way his touch lingered. She withdrew her fingers and returned to the problem drawn on paper, a matter more easily resolved than what had grown between them.

Jace straightened. "As to squaring the triangle, it is the magick behind much of everything around us. Used by builders to reckon the slope of a roof and the position of walls. Sailorfolk tap its power to chart their course across the seas. Mappers do the same to draw coastlines and borders."

Inspired by his explanation, Nyx set about solving the problem with renewed vigor. She scratched her sums with her nub of charcoal and worried her way through to the end. Once done, she turned to Jace, who smiled proudly but with a slight sadness in his eyes.

"Very good," he said. "In no time, you'll be leaving me far behind."

It was her turn to reach to him. "Never," she promised. "I can't survive my ninthyear without you at my side."

"I failed my fifthyear," he reminded her, the smile dimming. "I think the girl who survived the poison of a Mýr bat can face anything."

She wanted to believe him, but this reminder of the attack, of the nightmares that followed, further unsettled her. Still, she sought to reassure her friend. "Jace, you're far more than your stumble in your fifthyear. Prioress Ghyle recognized your potential by keeping you here at the Cloistery, working at the scriptorium, aiding me these past years. I wager you know more than most of those who will be crawling alongside me to the top of the school."

His grin returned. "You are kind to say that. But of late, I've struggled to keep abreast of you. I know it. But I will admit that I *have* learned much on my own, not only by studying beside you, but also by copying faded ancient texts in the scriptorium, preserving them before their ink vanished. Some volumes were shockingly blasphemous. Others so raw in subject that it would make the vilest whoremonger blush. It's certainly been a tutelage very different than any path up the tiers."

"And no less important." She patted his knee. "And that is how you will get me through my ninthyear."

"But what after that?" Jace asked, his voice going softer. "Where will you go then?"

She heard the unspoken query: *What's to become of us?*

"I don't know," she answered, addressing all of those questions. "I hadn't dared look past what's in front of my nose. I would hate to leave my dah and brothers, so perhaps the prioress would allow me to continue my advanced studies here at the Cloistery."

Jace drew taller in his seat, hope brimming in his eyes. "I would like—"

A blast of horns cut him off. They both turned to the window of her borrowed room. A steamy drizzle hung in the air, all that was left of a storm that had been blowing through the swamps for several days. As they stared, another bright trumpeting echoed across the breadth of the school.

"What is it?" Nyx asked.

Jace gained his legs with a heave. "Let's take a break and find out."

She happily stood. Jace crossed and grabbed her cane, but she waved it aside. She would need to learn to walk on her own. She had to adjust to the strange dimensions and sights of her new sighted world. Plus, she had Jace if she became too overwhelmed.

They abandoned her little cluster of rooms and headed through the physik's wards. They drew more of the curious in their wake. Once they reached the open air, they crossed toward the tier's main stairs. Further bursts of horns urged them onward, now clearly rising up from below.

Nyx swiped her wet brow. Under the low weeping clouds, the heat smothered. Over the past days, it had quickened tempers and slowed everyone's pace. But the strident blaring could not be ignored. The novelty pulled everyone out of hiding.

"This way," Jace urged.

He guided her through the worst of the gathering throng and over to a terrace just off the steps. It offered an expansive view to the town of Brayk below. The sight and spread of the world transfixed her and terrified her. In the past, her clouded eyes had always kept the world tight around her. Now it spread endlessly in all directions.

Another blow of horns drew Nyx's attention down to the swamps. "Look!"

Bright torches flickered through the shadowy bower. Scores and scores of them, all slowly drawing toward the island of rock in these drowned lands. The faint beat of drums rose, along with the deeper lowing of bullocks. Hard snaps of whips echoed up now, sounding like the crackling pops of a log in a hearth.

"It seems we're being invaded," Jace mumbled.

Nyx glanced sharply at him, all too aware of the tensions with the lands of the Southern Klashe.

He gave her a consoling shake of his head. "This morning at the scriptorium, I overheard talk of a large hunting party coming through Mýr. The teeth of the storm had kept them holed up in Fiskur for a while. Still, never imagined there'd be so many."

The first of the torches reached the edge of the swamps. Crimson oilskin banners were raised, but with no wind to unfurl them, their bearers had to wave them loose. Though the distance was far, Nyx recognized the black crown against a gold sun.

"Sigil of the king," Jace said.

Despite the heat, Nyx shivered with dread.

What is going on?

A commotion on the neighboring stairs drew their eyes. A long-legged figure flew up the steps, taking them three at a time. Nyx recognized one of her former seventhyears, identifying him by his lanky form and flailing gait. His face now glowed with excitement, practically bursting with barely suppressed glee. She also knew this particular student was the class's chinwag, always ripe with gossip.

"Lackwiddle!" she called out to him.

The damp-haired youth nearly tripped over himself trying to stop. He glanced around and spotted Nyx. He gave her a hard scowl. With that one look, he revealed what all her former classmates likely thought of her.

"What's happening down there?" she asked.

He gestured rudely and braced his legs to continue his flight upward.

Before he could, Jace thrust out an arm and grabbed him by the collar, pulling him closer and anchoring him in place. "Answer her!"

As wet as Lackwiddle was, he probably could have broken free, but he was clearly incapable of keeping what he knew bottled up any longer. "It's the king's legion, I tell ya! A full mess of 'em. Even some red-faced Vyrllians. Can you believe it?"

Nyx's chill sank deeper to her bones.

But Lackwiddle was not done. "And who's marching with 'em? It's Kindjal and her father, the highmayor of Fiskur. I'd give up one of my hairy bollocks to be sitting there with 'em."

Nyx shared a worried look with Jace. Her heart pounded. She again felt the weight of Byrd's headless body atop hers, the spill of hot blood.

Jace finally let the boy go and moved closer to her.

Though freed, Lackwiddle dawdled, his eyes bulging with one last bit of gossip. "And best of all, I heard they captured one of those winged bastards."

Nyx stiffened, picturing the lurker in the rafters. "What?"

"A big 'un," Lackwiddle said, holding his arms wide. "All arrowbit and caged. Heard they're dragging it up top. Gonna burn it alive in the pyre. As fitting vengeance for Byrd."

To hide her reaction, Nyx turned to the twin fires ablaze in the drizzle. The taste of sweet milk again filled her mouth. She felt the enfolding warmth of protective wings. A keening filled her head, full of grief.

"Can't wait till that beast be flopping and screaming in those flames," Lackwiddle said, and darted away, anxious to spread what he knew.

Nyx continued to gaze upward, but she fell back into a smoke-shrouded world of screams and thundering war machines. She found herself again on a mountaintop, running toward a huge winged beast nailed to a stone altar. Her foremost desire in that moment fired through her again.

To free what was captured.

Then she snapped back into her own flesh, standing in the drizzle. The keening remained—both past and future—but it had grown into the buzz of an angry hive inside her skull. It spread through her bones, sharpening her certainty.

She turned to face the approaching legion.

She didn't have a plan, only a purpose.

I must stop them.

15

KANTHE STOOD SULLENLY in the rain.

He could have sought shelter in the covered livery sledge, where the high-mayor of Fiskur and his daughter were offloading a mountain of the girl's chests and crates. The pair of bullocks at the front looked no happier than him, with their pelts sodden and dripping, huffing heavily and stamping the splay of their three-toed hooves.

He saw no reason to be over there. His breeches were already soaked to the skin. His boots squelched with mud and bogwater. His hair was pasted to his scalp. It seemed like ages since he'd been dry, though it had only been a dozen or so days. Not that he was confident in his accounting. The large company had left the port of Azantiia during a lull in the stormfront. Still, winds had tossed the seas into frothing white peaks. His stomach still had not fully settled from the voyage.

When they finally made landfall at Fiskur, the squall strengthened again. The skies blackened, split with jagged spears of lightning. Thunder boomed loud enough to shake the stilts that held up the town. They had been trapped in Fiskur for four long days, where the only fodder had been salted, dried fish and equally briny ale.

Kanthe had initially been relieved to escape Fiskur as the black skies turned gray and the worst of the storm blew off to the east. Then came days of sucking mud, bellowing beasts, pushing through clouds of bloodsucking meskers or stinging botflies that left worms under the skin. All along, whether they were on foot, huddled on sledges, or poled on rafts, the swamps tried to trap them. Thorny vines tugged at clothes or pulled caps from heads. Then again, better that than be grabbed by the fanged jaws of the multitudinous adders and pit-vipers that draped from mossy branches or slithered across the water.

Kanthe cursed his father with every hard-earned league. He now wished he had allowed Mikaen to intercede on his behalf and convince the king to spare him this torturous trek.

Their group's only advantage lay in their numbers. The passage of a hundred knights and a score of Vyrllian Guards had kept the worst of the swamp's denizens away. And the storm god Tytan—perhaps apologizing for his temper—had granted them a rare boon with a well-aimed bolt of lightning.

Kanthe looked past the livery sledge to a raft being poled toward the rocky shore. A large wrapped cage rested atop it. The two bullocks nearby lowed a note of distress and shifted away from the approaching raft, dragging the livery to one side. The driver had to crack a whip over their haunches to root them back in place. Still, the beasts shivered their flanks in anxiety.

Despite the bullocks' warning, Kanthe found himself crossing in that direction. It felt good to feel solid ground under his feet. Plus, he didn't want to be conscripted into setting up the tents or gathering firewood. Out in the swamps, his princely status had held no sway. It was hard to maintain a royal decorum when groaning as one shite over the edge of a sledge.

Curiosity also drew him toward the raft and cage. He had barely caught a glimpse of the large Mýr bat as it had been dragged in a tangle of ropes and chains from the swamp. The victory had been celebrated with boisterous cheers and the battering of swords on shields, as if a major battle had been won. Though, according to the fireside chatter later, it wasn't much of a fight. A chance lightning bolt had shattered the cottongum where the beast had unfortunately roosted during the storm. A clutch of six Vyrllians had stumbled upon it, discovering it weak and dazed, a wing burned clean through. Still, they had peppered it with a flurry of arrows before netting and roping it.

Kanthe had watched the beast be caged with a pang of pity. The captured bat was the size of a small pony. And even bleeding from wounds and pained by burns, it had thrashed and screeched, struggling for freedom.

He had understood that desire all too well. And maybe that was what drew him now. A mix of guilt and pity. Unfortunately, he was not the only one who gathered toward the caged prize.

"Let's take a look at it," Anskar said, hopping deftly onto the tall raft. "Before we drag it upward."

Anskar vy Donn was the head of the Vyrllian detachment. Kanthe's head barely reached the height of the man's chest. And the vy-knight was as muscled as an ox. He had not only inked his face and shaved head in crimson, as was traditional, but also his legs and arms, both of which were also tattooed in black thorny vines. Kanthe had heard he added another thorn for every man he killed.

Maybe that's why the king had secretly assigned the vy-knight to be his bodyguard, though it was never stated as such. Still, Anskar had been his shadow throughout this journey, seldom letting him out of his sight, even when Kanthe was wiping his arse. Despite that, Kanthe had come to respect the man's hard, but amiable nature. By now, Anskar already felt more like a stern older brother than a bodyguard.

Kanthe climbed up onto the raft to join the knight.

Anskar lifted a flap of leather covering tied around the cage. Kanthe bent to peek under it.

"Not too close," Anskar warned.

"No worries there. I'd like to keep my nose where it's at."

From two steps away, Kanthe peered into the shrouded darkness. It took him a breath to discern the darker shadow within. He spotted no movement. *Maybe it's already dead, succumbed to its injuries.* It would be a mercy, considering its fate from here.

He glanced to the top of the school. The Cloistery was similar in shape to Kepenhill, only a quarter smaller. Twin flames smoked at the top. Alchymist Frell had already abandoned his pupil, climbing toward the summit. Frell had wanted to meet with the head of the school, a prioress who had once taught the man. Kanthe had tried to follow him, but Frell asked for his patience, abandoning the prince on this rocky shore.

Kanthe returned his attention to the cage—only to discover a pair of red eyes glowering back at him.

So not dead. But more likely—

The shadow burst toward him, crashing into the ironwood bars and rocking the entire pen. Kanthe fell backward, landing on his backside. He scooted farther away as teeth snapped and gnashed at the cage. A slavering poison, glowing in the darkness against the black wood, seeped down the bars' lengths.

Anskar laughed and jabbed his sword at the face of the beast, driving it into the shadows again. Once it retreated, he let the flap of leather fall back over. He then faced Kanthe, towering over him.

"Looks like our guest is mending itself right smartly, don't ya think?" The vy-knight held out a thick, calloused hand. "Up with ya. Can't have a prince of the realm sitting on his arse in front of half the town here."

Kanthe accepted the offer and allowed himself to be pulled back to his feet. "Thanks," he mumbled, his cheeks heating up.

He turned to discover the commotion had drawn others to the raft. A circle of faces stared; a few heads whispered to one another. They were mostly townspeople, but their attention was not on the cage or the prince, but on the pair who had approached and stood silently next to the raft.

It had to be a rare sight.

A boulder-shouldered Gyn from across the seas stood bare-chested in the rain, his flesh branded with strange sigils. The mute made even Anskar look like a dwarf. He stood glumly, his heavy brows shadowing small, dull eyes. He held aloft a canopy over the head of his companion.

The Shrive leaned on a gnarled length of silvery bane-alder, whose sap was said to weaken the borders between this world and the mysteries beyond. Its length was as equally branded with sigils as the massive Gyn.

During the journey, Kanthe had kept well clear of the man, sensing both enmity and danger curled within his withered form. The Shrive's tattooed brow looked especially dark under the drape of his cloak's hood and set against his pale skin. And though the man was thin-limbed, saggy jowls hung from cheek and chin, as if all the fat and flesh had been sucked from him, leaving only this wrinkled drape of skin over bone.

No doubt an Iflelen, Kanthe thought, *but at least it's not that bastard Wryth.*

The Shrive's eyes, ashine with avarice, were not on Kanthe or the cage, but on the poison pooled atop the raft's planks. He pointed his cane. "Do not wash that away," he rasped to Anskar. "I will bring my vials to collect what I can. Though I'd prefer to dissect the venom glands while the creature still lives."

"If you wish to wander in there, Shrive Vythaas," Anskar said, "you are more than welcome. But I'm not risking any of my men. Besides, this beastie is already claimed in the name of vengeance, and I made a blood oath to honor it, to burn the first bat to the gods. Especially as the thunderous god Tytan so graciously dropped this sacrifice in our path."

The Shrive lowered his cane, looking none too happy.

Kanthe knew the holy man had been sent here by will of the king, to gather poison and distill it into a weapon of great malignancy. But once their party dispensed with their first obligation—to deliver the highmayor's daughter here and make a blood sacrifice atop the school's pyre—then the great hunt could begin in earnest. They would slaughter as many of the Mýr bats as they could over the next turn of the moon. By that time, Vythaas should have a mountain of poison glands with which to perform his experiments.

But patience was running thin, and not just for the Shrive.

A gruff voice shouted at them, "What are you all waiting for?"

The crowd skirted apart for a portly belly. The man who approached could pass for a wine cask that had sprouted legs, arms, and a gray-whiskered face. It didn't help that he wore a set of oiled breeches and tunic that was a smatter too small for his bulk, allowing an edge of his hairy stomach to protrude over a thick leather belt, which tried its best to hold back the rest of his ale-swelled gut.

Highmayor Goren shoved between the Shrive and the raft. "Day's a-wasting. We need to get that foul cur to the blasted top of this rock. I want that beast charred to smoking ash before the last clang of Eventoll."

The man was accompanied by his daughter, a gangly-limbed girl about Kanthe's age, with mud-brown hair that she tried to brighten with a few silk ribbons. Though only a smidgen above homely, she carried herself as if a stick had been planted square up her arse at birth. During the trek here, she had never dared to extend a slipper out of the sledge. Instead, she stayed nestled among her tall stack of chests, likely full of dainties and perfumes.

Unfortunately, someone must have alerted her that a prince was among them. She had spent considerable time in her covered livery doing her best to shove her surprisingly generous breasts high whenever he happened to pass. Still, even if the two weren't distantly related, those were two peaks he would never climb.

Anskar cast his gaze up the tiers of the school, eyeing the twin pyres with a scathing glare. He swiped one palm over his crimson scalp and scratched his nethers with the other. "That's a long haul, especially with bullocks balking at even getting their horns near that cage."

"I had considered as much," Goren said. He lifted an arm and motioned off to the side, past the raft. "I sent a man to fetch someone who knows bullocks right better than anyone else in these swamps. Here he comes now."

Kanthe turned as a well-weathered swamper crossed through the crowd, thumping along on a cane. The man looked like he had spent all of his life here, along with generations before him. Kanthe half expected moss to be growing in his beard. And though the fellow was aged and worn, he carried himself with a measure of stubborn strength. He was accompanied by a taller and stouter young man, hale of limb and brighter of eye.

No doubt his son.

Goren crossed to the old swamper. The two gripped each other's forearms, not warmly, more in a greeting of respect. Both had likely managed the breadth of these swamps all their lives.

"This is Trademan Polder, the best bullock drover in all of Mýr."

The swamper merely shrugged, accepting the compliment as fact, not bothering with any false modesty. "I a-heard your problem," he said, leaning over to inspect the cage on the raft. "Bullocks know to keep clear of those winged daemons. Nothing but problems them are. Somethin' I know all too well."

Anskar grunted his disappointment. "Then looks like we'll have to shove poles through the cursed cage and try to haul it upwards ourselves." He turned to the highmayor. "Or we can stoke a bonfire on these rocky shores and burn the beast, cage and all, right here. And be done with it."

Goren's face darkened to an angry bruise. "Sard that!" he swore. "My son died up there, so will that bastard."

Anskar looked like he wanted to argue, but clearly he was under an order to appease Goren. Not only was the highmayor distantly related to the king, but trade with Fiskur—a town that culled a rich bounty of hides and salted meat from the swamp's wilderness—was important to Azantiia. A small measure of courtesy and accommodation here would serve the realm well.

The impasse was broken by Trademan Polder. "I didn't say I couldn't get no bullock to help. I got an old 'un that fears nothing. I can put blinders on 'im and hang a bag of fresh-ground bitterroot under his nose to mask any scent." He thumbed at his son. "As extra measure, I'll have Bastan guide him up by hand, too. To help keep the bullock calm."

The big lad nodded his assent. "Gramblebuck won't disappoint."

The old man added one warning: "'Course, best you keep that beast bundled up right tight."

Goren crossed his arms and sneered at Anskar. "What'd I tell ya."

Anskar shrugged. "Then we better get things moving if we want to be done by Eventoll."

The two swampers turned and headed back the way they'd come.

Kanthe started the other way, only to note Goren's daughter lift up on her toes and whisper in the highmayor's ear. She pointed at the departing pair.

Goren's eyes went wide, and he scolded the girl under his breath. "Trademan Polder's daughter? You're saying *she* was the one up there with Byrd? Why didn't you tell me this before?"

She cowered before his anger and shook her head, clearly having no answer.

Goren glanced over to the old man and his son. The highmayor's eyes had narrowed, glowering and angry. "Then I swear by all gods above, I'll burn the lot of 'em."

Kanthe backed from that fury. He slipped away before the highmayor realized his threat was overheard. Still, he stared after the two swampers, baffled by whatever politics were at play here. It seemed in a heartbeat old colleagues had become enemies. At least, on one side.

Kanthe sighed. What did it matter?

I'll be gone by the morrow.

He headed toward a fresh bonfire blazing along the shore, promising the possibility of dry clothes. As to everything else going on here . . .

Not my problem.

16

WHAT AM I going to do?

As the fifth latterday bell rang throughout the Cloistery, Nyx stood at a rail atop a crowded balcony on the fourth tier. The perch offered a view across the breadth of the main stair that climbed from the gates of the school to its summit. At long last, the drizzling skies had dried out, and the scud of gray clouds had broken in places, letting through spears of bright sunlight. The mist in the air even glowed in brilliant bows.

A nonne on her left pointed skyward. "It's a blessing of the Father Above. He smiles His grace upon us all."

Nyx glanced to the shining arches in the air, marching off into the distance across the emerald of the swamp. She could not discount the nonne's words. Nyx had never viewed such majesty, such divine radiance. The shimmering azure, the rosy reds, the glowing yellows.

How could it not be a blessing of the gods above?

Still, as joyous as this display was, it could not dispel the misgivings in her chest. She gazed from the sky down to the procession slowly winding up the steps. First had come rows of knights. They had donned light armor that glinted in the sun, their helms topped by bristled horsetail plumes. They carried shields strapped to their left arms, bearing sigils of different houses. The clinking of their armor sounded like the ticking gears of the school's bronze orrery, as if the procession was a vast machine set in motion, one she had no hope of stopping.

Behind the knights now came a large hump-backed shaggy beast with his head down low. It was led by a tall figure marching alongside it, leather lead in one hand and a grip on a bridle in another.

"Isn't that your brother?" Jace asked on Nyx's other side.

Nyx swallowed. "And Gramblebuck."

The bullock shouldered into his harness, the straps digging deep into his pelt and muscles. Behind him, a flat wagon bumped up the steps on iron-shod wheels. A tall cage, wrapped in leathers, had been lashed atop the cart.

Nyx pictured the wounded bat inside. She swore she could hear a faint wailing of its distress. Or maybe it rose from her memories. Still, she rubbed an ear with a shoulder, trying to ease the itch deep in her skull.

Around her, the crowd whispered at the sight of the cage. Some sounded awed, others frightened. Several kissed their fingertips and touched each ear-lobe in a ward against evil. A few even glanced her way with sympathetic expressions.

No one suspected what lay within her heart.

Earlier, she had entertained a hope to somehow free the bat, to pay back a debt long overdue. She now recognized the futility of it all. It was the fancies of a silly girl, one who had deluded herself into thinking she was capable of such a defiant act. She only had to stare at the long line of knights that would encircle the ninth tier to accept defeat already. Only a handful of people would be allowed atop the summit where the cage was headed—and certainly not any student.

Nyx had trespassed up there once and brought about much misery. She dared not do so again, not after all the efforts of the prioress to secure her spot among the ninthyears. Even her own family was participating in the sacrifice to come. How dare she consider sullying their efforts with some rash ploy?

"I'm such a fool," she whispered to herself.

Jace glanced her way with pinched eyes, but she waved away his concern.

As the wagon trundled across the fourth tier, a pair of men followed the wagon. One bore light armor, but carried his helm under an arm, exposing the shining crimson of his station as a member of the Vyrllian Guard. The vy-knight towered over a slimmer, darker figure hidden under a hunter's green cloak, with a bow strapped across his shoulders. From this last one's position of prominence in the procession, Nyx wondered if that squint-eyed hunter had been the one who had shot down the bat.

Anger stoked in her breast at the sight of him.

Behind the pair followed two dozen more of the hardened Vyrllian Guard.

The nonne on her left leaned toward a neighboring hieromonk. "I heard the king's forces intend to finally rid us of the scourge of those daemon bats. To slaughter a path all the way to the volcanic flanks of The Fist where those monsters roost and breed."

The monk nodded sagely. "I heard the same."

Nyx's fingers tightened on the rail. She pictured dark shapes tumbling from the skies, crashing into marsh and bog. Her vision grew blood-tinged with swords and axes swinging, hacking into broken bodies.

The nonne pointed below. "And it's high time Goren called for such a hunt."

Nyx stared down as a final pair climbed behind the crimson-faced guards. The highmayor of Fiskur waved at the crowd as he huffed his way toward the summit. His round face, shining bright red, dripped with sweat. Beside him strode a figure Nyx had dreaded to see again—Kindjal, twin sister of Byrd.

Nyx clutched harder to the balcony rail as her legs trembled. The sight of Kindjal stoked the guilt and worry inside her. Byrd was dead in part because of her own cowardice. She had fled where she should not have, luring her classmate to his doom.

And more death would follow.

She again pictured the slaughter to come.

All the bloodshed and misery will be because of me.

She stumbled back from the rail, barely able to stand, gutted by despair.

Jace drew closer. "Nyx?"

She looked to him. "Get me out of here."

He scooped an arm around her and helped her away from the rail. He half carried her across the crowded balcony toward the doors. Her hurried departure did not go unnoticed, especially the way she hung on Jace's arm.

Voices followed in her wake.

. . . poor girl will soon be avenged.

. . . her suffering will fuel the flames as that monster writhes.

. . . no doubt, the Mother has twice-blessed her.

Nyx fled from their words, from their misplaced concern. Shame strengthened her legs. She pushed free of Jace's arm and rushed through the narrow halls and past the wards. He followed behind her, but she wanted to flee everyone. She did not deserve his friendship.

I'll only doom you, too.

She reached her set of borrowed rooms and stumbled inside. She tried to close the door on Jace, but he would have none of it. He pushed through after her.

His worry rushed out of him, his eyes huge, his breath panted. "Nyx, what's wrong? Are you feeling ill again? Should I fetch Physik Oeric?"

She turned to him, ready to batter him back outside, but instead she fell into his arms. She pressed her face into his chest, smelling bitter lime and musky sweat. She shook there, trying to find comfort, to settle her pounding heart. Her body quaked with sobs. She had no words to express her anguish and guilt.

Instead, she felt a darkness closing upon her.

As if from far away, Jace's voice reached her. "What's that noise?"

Only then did she hear the sharp keening past the pounding of her heart. It cut through her misery. She stared into the rafters of the study—and spotted tiny eyes, glowing a furious crimson from the shadows. Her lost brother's ululating cries filled her head, vibrating the bones in her ear, in her skull, and firing across her brain.

Under that barrage, the world began to shiver away.

Nyx gasped, clutching to Jace. "Hold me."

Then she was gone.

She stands amidst flames. A shadow thrashes and writhes inside a burning cage. Pain is carried on smoke and wind. Before her, wooden bars turn to coal. Flesh to cinders. Bone to ash. The flames cast higher, lifting her. She becomes a fiery ember carried aloft, swirling skyward toward gray clouds.

High enough now, she spots a black storm building at the horizon, stacking higher, roiling with dark energies. It rolls forth from a mountainous shadow in the distance. But no thunder flows from that stormfront, only a wail of fury. The blackness breaks apart into a thousand wings that come crashing toward her.

No, not her.

Bathed in the smoke of charred flesh, she stares down from her height.

Below, the breadth of the school lies quiet and dark, unaware of the savage storm about to break upon it. She tries to cry a warning to those below, but all that comes out of her mouth are the screams of a thousand bats.

With a shudder, Nyx fell back into herself, still in Jace's arms.

"They're coming," she moaned to his chest.

Jace shifted her higher. "Who . . . Who's coming?"

A snap of wings drew their attention to the rafters. A dark shape dropped toward them.

Jace yelped and sheltered his body over hers.

The bat dove across their heads and swept out the open window.

Jace kept low. "Stay. There could be more."

She knew there were *many* more. She pushed out of his arms. She understood the reason for this visit from her long-lost brother. He had come with a warning and a threat. She shared it with Jace.

"We have to stop the sacrifice, or all will be lost."

Jace's face scrunched with bafflement. "What're you talking about?"

She faced the door, knowing she could not do this alone. "I must speak to Prioress Ghyle. Before it's too late."

NYX STUCK TO Jace's shoulder as he slipped a key into the lock of a forbidden door. He glanced back at her. "Maybe I should go alone."

She chewed her lower lip and stared at the brand in the door bearing the vine-wrapped sigil of the Cloistery. A small silver crucible and pestle adorned it. Tension kept her shoulders by her ears. At any moment, she expected to hear the final latterday bell. After that, with the first bell of Eventoll, the fiery sacrifice was due to begin.

She took a breath, then shook her head. "No. We have too little time. I must risk this path."

"But why?" Jace pressed.

"I don't have time to explain."

Certainly not time for you to believe me.

He sighed, keyed the lock, and opened the way to the private stair up to the ninth tier. Jace—no longer a student—had been given access to haul precious books up to the scholars, which included Prioress Ghyle's chambers atop the school. Such dispensation did not apply to guests. Nyx knew she was putting Jace's position and livelihood in danger by this trespass. If caught, she intended to deny his involvement.

Jace led the way over the threshold. There was not enough time for him to run up from the fourth tier to the ninth, convince the prioress of the urgency, and return with her back down here. Nyx knew she had to press the matter directly with the head of the Cloistery. No other would believe her.

"Hurry now," Jace warned. "It's still a long way."

He took off up the steps with her in his wake. She found herself holding her breath for long stretches, expecting to be accosted by an alchymist or some other scholar on these steps. But as they wound around and around the narrow stair, they encountered no one. Most likely everyone was out watching the last of the legion marching toward the summit.

"Almost there," Jace gasped out, his cheeks ruddy, his back soaked with sweat. She suspected a significant amount of that wetness came from fear. He slowed, pausing at a landing, and nodded toward the door there. "This leads out to the eighth tier."

He was giving her one last chance to take another path. She could escape out that door and no one would be the wiser. "If you hid on this tier, I could fetch the prioress to you," he offered.

She considered it, swiping her damp brow.

Before she could answer, a bell clanged loudly, muffled by stone, then growing louder as its ringing spread throughout the school.

The last of the latterday bells.

She stared at Jace and waved for him to continue. But he suddenly lunged at her and shoved her behind him. He leaned back to pin her against the wall. She panicked for a breath—then heard the rasp of a lock and the creak of a door being opened. Brighter light bathed them both.

Hidden behind Jace's bulk, she could not see who entered.

"What are you doing here, Journeyman Jace?" a woman asked with a note of accusation.

Nyx cringed as she recognized the nasally voice of Sister Reed, the noviatiate who taught the seventhyears.

Jace stammered for a frightened breath, then straightened but kept Nyx hidden behind him. "I . . . I was summoned by Prioress Ghyle, to pick up and return a copy of Plentiarorio's *Doctrine of Seven Graces* to the scriptorium."

Sister Reed groaned, "Then get about it, rather than blocking my way."

Jace scooted to the side. Nyx matched his step to stay behind him. Sister Reed scuffed past them both, likely with hardly a second glance at someone as lowly as Jace. Still, they waited until her footsteps had faded before hurrying upward again.

The rest of their flight was a blur. Jace led Nyx up to the ninth tier, across a cavernous room under a candelabrum smoking with strange alchymies, and down a long, curved hallway. They encountered a handful of scholars, but Nyx kept in Jace's shadow. Luckily, the others all appeared to be too involved in their own affairs or with what was happening outside to even note Jace's hurried passage.

Finally, their trek ended where the black volcanic rock of the alchymists' towers brightened into the white limestone of the hieromonks'. Between those two, a tall arched doorway stood to one side of the hall, plated half in iron and half in silver.

Jace rushed forward and used a hinged knocker to rap loudly.

Nyx winced at the noise, expecting knights to rush down upon them from all directions. In truth, she couldn't even be sure the prioress was still in her chambers. If not, Nyx was prepared to go shouting up and down these halls if need be.

I have no more time.

Finally, a faint shuffle sounded, and the door opened on well-oiled hinges.

Nyx exhaled her relief when she spotted the familiar countenance of Prioress Ghyle. The woman's eyes narrowed curiously at the sight of Jace, then widened when her gaze discovered who stood beside him.

"Nyx?" Ghyle must have immediately surmised that something dire had happened for Nyx to be standing at her threshold. "Get in here."

The opening was pulled wider, and she and Jace rushed through. The prioress closed the door after them and stepped to follow—then turned back and twisted the bolt in the door.

"What's this all about?" Ghyle asked.

Nyx struggled with where to begin. She took in the room, which was circular in shape, lined by shelves of ebonwood on one side and white ash on the other. Dusty books, cubbied scrolls, and strange arcane artifacts filled the shelves. In the center was a table halved by the same woods. Nine high-backed chairs stood around it: four white, four black, with the last and tallest split like the table into ash and ebonwood.

Nyx realized here must be where the Council of Eight deliberated and discussed matters pertaining to the school, presided over by the prioress in the ninth seat. Nyx also took in the four tall hearths, presently cold, and noted other doors that must lead into the prioress's private chambers.

Ghyle drew her toward the table. "What has you so distressed to risk trespassing up here?" she pressed.

Nyx opened her mouth to speak—when a stranger, seated with his back to them in one of the tall chairs, stood and faced them all. The man wore the black robe and crimson sash of an alchymist, but Nyx had never seen him before. He looked a decade or two younger than the prioress, with dark auburn hair tied in a tail and bright hazel eyes.

Nyx took a step away from the stranger, only to have the prioress hold her from retreating farther.

"This is Alchymist Frell hy Mhlaghifor. From Kepenhill in Azantiia. A former student of mine. You can speak freely in front of him."

Nyx realized the man must've come with the king's forces. Despite the prioress's reassurances, Nyx didn't know if she could trust a man who had arrived with the same legion who intended to sacrifice the captured bat.

The alchymist approached with a smile that seemed genuine. "Ah, this must be the miracle girl. Survivor of poisons. And the bless'd of the Mother. And someone the king demands we secure and take to Highmount."

The blood drained from Nyx's head at his words, dizzying her for a breath. "Wh . . . What?"

Jace looked equally shocked and turned to the prioress. "You can't let that happen."

Ghyle turned to the both of them. "Trust me, I will do everything in my power to keep Nyx here. Alchymist Frell was kind enough to alert me in advance, so I might ready my arguments."

Nyx pictured herself being trussed up in chains and dragged to some dungeon in Highmount. She might never see her father or brothers again. But even that heartbreak paled in comparison with what was to come.

"I . . . I must tell you something," Nyx whispered, finding it suddenly difficult to breathe. She cast a guilty look at Jace, then concentrated on the prioress's kind but firm face. "Something I've kept from all of you."

"What does it pertain to?" the prioress asked.

"Moonfall."

A gasp rose—not from the head of the school, but from the strange alchymist. He shifted closer. "What do you know?"

Nyx didn't have an answer to his question.

Everything, nothing.

She slowly related all that had happened during that strange visitation, about the nightmare, about the disturbing visions—both in the past and atop some blasted mountaintop. She finished with, "I think I was rescued in the swamps by one of the Mýr bats, raised as one of her own, alongside the one who visited me."

Jace looked aghast, even stepping away from her.

Nyx sniffed back tears. As she fought against them, the alchymist leaned closer to the prioress. Nyx heard his whisper.

"You don't think she could be the same child. Graylin's—"

"Not now, Frell." Ghyle held up a hand. "Such speculations can wait. But it is now clearer than ever that we cannot let this girl fall into the shadow of the king. That must not happen."

The alchymist straightened with a nod. "From her story, the bats must have sensed their milk was tainting the child, blinding her, and so returned her to her own kind."

"Which suggests a level of intelligence far superior than anyone ever imagined." Ghyle grew silent as she contemplated this, then spoke again. "Is it possible that they poisoned the girl a fortnight ago on purpose? Reawakening her—both in sight and knowledge—to serve as a vessel of warning to the greater world? Do we dare place such reasoning and cunning upon those winged beasts?"

The alchymist rubbed a finger in the crease of his chin. "I reviewed several texts after receiving your missive, to better understand the venom that had afflicted the girl. Justoam's *Anaticum Plenary.* Lakewright's *Historia Animalium.* Even the oft reviled Klashean tome Fhallon's *Dialogues of Biologica Variations.* We know other bats—like the eyeless fruitwings that inhabit the shadowy depths of Cloudreach—navigate somehow via their near-silent cries. Surely the Mýr bats must do the same, experiencing the world in such a manner. A handful of alchymists suspect these kings among their kind also use their high-pitched calls as a means of communication, binding one to another, like bees in a hive, ants in a nest. Perhaps even magnifying their entire genera's intelligence."

"The whole greater than its parts," Ghyle said.

Frell nodded. "Fhallon's *Dialogues* goes so far as to conjecture that their knowledge, shared and communed, might go back generations, farther than our own histories. We also know other genera of bats, especially those in the dark western fringes of the Crown, prefer the dark of night, as if binding their behavior and patterns to the cycles of the moon. If so, surely our Mýr bats would be equally sensitive to changes in the moon."

While Nyx was lost by most of this, Prioress Ghyle's eyes narrowed with intent on her former student. "Frell, are you suggesting the bats have somehow intuited what your research has shown?"

He nodded. "That the moon has been growing larger over the centuries, and more quickly now."

Nyx put herself back on that accursed mountaintop, watching a moon swelling, crashing toward her, its edges on fire. "Moonfall," she whispered.

Frell turned toward her. "Mayhap that is what they were trying to show you, to warn you in their own way."

Nyx knew his explanation did not illuminate everything. Her vision atop the mountain had been too detailed. Even now screams echoed in her head. She remembered the name shouted from her own lips. *Bashaliia*. Still, she set aside such mysteries for now and addressed a question that had been plaguing her since that nightmare-riven day.

"Why me?" she asked, glancing over to Jace, then back to the two scholars. "Why am I the one beset by their calls?"

Frell shrugged. "I think it's obvious."

Nyx frowned. *Not to me.*

Frell explained, "You lived your first six moons under their tutelage, when your mind was soft clay, still pliable, far from fully formed. Your brain grew while under a constant barrage of their silent cries. Under such persistent exposure, your mind may have been forever altered by their keening, as a tree is gnarled by winds."

She glanced to Jace, whose eyes had grown even larger, shining with fear.

Of me.

Frell continued, "I believe, in some small way, that you joined the greater mind around you. And though grown now and diverged on a new path, you still remained attuned to that pattern ingrained upon your spirit."

Nyx shivered, wanting to argue against the alchymist's words. Still, she remembered those moments when she saw herself through another's eyes, through her lost brother's eyes.

Ghyle spoke up. "If Alchymist Frell's suspicions are true, then it suggests your recent poisoning awoke more than just your eyesight. It opened an inner eye long closed since you were left in the swamp."

Nyx swallowed, her stomach churning sickly and hotly.

Then what am I?

Jace must have sensed her distress and pushed through his fear to step closer. "Nyx, is that what you came here to tell the prioress?"

She stiffened, realizing what she had forgotten. "No," she blurted out, and turned to Ghyle. "I had another visit from my lost brother."

Jace took her hand. "I saw the bat, too."

She looked gratefully over at him. She took strength from the firmness of his grip, fighting back tears at his simple gesture, at his show of support and friendship.

"I had another vision," she said, and explained about the coming storm, an attack by thousands of bats to avenge the sacrifice about to happen. "We must stop the others from burning the creature they captured, or we'll be attacked from the air."

Jace's brows pinched. "But how could the bats know what we intend to do here, when it's not even happened yet?"

As much as it disturbed her, Nyx knew the answer. "If I know that greater mind, then perhaps they also may know mine."

She again pictured the switching back and forth of her vision. She also remembered the fury that had grown inside her upon learning about the sacrifice and the fervent stirring to do something about it. It was a rescue that her normally meek self would never have contemplated or risked.

Where did that desire come from?

She lifted a hand and touched between her breasts.

Was it born of me? Or stoked by them?

Before she could decide, a ringing rose from beyond the walls, clanging louder with each heartbeat. She cringed at the sound.

The first bell of Eventoll.

She gaped at the others, her breath seizing in her chest.

I took too long.

It was already too late.

The prioress turned to Frell, plainly not giving up. "We must intervene, but I'm not sure my word alone can cast aside a king's order."

The alchymist nodded. "Then it may take that of a prince. If I can convince him."

A prince?

Ghyle crossed and took hold of Jace's arm. "Nyx has already drawn the king's attention, and I fear her situation will soon be far graver. You must get her somewhere safe."

"Wh . . . Where?" Jace stammered.

"Out of the school. It is no longer safe for her here." The prioress looked at Nyx. "For now, get her back home."

Nyx did not resist as the two of them were rushed toward the door, but an unsettling question chased her heels.

Where is my true home?

17

KANTHE SNIFFED AND rolled his eyes.

I thought I *reeked of the swamp.*

He shifted farther across the top of the school, trying to get upwind of the great shaggy bullock, but the cloud of flies hovering around the phlegmonous, farting beast buzzed after him.

Its caretaker—Bastan, the old swamper's son—seemed oblivious, shifting within the muck of it all, checking the wagon's leather traces and breeches. The young man kept his gaze away from the bundled cage atop the wagon. Having reached the ninth tier, the bullock was nearly done. It only had a few paces to go to complete its trek.

The plan was simple enough. The bullock would haul the wagon between the twin pyres atop the school, then the cart would be unhitched and left there. More kindling would be shoveled between its wheels and lit with torches. Then the wagon and wooden pen would be set aflame, briefly joining the two fires into one.

To Kanthe, it struck him as far easier to simply back the wagon into one of the two pyres and be done with it. But apparently both the hieromonks and alchymists believed their honor would be tarnished if their fire missed out on this opportunity to exact divine retribution atop the Cloistery.

So, this was the solution worked out.

He huffed his irritation.

Let's get on with it already.

On the far side of the pyres, the highmayor stood atop a stone dais and finished some grand speech. Thankfully the roar of the flames muffled the worst of his pontification. From all the *Glory be*s and *Blessed He*s and *She*s, Goren wanted his son properly mourned, but just as ardently, he clearly wished to polish his own image before the scholarly elite and the Vyrllian Guard gathered here. For those outside the school, it was a rare opportunity to stand atop the ninth tier. Even the century of knights had to remain one level below, encircling the summit.

The winds shifted, and the smoke of the pyres washed over Kanthe. He choked on the cloying mix of bitter alchymies and sweet incense. Coughing, he retreated back into the stench of the bullock. A fat fly took the opportunity to gouge a chunk from his arm. He slapped it away.

When will this be over?

As if summoned by his thought, a tall set of doors opened behind the highmayor, where the black towers of the alchymists ground against the white spires of the hieromonks. Two figures appeared and hurried forth, though the pair quickly parted in opposite directions.

Kanthe recognized Frell, who set about circling the pyres toward him. The other was a woman with a crown of white braids dressed in a stately robe with a black-and-white stole over her shoulders. She headed toward the raised dais, where the highmayor stood with his arms lifted to the sky, preparing to once again extol the gods. The woman—who had to be Frell's old teacher, the Prioress Ghyle—stepped to Goren's side and whispered in his ear. The highmayor's arms sagged, like the sinking wings of a deflating wyndship.

Closer at hand, Anskar shoved toward Kanthe—or rather toward the wagon, brushing past the prince. "'Bout sarding time," the vy-knight grumbled over to him. "Thought that fartbag would never stop blowing. Gimme a hand unwrapping the cage. Bastards will want to watch the beastie writhe and burn before their eyes. Then maybe we can get away from here."

Gods be, I hope so.

Kanthe turned to follow, but the prioress spoke to the gathering, drawing his eye. "Thank you all for joining us here." Her voice easily carried to Kanthe, though she did not have to holler and bellow like the highmayor. "It is with great regret that we must delay this Eventoll sacrifice."

Murmurs of surprise rose around the smoking pyres. Voices were raised. Goren stalked over to her, looking ready to grab her, but a stern look rebuffed him.

Goren still insisted on being heard. "It is the king's order! His Majesty's sworn word under his personal seal. You cannot refuse it."

Anskar groaned. "The god-blighted bastard is right. Let me see what this is about."

The vy-knight stalked away, his crimson face glowering darkly.

Anskar was replaced by another. Frell had reached this side of the pyre. He rushed to Kanthe's side, grabbed his arm, and drew him closer to the wagon. "We have a problem. One that requires a prince to resolve."

Kanthe pulled his arm free and pointed toward the far dais. "I'm supposing it has something to do with that."

"It does. We must stop this sacrifice. If the bat is burned atop the school, all will fall to ruin."

Kanthe cast a skeptical eye. "To ruin? The Cloistery has stood here for nearly as long as Kepenhill. Who would dare attack this place?"

Frell nodded to the cage in the wagon and what was hidden inside. "That creature's brethren. They gather into a storm as we speak."

"How can you possibly know that?"

"The story is a long one, too long for now. Suffice it to say, it ties to the young woman whom your father wanted taken back to Highmount."

Kanthe gave a shake of his head, struggling to make sense of it all. "The one who survived the poison and regained her sight?"

"The same." Frell glanced back as more shouting rose from beyond the fires—then back to Kanthe. From the set of his lips, the alchymist struggled with how to convince his young pupil. With a sigh, he settled on an argument. "Prince Kanthe, a fortnight ago you pressed me with a story of Graylin sy Moor, the Forsworn Knight. You used that tale to sway me from taking my fears to your father."

Kanthe squinted. "What of it?"

"I believe that girl is the very babe that Graylin sy Moor sought to protect by breaking his oath. Maybe the knight's own child." Frell stared hard at him. "Or maybe your half-sister."

Kanthe scoffed at such a proposition. "That's impossible."

"Perhaps I could be wrong about her, but I'm certain about the danger. Her life—all our lives—will be forfeited if this sacrifice commences."

Kanthe took the alchymist's wrist. "Frell, you're more of a father to me than my own blood. So, I want to believe you, but what you ask? You want *me* to break the king's sworn oath. After my father has only just begun to trust me again, to put his faith in me. Do I look like some hero out of bygone stories?"

Frell smiled. "I won't burden you with such a fate. It usually ends badly for such heroes."

"Then you know I can't do what you ask."

Frell sagged and gave a shake of his head. Kanthe stared at the man who had mentored him throughout his years, who too often had held him when he was a first- or secondyear—a heartsick young prince who needed comfort. He read the disappointment in the man's face, which wounded him far more than any fiery admonishment by his father.

I'm sorry . . .

Kanthe turned away and headed toward the back of the wagon.

Frell followed, refusing to give up—on this cause and on him. "Prince Kanthe, the prioress is only securing us a little time. Only *you* can dissuade the others."

Kanthe reached the rear of the wagon and faced his mentor. "Frell, you again think too highly of me. The highmayor, the Council of Eight, even

Anskar, none of them will heed the word of the Dark Trifle. The drunken Tallywag. A mere Prince in the Cupboard."

Kanthe turned, hiked his bow higher on his back, and leaped into the rear of the wagon. Only then did he face the disappointment of his friend with a smile. "But they dare not shoot me in the back."

He rushed to the front of the wagon, scooting past the wrapped cage.

Frell clambered up after him. "What do you—"

"You there!" Kanthe called down as he reached the cart's seat.

Bastan dropped a curry brush in surprise and swung around at the bull-ock's side. He stared up at the prince in the wagon.

Kanthe circled an arm around his head. "Turn this cart around."

Frell joined him. "What are you doing?"

"They can't burn a sacrifice that's not here." Kanthe tried again with the young man, pointing down the tiers. "Turn that big beast of yours. Gram-blebuck, you called him. We're heading back to the swamps."

Kanthe pictured breaking the cage open and letting the wounded creature escape back into the watery bower of its home.

Bastan simply gaped up at him.

Kanthe leaned over to Frell. "See. I can't even convince a swamper's son to listen to me."

Frell called over the cart seat, "Young man! Your sister Nyx is in danger!"

Kanthe glanced hard to the alchymist. *His sister?*

Bastan looked equally baffled but drew nearer. "What about Nyx?"

"She may have survived the bat's poison, but she won't live until the dawn bell if we don't escape and free the creature here."

Kanthe's mind spun to catch up. *Again with that girl.* He remembered Frell's speculation on her past, about her possible shared lineage with a cer-tain prince. *Is she everyone's blasted sister?*

Bastan considered the alchymist's words, then turned swiftly, snatched the bullock's lead, and dragged its nose away from the pyres and toward the steps leading down. Kanthe grabbed the back of the cart seat to keep his feet as the wagon lurched on its iron-shod wheels.

The commotion began to turn heads. While most eyes were still on the fiery discussions on the far side of the pyre, those closest glanced over shoul-ders to stare at the wagon. A few of those faces were stained crimson. Hands lowered to swords. Crossbows were swung off of backs.

"Move that shaggy arse faster," Kanthe hissed below.

Bastan hauled harder on the lead.

As the wagon turned, another pair of faces watched from only steps away. Though the rain had stopped, Shrive Vythaas still stood under a canopy carried by the hulking form of his personal Gyn. The holy man's eyes were slits. Yet, the Shrive raised no alarm. He could have easily sent the craggy-faced Gyn to stop them, to block them, to even drop the bullock with the strike of the Gyn's stony fist. Instead, the Shrive simply stared.

How much had the bony bastard overheard?

The wagon finally got hauled full around, with the bullock's nose pointed at the steps.

"Quick now!" Kanthe urged.

Bastan tugged the lead, trying to get Gramblebuck to head for the stairs, but the beast balked at the sight of the long flight back down.

Can't blame the poor brute.

Still . . .

Kanthe waved to Bastan. "Whip 'im if you must! Get us moving!"

The swamper scowled, as if the prince had asked the man to beat his own mother. Instead, Bastan grabbed a firmer hold of the bridle and yanked, digging in his heels. The bullock did the same with his three-toed hooves.

Kanthe blew an exasperated breath at the stubborn standoff.

Bastan's face purpled with frustration. "Git clomping, Gramble. Nyxie needs us."

The girl's name managed to get the beast to shift one leg, then another forward. The wagon lurched—but far too slowly. Kanthe looked back to the gathering atop the ninth tier. All eyes had swung their way. A cadre of Vyrl-lian Guards shoved toward them.

Kanthe cursed and worked his way toward the rear of the wagon. He needed to buy the others a few more breaths. As he sidestepped around the cage, a low hiss from the beast inside followed him.

"I'm trying to save your hairy arse," he grumbled back at it.

Kanthe reached the back of the wagon and shifted to stand behind the wrapped cage. He braced his legs and waved his arms. Angry shouts erupted. The highmayor hollered, "Stop 'em already, you louts!"

The vy-knights pulled their swords.

Kanthe suddenly had doubts about the impenetrable shield of his princely standing. This was made all too clear with the sharp *thwits* of crossbow bolts. One skimmed his ear; another laid a fiery line across his left hip.

He ducked and scrambled back toward the front of the wagon. "Now or never," he screamed. Everything was going too slow.

He passed Frell, who sheltered behind the cage—but the alchymist wasn't hiding. Frell tugged at a knot in a rope. Another cord dangled loose beside the man.

What is he doing?

Frell then stood and ripped away the flap of leather that he had untied. The alchymist fell back as the bat slammed into the bars, gnashing and spitting poison. Frell herded Kanthe to the cart's seat.

Kanthe spluttered, "Why did you do—?"

The bat screamed at them, its piercing cry like a wind in his face. Kanthe was not the only one to hear it. The wagon bolted forward, nearly throwing Frell and Kanthe back into the cage bars. The old bullock suddenly knew what was hidden atop the wagon and fled from it.

"Hang on!" Kanthe yelled as the beast thundered in a bellowing panic toward the steps. He hooked an arm around a plank of the cart seat.

Frell followed his example.

Over the humping back of the bullock, Kanthe watched Gramblebuck reach the top step and leap headlong. Bastan miraculously kept hold of the beast's bridle and used it to swing onto the bullock's back.

And not a moment too soon.

Gramblebuck crashed back to the steps, deftly landing on all four legs. The wagon followed, the rear end bucking high. It hung there for an impossible breath—then hit the steps with a teeth-shattering impact. A rope snapped behind them, and the cage bumped toward them with a savage hiss of the bat inside.

As they bounced and rattled toward the eighth tier below, more bolts pursued them. The iron quarrels ripped through the air and through the wooden pen. Several bolts must have struck the beast inside. The bat's scream sharpened to a pitch that threatened to burst his ears. It certainly goaded the bullock to a faster clip.

Ahead, a group of knights in light armor stood clustered at the bottom of the stairs. More gathered from their stations around the eighth level, drawn by the noise. Kanthe lifted high enough to flag an arm at them.

"Get out of the way!" he bellowed.

Gramblebuck did the same with a frightened lowing.

The knights obeyed them both and scattered to either side. Sharper shouts rose behind the wagon. A glance back revealed the charge of crimson-faced figures down the stairs. The vy-knights leaped several steps at a time, led by Anskar, whose face had gone far redder.

Bullock and wagon reached the eighth tier and struck it hard, showering fiery sparks from the ironclad wheels. Several spokes shattered away. Still, the cart continued clattering toward the next set of steps leading down.

The Vyrllian Guard gave pursuit, leaping like a flight of deer to the tier and chasing after them. Anskar sped ahead of the others, flanked by his two best men. He yelled something to the pair, the words lost in the rattling.

Without slowing, the two dropped coils of ropes from their shoulders to their hands. They snapped their weighted ends and barbed hooks unhinged to form grappling irons.

Sard it all.

Kanthe swung around, judging the distance to the next stairs.

We can still make it.

Then the left rear wheel broke free. With a scatter of sparks, it bounced and rolled away, as if escaping on its own. Still, the wagon sped ahead, balanced on the remaining three wheels.

But for how long?

The bullock reached the edge of the tier and dashed down the next set of steps. The wagon followed, its rear end rocking wildly on the remaining wheel back there. More ropes snapped away from the cage—then the entire pen slid toward Kanthe and Frell. The bat howled at the bars, fangs snapping wildly.

Kanthe dropped to his bottom, braced his back against the cart seat behind him, and caught the cage with his legs, his feet balanced on ironwood bars. The pen's weight still crushed toward him. Frell tried to help, grabbing for the cage.

"Don't!" Kanthe gasped out, fearing his mentor would lose fingers, if not his entire hand. "I got this."

He didn't.

His muscles gave out, and the cage fell toward them both. One of his legs slipped between the bars and into the pen. The front of the cage smashed into them both, pinning them in place. The bat slathered poison over Kanthe's upturned face. Claws tore through his breeches and into his thigh.

So this is how I die.

It was a far more dramatic end than he had ever imagined for himself.

Then the wagon bucked, and the cage lifted high—and it inexplicably flew away from his face, stripping his leg back out of the pen. As Kanthe watched, the cage sailed out the back of the wagon.

He rolled to his knees to try to comprehend this miracle.

At the top of the stairs, Anskar's two men had anchored the ends of their ropes around statues to either side of the stairs. The ropes' lengths stretched to the flying cage, where grappling irons had hooked into the pen's bars. The snagged cage tilted sideways in midair and crashed to the steps, shattering open.

Anskar must have prepared for this. He rushed down the steps, swung a net, and tossed it high. The net spun through the air toward the remains of the cage and the prisoner inside. The bat thrashed to break free. Its wings cracked more bars; claws shredded scraps of leather. Finally, it managed to shove its head out, snapping everywhere, its belled ears flat to its skull. It fought to extract itself. Its neck stretched with a wail of despair, as if it were drowning in the wreckage.

Then the heavy net, knitted through with thorns, fell over all.

As the wagon continued down the stairs, Kanthe accepted the inevitable. He had failed. The bat strained toward him, desperation written in its every thrash. It was a futile battle. Once subdued, it would be dragged back to the fire and burned alive.

Kanthe faced his defeat, refusing to look away.

Still, I'll not be the one to suffer for it.

Across the distance, the bat stared at him. The fear and misery in its red eyes was easy to read.

"What are you doing?" Frell asked.

Kanthe couldn't answer as he shifted higher, one knee still braced under him. He lifted the bow already in his hand and notched an arrow. He pulled the gut string to his cheek. The arrow's fletching tickled his ear as he took aim.

Better this.

He inhaled one deep breath, then released the bowstring.

The arrow shot up the steps.

And pierced clean through a fiery red eye.

NYX CRIED OUT as agony shattered into her skull. She slapped a palm to her left eye. The world suddenly went dark. She missed the next step and fell headlong down the last of the forbidden staircase.

Jace caught her before she struck the stone floor. "What happened?"

The burning pain spiked for another breath, then faded to an icy coldness. She lowered her hand, and her sight returned.

"I . . . I'm not sure," she said.

But she was.

As she read the worry in Jace's pinched face, a dark storm grew in the back of her mind. With every breath, it grew larger, stoked by fury.

She quailed before it.

Jace helped her to her feet. "Nyx, what's wrong?"

She turned and stared upward, knowing the truth.

"We failed. They're coming."

Arkival limne of
Bullock
(Swamps of Mýr)

SIX

WISDOM WRIT
IN BRONZE

The treuest wisdom lies in accepting that you know noht,
while the grettest folly lies in beleafing you know all.
—Aphorism of Hestarian the Elder

18

RHAIF HATED SUMMER, especially in the sweltering stifle of Anvil.

As the first bell of Eventoll rang throughout the city, he hurried down a shadowed alley that cut from one street to the next. He huddled under a mud-beige light-cloak that brushed his ankles and wore sandals to keep the heat of the cobbles from burning his soles. He hurried along with the cowl of his cloak's hood low over his eyes. He looked like many of the day-laborers hunching their way home, or night-staffers sullenly heading the other way.

Few, if any, lifted their faces.

Like him, the entire town sought to hide from the Father Above. The sun sat near to its highest point in the eastern sky as midsummer approached. Though that significant moment was still another three days off, a few houses already had bright bows framing windows or were decorated with oil lamps glowing behind glass shades tinted in crimson and purple, trying to bring a measure of cheer to the gloom. The celebration to come—the Midsummer Bloom—was an attempt to falsely brighten the grimmest time of the year. For Rhaif, it always struck him as the height of submission, marking how readily the townspeople accepted the sullen order of Anvil.

What're ya gonna do? was as common as *Good morrow* or *Sard off* here in Anvil. Like an ox beaten so often that it learned to ignore the strike of a driver's club, the townspeople simply grew hardened to their sorry state. They trudged from one day to the next, until they were finally laid low in an early grave in the burning sands. It was a small mercy that few of them ever lived past their fortieth birthyear.

And the cause behind such an early demise was plain with each breath.

Rhaif tugged the linen scarf higher over his mouth and nose, a veil that all the townspeople wore to filter the soot and smoke that threatened to prematurely blacken a lung. The deathly pall hung most heavily during the stretches of summer, when there was nary a breeze off the sea. And rather than shade the sun's heat, the black blanket only trapped it closer, smothering the city.

Rhaif cocked an ear to the low roar that continually sounded throughout the city, what was dubbed the Grumble of Anvil. Its source was the same as the pall of soot and smoke. Hundreds of huge belching chimneys and flaming stacks—like the war-towers of some great siege—rose all around. They marked the city's countless smelters, refineries, forges, and gas distilleries. All of the mines across the Guld'guhl territories shipped their wares to Anvil. The city was the hard iron upon which the raw ores, rocks, and salts were hammered against—before finally being shipped around the Crown.

Rhaif reached a larger street and slipped into the sullen drift of the crowd, picking the side heading upward. Here, bright Bloom garlands were strung across the way. Many were lined by tiny upraised flags, representing the sails of the thousand ships coming and going from Anvil, whether by sea, like the thick-beamed ore-trawlers, or by ethereal winds, like the gas-filled giants that safely ferried precious jewels over the pirate-riven waters.

As if summoned by this thought, a wyndship passed overhead, gliding through the black pall. It was headed toward the docks of Eyr Rigg, the tall ridgeline marking the easternmost border of Anvil. He gazed longingly for several steps.

If only . . .

He lowered his face again from such lofty heights and returned his gaze to the street. He knew the homes and shops to either had been constructed of white marble and topped by roofs of clay tiles in shades of blue and deep reds, all the better to reflect the shine of the Father Above. Though that was no longer the case. Centuries had layered soot over the walls and muted any brightness to a drab dullness. Only during the all-too-brief midwinter Freshening, when the winds would finally kick up and blow the worst of the pall away from the city, did any of the townspeople try to scrub away the filth. Still, it was a futile effort, as the winds always died and the pall returned to settle heavily again. While most sang their relief to the gods during each Freshening, Rhaif was not fooled. To him, the winds were merely the gust of a bellows, which cleared the smoke only to allow the fires to burn hotter.

As he zigzagged through streets and alleys and up crumbling steps, he climbed higher and higher away from the port. Finally, just as the second bell of Eventoll rang out, he passed under a pointed arch formed by the crossing of two large hammers and entered the large central square of Anvil. Tall buildings towered on all four sides. To the left was the Crown Mynt, where coins of the realm were forged and protected behind walls of iron and steel. Directly ahead was Judgement Hall, which was the bailiwick of Anvil's sheriffdom. Flags hung to either side of its doorways, one emblazoned with the Guld'guhlian crossed hammers and the other with the crown and sun of the Kingdom of Hálendii.

Rhaif kept his face even lower as he skirted to the right, keeping to the milling throngs as shifts changed from day to night. He also hunkered lower, with a hunched back and a slight bend to his knees. He didn't want his above normal height—due to his mixed blood—to make him stand out among the squat Guld'guhlians around him.

Still, he swore he could feel the piggish eyes of Archsheriff Laach peering down from his high office at those gathered below, searching for a certain thief in the city.

Just your imagination, Rhaif. Quit your shivering already.

He reminded himself that he had escaped discovery for nearly a fortnight after the train from the mines of Chalk had finally ground to a halt in Anvil's yards. During the chaos of its unloading, he had stolen away, hurrying along the length of wagons, passing the two giant sandcrabs who steamed amidst the chaos of the yards as their armored carapaces were washed down to cool their heat. Their driver calmed them further with the soothing melodies of bridle-song, each gentle note winding its control down to the knot of brain beneath all that armor and muscle.

It had been a sad, plaintive melody, fitting for Rhaif's return to Anvil. He had even paused to listen, to eavesdrop, recognizing the loneliness etched in the driver's refrain. It had momentarily captured him, as surely as it had the pair of giant crabs. While such a talent was rare and well compensated, the bearers of such a skill were often shunned by others. As cities spread and lands were consumed, such a gentle connection to nature, to the wild corners of the world, was something to be scorned, a remnant from another era, when men struggled against tooth and claw, against ice and fire.

After a time, under the cover of steam and song, Rhaif had slipped off and vanished into the smoky shroud of Anvil. Of course, he had not arrived alone. The mystery that was the bronze woman had followed his steps, sticking to him like lodestone to iron.

She continued to remain as much of a riddle as ever. It didn't help that he had to keep her locked in his room at a whorehouse near the port, where few questions were asked and no one bothered to look too closely at one another. She had also grown strangely sluggish, not speaking a word, barely moving, the glow in her eyes ebbing to a dim shimmer. He suspected it had to do with the smoky pall blanketing the city, shielding the sun's blaze. As far as he could tell, the Father Above fueled her in some arcane way, and with His face mostly hidden here, she had faded like a Klashean rose in winter.

Her state was worrisome, but not as concerning as the threat of their recapture. He had considered simply abandoning her. It would have been far easier for him to escape Guld'guhl without that bronze anchor dragging behind him. But he could not. He would not be free now without her aid back in Chalk. He pictured what would have happened if he'd been caught: his impaled body staked outside the mine, being burrowed through by vermin and pecked at by carrion birds.

I owe her my life.

Still, that was not the only reason. Even when she was sluggish and dull, he caught her staring at him many times, studying him with unblinking eyes, as if continually evaluating him. But it was not a cold inspection. In the subtle pinch of brow and downturned lips, he recognized a deep sadness. He knew that look. When he was a boy, still an apprentice at the guild, he came across a bony dog that had been half-trampled by an ore cart. It was still alive, but near unto death. Still, he took it to his room in the Guildhall, bundling it up, using a soaked rag to ease its panting thirst. He could not say why he did that, and certainly Llyra, the guildmaster, questioned him, insisting there was nothing he could do. She was proven right a day later. The little cur died in his lap, nose tucked under an arm, but those amber eyes had never looked away from his face, even as the life faded from them. He knew his expression then was not dissimilar to the bronze woman's now as she contemplated him, some mix of grief and worry rising from a well of tenderness.

So, how could I abandon her?

At times, he even wondered if she was silently emanating some version of bridle-song, entrapping and binding him to her. Or maybe he was romanticizing it all just to cover up the real reason: his own greed. She was undoubtedly of great value and could likely be ransomed for her weight in gold.

Ultimately, no matter the reason, he refused to leave her behind. It was why he had crossed the breadth of Anvil to reach the central square. He lifted his scarfed face to study the windowless towers to the right of the Judgement Hall. It was the city's main gaol and dungeons.

He headed toward the steps leading to its arched doorway. An iron portcullis stood presently open, its bottom edge lined by sharp spikes, like the fangs of a great beast. He gulped at the sight, unnerved, fearful of being swallowed once again by that monster. Two years ago, he had languished in a hot cell for nearly an entire moon as he was tried and eventually sentenced to the mines of Chalk.

Still, he continued toward the steps.

Can't be helped.

As he passed behind a soot-blackened statue of the chained god Yyrl, he shed his light-cloak and let it drop behind him. He continued back into view of the square, regaled now in black breeches and tunic, including a matching half-cloak that bore the crossed gold hammers of Anvil. It was the habiliment of a prison gaoler. It had not been hard to acquire. He had simply followed a turnkey into one of the portside's many whorehouses. Rhaif had waited until the man was grunting in rented passion, then slipped into the room and took what he needed. Not even the bored woman on her hands and knees, skirt around her waist, had heard his soft-footed entrance into the room. Luckily, the years in Chalk had not tarnished his skills to move unseen and unheard.

Still, more skill was needed from here.

Rhaif reached the steps and climbed toward the open portcullis. He finally shed his scarf, knowing faces could not be masked in the gaol. Shortly after arriving in Anvil, he had dyed his hair to a straw-blond, and during the past fortnight, he had grown a crust of beard, presently oiled and also dyed.

Still, as he crossed under the spears of the portcullis, he fought down a shiver, recognizing the irony of his trespass.

After escaping one prison, here I am breaking into another.

Standing at the bars, Rhaif took in the sight of the gaunt figure inside the cell. It was as if a shadow had been given form, a sculpture of polished ebonwood. The man, who had to be several years younger than his own thirty years, stood with his back to the cell door. He had been stripped naked, except for the collar of iron forged around his neck. His black skin, from buttock to shoulder, bore a map of white scars from the bite of whips. His head was darkly stubbled. He was plainly not allowed to keep his head shaven here, which was typical of the Chaaen, both men and women.

Rhaif glanced right and left to make sure no other gaolers were in this remote corner of the dungeons. "I would speak with you," he said gruffly, doing his best not to sound conspiratorial.

The man sighed and turned, revealing eyes of a mesmerizing violet— along with a feature unique to the Chaaen. Between his legs was nothing but a tuft of hair and a mutilation. All such men of his order were cut, disfigured into eunuchs. The women were equally marred in their own way, so as to never bear children, to never experience the pleasure of union.

"What do you want?" the Chaaen asked. His voice was calm, showing not the slightest fright, which, considering all he had been through in life, was not surprising. The slight lilt in his voice revealed his Klashean origins.

Rhaif shifted closer to the bars. "Let's start with your name, so we might know each other better."

"I am Pratik, chaaen-bound to Rellis im Malsh."

"And as I understand, your master is also detained here, accused of being a spy for the Southern Klashe."

Pratik simply stared.

Rhaif, like much of Anvil, had heard of the incarceration of many Klashean traders, brought here to be questioned as spies, which was likely true of most of them. Besides being a major mining port, Anvil had sprouted a score of great alchymical houses, some centuries old, that delved into the design of arcane machines and other geared works. Still, the Southern Klashe far outstripped Anvil's feeble efforts in such pursuits. Rhaif knew there were just as many, if not more, Hálendiian traders who doubled as infiltrators when they traveled south, seeking to steal knowledge from Klashean establishments. In fact, it was well known in Anvil that the trade in secrets was as important here as its shipment in rock and salt. Coins rolled from north to south and back again. Occasional hands were slapped if there was too much overreach, but in the end, it served all to turn a blind eye upon such clandestine enterprises.

Until now.

Archsheriff Laach had gathered up the Klashean traders for one simple reason: to trap Rhaif in Anvil. Laach could not risk losing the bronze prize stolen from him, especially with the malignant Shrive Wryth clutching the man's neck. Like Rhaif, the archsheriff knew the northern Crown would offer no refuge for the escaped pair. The only hope for them was to barter for passage to the south. To thwart that, Laach had imprisoned anyone who might strike up such a bargain—both to question them and to keep them locked away from Rhaif.

So, with no other choice, Rhaif had to come to the prison in person to plead his case. Even Laach—bursting with his own high opinion of himself— would never suspect such an attempt.

At least, I hope not.

Pratik finally spoke. "And who are you?" One brow lifted. "Someone I suspect is more than a simple turnkey."

Rhaif considered how best to answer this. He knew any deception with a Chaaen would likely fail. It was said such men and women knew another's inner truth with a glance. So, he opted for the truth. "Rhaif hy Albar."

The only sign of recognition was the lowering of the Chaaen's one brow. "You risk much, but I fear for little gain. My master will be of little use to you."

"I didn't come here for your master."

Rhaif knew the traders themselves were under much closer watch in the gaol's upper towers. This was not true for their chaaen-bound, whom most considered little more than slaves. They were barely worthy of note; as such, they had been tossed down into the sparsely guarded dungeons—which suited Rhaif just fine.

Rhaif lifted the heavy circle of iron keys that he had pilfered from the dungeon guardroom. "I came to free you."

Pratik narrowed his eyes and finally stepped closer. "At what price?"

"To help me escape Anvil in one of your wyndships."

The prisoner shook his head. "Impossible. Besides, even if I don't shout and expose you now, my freedom will come eventually. They cannot keep my master for long, not without further offending our emperor. So, as you see, your price is too high."

"Ah, but that is not all I came to bargain with." This time Rhaif lifted a brow. "You know what I stole."

A shrug. "What is *rumored* that you stole."

"It is more than a rumor, I assure you." He let the Chaaen read the truth in his face. "I will take you to her, and if you are dissatisfied, you can turn me in to the archsheriff. But you will not be disappointed. The Klashe will want what I possess, especially with war drums pounding in the distance, with armies gathering at the borders. And who knows? Such a prize may not only earn my freedom—but maybe yours, too."

Pratik's eyes narrowed further. The prisoner lifted a hand and fingered the iron ring fused around his neck. His gaze steadied on Rhaif. "Show me."

Rhaif grinned. It took him a few tries to fit the right key into the lock, but eventually he hauled the door open and tossed a bundle at the naked man. "Put these on quickly."

Pratik obeyed, slipping on a turnkey's habiliment that matched his own. Rhaif had stolen it from the same guardroom, where the only gaoler present had been some fat lout snoring at a scarred table.

Rhaif pointed to the half-cloak's hood. "Pull that high and keep your face low. Let me do the speaking from here."

With a nod, Pratik tugged the hood over his stubbled head.

Rhaif gave his look a final inspection, then set off. He wanted to be out of here before the next bell, to lose themselves among the gaolers heading home.

He glanced back to Pratik, trying to judge if the Chaaen would betray him, but such men and women were known for their word, not necessarily out of honor, but because any deception had been beaten and whipped out of them long ago.

Rhaif had a hard time swallowing the cruel practices of the Klashe. Their lands were ruled over by a single caste of royalty, known as the *imri*, which meant *godly* in their tongue, led by the Imri-Ka, the god-emperor of the Klashe. Only those of his bloodline were allowed to show their faces when abroad in their lands. All other baseborn castes—which numbered in the hundreds—had to remain cloaked from crown to toe, deemed too unworthy for the Father Above to gaze upon them. An admonition that included the Chaaen, who were trained and schooled at *Bad'i Chaa,* the House of Wisdom.

Where the northern Crown had a half dozen schools, the *Bad'i Chaa* remained the Southern Klashe's sole place of learning. It was said the House of Wisdom was a city unto itself. It was divided into nine tiers like the Hálendiian schools, but the House of Wisdom was far crueler. There was also no choice in attending. Young boys and girls were culled from across their lands, from all castes, except the *imri.* While Hálendiian schools discouraged trysts and unions, demanding purity, the House of Wisdom enforced it beforehand by clipping their firstyears. Worst of all, those who failed to move upward were not simply sent home, but were executed and their bodies burned in the pyres atop the school as both a warning to the tiers below and a sacrifice to the Klashe's pantheon of gods, who were far more bloodthirsty than those to the north.

As Rhaif reached the stairs leading up from the dungeons, he searched for those years of terror and horror in Pratik's face, but the man's features were placid, as if he had accepted such cruelties as a part of life. Then again, the young man had eventually made it through that school, earning the iron collar of alchymy. Other Chaaen bore the silver collar of religion and history. Afterward, those who survived the school were bound in pairs—one wearing iron, the other silver—to one of the *imri.* The Chaaen served as counselors and advisers to their masters. And sometimes objects of pleasure, as was whispered. In public, ceremonial chains ran from a Chaaen's neck-collar to his or her master's ankles. The higher you were ranked among the *imri,* the more Chaaen were bound to you, the pairs linked from one to another. It was said the Imri-Ka had sixty-six Chaaen chained to him, thirty-three pairs, the same number as their pantheon of gods. Whenever he walked about, he dragged a veritable train behind him.

Rhaif tried to imagine such a sight as he finished the climb out of the cooler depths of the dungeons and back into the swelter of the day. The air became smudged and reeked of burning oil. They passed a few gaolers heading down for their shift, but beyond a grunt or a nod, no one heeded anyone else.

At the top of the steps, Rhaif hissed back at Pratik, "Stay close to my back. Eyes down."

Ahead, the main hall bustled with turnkeys coming and going, some leading chained prisoners. A handful of red-capped boys darted throughout the throng, whisking messages up and down the towers.

Perfect.

Rhaif led Pratik into the bedlam. He drew them into the flow of gaolers leaving for the day. In short order, the spikes of the portcullis appeared. All was going well until the crowd ahead eddied in confusion. A few shocked voices echoed back to them.

Rhaif shifted to the side to determine the cause of the commotion.

He groaned when he spotted a familiar figure in a gray robe who sported a noose of silver braids around his throat. Shrive Wryth scaled the steps toward the gaol. The rarity of such holy men, especially one traipsing into a prison, had stopped everyone, drawing all eyes. The sea of boys and gaolers parted before the Shrive, both out of respect and fear.

Worst of all, the divide seemed to be aiming straight for Rhaif.

He herded Pratik back, swearing under his breath.

The gods must hate me.

He grabbed the Chaaen's arm and turned him away. *What is Wryth doing here?* The answer appeared directly ahead of them as a pair of turnkeys were shoved to either side. Two familiar figures strode forward, the same pair who had damned Rhaif to the mines of Chalk.

Only steps away from Rhaif, Archsheriff Laach waved an arm in greeting toward the gaol gate. "This way, Shrive Wryth!"

The sheriff, seemingly blind to his surroundings, had not even noted Rhaif standing there. Unfortunately, the same could not be said of Laach's companion. Little escaped the attention of Llyra hy March, the guildmaster of thieves. Her face froze for a breath in shock—then her lips thinned, and her eyes sparkled with dark amusement as she stared over at him.

Rhaif groaned.

The gods definitely hate me.

19

RHAIF'S VISION NARROWED as he struggled for a way to escape.

Llyra met his gaze in that strained moment. Her fingers rested at her wrist, where the edge of her sleeve hid a bracelet of sheathed throwing knives. He had once watched her impale three rats—to a wall, a rafter, and a keg—with one sweep of her arm. And she hadn't even bothered to look in the vermin's direction.

But that was not her truest threat. There was a reason she had been the guildmaster in Anvil for over a decade. He had learned long ago that her mind was as slippery as greased cobbles in the rain. Such cunning made it nearly impossible to keep one's footing when pitted against her. Her skill was so daunting, he sometimes wondered if her talent was spyllcast or fueled by alchymies. In the past, he had often challenged her to a game of Knights n' Knaves, but she trounced him every time, toppling his king on the board with nary a sign of effort.

So, what hope do I have now?

No doubt she was already thinking a dozen steps ahead of him, preparing to countermeasure any of his flight attempts. With every pound of his heart, he felt the iron jaws of a trap closing on him.

She narrowed the distance between them, her gaze never breaking from him—then she brushed past with a bump of her elbow. She spoke to the sheriff and nodded toward the commotion at the portcullis. "Laach, we should get that braided bastard up to the tower before all these gaolers start bending a knee and begging a blessing."

The archsheriff grunted his acknowledgment and forged a quicker pace across the hall to meet Wryth.

Llyra cast one last glance back at Rhaif, but her features were inscrutable. *What new game is this?*

Despite the danger, he was struck by the severity of her beauty. Her blond hair was cut straight at the shoulder. Her eyes glinted an icy copper, framed by sharp cheekbones. The only thing soft about her was the bud of her lips. And though she had taken him into her bed many times, she had never let him taste those lips.

As she turned and strode away, it was clear she had dressed to accent her curves. Her linens and leathers were corseted tight at the waist, her leggings hugged her like a second skin. And while she had the short stature of most Guld'guhlians, she was lithe of limb, sculpted of muscles so hard and wiry that he swore they were threaded through by steel. He especially remembered her strong legs wrapped around his buttocks, demanding he perform better.

But what does she want now? Why didn't she raise an alarm?

All he knew for sure was that he could never outwit her in the past, let alone untie her elaborate plots. Instead, he took advantage of this mysterious reprieve to grab Pratik's arm and guide him to the side. Rhaif picked a path that skirted the clot of onlookers around the Shrive, and once clear, he hurried under the portcullis and out into the open square.

He didn't know if Llyra ever looked his way again.

He didn't care.

As long as I'm still free.

He kept moving, forcing himself not to run. "Keep with me," he warned Pratik. "We have a ways to go."

And likely a trail of shadows to shake.

It was the only possible explanation. Llyra surely knew the value of what Rhaif had stolen and wanted it for herself. She must hope that he would guide her hounds to his hiding spot. As Llyra and Laach reached the portcullis ahead of Rhaif, she had likely already signaled lurkers out in the square. And she certainly had the entire breadth of the guild from which to choose the best trackers.

But not the very best, Rhaif thought with a matter of pride—which he prayed was not misplaced. As he headed toward the crossed hammers of the square's main arch, he searched around him. He sought eyes that lingered too long, or bodies that shifted course in his direction. He identified a half dozen suspects, but he was equally sure there were more. Worst of all, he had no doubt that word of his sighting was rapidly spreading ahead of him.

With Pratik in tow, he did his best to navigate back to the port. He knew the city well. He chose the narrowest alleyways, empty of any others. He crossed into shops and out back patios. He sought crooked paths and backtracked often. He entered a smoke-choked smithy, where one could barely see the fingers of an outstretched arm. There, he tossed the blacksmith a silver eyrie and retrieved a pair of cloaks to hide their gaoler garb.

Back out on the streets, he continued his winding route homeward. Finally, the stinking air turned salty, and the squabbling screams of sea terns cut through the ever-present Grumble of Anvil.

"This way," Rhaif urged.

By now, they had reached the Boils, a cramped dark warren in the shadow of the city's largest chimneys. Here, the air was just soot and cinder, while underfoot, muck and shite coated the cobbles. In the Boils, all manner of ill repute found their home. He led Pratik into the maze of squeeze-thrus and narrows that made up the whoremongers' yoke. He finally reached a door and shoved inside.

He paused long enough to remind Pratik, "Not a word."

It was rare to have a Klashean—let alone a clipped Chaaen—in such a place. Rhaif dared not let the man's lilting accent raise any suspicions.

As they entered, the stink of sour ale and piss greeted them. A heavyset matron heard the telltale creak of the door and began to stir a few languid forms draped about the room, most of whom were smoking snakeroot or stronger leaves. Rhaif waved leadenly at the matron, who scowled in recognition of her renter. She settled back over a tankard, likely already forgetting him.

Rhaif climbed rickety stairs and passed down a hall where closed doors did little to mask the grunts, gasps, and spats of laughter, some genuine, more feigned. He reached his room and rushed Pratik inside.

Once the door was closed and barred, the Chaaen inspected the cramped space. The bed was a flat board with a thin spread of hay atop it. The privy was a bucket in the corner. Nothing had been freshened in several days.

Pratik's face pinched with disgust. He covered his mouth and nose against the stench. He mumbled between his fingers, "I now regret leaving the dungeons."

Rhaif grinned. "Oh, fear not, we're not home yet." He crossed to the wall, dropped to a knee, and lifted away a section of planks to reveal a tight squeeze. He had secretly sawed this opening shortly after securing the room. "You'll need to crawl the last of the way."

Pratik bent down and inspected the dark pass-thru between old beams. "Where does it lead?"

"To both our freedoms," he said, voicing his best hope.

RHAIF DUSTED OFF his knees and helped Pratik out the far end of the cramped passageway. It emptied into a larger rented room in a neighboring whorehouse. This one backed upon the first and opened onto a different corner of the Boils, one slightly less tawdry. He had prepared this arrangement early on, anticipating trouble, because it always found one eventually.

He had also been following a creed ingrained into any rogue.

Never trap yourself in a room with only one door.

In this case, such an extra measure served an additional purpose. If any of

Llyra's hunters had managed to shadow Rhaif across the city, they would believe their mark had holed up at the other establishment. If Llyra attempted a raid there, the commotion through the thin walls would alert him in time to make his escape from here.

At least, I pray so.

Once Pratik was out of the tunnel, Rhaif refitted the section of planks on this side back into place. He rubbed grime and dust over the outline in the wall, doing his best to mask the secret door.

Once satisfied, he rolled to his feet.

Pratik had used the time to inspect the new room. His expression looked relieved. The chamber had a single thin window, presently shuttered. A small hearth glowed in a corner, its ruddy coals sprinkled with incense, casting a spicy hint to the air. The bed was far more stout with a pillow and mattress, both stuffed with sweethay, and all covered with a light blanket. A clay washbasin sat atop a table, and the privy had its own closet.

Pratik passed his judgement. "A slight improvement on the dungeon. But . . ." The Chaaen glanced full around the room, even stepping to peek past the open door into the privy. His brows were pinched when he faced Rhaif again. "Where is the bronze artifact you promised to show me?"

Rhaif grinned and crossed to the other side of the bed. While the room's hall door was barred against any unwanted trespass, he had taken one extra precaution. Along the far wall, he found the carved fingerholds and revealed his last bit of carpentry. He lifted free yet another secret door—this section far taller than the others—and exposed a cubby between dry beams.

Pratik came to stand at Rhaif's back.

Inside the niche, the bronze woman stood as if a statue. Her eyes were closed, and her hands were demurely folded at her waist. She still wore the yellow linen robe he had bought with coins pilfered from the milling crowds of the port.

"Mes wondres," Pratik murmured in his own tongue. He drew closer. "I've never seen such perfection in forge and mold. It looks as if she is about to take a breath at any moment." He glanced to Rhaif with wide eyes. "Such a sculpture belongs in the finest *imri* garden or among the House of Wisdom's collection of ancient treasures. Even the Imri-Ka himself would pay dearly for her."

Rhaif chuckled, realizing how little this Chaaen knew about how truly *mes wondres* this statue was. But the man's ignorance made sense. Of course, Laach, Wryth, and Llyra would have shared as few details as possible about the discovery in Chalk, restricting such knowledge to themselves.

"Why do you laugh at me?" Pratik asked with a frown.

Rhaif pointed to the cubby. "Maybe she can explain."

Pratik turned in time to see the woman's eyes open. The cold glass glowed brighter as the fires inside her form stoked her back awake. Her gaze quickly warmed and softened under that heat, finally shifting to linger on the stranger.

The Chaaen gasped and stumbled back a step.

The woman's head cocked to one side, her attention still following him. Rhaif lifted an inviting arm toward her. She responded by unfolding her hands and gently lifting a shapely leg to step free of the cubby.

Choking in shock, Pratik retreated until he reached the bed and dropped heavily atop it. He stammered, leaning farther away, "Wh . . . What magick or alchymy is this? Or is it some form of artifice?"

"No, it's far from trickery. And in truth, beyond anything that I understand."

In order to win over the Chaaen, Rhaif knew he would need to reveal all. He started by explaining about the quake deep in the mines of Chalk and the bizarre discovery even deeper. He described the blood sacrifice that revived the artifact, including the Shriven's seeming knowledge of it.

Pratik interrupted with a smattering of questions, but there were few that Rhaif could answer.

Rhaif finally finished the tale with his escape and arrival in Anvil. "But we can't stay here. I must find a way of absconding with her. Hopefully to the lands of the Southern Klashe, where those hunting us will not follow."

Still seated on the bed, Pratik spent much of Rhaif's story studying the bronze woman. Though calmer now, he was clearly fearful of drawing any nearer to her. She had crossed to the thin window and opened the shutter. She stared up at the sooty skies, toward the wan glow to the west that marked the moon. From the slump of her shoulders and doleful bend to her back, she was a bronze sigil of sorrow.

I'm doing what I can, he silently promised her.

Over the past fortnight, he had come to sense a desire in her. Though sluggish, she would drift around the room for a spell, then eventually come to a halt somewhere, but always facing to the west, like a lodestone in a broken wayglass that could only point one direction. Plainly she fretted upon some concern known only to her.

As he stared at her now, he could not forget the one mournful word she had spoken on the train, staring up at the full face of the moon. It haunted him.

Doom . . .

Over the past fortnight, her trepidation had seeped into his bones. He knew he could not discount her warning.

But what could a petty larcener from Anvil hope to accomplish?

It was why Rhaif had chosen to free a Chaaen with an iron collar, one steeped in alchymical lore. He needed an ally to help him understand what he had stolen and to perhaps discern what mystery lay buried in her bronze heart.

Yet, there was another reason he had needed the Chaaen, but that could wait for the moment. Right now, a more pressing question required his attention.

He faced Pratik with a challenge. "Will you help me?"

20

RHAIF FUSSED WITH his robe's headgear, which consisted of a leather helmet and a mesh of linen draped across the front. The only opening was a narrow slit across his eyes. Each inhale sucked the cloth across his mouth and nose.

Blast it all, how does one breathe under all of this?

"Calm yourself," Pratik scolded.

The Chaaen reached over and tucked the helmet's loose drape under the faux iron collar around Rhaif's neck, drawing the linen tauter so it no longer suffocated him.

"Thank the gods," Rhaif gasped out as he turned to inspect the others.

Beside him, the bronze woman was similarly attired in a Klashean *byor-ga*. The embroidered length covered her entire body, outfitted with a matching pair of thin gloves. The only difference from Rhaif's attire was the silver collar around her neck, mostly hidden by the high collar of her robe.

Pratik shifted over and tucked her headgear's drape into her collar, then stepped back and nodded. "We're not allowed to speak to another when shadowing a master on the streets, so her reticence will not be a difficulty."

"And what about everything else?" Rhaif asked. He waved to the woman. "Do you think we can pass as a pair of chaaen-bound?"

Pratik shrugged. "Few in the Klashe pay any heed to the chaaen-bound. I fear my role will be the most challenging—and dangerous."

Rhaif eyed the Chaaen. Pratik had stripped out of his gaoler garb, showing a surprising shyness in the presence of the bronze woman. He had hurriedly donned the final raiment purchased by Rhaif at a Klashean dressmaker. The boots were polished snakeskin. His tight breeches and sleeveless tunic were a crimson silk stitched in a zigzag of gold along the seams. Over it all hung a white robe—what the Klasheans called a *gerygoud*—that reached his knees and splayed out wide at the sleeves. A cap of gold finished the outfit.

Except for the thin scarf that hid the man's collar, it was the typical raiment for an *imri* trader of the Southern Klashe. The habiliment alone had cost Rhaif nearly all of the coins he had pilfered over the past fortnight. But for the ruse to work, only Pratik—with his dark features and violet eyes—could pass as a member of the ruling caste. Rhaif and the bronze woman would remain fully hidden away until they reached their cabin aboard the wyndship, which was due to rise with the last bell of Eventoll.

With the fourth bell having already sounded a moment ago, there was little time for mistakes or interruptions. They still needed to cross Anvil to reach Eyr Rigg, where the wyndships were moored. If they missed their ship, they would have to wait until the next day—which Rhaif knew they could not risk.

Not with Llyra's nose on our scent.

While short-haul wyndships traversed the territories throughout the day, those scheduled to travel farther left only at Eventoll, due to some vagaries of pressures, winds, and magnes energies that were beyond Rhaif's understanding. All he knew for certain was that they needed to be on that ship before the last bell.

He gave the group one final glance, noting the thin coiled chains in Pratik's hands. When their livery reached Eyr Rigg, those lengths would connect their collars to the bands around the Chaaen's boots.

Pratik shifted those coils from one hand to the other, nervously jangling their links. If the Chaaen was exposed before he could bring the bronze treasure to the foot of the god-emperor's throne, his impersonation of a royal trader would likely end with his death.

"Are you ready?" Rhaif asked.

The answer did not come from Pratik. A muffled crash drew their eyes to the secret door in the far wall. They all froze as shouts reached them, followed by one blood-edged scream.

Pratik turned wide eyes toward Rhaif.

Llyra . . .

Rhaif pushed the Chaaen toward the door, then swung to the bronze figure. He took her gloved hand, fearful that she might have already returned to her sluggish slumber. But her palm was still warm through the thin silk. Soft fingers closed over his.

"We must go, Shiya," he whispered, using the name he had given her.

He didn't know if it meant anything to her, but to him, it ran back to his mother, or rather to her homelands that she often told stories about. The shiya were small birds in the greenwood of Cloudreach. They were plumed in shimmering shades of copper and gold and piped sweetly in the dark depths of the endless forests. But they were also savage—like most creatures who survived those misty highlands—defending their nests with sharp talons and hooked beaks.

He thought it a fitting name.

She turned to him, her eyes softly glowing through the meshed drape of her mask. She gave him a small nod and followed after him as he guided her to the door. Pratik had already lifted the bar and set it aside.

"Hurry," the Chaaen urged, cringing as more crashing and shouts echoed to them.

"No." Rhaif pictured Llyra and her crew smashing through the rooms, searching for him. He cautioned Pratik, "We move as if nothing concerns us."

He waved the Chaaen out, knowing even now Pratik must play his part by leading them. Not the other way around. With one last shudder, the man headed through the door and out into the hall. As they traversed toward the stairs, Pratik's pace quickened, likely fired by his apprehension.

"Slower," Rhaif warned him.

The man obeyed.

They reached the stairs. As they set off down, the steps creaked under the weight of the bronze woman. Rhaif feared they might break. But they safely arrived in the commons, which was better appointed with pillowed couches and tint-shaded lamps that cast a rosy glow all about. The wenches here sat straighter, with bosoms pinched higher. The matron of this establishment noted their arrival. She showed not even a hint of astonishment at the sudden appearance of a trader and his pair of chaaen-bound. Rhaif was not surprised. Curiosity did not serve one well in the Boils.

Without a word, Pratik led them out the main door and onto the street. A closed livery carriage awaited them, already arranged by Rhaif.

The driver rushed toward them from his post beside a pair of stout Aglero-larpok ponies. "Right here with ya," he said, and hurried to open the carriage door.

Pratik played his role well, refusing the man's proffered hand to help him into the livery. Instead, he cast the driver a look of lofty disdain. No one dared touch an *imri*.

"'Course, 'course," the man mumbled.

Pratik ducked inside, scooting over to allow them to join him.

Rhaif guided Shiya to follow. She craned her neck, taking everything in as she approached the carriage. As she climbed inside, the livery tilted under her weight, but the driver didn't seem to notice.

The man was still scolding himself under his breath. "You're a daft gudgeon, that's what you are."

Rhaif took an extra moment to survey the narrow street. He allowed a heavy breath to escape, fluttering his mask. There was no sign of Llyra or any of her crew. Satisfied, he clambered aboard.

As he leaned back to pull the livery door shut, a chest-bumping boom erupted, fierce enough to knock a few slate tiles from atop the whorehouse. They shattered to the cobbles. Overhead, the clouds brightened as flames spiraled up from beyond the roof ridge.

Rhaif pictured the establishment on the other side blasted and burning.

He knew all too well that Llyra had a temper, as fiery and explosive as any combustible. If she thought she'd been thwarted of her target—unable to find Rhaif—it was easy enough to imagine her exacting her revenge. But he knew better. Llyra's actions always had twice the purpose. Besides venting her frustration, she was trying to flush him out of where he might be hiding. It was a judicious ploy. Even if Rhaif died in the fire, she must know she could always sift through the building's ashes for a treasure that would not burn.

With a shake of his head, Rhaif tugged the door closed and looked across the livery at the bronze woman. He then pounded on the front of the carriage, signaling the driver to set off for Eyr Rigg.

A whip snapped, and with a jerk, the livery rolled away.

Rhaif leaned back into his seat with a smile. *I finally outwitted her.* He pictured his finger tipping over a king on a board of Knights n' Knaves—then more blasts and booms shook the carriage. Outside, the horses nickered and neighed in terror. The livery bobbled wildly until the driver could whip his charges back under control. Still, the frightened beasts sped at full gallop. The livery bounced and rattled behind their clattering hooves.

"What's happening?" Pratik yelled.

Rhaif shifted to search out the small window, then out the other side. All around, fires erupted, choking smoke into the dark skies. Even as he watched, they grew and spread across the grease of the Boils. Rhaif gaped at the damage. He understood who had orchestrated this firestorm and how much he had underestimated her.

Clearly, Llyra was not content to just burn down one whorehouse to flush him out.

She's willing to take down all of the Boils.

Outside, the driver hollered and cracked his whip, but his ponies needed little guidance to flee the smoke and fire. The carriage crashed back and forth, tilting on two wheels to round sharp corners. Still, more booms chased them.

Thick smoke, glowing with cinders, choked the streets now. The livery rushed past a flaming shop, the roof tiles popping and flying high from the heat.

To either side, people fled all around. Several of them tried to clamber onto the carriage, but the driver turned his whip upon them. He dared not let any added ballast weigh down the carriage. Several bumps and screams suggested an unfortunate few were trampled or ridden over.

Rhaif hunkered with the others. He had to trust the driver's knowledge of the Boils to get them out in time. Unfortunately, the man was not the only one who knew this squalid corner of Anvil well.

"Ho now!" the driver screamed.

The carriage abruptly slowed, throwing them all forward. Rhaif twisted to get his head out of the open window. As the livery cleared the worst of the smoke, the street ahead was packed with a panicked crowd, which ran up against a line of men in armor and mail, carrying swords and axes. They were inspecting everyone who passed.

Rhaif cursed the woman behind all of this. Llyra had always been coldly clever. He knew her fires had not been haphazardly placed, but instead they had been ignited strategically, to force survivors to guarded chokepoints.

Like this one.

Rhaif struggled with what to do. He feared their disguises might not hold up to close inspection. A simple lift of either veil would expose the subterfuge beneath. Plus, he could not know for sure if Llyra had spotted Pratik standing beside him in the gaol's main hall.

Still, he had no other choice. The fires raged behind him, and the wyndships would soon lift off Eyr Rigg. Worst of all, the bronze woman had grown ever more listless. They did not have the time to seek another way out of the Boils.

The driver leaned over and spotted Rhaif's head poking out the window. "What to do?" he called down from his seat.

"Push ahead," Rhaif ordered. "Whip a path through if you must. I'll pay you another gold march if you get us to Eyr Rigg in time."

The driver's eyes widened. "Aye. That I'll do."

Rhaif settled back inside the carriage as it lurched faster again. He glanced to Shiya, who had not moved even with the jarring and rocking. He placed his palm atop her gloved hand, testing for any warmth. He discovered only a disconcerting coldness. He searched her face but could no longer discern any glow of her eyes behind the meshed veil.

He gave her unyielding hand a squeeze.

Hold on, Shiya.

Outside, the driver's whip cracked over and over. Townspeople cursed and shouted. A few spat through the window as the carriage barged toward the line of armored men. Angry fists pounded on the livery's sides and back.

Pratik shifted to the center of his bench across from Rhaif. "What do we do now?"

"I'm going to sit here quietly." He pointed toward the line of men ahead, surely Llyra's crew in borrowed armor or other well-paid brawlers. "You, on the other hand, get your first chance to impersonate an *imri*."

Pratik visibly swallowed and ran his palms over his outer cloak.

Finally, the livery slowed, and the driver pulled his ponies to a stop at the guard line.

A gruff voice approached. "Out with ya!"

Rhaif nodded for Pratik to obey. The Chaaen scooted across his bench to the door and after two attempts got it open. He was immediately confronted by a barrel-chested larcener in rusty mail and balancing an ax on a shoulder.

He shoved his crook-nosed bullock head into the carriage. "Whatda we got here?"

Pratik leaned away, cringed, then tilted forward again. "How . . . How dare you?" he said with haughty ire. "This livery is Klashean territory as long as we are in it. Trespass and I will have your skin flogged from your bones at such an affront to the honor of the Imri-Ka."

The bullock retreated from the storm of his arrogance and hauteur. From the door, the man glanced quickly throughout the carriage, his gaze lingering first on Shiya's robed form, then over to Rhaif. Rhaif lifted a gloved hand and fingered the faux iron collar around his neck, feigning nervousness, but mostly to expose his status as an enslaved Chaaen.

"Your breath offends me," Pratik continued, "and pollutes the sanctity of my private space. Be off before I get truly angry."

The bullock's face darkened, but he made no further effort to enter. Instead, he hollered to a pair of brawlers behind him, "Look about. Make sure there be no stowaways hitchin' along here."

As the two circled the carriage, Rhaif stared past the bullock's shoulders. The frightened crowd pressed the line. Sweating and cursing, Llyra's men fought to hold them off. They yanked back hoods, knocked wet rags from mouths and noses, and searched each face before shoving the person past the blockade.

Then the line of men shifted. Rhaif stiffened in his seat and cursed his luck.

Of course she'd be at this chokepoint.

He watched Llyra use a dagger to slice away a scarf from a hunched man. She tilted his chin up with the point of her blade, scowled at what she saw, and pushed the man behind her. Her lips moved in a silent curse as she grabbed the collar of the next man who looked a match to Rhaif's build.

Rhaif's hand balled into fists.

All of this because of me.

Finally, Llyra swiped a sooty brow as she let a woman and boy hurry past her. In that moment, her gaze swept to the carriage. She took a step toward it.

The bullock noted her interest as his men finished their inspection with shakes of their heads. He lifted an arm, waved to Llyra, and hollered, "Black Klashers!" He spit his distaste on the ground. "The lot of 'em. Nothing else."

Llyra's eyes squinted. For a moment, she stared straight at Rhaif's masked face. Then the mob surged the line all around. A few desperate figures broke through and ran. With the fires spreading rapidly through the greasy Boils, the frightened crowd had begun to decide the flames were the greater danger than the swords. Llyra snatched the hood of a man who tried to bowl past her and dragged him back.

The bullock took her diverted attention as satisfaction. He shouted up to the driver, "Get on with it!"

The driver needed no further encouragement. A snap of the lead got his ponies pulling again. The carriage swept past the blockade and away from the Boils. They were soon trundling into the broader breadth of the city.

"We made it," Pratik said, sagging in his seat.

Rhaif frowned at him for daring to state such a hope out loud. Instead, he held his breath until the fires faded to a dim glow behind them. Only then did he finally exhale. He even allowed himself a moment of silent celebration. He again pictured his finger tipping a king atop a board and toppling it over. This had been a game he had longed to win for ages.

Finally . . .

He turned back to the fiery glow.

With Llyra behind him, no one could stop them from here.

FROM THE BALCONY outside of the archsheriff's office atop Judgement Hall, Shrive Wryth watched the spread of fires near the town's port. The distant blasts and booms had drawn him and Laach through the doors, but the sheriff had already returned inside. Laach shouted and bellowed orders. Messengers and guardsmen came and went as the sheriff coordinated with Anvil's highmayor to respond to the flames before they spread wider.

Wryth remained outside, trying to read meaning in the swirling cinders and flaming embers. Unlike Laach, he refused to assign this conflagration to misfortune and mishap. He divined purpose behind each spiral of flame.

His hands rose to the leather bandolier—his Shriven cryst—strapped across the chest of his gray robe. His fingers ran over the sealed pockets along its length. Most of his brethren's crysts held nothing but mawkish charms and oversentimental detritus, each pouch intended to venerate and memorialize one's long path to the holy status of Shriven.

Not so his own cryst.

His fingertips read the symbols burned into the leather. Each of his bless'd pockets hid dark talismans and tokens of black alchymies. He carried pouches of powdered bones from ancient beasts who no longer walked under the Father Above but whose dust was rife with ancient maladies. Other pockets held phials of powerful elixirs leached from the hard creatures who survived the frozen reaches of the far west. Others hid ampoules of poisons sapped from the beasts who crawled, burrowed, and slithered across the burnt wastes of the distant east. But the most treasured of all were the scraps of ancient texts scrolled into pouches, their faded ink indecipherable but hinting at the lost alchymies of the ancients, of the darkest arts hidden before this world's histories had been written.

Wryth cared little for the here and now, only so much as it served his ends. He sensed this world was but a shadow of another, a place of immeasurable power, and he intended to collect that power for himself. No knowledge would be forbidden to him. No brutality too harsh to acquire it.

Even now, he remembered how bronze had melted to life before his eyes, the miracle fueled by his bloodbaerne sacrifice in the caverns of Chalk. His fingers clenched into fists at what he had lost, at what he must find.

He stared again toward the fires and could guess the culprit behind it. It had to be Llyra hy March. The guildmaster of thieves had vanished with the midday bells, making excuses that seemed feeble now, burned away by the flames in the distance. She had learned something, kept it from him, even from her consort, Archsheriff Laach. Wryth thought he had fathomed the woman's greed, but clearly he had vastly underestimated her.

A fresh commotion drew him away from the flames and back to the sheriff's office. Wryth's eyes narrowed upon Laach. *Had he played a role in the woman's deception?* From the purple anger in the man's face, Wryth guessed not. The bastard was also too dim-witted for such a cunning feint as this.

In the office, a steely-eyed guardsman burst into the chambers and rushed to the sheriff's desk, breathless but intent. "Archsheriff Laach, I've just received word from the dungeons. A prisoner has gone missing, maybe escaped."

Already standing behind his desk, Laach glared across to the guardsman. He pointed a stiff arm toward the balcony. "A missing prisoner? That's what you trouble with me right now? When the city is burning?"

The guardsman blathered and hawed, plainly not sure what to say.

Again, Wryth refused to treat this bit of misfortune as insignificant. He strode from the balcony to the office, an ostentatious chamber of imported woods and rich tapestries.

"When did this prisoner escape?" Wryth asked.

The guardsman jerked straighter, having failed to note the Shrive's presence until now. Apparently, Wryth decided sourly, much was missed in Anvil that was standing in plain sight, a heedlessness that no doubt seeped down from the very top.

Laach waved for the man to answer. "Speak up already."

The guardsman nodded, bowed to Wryth, then nodded again. "We can't say for sure when he went missing, Your Holiness. Late in the day, as best we can determine."

Wryth absorbed this information. *So shortly before Llyra hy March made her excuses and vanished.* Another blast echoed to them from the city. "And who has gone missing?"

"It was one of the many slaves we stored in the dungeons while you finished your questioning of their masters, the Klashean traders."

"So, one of the Chaaen?" Wryth said.

"Aye, Your Holiness. I know those Klashers won't take to us misplacing one of their own. That's why I rushed up here myself."

Wryth took this into consideration. He faced the open balcony doors and returned to reading the message written in cinder and ash out there. He had to assume these two misadventures—a burning city and a vanished prisoner—were connected, all tied to that clever rogue Rhaif hy Albar.

But how? Of what use was a Chaaen to such a thief?

He closed his eyes and lifted a hand to touch a sigil burned into one pocket. A fingertip traced the curled outline of the *horn'd snaken.* Its pouch held the dried tongue severed from Wryth's first blood sacrifice. He willed the tongue to speak to him with the wisdom and cunning of Lord Ðreyk.

As he prayed to his dark god, a calming slowed his heart. The knot in his head—formed by tangled threads of these mysteries—loosened. New patterns came and went until finally a picture formed in his mind's eye.

A Chaaen leading two robed and cloaked figures.

His eyes snapped open.

Of course . . .

He dropped his arm and swung toward Laach. "Rally your best swordsmen and archers. Saddle your swiftest horses."

Laach straightened, glancing toward the smoke and flames. "And go where? To help with the fires?"

"No." Wryth pointed in the opposite direction. "To Eyr Rigg."

21

RHAIF CLUTCHED HIS livery's seat as the carriage carted around yet another tight switchback. They were halfway up the Jagg'd Road toward the ridgeline of Eyr Rigg. From this height, the spread of Anvil glowered under a bank of soot and smoke.

Off in the distance, the Boils continued to smolder, casting occasional flames higher, as if daemons worked bellows to stoke those blazes. The firestorm continued to spread. One of the trading ships, a triple-sailed ore-trawler, was aflame, a bright torch floating on the sea.

Rhaif wondered how many had lost their lives to those fires. He wanted to blame it all on Llyra, but he could not.

I'm also to blame.

Still, fear burned through his twinge of guilt. He stared over to the bronze figure of Shiya, gone cold and still. He wondered if they'd be able to stir her enough to board the wyndship. And that's if they even reached the docks above in time. The fifth bell of Eventoll had rung out as soon as the carriage had reached the ridge, competing with the distant alarms from the port. He expected the last bell to sound at any time.

Pratik stiffened by the opposite window. "Come look," he gasped out.

Rhaif shifted across his bench to join the Chaaen. "What is it?"

Pratik pointed toward the low sooty clouds that hugged the top of Eyr Rigg. A large shape pushed through the pall, like a massive white orcso gliding through dark seas.

Rhaif tensed.

A wyndship was already departing.

Fearing the worst, he craned up. Its lower hull and keel sliced through the clouds, like the sky-god Pywll's mighty sword. Only this blade was sculpted of wood and batten and held together with glue and studded bands of draft-iron forged to an airy strength with alchymies known only to a special caste of shipwrights. The craft's shape was not unlike that of any wide-bellied barge, but instead of masts, draft-iron cables vanished into the clouds above, which hid the sleek gaseous balloon from which the ship was suspended.

Rhaif searched for flags at the winged stern, trying to identify the craft, but before he could do so, the ship rose higher and vanished into the gloom.

He turned and met Pratik's face, both of them sharing the same worry.

Was that our ship leaving early?

Rhaif clambered to the other side and stuck his head out the open window. He quickly ducked back, coming close to losing his skull as an ox-driven cart trampled past, heading down the steep road, returning after offloading its cargo above.

Taking heed, Rhaif peered out more cautiously.

A long line of supply wagons and carts slowly worked their way up the Jagg'd Road toward the summit. Even more rushed downward, having discharged their duty. Their driver did his best to occasionally—and terrifyingly—pass those ahead of him. The extra gold march that Rhaif had promised the man clearly fueled such daring.

He sank back to his seat, recognizing there was nothing else he could do. It was up to the gods from here—not that any of them had smiled on Rhaif of late.

After another four switchbacks, the carriage finally righted itself and pulled out onto the flat summit of Eyr Rigg. The air here was as bad as the Boils, heavy with soot, barely breathable. All around people bustled with cloths over noses and mouths.

Rhaif ignored them as the carriage wheeled around and lined up with the other wagons and carts. He searched the breadth of the place. Most days three or four ships left Anvil at Eventoll. The murk made it hard to discern which ship had already departed. Even this close, the ships remained misty titans in their wooden berths, their gassy heights lost in the gloom above.

He read the marks painted on the hulls of the closest two: the crown and sun of Hálendii and the curled horns of Aglerolarpok.

No, no, no . . .

Then Pratik called to him. "Over here!"

Rhaif hurried to his side. The Chaaen pointed to a flag stirring in the firestorm-blown winds. He recognized the two curved swords crossed against a black background.

"The Klashean Arms," Pratik said, his eyes moist with tears. "We got here in time."

Rhaif intended for that not to change. "Out then. Quick about it." He pressed a gold march into the Chaaen's palm. "Pay the good man outside. He's earned every pinch of it."

As Pratik stumbled out of the carriage, Rhaif turned to their last passenger. He took the bronze woman's hand in his own. None of her fingers moved in response to his touch.

"Shiya," he urged, "we must go."

She ignored his pleading and continued to sit like a statue come to rest.

He took his other palm and rubbed her hand between his own, trying to warm her back to life. When that failed, he stripped off their respective gloves and buffed her bronze skin even harder.

"Please," he whispered.

He finally abandoned her hand and lifted her veil. Her eyes were open, but they were cold glass. He rested his warmed palms on her cheeks.

"Shiya, I know some fear fuels you. Draw upon that now. We must go."

He waited a breath.

Still nothing.

He considered abandoning her and escaping with Pratik.

No . . .

He pressed his palms more firmly. "I won't lose faith in you. So, you don't lose faith in me."

At long last, a soft glow returned to her eyes. A hand rose to cup his hand to her cheek. Her lips moved, but no sound escaped. Still, he imagined what she said, wanting to believe it.

Never . . .

In short order, they were all out of the livery and moving toward the row of berthed ships. The behemoths towered into the skies, cables groaning. Laborers and dockworkers scurried all about in final preparations.

Pratik stopped and swung around.

"What's wrong?" Rhaif asked.

The Chaaen showed his empty palms, then pointed from his boots to their collars. "I left the binding chains in the carriage."

Rhaif frowned and glanced back in time to see the livery vanish over the edge of the ridge. Clearly the driver was taking no chances that Rhaif might reconsider his reward of a gold coin.

With a grumble, he turned back around. Ahead, docking lanyards were already being loosened from stanchions. He pushed Pratik forward, knowing the truth.

"At this point, it won't matter," he said with a sigh. "We must push on."

ATOP A STRONG steed, Wryth galloped alongside Archsheriff Laach. Ahead of them, a clutch of a dozen riders in leather armor led the charge up Jagg'd Road. The swordsmen forced aside any impediment to their group's swift passage. Another dozen men, mostly archers, trailed behind on horseback. The clanging din of the last bell of Eventoll drove them onward.

Wryth's hood flagged behind him, so did one of his braids that had loosened from its tie around his neck. Such a disheveled state was unseemly for a Shrive, but he did not slow. He stabbed his steed's flanks with his burred heels. The cavalcade pounded around the last switchback and up onto the summit of Eyr Rigg.

The hooves of their two dozen horses stirred a cloud of dust and sand as the group spread wide and skidded to a stop. Several legionnaires dropped swiftly from their saddles and shoved startled dockworkers out of the way. The others stayed on horseback, dancing their sweating steeds, ready to act.

Standing in his stirrups, Wryth waved an arm to clear the worst of the dust. Laach did the same, coughing to clear his lungs. It took a breath or two for Wryth to discern the conditions atop the soot-clouded summit.

High overhead, a wyndship rose into the darkness, its outline misty and faint. To the left, another balloon rose with a groan of strained cables. It, too, followed the first toward the gloom.

"There!" Laach said, his younger eyes far sharper than Wryth's. He pointed to the right where a third ship was already off its cradle-berth, rising quickly skyward. "It bears the Klashean Arms!"

No . . .

Wryth could not let the bronze treasure—a weapon of inimicable power and mystery—fall into the hands of his enemy. Beyond his own desires for lost knowledge, he knew that the Kingdom of Hálendii had to be protected against the iron fist of the Klashe, where freedoms would be strangled, where knowledge would be forbidden. Wryth had spent decades gaining his lofty position here, committing himself fully to these lands, knowing in his heart he could guide the kingdom to an even greater glory. With the king's ear at his lips and the Shrivenkeep nearly under his control, he was in position to wrest the secrets out of the past and raise the sigil of Lord Đreyk on high.

He also knew another certain truth.

The kingdom's fate is my own.

Understanding this, Wryth spurred his horse toward the Klashean wynd-ship. He drew the others in his wake as he trampled and knocked workers to the side. He led the charge toward the rising ship. Still, by the time he was near enough, its keel was far overhead and beginning to turn south.

Laach clattered up to him. "We're too late."

Wryth turned his fury upon the archsheriff. "No. We do what we must."

Laach shifted in his saddle. He was plainly uncomfortable with what had been worked out earlier, an eventuality that they had both hoped to avoid.

"If the king finds out you let that potent artifact of malignant power fall into the hands of his enemy," Wryth warned, "it will be your head."

Laach sank more firmly atop his horse, recognizing the truth in Wryth's threat. He twisted and bellowed to his men, "Archers to the fore!"

A cadre of bowmen separated from the others, pounding forward and slipping from saddles, their longbows already in hand. A torchbearer ran across the row with a fiery brand, lighting the oil-soaked wraps knotted below each iron tip. One after the other, the archers dropped, bending knee and bow, strings pulled to ears, flaming points aimed skyward.

"Let loose!" Laach ordered, chopping an arm down.

Strings twanged, and bows sprang. A volley of streaming fire shot through the smoky air. Several hit their mark, piercing the skin of the balloon and winking out. Even before those struck, the torchbearer ran the line once more, and another dozen fiery tips pointed high.

"Again!" Laach hollered.

More arrows peppered into the balloon with hardly any more effect. As a third volley was prepped, Laach looked at Wryth. The sheriff's face vacillated from apology to fear. Maybe even a little relief. What they were doing could ignite far more than a wyndship.

Then Wryth heard it. A muffled blast from above. He stared high but saw nothing. The wyndship continued to rise, the gasbag drawing it ever upward. The balloon faded into the bank of low clouds—which suddenly flared brighter, as if run through by lightning. Thunder followed in booming blasts. Gouts of flame shredded apart the gloom. The bow of the wyndship tipped downward as loose cables drizzled out of the fiery cloudbank.

"Back!" Laach yelled, swinging an arm overhead. He yanked his reins and tugged his steed around. "Go!"

To either side of Wryth, the guardsmen fled, some on horseback, others on foot. Laach galloped past him. Wryth kept his horse rooted in place. He watched the fiery spectacle above.

I must be sure.

Overhead, the ship canted steeply down, first slowly, then faster. Wryth searched for any billowing dispatches of sailrafts from its flanks, in case anyone on board tried to make an escape from the plummeting ship. He saw none. The destruction had happened too fast.

As he watched, the few cables still attached to the ship dragged the flaming remnants of the blasted balloon out of the black clouds. The ship plummeted even more swiftly, diving toward its doom.

Wryth swore he could hear faint screams of terror, but maybe it was only his own heart's desire given voice. He cursed the thief for causing him so much grief, for requiring such rash action. But he dared not let that ancient bronze mystery fall into the clutches of Klashean alchymists. For the sake of the kingdom, that must not happen. No matter the consequences.

Better for it to crash to ruin here.

He finally tore his horse around, dug in his heels, and galloped away. A splintering boom exploded behind him. He twisted back to see the ship shatter against the rock, cracking in half, blasting a wave of sand toward him. He raced it to the ridge and finally reined in his steed alongside the others.

Sand washed over the group and rolled past the ridgeline. Debris rained and pelted all around. Finally, the flaming remains of the balloon drifted down and settled over the broken ship, like a fiery death shroud.

Wryth faced the destruction with one goal.

To sift through the wreckage for the treasure that is mine.

FROM A QUARTER league above, Rhaif stared out their cabin's window down to the fiery crater atop Eyr Rigg, where the flaming husk of the Klashean wyndship smoked and burned. He and Pratik had watched the flaming attack upon the other craft from the safety of a wyndship flying the curled horns of Aglerolarpok.

"Clearly your precautions—as deceptive as they were—have proven wise in the end," the Chaaen said dourly.

Rhaif heard little praise in the man's words, and he certainly felt no satisfaction himself, only a pain in his chest that he rubbed with a knuckle. "I did not expect my ruse to lead to such a fiery end, to more lives lost."

As their wyndship was drawn farther into the clouds, the view below grew obscured. Rhaif turned his gaze out to the smolder of the Boils in the distance.

So many dead . . .

He shook his head. "I only wanted to fool the others into thinking that I'd fled to the Southern Klashe, to draw their eyes that way, instead of west." He glanced to Shiya, whose bronze face was exposed after he had removed her veiled helm in the privacy of their cabin. He looked at Pratik. "I hadn't imagined they'd have connected your escape from the gaol to me so quickly. I thought it would take them a day or two at the very least."

He hadn't even explained his ruse to Pratik until they were marching toward the wyndships. He had wanted everyone—including the Chaaen—to believe the other ship was his goal. Days ago, when Laach's men had begun rounding up Klashean traders, Rhaif had come up with his plan. In order to reinforce the assumption that he would flee to the Klashe, he had plotted to break a Chaaen out of the dungeon, knowing eventually someone would realize who had orchestrated that escape. Especially as Rhaif had left behind clues at the whorehouse, connecting him to the crime. He needed everyone to believe he had persuaded the Chaaen to help him board a Klashean ship.

But I had underestimated who pursued us.

He knew the fiery wreckage could not be laid at the feet of Llyra hy March. He pictured the tattooed countenance of Wryth. From the air, Rhaif had spotted the Shrive ride up with Laach in a flurry of horses. Then the flaming arrows had flown, surely directed more by that accursed Iflelen than by the archsheriff.

Pratik looked ill. "Let us hope they do not realize too quickly that we were never aboard the other craft."

Rhaif was not overly concerned in this regard. "It will take them some time for the fires to be snuffed out, for the ashes to be sifted through, before they realize that Shiya's bronze form is not in the wreckage. Even then, they'll still have to judge if we backtracked to Anvil or took one of the two wyndships. Hopefully, by then we'll be across the seas and well on our way to the lands of Aglerolarpok."

Pratik nodded. "Despite the tragic outcome, there was wisdom in your plan."

Rhaif sighed and stared down through the dark clouds at the ruddy glow still faintly visible. He remained unconvinced if the steep cost in lives and misery was worth the freedom of one thief. The Chaaen's next words reinforced this.

"There will be consequences," Pratik warned. "This attack upon a wyndship flying the Klashean Arms, along with the fiery deaths of so many of my people, it will not go unpunished. The honor of the Imri-Ka will require swift and bloody vengeance."

Rhaif swallowed hard, his stomach churning with the implication. Everyone knew of the escalating tensions between the Kingdom of Hálendii and the Southern Klashe. Any spark risked blowing both sides into a raging conflagration. He pictured the fiery arrow igniting the volatile gasses filling the other balloon.

Was that it? Did I just ignite a war that could consume half the Crown?

Rhaif quailed, imagining the many deaths from such a war. All the bloodshed and grief. He pictured cities burning, armies battling across mucked fields, innocents put to the blade. Aghast at such a fate, he stumbled back from the window.

Pratik caught his arm. The Chaaen's eyes pinched with concern. He clearly sensed Rhaif's dismay. "Do not draw that blood to your heart. Even if what I say comes true, you will not be the cause—only the excuse. And if it wasn't you today, it would be another tomorrow. This hostility has been brewing long before either of us was born. It is rooted far into the past, tied to ancient animosities, clashing creeds, even differing gods. You cannot take all of history's burden upon your shoulders."

Rhaif heard the wisdom in his words, but it still failed to reach his heart. He shook his arm free from Pratik's grip. *Whether a scapegoat or an excuse, it's still my hand that lit the fuse, not yours.*

Pratik stepped toward him, ready to press his case, but a sudden flash of bright light flared all around, growing to a stinging blindness. He gasped and shielded his eyes.

Rhaif squinted against the glare as he turned to the cabin's row of windows. The balloon had finally lifted free of the black shroud over Anvil. Raw sunlight streamed through the windows with all the force and vigor of the Father Above.

Rhaif drew it all in with a breath. For a moment, the brightness helped dispel the gloom inside him. Or maybe it was that the world below was now nothing but a rolling black sea, hiding all the fire and death beneath it.

He was not the only one affected by the change.

Movement drew his attention to the bronze figure of Shiya. Her face swiveled toward the radiance. She lifted her palms toward it, too. Her lips parted as if trying to inhale the potency in the sunlight. She took a stiff step toward the windows, then another. As she continued, her movement melted into a smoother stride. The bronze of her face and hands softened, their surfaces swimming in swirling patterns of crimson and copper.

Pratik retreated from her. Rhaif realized that the Chaaen had only witnessed her in a muted, stiffened state, never at her most glorious luminosity.

She reached a window and placed a palm against it. Her eyes—whether reflecting the brightness or fueled by it—turned to fire.

Rhaif drew next to her. He realized two things at that moment.

She was again facing west, as she had for days. And her gaze was fixed to the half-moon shining near the horizon, as if it beckoned her. Her expression turned pained, even anguished.

"Shiya," he said. "What's wrong?"

She finally found her voice, though it was only a whisper, like wind through crystals. "I must go there."

Rhaif touched her arm. "Where? Why?"

She turned to him, her eyes still afire. "To save you all."

SEVEN

BLOOD & FURY

*I saw the grett beast flie ouer the quaggy clime. Ah! such
was the terror that I barely ken the breadth of leather'd
wing & mighty cry & how it wrought upon me such won-
dre. It is poison on the air, yet beautuous, too. How I
wyssh I could read its heart as my own. But be warn'd
most soundly. Its cry is death.*

—From *The Illuminated Bestiary,* by Alkon hy Bast

22

NYX STRUGGLED TO convince her father about the storm of wings due to crash upon the town of Brayk and the Cloistery. "Dah, you must believe me."

He stood before the hearth, where a thick stew bubbled in a kettle that hung above bright coals. He held a large wooden spoon in hand, ready to keep his late Eventoll meal from burning. During the telling of her tale about the coming danger to all, his eyes had narrowed, but the lines of his face remained etched with doubt.

"We must seek the stoutest cover." She pointed to the roof. "Our thatch will not hold back the beasts."

Jace stepped forward, adding his support. He still panted hard from their flight across Brayk to reach her homestead at the swamp's edge. His cheeks were as ruddy as the hearth's coals. "She's right. You must listen to her."

Her dah remained incredulous. He gave the kettle another stir. He had been preparing a late meal for Bastan, who had taken Gramblebuck to the top of the school, and Ablen, who was bedding down the herd in the back paddock. Her dah shook his head as he slowly scraped his spoon around the kettle. A tale of death and vengeance on the wing was clearly too fanciful for a man who had spent all of his days tied to the ageless tides of the wetlands, to the slow rhythms of a bullock pulling a sledge, and to the pace of one day bleeding into another. Even the aroma of bubbling potageroot and marsh hare in the kettle sought to squash her urgency with its promise of familiar comfort.

"Don't see no need to get all fluttered," her dah said. "This ol' place has stood pat through spit and gristle. Going back near unto two centuries. It'll weather any storm just fine."

"Not this time," Nyx stressed. Like a black shadow building in the back of her skull, she sensed the fury of the tempest about to break upon them all. "We could hole up in the winter bullock barn." She pictured the thick-walled structure, where the calves and yearlings were housed. It had a stone roof, only slits for windows, and beams timbered from trees older than Brayk. "If we bar its doors, we can withstand any attack there."

Jace nodded. "I don't fully understand how your daughter knows what's to come, but we should take heed. Especially with the king looking to steal Nyx away to Azantiia. Regardless of the strength of your home here, it might be better if we were elsewhere, and Nyx tells me the winter barn is buried deep in the fen."

"Aye, lad, 'tis indeed. But I can't see what King Toranth would e'er want with little Nyxie. You must've not heard it right."

She shared an exasperated look with Jace. She wished Bastan and Ablen were here. She knew her dah's stubbornness was as much a part of the old man as his bones. To move him from his ways often took many hands, like pulling a mired sledge free of sucking bog muck.

Jace tried one final gambit. "Trademan Polder, please trust your daughter. Even Prioress Ghyle believes her story."

At the mention of the prioress, a crack appeared in her dah's high walls. He turned to them both, looking both worried and stupefied. "She does, does she then?" He thought for a moment, then straightened, clearly coming to a decision. "Then, big lad, you best help me with the stewpot. We'll want something warm in our bellies when we get to the old barn."

Nyx sighed with relief.

Finally . . .

Before her dah could swing the pot from the coals, a resounding clatter from outside drew all their eyes. The door crashed open. Nyx cringed back, and Jace stepped in front of her.

Bastan burst inside. Red-faced and sweating, he cast a harried glance around the room. "We must go!" he blurted out between gulps of breath. "Now!"

Nyx struggled to understand her brother's sudden appearance. Past his shoulder, the hulking silhouette of Gramblebuck chuffed and steamed out on the street. The great beast was tied to a teetering wagon that had no back wheels and a broken rear axle.

What had happened?

The answer came when two more figures barged in behind Bastan. She recognized the black robe and crimson sash of the alchymist from Kepenhill. He came with another: a slender young man with a dark complexion and gray eyes who wore a green hunter's cloak clasped with a tiny silver arrow. He also carried a bow and quiver over his shoulders. Nyx recognized him from the procession up the school's steps. He had been marching behind the wagon pulled by Gramblebuck.

"Bastan is right," Frell gasped out. "It won't be long before we're overrun by knights and Vyrllian Guards."

And that's not all, Nyx thought. *There's far worse coming.*

She could already hear the cries of the thousand bats sweeping toward the town. The edges of her vision had begun to frizz with their sharp whining.

Still, from the lack of any reaction, the others appeared deaf to the rising chorus.

"Where's the rest of the bullock herd?" Bastan asked her dah, breathing hard. "Saw the paddock was empty on my way here."

"Aye, Ablen moved 'em to the back yoke for the eve."

Bastan winced. "Then it'll have to be Gramblebuck," he said. "I'll get the brute around to the marsh dock and switched over to a sledge. We must get deep into the swamps."

With that, her brother dashed out the door and crossed to Gramblebuck's side. He used a knife to slash the traces and free the old bullock from the wreckage of the wagon.

As he led Gramblebuck away, Nyx's dah stepped forward and addressed the other two men. "What's this all about?" Confusion and dread sharpened his voice. "Why be knights coming here? Are they meaning to take Nyxie?"

"Possibly," Frell admitted. "But right now, the highmayor will demand satisfaction for the death of his sacrifice." The alchymist glanced to the hunter with a forlorn look. "I understand why you dropped the beast with your arrow, Kanthe, but there will be blood to settle before it's all over."

Nyx stiffened. She remembered the searing pain in her left eye. Fury burned through her fears as she realized the source of that attack. She swung to the hunter. "You . . . it was *you* who killed the bat?"

The hunter stood his ground against the heat of her anger. His face hardened with a stony disdain, as if he had weathered far worse than her tirade.

Frell came to his defense. "Trust me, lass, it was not a cruel killing. Prince Kanthe acted out of mercy, to keep the beast from the agony of the flames."

Nyx struggled to put this explanation in perspective, to quash the fire inside her. But shock made it difficult. She stared harder at the hunter.

He's a prince?

Her dah gasped, looking near to dropping to a knee. "Prince Kanthe ry Massif, the king's second son."

As confusion and astonishment snuffed out the last of her anger, Nyx again heard the approaching cries of the winged horde. She squinted against the fiery buzzing in her head. It grew with every breath. Her sight narrowed toward a pained pinpoint. She pressed her palms against her ears, both to try to muffle the shrillness and to hold her skull together.

Frell frowned at her. His voice sounded far away. "What's wrong?"

She gasped her answer. "They . . . They're almost upon us."

As if summoned by her words, a small shape dove low over the abandoned wagon and through the door. It swept the room, driving everyone down, except for Nyx. Then with a snap of its wings, it flipped through the air and vanished into the shadow of the rafters.

To her side, the prince had dropped to a knee. He had his bow out, with an arrow already nocked. Its steel point aimed at the thatched roof.

"Don't!" Nyx warned.

Jace reached and pulled the prince's bow down. "Listen to her."

"He means us no harm," she said, staring up. "It's my lost brother."

Prince Kanthe scowled. He relaxed his bow but kept the arrow tight to the string. He mumbled under his breath, "How many blasted brothers does she have?"

Nyx had no time to contemplate his odd words. Her skull still vibrated with a thousand cries of fury, but a sharper note cut through it all and arrowed deep inside her, taking the world with it. Two watery images, one lapping over the other, filled her vision.

First:

A dark body burns in flames. Wings smoke and curl. Flesh chars and splits, exposing bones. Through the black pall over the pyres, red eyes glow—at first several, then hundreds, then more. A moment later, the two pyres shatter under a blast of furious wings. Burning wood and embers cascade high, falling like fiery rain over the school, followed in turn by dark bodies diving everywhere.

Second:

A winged shape lies broken across the steps to the ninth tier, slowly being dragged by hooks and nets. Then it is freed, abandoned on the steps, the thorny nets yanked away. In the sky above, a pair of monstrous bodies circle once, then claws descend and gently dig into dead flesh. With a rush of air, the body is carried off the steps and lofted high. It wafts through the smoke of the pyres and is drawn even higher. It now sails through the clouds, on one last flight, toward the distant shadow of a mountain misted in steam, where it will find its final rest. Behind it, the dark storm follows in its wake, leaving the school unmolested.

Nyx dropped back into her body with a gasp, back into the warmth of her home. The aroma of bubbling stew replaced the terror of burnt flesh and the sulfurous steam of a distant mountain.

Jace caught her before she fell. "Nyx . . ."

She gulped a breath, then turned to the others. The bones of her skull still trembled with the energies buzzing inside. She squinted against it to speak.

"There is hope. Buried in a warning." She searched the rafters for red eyes, but her winged brother remained hidden. She glanced over to the prince, who looked upon her with a measure of horror. "Maybe they sensed your merciful heart and now offer some mercy of their own. Yet, their forbearance only extends so far. If their brethren's body is burned, they will still exact their vengeance upon us all. But if we let them recover its remains without interference, they will depart and leave us be."

Frell gaped at her as much as the prince, but his gaze shone with fascination and wonder. Still, he understood. "Then we must stop the others from casting the bat's corpse into the flames."

"Is there enough time?" Jace asked.

"We must try." The alchymist grabbed the prince's shoulder. "Maybe you can convince them that the death of the bat is enough."

Kanthe stared toward the open door and blew out a pained breath. "In other words, you want us to run all the way back up there? After coming all the way down?"

Jace reached to his tunic pocket and fumbled out a key. "Maybe this will help. It's for the alchymists' stair." He offered it to the pair. "You'll find swifter passage that way with fewer folks to block you."

Frell took it. "Thank you. I know that path well from my time here at the school." He faced Nyx and the others. "Whether we succeed or fail, you should all seek refuge in the deep swamp. Bats are not the only danger to Nyx or anyone else who aids her."

"It will be done," her dah said. "We can go to the winter barn on the shores of Fellfire Scour."

"Perfect. I know that lake," Frell said. "If we can, we will look for you there. But be wary. Be ready to flee farther if you must."

"Aye," her dah said. "You don't survive the Mýr for long without being wary." He glanced to the little altar in the room's corner, aglow with a score of candles. He kissed a thumb and tapped it against his forehead in a silent plea to the Mother Below. Then he nodded to Frell. "Do what ya kin, and we'll do the same."

Frell firmed a fist around the key and waved to Kanthe. "You proved your marksmanship earlier. Maybe spared the school with your effort. We cannot lose this chance. We must get them to listen."

"I'll try." The prince gave a small shrug. "But my tongue is not nearly as sharp as my arrows, nor its aim as true."

Frell clapped him on the shoulder. "We shall see."

As they headed out, the prince gave Nyx an appraising look, as if searching for something in her face—then he turned and dashed through the door.

Jace urged Nyx the other direction, toward the rear of the house that led out onto the length of the marsh dock. "Hurry. We must join your brother and put as much distance as possible between us and what comes—whether that be bats or the king's legions."

KANTHE HURRIED IN the wake of Frell's swift passage through the streets of Brayk. Even this late, people crowded about, still celebrating the parade of the king's knights and guards. Drunken singing echoed down alleyways, along with boisterous cheers and laughter. A few brawling fights tumbled across their way and had to be skirted past. Children ran hither and yon, waving tall sticks with paper bats fluttering from strings. Throughout the merriment, hundreds of braziers smoked with fish, broiled meats, and steaming bread.

The latter reminded him that he hadn't eaten in half a day. Still, terror and worry knotted his stomach. As the Cloistery gates appeared ahead, he searched up the length of steps, expecting to see a clutch of knights or crimson-faced Vyrllians rushing down. But he spotted no armor-clad figures or raised swords. Apparently, with the dead bat in hand, the king's legion had returned to their assigned task, determined to finish the sacrifice before directing their attention to a lawless prince.

Still, the stairs ahead were even more packed than the streets. The crowds had refilled them after the broken wagon had crashed downward from the heights. It appeared as if the entire town had come out to witness the burning of the winged terror.

The press of bodies on the steps made him appreciate the key in Frell's hand. Hopefully the private stair would offer an easier climb to the top. Still, as he and Frell elbowed and wiggled through the school gate, Kanthe struggled for the words he would need to convince the others not to toss the dead bat into the flames. Especially Anskar and Goren. Presently, such an argument still escaped him.

Once clear of the archway, Kanthe divided his attention between Frell's charge through the pack of onlookers and the twin pyres flaming and smoking high above. Then movement drew his eye to the left, where a commotion centered around a craggy mountain. It was the hulking figure of the Gyn. The beast of a man shouldered back the crowd. People retreated in a stumbling, elbowing rush—though, it was less due to the threat of the Gyn than the gaunt hooded shape he guarded over. Shrive Vythaas hobbled out of a door, likely exiting from the hieromonks' secret stair on that side. The Shrive fell into the Gyn's protective shadow, using his cane to ward off anyone who dared get too close. But the sight of such a holy man was ward enough. Everyone backed away a respectful distance.

As Kanthe stared, the tattooed band over the Shrive's eyes swung unerr-ingly toward his position. He shivered and ducked farther into the pack of people around him. Luckily, Vythaas seemed not to have spotted him. The Shrive turned and followed the Gyn as he forged a path to the gates. The pair were likely returning to the black livery sled that had carried them through the swamps.

Good riddance.

Kanthe turned in the other direction and hurried after Frell. He joined the alchymist at a stout door studded in iron—when a loud cheer resounded from on high. In moments, the triumphant cry swept down through the gathered onlookers, spreading like a flame through dry tinder. Kanthe re-treated a few steps to get a better view to the top of the school.

He feared the worst—and was not disappointed.

His heart sank at the sight of a thick column of dark smoke rising from the twin pyres. Fiery embers, like a thousand furious eyes, spiraled through the heart of the black pall. Bright horns blew from on top of the school, sounding the victory, which raised more raucous shouts from those packed below.

Kanthe stumbled over to Frell. The alchymist had frozen with the key in the door's lock. "We're too late," Kanthe warned.

Frell swore—something Kanthe could not recall the alchymist ever doing in his presence before—and yanked open the door. He stared hard at Kan-the. "I must warn Prioress Ghyle. You go after the others."

Before Frell could cross the threshold, a long, piercing cry—as sharp as broken glass—shattered through the blare of the horns. It immediately silenced the cheers, smothering the crowd to a tense uncertainty. People shifted nervously. Then a chorus of shrieks joined the first. They seemed to come from everywhere and nowhere, the cries echoing and reverberating off of every surface.

Kanthe clamped his hands over his ears, but he could not escape the an-ger and fury in those cries. The noise shook his teeth, tremored his ribs. He squinted against a force that felt like a wind.

To the south, darkness swelled into the sky, blowing up into a black thun-dercloud. The storm swept against the winds toward the school. Then sud-denly the piercing screams died all at once as the silent black wave crested high, about to fall upon the school.

No one moved. Faces stared upward.

Kanthe knew they could not wait. He grabbed a fistful of Frell's robe. "Surely the prioress now knows we failed." He tugged Frell away from the door. "And I don't know these swamps like you do. If you want me to help that accursed girl, you're coming with me."

The alchymist resisted for a long breath—then relented. "You're right." He shoved Kanthe toward the school gate. "And the prioress tasked me with another duty if all else failed."

Kanthe couldn't imagine what that might be and didn't care. Right now, he wanted to be far away from this place. They set off for the gates and not a moment too soon. The frozen tableau around them finally shattered as the realization of the threat spread through the crowd.

Screams and shouts erupted. People snatched children off of steps. Fear and terror drove everyone to seek the nearest shelter.

Kanthe and Frell were buffeted by the panicked crowd, but they made it through the school's gates and out onto the streets of Brayk. Chaos followed in their wake. The pair fled, trying to stay ahead of the worst. Frell led the way, knowing the town well. Still, a couple of times Kanthe lost sight of his fleet-footed mentor, only to spot him again. They raced and zigzagged, elbowed and shoved, until finally the glassy black waters of the swamp shone ahead.

"Over here!" Frell yelled, and rushed toward a small punt with a set of crossed oars atop it.

Kanthe followed, but he stumbled when an earsplitting chorus of savage cries erupted behind him. He ducked from the onslaught, cringing against its sharpness. He swore he could see the very air shiver with their fury.

He glanced over a shoulder to see the black wave crash atop the school. It shattered into a thousand wings. Into that dark chorus, new voices joined. Hundreds of screams full of blood and pain. Horns blared from out of the darkness, sounding bright but feeble against the horde's assault. Nearer at hand, a pack of panicked townspeople surged toward the swamps.

"Kanthe!" Frell hollered, drawing back his attention. The alchymist struggled to push the flat-bottomed boat into the water.

Kanthe raced over and joined Frell. Together they shoved the punt off the strip of rock and into the water. As it floated away, they waded over to it and clambered aboard.

Panting hard, Kanthe dropped to the seat. He fumbled with the oars, while Frell found a long pole and pushed them farther from shore. With his back to the swamp, Kanthe rowed away from Brayk. He watched others along the beach seeking the same escape. People scrambled and spread, going for anything that might float. Some even simply took to the water, braving what might be lurking under the black mirror of the swamp. But he understood that decision: *better the unknown below than the certainty above.*

The point was made all too clear when a huge dark shape—twice the size of a horse—swept low over the panic. It dipped down. Claws snatched a man running toward a raft and plucked him high. The bat bunched around its captured prey, spinning and somersaulting through the air—then wings snapped wide, and it shot upward, raining blood, meat, and broken bones over those below.

Sard me . . .

Kanthe rowed harder. Frell abandoned his pole and dropped low. They crossed gazes, both their faces aghast. Past the alchymist's shoulders, Kanthe watched the black, battering mass atop the school start to flow down its flanks. More winged shadows swept the beach.

At least we made it—

The punt burst upward with a loud splintering of wood as something struck them from below. They were tossed high into the air. Kanthe managed to keep hold of one oar. Frell tumbled the other direction. They both splashed heavily into the dark waters. The small boat crashed into a nearby tree and broke in half.

Kanthe sputtered up, coughing, his heart hammering hard—then lunged to the side as a large scaly back hunched out of the water, flaring a spiny fin, then vanished away. The beast ignored him and hurried toward the shelter of the deep swamp. Apparently, more than the townspeople were trying to escape the attack.

Frell kicked over to him, fighting his waterlogged robe. His friend's face was a question easy to read. *What now?*

Kanthe spun to the shoreline again. He pointed down its bank, toward a set of bonfires clustered and smoking amidst a few planted banners bearing his family's sigil. A knot of knights gathered in the center with pikes and raised swords. So far, the heat and steel seemed to be keeping the bats at bay. More of the king's legion would likely rally there, too.

Though reluctant to return to his father's men, Kanthe considered the situation and decided to take heed of an old adage.

Any port in a storm.

He began to swim in that direction. Still, he gazed one last time toward the deep swamp, wondering about the fate of the others and sending them a silent prayer.

I hope you're all faring better than us.

23

NYX COWERED IN the rear of the sledge with Jace. She had her palms clamped to her ears. She winced as her head rang with the cries of the assault. She swore she could taste blood on her tongue. As she sat, guilt drove her knees close to her chest, as if her bones could shield her from what was happening back at the town.

Jace kept at her side, an arm around her. Both of them had their backs to the drover's bench, where Bastan manned the reins next to her father. Gramblebuck's long legs waded slowly through the water, drawing the floating sledge behind him. The craft's bottom also had a pair of smooth ironwood runners for dragging the sledge through reed-choked shallows or across grassy hummocks. But this route from the marsh dock had been dredged of chokeweed, so the nearly empty sledge drafted easily behind the tired beast. They were traversing along the edge of the thousand yokes that made up their farm, heading toward the rearmost paddock to pick up her brother Ablen. From there, they would head even deeper, to the black expanse of Fellfire Scour and the homestead's winter barn.

As the sledge was dragged deeper into the swamp, Nyx searched for what was happening back at the town and school. But the gnarled boles of trees and mossy branches blocked any view. All that reached her was the savage keening and distant screams. From the furious rage on the wind, she and the others knew the alchymist and the prince had failed to stop the dead bat from being burned.

She panted, trying to cast out her fear and shame.

This is all because of me.

Jace tightened his arm around her, as if sensing her distress, but it was not that. His face turned to the shadowy canopy overhead. It was dappled in lighter shades of emerald where the leaves thinned.

"It's returned," he said near her ear.

She followed his gaze and spotted a darker shape as it winged over the sledge. Her little brother fluttered, then circled back again. He did it over and over again, growing clearly more agitated, as if trying to signal her. He finally swept lower to reveal himself fully. His wingspan was the length of her arm, the leather so thin she could see the dapple of the canopy through it. The body cradled between the wings was a sleek black mass, fronted by two belled ears.

As if noting her attention, red eyes turned and gazed down at her. A sharper whistling sliced through the larger cacophony. Her vision went dark, and a new view opened in her mind's eye.

—*a woman runs before a diving shadow. Then sharp claws snatch and tangle into her flagging hair. The shadow sweeps over her, then wrenches upward. The crisp snap of neck bones follows the flight upward. A limp body is dropped in the shadow's wake.*

The image broke away as her brother flitted past. Then he tipped on a wing and returned, keening his way over to her.

—*a young boy in the robes of a fifthyear cowers under a balcony. A shape sweeps past him under the shelter. The edge of a wing, tipped by a blade-sharp talon, grazes him, slicing his throat open. Blood sprays high as knees buckle.*

Again, the world returned to Nyx, only to be taken away in the next breath with another pass of her brother overhead.

—*a bat the size of a bullock calf struggles on its back, a wing broken. Men in gray mail and silver armor stab down with swords and hack savagely with axes.*

She snapped back to the sledge, but she saw nothing. Her hands had moved from her ears to cover her face. It did not help. More and more, visions of the attack whelmed through her, one after the other, from scores of eyes, all frosted over with screams and scented by blood.

—*a shape crashes to the steps, shattering the shafts of the arrows already peppered across its chest.*

—*another stalks a hall, wings tucked, crawling over the writhing bodies of the fang-torn and poisoned.*

—*a screaming knight, arms wheeling, drops from claws and crashes into the heart of a pyre.*

—*higher still, a sweeping view from on high as a section of Brayk burns amidst flames and smoke.*

—*then closer, a child weeps over a woman's body in the street, tiny fists knotted in her shredded cloak.*

The last image finally shattered through the storm in her mind, leaving her gasping. Hot tears streamed through cold sweat.

She stared toward the canopy.

Please, make it stop, she willed to her winged brother. *You've had your blood. Is that not enough?*

Jace stood next to her and waved an arm through the air. He yelled at the bat. "Leave her be! Off with you already!"

Perhaps heeding his command, her brother swept higher and slipped into the deeper shadows of the canopy. Still, the bat did not leave. Dark wings glided in slow circles above them.

Jace dropped next to Nyx. "Are you all right?"

She shook her head, unsure. She didn't trust herself to speak, lest she end up screaming. Still, she took Jace's hand and squeezed his fingers, letting him know she was unharmed, only shaken. She needed a few breaths to root herself back into her body after the dizzying panoply of the town's attack. It was as if she had been living it—through sight, sound, and scent, viewed through a hundred eyes.

It was too much, on too many levels. She felt dizzied and sickened. More than ever, her newly returned vision felt more like a curse than a miracle.

She gazed back up at her lost brother, knowing he had merged her into that battle, joining her to the great mind shared by the tribe of Mýr bats. With the pound of her heart quieting, she remembered something more, something she had sensed throughout the terrifying experience. It was as if a larger pair of eyes had been staring back at her throughout the ordeal, far more intent than the little red embers of her brother's gaze. In those moments, she caught the barest glimpse of something far older, ageless and dark, cold and unknowable. That brief brush against that vastness terrified her, but it also left her feeling hollowed and empty when it ended.

What did it mean?

She shivered and moved deeper into Jace's arms.

As she sought his comfort, the distant cries changed in timbre, slowly growing quieter, though interrupted by occasional sharper spats. Then even those faded over the course of several breaths. What didn't stop were the screams of the dying and wounded echoing across the water.

She looked to the pair of dark wings circling across the dappled canopy.

Is it over? Please let it be over.

There was no answer from above.

Instead, her father leaned back without turning around. His voice was low and urgent and full of warning. "Git down, the both of you. Right quick now."

NYX STAYED LOW in the sledge, shielded by the high back of the drover's bench. After heeding her dah's warning and dropping into hiding, she had peeked out long enough to see a wide raft being poled in their direction, coming from ahead.

Jace crouched next to her.

She understood her dah's urgent instruction. The raft was crowded with a clutch of hard-looking men. From their ragged wear and knotted beards, they were deep swampers, the whole lot of them.

With the exception of one figure who was held at knifepoint at the front of the raft.

"Hey ho," her dah called over. "What're you bastards doing with my son over there?"

It was Ablen, her eldest brother. One of his eyes was swollen and bloody. He had a dagger at his throat.

The raft poled closer, moving to block their path. Gramblebuck could have easily crashed through them, shrugging the raft aside, but Bastan whistled and nickered for the old bullock to slow and hold. The men on the raft carried rusty fishhooks and long hunting spears.

The one threatening with the knife called past Ablen's shoulder, "Where be your daughter, Polder?"

"My lass?"

"Aye."

Her dah scrunched his face and swung around the bench. He pointed back the way they had come. "Up at school. Whatdya think, you sarding arse? She's not mucking about these swamps any longer." With his back still turned to the raft, he secretly pointed to the left and whispered to Nyx and Jace, "O'er the side when we pass 'em. Hang from the rail."

She nodded her understanding.

Her dah faced the raft again, raising his voice. "What's all this bloody business about anyway?"

"Goren wants you. *All* of you brought before him."

Nyx cringed at the mention of the highmayor's name.

"What for?" her dah called back.

"It's none of your business what for. We been paid to git you all to 'im."

Her dah shrugged heavily. "Sard that. Nyxie ain't here, and I got a herd of bullocks to git boxed up before those winged daemons spook 'em clear to the coast. And don't think I don't know you, Krask. I can right near tell who you are from your stank. If I lose any of my herd cuz of this, you'll be a-paying, let me tell you." He swung an arm. "All youse will."

"That ain't our prob—"

"It will be when I bring it up to the Council of Eight."

Silence followed, except for some furtive muttering.

Her dah, ever the negotiator, clearly decided to take advantage of their hesitation. "Tell ya what, Krask. Let my two boys take the sledge to the rear paddock and get everything squared away. I'll go with ya all instead and pull that thorn out of Goren's fat arse. How 'bout that?"

More muttering followed. Finally, Krask yelled over, "We take you *and* this here boy. That other 'un over there looks big enough to handle the paddock himself. That's what I say, Polder."

Her dah rubbed his chin in a familiar posture of deep pondering, then lowered his arm. "Fair enough." He spat over the side. "Let's git to it then."

Bastan looked hard at the old man, who waved him onward. With a muttered complaint, Bastan gave a light snap of the reins to get Gramblebuck ambling forward and skirting to the right.

Her dah whispered out of the side of his mouth to Nyx and Jace, "Off with ya both."

Nyx stayed low behind the high back of the drover's bench and scooted with Jace to the rail. She hiked over the lip and lowered herself over the side until she was hanging by her hands from the ironwood rail. Her legs dragged through the dark waters below. Jace did the same with some grunting that was covered by a loud belch from Gramblebuck.

The swampers poled their raft up on the sledge's other side.

Her dah shifted across the bench toward them and called down to Ablen, "How ya doing, boy?"

"Ah, ya know, Dah," he answered drily. "If a bullock ain't pissing on your head, it ain't a day's work, is it?"

"True, very true." Her dah hopped off the sledge and onto the raft, then called up to Bastan, "I'll see ya back at the house."

Bastan waved and got Gramblebuck moving at a faster clip. He kept the sledge angled to keep Nyx and Jace hidden from view. Once they rounded a dense copse of tanglepine, the raft fell out of sight. Nyx and Jace finally climbed back up.

Her brother frowned at her. "Whadya think that was all about?"

Nyx glanced toward the town buried behind them. "It's because of me. Because of the death of the highmayor's son." She swallowed hard. "I fear he means to turn the blame on me."

And he might be right to do so.

Jace shook his head, his face worried. "Not just you, Nyx."

"He's looking to all of us," Bastan added. He scowled back to where the raft disappeared. "I don't like it none, not at all. Especially a-hiring that rank lot."

Nyx followed his gaze, finding it harder to breathe.

Gramblebuck turned their path slightly, aiming toward a wide hump of wet mud fringed by reeds and thistlegrass. Bastan turned his attention forward and tried to guide the old bullock back into the main channel. Gramblebuck wasn't having any of it. He lowered his horns and continued on his course. He climbed out of the water and up the muck slope, his splayed hooves gouging deep.

"Hang tight," Bastan said.

Both Nyx and Jace gripped the back of the bench. The front of the sledge lifted as its length was hauled out of the water by the bullock. Dragged forward, it slid atop its runners across the slick mud. The reason behind Gramblebuck's determination appeared ahead. A spread of blushberry bushes crowned the weedy hillock. Clusters of rosy, ripe berries draped from its branches.

Gramblebuck hauled up to them and used his lips with surprising delicacy to pluck the bunches from each leafy branch. He let out a huffing, rattling sigh, and one long fart of contentment. With a tail swishing back and forth, he set about taking his fill of the ripe bounty, a treat the poor fella sorely needed after his hard day.

Bastan lowered the reins and slouched on the bench. He let the great beast graze. Nyx tried to settle, too, but screams and shouts still carried across the watery breadth of the swamps, keeping her on edge.

Jace stood up and stretched a kink from his back. "Maybe we should—"

A distant blaring of horns silenced him, sounding bright and urgent. Nyx drew to her feet, so did Bastan. They all stared toward the source. From the top of the hillock, the upper tiers of the Cloistery were visible through a break in the trees. Even from this distance, a silver river could be seen flowing down the school's steps. It was armor reflecting the sunlight of the dying day.

The king's legion.

With the sacrifice over and the battle ended, it appeared the knights and guards were abandoning the school's heights, maybe even the entire battered town.

Bastan grumbled under his breath. "I don't like it none," he said, repeating his earlier admonishment. "Not at all."

Nyx looked at him. He met her gaze.

"I'm going back," he decided aloud.

She clutched a fist to her throat. "What?"

"Gramblebuck will mind you. And you know how to run a sledge right good. You git yourself and this big lad over to Fellfire Scour. I'm going to see what I can do to help Dah and Ablen."

She understood why he had come to this decision.

He voiced it aloud. "I have a sour pit in my gut about all this."

She did, too. But she stared from the distant town to the deep swamp. These drowned lands had always been her home. Only now they felt dark and dangerous. Especially on her own.

"You can do this, Nyxie," Bastan said. He pointed to the tiny raft lashed near the rear. "I'll take the pole-skiff and do my best to free Dah and Ablen. We'll meet you at the winter barn."

She forced her head to nod, recognizing he was going whether she objected to it or not. He climbed over the drover's bench and left the reins hanging over its back. As he headed past her toward the skiff, she grabbed him and hugged him around the waist. He smelled of sweat and silage—of home.

"Be careful, Bastan."

He squeezed her back. "Ock, our family . . . we're all part bullock. You know that. Nothing can stop us once we get our shoulders into it." He pulled out of her grip and leaned to her face. "And same goes for you, too, Nyx."

She smiled, this time without any effort.

He gave her a final hug, then clapped Jace across the back, nearly knocking her friend over. "Ya watch over my sister, or ya'll answer to me."

Jace nodded and stammered, "I . . . I'll do my best. I promise."

Satisfied, Bastan freed the skiff, pushed it off the back, then leaped atop it. The skiff skidded down the mud-slick slope and slipped smoothly into the water. Bastan never lost his footing as he rode atop it. Once in the water, he saluted with his pole and set off toward Brayk.

As he disappeared from view, Nyx climbed into the drover's seat and picked up the abandoned reins. Jace joined her. She gave him a shy smile, grateful for his presence, his friendship.

By now Gramblebuck had finished his feast. With a grunt and belch, he continued over the hummock and down the far side, wading back into the brine. In moments, they were gliding across flat black waters. The channel grew ever narrower. The trees pushed closer. Drapes of moss brushed the tops of their heads.

"How long till we reach the winter barn?" Jace asked.

"Another bell at least," she whispered, fearful of disturbing the constant low drone and twittering birdsong of the swamplands. But that was not the main source of her anxiety.

She glanced over a shoulder. With Ablen taken and now Bastan vanished, both of her brothers were gone.

Still . . .

A dark pair of wings swept past overhead.

I do have one brother left.

She found odd comfort in the small bat's presence, but it did little to stanch the rising dread inside her. She remembered Bastan's words: *I have a sour pit in my gut about all this.*

She felt the same, only it grew worse with every league gained. It was as if she was being dragged farther and farther from all she knew, all she loved. Through breaks in the canopy, she caught glimpses of the pale moon low to the west, reminding her of the danger far above.

Moonfall . . .

She did not want this burden. She had already told the prioress of her dreams and visions. Wasn't that enough? Surely it was up to leaders and scholars to determine if the threat was real or not. And if it was real, they were also the wisest and best prepared to do something about it.

Not me.

She shoved such lofty fears aside. Instead, she turned her gaze from the mysteries of the sky to the slow trudge of Gramblebuck through the dark waters. A larger and more immediate concern kept her breathing shallow and her heart pounding hard.

She cast one last look over her shoulder.

What is happening back there?

24

STANDING WITHIN THE circle of bonfires, Kanthe considered all the places he could hide. His options were few and growing scarcer. Knights in bloody armor and crimson-faced Vyrllians continued to flow out of Brayk and crowded into the king's encampment at the edge of the swamp.

Bodies lay strewn all around, dragged or carried here by others. Many had limbs torn off, the stumps field-wrapped in bloody, seeping bandages. Others writhed in poisonous delirium, with skin blackening around deep bites. Even more simply lay on their backs with small strips of cloth over dead, glassy eyes.

Clouds of black flies swarmed thick in the air, drawn by the blood. A handful of knights waved torches, their flames burning with bitter incenses. They tried to smoke the buzzing masses off of the wounded. It was a losing battle as more injured were hauled into the camp.

All around, groans, sobs, and cries echoed—here and across the breadth of the town and school. The misery rose like smoke toward the darkness overhead, where the hordes of bats still massed, winging about in plain threat. Like the knights and guards, the bats were collecting their dead and wounded, carrying them away. Anyone who dared to thwart them were met with savage attacks.

No one bothered any longer.

Kanthe gazed at the swath of flames burning through a section of Brayk. Smoke roiled into the sky, chasing embers upward, only to be churned by the flurry of wings above.

He had come to one firm conclusion about all of this.

I should've tried harder. He pictured his mad flight down the steps atop the wagon. *Maybe I should've argued for the beast's release, instead of running.* But he knew that was his usual nature: to flee what was difficult rather than stand his ground.

A hard voice broke through his despair. "There you are!"

He turned to find the head of the Vyrllian detachment stomping toward him. Anskar carried a broad-ax in one hand, his arm bloody to the shoulder. Gore spattered his skull and drenched his light armor. His face was a storm of fury. He came straight at Kanthe—then pulled the prince into a fierce one-armed hug.

"Thank the Father Above, you're still breathing." Anskar pushed him back and held him at arm's length, his gaze sweeping up and down. "And unscathed as best I can tell."

"I'll live," Kanthe admitted, baffled by the Vyrllian's greeting. He had expected to be reproached and castigated, maybe even restrained for his earlier actions. Instead, from the relieved grin splitting the hard man's face, Kanthe suspected the Vyrllian's concern was genuine.

Anskar's crimson brow wrinkled. "But what were you thinking before, lad? Running off with that accursed bat?"

Kanthe sighed. *Clearly my plan had not been well thought out.* Still, he swept an arm to encompass the dead and dying. "I was trying to prevent all of *this*. I knew if the bat was sacrificed that the town would be attacked."

Anskar's wrinkles deepened. "How could you possibly know—?"

The inquiry was cut off as Frell coughed and rose from beside a young knight whose face was shredded. Since wading out of the swamp, the alchymist had been attending to the wounded alongside two harried physiks. Frell looked like he had aged a decade. His black robe hung heavy with soaked blood. As he stood, he shook loose a coat of black flies and waved them away with an arm.

"We received word of bats massing in great numbers to the south," Frell explained, lying to the vy-knight. "It was not hard to surmise that such a horde might be coming to the aid of one of their own."

Anskar turned to the school. From the third tier, a huge shadow rose with a heavy beat of wings, drawing up a broken form in its claws. "If only we'd known. Plainly there be a noble savagery to their nature."

Frell's gaze followed the rise of those dark wings. "Is it any wonder that no one ever returned with one of their kind—alive or dead?"

Kanthe had a more important question and asked it of Anskar. "What now? Where do we go from here?"

Anskar shouldered his ax, balancing it there. "Don't know for sure, but we're definitely done with hunting bats." He scowled over at a clutch of men, all from Fiskur, who stood outside the ring of bonfires. "We should have never appeased that bloated cur."

In the middle of the group, Highmayor Goren was planning something. He and his men had their heads bent together.

"That bastard got his sacrifice," Anskar rasped, "but it cost us a quarter of our force. It's clear now we'd never survive bringing the fight to the swamps, let alone to their steaming mountain home."

Frell drew closer. "What about the king's desire to gather the beasts' venom, to distill it into a malignant weapon?"

The Vyrllian shrugged. "King Toranth will have to be satisfied with the glands we already collected."

Kanthe frowned. "What glands? From where?"

Anskar clapped him on the shoulder. "From that bastard you so finely shot, my young prince. Shrive Vythaas cut free a pair of glands, each the size of my fist, from that beastie before its body was tossed into the flames."

Despite the heat from the bonfires, Kanthe felt a cold chill. He remembered the Shrive and Gyn sneaking away before the attack. *Where are they now?*

Anskar continued, "Hopefully with that prize in hand, we can pack up and haul out of here once and for all. 'Course, we still have one last task to complete. We can't return to Highmount without one final trophy."

"What's that?" Kanthe asked.

Loud voices, rife with triumph, erupted from the group gathered around the highmayor. Goren shoved his way clear of his men and lifted an arm and hollered toward the swamp, "About time you got here, Krask, you quaggy ort!"

Kanthe spotted a wide raft being poled toward shore. Atop it, a bedraggled band of bearded men brandished hooks and spears. One of them was pissing off the back.

Anskar nodded toward the highmayor. "The only reason I escorted that bastard down to our camp was that he promised he could fetch us that lass your father wants so badly, the one who survived the poison and regained her sight."

Kanthe shared a glance with Frell.

Nyx . . .

Goren crossed toward the water's edge with his men.

Anskar pushed for Kanthe to follow. "Let's see if that rangy lot of fisherfolk caught anything worthwhile. Word is that the girl was spotted leaving the school and heading across Brayk with some fat lad."

Kanthe dragged his feet, letting Anskar take the lead. He drew next to Frell. "What are we going to do?"

Frell grabbed his elbow. "Stay silent. That's all we can do. We'll have to see how this plays out."

By the time they reached Goren's men, the raft bumped into shore and was poled farther aground. A broad-shouldered ruffian in clothes that looked like they'd been woven from old nets pushed to the front. He hopped off the raft, ran a hand down a knotted beard to clean the filth from his palm, then grasped Goren's forearm.

The highmayor returned the greeting, while eyeing the others on the raft. "Well?"

Krask stepped to the side. "Got a little something for ya."

Behind him, the clot of swampers shoved two men into view. One looked like an older version of Bastan, only with an eye swollen shut. The other elbowed his way forward and stepped onto shore, his face blustery and red.

It was Nyx's father.

Holding his breath, Kanthe searched the raft but saw no sign of the girl.

The old man stalked forward to confront the highmayor. "What's this all about, Goren?"

The highmayor faced the anger in the other's face without balking. "Where be your daughter, Polder?"

The old man ignored him for the moment. His gaze swept the sprawl of dead and dying. His face paled, likely only now recognizing the bloody magnitude of the attack.

Goren got nose to nose with Nyx's father, drawing back his attention. "Your daughter, Polder."

The old man gave a small shake of his head. His answer was dulled by shock and horror. "Up . . . Up at the school."

Goren lunged and snatched Polder by the collar. "No, she ain't. And you know it. Your little fen-whore was eyeballed running through Brayk. No doubt going home."

Polder knocked the man's arm down with surprising force. "Then look for her there, you bastard. My boys and I been out working the paddocks all day."

"We already searched your house. And once we're done with ya, we're going to torch that lice-ridden place." He leaned closer. "And we'll do worse to your daughter."

By now, Kanthe's group had reached the others. He remembered over-hearing Goren's earlier threat, directed at Nyx's whole family. Clearly the highmayor intended to carry it out, to exact vengeance for the death of his son in all ways he could. Luckily, there was another who represented the king's order.

Anskar barged through the highmayor's men. "You'll do no such thing, Goren. The lass is wanted by the king. You even bruise such a prized plum, and you'll face His Majesty's wrath." The Vyrllian hefted his ax from his shoulder to his other palm. "And mine."

Goren sneered, his face darkening with fury. "So be it," he muttered through a clenched jaw. "But the king's shield does not defend all."

The highmayor swung around, and with a flash of silver in one hand, he stabbed a long dagger into the old man's belly. Surprise, more than pain, burst across Polder's face. Goren reached his other hand to better grip the dagger's hilt and shoved high, driving the point of the blade deep into chest and heart.

Kanthe lunged forward, though he knew it was already too late. A cry rose from the raft, from Nyx's brother, but he was clubbed to his knees before he could act.

Anskar knocked Goren to the side. "What have you done, you beef-witted fool?"

The highmayor glared back at him, triumphant.

Polder stumbled back, cradling the dagger still plunged in his belly. Then he slowly slumped downward. As he did, he continued to stare at the sky. Agony etched his face, but he did not cry out.

Instead, his pain screeched down from above, rising from a thousand throats, shivering the very waters with its might.

As terror welled inside him, Kanthe suspected the true source of this shrieking chorus—along with the fury behind it.

NYX CLUTCHED HER belly, bent in half by pain and shock.

A moment ago, her winged brother had swept down, wheeling in clear panic. His keening shattered her world, erasing the slow trudge of Gramble-buck and deafening the words of Jace sitting next to her.

Instead . . .

She stares from on high. Her scrutiny snaps from one pair of eyes to another and another, spreading into a dizzying view of the scene below. Men cluster at the edge of the swamp, near a raft she recognizes. Fear incites her. She needs to see more. Demand becomes intent. One set of eyes sweeps lower.

Below, someone falls to his knees, holding his belly, his eyes gazing up at her as she rushes down. She smells his blood, his pain, his shock.

Dah . . .

She cries, louder and louder, until it fills the world.

Below, frail hands fall away, revealing the hilt of a dagger. Life flows out around it in a wash of crimson. Then the body slips to the side, as if exhausted by all the hatred and cruelty of this harsh world.

No, no, no, no, no . . .

With a breath, her grief sharpens to a blood-tinged fury.

Movement flicks the gaze of the predator to the side, to a wide-bellied figure. Triumph is on his lips as he laughs, on his scent as he gloats. The man's hands are bloody, drenched in the life of her father.

She dives down as he looks up. His joy turns to terror in a flash. Wings buffet wide as she slows, leading now with her claws. Others scatter to all sides. She strikes Goren in the chest. Talons dig through leather and flesh. Claws hook into ribs. She beats her wings and lifts him off his feet and into the air.

Goren screams, pouring blood from lips and lungs. She carries him higher still. Shadows dive past, her fury spreading as far as her screams, igniting a thousand fiery hearts.

She sweeps into a roll, tossing Goren's body high. He cartwheels, limbs spread, blood spraying from his torn chest. But he still lives.

Good . . .

She whips around. Talons catch him again, piercing his back, snagging his spine. He still wails. She bends to bring her prey closer. Fangs flail flesh from bone, limb from body. She guts and hollows until finally there is nothing but dead meat in her claws. She throws him far into the swamps, to feed what slithers and lurks below.

She dives again, her anger far from slaked. Her gaze multiplies and spreads. Her bloodlust stretches across the breadth of the sky. Below, men scream and die. Instinct demands she joins the fray.

Then her gaze—fueled by her own heart and memory—fixes on the raft, on a familiar figure that momentarily dims the predatory fire. She knows that face, her nose scents the swamp and bullock on him.

Ablen . . .

She struggles to beat back the savagery still raging inside her and across the sky. She begins to drown in that darkness, losing control. On the raft, her brother fights with four men. They stab and threaten with spear and hook. He bleeds from a score of cuts. As he falters, a man runs at his exposed back with a raised dagger.

She struggles to go to her brother's aid, but bloodlust has burned away her control. Even her vision darkens.

No . . .

Then the attacker with the dagger falls to the side, an arrow impaled through his throat. Her gaze shifts as the predator inside senses another hunter. Kanthe, down on a knee, snaps arrow after arrow toward the raft, defending her brother.

Ablen breaks free. He rushes and dives headlong into the swamp. He vanishes under its black mirror and escapes. She sees herself reflected for a breath in those waters, a shimmering winged shadow that sweeps past overhead.

Shock loosens her control further.

Unable to stop, she rolls in the air, drawn by the blood and screams.

Her vision dims as she drowns in the otherness, in the vastness around her. Again, she senses ageless eyes staring back at her out of the depths of the darkness. The intensity of the gaze shoves her away, as if finding her unworthy, disapproving of her blind fury.

She is cast aside, a gnat before a gale.

Nyx tumbled back into her body with such force that she nearly toppled off the bench. But Jace caught her, pulled her back into the seat. He took her, held her close. She shook and trembled, balanced still between fury and grief, unable to settle. Tears blinded her, soaked her cheeks, filled her nose and mouth.

Jace squeezed her. "Nyx, I've got you."

She sobbed a refrain, "Don't let me go, don't let me go . . ."

"I won't."

She felt his heat, the press of his muscles, took in his sweaty scent. She used his familiarity like a muck-anchor, to draw herself back into her own flesh. She sensed how close she had come to losing herself to the savage otherness, of being lost forever in that darkness.

As she came back into her own body, the grief inside her ached more sharply.

Dah . . . no . . .

Her anguish grew quickly, becoming too much to bear, to carry in a single heart. It seemed impossible she could survive it.

Then a quiet peeping reached her. Its plaintiveness drew her eyes open.

Over Gramblebuck's rump, her winged brother hovered. She met those crimson eyes glowing nearly golden under the shadowed bower. As if drawn by her grief, wings tipped lower, and he glided toward her.

She straightened out of Jace's arms. Her friend also caught sight of the bat's approach and gasped. But she held her place and lifted a hand, her fingers trembling.

The bat drifted and sniffed at her fingertips. Whiskers tickled for a breath, then the little creature soared up her arm. He reached her shoulder, and tiny talons found a roost. Wings battered her head, then folded tight. Claws shifted and tucked the softness of his fur against her cheek and neck. His body was a furnace. His panting like tiny bellows. Tall ears rolled to touch their tips together.

She lifted her other hand, realized it was too much, and settled on a single finger. She slowly reached and rubbed under the tiny chin. The bat stiffened, wings shifting wider, wary and nervous—then with a final tremble, his body relaxed and leaned into her touch. She offered her palm, and he scooped his head against it, rolling one cheek, then another. A raspy tongue tested the salt on her skin.

Then he shifted even closer. He tucked his velvet ears and ducked his head under her chin, rubbing her as she had done to him a moment before. Finally, he settled against her. His gentle peeping softened to a note heard only in one ear.

For a moment, she flashed back to something similar.

Two figures snuggled together in the cradle of warm wings.

She knew this glimpse was not memory fired from any keening, but simply born out of his soft touch now, the shared heat, the quiet murmur of two who had known each other all their lives.

Nyx leaned a cheek closer, allowing her eyes to close again.

Grief still pained her, large and bottomless, but she no longer had to carry it in one heart. While she no longer had the breadth of a thousand hearts to disperse the agony, she sensed the truth.

For now, two is enough.

25

"Off with you both," Anskar ordered.

With the attack seemingly over, the Vyrllian herded Kanthe and Frell toward the swampers' raft. The rocky shore was a charnel house of torn bodies, steaming bowels, and pools of black blood. The neat circle of the camp's bonfires had been shattered into a hundred smoldering piles along the bank. Elsewhere, banners lay broken; the legion's score of sledges and liveries were either smashed or burning.

Only a few of the latter still looked salvageable, though they were probably enough to handle the number of knights and guards who still breathed. Anskar had already sent one of the legion's physiks running to the school. The plan was to leave the worst of the wounded here, while the rest of them headed back to Azantiia.

Anskar was taking no more chances with the horde above. After this last attack, it looked as if the mass was finally breaking up and starting to wing back toward their mountain home.

Kanthe stared up at the dark storm slowly blowing south.

It seems both sides had enough bloodshed for one day.

Anskar shoved him forward at the raft. "Quit your gawking and get your arses aboard." He called over to the four vy-knights standing on the raft, two leaning on poles. "Mallik, get the prince and Alchymist Frell deep into the swamp, under as much cover as possible. In case those fanged bastards decide to attack again."

Mallik nodded sharply. He was the detachment's second in command, towering the same height as Anskar. While shaven-headed and crimson-skinned, like all Vyrllians, he kept a strip of black beard trimmed along his jawbone. His cold eyes appraised Kanthe as he approached. From the set to Mallik's scowl, he did not like what he saw.

"Quick now," Mallik growled. "Both of you."

Frell hopped onto the raft. Kanthe had no choice but to follow. Not that he would've objected. He wanted away from the flies, bloody shite, and ripped bodies. After they left, Anskar would lag behind long enough to square away the rearguard for the trek back to Fiskur, then home.

There was nothing more Kanthe could do. The girl Nyx was still off in the swamps somewhere, and with her brother safely escaped, there was no one in town who knew where she went.

So, she's safe.

Amidst all the horror and losses, he would take this as victory and be happy about it. Plus, the disappearance of the supposedly bless'd girl would irk his father. Kanthe could savor that. Still, the trek had not been an entire waste of life and limb. The legion would return to Highmount with one significant prize. Shrive Vythaas had managed to secure a batch of the bats' poison.

Kanthe stared across the swamp to the Shrive's black livery. Its outline could be seen in the distance. Prior to the onslaught, a pair of bullocks had dragged Vythaas's sled away from shore where it took refuge under a thick protective canopy. Kanthe noted a thin iron chimney atop the livery puffing with black smoke and imagined the Shrive was already working on those stolen sacs of poison.

He gave a sad shake of his head as the raft poled away from the bloody wreckage along the shore. *So much misery for so little gain.*

He turned his back on Brayk, hoping to never set foot there again. He settled to a seat next to Frell. The breadth of the dark swamp stretched ahead of them. It buzzed and nattered. It squawked and croaked. Black branches draped to the sluggish currents or hung heavy under matts of yellow-green moss. Clouds of suckers and flies drifted like mist on the water.

As they were poled deeper, the Mýr closed around them. The cries and occasional screams soon faded behind them, muffled by the weight of the drowned forest. The boles of the trees thickened. The canopy stretched higher, even the waters blackened. As much as he hated this place, he had to respect its brutal beauty. It was forever changeable with each tide, but still ancient and eternal, its roots dug deep into these lands.

At the front of the raft, Mallik nicked out with his sword and sliced through the churning coils of a pit-adder that draped from a tree branch. The snake's lengths loosened and dropped heavily to the raft, still twisting and twining in death. Jaws snapped at empty air. Kanthe felt a measure of pity for the creature. Another crimson knight kicked its remains into the water. The loops stirred atop the blackness—then the surface roiled, and the snake vanished into the depths, its flesh returning to nourish the swamp.

Kanthe shivered and stood, no longer able to sit.

Frell followed him up, but he stared behind the raft. "It seems we've left the others far behind."

Kanthe glanced back, peering between the two vy-knights who manned the poles. A handful of skiffs and punts had followed them from shore, seeking the safety of the swamps. Farther back, even the bullocks had begun to haul sledges into the water. Now there was nothing but dark forest behind them.

Kanthe turned to the front. "Shouldn't we wait for—"

Mallik stood a step away—and plunged his sword at the prince's chest.

NYX DROPPED HEAVILY out of the sledge and onto the sandy banks of Fellfire Scour. Tiny crabs scurried from the impact of her sandals, clacking their irritation at the intrusion, heading toward the lake.

She stretched her limbs and stared leadenly across the flat expanse of the Scour. It stretched a full yoke around, and though its black waters looked like much of the briny swamplands, a sharper eye could note a cast of blue under the open sky. Fellfire was one of the few spring-fed lakes. Its waters were fresh, clean of any bitter salts. It was this feature that drew the family's ancestors to build the winter bullock barn way out here.

Jace came around the back of the sledge to join her. "It looks like an ancient fortress," he said, his back to the lake, craning up at the barn. "Yet, also like it grew straight out of the swamp."

She turned to the barn, better appreciating it under the glow of Jace's admiration. The stout stone barn, five centuries old, climbed twice the height of a bullock. Its walls were stacks of gray boulders, its roof plated in tiles of the same rock, all of it coated in layers of moss and lichens. It did look like the massive structure had been pushed forth from the swamps, a gift to their ancestors. The high doors were timbered in wood so ancient that they had turned to stone themselves. It took a bullock to pull them open and closed.

The barn had served generations of both Polders and bullocks. Countless calves had been born here and yearlings raised, safe from the savage storms that wailed through the Mýr in winter, tearing down trees, stripping thatch from roofs. There remained a stolid practicality to the construction of the place, but also a simple beauty.

She faced the lake again, her heart growing heavy. Their family had spent every winter here. Memories overlapped the view: hauling in woven traps full of tiny armored kryll or larger pincered siltclaws, fishing the depths for whiskered mudfins, or fighting to haul in the sleek karpbows. She remembered those autumns when the lake's surface would be covered by winter geese, their honks deafening. Or those rare frigid snaps in the depths of winter that would rime the edge of the lake with ice.

Still, as familiar as this place was, she felt a distance from it now. She had always known in her heart what Fellfire Scour must look like. Over the years, she had filled in the blanks that her clouded eyes could not see.

Only now her new eyes erased those spots and refilled them with details she had never imagined. What was once home now seemed both familiar and strange. She felt no longer a part of it, and it broke her heart even more.

Saddened at the loss, she closed her eyes and listened to the rising chorus of croaks instead. That had not changed. She picked out the different calls. Her dah had taught them to her. The *pluck-crunk* of emerald-green sprig-frogs, and the heavier *gronking* of platter-sized wartoads. Above that noise, as if scolding the chorus, the clacking of stiff reeds sounded all around as the rods swayed in the breeze.

She sighed and finally opened her eyes. Tears blurred her vision, which was just as well. The loss of detail brought her closer, to this place and to another.

"How my dah loved the Scour," she whispered. "We all promised to bury him in the sands here."

Jace pushed closer. "We can still do that. I'm sure the prioress will attend to his body until we can manage to return."

Nyx wanted to scoff at his words but kept silent. She knew in her heart that would never happen. She turned from him and crossed to the front of the sledge. "I should see to Gramblebuck. Get him untethered so he can properly graze."

Jace followed. "I think he's doing fine on his own."

Gramblebuck had his nose buried in a field of blooming honeyclotts, disturbing fat bees, which he flapped his ears at. He munched on the flowers and rooted his curled tusks in the sandy mulch, digging for the richer musty tubers. The vast fields that circled the lake and stretched a distance into the forest were another reason this site had been chosen for the barn.

She ran a hand over the old bullock's flank, feeling each chew and grind under her palm. She checked the straps, bellybands, hame, and bridle. She searched for rub-sores at the bindings, but a century of hauling sledges had toughened those spots. A pang of guilt spiked through her, knowing her friend would never have been so calloused if not for his labors all these many years.

Gramblebuck noted her approach and turned his damp snout toward her. He snuffed and licked phlegm from his nostrils. He nosed and huffed at her. She noted the gray fogging in his eyes, marking his age. She took his horns and pressed her forehead to him. She inhaled his sweet musk.

"Thank you," she whispered to him. Her words were too feeble to truly encompass her gratitude.

Still, he nudged her back, licked her hand, then with a final chuff, he returned to his grazing. She stepped back and started to free him from the sledge.

"Maybe you'd better keep him tied," Jace said. "At least until Ablen and Bastan return. We don't know if we may need to leave in a hurry."

Nyx remembered her brother diving into the black waters. She straightened and nodded. Gramblebuck shifted a few steps, dragging the sledge behind him to reach a fresh patch of honeyclotts. He plainly had no problem grazing while hitched up.

A gentle whining reminded her that the old bullock was not the only one using this reprieve to fill his stomach. Her winged brother sped silently overhead, sweeping through the droning clouds of gnats and suckers. The bat had left her shoulder's perch as soon as the Scour opened up, drawn by the steaming bounty that buzzed heavily over the water.

She watched his path until he vanished into the shadows.

"Perhaps we should eat, too," Jace said. He had shifted to the back of the sledge. "No telling how long we might be waiting here."

He lugged out a large black kettle that had been roped in place, his face reddening with the effort. He stumbled to the side and carried it a few steps and then lowered it to the sand.

She drifted over as he lifted the lid. The familiar aroma of stewed potageroot and marsh hare carried to her, stopping her. She trembled where she stood.

"It's still warm," Jace noted aloud. He tested with a fingertip, then licked it clean. "Oh my, that's good."

Overcome, Nyx fell to her knees. She pictured her dah stirring that pot, recognizing now it was the last stew he would ever make. The smell—which always meant home—now churned her stomach to a roil. She lurched over. Her belly clenched, and she heaved a stream of bile into the sand. She gasped and coughed, until finally all she could do was sob, bent in half, bitter bile on her tongue.

Jace was there, dropping beside her. "I'm sorry. I'm such a feckin' mooncalf. I wasn't thinking."

She covered her face and straightened. "No," she moaned, still quaking with sobs. "It's not your fault."

It's all mine.

She lowered her hands. Jace had resealed the kettle, but the aroma still seasoned the air. She stared off into the swamp beyond the Scour. She needed Ablen and Bastan, maybe even the dark prince and the alchymist.

What is taking everyone so long?

KANTHE TWISTED TO the side as Mallik's sword stabbed at him. If not for his thin form and his unexpected turn toward the vy-knight at the last moment, he would have taken the full length of the blade through his body. Still, the sword's edge knifed through his tunic and sliced a fiery line across his chest.

Kanthe continued to spin away from the sword, only to fall into the arms of the second knight posted at the front of the raft. Before the man's grip could tighten, Kanthe used panic to fuel a speed honed from his many years hunting. He snatched an arrow from his quiver and stabbed at his captor's eye. The steel point struck soft flesh and hard bone. A sharp scream followed, freeing him.

He ducked, shoving his attacker back with his arse. Mallik came at him, swinging his sword in a double-fisted grip at Kanthe's head. Already tucked, Kanthe leaped to the side and rolled over one shoulder. The sword struck the half-blinded vy-knight in the meat of his calf, nearly taking his leg off. With a cry, he toppled into the swamp.

As Kanthe finished his roll, he smoothly freed his bow and brought it to bear. He skidded on a knee, with his other foot planted. It was a skill taught to him by a Cloudreach scout, the revered hunters of the misty greenwood. He had practiced it over and over, hoping to one day traipse that dangerous forest on his own.

Mallik hollered his rage, clearly never expecting such a move from the Prince in the Cupboard, the drunken Tallywag. He rushed at Kanthe, who had an arrow in hand but struggled to fix it to the bowstring. Panic apparently only carried one so far.

Then a loud boom shook the raft, accompanied by a bright flash.

Mallik stumbled to a wary stop.

From a corner of an eye, Kanthe watched one of the two polemen go flying off the rear of the raft, his chest on fire. The other had already dropped his pole and lunged at Frell with a dagger. The alchymist flung a hand high, as if defending himself, but something shot free of his loose sleeve and into his palm. With a squeeze, a tiny flame spurted from one side. Frell flung the arcane object at the other's face. A blinding blast blew the vy-knight's head back, cracking bone and searing skin.

By now, Mallik's visage had become a narrow-eyed mask of crimson fury. He ignored Frell and leaped at Kanthe. But his mentor's success had firmed Kanthe's hand. He seated his arrow and pulled the bow. He didn't bother to aim, trusting a talent that was now more instinct than thought. He let loose the string.

His arrow crossed the short distance and pierced the man's chest.

Still, Mallik came at him, but Kanthe tucked low. As the vy-knight tackled over him, he burst to his feet and tossed his body high over his shoulders.

A large splash followed. Kanthe turned around in time to see Mallik sputter up in the water, his sword still in hand.

Malice shone in the vy-knight's eyes.

Still, there was already too much blood in the water. Before the man could kick toward the raft, a huge shape lurched out of the depths. A long, scaled snout snatched Mallik, clamping yellow teeth into flesh and bone. It rolled, showing a glimpse of an armored back fringed with glowing moss—then both vanished into the dark depths.

Kanthe turned to Frell. Only the two of them were left on the raft. "What in Hadyss's arse just happened?" he asked, suddenly unable to stop his limbs from trembling.

Frell joined him, his lips thin and bled of color. The alchymist stripped back his robe's sleeves to reveal some mechanism strapped to his forearms. It was plain they were the sheaths for whatever alchymy the man had used to dispatch the two polemen.

"I had suspected something like this," Frell said, shaking his sleeves back down. "Though, I had hoped it wouldn't come to be."

"Suspected what?"

Frell stared out at the only body still floating in view. Still, the corpse shivered as something picked at the flesh. "I feared you were never supposed to return from the swamps." He glanced back to Kanthe. "Did you not find it odd that your father would send you on this trek, after ignoring you for so many years?"

"Maybe, I guess." Kanthe shrugged, trying to mask both his anger and his own foolishness. "I attributed it to him just wanting me out of Highmount for my brother's nuptials. Maybe also offering me a chance to prove myself."

"You are right about Mikaen's marriage. It probably *was* the impetus for this rash act. To clear the slate for a future heir."

Kanthe sighed.

Which means I'm just mud that needed to be wiped away.

Frell crossed and picked up the abandoned pole. "The plan must have been to wait until the legion could dump Goren and his party over at Brayk. Once free of any prying eyes, you were to meet a bloody and untimely end in the swamp."

Kanthe gazed back in the direction of the town. He pictured Anskar sending him off alone, ahead of the rest of the legion. *How many of them had known what was planned for me?*

Frell pushed the raft toward the other pole floating in the water. "Grab it but take care. With all the blood and torn flesh—"

"I got it. At least, it's not our blood and torn flesh."

He gingerly collected the long rod, fighting the despair in his heart. He knew his father had held him in little esteem, but he had never imagined the depths of the king's disdain. As he straightened, sharper voices carried over the water, sounding distant, but one could never tell out here.

Frell waved him to the far side of the raft. "They must have heard the blasts from my chymical bombs. We must be well away before anyone reaches here. It won't take the others long to suspect you might still live."

Kanthe firmed his grip on the pole. Together they got the raft moving. "Where do we go?"

Frell nodded ahead. "First, to Fellfire Scour."

"And then?"

Frell glanced over to him. "There is much you don't know."

Kanthe rolled his eyes and turned away. "Sometimes, Frell, you are the master of the obvious."

"WE CALL HIM the King of the Scour," Nyx said.

She sat in the sand next to Jace and pointed toward the island in the flat expanse of the lake. The round shape was half the size of the sledge. Its arched surface glimmered in the sun, running with every color, as if a storm-bow had come to life and settled to the Scour.

Even through her despair and exhaustion, the wonder of the sight—something she had never been able to fully appreciate with her beclouded eyes—gladdened her heart. It was as if the Mother were blessing her with the king's presence. She knew her dah would certainly ascribe it as such.

So, I will, too.

The island drifted toward one of the banks, occasionally lifting its head into view atop a gray stalk of a neck. She and Jace had been watching its path for over a half-bell, ever since the king first surfaced, revealing its royal presence.

According to the story shared by her family, the dappleback turtle had been released as a baby into the lake after the foundation stone of the winter barn had been set in place five centuries ago. It was the family's gift of thanks to the gods. All believed that as long as the king lived here in the Scour, the winter barn would stand.

She didn't know if this story was true or if this was even the same turtle, but she wanted to believe it now more than ever. She needed some hope that her family would survive the ordeal, that Bastan and Ablen would rejoin her soon.

As if jealous of the attention, her winged brother returned, darting and dancing overhead. He pinged and squeaked at her. This time his piping call was not riven through with visions and sights, only warning.

She stood. "Someone's coming."

Jace pushed up and searched back at the barn. "Maybe we should get inside."

Before they could move, faint voices carried to them. Words could not be discerned, but notes of complaint were interrupted by firmer scolds. She bottled her disappointment, trusting the sharpness of her hearing.

She glanced over to Jace, who still looked worried. "I think it's Alchymist Frell," she said. "And the prince."

Still, she listened, straining for other voices.

Ablen's grouse or Bastan's glumness.

But it sounded like the prince and alchymist had come alone. Before long, their voices became words, and a raft poled out of the deep swamp and into the open lake.

Jace waved to them.

The raft turned and aimed for their spot on the sand. As it beached, Frell hurried over to her, his face ashen. "Nyx, your father . . ."

"I know," she said, not ready to talk about it. She turned to Kanthe. "And I saw you save Ablen. I'm in your debt."

The prince frowned. "How did you—" The small bat sped past his head, causing him to wince and duck. He then straightened and followed her small brother's course over the lake. "Ah, I see. Definitely a nosy little bugger. Too bad he couldn't have warned me of my father's ambush."

Jace looked between the two men. "What do you mean? What ambush?"

Frell quickly explained all that had befallen the pair. As he did so, fear began to replace Nyx's despair. It centered on the two men still missing.

"What about Ablen and Bastan?" she asked.

Frell sighed. "We do not know. We saw no sign of Bastan on our route here. And as far as we know, Ablen escaped before the bats attacked. As I understand it, both your brothers know these swamps far better than any in the king's legion. We must trust that they can follow us from here."

Nyx balked. "What do you mean *follow us from here*? Why do we not wait for them?"

Kanthe answered, "The Vyrllian Guard are as pernicious as your little brother's horde. With the assassination failed, they will seek to correct that mistake—and to avenge their fallen."

"No doubt they already suspect what happened." Frell pointed to Gramblebuck, who had finished his grazing and snored contentedly within his traces, his large head hanging low. "We must continue to add distance from the force that follows. Not only do they seek the prince, but if they discover you here, lass, you will be dragged to Highmount."

Frell stared hard at her, silently reminding her that more than her own freedom was at stake. In the back of her head, she heard the grind of war machines and the screams of the dying, all ending with a resounding crash that erased everything.

Moonfall . . .

Jace gripped Nyx's arm. "We can't let them take you. We must go."

Nyx wanted to argue. Her brief time here—wrapped in fond memories—had been a balm on her grief. She had even felt the stirring of the first embers of hope, imagining a reunion with Ablen and Bastan.

She stared across the Scour. As she watched the king sink back into the black depths, his radiance vanishing, those hopeful embers inside her died. She knew she could not stay here and would likely never return home.

But that didn't answer a larger worry.

She turned to Frell. "Where do we go?"

"Before I left the Cloistery, the prioress had instructed me on a course, a path to take if matters turned sour and these lands became too dangerous for you."

Kanthe looked to his toes—but not in time to hide the strange sadness in his gray eyes.

He knows . . . Frell must've already told him.

"Where?" she asked, her heart pounding harder. "Where am I supposed to go?"

Frell swallowed, then answered, destroying all she knew about herself. "We must find your true father."

EIGHT

THE
FORSWORN KNIGHT

KNIGHT: *What dare we hope to gain from such a tryst when my heart is twice forsworn to another—to my betroth'd and to my king?*

WOMAN: *Whiche of the two do you hold in the heyest esteem?*

KNIGHT: *Neither—when I look into your eyes.*

—A duologue from the third act of
The Brokyt Oath, by Galiphaestii

26

GRAYLIN HUNTED THE Rimewood with his two brothers.

He had been following the frost-elk for most of the day, passing deep into the eternal twilight of the far western forest. He stepped with care, settling each hide-boot into the litter of dry needles without a rustle. His fingers reached high to test a deep scrape in the bark of a silver cedar. He felt the sticky fresh sap. He brought his hand down, smelling pitch and the musk of the bull's mark.

Close now . . .

He had not planned to travel this far into the forest. Few dared to risk the western ranges of the Rimewood. While the eastern edges, closer to the sea, were green and bright, the western forests remained forever locked in twilight. Forbidden the warmth of the Father Above, the trees sapped what strength they could with wide splays of dense needles and survived due to roots that dug deep, lined by large sulfurous galls that fed them. And despite the lack of His grace, the ancient heartwoods of the western Rime grew into giants. Some were so large that it would take twenty men with outstretched arms to encircle their trunks.

Only once had Graylin dared venture into those huge woods. It had been a decade ago, shortly after he had been banished here, back when he was too foolish to know better. He never intended to trek that far again.

Not that there weren't enough dangers in this deep wood.

With a grind of his teeth, he concentrated on his current hunt. The shred of claws on a black pine reminded him to take heed. The ironhard bark had been gouged deep. It was the mark of a knoll-bear, whose sows grew to the size of black-furred boulders twice his height, and the boars even larger.

He ran a hand over the scrapes.

Mayhap it's best if I abandon this trail . . .

His gut-sense warned him that he had traveled too far. Still, the mark in the pine was an old one, crusted with stony sap, and in the distance a mournful lowing drew him onward, rising from the throat of the frost-elk. He had picked this particular bull after watching a herd move through the valley near his cabin. From the spread of the bull's antlers—with broken points and covered in fringes of moss—it was an old one. He had watched it hobble on one hindlimb. The leg had been scarred long ago from what looked like an old lion attack.

Graylin related with this noble beast, as he bore many scars of his own. He also knew, come winter, how the frigid cold would pain the creature. He imagined this was the bull's last summer, a summer already half gone. With the first snows, the hobbled bull would not keep up with the rest of the herd as it moved to warmer pastures. Abandoned, the beast would starve or be savagely mauled.

Then this morning, as Graylin spied upon the herd from a deadfall, the bull elk had headed away from the herd, drifting west on its own. Maybe it would've eventually returned, but Graylin sent his two brothers to further divide it, to drive it farther away.

With the choice made, Graylin had tracked after it. Though the elk was old, the bull proved its craftiness, honed from its decades in the bitter Rime. Even with his two brothers tracking it, he nearly lost the bull's trail twice. Graylin also suspected the frost-elk's path toward the ice-fogged bowers of the deeper wood was intended to shake off the hunters behind it, as if daring them to follow. But Graylin continued his pursuit, feeling a responsibility for separating the bull from the herd.

As he stalked deeper, he came upon a heartwood. It was a small one, maybe a century old, still white-barked, a lone outcast from the greater forest to the west. He kissed a thumb and placed his palm against its trunk, feeling an affinity with this lonely sentinel. He also took it as a signpost and read its meaning.

Pass no farther.

He stopped and eyed an open glade ahead, split by a silvery stream. He whistled like a woodthrush to his brothers. He knew the pair had already ventured far ahead, circling past the old bull. He rushed forward, still minding dead branches and brittle needles. From off his shoulder, he rounded his ash bow into his hands. As he closed on the misty glade, he slipped an arrow from his quiver and placed its haft between his lips. In the meadow, a large antlered shadow drank from a stream whispering over polished stones.

He crossed to the tree line and stayed in the shadows, keeping downwind.

The elk lifted its head with no sign of panic. Still, its ears stood tall, facing toward the dark woods ahead. Velvety nostrils flared as it huffed. It surely scented the danger but remained in the open, only roughing a forehoof in the grass. It shook its antlers, challenging what hid in the forest's shadows, ready for one final battle, too proud to run any farther, showing no fear, only a tired resignation.

Graylin also understood this stance and would honor it as best he could.

He reached to the arrow at his mouth and drew its fletching across his lips, wetting the feathers. He bent his knees, nocked the arrow, and drew the string until his fingertip found the corner of his lips. He tilted the bow slightly away from the arrow, aimed for the whorl of fur behind the elk's front leg, then gently released the taut string.

The arrow shot away. Graylin followed it with his hunter's sense. He could almost feel the impact of the bolt through fur and skin, sensed it cross ribs and impale a proud, tired heart. The elk only shuddered, took a single step, then with a great majesty, toppled to the grass beside the stream.

Graylin straightened and walked out of the woods toward the bulk of the downed elk. He silently thanked the Mother Below—both for the bounty given to him and for the long life bestowed upon the old bull.

He loosened a pack slung low to his hip and removed knives and unfolded roughspun sacks. He set about quartering the elk. It was cold enough that he kept the skin on the meat. He had a long haul back to his cabin, so he stripped out the bones to lighten his load. As he worked, he built a steaming pile of bowels beside the stream to feed the forest after he left.

Unfortunately, these woods had little patience and far more hunger.

A rumbling growl was the only warning.

He froze, skinning knife in hand.

Beyond the stream, a huge shadow separated from the forest. The knoll-bear ambled toward him. It was a rounded hill of shag and rolling muscle. Its head was a stony crown topped by round ears. Thick jowls rippled back in tune with a grumbled threat, exposing fangs as long as his forearm. He remembered the deep claw marks in the black pine and suspected here was the culprit, a full-grown sow. Off to the side, he noted a pair of eyes glinting deeper in the wood, surely a summer cub.

The bear's shoulders shifted, its haunches bunching, readying for a charge.

There was nothing more dangerous than a sow with a hungry cub. And nothing that these giant monsters had to fear in these woods.

But Graylin hadn't come alone.

And his companions were not from these forests.

Out of the shadows to either side of the bear, his two brothers stalked into view. They looked like wolves, only a handsbreadth taller in the front. No growl marked their approach. No fangs were bared. They slunk low, a staccato chittering flowing from them. It escalated in volume and pitch, raising hairs on his neck.

The bear stopped with a tremble. Its large head swiveled between the two approaching beasts. It recognized the threat, as did all who lived here.

The vargr were the scourge of the heartwoods. Their dark-striped fur was nearly impossible to discern amidst the fog and darkness. Some considered them more spirits than flesh, just shadows with teeth. The vargr seldom roamed east of their shrouded forests, but when they did, no one dared cross them.

The sow heeded this warning and backed step by step. Even if she chanced taking on the pair, she had her cub to consider. Wisely, she retreated into the forest, and a moment later her large bulk could be heard barging away.

The two vargr finally bent their necks, ruffed by short manes, toward him. Two sets of amber-gold eyes stared at him. Still, his brothers' tufted ears remained turned back toward the forest, continuing to listen to the bear's retreat.

Born of the same litter, the two looked identical, but Graylin could pick out subtle differences that seemed glaring to him after so long. The mischievous Aamon was a fingersbreadth shorter than his brother, with one ear that always hung slightly crooked when relaxed. The more stoic Kalder had thinner stripes across his haunches and a bushier tail.

Still, they were two kindred spirits bearing one heart.

And they allow me to share it for now.

Graylin pressed a hand to his chest, then turned the palm toward them, silently thanking them. He owed them his life, not just now, but many times over, especially a decade ago. As he worked on dressing the elk, he fell back into that darker time. He remembered a glint of moonlight on snow, marking where the Crown ended and the endless frozen wastes began.

I'VE REACHED THE end of the world.

With the day over, Graylin gazed at the full face of the moon hanging bright in the sky through the thin, high branches of the heartwood forest. He stood mesmerized. A swath of stars—a rare sight in his homeland in Hálendii—spangled the dark arch above, sparkling like a crush of diamonds. And farther to the west, a serrated line of silver marked the jagged peaks of the Ice Fangs. They glowed as if lit from within, a jagged rampart that marked the Crown's westernmost border.

He tried to imagine the frozen lands beyond that snowy range, but all he could picture was an endless plain of broken ice.

And maybe that's all there is.

He was new to the lands of Aglerolarpok. Three fortnights ago, he had arrived on a prison ship. He and a handful of others had been dumped in Savik, banished and forbidden from ever setting foot in Hálendii again. He had barely healed from the tortures in the dungeons of Highmount. His flesh was knitted with raw sutures; more wounds had been burned closed. His broken arm had healed crookedly and still hurt to move. Still, if not for the compassion of the king for a former friend, he could have lost toes, fingers, an eye or two, and likely both bollocks.

He knew it was that same mercy that led to his banishment across the seas. He understood the punishment. *King Toranth could no longer look at me—yet, couldn't bring himself to kill me.*

So, after his tortures, broken inside and out, Graylin had been stranded here, a knight forever prohibited from carrying steel. Some might call it mercy. He considered it one final torture that was intended to last a lifetime. He was sentenced to forever remember his broken oath and what it had cost him. Even now, with the wondrous spread of stars in the sky, he could picture the remains of his lover, Marayn, thrown into his dungeon cell. Her body—the little that was left of it—had been discovered in the swamps of Mýr. They left her remains in his cell, flybit and maggoty, to serve as a horrific testament to his broken oath.

As he stood in the dark heartwood, he took a deep breath of the cold air. He lowered his eyes, feeling unworthy to gaze at the pantheon above. Still, the natural beauty around him could not be ignored. Here at the edge of the world, the heartwood trees were giant gray columns, enshrined in wisps of ice fog. The march of their trunks glowed with rafts and conks of phosphorescent fungi, while the bowers created lofty vaults overhead, allowing peeks at the sky's splendor.

It was as if he had trespassed into a living kath'dral, a holy shrine to the Mother, hidden away from the gaze of the Father Above.

He came to one firm conclusion.

This is a good place to die.

From deeper in the woods, this desire was given voice. A single ghostly cry, eerie and high-pitched, echoed to him. The birdsong fell silent. Even the *chirp-chirp* of beetles in the low bushes hushed in respect. Then another throat joined the first, then another, until an entire chorus wailed at him.

Every hair on his body shook. His heart pounded in an age-old tympani of the hunted. He had heard tales of the predators that haunted the deep heartwood. The shadows with teeth. But he had not truly believed them, dismissing stories of their bollock-icing cries, their savage cunning, of jaws powerful enough to crush an ox's skull. He thought such tales to be just fancy and boast. Especially as Graylin had raised war dogs at the Legionary himself, even some who bore the blood of wolves. So, tales of the shadowy monsters in the mists sounded preposterous to him.

Now, Graylin knew all those stories to be true. It had been foolhardy to trek this far. Though, in truth, it was not foolishness, but despondency, that drove him westward. Deep down, he knew he had crossed to the edge of the world to find his own end, to seek a death that had been denied him.

And now it comes for me.

Only in that moment, faced with the inevitable, did he recognize an even deeper truth about himself: how quickly a longing for death could be dashed by a dagger at one's throat.

He turned and fled through the heartwood, finally seeing what had been buried under his grief and shame.

A will to live.

But it was a realization that had come too late. The pack howled and screamed their eerie cries, chasing after him. It was impossible to know how far back they were. He simply ran wildly through the wood, stumbling over dark bushes, bouncing off trunks. His heart pounded; his vision narrowed. He aimed for the distant brighter forests, but he knew he would never make it. The pack went ominously silent behind him. He expected the mists to shatter into lunging bodies and snapping teeth at any moment.

Then the dark Daughter, the eternal Huntress, showed him mercy.

From ahead, a plaintive mewling rose out of the lightening mists, a forlorn piping of distress. His path veered toward it. It was not a conscious act, but more as if the crying was a form of inescapable bridle-song that pulled at his bruised heart. He thrashed in that direction—only to fall headlong over a body in the brush.

He sprawled hard and rolled around.

Panting and wild-eyed, he discovered a mound of striped fur draped across the forest floor. Though he had only seen a single pelt, he knew it had to be a vargr, one who had died recently. The mewling rose from its far side. He peered over and discovered two squirming cubs, maybe a moon or two old, struggling for cold nipples. He also saw the clamp of iron jaws on the mother's hindleg, the limb plainly broken and soaked in blood. The tale was easy to read. The she-vargr must have ventured into the brighter woods to hunt for her young, only to fall prey to the cruelties of a Rimehunter's trap. Still, the beast had pulled the chain's stake free and dragged herself back to the heartwood, back to her litter—where she eventually died, but not before offering her cubs one last meal.

He couldn't explain his next act. Maybe it was to honor her efforts before he died himself, or maybe his action was born out of the guilt for a child he could not save.

No matter, he grabbed for the cubs. They hissed and snapped, savage even at such a young age. One caught the meat of his thumb and nearly took it off. The pair then darted into a nearby den in the hollow of a moldering log.

He considered abandoning them, especially with the hunters surely closing in on him. Instead, he swore under his breath. He reached to the she-vargr and squeezed cold milk across his hands. It was a trick he had learned in the Legionary's kennels. He crawled to the log, draped his cloak across the mulch, and opened his palms. He used the scent of milk and mother to lure the cubs out of hiding. One crept forward, growling, shadowed by the other. They had to be starving.

Once the cubs were close enough, more sniffing than snarling now, he snatched one in each hand. He quickly bundled them up in his cloak. The pair fought and tore and bawled, trying to rip their way out, and were likely to succeed.

He searched around, then yanked his hunting knife from its sheath and sliced off the she-vargr's tail. He rubbed it across the weeping teats and tossed its length inside his cloak. He cradled the bundle up in his arms. The thrashing cubs had already begun to settle to a wary rumble. The fur of their mother and the soak of her milk calmed them enough for exhaustion to set in and subdue them.

Lucky to still be alive, he stood up.

But it wasn't luck.

He found an arc of glinting eyes staring out of the heartwood at him. His heart pounded harder. He cursed his foolishness at stopping, but he also did not regret it. He had once failed another desperate mother.

Let this be a small act of atonement before I die.

But the eyes just continued to shine at him. He held his ground, accepting what was to come, maybe even welcoming it now.

Then one pair of eyes vanished, then another, and another. Soon the forest was dark and silent. He took a shaky step away, waited, then risked another. But those eyes never reappeared. He did not know if the vargr were mystified by his strange act of mercy. Or maybe it was the scent of milk and cubs that masked him, confused them.

For whatever reason, they allowed him to go.

He accepted their gift of his life and fled back to brighter woods.

FINISHED DRESSING THE elk, Graylin let go of the past and stared appreciatively at the pair of full-grown vargr, his brothers of the hunt. Not only had he survived that fateful brush with death in the heartwood, raising the pair had given him a reason to live.

He straightened from his labors. With still no sign of the knoll-bear's return, he called them.

"Aamon, Kalder, to me."

They trotted over, leaping the stream to join him. He bent down and split away two lobes off the elk's liver and tossed one to each. They savaged into the raw flesh, then returned to patrolling the edges of the forest while he fashioned a crude travois out of roped branches. He piled his meat on top of it and set about for home, dragging the sled and whistling for his brothers to follow.

The path back was thankfully downhill. It took half the time to return to within a quarter league of his cabin. He stopped long enough to strip his clothing and dive naked into an icy blue tarn. He rinsed the blood, sweat, and bile from his body and used the cold to numb the ache in his limbs and joints. With a final quake of frigid limbs, he climbed out and buffed himself dry with an empty roughspun sack.

As he did so, he caught a glimpse of his reflection in the slowly settling lake. He read the map of his scars, the veins of gray in his black hair and scruff of beard. But as the waters shimmered, he allowed himself to imagine how he had once looked, before he broke an oath. A hale knight of strong muscle, straight limbs, and with hair as black as oiled soot and eyes of a silvery blue.

On the bank, he ran a palm over the ruff of his chest hair, trying to remember his former self. He still felt strong muscles, but they were leaner and harder now. His fingers traced the gnarled scars, the broken nose, the knot in his jaw. His hip joints ached, and his left forearm had a crook to it.

This is who I am now, disgraced and banished and broken.

With a scowl, he turned his back on the illusion in the water. That shimmering knight was long dead. And to most of the world, so was the *man.* And in some ways, he had died in that heartwood a decade ago. The hunter who returned with two squalling vargr cubs was not the same one who had entered that dark wood.

He found Aamon and Kalder sitting on their haunches, staring back at him. Aamon gave a sweep of his tail, and Kalder simply narrowed his eyes. He met their uncompromising regard. Their gazes were not so much loving as tolerant. He knew these two were not lapdogs. Despite heeding his command and learning a hundred hand signals, they remained beasts of the field, as likely to turn on him as not, if the winds should shift. He accepted that as part of their pact and would have it no other way.

May you always hold me to a hard account, my brothers.

Still, he found himself grateful for their attention and company. It was difficult to remain morose when he had such stalwart companions.

"At least someone still finds value in me," he muttered to them, donning his clothes. "Even if it's just to fill your bellies."

He got them all moving again. He followed a stream that drained the tarn. It ambled a meandering track through bosky wooded hills. The forests grew slowly greener, going from dark pines to a mix of oaks, mountainash, and maples. The stream became dotted with large willows. The bushes thickened with juniper and peashrubs. The ice in the mists melted to a simple chill in the air. Even with the day nearing an end, it brightened as they climbed the last hill toward home.

The cabin he had built from local timber stood atop the next rise. He had chosen this spot as it balanced between the greener woods that stretched to the sea and the twilight forests thick with freezing fogs to the west. It was also remote enough that few, if any, ever chanced upon his cabin. And no one ever visited.

So, he stopped at the bottom of the hill, studying the sod roof of his cabin. A thin stream of smoke rose from the stone chimney, promising the warmth of home and a hot meal.

Still, a chill of trepidation swept through him.

When he had left this morning, his hearth had been cold.

27

GRAYLIN CROUCHED AT the edge of his homestead, sticking to the shadows of the tree line. He searched the back gardens, already sprouting with a summer's leafy bounty of lettuce, purple squash, ripe bloodapples, along with a patch of stalky hardcorn. He eyed the smokehouse to the right of his one-room cabin and a small barn where he kept a lone pony and wagon for trading down in the town of Savik near the coast.

He spotted no one skulking about, but the chimney continued to smoke.

Graylin signaled his brothers who guarded to either side. He softly nickered for their attention, then placed his palms together and opened them, spreading his arms wide before bringing his palms together. It was a command they knew well: CIRCLE AND GUARD.

The pair split off, going opposite directions, keeping to the forest's edge. Their senses were far sharper than his. If there were any strangers hidden, they would soon regret their trespass.

With his back guarded, Graylin ran low to the barn and peeked inside. He saw his Aglerolarpok pony drowsing in his stall, but another horse had been tethered at the gate. It shifted nervously, maybe scenting the circling vargr.

He sidled over to the smokehouse, fingered the door open, and except for the slabs of salted, dried meat, it was empty. By now, he was less nervous and more irritated. He reached the timber-framed cabin and peered through a window. Lit by the hearth, a cloaked figure sat on a chair near the fire. His chin rested on his chest as if asleep, but the puffs of smoke around the glow of a pipe suggested otherwise. The trespasser's arm lifted, and without glancing up, the man waved at the window, plainly inviting Graylin into his own house.

Spotting no one else in the cabin, he cursed aloud and crossed around to his front door. He kept a dagger in hand as he entered. The scent of woodsmoke and smoldering rakeleaf greeted him back home. The room was simply furnished with a thick oaken table to one side near a rise of shelves stacked with dry goods and other necessities. The bed was a frame with a thick mattress stuffed with goose feathers and blanketed in furs, the only bit of luxury about the place. A few dark oil lamps hung from hooks.

The figure shifted, stretching in the chair, like a lazy cat waking from a half-slumber. He was a firm-bodied man with a slight paunch to his belly from too much ale. He had slate-gray hair braided to the back and a scruff of several days' growth of the same over cheek and chin. Under his heavy traveler's cloak, he wore baggy breeches and a stained tunic laced to his throat. He had removed his boots, which he had set by the fire. Both his woolen hosen had large holes at heel and toe.

"I see you made yourself at home, Symon."

The visitor's green eyes sparkled with amusement at Graylin's exasperation. "How could I not? You expect me to freeze my bollocks off while I wait for you all day?"

"Why are you here?"

"How're the pups?" Symon asked, shifting around to stare out the window.

"I'm more than happy to have them greet you if you don't answer my question."

Symon held up a palm and took a long puff on his pipe, ripening the glow in the bowl. "That's okay. No reason to bother the boys. I'll trust the pair are doing fine."

"What's this all about? Why are you here?"

Symon waved for Graylin to bring the stool from the table, as if he owned the place. Graylin had never bothered with a second fireside chair as he didn't invite or tolerate visitors. He had company enough with Aamon and Kalder.

Still, he dragged the stool closer to the hearth, curiosity getting the better of him. Symon hy Ralls served as his trading partner in Savik, helping him barter for goods he needed up here in the wilds—which made him as close to a friend as one could muster out here. Symon was also one of the few people who knew Graylin's true identity, something he kept obscured by using a false name, which he changed regularly.

Such a deception would have never worked with Symon anyway. While Graylin plied his trade in furs and dried meats, Symon dealt in secrets and whispered words. Also, the two knew each other long before Graylin's arrival, going back two decades. Symon had been an alchymist at Kepenhill, and their paths had crossed periodically, mostly in taverns. But Symon had eventually been stripped of his robe and cast out due to his preference for wine and spirits over books and teaching.

Or so the story went.

When it came to Symon, much of his history was dubious. Graylin suspected there was far more to the man. Even deep in his cups, Symon seldom appeared drunk. Instead, there remained a glint of hard steel buried under his feigned merriment, and a sharper intent hidden behind his idle banter.

Still, the man had kept Graylin's secret all these years, and for that, he tolerated the former alchymist. But there were limits to his largesse.

Graylin dropped his stool near the fire and sat atop it. "Explain yourself."

Symon shifted and reached inside his heavy cloak and removed a curl of parchment sealed with wax. He offered it over, but Graylin simply folded his arms. He recognized the missive of a skrycrow and had no interest in reading what might be written there. His world was now this cabin, these woods, and his stalwart brothers. He needed nothing else, *wanted* nothing else.

Symon studied him for a breath, then rolled the scroll between his fingers until the red wax seal faced Graylin. "This is pressed with the mark of the Cloistery."

Graylin's heart clenched in his chest.

"From the Mýr," Symon added.

"I know where the Cloistery is," Graylin grumbled darkly. "Why does this concern me?"

Symon leaned back, fingering the scroll around and around. "The skrycrow arrived a day ago," he said. "Sent to me—but meant for you."

"If so, then you failed to keep your word. For anyone to know I still live, to know you could reach me, then you must have shared what you swore to keep secret."

Symon shrugged. "Breaking an oath to an oathbreaker. Surely you can't hold that against me."

Graylin stood up, tightening a fist.

Symon sighed. "Calm yourself. There were a few who needed the truth and could be trusted with it."

"Like you?"

"Like the prioress of the Cloistery."

Graylin knew the woman and respected her. He slowly settled back to his stool.

"You are not a fool, Graylin. Nor a naïve sop. Surely you must understand that some matters overrule even a sworn word. You certainly demonstrated that amply in the past. Did not love break your oath?"

Graylin felt his face heat up, not with shame, but with rising anger. "You think you need to remind me of—"

Symon cut him off with a raised hand. "Fair trade."

Baffled by his words, Graylin took a breath, then sputtered, "What do you mean?"

"Since I gave away your secret, in payment I will give you one of my own."

Graylin frowned. He did not care about any of the confidences that Symon kept, but he was intrigued enough to wave to the man.

Symon planted his pipe between his lips and bent over. He used a finger to pull the worn hose from his left foot and tossed it aside. He then lifted his leg to expose his sole to Graylin. "What do you think about that?"

Graylin leaned closer and came to a firm conclusion. "You need a bath. With plenty of lyeleaf soap to strip that reek from your flesh. If that's even possible."

"Look closer, near my heel."

Holding his breath, Graylin pushed forward. He squinted and spotted a small raised scar. It looked no more than what one might get from stepping on a hot coal rolled from a fire. "Are we comparing burns?" he asked.

Symon tilted his foot slightly, and the scar transformed from a knot of thickened skin to a vague outline of a rose. Graylin shifted back.

No . . .

Symon lowered his foot.

Graylin studied his former alchymist anew. "You're not suggesting you're part of—"

"The Razen Rose?" Symon lifted a brow.

He scoffed. "They're just stories, concocted by those who see shadows where there are none."

"You've heard me belch and fart. Is that not real enough?"

Throughout his years in the Legionary and beyond, he had heard rumors of the Razen Rose, a confederacy of spies aligned to no kingdom or empire. They were said to be stripped alchymists and hieromonks who had been secretly recruited to use their skills to a greater purpose: to protect and preserve knowledge throughout the rise and fall of realms. Some suspected their true agenda involved steering history, believing the Rose was the hidden hand that ultimately moved the gears of the world.

Graylin stared over at Symon.

If this man is part of that hand, the Urth is doomed.

"Does that not pay my debt?" Symon asked.

"Assuming what you say is even true."

Symon shrugged. "A secret sold does not require a buyer's belief. It's a value unto itself."

Growing exasperated, Graylin stood. "Consider your debt paid, but I want nothing to do with the greater world."

Symon remained seated, even leaned back. "It's not the greater world that you need care about." He puffed hard on his pipe, then lifted the scroll over the smoldering bowl. "This missive concerns Marayn's child."

Graylin went cold. All the blood drained to his legs. The unquiet peace he had settled upon suddenly fractured into a thousand painful shards.

"A daughter, as I understand it." Symon lowered the parchment toward the pipe's fiery bowl. "But if you don't wish to involve yourself . . ."

Graylin lunged and snatched the message. He clutched it as his past overwhelmed him.

KNEELING IN THE sailing skiff, Graylin clasped Marayn's shivering hands between his warm palms. It was the only way he could keep her from speaking, to stop her from refusing what he asked of her.

He felt her tremble. She tried to free her hands, her eyes forlorn, tears running down her cheeks.

"You must go," he insisted.

He nodded toward the strip of grassy sand where he had nosed the skiff after poling it as far as he could into the swamps. He could traverse no farther. Marayn's best hope for her and her unborn child was to hide in the swamp while he tried to lure away the legion's ships that closed down upon the coastline of these drowned lands.

She tugged her hands free and clenched a fist to her chest, then opened her fingers like a budding rose. [*I love you.*] She motioned quickly, nearly too fast for him to interpret, but her frantic face was easy to read: [*Let me go with you. We must stay together. Even if it means our deaths.*]

He placed his hand on her belly, believing he could feel the babe stir under his palm. Even now he didn't know if the child was his or the king's. "And what of the baby here?" he asked. "Would you risk its life for another few breaths together?"

She covered his hand with her own. He felt a determined kick under his palm. *Must be my child.* Despite his terror, he found himself smiling. He looked up as Marayn offered a sad version of his same expression. He leaned his forehead to hers.

"You must go," he whispered. "If only for the sake of your child."

She pulled back, pointed to his chest, then cradled her fingers together. [*Our child.*]

He nodded. They had come to this decision with the first swelling of her belly. He didn't care who the father was, only that the child would be his. It was why they planned this flight. The king had waited this long to decide if the child would live or die. Toranth already had two boys, but he considered a third heir, even a bastard, could cement his throne in case his elder sons should die. Then a scryer threw bones, tested Marayn's chamber pot, and deemed the child to be a girl. As Toranth placed great stock on his soothers and bone-readers, he ordered Marayn's babe to be expelled through draughts of Bastard's Herb tea, and failing that, through knife and blood.

So, they fled that same winter night.

"We dare wait no longer," Graylin said. "If I'm to lure them away, I must set off for the open water now."

She finally relented, weeping silently, her shoulders shaking. He helped her out of the boat and onto land. He drew her into one last kiss. He tasted the salt of her tears on her lips. He wished he could stay there forever, but it could never be.

He pulled back, fighting his own tears now. As she stood there trembling, he pressed a knife into her hands.

"Travel as far as you can," he instructed. "And hide. If I can lose the others, I will find my way back to you. I swear it."

She nodded, clutching the dagger.

He returned to the skiff and poled off the beachhead. He glided across the black brine, staring back at her.

She stood with a fist at her chest and bloomed her fingers.

He repeated the sign, knowing that was where all their troubles had begun. A year ago, Marayn had been offered to Graylin to serve as a private tutor, so he might learn the gesturing language shared by the tongueless pleasure serfs. As captain of the king's guard, he had hoped to learn that means of communication, to employ it as a tool for the legion to correspond silently among them or even across battlefields.

Graylin thought himself so clever for considering this tactic.

And so did King Toranth.

Graylin and Toranth had been friends for ages. They had gone through their nine years in the Legionary together, growing into bosom companions through hardship and strife. Graylin could still remember a young prince thrust into training from his pampered rooms at Highmount, a waif with girlish blond curls. Though he was destined for the throne, the teachers offered the prince no special favor, as was tradition. The coda of the legion's school was a simple one: *It takes the hottest temper to forge the toughest steel.* And their teachers—all hardened soldiers—beat that into them on a daily basis.

To make matters worse, Toranth had been equally bullied by the other recruits. Graylin—a head taller and instilled by his parents in the Brauðlands with a strong sense of justice—shielded the prince, not to curry favor, but because it was right and fair. He also worked with Toranth to hone the young man's skills, to learn to defeat others older or larger than him. In the process, the two added a new caveat to the school's coda: *The toughest steel of all comes when two metals are folded into one.*

Their friendship grew to be unbreakable.

Even years later when Toranth assumed the throne, and life drew them in different directions, their love for one another continued, until finally Graylin bent a knee to the king and took over his personal guard, swearing undying fealty and loyalty.

So, years later, when Graylin brokered interest in learning the silent language of the pleasure serfs, the king invited him into his personal palacio. The king was not possessive of his serfs. He shared them freely, all except for one.

Marayn.

Graylin knew *why* when he first gazed upon her. She was a beauty unlike any of the others, a goddess carved of marble. Her hair was dark gold, as if spun by the Father Above. She was shapely of form and generous of bosom, but more than anything, she was quiet and calm, warm and inviting. Her eyes were so deep a blue that one could get lost in them forever.

Toranth trusted Graylin with Marayn due to their long friendship, reinforced by sworn oaths. Also, Graylin had recently been betrothed to a young woman from his family's town, a match that did not warm his heart but was well suited to all back home.

Over many moons, he met with Marayn and learned her unspoken language. It involved much touching: how to fold one's fingers, where to shift a hand, when to move from one gesture to another. The training involved plenty of laughter between the two, then quieter conversations spanning words and gestures. He slowly learned the inner lives of the serfs, what the women never shared, what they held close to their breasts, their fears, their despairs, their boredoms, and their hopes.

It broke his heart and challenged his sense of justice. More so, he read far more in Marayn's face than she ever expressed with her hands. He sought to help her and the others by leaning on his friendship with the king, but his efforts proved futile and fruitless, which only frustrated him more. He felt as if he were rolling a boulder up a hill that only grew steeper.

Still, Marayn had never held him at fault for his failings. Instead, one night she had drawn him to a silver cage where she kept a tiny lyrebird. It had chirped and sung sweetly, hopping across its perches, though she kept the door forever open.

She had signed to him. [*We all live in cages of some making.*] She smiled sadly. [*Knowing this, we must sing when we can.*]

Over time, something finally cracked inside him.

Without ever kissing her, he had fallen in love with her.

Eventually, neither of them could deny the truth silently held between them.

As he poled away now, he remembered their first night together. Fear had made him gentle, knowing how much she had been hurt in the past. He entered her slowly, allowing her to pull him deeper. Soon their passion grew to a fiery heat that could not be resisted or denied. She shook under him for the longest time afterward. Only once she let him go did he see how her pleasured trembling had become quiet sobbing.

She had explained her tears, how they were stirred forth by joy and sorrow. In all her life, she had never been taken with such love and tenderness before. Afterward, they enjoyed many nights together, locked in each other's arms, discovering more about each other than words could express—until eventually her belly swelled with a child. He did not know if the babe was his or the king's. But when Toranth ordered its expulsion, like so much shite from a chamber pot, Graylin knew what he had to do.

He had to break his oath.

He stared now at Marayn, standing forlorn at the swamp's edge, and he knew the truth in his heart.

I ruined us all.

GRAYLIN TREMBLED AS he held the curled scroll in his hand. He gazed down at it. *What did it contain? Was it hope for redemption or a cruelty that I will never survive?*

As much as it unmanned him, he had to know.

He broke the wax seal and unrolled the missive. The first words, written in a handsome script, tore open a wound long scarred close.

To Graylin sy Moor . . .

The honorific—*sy*—signified his status as a knight. Over a decade ago, it had been stripped and forbidden to him. Even among his many false names, he had never dared to use it. Those two letters were full of pain, both of body and heart. He wanted to toss the scroll into the hearth, but his fingers clenched.

I've come this far.

He read the rest of the message. It was brief, yet the implication so large he could not hold it all in his broken body. It was too poor a vessel.

Marayn's child lives, or so we have come to suspect.

Tears blurred his vision as he consumed the rest.

Get to Havensfayre between The Twins. Wait at the Golden Bough.
I will do my best to get her there or send word elsewise. Fetch her to the
Rime, hide her there.

It was not signed, but Graylin believed Symon concerning the missive's author. If Marayn's child had miraculously survived the swamps, it was possible that the babe had ended up at the Cloistery.

He lowered the scroll. "Could it be true?" he asked both himself and Symon.

The former alchymist—perhaps a member of the Razen Rose—grabbed the scroll and tossed it into the hearth's fire. "As I said before," Symon intoned, "a secret sold does not require a buyer's belief. It's a value unto itself."

Graylin stared into the flames as the missive curled to fiery ash.

"In the end," Symon continued, "all that truly matters is how *you* respond."

Graylin struggled, balanced on a sharp edge. He knew of Havensfayre, a town located between The Twins, a pair of lakes at the heart of Cloudreach. But he also knew what it meant to try to reach there.

"I broke an oath and swore a new one," he said, his voice hoarse with misery. "To never set foot in Hálendii again on penalty of my life."

Symon leaned over and lifted something hidden on the far side of the chair. It took both his arms to rest its wrapped length across his knees. "That is not *all* you swore. You also bled an oath never to touch steel again, to never carry a knight's weapon."

The alchymist folded back the cloth and revealed a scabbarded sword. He unsheathed its silvery length, shiny and bright. Inscribed upon it were twining vines heavy with grapes. The decoration celebrated Graylin's county in the Brauðlands, a roll of hills cooled by the shadow of Landfall's cliffs where his family's vast vineyards spread.

"Heartsthorn." Graylin took a step back, recognizing the blade. "I thought it had been melted to ruin."

Like my life.

"Only lost for a time," Symon corrected. "The Rose believes some artifacts are worth preserving, of being treasured away."

Symon returned the sword to its scabbard.

"My oaths . . ." Graylin whispered. "How many can I break and still be the same man?"

"As I see it, you forsook that first oath in the hope of saving Marayn's child. Thus, it holds precedence over those that came later. If you return, you are merely continuing that same violation, one you set aside for a time and for which you have already been punished." He shrugged. "The most honorable act from here is for you to see that first bit of treachery through to its proper end."

Graylin's head ached from Symon's twisted path to this conclusion, but his heart hurt far worse. Still, he knew what he had to do.

He crossed to Symon, grabbed the scabbard, and strapped Heartsthorn around his waist. He stood and tested the weight of its steel on his hip. It felt right, as if a severed limb had grown back.

Symon grinned at him. "Welcome back to the living, Graylin sy Moor."

28

GRAYLIN DROVE HIS small wagon swiftly through the woods. He followed a trail that was not even rutted, only an unmarked path twining through a forest of white-barked alders. Ahead, Symon rode atop a foul-tempered mare who kicked at Graylin's pony if it dared get too close.

Graylin suspected the mare's nervy disposition was in large part stoked by the pair of shadows sweeping the trail to either side. Aamon and Kalder easily paced the horses, even after hunting all day. But Symon had insisted that Graylin had one hope to barter for passage back to Hálendii, and it meant traveling throughout Eventoll to get there.

Despite Graylin's misgivings, he allowed Symon to guide him south of the town of Savik. They headed toward a breadth of coastline where few dared to venture. It was a broken scape of deep fjords packed with towering jagged rocks. Its waters were run through with dangerous shoals and unpredictable riptides. All along, sea caves pocked its cliffs, rumored to form a subterranean maze twice the size of Savik.

This swath of broken coast was home to various clans of pirates, cutthroats, and brigands of every ilk. They preyed upon the seas of the Crown, though most often on the pleasure crafts gliding from Hálendii to the terraced homes and palacios stacked along the cliffs of Lyria, north of Savik. It was where the kingdom's richest escaped the summer's scorch and sailed to the cooler climes of Aglerolarpok's coast, whiling away the hottest time of the year.

After a long stretch, with Graylin close to drowsing off, Symon finally lifted an arm ahead. He reined his mare and dropped back alongside the wagon. His horse nickered and huffed irritably at Graylin's pony, who merely swept his tail and smacked the mare's side.

Around them, the straight alders had been overtaken by darker pines and twisted cypresses. Graylin shifted higher. The seas salted the air now. Even past the rattle of wheels and clap of hooves, his ears picked out a distant rumble of heavy surf against broken rock.

Symon twisted in his saddle to face the wagon. "With care now," he warned. "Stay close. They're as liable to shove a spear in your gut as say g'morrow."

"And these are folks you believe we can trust?"

Symon frowned. "Of course not. But that scoundrel Darant will honor a pact, insomuch as the reward outweighs the price of a betrayal."

Graylin craned back to his wagon. It was loaded with bundles of hides and furs and enough salted, dried meat to feed a small village through winter. It was more than enough to barter for passage across the sea, but was it enough to keep his secret? He could not take any chances, so he had emptied his homestead of all its worth.

"Let's go," Symon said, urging his mount forward again.

As Graylin followed, he squinted at the woods. He spotted no lurkers, but he heeded Symon. He even whistled for Aamon and Kalder to draw closer. He didn't need to start a war before they even reached the coast.

A quarter league later, he realized they weren't approaching the coast. *We're already there.* A crack to his left suddenly billowed with salty spray and a great gust of air.

A blowhole.

He surveyed the terrain around him with a sharper eye. While the forest seemed to stretch flat ahead, the ground was split with dark cracks, echoing with churning water and steaming with mists. As they continued, those crevices merged into deep-cut channels, eventually building toward the fjords facing the sea.

Symon stopped, lifted in his stirrups, and searched a moment.

"Are you lost?" Graylin huffed at him.

"No," he answered, but he did not sound all that sure. "Better to be cautious than ride yourself straight off a cliff or down a watery hole. There's a reason no one has ever been able to root these hard folk out of even harder rock."

Worried by the alchymist's words, Graylin whistled again and signaled Aamon and Kalder to join the wagon. Two shadows slipped out of the woods behind them. The vargr panted, tails swishing, tufted ears cocked high.

Symon's mare whinnied in fear and bucked. Only a grab at the pommel kept the alchymist in his saddle. He swore and fought his mount to a nervous shifting of hooves.

Graylin's brothers stayed put, though Kalder lowered his muzzle and eyed the horse's dance. The pair were surely hungry.

Symon glared over at Graylin. "Warn me next time. Nearly pissed myself."

"What?" Graylin enjoyed his companion's irritation. "Did you not hear my whistle?"

Symon grumbled and twisted forward in his saddle. "This way."

They set off again, winding a path that only Symon seemed to know.

Or at least, *pretended* to know.

AFTER AN ENDLESS course that meandered one way, then the other, a low growl rose behind the wagon. Graylin stiffened in his seat. As if summoned by that rumble, a clutch of a dozen men in dark green cloaks appeared out of the woods, blocking the way ahead.

"Stay here," Symon ordered, and walked his mare forward to meet them.

Graylin could not hear what was said, but he noted an occasional branch crack to the right and left, indicating there were others hiding in these woods. Behind him, his brothers' ears swiveled, tracking the noises while not moving their heads. Furry hackles rose down their spines, as if testing the air for threat.

Ahead, Symon turned high in his saddle and waved him over. Graylin tapped the reins and got the wagon trundling to join the alchymist. The cloaked group faded back into the woods, except for a pair who led the way from here.

As they continued through the broken woods, Graylin caught peeks of the blue sea, ruffled by ridges of white. But they weren't traveling that far. The escorts took them to a wide crack, bordered by a precarious road descending along one side. Over its edge, black water gurgled and thrashed far below.

Symon showed no hesitation as he headed down. Graylin followed, easing his wagon onto that narrow path. Aamon and Kalder padded behind, drawing closer.

The road diverged from the crack and crossed into a damp tunnel lined by torches. The scent of the sea filled the passageway, stinging the nose with salt and a faint taint of tangleweed bloom. He pictured the choked seas a hundred leagues to the south. The thick mass of floating weed ran in a continuous wide swath from this coast over to the swamps of Mýr, creating a natural barrier against any swift invasion from the south, not unlike the broken shoals and atolls of the Shield Islands on the far side of Hálendii. Those natural barriers had protected the kingdom for ages on end, thwarting any unwanted encroachment.

Graylin hoped one tiny trespass would go unnoticed. He could still feel the scroll of parchment and crumble of wax in his fingers. The words written there blazed in his head.

I must not fail.

He knew he could never survive this second chance if it proved fruitless.

Finally, after a long winding descent, the way ahead brightened with blinding light. In short order, the tunnel emptied out onto a wide sandy beach that framed a silvery blue pool, open to the Eventoll sky. To the right, a languid river flowed away, coursing between towering walls toward the sea. On the left, a huge waterfall thundered into the water, casting up a mist that filled the scalloped valley. All around, the cliffs were damp, coated in dripping ferns and thick matts of emerald moss.

Graylin followed Symon and his escorts out onto the beach. Men and women bustled about. Crates were piled at the pool's edge. Along the cliff walls, overhung by a lip of rock, rose a ramshackle wooden village. It stacked haphazardly upward, traversed by ladders, wooden steps, swaying bridges, and rope pulleys. A merriment of drums, pipes, and strings carried from there, along with rough laughter, shouts, and barked orders. The place hung with smoke from scores of stone hearths and sizzling iron braziers.

He and Symon headed across the strand toward the pile of crates alongside the pool. As they passed, heads turned, barely showing any interest—then turned again, upon spotting the pair of vargr trailing the laden wagon. People froze. Children were tugged behind parents. A few of the bravest risked stepping closer; most retreated back warily.

A loud voice cut through the thunder and bustle. "Here with you!"

Graylin turned from the village to the high stack of crates and barrels. A tall figure swept through the men working there and strode forward to meet them. He wore a dark blue half-cloak that flagged behind him. It matched his tunic and breeches, which looked to be belted in eelskin, with calf-high boots of the same leather.

He wore a huge smile that Graylin did not trust.

No one is that happy.

Symon slid from his mare and gave the man a big hug and a slap on the back for good measure. "Well met, Darant."

The two spoke for a bit, catching up, speaking about the weather and rumors of war.

Graylin used the time to size up the stranger, who, according to Symon, led one of the rough clans that made this shattered coast their home. The brigand's hair, cut to the shoulder and loose, was so black that it appeared nearly blue, a close match to his clothing. His eyes were black diamonds, glinting from the salt-scoured hard planes of his face, which he kept clean-shaven.

Graylin tried to surmise his age. The pirate appeared to be a few years younger than him, but he could easily be a decade older. It was something about his eyes that seemed to age him. But Graylin paid particular attention to the two swords at his waist. The scabbards were too thin, tellingly so.

Whipswords.

Such Klashean blades were as thin as his finger at the hilt and stretched to a point so fine as to be nearly invisible. The steel was crafted by alchymists in some arcane method that made the swords nearly unbreakable, yet still flexible. In the hands of Klashean sword-dancers, they could transform from piercing steel to thrashing whips in a blink. Only the truest masters dared to wield two at the same time.

Graylin took this fact into account about the pirate.

Despite the ongoing banter, Graylin knew Darant was appraising him as well. His dark eyes flicked toward him, taking in much with each glance. The brigand's face was unreadable, a mask of merriment. The only break was when Aamon and Kalder hopped onto the wagon and set about sniffing the dried slabs of salted game. As Darant eyed them, something darker broke through his bright demeanor, then just as quickly it vanished.

Finally, Symon turned and pointed at Graylin. "This is the man who needs passage to Hálendii."

"To Havensfayre, you mean," Darant corrected. "While I might only be a seafaring man, I know that town is farther afield than the coast."

Graylin glanced sharply at Symon. *How does this brigand know my final destination?*

Symon ignored his expression. "True," he admitted to Darant, and handed the man a folded paper. "Here is a list of all the goods we have to barter. The load should easily fetch two gold marches and a fistful of silver eyries, more than enough for passage on your swiftest ship."

"My swiftest ship?" He cocked a brow at Symon. "She's already underway, mark my word. But I'll be the judge if this bill of sale suffices."

Graylin stewed as the brigand inspected the list. Darant eyed the wagon every now and then, as if making sure what was written matched what was loaded. Graylin had no fear of any discrepancies. He would not cheat the man.

With a final harrumph, Darant lowered the sheet and reached an assessment. "I also want the pony."

Graylin stiffened, glancing over the rump of his stout beast. He had bought the pony four winters back and could find no fault with the animal. The plan was for Symon to guide the pony and wagon over to Savik and stable the horse until Graylin could return.

If I return.

"Hold on," Symon said. "That's no slouch-backed nag. That's a pure Aglerolarpok in his prime. He's worth as much as what's in that wagon *and* the wagon itself."

Darant shrugged, crossed his arms, and waited.

Symon glanced toward Graylin, leaving the decision to him.

"Done," Graylin said.

"Mes wondres," Darant said in Klashean, and clapped his hands smartly and held his palms toward them, declaring the deal done.

Symon shook his head, and Graylin glanced toward the river flowing to the sea, anxious to be underway.

Darant cleared his throat. "Now to the *true* identity of my cargo. You're Graylin sy Moor, I believe."

Graylin whipped around so fast, his neck pinched with pain. He glared at Symon, but the alchymist looked equally shocked.

Darant merely smiled, his expression just as merry, but maybe a tad harder. "You are not the only one who trades in secrets, Symon. The clans also have eyes and ears across this coast. We collect secrets and keep them as preciously as jewels. It was not hard to discern who arrived under a false name. Especially with two vargr in tow and needing passage under such secrecy. Do not count me a fool."

Symon sagged.

Graylin's heart pounded, his face burned with fury. "What do you want for your silence?"

Darant shrugged. "Nothing you don't have plenty of. I'm sure you can spare one."

Graylin's fists tightened on his reins, knowing what the bastard would say next.

"I want one of your vargr," Darant confirmed. "I'll let you pick which one."

Never.

He glanced over his shoulder to his two brothers. The pair were as much a part of his heart as what beat in his chest. "Anything else but one of them," he said through gritted teeth.

"Fair enough," Darant said. "What else do you have to trade instead?"

Graylin shifted his palm to the sword lashed to the back of the wagon's seat. Heartsthorn had been in his family for countless generations. But it was just steel. Apparently, Darant thought so, too.

"I have no need for another blade," the pirate said. "And if you draw it, I will prove the two I carry are more than a match for your one."

Graylin withdrew his hand.

Symon stared up at him with pained, apologetic eyes. Graylin remembered the alchymist's earlier admonishment in dealing with this man: *Darant will honor a pact, insomuch as the reward outweighs the price of a betrayal.*

Graylin knew he needed the brigand's loyalty, no matter the cost.

He turned to his brothers in the wagon. Amber-gold eyes stared back at him. Though it tore his heart, he answered while never breaking their gaze. "Done," he said. "But I will choose which one, as you offered."

"So be it."

Graylin turned back to the pirate, binding the man to the only cause that was worth this price. "But only when I return. Until then, they remain mine."

Darant turned one eye toward him, then another, like a curious hawk. Then he gave a nod, clapped his hands, and bared his palms. "Done."

Graylin turned back to the river. "So where is this ship of yours?"

"It's already here," Darant said. "Just waiting for us all to come to a satisfactory conclusion."

Graylin faced around in time to see the blunt nose of a large ship push through the waterfall from behind. He now understood why Symon had shared Graylin's destination of Havensfayre, a town buried in the highlands of Cloudreach. The passage that Symon had booked for Graylin was not just to the *coast* of Hálendii.

Graylin gaped as the craft edged out of the cascade, parting through it, revealing the breadth of the balloon and the ship cabled below it. It was not one of the colossal wyndships that plied the skies with cargo and passengers, but a smaller attack craft—a swyftship—used by many armies of the Crown. It had special ballasts of obscure alchymies that when set aflame could drive the ship far faster, allowing it to defy the winds and maneuver deftly during battles.

Darant nudged Symon. "You said you needed a *swift* ship."

"You are a man of your word."

Graylin climbed down from the wagon, signaling Aamon and Kalder to his side. The two vargr watched the ship pass out of the falls, its balloon continuing to shed water that rained into the pool below. A spate of fire, nestled within paddles of draft-iron at the stern, burst forth, and the craft glided smoothly over to hang at the beach's edge.

Mooring lines were quickly secured. A gangplank pushed out from the portside of the ship and dropped to the sand. Crates, barrels, and casks were loaded.

Darant returned after overseeing his crew. He kept a few steps back from the two vargr. "We're ready to go."

Symon turned to Graylin and clasped his forearm. "May the gods bless your path, my friend."

"Where will you head from here?" Graylin asked.

"Ah, I have other matters that need attending. The Rose is a prickly master." He wet a finger and stuck it in the air. "Can you not feel that shift in the wind?"

Graylin frowned. The low winds blew ever eastward, the high streams ever westward. That never changed.

Symon lowered his arm with a grin. "Something tells me your actions are but the first move in a much larger game of Knights n' Knaves."

Graylin sighed, tired of the enigmatic man. *Maybe it's best from here that I deal with allies who are less cryptic.* He finished his good-byes and headed toward the gangplank. Aamon and Kalder trotted to either side, sticking close to his legs.

Only when he neared the beach's edge did he realize another followed. He turned to find Darant trailing him, hiking a pack higher on one shoulder.

Graylin stopped. "Are you coming with us?"

Darant grinned. "Aye, I plan on keeping an eye on my bounty." He waved to the two vargr. "Besides, the voyage will allow these fine brothers of yours to warm up to me."

Both Aamon and Kalder growled, baring fangs.

Darant appeared undaunted by the challenge and passed them both, but not without giving them a wide berth. "Let's get aboard and underway."

Graylin stared at the brigand's back.

So much for ridding myself of cryptic allies.

Arkival limne of the
Vargr (Rimewood)

NINE

THE PATH OF
THE FALLEN

*The towering cliffs of Landfall split the land of Hálen-
dii like a cruwel knyf, dropping the lands to one side &
lifting the other toward the godes. All to keep the highland forest virgine & pur, away from the corruption of
man. Onli 3 passes, all rife with cascades and brokyt with
treacherous steppes, offer passage to those blessedly wyld
lands. To the north, middle, and south. Beware of the
latter, for it is curs'd.*

—From *The Sylvan Dreme*, by Queen Praa ry Fai,
written one year before her assassination

29

TWO DAYS AFTER abandoning the winter barn, Nyx stood at the edge of her world. She stared off into the steam of the swamps and listened to its croaking, buzzing, and twittering birdsong. She inhaled its mossy, musky brume. She tasted its dark brine on her tongue. It was all she had known her entire life. She hugged her arms around her chest, trying to hold in the strength necessary to leave it.

She turned and craned up at the sheer white bluffs, which disappeared into gray mists far overhead. The cliffs of Landfall marked the eastern edge of the swamps. Directly behind her, a chasm cleaved the wall, carved through by a river that drained out of the highlands of Cloudreach. It descended in a rumble of silvery cascades and a roar of blue falls to finally flow leadenly, as if in defeat, in to the salty murk of the Mýr.

Frell and Prince Kanthe gathered at the silty wash to the left of the river, whispering about how best to ascend the Path of the Fallen. Jace waited a few steps back from her, allowing her a private moment to say good-bye.

But it wasn't just these drowned lands that Nyx would have to forsake.

She crossed the sandy beach and through stiff reeds to reach Gramble-buck. The old bullock stood fetlock-deep in the dark waters. He ripped out a sodden length of pickleweed, shook away the worst of the salty water, and slowly chewed and ground the leaves. He noted her approach with a heavy chuff and waded over to meet her. She had freed him from the sledge earlier and left him to graze at will.

As he reached her, he lowered his huge head, and she lifted her arms to take him in. She hugged her cheek to his forehead, feeling the rumble inside him as much as hearing it. More than anything, he was her home. It was Gramblebuck who had first heard her bawling in the swamp, who had dragged her dah over to the raft of fenweed where she lay. He was the one who had so often comforted her, who had suffered her complaints as they traveled the swamps together. He had been a constant in her life.

And now I must leave you.

She tipped on her toes, high enough to whisper in his ear, "I love you so much. But it's time for you to go home." She knew Gramblebuck could trek back on his own to the paddocks. "Find Bastan," she urged. "Or Ablen."

Even saying her brothers' names pained her, threatened to set her shoulders to shaking, to once again wrack sobs out of her. Over the past two days, grief had struck her at unexpected moments. Even when she thought herself wrung and emptied, she would see the bloom of her dah's favorite sea lavender or hear a loon's forlorn call, and tears would flood through her, near to drowning her.

She hugged tighter to Gramblebuck. One hand ran down his thick neck, reaching the thick ring of callus where the sledge's yoke had scarred him. She rubbed there, as if trying to erase that mark.

"Or don't go back to the paddocks," she offered to him. "Be free. Find your own heart's path. You've earned it."

She leaned back and stared into the milky age of his eyes. He nudged her as if to say, *My heart is here.* She silently answered with, *And mine is in yours.*

She pressed her forehead to his one last time and made him a solemn promise. "No matter where you go, I will find you again. This I swear."

Off in the distance, horns resounded across the swamp, echoing off the high cliffs behind her, persistent in their reminder that she could no longer stay.

Gramblebuck bent his neck to the strident blaring. It was also accompanied by the hunting howls of thylassaurs, likely brought over from Fiskur to aid the king's legion in tracking their group. Those blood-scenters could not be shaken from their trail, but at least the waters kept the curs from running their group down. Thankfully, those beasts—native to the deserts of Guld'guhl—were not good swimmers.

Still, that advantage would soon end.

She glanced back to the chasm, cut with ancient mossy steps that climbed alongside the river. They needed to put as much distance as possible from those others. Even now, she could pick out faint shouts carrying over the flat waters.

Jace called to her, "We can't wait any longer."

She understood. Gramblebuck seemed to, too. He had his rump to her now, huffing at the howls. He turned his ponderous head at her.

She waved to him. "Go now, off with you."

He still simply stared, looking ready to defend this beach, even if it meant being mauled by a pack of thylassaurs or peppered with arrows and spears. She knew he would do it if she asked it of him.

"Go," she said more emphatically.

Her command was reinforced by a sweep of wings through the air, accompanied by a high-pitched cry directed at the beast. Nyx's little brother harried the huge bullock, until Gramblebuck finally harrumphed, turned his head, and lumbered toward the dark bower of the swamp.

Nyx waited until the bullock vanished. Once he was gone, she felt as if an anchor had been cut loose. She could finally turn and cross back to Jace. She gathered her friend in her wake and headed over to Frell and Kanthe.

Jace dubiously eyed the endless climb of steps as they joined the two. "How long will it take us to reach the wild forests at the top?"

"All the day," Frell said. "At the very least."

"If we keep a good pace," Kanthe added, raising a brow toward Jace's girth.

Nyx scowled at the prince. Jace placed a protective hand on his belly, looking wounded, but Nyx gave her friend a reassuring touch on his elbow.

Kanthe shrugged and turned haughtily away.

She studied his back, trying to fathom if this prince could truly be her half-brother. She didn't want to believe it for many reasons. Frell noted her attention, his expression both apologetic and maybe guilty for shattering her past. After so many years, she had come to an uneasy peace, embittered though it may be, with the faceless father and mother who had left her in the swamps, abandoning her until a new mother, one with wings, rescued her.

Over the past two days, she had struggled to fit this new history into what she knew about herself. Alchymist Frell had explained his belief—one shared by Prioress Ghyle—that Nyx's history of abandonment in the swamp might tie to a story that ended in these same swamps, the tale of the Forsworn Knight, a cautionary fable of broken oaths and forbidden love.

Whether true or not, she suspected the alchymist had kept certain details from her. She caught Frell and the prince sometimes whispering to each other, sneaking glances at her, while she pretended to drowse in the back of the sledge. She overheard something about prophecies spoken by a dark Shrive, something tied to this same tale.

And maybe to me.

She followed the others toward their meager supplies at the base of the steps. Jace had already filled their waterskins from the freshwater flow of the river. The prince had managed to shoot a summer-fat duck and three marsh hares. She had showed him how to salt-pack his game by soaking gunny sacks full of meat in the swamp's brine and sun-drying them. By repeating this a few times, the hunter could ensure the salt coated and penetrated everything.

They gathered their packs and skins and readied for the climb. From the corner of her eye, she studied the prince, searching for any features she might have in common with him. She certainly lacked his ebonwood complexion and gray eyes. While both had dark hair, his was far blacker. Their noses were both thin, similarly tipped at the ends. But the same could be said of many.

She gave a shake of her head and turned her attention away.

Her tiny brother winged low over her head and flew up into the chasm,

as if urging them to follow. But the bat's true intent was plain as it rolled
and dived, catching the last of the swamp's buzzing hordes, which the river's
flowing mists held at bay.

Finally, another blare of horns pushed them all toward the chasm.

Frell led the way, climbing onto the first mossy step. "Take care," he
warned. "Any slip means death."

"Maybe that's why they call it the Path of the Fallen," Kanthe said sourly,
following behind the alchymist.

Jace waved her ahead, then continued behind her. "According to Plebian's
Annals of Lost Ages," he said sternly, "the pass was named long before our
histories were written. Possibly by those who carved these very steps. No one
really knows where the name came from. But what *has* been carried forward
out of the mists of time is how dangerous and treacherous this path can be.
Some believe it's cursed. Others that it's haunted or daemon-riven."

"It certainly looks like no one has trodden here in centuries," Kanthe admitted. "I see no crush to any of these moss flowers."

As they climbed, Nyx noted the tiny white blooms in the emerald, shiny
and pearled with mist droplets. She caught a hint of minty oils rising with
their treadfalls.

"I doubt the tales of spookens and curses are what kept people away,"
Frell said. "The other two passes to Cloudreach—near Azantiia and up in
the northern Brauðlands—are far more accessible and better groomed for
travel. You'd have to trek half the swamp to reach this pass, one overgrown
and crumbling with age. It's why I chose this nearly forgotten route to get us
to Havensfayre."

Reminded of their goal, Nyx raised a question that nagged. "Do you truly
think the knight, Graylin sy Moor, will meet us there?"

A man who may be my father . . .

"We must hope," the alchymist answered. "We need a strong ally—one
we trust absolutely—to get you out of Hálendii and somewhere safe. And
if Graylin doesn't show up, the misty forests of Cloudreach will offer some
refuge all on its own."

Nyx knew little of those highland woods. They were wild and untamed,
one of the rare stands of untouched ancient forests. Few made their home
there, only a handful of pale-skinned nomadic tribesmen, said to be as wild
and untamed as their woods. Even Havensfayre was less a town than a part
of the forest that had been carved into a trading post.

As they continued up the chasm, the way became steeper, sometimes requiring them to crawl on all fours to keep their perch. Exertion and concentration soon silenced them, while the roar of the falls, trapped between the

high chasm walls, grew deafening. Still, it was not loud enough to block out the occasional blare of hunting horns behind them.

Frell stopped ahead on the stairs.

Though anxious to keep going, Nyx gasped in relief, needing a break. A glance back showed Jace panting, his red face streaming with sweat and spray. His clothes were plastered to his body as if he had fallen into the river.

Kanthe swore ahead of them, drawing her attention forward.

Frell shifted, revealing his halt was not a mercy but a warning. Past the alchymist, a section of the steps had broken away long ago and tumbled into the churning cascade. Only mossy stubs were left sticking out of the wall. Frell glanced back to them with a forlorn expression.

"I can make it," Kanthe said, and tried to shift past Frell on the stair.

The alchymist blocked him with an arm. "It's too dangerous."

Kanthe waved back at a faint blast of horns. "Is it any less perilous than the Vyrllian assassins on our trail?" He pushed Frell's arm down and brushed past him. "I'll cross and rig a line."

The prince dropped his pack and fished out a coil of rope stripped from the sledge's rigging. He tossed an end to Frell, then crossed to the collapsed section of stairs. He paused at the brink. He rubbed a chin, clearly conspiring how best to traverse the span, likely anticipating his every move.

How can I get out of this? What was I thinking?

Faced with the task ahead, Kanthe realized the absurdity of his boast a breath ago. His heart pushed into his throat and pounded there, as if scolding him for his foolishness. Not only had most of the width of the narrow stairs broken away, but in the middle, two steps were completely gone. It looked like the gap-toothed leer of a villain mocking him for his false bravado.

"We can find another way," Frell whispered to him.

Kanthe firmed his grip on the rope. He felt all their eyes upon him, especially the girl who might be his sister. His face heated up. In the past, shame could never touch this Prince in the Cupboard. He had heaved his stomach empty in taverns or woken in beds fouled by his own piss and filth. Back then, he had simply wiped his mouth or arse and carried on, caring little what others thought. But over the course of this trek, somewhere along the way, something new had taken root inside him. Maybe it was being free of his brother's shadow, or away from the king's ridicule, or maybe it was simply the nobility of the others that had stirred what was inside him all along.

No matter, he refused to back away from the challenge. Whether it was newfound pride or some anger at his father for trying to murder him, Kanthe took a step to the edge. He turned his back to the wall, reached a boot to the first broken step, and tested his weight on the short stub of rock. Satisfied, he moved to the next, then another. Slowly he scooted his way until he reached the gap of missing steps. He closed his eyes and took a deep breath, knowing he would need to leap that open stretch to reach to the far stub.

I can do this.

He opened his eyes and glanced back to the others. They stared at him, unblinking, likely all holding their breath. The girl's blue eyes shone with a confidence he did not feel. She gave him the barest nod.

He sapped what courage he could from her and turned away with a swallow. He lifted a leg, bent the other, and hopped sideways across the gap toward the next stub. He landed one-footed, expecting it to give way, but it miraculously held—which could not be said of his balance.

He teetered away from the wall.

This is how I die . . .

Then a dark shape dove out of the mists and slammed into his chest. The bat bounced off of him and battered back with a frantic flap of wings. Whether it was the impact or simply his own startled terror, Kanthe tilted back to the wall and firmed his poise, bringing his other foot down.

He panted for three breaths on the lone stub, before hurriedly scaling the last of the broken steps to reach an intact landing. He dropped to his knees there and began shaking all over.

So much for a brave front.

Still, no one mocked him. Finally, he rolled to his rear, searched around, and found a small stunted tree rooted in cracks in the wall. He tested its hold, then wrapped his rope's end around the gnarled trunk. Frell took out the slack and did the same, but around a spar of rock jutting overhead.

With a hand bridge in place, Nyx scurried across next, so surefooted it didn't look like she even needed to run her hands along the rope. Kanthe caught her on the other side and drew her into a hug. She stiffened but didn't fight him.

"Thank you," he said.

She frowned, misunderstanding. "I wasn't the one guiding the bat, if that's what you think. He did that on his own."

He rubbed his chest, doubting if that was entirely true. Over the past two nights, he had noted how the creature, surely lice ridden and fraught with diseases, had nestled with the girl as she slept. He had heard it gently cooing and squeaking, which she seemed to imitate in her sleep, as if the two were knitting further together, binding one to the other. So, though she might not have willed the bat to his aid, maybe it was driven by her desire anyway.

Still, that was not the reason he thanked her. He remembered her small nod to him, the confidence shining in her eyes.

For me.

It was something he couldn't remember ever seeing in another's eye, certainly not directed at him. That look, more than anything, got him across that damnable gap.

She brushed past him and waved to her friend, the journeyman from school.

"You can do it, Jace! I know you can!"

There was that confidence again in another. He felt a stab of irritation. *Maybe she throws it around to everyone.* His face reddened, knowing his thought had been uncharitable and mean.

To make up for it, he called over to Jace. "It's not that difficult. Even my sister did it easily enough."

Nyx scowled at him, clearly assuming he was mocking both her and her friend.

Kanthe started to explain, then gave up.

It's got to be my tone. I have to work on that.

Still, the trepidation in Jace's face firmed to determination. Sometimes anger was better than courage. The journeyman grabbed hold of the rope and accepted the challenge. He was not as deft as Nyx, needing the rope to keep his balance, especially over the gap, but he managed to reach them.

Nyx hugged her friend.

Again, Kanthe felt that flicker of irritation.

Sard them both.

Frell soon joined their group and clapped Kanthe on the back. "Well done."

He accepted the praise sullenly. Frell shifted to the front and started off again. Kanthe lagged behind to shake the rope and loosen the loops around the spar of rock. He gathered the freed rope and continued after the others.

The bat sped through the mists alongside him for a breath.

He glowered at it. "If you're waiting for thank you, too, you can feck off."

As they climbed, the mists thickened, making the steps even more treacherous. It wasn't just due to the dampness alone. The mix of fog and spray watered a riotous garden. Thorny vines draped from walls or snaked underfoot. Flowering shrubs sprouted everywhere, both on steps and walls. The stunted trees of the lower chasm grew into giants here, with their roots kneeing everywhere, as if trying to push them off of the steps.

Their trespass disturbed scores of rooks nesting in burrows in the walls and a handful of hawks perched in the branches above. Furry weasels and other vermin scurried from their path. A few snakes hissed and spat. He even spotted a dwarf deer bound away, leap to a rock in the river, and vanish into a copse on the far side.

It appeared the forests grew even thicker as the stairs vanished into the mists ahead. Somewhere up there a leonine yowl warned them away. Kanthe pictured the distant forests of Cloudreach spilling down into the chasm as fiercely as the river roaring next to the stairs.

They finally reached a wide landing next to a waterfall. Frell lifted an arm and called for a stop. They all needed a rest before tackling the remainder of the forest-choked chasm. No one complained.

Jace looked like a drowned dog. He stood with his back to the climb, as if unable to face it. But that was not the reason. He pointed back the way they'd come. "Nyx, look."

They all turned.

Through the mists, the chasm walls framed the last glimpse of the swamps of Mýr. Nyx's expression turned desolate, and Kanthe wanted to shove Jace into the river for reminding the girl of all she was leaving behind, especially *who* she was leaving behind. He didn't know if he shared any of Nyx's blood, but he knew two men—Bastan and Ablen—who did not, yet they remained her truest brothers.

Them and one other.

The bat, as if sensing Nyx's distress, swept a circle over her head. Or maybe the creature was equally distraught. The view to the swamps centered on the dark mountain rising from the emerald expanse. The Fist wore a crown of steam and vents along its flanks shone crimson with the fires of Hadyss.

Even from this height, Kanthe could discern darker shadows plying the hot updrafts around its summit. Closer at hand, the tiny bat keened sharply, raising the hairs on his neck, as if calling to its brethren.

Frell shaded his eyes and stared up at the winged beast. "Apparently, Nyx, your friend intends to stay with us rather than returning to his flock."

She didn't respond, still gazing outward.

Kanthe tried to distract her from her misery. "If it's going to stick with us, maybe we should give it a name. Just so I can curse it properly."

Jace nodded, looking at Nyx with concern. "What do you think we should name it?"

She continued to ignore them.

Kanthe remembered the bat snapping at him when he had once tried to touch it. "As churlish as the bastard is, the name should be something that warns of its savage nature. Maybe *arse-wing.*"

Jace glared at him. "He's not just a *beast*. There is a grace to him, too. Something you clearly can't appreciate."

Kanthe rolled his eyes. "Let's see *you* try to pet it."

Still, he remembered Anskar expressing a similar sentiment about the beasts in general. *There be a noble savagery to their nature.* The reminder of the Vyrllian captain only soured him further. He tired quickly of this game already.

Frell did not. "I think you're both right. Savagery and grace are distinct sides to his character and comportment. Maybe a name tied to the Elder tongue, as their kind have been around long before our histories were written. In that dead language, *bash* means savage."

Jace brightened. "And if I recall, grace is *aliia*."

"That's right." Frell smiled. "I think it's a fitting name."

Jace tested it aloud. "Bash Aliia."

Nyx flinched away from her friend, her face horrified. "No . . ."

30

NYX HAD BARELY heeded the whispering behind her—then a name cut through her misery and stabbed her heart.

Bash Aliia . . .

She fell back into that nightmare atop a fiery mountain. War drums echoed in her head, along with a rising crescendo of screams. She again raced across the dark mountaintop, toward a winged shadow nailed to an altar. A name burst from her throat, ripping forth with a stone-shattering power, naming the tortured beast atop the rock.

Bashaliia!

"No . . ." she moaned to the others.

She had never shared that particular detail of her vision with Ghyle and Frell. It had seemed unimportant, especially as she had dismissed that mountaintop view as a fevered dream born of poison and terror.

Frell stared at her. "Nyx, what's wrong?"

She ignored him and turned to her tiny brother in the mists. In her vision, he had been as large as a full-grown bullock, with wings huge enough to lift such a beast into the air. Surely the two could not be the same.

But the name . . .

Jace misinterpreted her distress. "Nyx, I'm sorry. Of course, *you* should be the one to pick the name."

She continued to stare up at her winged brother and admitted what she knew to be true in her heart. "He is Bashaliia," she whispered, as much as it also terrified her.

As if catching wind of her distress, the bat winged through the mists, cartwheeling and whistling. Her vision frizzed at the edges. No images burned across her mind's eye, but her heart pounded, fired by his agitation, stoked by his cries.

Even Kanthe noted her brother's display. "What's wrong with him?"

The answer came from behind them, rising from the lower chasm. A sharp howl echoed off the rock walls, joined by others. They all froze.

"Thylassaurs," Frell said.

Kanthe turned back toward the swamps. He shaded his eyes, searching the chasm below, then pointed. "There."

Nyx shifted next to him. Movement caught her eye. Sunlight glinted off of armor as a long line of knights climbed the steps. The legion moved quickly, but not as swiftly as the dark shadows that raced ahead of them.

Jace drew nearer. "What about those broken steps? Do you think they can make it past there?"

Frell answered, "It may delay the king's men. They'll need to rig a rope ladder."

"But not the thylassaurs," Kanthe added. "I've seen them hunt. They'll leap that gap in a bound and be on us before long."

The howling continued, growing in volume and numbers.

The prince cocked an ear in their direction. "I'd say there's at least ten of the beasts, maybe a dozen."

Frell pointed up the steps. "Quickly then. We must reach Cloudreach before they close on us."

"Then what?" Jace asked.

"We'll figure that out later." Kanthe herded both Nyx and Jace after the alchymist. "Right now, we don't want to be caught on this narrow stair."

They all returned to the foliage-crowded steps and hurried upward. Every step was a battle. Thorns ripped at their clothes and tore skin. Roots and branches sought to block their way. It was as if the entire damp forest intended to trap them and keep them from ascending any farther.

And it wasn't just the riotous growth.

After fording a score of steps, the group approached a limestone arch that bridged the chasm overhead. Bashaliia sped to it and spun and cartwheeled under its span. He dove and winged in a clear sigil of panic.

"Wait!" Nyx called out.

Everyone turned to her.

She pointed to Bashaliia. "He's trying to warn us."

Howls rebounded all around them, filling the air.

"I don't think we need your brother to deliver that message." Kanthe waved back down the path.

"No. It's not the thylassaurs." Nyx pushed forward and grabbed Frell's arm. "It's *never* been the thylassaurs. Bashaliia does not want us to continue past that arch. It's what he's been trying to warn us all along. He senses something higher in the pass."

Jace crowded with them. "What?"

Nyx shook her head. She didn't know the answer, but she was certain of one thing. "It's worse than the thylassaurs."

She got support from an unexpected source. "I think that little bastard might be right after all," the prince said.

KANTHE STOOD AT the edge of their small landing. He drew the others' attention to a deep blue pool in the river far below. A chattering cascade flowed into it from one side and a misty waterfall raged out the other. Between the two, the pool was shimmering glass, clear enough to reveal its bottom. Smooth river rock lined its surface—but that was not all that the current had polished.

Bones formed cadaverous mounds in the crystalline depths. Skulls of every size were heaped below, from giants with broken horns to tinier domes with pointed beaks. Leg bones crisscrossed throughout, some ending in yellowed claws or bleached hooves. Hundreds of shattered ribcages lay tangled together like woodland deadfalls, home now to scuttling crabs and a few silvery fishes.

Worst of all were the hollow-eyed skulls of dead men, some still wearing bright helms. A hundred swords stuck out of those piles, a few clutched in skeletal hands.

Kanthe turned to the others. "I think we now know why this pass was named Path of the *Fallen*."

They all turned to the archway and the frantic bat's efforts to ward them away.

"What's up there?" Jace asked.

All around, the howls of the thylassaurs turned to savage wails, close enough to hear the hunger in those hunting cries.

"We don't know," Kanthe said, "but we *do* know what's back there."

"We keep going," Frell decided. "We have no choice. Maybe those bones are centuries old."

No one objected as the thylassaurs' fury grew. It was death to remain on the stairs with that savage pack approaching.

As they headed toward the arch, Kanthe was not fooled by his mentor's words. He eyed the bat dancing in the air above and took heed of that warning. He slipped his bow into his hand and drew an arrow to his fingers. Still, he felt no conviction his preparation would help. He pictured all those silvery swords in dead men's hands.

Weapons certainly hadn't helped them.

They crossed warily under the archway, all holding their breath. But the steps beyond the span looked no different than the ones behind them. The forest filled the breadth of the chasm ahead. They fought their way higher, step by step, landing by landing. Still no threat revealed itself.

Maybe Frell was right . . .

Nyx was the first to notice the change. "The birds are gone," she whispered.

Kanthe stopped. He cocked both eye and ear, searching and listening to the tangles of forest. No hawks screamed down at them. There was no chatter from the rookery burrows. He realized it had also been a while since he had spotted any vermin or had to dodge the fangs of a striking serpent.

Frell waved for them to keep going.

As Kanthe continued, he searched for any sign of life that wasn't green and thorny. He eyed the walls, noting the nesting burrows high up the cliffs, but they all appeared empty and deserted.

Where did they all—

Movement from one of those holes caught his eye. Something fell out and rolled down the cliff face. It vanished into the undergrowth.

He stopped, letting the others pass. He squinted at the other holes, but he failed to spot any other such occurrence. He began to turn away, ready to dismiss it as a displaced rock, when another gray-black ball popped out of another old rookery nest and bounced and rattled down the wall.

Then another.

And another.

He tried to fathom this mystery, until a cry burst ahead of him. He barged through the leafy brush to join the others. On the next landing, Nyx stood with a hand over her mouth. Jace drew her back a step, while Frell leaned forward.

Something sprawled across the rock ahead.

Kanthe pushed forward to see.

Nyx mumbled, "Poor thing . . ."

Kanthe joined Frell. The body of a dwarf deer lay stretched on its side across the landing. Its legs stuck out stiffly in death. Its glassy eyes stared at them. Its belly was distended with bloat.

"What killed it?" Jace asked.

With the eye of a hunter, Kanthe looked for any wound, for a spot of blood.

Frell's next words sent a shiver through Kanthe. "It's not dead."

"What?" Nyx backed another step, sounding as horrified as Kanthe felt.

But Frell was right. As Kanthe stared, the deer's eye shifted toward the alchemist as he spoke. From its nostrils, a tiny pained breath escaped, so weak it didn't appear to move its chest.

Kanthe cringed in pity at its state.

It's alive but unable to move.

With the macabre interest of an alchymist, Frell bent a knee closer. He mumbled, "Are those black thorns in its neck?"

Kanthe had no interest in answering that riddle. He swallowed hard and shifted his gaze away—but where his eyes ended up settling was far worse. The deer's bloated stomach had begun to ripple, like a stew at a slow boil.

"Frell . . ." Kanthe warned, and pointed.

The alchymist grabbed his shoulder and drew them all away. "Stand back."

The churning of the deer's belly grew intense. A plaintive bleat escaped the beast's throat. Then its stomach burst in a wash of blood, releasing a squirming mass of white worms, each as large as his smallest finger. They roiled and rolled across the landing, swimming through the bile and blood.

The group fled backward with gasps and cries of shock. But the blind worms ignored them, writhing off into the leafy brush, shying from brighter patches on the rock.

"What are they?" Nyx asked.

Frell looked at her, his face ashen with knowledge. But before he could answer, a clattering rose from all directions. It sounded like hail striking a slate roof.

Kanthe remembered the strange sight a moment ago. He straightened and turned to a break in the forest. It offered a glimpse to the cliffs to either side. From the old rookery nests, armored balls, each the size of his fist, surged from those holes and rattled down the rock. Hundreds of them. From ahead and behind. Even from the cliffs on the far side of the river.

The clattering rose into a hailstorm.

As he stared, one of the spheres bounced off a wall toward them. It unfolded its armored segments, flaring black spines along its back and spreading fluttering translucent wings. It flew through the air with a menacing buzz.

What in Hadyss's fiery prick is that?

Frell answered his silent question.

It sounded like a curse.

"Skriitch . . ."

NYX SEARCHED THE misty forests in horror. The dry-bone clattering around them transformed into the rising drone of wings. The noise spread all around like a brushfire through dry sedge. With her heart hammering, she readied to run, but Frell caught her eye and shook his head.

The alchymist grabbed Kanthe and drew the prince low. "No one move," he warned in low tones.

Jace snatched Nyx and pulled her down. He dropped his voice to a whisper, directed at Frell. "Skriitch. I thought they died out centuries ago."

"What is inscribed in ink is often written more with hope than certainty." Frell faced them as they hunkered. He spoke rapidly to share what he knew, knowledge they needed to survive. "Skriitch are an ancient scourge. They're paralytic with their stings, flesh-eaters who nest in the living to feed their young. They hunt blind, drawn by loud noises and the smell of a prey's breath."

Nyx stared over at the ruins of the tiny deer. It was mercifully dead, gutted and bled by the horde of voracious maggots. Most of the worms had squirmed into the shadows, but a handful still delved the torn cavity or writhed in the blood. The stench on the landing was not the clean smell of a fresh kill, but the malignant reek of corruption and putrefaction.

Frell pointed past the carcass. "Up. It's still our only hope. But we must move with care. Shield our breaths." He demonstrated by using the loose cuff of his sleeve to cover mouth and nose. His voice was muffled. "Pray their queen remains in slumber."

With those cryptic words, he led the way forward.

Jace stopped them at the remains of the deer. "Wait," he whispered through the edge of his cloak. "I once copied a moldering edition of Haasin's *Primordia Biologicum*. From four centuries ago. It spoke of the skriitch. And a possible warding. According to Haasin, the grubs infuse some scent into their kills, marking their fleshy nests. Maybe to keep other skriitch from skewering more eggs into already occupied flesh."

Frell looked at Jace with sharper eyes, plainly seeing her friend in a new light. Nyx remembered her conversation with Jace, back when she had tried on her Ascension robe, which seemed like a lifetime ago. She had told Jace that his education in the scriptorium was unique and important in its own right.

"How does that knowledge help us?" Kanthe asked, staring all around.

Jace knelt and dragged his cloak through the pool of blood and bile. "Daubing such signaling scent on our bodies could further discourage their attention, make them think we're already afflicted."

Kanthe nodded at this suggestion. "Why not? I've certainly smelled worse in the past."

They all quickly soaked and coated the gore on cloaks, robes, breeches, and smeared the same on their cheeks. Nyx fought to hold her stomach down at the stench. Kanthe reached toward her with a befouled hand. She flinched away, but he plucked a fat worm from her shoulder, near to crawling into her hair. She frantically searched the rest of her body for any others but found none.

Once they were all finished, Frell glanced around at the horde buzzing throughout the forest. "I think the only reason we've not already been assaulted is the reek of this corpse. We'll have to pray that sickly miasma carries with us long enough to cross out of their territory. Let's go."

They set off again through the forest as the mists thickened. The canopy of the trees vanished above them. The drone of the skriitch haunted their path. Leaves stirred with their winged passage. The mists shivered. They crept upward, step by hard-earned step.

The skriitch continued to ignore them. After a time, with her arm over her mouth and nose, Nyx spotted several of the creatures roosting in shrubs, their weight bobbing the tiny branches. More clung to gnarled trunks, nearly blending into the bark. It seemed the horde was growing exhausted.

Then something struck her upper arm.

She winced and twisted her shoulder to look. A skriitch had landed there. She froze and stared. Eight pairs of jointed legs clasped to her sleeve. Its body was broken into the same number of armored segments, while the two centermost were hinged open, bursting forth with two wings on each side, an upper and lower wing, threaded through by tiny veins. Its foremost sections reared up on her sleeve, waving fringed antennae, testing the air. It also exposed a gnashing of four mandibles. As it perched there, it breathed heavily, the segments expanding and contracting. Each breath also lifted and lowered a ridge of black spines.

She pictured those same spikes impaled in the throat of the dwarf deer.

The skriitch lowered back down and crawled up her arm. It traipsed through the bloody gore on her shoulder. It dabbled there as she held her breath—then finally leaped away and flew off.

She shivered, both in terror and relief. She found the others staring back at her, but she waved them on. Sweat soon coated all their faces, threatening to wash the smears off their cheeks. They continued in silence, doing their best to avoid the buzzing horde that continued to settle all about the forest. Still more droned and hunted the mists and foliage.

With his gaze above, Jace's boot snapped a dry branch underfoot. He ducked as a pair of skriitch immediately sped at him from the canopy. They passed over the crown of his head, then circled blindly back, clearly searching for the source of the noise. He clamped his cloak harder over his mouth. The pair circled twice more, then finally whizzed away.

Frell lifted his brows at Jace, silently warning him to be wary.

On they went.

No one knew how far the skriitch's territory extended, but Nyx imagined there had to be a limit. The horde had not spread and infested the lower chasm over the centuries. It was as if something was bottling them up here. Maybe it was the thicker mists; maybe it was some scent in the air, like what wafted from their fouled clothes.

Frell stopped ahead, his shoulders slumping.

They gathered to him and saw the reason for his halt. The river cut across their path. The steps upward continued on the far side.

"We'll have to swim," Frell whispered dourly.

They all knew the danger was not the river's current. This stretch of the chasm was relatively flat, so the stream looked sluggish and manageable. But the forest on the other side buzzed with more of the skriitch. The cliffs ahead were pocked with hundreds of their warrens, along with larger caves. If they swam across, the gore would be washed from their clothes and bodies, leaving them exposed and defenseless.

"We have to risk it," Frell said.

No one argued.

One after the other, they slipped into the cold stream. They tried not to splash and draw attention. Nyx stayed alongside Jace. Kanthe trailed, clutching his bow in one hand and kicking low with his legs. Their eyes remained on the sky, on the air above them. Skriitch buzzed past their heads. A few even crashed atop the water, roiling and fluttering, only to be swept past them.

Finally, they reached the far bank. Frell discovered steps under the water that led out of the river. He crouched there. "We must move quickly. Pray we're close to the end of their domain. If stung, keep running for as long as you can. Be ready to help each other if someone falters."

Nyx swallowed and nodded.

Frell turned back to the steps—but Kanthe grabbed his arm.

"Stay," the prince warned.

Frell frowned. "I know it's danger—"

"No." Kanthe turned to the other side of the river. "Listen."

With her heart pounding and the terror in the air, she had gone deaf to the echoing howl of the hunting thylassaurs. The pack wailed and screamed, likely scenting how close their prey was.

Kanthe faced them, his eyes huge. "Wait," was all he said.

The triumphant cries of the hunters grew louder, more excited, echoing everywhere. But Nyx and the others weren't the only ones listening. Skriitch streaked past overhead, all racing toward the howling pack, ready to paralyze the trespassers, each vying to be the first to lay its clutch of eggs into these new warm nests. The skies above the river briefly thickened with their forms as the horde swept down the chasm.

Nyx lowered warily in the water as she watched them pass. Finally, the river cleared of their buzzing wings, until only a few leaden skriitch traced the mists. These last wobbled, a few falling into the current, clearly too old or enfeebled to offer much threat.

"Now," Kanthe said.

They climbed out of the stream, their clothes heavy and shedding water with each step.

Kanthe glanced across the river. "I've never been happier to be hunted."

"We still must hurry," Frell warned. "And heed what I said before."

They took off, not bothering to remain silent any longer. The baying cries of the thylassaurs covered the occasional snapped branch or tumble of loose rock. As they fled upward, those victorious howls transformed into pained, terrified wails and yelps. Nyx pictured the slinky beasts coated in clinging skriitch, being stung and bit, impaled and seeded. Pity for them flickered through her, especially remembering the tortured state of the tiny deer.

No creature deserved such a cruel end.

Half focused behind her, she ran square into Frell, who had skidded to a stop ahead. She bounced off of him, only to be pushed even farther back.

She spotted the reason for his sudden retreat.

Ahead, the woods broke open to expose a section of chasm wall and the mouth of a large cave. The forest looked as if it had been tunneled through to that spot, the branches coated in mats of silvery webbing.

From the cave, the source stalked into view on long jointed legs. It was the size of an ox, only with armored plates across its back. It dragged a long bulbous abdomen behind it. Segmented antennae swung through the air toward them. Each stalk ended in eyes that looked like faceted black diamonds.

As the creature raised its front carapace higher, a triangular head gnashed the air with sharp mandibles. It crawled to the stair and blocked their way.

Frell moaned as he backed them all away. "It's a skriitch queen."

31

KANTHE LET THE others retreat behind him. He knew there was only one path open to them, one way to go.

Straight through that fecking monster.

He dropped to a knee, bow held out, and fitted an arrow to the string. He fought down the horror of the sight before him. Half spider, half wasp, it looked like some creature cobbled together and dredged from the depths of an Iflelen crypt, or maybe a daemon conjured by their dread god, Ðreyk. It hissed at their group, while some noxious gas escaped from puckering pores along its oily flanks. He didn't know if that pall was poisonous, but it smelled of the rotted bowels of a sun-bloated corpse.

It trundled toward their group, stabbing rock with its skeletal legs, the backs of which were lined with rows of sharp chitinous hooks.

Kanthe held his ground. He pulled the string to his cheek, the arrow's fletching tickling his ear. He cast his gaze toward its dark triangular head, half-hidden by the edge of its crowning segment, and loosed the string. The bow sprang, and the arrow flew. As if anticipating the shot, the queen tipped the edge of its crown, and the bolt's steel point glanced off the armor shell.

But Kanthe was no inexperienced hunter. He remembered a lesson from the Cloudreach scout who had served as his first teacher: *Often it's not your first shot that kills, but the one already in the air after it.* He had been taught to never count on the first arrow, to never stop to savor his marksmanship. Once an arrow was loose, it was best forgotten.

As the bolt *tinged* off the carapace, he already had another arrow nocked and pulled. He let it loose, so when the queen lifted its crown, the next bolt was there and struck it square in the center of its head. Still, he didn't stop to relish that strike—especially as the creature screamed and charged.

He kept his post as another arrow flew and another.

All striking true.

Still, it came at him.

He leaned his cheek, fixed the point, and thrummed the string.

The next bolt swept through its jaws and struck into its dark gullet. Mandibles snapped the haft in two, but a second arrow followed the first.

Have another taste.

The queen's charge faltered, its legs wobbling like a mummer's stilts on cobbles.

He continued to unleash his fury, peppering its head, a few aimed at its exposed chest, searching for its blasted heart, if it had one.

Finally, the beast crashed to the steps, skidding toward him.

Only then did he push off his knee and retreat. Still, he reached over his shoulder for another arrow, but he felt no feathers. He had emptied his quiver. He yanked out a dagger instead, ready in case it showed any sign of life.

Thankfully, the mountainous bulk remained unmoving. Even in death, noxious gas steamed from its bulbous abdomen, forming a cloud around it.

Kanthe fled from it.

Frell joined him, drawing the others. Kanthe expected praise and cheers, but all he got was a worried look from his mentor. The other two stared back across the river. From the mists, the low drone of the skriitch had risen to a furious whine. Focused on the kill, he had failed to notice the change in the horde's timbre.

"They're coming," Jace said.

Whether drawn by the scent of their queen or its earlier hissing screams, the skriitch plainly intended to avenge their fallen ruler.

"Run," Frell said. "And keep running."

The group sped away from the river, giving the steaming hulk a wide berth, and continued up the ancient steps. Kanthe led—so he was the first to see their mistaken assumption.

Ahead, another four or five webbed tunnels branched off the foggy stairs. Large dark shadows clambered into view.

Kanthe glared back at Frell, scolding his friend for not knowing the truth, an ignorance that would kill them all.

The skriitch didn't just have *one* queen.

They had many.

NYX GAPED AT the dark shapes piling onto the stairs ahead of them. Behind her, the furious droning of the horde rose toward a dreadful crescendo, shivering the mists with their approach. She felt that buzzing on her skin, in her bones. She shook her head as the noise became a hornet's nest in her skull.

Only then did she realize it wasn't the skriitch who plagued her so, but something more familiar. Her ears sharpened on a keening that sliced through the feverish whirring of the skriitch.

She looked up as a winged shape dove through the branches and sped past overhead, then shot skyward, as if trying to draw her up and away—and succeeded.

She still felt the rock under her boots, but she also flew skyward. Images lapped over one another. She still saw the forest around her, but she also watched the chasm open up under her as she skated high above. Even the mists failed to challenge her new sight. Her acuity stretched the breadth of the chasm, carried by the keening, which sharpened every nook, branch, leaf, and cranny. She saw the skriitch sweeping over the river. With focus, she could pick out individuals among the many.

She remembered a similar moment like this, during her frantic flight away from Byrd and his cohorts at the Cloistery. She recalled how for a brief time the ringing of the school's bells had somehow revealed a gauzy map of her surroundings. She had used that sight to flee more surefootedly across the revealed tier.

Now she suspected the truth.

Maybe it wasn't the bells.

Had Bashaliia already been there? Had he been the one who summoned the larger bat who killed Byrd?

But she had no time to dwell on this.

Through her real eyes below, she saw the dark queens stalking toward her and the others. Panic pounded her heart, pulling her out of the mists, down to her body. But she never made it. The keening grew sharper in the air, erasing the view of the steps, drawing her back up. She fought it.

I must help them.

She was ignored. Instead, her gaze was forced toward the swamps. She felt power in the air, like before a thunderstorm. Its strength gathered and coalesced around the fiery mountain of The Fist, shadowing the swamps around it. Then it surged toward the chasm, flooding up its length, sweeping faster and faster toward her.

Through her other eyes, she saw Frell pulling them all back down the steps. She heard him say something about a cave, a place to flee the approaching horde.

She knew that would not work.

Viewed from on high, she watched the black wave thundering toward her. Out of the depths of that darkness, a pair of eyes shone back at her. She quailed from that gaze, sensing its immensity, its unfathomable nature, its abiding agelessness.

She wanted to flee from it.

But something whistled and pinged in her ear, the tiniest spark of that vastness, something tangible and comprehensible. *Bashaliia.* She fell back to the taste of warm milk, of another sharing her warmth. Here was something she could grasp, maybe even love.

She clutched to it as the storm fell upon her. She was cast about like a twig in a flood. The current spun her out of the sky and back into her own body. Even then, power continued to pour into her, flowing through Bashaliia in the sky and down to her.

She gasped as her body burned with those energies. It filled every bone, every vein, every organ. She sensed those ancient eyes staring at her from afar, coldly judging what she would do. And still the power flooded into her, until it could no longer be contained.

She had to let it out.

On the steps, she grabbed her skull with both hands and screamed, casting out that force. It burst forth in all directions, stripping the world of its secrets. Nothing could be kept from her sight now. In a blink, she saw every vein of leaf, every weevil that burrowed in bark, every tendril of fungus in soil. The others around her became bones, beating hearts, rushing blood.

But what erupted from her was not only amplified sight. Her scream resonated with all the force of Bashaliia's brethren, forged into something far greater.

She remembered her nightmare atop the mountain, when that same force had broken stone. She had no such control now.

As the wild wave surged out of her, she was lifted to her toes, maybe even off the stone. Its force blasted away the mists and buffeted the encroaching horde back down the chasm. Her companions tumbled to either side, blown into the shrub and trees.

The nearest queen crumpled on the stair, like a spider burned by a hot ember. The other dark shapes fled as leaves were ripped and branches broken, battering after them. Her new eyes watched the creatures' rows of tiny hearts squeezing in terror as they abandoned the stairs, seeking the refuge of shadow and rock.

Then it was over.

The strange force emptied out of her, and her heels settled back to the stone. But she had no strength. Her legs could not hold her. Her sharp vision collapsed to shadows, to patches of brightness and darkness, as if she had returned to her beclouded self. Weak, she toppled toward the hard stone, but arms caught her.

"I got you," Jace said out of the murk.

Then another arm scooped her and lifted her higher. "We can't wait," Kanthe warned.

Frell confirmed this. "The queens could return once their initial fright subsides."

Nyx felt herself carried between the two. Jace on one side, Kanthe on the other. She did not fight them or pretend strength she didn't possess. She was hauled up the steps, her toes bumping along behind her. She passed out for a stretch, only to be stirred awake again, confused and panicked.

But Jace reassured her.

It also helped that her vision slowly returned. First, the depth of green forest, then details of leaf and branch. Her strength took longer to restore. Her head lolled between the two young men.

Finally, Frell drew them to a stop. "I think we made it. We should be able to rest for a moment."

Jace helped her over to a fallen log. She struggled with her legs but managed the last few steps on her own. She gratefully collapsed to the makeshift seat. She gazed dully around her at giant trees that vanished into the low clouds. She spotted no sign of cliffs or rocky walls. She realized that Frell must have run them far into the woods beyond the chasm before risking a halt.

Thank the Mother . . .

Kanthe stared around, too. "We made it to Cloudreach. All my life, I've wanted to get my arse up here." He shrugged. "'Course, maybe not like this."

"We can't rest long," Frell warned. "We still have two or three days of trekking to reach Havensfayre. And these woods can be just as dangerous."

Jace stared back the way they'd come. "What about the others? Surely the king's legion isn't going to be able to breach that chasm." He glanced at Nyx, his face pale and nervous. "At least not like we did."

Kanthe answered, "That may be true. But I know the head of the Vyrllian Guard. Anskar has surely dispatched a skrycrow to Highmount. Knowing the path we took means he knows where we're headed, and it wouldn't take much to guess we might strike for Havensfayre."

A sullen silence followed.

She caught the others eyeing her.

Frell began to ask her something, even stepping forward, but Kanthe drew him back with a stern look.

"Later," the prince urged.

Frell nodded.

She knew they all wanted to inquire about what had happened back there, but they also recognized her exhaustion. *Not that waiting would matter.* She wasn't sure she had any answers to give them.

She craned her neck and searched the cloudy treetops.

Jace noted her attention. "We've not seen any sign of your brother. Not since when . . ." His voice trailed off.

"Bashaliia," she whispered.

As if summoned by his name, a winged shape circled out of the mists overhead and descended toward her. He dropped silently, with no keening or piping.

He must be as exhausted as I am.

Then her brother tipped sideways, fluttered weakly, and toppled toward the ground.

Nyx lunged to her feet and stumbled forward. Kanthe crossed from the other direction. Together, they caught Bashaliia in their arms, careful of his wings, and cradled him to the ground.

She knelt down, her heart at her throat. Bashaliia lay on his back, his chest barely moving, his neck stretched and twisted to the side.

Frell and Jace hurried to them.

"What happened to him?" Jace asked.

Kanthe turned Bashaliia's head. "The poor bastard never had the protection of that stinking bile like we did. Still, he stayed with us. And suffered for it."

The prince exposed the row of black spines impaled in her brother's neck. Frell thumbed a bloody patch of fur, revealing a jagged stinger.

Kanthe looked up at Nyx. "I'm sorry."

Arkival limne of the
Skriitch
(Path of the Fallen)

TEN

TACKING INTO
THE WIND

Do not fear beyng wronge. But do fear beyng righteous.
—An admonition found in
A Boy's Gentle Book of Wysdoms

32

Dressed again in a Klashean *byor-ga* to hide his face and form, Rhaif strode down the central passageway of the wyndship. He carried an empty woven basket and headed toward the ship's cold kitchen to collect their cabin's midday repast. As with all their meals, it was usually hard cheese, harder bread, and a small bottle of wine to wash it all down.

But Rhaif's trip to the kitchen now was less about filling his belly than about gathering information.

He and his two companions—the chaaen-bound Pratik and the bronze woman Shiya—had been aboard the wyndship for two days, a craft dubbed *The Soaring Pony*. Then this morning, word had been tacked to their door, announcing a change to the ship's route. Originally, the *Pony* had been slated to travel directly to Trader's Ferry, a sprawling city at the center of the vast grassy plains of Aglerolarpok. It was a wild, lawless place and offered Rhaif plenty of directions and methods in which to vanish, to maybe even start a new life.

Only now the ship was scheduled to stop in Azantiia in another two bells. *Why?*

That's what drove him out of his cabin, leaving Pratik with Shiya. The change plagued and worried Rhaif, especially as the brief message had not stated how long they would tarry in Azantiia. His entire gambit in escaping Anvil depended on no delays.

He pictured Shrive Wryth sifting through the ashes of the downed Klashean ship and the man's fury when he discovered the wreckage held no bronze statue. Wryth would surely send a flock of skrycrows in every direction, paying particular attention to the two ships that had left that same eve from Anvil.

Rhaif could not risk one of those crows winging ahead of the *Pony* and spreading word of a possible thief aboard, along with a bronze treasure like no other. He also worried about the timing of this change. Was it just bad luck—a state he was well familiar with—or something more nefarious?

He hurried down the ship-long corridor toward the stern. He wasn't going that far. The common room, which included the cold larder and kitchen, was at midship, basically a widening of this same passageway. He reached the swinging door and shoved into the larger space. His nose was immediately assaulted with the smell of sweaty bodies and musky cheeses—though it was not clear which was which.

Ahead of him, the commons was broken into two halves. To the right were the shelves and cupboards of the ship's larder, fronted by a long bar where a servitor in sky-blue livery stood alongside a sullen-eyed scribe who tallied each passenger's allotted fare. Of course, for an extra silver eyrie or two, indulgences could be bought: dried fruits, cold sweet-curdles, salted meats. There was even a small oven of draft-iron heated with coals to warm bread or cheese, but that cost an extra ha'eyrie. Rhaif, with his purse nearly empty after booking a cabin fit for an *imri* trader, could not waste his last coins on such meager luxuries.

Even with his head covered in the leather helm and silk drape of his *byor-ga* habiliment, he kept his face down as he entered. As he crossed toward the larder bench, he surreptitiously searched the room.

To his left, the other half of the commons was a mirror to the first. Only the bar on that side protected shelves that held dusty bottles strapped in place, along with a row of casks and barrels along the floor. The crone of an alewife stood there, doling out drabs of spiced spirits, tankards of heartier beers, and flagons of fruity wines. She even offered an assortment of pipe leaf, which could only be partaken in the commons, where every flame was guarded over by a wary watchman. No one resented such beady-eyed attentiveness. All knew the danger floating above their heads.

As Rhaif crossed the room, he attended to the other passengers here, a dozen or so, mostly bowlegged Guld'guhlians, but also a few leather-faced, lanky Aglerolarpoks. The latter had patches cut out of their upper sleeves, baring the seared brands of their various ranches. Faces swung his way. Of the hundred or so riding this gasbag to the far west, his party was one of only a handful of Klasheans—at least, as best as Rhaif had been able to discern so far.

Eyes narrowed upon him as he crossed the room, varying from wariness to outright hostility. Over the past two days, Rhaif had usually sent Pratik to collect their meals. It was a necessity to maintain their cover. The Chaaen—posing as a member of the *imri* caste and fluent in Klashean—could engage in conversation if any of his people should attempt to speak to him. Rhaif, on the other hand, only knew a few words of their lilting tongue. Though, in the end, it proved a needless precaution. None of the other Klasheans on board ever approached Pratik.

The reason behind that segregation was obvious. Tensions and hostilities were running high aboard the wyndship. Everyone had witnessed the fiery destruction of the Klashean ship at the docks of Eyr Rigg. Suspicions abounded. Most had come to believe there must be a justifiable reason for such an attack. Why else risk riling the empire of the Southern Klashe? Furthermore, as the *Pony* traveled the breadth of the sea, fears grew, stirred by speculations of retaliation, of war breaking out. All that anxiety needed a focus, which ended up being directed at the Klasheans on board, with their foreign tongue and reclusive natures.

Pratik had even reported one passenger spitting at him, which was an affront no *imri* would normally tolerate. Still, Pratik bore it silently, not wanting to draw undue attention. This sour attitude of their fellow passengers was surely noted by the other Klasheans, too. To avoid raising further suspicions, the foreigners mostly kept to their cabins and mingled as little as possible.

Unfortunately, Rhaif saw now that this sudden unexplained stop in Azantiia had stoked tensions to a feverish degree. Distrust shone from all the faces that followed his path across the commons. Eyes glinted with anger, as if he were to blame for everything, even their own fears.

Rhaif had come here to circumspectly inquire if anyone knew the reason for the *Pony*'s sudden need to land at Azantiia's port. In just the few steps it took to reach the bench before the ship's larder, he read the room and recognized not only the futility of such an endeavor, but also the likelihood of his arse being thrown from the sailraft deck at the stern of the ship if he should draw too much attention his way.

He weighed if it might be better to simply disembark in Azantiia. Maybe his group should take their chances hiding under the noses of those who hunted them versus taking the risk of traveling the rest of their passage to Aglerolarpok.

"What'll ya have?" the servitor asked as Rhaif reached the man's station at the kitchen larder.

Rhaif set his basket atop the bar and slid his slip over. "Just the usual fare," he said, speaking stiffly to pretend that Hálendiian was not his native tongue. "Thank you most kindly," he added with extra politeness.

Such civility only earned him a scowl as the man took the basket and turned to his shelves to collect their foodstuffs. The servitor moved with a slowness that clearly took effort, an unspoken affront. The man's hand shifted from a fresh-cut slab of yellow cheese to one that had crusted over, its rind mildewed to a dark green. He dropped the old chunk into the basket. The loaf of bread that followed had patches of frothy black mold.

Rhaif pretended not to notice. *Now's not the time to raise any objections.* He heard grumbles rising behind him from the other tables near the bar. A few louder voices sniped purposely at him.

   . . . fecking Klashers . . .

   . . . oughta burn 'em all, I say . . .

   . . . cast the lot straight off the ship . . .

The old scribe behind the bench—whose face was forever fixed in a knot of tired disgust—took Rhaif's slip and marked off what was collected. From the open patch in his sleeve, he was an Aglerolarpok. Only his brand was crossed out by another scar, indicating he had been banished from his ranch. The skies were likely the only refuge afforded him.

"Anything else?" the man asked leadenly, a rote inquiry he must've asked countless times. "Warm your cheese, mayhap?"

Rhaif shook his head. Even if he had the coin for it, he sensed it was better to get out of here without waiting for that stone-hard cheese to melt.

A muffled lilting voice rose behind him. "Please do," she said. "I will be happy to pay."

He turned to find another figure outfitted in an embroidered *byor-ga* standing at his shoulder. She shifted next to him, a bit too closely, clearly seeking companionship amidst the storm behind them.

He inwardly cringed. *"B . . . Ben midi,"* he stuttered out, greeting her in Klashean, while trying his best to mimic her lilt.

He wanted to refuse her largesse, but he was not fluent enough to do so. And he certainly dared not be exposed here. He could only imagine the reaction of the already twitchy group in the commons if it was revealed he was in disguise. He pictured a long fall from the stern deck to the forests of Cloudreach below. The *Pony* had nearly crossed the breadth of those greenwoods. Such a plummet would certainly mark a dramatic return to the homelands of his mother, an unexpected visit he'd prefer not to make.

Next to him, the Klashean woman placed an eyrie on the table. Her gloved fingers pushed the silver coin toward the scribe and waved away any attempt to return the ha'eyrie she was owed back. "For your troubles and kind service," she intoned.

The scribe snatched the boon and flashed his treasure at the servitor. Rhaif's moldering rind was quickly exchanged for a riper slice, and both men moved to the draft-iron oven.

The chaaen-bound woman leaned closer. "Since we must wait for your cheese to warm . . ." The lilt faded from her whisper. A sharp point stabbed into his side, expertly positioned at his kidney. "Perhaps we can talk."

He turned enough to spy through the slit in the silk that hid her face. The coppery eyes that glared back at him, though, were familiar enough.

He closed his own eyes in defeat, at the impossibility of his circumstance.

It was Llyra hy March.

STANDING AT THE cabin window, Pratik wondered for the hundredth time what he was doing here. He had agreed to accompany the thief and his stolen treasure with the hopes of presenting such a valuable trophy to the Imri-Ka, to use such a prize to possibly win his own freedom.

He fingered the iron collar around his neck. He still remembered both the happiness and terror when the band had been fused around his throat. He still had a scar from the hot metal, which burned his tender flesh despite the insulation of a ceramic neck shield. The collar marked his esteemed accomplishment of earning the Highcryst of alchymy, but it also forever bound him to his master, Rellis im Malsh. He tried to imagine what it would be like to be free of this weight. He imagined he'd float off his toes if this anchor was ever cut away.

Even that dream was mixed with both hope and dread.

He lowered his hand.

Back at the Anvil docks, Rhaif had not warned him about the change in ships until the last moment, leaving Pratik no choice but to follow. But where did this new path lead? Would it still end at the throne of the Imri-Ka? Or would he forever be an outcast, a Chaaen who had broken his bind, always on the run?

He had tried to raise these concerns with the Guld'guhlian thief, but any real answers were rebuffed. *Too much remains up in the air,* Rhaif had said with a wave at the wyndship, trying to use mirth to blunt the ambiguousness in his words.

Pratik had even considered approaching one of the other Klashean groups on board, to reveal the subterfuge, to beg for forgiveness. But he knew such a path would likely end in his death, especially after the fiery destruction of a ship bearing the Klashean Arms. He had been partly to blame for that tragedy.

Then there was the one other matter, the truest reason he stayed silent.

He turned to the bronze figure.

Shiya stood before the other window. She had seldom strayed from that spot for the past two days, bathing in the bright sunlight. She had even stripped off her *byor-ga* and remained unabashedly naked, exposing as much of herself to the Father Above as possible. Under His bright gaze, her bronze had melted, turning impossibly soft and warm. Her plaits of hair had shivered into loose filaments so fine that they could be brushed from her cheeks or tucked behind a curl of ear.

Someone, with a casual glance, could easily mistake her for any other tanned woman, one of exceptional beauty. It was only her eyes that gave her unnaturalness away. They were distinctly glassy and glowed with an inner fire that could not be ignored. The energies turned her azure eyes into the deep blue of a lightning-struck sea. He found her gaze, whenever she deigned to look at him, to be frightening and inexplicable, yet also mesmerizingly beautiful.

Pratik did not understand any of the alchymy that fired through her, that gifted her with life and vigor. A debate warred in him. *Is it even alchymy? Or is she truly god-touched?* It was this wonder that kept him alongside her and Rhaif. No matter the answer, he sensed she was a creation from beyond their oldest histories, maybe even before the Crown was first forged in fire and ice, what the Elder tongue called *Pantha re Gaas,* the Forsaken Ages.

So how could I possibly forsake you myself?

He shifted to her window, to study her closer. Something of late had troubled him about her, but he could not narrow down what it was.

With her face in the full sun, her cheeks stirred in hues of rich coppers, from pinkish to a darker red. Her lips gathered those hues, creating a rosy aspect that accentuated the bow of her mouth. Her lower belly and legs, partially shaded below the windowsill, remained a deeper bronze, swirling in tones of browns and murky yellows. The back half of her, turned away from the sun, was equally dark, accentuating the breadth of her hips and curve of her buttocks. His gaze drifted around and up to the swell of her breasts, no larger than ripe plums, but perfectly formed with dark bronze areolas and nipples lifted to the sun.

He continued to stare at the full breadth of her sculpted beauty. It would be easy to accept how a goddess might want to instill her essence into such a form. He wanted to run his hands down her curves, but not how a man might wish to fondle such a woman, more like a scholar wanting to explore and understand the mystery standing there.

Confused by her, by his own feelings, he turned from her to the window.

Below, the cliffs of Landfall fell behind the stern as the wyndship abandoned the heights of Cloudreach and sailed high over the Bay of Promise. Ahead, the vast sprawl of Azantiia hugged the coastline to the north. From this height, he could make out the star-shaped castle ramparts of Highmount. Stretching from the city's harbor, thousands of white sails dotted the blue seas. On the opposite side of the city, scores of balloons rose and fell from the mooring docks that spread over thousands of acres. Some of the ships were as large as *The Soaring Pony,* many others smaller. Then there were warships that dwarfed their own craft, moored in their own yokes to the northeast.

Pratik had visited the city a few times with Rellis on trade or diplomatic missions, but he had found the place chaotic and unruly. Nothing like the empire's capital of Kysalimri, which meant *kissed by the gods,* which the city certainly appeared to have been. He pictured its flowing gardens, its white palacios, and its thirty-three spires topped by golden figures of the holy pantheon. Under the obsidian fist of the Imri-Ka, order was vigilantly maintained. All the baseborn castes had their role to play, like the cogs of a great machine, and no one dared step from their assigned tasks.

Except for me.

This new role, free of caste and rule, both excited and frightened him in equal measures. He had always dreamed of his freedom, to rid his neck of its iron collar, but where would this path lead? The danger was great, but he did not fear death. He had lived all his life with a dagger at his throat, where any misstep would end him. No, what truly kept his chest tight was to imagine a life of self-determination, to be truly free of the great machine that was the Klashe—and then have such a hope dashed in the end.

That would be worse than any death.

He stared out the window as the wyndship lowered toward Azantiia's docks, tacking against the winds that blew forever east at this low height. Over the past days, as the *Pony* had crossed the seas from the Guld'guhl territories, the ship had ridden the two streams that flowed in opposite directions across the Crown. The ship would rise high and brush into the hot winds that blew forever west, carried along by that steamy current until the heat grew too much, then the ship would lower into the colder streams flowing the other way, tacking against that tide. Then, once cooled, back up they'd go. Over and over. Lifting and lowering. Like a sailing ship across the swells of a sea.

But now it looked like they would rise no more.

The *Pony* circled toward the fields north of Azantiia, preparing to dock.

As the ship turned, so did Shiya. The bronze woman's face swung in the opposite direction. She even shifted to the other window, forcing him to stumble out of her way. She fought to keep staring toward the cliffs of Landfall.

What is she doing?

Then it dawned on him. He finally recognized what had been troubling him all morning. Throughout this trip, she had seldom said a word, a few one- or two-word comments, mostly expressing urgency toward some goal known only to her. For the past two days, she had always stared to the west.

Rhaif had told him about this peculiarity of her behavior and his belief that whatever Shiya was seeking lay in that direction.

Only over the course of this long morning, Shiya had begun to turn, like the shadow of the sun shifting across the dial of the yearlong clock at the center of Kysalimri. Her face had swung, tick by tick, shifting from due west until now she looked to the east. It was even more apparent as the *Pony* circled to land.

What had changed?

He approached her as she stood at the window. She stared off past the cliffs toward the ancient greenwood of Cloudreach. Farther in the distance, he could just make out the highest tier of this land, nearly swallowed by the clouds, the Shrouds of Dalalæða.

As the wyndship circled to land, Shiya continually turned to maintain her view east.

"What's wrong?" he muttered, more to himself than her.

Still, she answered without looking his way. "We must go back."

"Where?"

She went silent again.

"Shiya, where do you want to go?" he pressed.

She continued to ignore him. Still, the hues of her naked skin stirred more fiercely, expressing her agitation.

Fearing something was dreadfully wrong, Pratik turned to the cabin door.

Where is Rhaif?

33

"**How?**" **Rhaif asked** as he was marched at knifepoint down the *Pony's* central corridor toward his cabin. That one word held a number of questions: *How could Llyra be here? How had she found him? What was her plan for them all?*

Llyra kept behind him, keeping the point of her dagger at his left kidney. She had forced him out of the commons after collecting his basket of warm cheese and bread, which she carried in the crook of her left arm. She clearly didn't want him attempting to use the basket as a weapon.

As he continued down the passageway, a stream of blood ran down his back and along the crack of his arse cheeks.

"How did you find us?" he asked, settling on this one question among the many rattling in his head. The last time he had seen the guildmaster she had been manning the blockade at the edge of the Boils.

"I nearly did not, not until the last moment," she said with an irritating level of calmness. "Over the years, I had forgotten how shrewd and slippery you could be."

"Years I lost because you betrayed me to Archsheriff Laach."

She shrugged, dragging the blade higher, slicing deeper. "Such a betrayal served to further ingratiate me with Laach, a relationship that has served the guild well over the past two years."

"Ah, then I should be grateful I was so helpful," Rhaif said, almost respecting her ruthless practicality. He half glanced back at her. "But you still haven't told me *how* you ended up here."

"Back at the Boils, word reached me about a clutch of Klasheans leaving a whoremonger's house, a place that backed against the one I torched. Only then did I recall a dark face hidden next to yours when I ran into you at Anvil's gaols. I was so startled at the time I failed to add weight to that circumstance."

Rhaif pictured both Pratik's countenance and the flames dancing across the rooftops as they fled to the streets.

"Unfortunately, that word reached me too late, especially as a certain carriage had already slipped past my barricade. I only had time to mount a swift horse and dash after you. Gauging the time of night, I estimated you were trying to reach a wyndship. To stop you, I dashed headlong up Jagg'd Road toward Eyr Rigg."

Rhaif remembered how long it had taken their carriage to climb that path's switchbacks. Other horses had indeed swept past their foundering carriage, carrying lone couriers or late passengers.

One of them must have been Llyra.

"I ended up boarding the wyndship bearing the Klashean Arms, mistaking that for your destination." The dagger point dug deeper. "From that ship, I watched a group of robed figures rush from a carriage and aim for a craft bearing the curled horns of Aglerolarpok. I cursed you so loudly that I'm surprised you didn't hear me. Still, I disembarked and made it aboard here just before the mooring lines were tossed. And lucky I did."

Rhaif pushed down the rise of guilt at the fiery destruction of the other ship. But it seemed more lives were to be laid at his feet.

"To search this ship unseen," Llyra said, "I heeded your guidance. I followed a trio of Klasheans, broke into their room, and quickly dispatched them. I then borrowed a *byor-ga* to keep hidden."

Rhaif briefly closed his eyes, wondering how much bloodier his hands could get. "And this unscheduled landing at Azantiia?"

"I sent a ship's skrycrow diving toward the city last night, letting them know who was aboard. Word returned this morning, ordering the craft to land and prepare to be searched." Llyra shifted closer. "And until that happens, I intend to make sure you stay put and never leave my sight."

Rhaif had reached his cabin, recognizing he was defeated. But he held out one hope, and it lay beyond his door. He keyed it open and let Llyra shove him through. As she shadowed him inside, she kept hold of the neck of his robe and the blade at his back.

Pratik took a step toward him, his face lined with worry—then away again when he spotted the fully draped figure accompanying him. "What is this?" he asked, repeating the same in Klashean, mistaking Llyra's identity: *"Byr se quaan?"*

Llyra ignored him and gasped instead at the sight of the cabin's other occupant. She stopped Rhaif a few steps past the door's threshold.

Rhaif used her momentary shock at the naked figure of bronze to speak. "May I introduce Shiya," he said. "Shiya, this is Llyra hy March, guildmaster of thieves."

Pratik took another step away, now recognizing the threat standing behind Rhaif.

Shiya cocked her head toward them, blinked once, then casually turned back to the window.

So much for a bronze warrior queen rushing to my rescue.

Outside, the ship tilted enough to bring the approaching mooring fields into view.

Llyra never loosened her grip on his collar. She rapidly collected herself. "Amazing. I had no idea the breadth of this wonder," she muttered. "I see now why you stole it."

Rhaif heard the avarice in her words and tried to bend it to his advantage. "It's worth a king's ransom. A ransom even more valuable if we split such a bounty two ways." Pratik frowned at him, so he corrected himself. "Or even *three* ways."

Llyra remained quiet, contemplating his suggestion, surely weighing her options. She could kill them all and try to abscond with the treasure on her own. But she had already overplayed her hand by alerting Azantiia. For any hope of stealing this prize, she would need their help. She could always dispatch them later. Of course, the easiest and safest choice would be to stick to her current plan and hand the prize over to the legions in Azantiia, where she would collect some meager reward for her service.

Rhaif glanced over his shoulder, trying to fathom what her decision would be.

She studied the bronze treasure. He knew it was one thing to passively formulate a strategy of accommodation when the prize was not standing right in front of you. But Shiya now blazed in the sunlight, a torch shining with the promise of riches without end.

Llyra's stance firmed. "No . . ."

Rhaif wasn't sure what she was negating. Still, the dagger had not plunged into his kidney. Her gaze flicked toward him, as if to explain further—then the world exploded below them.

They all swung toward the windows, though the knife never left his side.

Across the mooring fields, wyndships burst with great fiery eruptions. Shredded balloons flapped amidst flames and smoke. Neighbors ignited neighbors. The *Pony* reared from its approach, rolling away from the carnage.

As it turned, Rhaif spotted a lone swyftship darting through the fiery field, spitting tinier flames to maneuver. It looked like a mouse trying to escape a burning house. Only it wasn't trying to flee. Tiny dark casks rolled out its stern and burst into flame. One barrel struck another moored wyndship, and a moment later, its balloon ruptured with a gust of fire. And still the swyftship sped across the field, sowing destruction in its wake.

Rhaif noted two details.

The tiny black flag flapping behind the craft carried the crossed swords of the Klashean Arms. He understood.

Here is the empire's retaliation for what happened in Anvil.

He glanced to Llyra. Other skrycrows—like the one she had sent—must have already been dispatched from the ship last night and spread word throughout the city about the death and destruction in Anvil, reaching the ears of Klashean saboteurs imbedded in Azantiia.

He turned back, focusing on the other detail of the swyftship. Its path, crooked though it may be, aimed to the northeast, toward the fortified corner of the fields where the great warships were moored. Their mighty balloons, adorned with the sun and crown of Hálendii, loomed over the destruction, ripe targets for the attacking ship.

It sped toward them, but Rhaif knew such an effort was futile.

As the tiny craft raced toward the moored warships, a flurry of fiery spears shot from a row of ballistas, giant crossbows positioned across the field's edge. The long bolts traced the air with flame and smoke. One steel point struck the Klashean swyftship and shattered it into splinters. Another ripped flames through its balloon, bursting it to ruin. The wreckage flew a quarter league onward before crashing to the ground in a skid of fire, never getting close to the berths of the colossal warships.

But the damage was done.

Half the city's mooring fields burned, swathed in smoke.

Sadly, that was not the only harm.

Pratik tumbled back from the window as one of the ballistas' fiery spears shot past him. It struck the *Pony*'s balloon hard enough to shake the entire ship. They all looked up, waited a breath, then heard a muffled boom.

A ball of flame shot into view high above, rolling away into a wash of smoke.

The *Pony* canted to the side, spinning away from the fiery ruins blow, revealing a brief glimpse of the Bay of Promise—then tipped toward a crash.

As they were thrown forward across the cabin, Rhaif accepted his fate.

The destruction I wrought in Anvil has finally caught up with me.

He remembered a lesson taught to him once by his mother: Right your wrongs before they rightly wrong you.

I should've listened better.

The next lesson was not as eloquent.

Llyra grabbed him and shoved him toward the door. "Move your arse!"

PRATIK UNDERSTOOD THE woman's order. He had flown enough wynd-ships to know her intent. She voiced it aloud.

"Make for the sailrafts."

Pratik also understood her urgency. Time was limited to make their escape. The small rafts were routinely used to ferry passengers or goods back and forth to the ground from the air, but they also doubled as a means of exodus in a foundering ship. He also knew the number of such skiffs was typically too few for everyone on board. Worse, the skiffs were all secured at the stern, across the breadth of the ship from here.

Rhaif ignored the guildmaster and called across the cabin, "Shiya, to me!"

Pratik turned, too. The bronze woman held her place at the window, her legs braced wide, one hand clamped to the window's edge. She swung her gaze to Rhaif. The thief was the only one she truly heeded.

Still, Pratik reached and took her other hand. Her palm burned in his. The hues of her skin roiled with anxiety. He tried to tug her along with him, but she slowly turned back to face to the east, inexorably pulled in that direction.

Llyra cursed sharply, turned, and fled out the door. She abandoned them, plainly deciding her life was more valuable than any treasure. With the door left open, people fled past their cabin, bellowing, many only half-dressed. They all rushed toward the stern as the ship's bow tilted more steeply.

Rhaif dashed over to the bronze woman. "Shiya, we must go. You may survive a crash, but we will not."

She ignored him, continuing to stare toward the cliffs of Landfall.

Pratik still had hold of her hand. "Come with us now," he urged. "I will take you where you want to go. This I swear."

She turned to him. Her fingers tightened on Pratik's fingers, as if silently holding him to his pledge.

"I will do all I can," he promised.

She finally moved along with him as he headed toward the door.

Rhaif kept to her other side. "We must get to the last sailraft before it's gone." When they reached the hall, it was empty of people, just littered with abandoned cases, some spilled open, one shining with a splash of jewels. Rhaif pointed to the stern. "Shiya, get us to the stern of the ship."

She gave a small nod and led the way, at first slowly, then gaining speed. He and Rhaif gave chase. The floor continued to tilt upward as cables groaned and the ship shuddered, throwing them side to side as they ran. Still, with the passageway empty, they quickly reached the commons at midship.

Unfortunately, a crush of people blocked the far side, bottlenecked in panic at the exit to the stern half of the *Pony*. Without slowing, Shiya bowled into them. She grabbed people by arm or nape and tossed them aside like stuffed dolls. It took an extra breath for the crowd to realize what attacked them: a towering naked bronze woman, fueled by the fires of the Father Above, her eyes blazing like furnaces. Screams of terror spread, sending people scrambling away, clearing the path.

She elbowed through to the far passageway. They followed in her wake, only to find the corridor ahead crammed tightly with passengers and crew. But those earlier screams had already drawn attention their way. The throng surged from the burning goddess among them. Some tried to climb over others. Most dove into cabins that were abandoned and left open to either side.

Shiya continued her charge through those that remained, leaving many broken and wailing behind her—which only encouraged those still ahead to desert the hallway.

Finally, they broke through to the stern hold. Screams and cries echoed across the cavernous space, piled to the rafters with roped crates and barrels. Several stacks had snapped their bindings and toppled, creating a broken landscape. Confounding the chaos, smoke choked the space, flowing in from the open doors at the back.

They fought toward the brightness. The stern deck had been cranked open to the skies. Flames and shredded flaps of balloon filled the skies outside. By now, the back of the *Pony* had been shoved up into the ruins of the airbag above as the bow sank. Another boom shook the ship and the *Pony* fell faster. The flames and scraps of the balloon momentarily whooshed higher, exposing the open sky.

Everyone lost their footing—except for Shiya.

"There!" Rhaif hollered, and pointed toward the open deck.

Shiya understood. She snatched Pratik and Rhaif by their arms and half dragged, half carried them up the last of the tilted deck. They reached the draft-iron stanchions, aligned across the opening, where the ship's sailrafts were normally berthed.

Only two of the six were left.

One of the rafts took advantage of the opening and shot out the back of the ship, propelled by the same mechanism as the giant crossbows below. The small raft, which looked like an enclosed skiff, arced high into the sky—then a small balloon burst forth from a dome on top, catching the raft before it plummeted like a stone into the sea far below. Tiny jets of alchymical fire spat out its stern, guiding the craft away from the burning *Pony*.

Shiya aimed them toward the last skiff. Its stern door was still open. A few stragglers rose from among those sprawled on the floor. One tried to crawl into the sailraft, only to fall back, clutching his neck. He toppled to the side, revealing a hiltless blade impaled in his throat.

Pratik saw now that those draped on the ground behind that raft weren't dazed.

They were dead.

A shout rose from inside. "'Bout time you got here!"

Shiya hauled them close enough to reveal Llyra crouched in the empty hold of the raft. She carried a short bloody sword in one hand and a silver throwing knife in the other. She hadn't abandoned them, only fled in advance to secure one of the sailrafts and hold it for them at the point of her sword.

"In here now," she ordered.

Shiya tossed them into the hold and followed inside. The only other occupant was a blue-liveried crewman, seated at the raft's wheel and pedals. He gaped in horror at what had just boarded his craft.

As soon as they were all inside, Llyra pointed her dagger at him. "Go or die."

Rhaif swung toward the pack of desperate people behind the raft. A few carried children on their shoulders. "Wait. We can take—"

The raft jerked forward hard, nearly throwing them out the stern door. Pratik managed to grab hold of a hanging loop of leather. Still, he lost his legs and hung breathlessly for a spell. Shiya had snatched Rhaif by the collar to keep him inside.

The skiff sailed high into the air, then tipped its nose downward.

Pratik still had not breathed—not until he heard a blast above. The balloon unfurled, snapped taut, and caught the plunging craft. Pratik's weight slammed him firmly to the deck. He coughed with relief.

Through the open door, he watched the *Pony* plummet away from them, its balloon trailing smoke through the air. It finally crashed into the sea with a great flume of water. The flaming ruins of the balloon followed and draped across the waves, where it continued to burn.

Grateful to have survived, Pratik turned to Rhaif. The thief's face was red with fury, directing his anger at Llyra, who had sheathed her sword but kept her knife in hand.

"We could've saved a dozen more," he said savagely, waving a hand back at the ruins of the *Pony*.

"Maybe, but I had to account for the weight of your bronze treasure." Llyra cast an appraising glance toward Shiya. "Her heft alone is surely that of several men."

Regrettably, Pratik recognized she was right. The raft's drover fought his wheel and worked his pedals, his brow pebbled with sweat. Even with just the four of them aboard, Shiya's weight was clearly a problem. Viewed through the thin window in front, the skiff was slowly sinking toward the seas below. The drover pulled a lever near his knee and flames spat out the back, just under the open door behind them.

Pratik retreated from that alchymical fire.

"We're not going to make it back to the coast," the drover concluded with a grimace as he fought to slow their descent.

Pratik searched the seas. The crashing dive of the *Pony* had taken the wyndship well over the Bay of Promise. Worse, their escape had shot their tiny skiff even farther out to sea.

The drover used his maneuvering flame to turn them toward the distant coastline. Still, the raft sank lower toward the sea.

"We're too heavy," the drover warned.

"What did I tell you?" Llyra drew Pratik's attention back. She had her sword out again, pointed at them. Its tip swung between him and Rhaif. "Looks like we must lighten our load."

34

RHAIF LIFTED HIS palms toward Llyra, which only drew her sword's attention his way. He scrambled for an argument to keep everyone on board. He considered ordering Shiya to toss the guildmaster off the ship, but to voice such a demand aloud would end any hope of accommodation. And in truth, he doubted Shiya would obey. Her will and actions had proven too capricious in the past.

Still, this thought offered him an argument.

Rhaif placed a hand on his chest and spoke rapidly, as if his life depended on it—which it did. "Listen, Llyra. Shiya will only mind *me*. If you hope to abscond with her, you'll need her cooperation, which means you'll need me."

She shrugged and turned her blade toward Pratik, who backed a step.

Rhaif shifted in front of the Chaaen. "And surely you know I had a reason in freeing Pratik, chaaen-bound to Rellis im Malsh, a bastard who you know traded in alchymical secrets."

This was a lie, but he suspected she would not admit to being ignorant of something he claimed to know.

He pressed the matter and pointed to Pratik. "This is his chief alchymist. He knows more about ancient mysteries and arcana than nearly anyone. He was the one who has kept Shiya moving, using alchymicals only he can craft to keep her fired and fueled."

Rhaif turned for acknowledgment, lifting his brows at Pratik, hoping the man would carry this lie forward.

The Chaaen understood and crossed his arms. "Creatures such as Shiya are known to a few in the Southern Klashe. My master keeps a librarie of great import at his palacio in Kysalimri, stacked with the ancient tomes, some written shortly after *Pantha re Gaas*. The librarie is even visited by the Imri-Ka's Dresh'ri."

"The Forbidden Eye," Llyra translated with a squinted expression of distaste.

Rhaif understood. Such a cabal was rumored to dredge through the ancient past, seeking dangerous knowledge. They were also said to employ cruel and bloody methods, even sacrificing infants, to achieve their ends.

Rhaif studied Pratik, wondering how much of what he had just revealed was true. He knew it was difficult for a Chaaen to lie. So, he suspected there must be some level of truth to Pratik's story.

Llyra reached the same conclusion and lowered her blade. "Then what do you propose we do?"

Rhaif was ready for this question. He pointed out the window. "We might not be able to reach the Hálendiian coast to the north, or even the swamps to the south, but the cliffs of Landfall are nearer at hand. With the wind at our back, we should be able to glide our way over to Cloudreach."

"To the east," Pratik mumbled, glancing at Shiya.

Rhaif nodded. "It might take time for anyone to realize a certain bronze treasure isn't sunk deep into the sea. In the meantime, if you wanted to lose yourself, those misty greenwoods might offer the perfect refuge."

She turned to the raft's drover. "Can we make it there?"

He sighed heavily and fired the nose of the craft toward the cliffs. "Maybe, but just barely."

Llyra sheathed her sword but kept the blade in her fingers. "If you want to live, you'll make that happen."

They all gathered behind the drover. The dark-haired man hunched his lanky form over the wheel, deftly working the pedals with small squeaks of hidden wires and gears. From the open patch on his upper sleeve, he was Aglerolarpok. His ranch brand was scarred over with an X, like the scribe at the larder. An outcast, banished to forever ride the winds. It was a sorry fate, but one that had honed a skill that Rhaif definitely appreciated at this moment.

The sailraft continued to sink toward the seas. The cliffs rose ahead, as if intending to block them. But as they continued, the drover proved his skill. He finally reached that rising rampart and used the draft blowing up the cliff face to shoot them high over the edge of Landfall. Soon the keel of the raft was sailing smoothly above the mists that hid the greenwood below.

Rhaif searched ahead, studying his mother's homeland. He ignored the peaks of black cliffs near the horizon, marking the distant Shrouds of Dalalæða. Instead, he fixed on a pair of closer breaks in the white, fluffy sea. They marked the location of two forest lakes, the green Eitur and the blue Heilsa, known simply as The Twins.

Rhaif pointed between them. "Can you reach Havensfayre?"

"Aye," the drover said. "With the winds blowing us toward there, we should just make it."

Llyra lifted a brow toward Rhaif. It was as much of a compliment as the guildmaster ever offered. Still, he was not fooled. While they might be uneasy allies at the moment, that could all change once they reached the woodland town.

He turned his gaze back to Shiya, who stared ahead, too.

Strange . . .

He recognized the oddity of this. He frowned over her shoulder toward the open stern, to the west, the direction where she had always cast her gaze before. Pratik caught his eye, maybe noting his confusion. The Chaaen tilted his head back to the east as if he knew something.

What does he know?

But now was not the time to address that question.

Llyra had a more important one. "Are you sure we can make it?" She leaned threateningly over the drover.

Rhaif focused forward again. The raft had drifted frighteningly lower. Its keel now swept through the clouds, like a ship sailing across a white sea.

"Don't fret. I'm seeking the strongest winds near the treetops," he explained. "I need every push I can muster."

The skiff did seem to be going faster.

Still, Rhaif reached to one of the hanging leather loops, expecting to hear branches scrape along their keel, for trees to grab their fleeing craft.

"Hang on," the drover warned.

What do you think I'm doing?

The ship suddenly shot higher, propelled by the winds out of the clouds. In another few breaths, they reached the northern break in the white seas and sailed high over the emerald waters of the Eitur, a lake that was said to be poisonous. Not a place they would want to crash into.

But Rhaif didn't worry about that.

Instead, he caught glimpses of lamps glowing south of the lake, marking the misty town of Havensfayre. It looked like they were going to overshoot it. He began to question their trajectory, when the drover hauled the wheel hard. As they cleared the far end of Eitur, the sailraft turned sharply. Its keel skidded across the clouds. The skiff swung full around until its nose was pointed back the way they'd come.

Rhaif recognized he should never have doubted the drover's skill.

The man now used the headwinds to slow them as he aimed back toward the hidden town of Havensfayre.

"Well done," Rhaif whispered, clapping the drover on the shoulder.

The man grinned proudly.

Another was not as enamored of his talent.

A low groan rose behind him. He turned and saw that Shiya faced the stern, which now pointed east. Her countenance—what little that he could see of it—was a mask of pain. As they glided toward the west, she took a step in the opposite direction, then another.

"No . . ." he called to her.

She ignored him, drawn by whatever force pulled at her.

He let go of his leather loop and rushed toward her.

But he was too late.

Without ever looking down, she walked straight out the back of the raft. He reached the stern in time to see her tumble away, toppling end over end, and vanish into the clouds.

Stunned, unable to speak, he turned to the others.

Llyra's lips were stretched in a line of pure fury. She pulled her sword, ready to exact vengeance, clearly believing this was some ploy.

"We have to find her . . ." he muttered lamely.

Llyra crossed toward Pratik, thrusting her blade at the Chaaen's exposed back. The only thing that stopped her from impaling the man clean through was Pratik's next words.

"I know where Shiya's headed."

ELEVEN

GRAVE SONG

Let us shadd our teres, until the dirt be salt'd by our
    greef.
Let us cast our laments heye, so the Father Above hears
    our sorrows.
Let us rip our hairs, so our payne reaches the shroud'd
    Modron.
Do all this—
So the Mother Below takes what you cherish in
Her warme embrace & preserveth it for all time.

    —Fourteenth Sonnet from *The Book of Lamentations*

35

AS THE GROUP rested in the depths of the cloud forest, Nyx cradled the limp form of Bashaliia in a thin blanket.

My little brother . . .

She knelt in a layer of brittle leaf litter and parted the wool to reveal a small furry face, his delicate nostrils, his fold of soft ears. She had carried him the past day and a half. He was so light, as if his bones were hollow or blessed with some magick that turned them to air.

Or maybe the life has already left him, leaving only this weightless husk behind.

She drew him closer and noted the barest flutter of those petal-thin nostrils. He still lived, which both broke her heart and warmed an ember of hope. She straightened enough to note Frell looking at her with concern. The alchymist had done all he could. He had plucked the poisonous spikes from Bashaliia's thin neck and pulled the jagged stinger from under a wing. He had smeared a balm of herbal medicum over those wounds but promised no miracle. *We can only hope the Mӯr bats have some natural ward against the malignancy of the skriitch,* he had offered.

Jace sank next to her, sitting cross-legged, his face forlorn, mirroring how she felt. "Is there any sign of him reviving?"

She shook her head and moaned, "No . . ."

Kanthe stood several steps to the side, his bow in hand. He had crafted a few crude arrows by sharpening sticks and using clipped leaves or stray feathers as fletching. He had learned such a skill from a former teacher, a scout of these same greenwoods.

Even Jace had fashioned a spear from a long stiff branch. It rested next to him. So far, they had encountered no dire threat in these woods, a misty forest said to be home to panthers and Reach tygers. On the first night, they had lit a fire, which might have helped ward off any predators. Still, distant yowls and screams warned of their presence. Otherwise, the only large beast spotted had been a curl-horned boar that had traipsed across their path, but it had run off when Jace yelled, his scream more of fright than anything.

Kanthe had offered an unpleasant reason for their safe passage: *Maybe the beasts know to stay clear of this corner of the Reach because of what lurks behind us.* He had glanced significantly at Bashaliia in her arms.

She swallowed down her grief, leaving only despair.

Frell approached. She closed her eyes, knowing what he had come to say. She drew Bashaliia closer to her bosom.

"Nyx . . ." He settled to a knee next to her. "It's been nearly two days since he was attacked. By now, the eggs inside his body are likely already hatching. We know his venomous slumber will not spare him the agony to come."

She also knew this. This morning Frell had pinched the tender webbing between Bashaliia's wing and body. While her brother had not moved, his breath had puffed harder, plainly feeling that pinch.

"What comes next will be unimaginably painful," Frell warned. "It is no mercy to keep him alive when we cannot help him."

"I understand," she said.

No matter how much she wanted to deny his words, she suspected she had waited too long already. She hadn't told anyone, but Bashaliia's breath had been growing more strained, as if the worst was already starting.

She stared down at his head, no larger than her fist. She could still picture those same eyes, glassy now, staring across at her from the warmth of loving wings. She had already lost so much. Her dah, her older brothers gone missing. Even abandoning Gramblebuck had torn a hole in her heart that had not mended.

Now this . . .

She feared she could not survive it.

Kanthe came over. He slipped his dagger from its sheath at his waist. "Let me take this burden from you."

Anger flashed through her despair. "He's not a *burden,*" she snapped at him. "Never a burden."

A sob shook through her. She regretted her words, knowing the prince had only been trying to be kind. But she hadn't the strength to apologize. It took all that was left inside her to lift an arm toward him.

"I will do it."

Kanthe hesitated. Her hand began to shake. She looked up at him. Tears blurred her sight. He nodded and placed the dagger's hilt into her palm. She firmed her fingers around it, anchoring her will to the heft of its steel.

"I . . . I'd like to be alone," she whispered.

The others didn't argue and retreated. Jace touched her shoulder in sympathy, then slipped away.

She took a deep breath and gently lowered the blanket to the bed of leaves. She peeled back its edges, revealing the fold of wings, cocooned around a frail body. Bashaliia's head lolled back, exposing his throat, as if asking for her help.

Tears dripped to the wool, to the fur of his chest.

She clutched the dagger, unsure if she truly could do this. Still, the image of the dwarf deer, the violation of its body, welled through her. She recalled her earlier admonition when she heard the thylassaurs being attacked: *No creature deserved such a cruel end.*

She reached a finger and brushed the velvet under Bashaliia's chin.

Especially you.

She continued to rub the spot that often made him purr in contentment when they had nestled together in the sledge. She lowered the knife's blade to his throat—and still hesitated. She remembered Frell pinching her brother's wing.

You still feel pain, so you will feel what I must do.

Her hand tremored. She knew a quick sting was better than a labored agony. But she hated to inflict even that. Bashaliia had saved her many times, maybe more than even she knew.

She lowered her chin, her shoulders shaking. She felt another wracking sob building. It rose from her throat as a low moan. When it reached her lips, it came out as a keening, a quiet song of grief. She did not fight it or question it. She sang to her brother, vaguely remembering doing this in a dream as they nestled in slumber together.

She closed her eyes, letting her song become her vision. She whispered into Bashaliia. Each note carried her down a dark well inside him. Somewhere deeper, he answered, a faint pining, like loonsong over still waters.

I hear you . . .

She keened back to him, not to draw him closer, but to gently push him farther away from his wracked body. She did not want him to feel even the sting of this blade. As she sang, he tried to stay, refusing to leave her, but she wrapped him in her song, letting her love and ache, her sorrow and joy, be his blanket now. She lifted him and carried him away.

As she did, ancient eyes opened at the well's dark bottom and stared back.

She ignored them, focusing all her love on the spark she cradled.

Find peace, my little brother.

Knowing he was free of this body, she slit his throat.

KANTHE HEARD HER footsteps stumbling toward them. He and the others had retreated to a nearby patch of briarberry, both to give Nyx privacy yet still be close at hand in case she needed them. He had intended to collect berries while they waited. But he didn't bother. No one did. They stood with their heads bowed, each in his own thoughts.

He had listened to Nyx keening, nearly singing, at her tiny brother. He recalled hearing something similar as the girl had drowsed with the bat in the sledge. Only now, it was more refined. He heard the love and pain in each note.

Finally, she returned.

Jace crossed to her, but his steps stumbled.

Kanthe saw why. Nyx's palms were covered in blood, as was her tunic and the edges of her cloak. He pictured her cradling her brother's slaughtered form.

"I . . . I need your help," she moaned.

As she stopped, she weaved on her legs, drunken with shock and grief. He hurried to her and caught her before she fell. She slumped in his arms but pointed back.

"I want to bury him, but . . . but . . ."

"We'll do it," he said, and glanced over her head to Jace and Frell. "We'll all do it."

He carried her over to the wrap of blanket resting in a bed of leaves. He lowered her to one side. He and the others parted through the leaves and mulch to reach soil. They dug a small grave. He reached to move the body to the hole, blanket and all, but Nyx shifted over, refusing to let anyone touch her brother.

She seemed to draw strength as she settled Bashaliia into the grave. She gave them a firmer nod and let them cover his body with soil and leaves. Once done, without anyone saying a word, they all gathered small stones and built a cairn atop it, marking the spot, honoring his sacrifice.

"Thank you," Nyx said, seeming to encompass them all with her gratitude.

Kanthe nodded to the large tree crowning the small grave. The trunk was white, with a bark that curled in paper-thin slices. The leaves were green on one side, silver on the other. These trees were rare. It was why he had asked for the group to rest here. The surrounding forest was a mix of dark spruce, green pines, but mostly giant golden-leafed Reach alders, which vanished into the clouds.

He placed a palm on the curled white bark. "The tribesmen of these greenwoods call this tree *Ellai Sha,* or *Spirit's Breath.*" He ripped a piece of bark off the trunk and held it out to Nyx. The curl looked somewhat like a skrycrow's scroll. "You carry this with you. If you wish to speak to those who have passed, you whisper into the curl, then burn it at a camp's fire, where the smoke will carry your message high."

Nyx took the curl, tears welling, and clutched it to her heart. She turned to the cairn and mumbled her thanks.

They gave her another few moments alone at the grave, then Frell finally spoke. "The day is already half gone, and we have a long way to trek to reach Havensfayre. We should continue while we still can."

Jace stepped to Nyx. "Or we can stay longer here, if you wish."

She faced them, her countenance sad but resolute. "No, Bashaliia gave his life for ours. I won't waste the gift he gave us. We keep going."

Kanthe studied her. He had long given up searching for any resemblance in her, trying to discern if she might truly be his half-sister. What did it matter? Only seeing her now, covered in blood yet still strong, he could not imagine she shared his lineage.

Not even Mikaen had ever shown such hidden steel.

Surprisingly, such a realization made him happy for her. And if he was honest, he hoped Nyx wasn't his sister. For more reasons than just—

"Let's go," Frell said, tugging Kanthe around. "If we make good time, we could be at Heilsa by midday tomorrow. Then Havensfayre by the last bell of Eventoll."

They set off again, following the sliver of lodestone in the alchymist's way-glass, and headed north.

Kanthe trailed at the back, bow in hand, an arrow already notched. He had heard many tales from Bre'bran—the Reach hunter who had instructed him two years ago—about the dangers hidden within the beauty of this ancient forest. Bre'bran had warned how Cloudreach lulled the unwary into lowering their guard—with the sweet piping of birdsong, the dabble of its silver brooks, the breath of wind through leaves. Even the unbroken layer of clouds stirred languidly above, casting a mesmerizing spyll, enhanced by wisps of mists drifting like the dreams of those below.

More so, the forest itself drew the eye with its beauty. It refused to be ig-nored. In all directions spread a march of huge alder trunks, each as wide as a full-grown ox. These eternal mist-giants were the white pillars of the forest. They held up the sky and vanished into the clouds. From their many layers of branches, golden-green leaves flickered with each breeze, whispering at them in the unknown language of the ancient forest.

Under that ghostly canopy, a patchwork of dark green copses marked stands of spruce and pine. Lower still, the forest floor was blanketed in leaf and needle, with stretches of pink fireweed poking through. Every rock and boulder was scribed with lichen in bright patterns of scarlet, crimson, emer-ald, and sapphire. The bushes were a mix of juniper, chokeberry, buckbrush, even scrabbly winterroses.

He watched a burst of a dozen ruby wings rush through high branches, long tails flicking black, then silver, as if signaling the forest ahead of their approach. Then, as if drawn in the flock's wake, smaller birds, plumed in copper and gold, arrowed after the others, piping down at the trespassers, scolding them.

Rustling to Kanthe's right drew his attention.

He looked down in time to spot a bevy of spotted pluck-quails race across the leaf litter, tiny dobbins bobbing atop their heads. He swung his bow up, hoping to spear one, maybe two. But they vanished into the underbrush before he could set his aim.

He began to lower his bow—then his heart pounded with recognition.

All the birds had been aiming in the same direction. *Ahead of us.* He glanced over his shoulder. The forest stared back, as blank-faced as ever. Had something roused them, panicked them into flight, more than the tread of their footfalls?

He turned to the group.

Nyx . . .

Her clothing was still damp with blood.

He breathed harder, his ears straining for any soft padding of paws or grumble of threat. He heard nothing but was not fooled. Whatever boon had kept the forest's predators away had ended, broken by the allure of fresh blood in the air. Something had picked up that scent and trailed them.

He rushed forward to the others. They sensed his distress and turned.

"We're being hunted," he warned.

Jace searched all around, clutching his spear to his chest.

Frell frowned back at their trail. "Are you sure? By what?"

Kanthe had no answer to either question, only a certainty in his bones. He had been a hunter for too long to ignore this instinct.

Nyx stared at him, seeming to accept his word. "What do we do?"

He winced and pointed at her. "You need to shed your bloody garb."

She stared down at herself.

"Everything," he stressed. "Anything with even a drop."

She didn't balk. She stripped her soiled cloak and loosened the cords on her tunic and yanked it over her head. She stood in her breeches, soft boots, and a sleeveless undertunic. The last was speckled with blood that had seeped down to it. With a huff, she reached to pull it over her head.

Jace dropped his spear, unfurled his own cloak, and hid her nakedness behind it. He kept his head turned away.

Kanthe nabbed what she had already discarded and ran to either side of their path and tossed one piece in each direction. He returned to catch her undertunic as she tossed it to him.

He lifted it to his mouth and clamped it between his teeth. The scent of her sweat and skin filled his nostrils.

Jace frowned at him. "What are you—?"

He brusquely waved the question away, turned to the nearest alder, and scaled its lower branches. He climbed as high as he could, then tacked the garment to the trunk with one of his arrows. He prayed that what stalked them might be deceived into believing its prey was hiding up the tree, at least long enough for them to get away.

He dropped back down and snapped a branch from a spruce. He handed it to Nyx, who now wore Jace's cloak. "Smear your hands with the sap, to mask any blood still lingering there."

As she did, Kanthe herded them all forward. "Swiftly now. I don't know how much freedom this will buy us."

They hurried off, with Kanthe hanging back, still watching the quiet forest. He held his breath for long stretches, straining for any sign of pursuit. He stopped with his bow up when he heard a faint snap of a branch far in the forest.

He listened harder but heard nothing else.

You're still out there, aren't you.

Scowling, he headed after the others, who had fled a ways. By the time he closed on them, he heard whispers of distress, along with a low burble of water. The others had reached a small river, running along stony banks and lined by yellow willows on both sides.

He arrived in time to see Jace down on one knee, filling a waterskin.

Frell's eyes widened as Kanthe joined them. "Anything?"

"Not that I could spot. The bastard's a sly one, I'll give him that." He pointed across the river. "Maybe once we're across, we can—"

Jace bellowed and fell backward from the river's edge, landing on his backside. The waterskin he had been filling drifted away from the bank, floating atop the current.

Nyx stepped toward him. "What happened?"

"Stay back," Jace warned. "Something leaped at me, tried to bite my hand, but latched on to the hide instead and pulled it away."

He pointed at the bobbing waterskin, which jerked and turned in the current, as if attacked from below.

Something's clearly in the water.

Kanthe tried to peer through the river's mirror into its depths. As he leaned, a heavy crashing of brush burst behind him.

He spun around.

Finally, it comes.

From the noise, it was large, aiming straight at them. His bow and small arrows would not be enough. He snatched the spear that Jace had left beside the stream. "Get back," he warned them all.

He shifted to the front, trying to judge the direction of the attack. He planted the butt of his spear in the dirt and braced it with a foot, leaning the sharpened end toward the forest.

He barely got it fixed before a giant boar burst into view, easily taller than Kanthe. It barreled toward them, tusks running low to the ground, froth flying from its lips. It charged at their group.

Kanthe put all of his weight into holding the spear, hoping he could impale it and leap to the side in time. He braced for the impact—only to have the boar veer away at the last moment. Kanthe cringed from its path as it crashed past them. The beast dove through the sweep of willow branches and leaped headlong into the river.

Kanthe straightened as it surfaced and kicked frantically for the far shore. Kanthe's heart still pounded in his throat. He turned back to the forest. Something had frightened that boar, bad enough for it not to bother with their group.

As if confirming this, a low chuffing growl flowed from the misty forest.

Kanthe's bollocks tightened in his loins.

No . . .

He knew that noise. Bre'bran had imitated that sound long ago. He warned Kanthe that if he ever heard such a call that death would follow.

The others gasped behind him. He turned, but they were all facing the river. A braying bellow rose from out in the water. The boar thrashed mid-river, caught in a churn of whitewater. A closer inspection revealed flashes of silvery fins within the roil. In a breath, the waters turned crimson. The beast's bulk rolled, exposing legs gnawed to bone, with scores of creatures leaping and snapping at muscle and tendon. The boar sank away, dragged alive into the frothing depths.

Kanthe knew what feasted in those waters. Bre'bran had warned of this danger, too. He watched the abandoned waterskin turning in the stream. Something leaped atop it. It looked like an oilskinned black frog with glowing purple stripes on its flanks. It was twice the size of Kanthe's fists and appeared to be all legs at the rear, except for a long, finned tail that draped into the water behind it. Large bulbous eyes stared back at them, as if challenging them.

"Away from the water!" Kanthe yelled.

He grabbed Nyx and pulled her back, which drew Jace and Frell.

The creature jumped to the bank and landed heavily. Its mouth gaped open, revealing a maw of sharp, pointed teeth, green with poison.

"What is it?" Nyx asked.

"A pyrantha." Kanthe nodded to the churn of bloody water. "Flesh-eaters. With venom in their bite."

Nyx and the others backed away—not that it would do any good. Pyrantha were not limited to the river. From the water's edge, more of the beasts surged to shore, clambering, hopping, and writhing toward them. They massed along the bank, piling over and atop one another.

Frell looked at Kanthe.

Behind him, the chuffing sounded again.

Kanthe winced with sudden knowledge. Bre'bran had warned about the predatory nature of this hunter in the woods, how its cleverness should never be misjudged, how it transformed the very forest into its jaws.

Kanthe turned to the misty glade, recognizing the truth now.

It herded us here, trapping us against this deadly river.

From the forest's depths, a pair of eyes finally revealed themselves, fiery and savage. The sight brought back the final warning from Bre'bran.

If you see the eyes of a Reach tyger, you are already dead.

36

NYX STOOD AT Kanthe's shoulder as the beast stalked toward them. The prince's ebonwood complexion had gone darker, his lips set in a harder line. He tightened his hands on the spear. She sensed the anger wafting off of him, but it seemed directed more at himself than what stalked through the woods toward them. They were trapped here and had no choice but to hold their ground.

Others were not as brave. Splashes sounded behind her, a growing chorus as the pyranthas fled back into the safety of the river.

Kanthe didn't have to name the beast in the forest's shadows. He had cautioned them enough on the first day of such tygers. But even his warning failed to capture the sheer ferocity closing on them.

The tyger padded into view. Though slunk low, it would still dwarf the largest bullock. Its white paws, split by dark yellow claws, spread as wide as Nyx's chest. Pointed ears, topped by feathery tufts, stood tall toward them, looking like furry horns. Eyes of dark amber shone at them. Its pelt was cloudy white, striped in shades of gold, darker along its back and lighter down below. Each step stirred those markings and shimmered its snowy fur, making it look more like a mirage of muscle and savageness, as if it were the heart of this ancient forest given form.

They all backed toward the river. It slowed, stalking slightly back and forth, revealing powerful haunches and a short thick tail. It lowered its head and stared at them.

Kanthe lifted his spear.

The tyger's eyes narrowed at the threat. It flattened its ears and rippled black lips to reveal fangs as long as Nyx's forearm. Its haunches bunched under it, tremoring with hard muscles. Its maw hissed open, building toward a scream.

Nyx winced—not at the attack to come, but at an underlying frisson in its escalating hiss, a crimson thread beneath the sound. It sang of fury and blood, of hunger and lust. It reverberated through her until she could no longer stand it. Somewhere inside her, she fought against it. She whined aloud and struggled to find the contrary notes to its savage chorus, but it was like someone deaf trying to write a masterpiece of strings, horns, and drums. She could not find even the crudest first rhythms.

It was beyond her.

But not others.

Behind her, a lone voice rose in song, heard half with the ear, half with the heart. Another joined the first, then another, until a score of throats built those layers she had sought. They became a force at her back, even pushing her a step toward the tyger.

Kanthe stopped her, glancing back to the river.

The tyger also felt that wind of song and power. It leaned away from it, hissing back at it. Its short tail swished. Its ears flattened so hard to its skull that they vanished into its mane. Its visage became one of fury and hate.

Still, the song pressed it back as the voices rose higher.

Finally, it gave a shake of its head, spat a yowl of frustrated fury, and leaped around. It bounded back into the forest, nearly soundlessly, chased by the final notes of that chorus.

Nyx turned as the song ended.

On the far bank of the river, a line of a dozen shadows, half-hidden in the willows, shifted closer, barely shivering the draping branches. They were all half-naked, wearing only loose hide or fur wraps at their waists. The women had additional thin strips banded over their breasts—though the latter appeared less about modesty than practicality, an aid to help them run through the forests with less hindrance.

They all carried bows or bone-tipped spears.

"The Kethra'kai," Frell whispered.

Nyx knew these must be the tribesmen who haunted these greenwoods from before any written history. Their skin was pale and white. Their long hair—which the men had braided, and the women tied back—ran through all the shades of gold, from a fiery bronze to a rosy blond.

Like the tyger, they seemed to be part of this forest, blending so well into it.

Nyx glanced back to the forest behind her, remembering the chorus. *Bridle-song,* she realized. She had only heard such singing a few times. In the Mýr, few ever demonstrated this ability, to use their voices to sway duller creatures to the singer's will. Clearly the tyger was no such dull beast, but the combined chorus had been powerful enough to drive it away.

She touched her own throat, remembering how she had felt, what she had heard when the tyger had hissed. It still echoed there, as did her weak attempt to respond to it. She recalled the intimacy she had shared with Bashaliia. Had the reunion with her brother woken something more in her heart, something always there?

Frell shifted closer to Kanthe. "Can you speak with them? We don't want to be here if that tyger should return."

The prince shrugged. "I can try. Bre'bran taught me a few words and phrases." He crossed over to the riverbank and lifted an arm. *"Ha'hassan,"* he called over. He pressed his palms together and lowered his brow to his joined fingers, then faced the others. *"Tall'yn hai."*

Nyx guessed he was thanking them, but a few of the Kethra'kai leaned closer to one another, silently whispering. Others tightened lips in plain disapproval.

Kanthe must have noticed. "It's been a while," he said to Frell. "I wager I'm not inflecting properly. Their language is more cadence than words."

"We need to get across the river," Frell pressed him. "Maybe they know a spot along its course where we could safely ford it."

The prince nodded, took a deep breath, and shouted again, *"Meer pay . . .* um *. . . pyranta krell nay?"* He gestured to the placid river and the danger lurking under its reflection of the forest. *"Nee wahl nay?"*

The line of men and women merely looked stoically back at them. A few retreated into the willows, vanishing immediately.

Kanthe cast their group an apologetic wince. "From the looks of it, I may have just told them I liked to sniff my own arse."

"Wait," Jace said, and pointed. "Look."

The few who had vanished returned with bows already nocked with arrows. But rather than tipped in bone or iron, taut melon-sized pouches were fixed to the arrows' ends. The Kethra'kai arched their spines, bent their bows, and shot high. The arrows dropped, one after the other, in a neat row from this bank to the other. The bags exploded upon impact with the water, wafting out a fine yellow powder across the river's surface.

One of the archers waved to them, motioning them over. *"Krell nay,"* he ordered.

Jace frowned. "Do they want us to swim over? Through those waters?"

Nyx pictured the thrashing boar.

Kanthe cocked an eye at the swirling yellow dust that was already sinking away. "Maybe they're seasoning the river. Making sure the pyrantha have a properly flavored meal."

"Krell nay!" the archer repeated with a scowl.

As their group weighed whether or not to brave those waters, another figure appeared among the Kethra'kai. An old woman leaned on a tall white cane, sculpted out of a wood that nearly glowed. Her hair was snowy, cleansed long ago of the others' golden hues. The wrinkles of her skin suggested a century of time in these woods.

The tribesmen parted before her. They offered small bows of their heads as she crossed through them to reach the riverbank.

She called across, her voice as pure and strong as the river at her feet. "The currents be safe. But only briefly. You must cross now."

As proof of her words, a lone pyrantha bobbed to the surface, belly up and unmoving. Then another. But that was all. Nyx knew there were hundreds more still below.

"Hurry," she urged, "before the spyll of addlemiff wanes."

Frell glanced at them. "We must trust her."

"Like we have any choice," Kanthe countered, looking back at the woods behind them.

They quickly waded into the river and swam across. Nyx kicked and paddled with her breath held. Jace's cloak billowed around her naked chest, trying to drag her back. The touch of cold water shivered her skin. Something bumped her leg. She flinched, picturing herself swimming through a mass of numbed purple bodies. Fueled by dread, she swam faster.

Upon reaching the far bank, she climbed out with the others. She did her best to drape Jace's sodden cloak around her shoulders, keeping her bareness hidden.

"Follow us," the crone ordered.

Only now did Nyx notice the elder's strange eyes. One was green, as bright as an emerald; the other was a dark blue, like that of a twilight sky. Both were piercing as they studied Nyx, then the elder turned and headed off.

The Kethra'kai marched away from the river. Nyx and the others kept close. As she pushed through the willow branches, an angry howl echoed from the far side of the river. She shuddered, imagining what would have happened if the tribesmen had not intervened on their behalf.

As she faced forward, with her heart finally calming, a question formed. She stared at the pale backs of the Kethra'kai, fading into and out of the woods ahead.

Why are they helping us?

IN A CLEARING in the wood, Kanthe stood naked with Jace and Frell. A clutch of tribesmen knelt or stood around them, cocking an eye at their bare flesh, parting their hair and searching their scalps.

A tawny-haired fellow named Jaleek picked at the scab along Kanthe's hip, where a crossbow bolt had grazed his flesh when he had attempted to steal the caged bat. Kanthe flinched as the man reopened the wound, setting it to bleeding again.

"Ow," he scolded. "Leave it be."

Though he had not spoken in Kethra, the tribesman seemed to understand and shifted his attention away from the tender injury. Kanthe was
relieved until the man's cold fingers grabbed his privates and inspected
the underside of his bollocks. His cheeks heated, equal parts anger and
humiliation.

He started to pull away, but Frell scolded him. "Let them search you."

Kanthe looked his mentor's way, realizing he had never seen Frell without his robe, which was piled with their packs and gear. The alchymist was
all wiry muscle over knobby bone. And from the significant handful being
examined over there, his friend could easily serve as a pleasure serf and not
disappoint anyone.

Good for you, Frell.

Kanthe turned away to find a man just as red-faced as him. Jace held his
palms over his privates as his examination was nearing its end. His larger
bulk had taken longer to inspect, especially with most of his skin pelted in
curled fur. Kanthe also saw that the journeyman was more muscular than
he had suspected.

A regular Brauð bear, that one.

"What are they looking for?" Jace eked out.

One of the Kethra'kai who had been searching their packs and clothes
turned sharply to another, speaking too rapidly for Kanthe to follow. He did
identify one word that was the same in both languages.

Skriitch . . .

The tribesman held forth an open fold of wool, taken from Frell's robe. It
held the four spines removed from Bashaliia's neck, along with the hooked
stinger of the skriitch. Others came closer to examine the vile trophies. All
eyes then turned toward them, squinting hard, casting gazes up and down
their naked bodies.

"I think that's what they are searching us for," Kanthe said. "Seeing if we
might be infected, bearing wounds that might suggest infestation."

"You may be right." Frell glanced behind them. "They would not want
that scourge to spread to the rest of their forest. The river is likely a natural
barrier, rife with pyrantha. Only birds would be a risk. Perhaps they scout
the river's edge for any attempt of the skriitch to spread here."

The tribesman who held the spines and stingers scowled at them. He lowered a palm to a bone dagger slung at his waist.

Kanthe held up a palm. *"Nay."* He shook his head and placed a palm on
his bare chest. *"Nee shell."*

He struggled for the proper words to explain. He formed wings with
his palms and wafted them about. He mimicked plucking the spines and

pointed to what the man held. He gave a firm shake of his head, returning his palm to his chest.

"*Nee shell,*" he repeated. *Not from us.*

The tribesman lowered his palm from his dagger. Another Kethra'kai joined him, carrying a wooden bowl full of gray powder.

"What's that?" Frell asked.

Jaleek, the tawny-headed one who had been examining Kanthe, seemed to understand. The tribesman straightened, pointed from the spines to the bowl, then crossed his arms into an X.

"*Kraal,*" he said with a reassuring nod.

Kanthe closed his eyes.

Oh, no . . .

Jace called to him, "What does that mean?"

Kanthe grimaced, refusing to answer, knowing he could never speak it aloud, especially to a certain grieving member of their party. He opened his eyes and stared over to the tall bushes where the old crone and a clutch of Kethra'kai women had taken Nyx to be examined in private.

She must never know.

He prayed none of the women shared that particular word's meaning with Nyx.

If only we had waited another half day . . .

He turned to Jaleek, who smiled with encouragement, as if assuring them that the skriitch were no threat.

"*Kraal,*" he repeated, pointing at the bowl of powder.

Kanthe shook his head, not in disbelief, but in despair.

Kraal meant *cure.*

37

Nʏx ʟɪꜰᴛᴇᴅ ʜᴇʀ arms as one of the Kethra'kai, a woman named Dala, wrapped a length of spotted fur across her bare breasts. The tribeswoman then snugged it securely and clasped it in back. Once done, Dala inspected her and nodded her satisfaction.

With the study of her body ended, Nyx donned her breeches and soft boots. They had warmed her clothes by a small fire. The heat helped calm her. Plus, the gathering around her was welcoming, if not somewhat reserved.

She reached to Jace's cloak, but the heavier wool was still sodden, so she left it drying beside the fire. She looked down at herself, judging herself to be adequately attired. She heard the men talking beyond the bushes. She didn't know if they had dressed, but from the way a few of the women peeked through branches and whispered with winks, she guessed they were still naked.

The elder Kethra'kai, the one held in highest esteem, stood up from a stump and crossed toward Nyx. The old woman had been present for the entire examination, but she had drawn no nearer. Her gaze never left Nyx's face. As she reached Nyx, she leaned on her cane. Its white length was adorned with a row of pearlescent white shells imbedded into the wood. Each had been carved into the changes of the moon, running from sliver to full, then back again.

She breathed harder, reminded of what had started her on this journey. As handsomely as the moon was depicted on her cane, the sight was wrought with too much bloodshed and heartbreak. She heard an echo of Bashaliia's keening, saw her dah fall to the ground. She pictured the cairn of stones in these woods. All of it drawn around a single word of dread and premonition.

Moonfall.

The elder seemed to read her sudden distress. The old woman lifted a hand

and placed a warm palm—withered but still as firm as the hardwood of her cane—on Nyx's cold cheek.

"I heard you, child," the woman whispered.

Nyx didn't understand, but the confusion drew her back from the brink of despair.

Dala bowed toward the elder, then spoke to Nyx. *"Xan. Dob van Xan."*

Nyx understood Dala was offering the elder's name.

"Xan," she whispered, testing it.

The elder gave a nod of acknowledgment. "You bridled so sweetly," Xan said. "How could I not be drawn by your song?"

Nyx swallowed. "What do you mean?"

Nyx remembered the tyger and her poor attempt to confront its savagery. It was nothing like the chorus of the Kethra'kai. The forest tribe's ability with bridle-song was unique, ingrained into their blood. Such was known throughout Hálendii and much of the Crown. A few others were so gifted, but even they often had some distant connection to these tribesmen.

None knew why the Kethra'kai retained such a talent. Nyx remembered some debate in her sixthyear class, between alchymists and hieromonks, on this very subject. The monks believed it was a blessing of the Daughter, the dark Huntress of the moon.

Nyx stared again at the cane's row of sculpted shells, depicting the Daughter's endless chase of the silvery Son, marking the moon's waxing and waning. But she also remembered what the alchymists believed: that the gift of bridle-song was not a blessing of the gods, but instead rose out of necessity. To survive in this ancient forest, rife with dangers at every turn, it would require more than a hunter's skill and woodland knowledge. The alchymists suspected bridle-song had helped the tribes survive, to bend a portion of the fauna here to their will.

She pictured the tyger leaping away.

Maybe the alchymists were right.

Still, such an explanation had not satisfied her back in her sixthyear and still failed to do so now. It didn't answer the fundamental mystery. *Where and how did the tribe acquire this bloodborne talent?*

"I heard your song," Xan repeated. "It was so full of grief, yet also love. Your call traveled far to reach me, to call me to you."

How could that be possible?

Nyx again felt brittle leaves under her knees, Kanthe's blade in her hand, a finger rubbing velvet fur. The cairn of stones was so far from here. They had traveled from midday and deep into latterday before reaching this river.

"How could you have heard me?" she asked aloud.

"Ah, the power of bridle-song comes not from the lips but from the heart." The woman placed her palm between her own breasts, then over to Nyx's chest. "It reaches those who know how to listen with their spirit."

Nyx did not want to believe any of it, certainly not that she might be gifted with bridle-song.

"But be warned," the elder said. "There are beasts, like that tyger, who will be drawn to your trail. They will seek to kill anyone who risks bridling them."

Nyx remembered the soak of blood in her clothes. If the old woman was right, it wasn't blood scent that drew the beast. *It was me.* No wonder Kanthe's attempt to misdirect the tyger by leaving false trails had failed.

"And it's not just beasts that you need to fear," the elder said dourly.

Nyx frowned for some explanation, but Dala interrupted, looking impatient. *"Nee crys wan jar'wren."*

Xan lifted a palm, calming the younger woman. "Dala is telling you we *all* heard your song."

"Wee jar'wren," Dala stressed.

"Ya, jar'wren."

Nyx struggled, looking between the two women. "Is something wrong?"

The elder smiled. "No, the opposite. Dala is honored to meet someone who the *jar'wren* bridled themselves to. The gods who inhabit them never listen to us, never sing to us."

"What are the *jar'wren*?"

The elder's expression turned pensive, maybe worried, then she answered, *"Jar'wren* are what the Hálendii call Mýr bats. But they are so much more. They were touched by the old gods long ago and—"

Xan was cut off by a shout from nearby. Nyx turned, recognizing Frell's voice. One of the tribeswomen posted at the bushes waved to Xan and spoke rapidly.

The elder patted Nyx's arm. "Maybe it's best if we leave this for now. I see how pale you grow from it all."

Nyx wanted to object. She had a thousand more questions, but she let the Kethra'kai women walk her back toward the others. As she did, her thoughts remained on Xan's words, on the possibility that she carried some aspect of bridle-song in her heart. She tried to fit this knowledge into the hollow spaces of her past. She pictured the naked squalling babe in the swamps. Had the large bat who had rescued her known about this ability? Had some nascent version of bridle-song already been in her cries, drawing the bat and maybe later even Gramblebuck? Was that why the bullocks seemed to always follow her about, why Gramblebuck loved her so—and she him?

Was it song that bound our hearts?

She remembered Frell's attempt to explain her ability to meld with the Mýr bats. *You lived your first six moons under their tutelage, when your mind was soft clay, still pliable, far from fully formed. Your brain grew while under a constant barrage of their silent cries. Under such persistent exposure, your mind may have been forever altered by their keening, as a tree is gnarled by winds.*

She now wondered if that was only part of the answer. Not only was her brain *unformed* back then, but so was her ability. Had the keening of the bats somehow tangled her with them, binding one to another, creating something unique and new?

She shook her head at these speculations. She could not know, could never truly know. Especially with Bashaliia gone.

As Nyx passed through a break in the bushes, she watched Frell grab at one of the Kethra'kai.

"That is mine," the alchymist warned sternly.

The tribesman ignored Frell, fascinated by the trophy in his palm. It was the alchymist's wayglass, the tool he had used to guide their party through the woods.

"I need that to help us reach Havensfayre," Frell demanded.

Kanthe pulled the alchymist back. "It's their way, Frell. The Kethra'kai share everything. What is yours is everyone's."

"Well, then it's still equally mine," Frell argued.

"Only once the other relinquishes it. If he sets it down, you can reclaim it. But only then." Kanthe grinned at his friend's frustration. "Considering how that guy is ogling it, like some big diamond, that's not happening anytime soon."

Jace offered a compromise. "Why not wait until morning? We have to be deep into Eventoll by now. Maybe by dawn, the hunter will have grown bored with his prize."

Nyx realized how exhausted she was, especially as more campfires were lit. The growing spread of bright flames circled their camp. Plainly the Kethra'kai were bedding down for the night.

By now, Nyx had come up behind the others in her group.

Jace was the first to note her return. He swung around with his mouth open, ready to greet her or maybe to seek her support. Then his eyes widened, and he quickly faced back around, looking down at his toes.

Kanthe and Frell turned to her with similar shocked reactions.

The prince's eyes flew wide, then narrowed with appreciation. His lips quirked crookedly with amusement. "I see the Kethra'kai adjusted your clothing, or at least lessened it. I have to say I approve. Though as your possible older brother, might I suggest a nice cloak to go with it?"

Nyx scowled at him and started to cross her arms over her bare belly— then dropped her limbs. She had nothing to feel shame about.

She motioned to the spread of fires. "Jace is right. We should start fresh in the morning."

Xan joined her and spoke to Frell. "Fear not, we will take you to Havensfayre. We were going that direction anyway. Until we heard the child's song. It drew us over to your path, one that we will share from here."

Frell glanced at Nyx for an explanation, but she shook her head. The alchymist squinted at her for a breath, then returned his attention to Xan. "So, you're all traveling to Havensfayre, too?"

"No," she corrected. "We head only north. To where another calls to us. We will pass Havensfayre and leave you there."

Frell nodded, plainly mollified and satisfied with this plan. He waved to Kanthe and Jace to set up their own little camp.

Nyx stayed with Xan, who remained leaning on her cane, staring forward but not leaving. It was as if she were waiting for Nyx to speak, expecting her to, maybe testing her. Nyx knew what the elder wanted her to address.

"Xan . . . you said someone else calls to you from the north."

The elder nodded.

"Who?" Nyx pressed.

"I do not know." Xan turned away with a thump of her cane and spoke as she left. "But someone sings darkly, in the voice of the old gods, a song of danger and ruin."

Nyx started to follow her, but the other Kethra'kai women closed behind Xan without a word being spoken.

Nyx stopped and stared after them.

Xan reached the break in the bushes and glanced back. As she turned away a final time, her thin fingers traced down her cane, along the row of moonsculpted shells, as if polishing them. But that was not the purpose of that last gesture. Nyx knew it was a confirmation of her worst fears.

Xan's last words stayed with Nyx long after the elder had vanished.

A song of danger and ruin.

While Nyx still doubted she had been gifted with bridle-song, she remained certain of one thing. She knew this particular refrain all too well. Especially its last, resounding note.

Moonfall . . .

38

Exhausted and bone sore, Kanthe stood atop a small wooded rise that afforded a view across the blue expanse of the Heilsa. The forest lake shone under the late latterday sun. After so long buried under the clouds and mists of the Reach, he was stung by the brightness of the open sky. He squinted at the brilliant mirror of the flat waters. A handful of sails scudded across the surface, marking the path of fisherfolk from Havensfayre, a town that lay hidden in fog on the far side of the lake.

He understood why the nomadic Kethra'kai had constructed their only town beside this lake. Rather than merely reflecting the blue sky, the Heilsa's water seemed to take that hue and concentrate it into darker shades of cobalt and indigo. The Kethra'kai called this lake *Meyr'l Twy,* which meant *tears of the gods.* The Heilsa was even shaped like a teardrop that had fallen from the skies.

Yet, that was not the only reason for this lake's name.

Jace groaned. He sat on a log so fuzzed with moss that not a speck of bark could be seen. He had taken off his boots and rubbed his ankles.

"What I wouldn't give to soak my feet in those waters," he said to Nyx, who stood nearby.

The Kethra'kai had certainly set a hard stride through their greenwoods. They moved tirelessly, including the old woman. And even then, Kanthe suspected they went slower to accommodate the pace of the lowlanders among them. Still, it had taken their party most of the day to reach the large lake. Frell's estimation yesterday that their group could reach the Heilsa by midday was dashed by the reality of both distance and hardship. Their path here had been circuitous, avoiding known hazards, aiming for spots to collect rare herbs, or diverging to hunt for fresh game.

Faint ringing echoed across the lake from Havensfayre. The distant bells sounded haunting and forlorn, marking either the last bell of latterday or the first of Eventoll.

Jace reached to his boots, preparing to don them. Their day's hike was not yet over. They still had to round the lake, which would take them near to the end of Eventoll. They currently waited for the Kethra'kai to finish some act of obeisance at the lake's edge. Frell was down there with them, observing a ceremony that involved much bowing. Palms were dipped in the water and placed to cheeks. He heard faint singing.

Nyx stared toward them with her arms crossed. She had donned Jace's cloak after it had dried overnight, but she had barely tied it, allowing glimpses of bare skin and the spotted wrap over her breasts.

Kanthe had caught Jace sneaking surreptitious glances her way as they trekked the forest. Not that he faulted the journeyman. Kanthe had done the same. And it wasn't just the peeks at her flesh that likely drew their attention, even Frell's—though the alchymist's glances were more studious than appreciative.

Instead, with each league hiked, an air grew about her, gathering like a cloak to her shoulders. Her skin shone with more than perspiration. The golden strands in her hair brightened, while the rest of it darkened into shadows. It was as if she drew some strange vitality from the woods. Kanthe doubted she was even aware of it.

Certainly no one mentioned it, but they all felt it.

Even the Kethra'kai, who snuck looks her way and whispered among themselves.

Nyx seemed blind to it all. During the long trek, she had hardly spoken a word, clearly dwelling deeply on matters she was not ready to talk about. She cast glances often toward the Kethra'kai elder, but any attempt of hers to move closer was rebuffed, not forcefully, more like a wind that kept pushing the women and elder away if Nyx drew too close.

Jace also kept protectively close to her, gasping and panting to keep up. Kanthe had come to realize how much he had underestimated both the journeyman's stamina and his boundless loyalty to his friend. The latter was certainly born of a stripling's love, which had yet to be spoken. Kanthe had harbored one or two such affections in the past and knew how much it ached one's heart, a wonderful anguish jumbled with hope, desire, and a large amount of insecurity.

Still, he sensed depths to Jace that, like Nyx, the journeyman was oblivious to. When Kanthe first met him, he judged the man to be slovenly, weak of muscle and wide of belly, stunted by his years of shelter at the Cloistery, truly no more than a man-child. But after these many days, he recognized the stinginess of his judgement.

And I should know better.

His ears rang with the many past jibes cast his way, by people who did not know him: the Tallywag, the Dark Trifle, and many other coarser titles.

Still, even with his newfound generosity for Jace, Kanthe sometimes wanted to slap him across his scruffy face. Like now.

Jace pointed to the lake after donning his boots. "It's said the waters of the

Heilsa hold miraculous curative powers. Many come here with dire ailments and swear that imbibing or bathing in these waters healed them."

Kanthe closed his eyes, biting back a groan. He remembered Jaleek's big grin and the word that the tribesman had spoken as he pointed to a bowl of powder. *Kraal.* The Kethra'kai apparently had a cure for what the skriitch inflicted.

A soft moan drew Kanthe's eyes open. Nyx had stepped from her post near the log and toward the lake. Whatever magick had infused her fell from her shoulders, leaving her back bowed. He knew what she feared, the guilt it sharpened. The promise of healing waters opened a wound barely closed.

He crossed over to her and cleared his throat, seeking for a lightness that his heart did not feel. "It's just legend," he scoffed. "The scout I knew, Bre'bran, laughed at such stories."

This was a lie, but one he knew Nyx needed to hear.

"The lake is no different than any other," he continued. "Truly. The people of Havensfayre suffer just as many ailments as any other town. Sure, it's pretty and all, but miraculous?" He blew sourly through his lips. "Preposterous."

Jace sat straighter. "But according to Lyllandra's *Medicum Priz,* the waters are said to be rich in—"

"In shite." Kanthe cut the journeyman off with a hard frown and a meaningful look at Nyx's back. "Flowing in from Havensfayre's sewers. And I know those fisherfolk sailing out there have pissed many a time in that lake."

Jace seemed to finally understand. He swallowed hard, his cheeks reddening, and nodded. "That's probably true."

"Then enough talk of miraculous waters," Kanthe said. "We still have a long trek to reach Havensfayre, and the Kethra'kai are coming back."

He waved to where the tribesmen climbed up the rise toward them, accompanied by Frell, whose face was flushed with excitement at observing a ceremony rarely witnessed by lowlanders.

Kanthe scowled at their approach.

If that skinny alchymist says one word about cures . . .

Still, the damage had been done. Nyx straightened, but she tightened the cloak around her body, as if she were suddenly cold. Or maybe she sensed the forest's charmed mantle had been stripped from her by Jace's ill-timed words.

Frell must have noted the shift in weather atop the knoll. He frowned around, saw nothing amiss, and waved back to the lake. "We should be in Havensfayre in another few bells."

Kanthe nodded. "Then we dare wait no longer."

As he followed the scouts of the Kethra'kai, he dragged his own shadowy fears along with him, which grew with every step. His hip ached from where the crossbow bolt had grazed it, a shot he had thought accidental, but now was suspect. He pictured the crimson-faced Mallik thrusting a sword at him. And the face of another vy-knight, the head of the detachment. Anskar would not sit idly by after allowing Kanthe to escape his assassination attempt.

Still, he cast a worried look toward Nyx. She had also survived an assassination long ago, one ordered by the same king. Maybe she was Toranth's daughter, as reviled as a certain despoiled son. But Kanthe also knew she carried a dark pall of prophecy, of doom laid at her feet, a warning whispered in the king's ear by a dark Iflelen. Kanthe had dismissed such divinations before, but he could not ignore a worry that had been growing of late, one just as rife with fear, especially with all that he had heard and witnessed these past days.

He stared over at Nyx.

What if that bastard Wryth was right?

Nyx watched the Kethra'kai vanish into the mists.

The final bell of Eventoll rang from the shadows of the fog-shrouded town to her right. The tribesmen had honored their promise and delivered her and the others to the outskirts of the woodland town. The two groups parted where a rutted road led toward Havensfayre.

At the forest's edge, only Xan and Dala still lingered in the mist, staring back at her, looking like ghostly spirits of these greenwoods. *And maybe they were.* Dala kissed her palm, held it toward Nyx, then backed into the fog and was gone, leaving only the elder.

Nyx did not understand why Xan had avoided her all day. *Had I done something to offend her? Or were there secrets the wizened woman was not yet willing to share?*

The elder's eyes—sapphire and emerald—shone out of the pall. It was nearly all that was visible of the snowy-haired woman's countenance. Only at that moment did Nyx realize how Xan's eyes matched The Twins, the two bright lakes that framed either side of the misty town: Heilsa's blue waters behind Nyx and Eitur's green spread, somewhere farther to the north, lost in the fog.

Before she could ponder this, Xan began to sing to her. With the woman's lips hidden, it was as if the elder's voice came from the whole forest. There were no words that Nyx could understand, but the intonations and melody, the lilt and rhythm, spoke of passing ages, of tiny seeds growing into creaking giants, of death's inevitability, and the joy of petal, leaf, loam, and all the creatures enjoying their brief spark here.

She pictured Bashaliia, winging through branches, chasing motes flashing in sunlight. Tears rose, which had always been there, held back in the false belief that they were no longer needed. The salt washed her eyes.

Xan continued to sing, but under her voice, another song wafted, stranded in golden notes. They bathed her until Nyx opened to them. She closed her eyes and fell back through the ages of the Kethra'kai in these woods. Images blurred. She tried to follow, but she stumbled, too raw and untrained for such travel. She caught a brief glimpse of dark cliffs, of ancient seas imbedded in those walls, of something stirring in the shrouds above.

Then she lost the rhythm and tumbled back into herself.

She opened her eyes as the song drew to an end. She stared ahead, but Xan was already gone. As she stared into the mists, she felt abandoned yet again, cast from a kinship that could never be hers.

Jace approached, moving with tender concern. "Nyx . . . ?"

She looked over to him, starting to shake. He reached to her, and she fell into his arms. He held her, letting her sob, staying silent, as if knowing there was nothing he could say. But his warmth, his scent, were enough.

I'm not abandoned, she reminded herself.

She waited for the last echoes of the song to fade out of her, to find herself back fully in her own skin, in Jace's arms. She finally hugged him back more firmly, letting him know she was all right.

She leaned back and stared up into his face. "Thank you."

He blushed, mumbled almost apologetically.

She slipped out of his arms but found his hand and held it. She stared over at Kanthe and Frell, who looked embarrassed.

Frell cleared his throat with a cough. "We should be going."

KANTHE KEPT NEXT to his mentor as they approached the edge of Havensfayre. "Do you know where you're going?" he asked Frell. "Have you ever been here before?"

"No," the man admitted. He nodded to the misty town, still barely visible through the pall. "But Prioress Ghyle gave me a name. The Golden Bough. An inn somewhere in Havensfayre."

As they marched along the rutted road, the fog thinned slowly to either side. More and more of the woodland town appeared out of the mists, going from hazy illusion to an undeniable sturdiness.

Despite his pretended worldliness, Kanthe gaped about at this forest trading post, aglow with a thousand lamps. It looked as if the entire place had been grown rather than built. And in many ways, it had. Here, an ancient grove of Reach alders climbed into the sky. The giant trunks had been hollowed out into homes, climbing many levels, with tiny windows shining and crooked stone chimneys piping with smoke. The highest homes vanished into mists, revealing themselves in the glow of distant windows.

Yet despite all of this, the trees still lived, spreading branches leafed in green and gold. Many of those limbs had been carved into bridges. And where those failed to span, hundreds of swinging wooden bridges crisscrossed throughout the town. Even the trees' massive roots, many as thick around as the trunks of the Reach's remaining forest, had been sculpted into natural staircases.

As their group passed under one such archway, Kanthe spotted stone steps that dug down, adding new meaning to root cellar. From the laughter and clinking of stoneware rising from below, he suspected a good portion of Havensfayre lay buried under this ancient grove.

Still, not all of the town had been carved from the forest.

As they continued, ordinary homes of stone and wood, of shingle and thatch, appeared, abutting against the trunks. These grew in number, stacking one atop the other, but still there remained a naturalness in the curve of walls, the layers of lichen on stones, the spread of circular windows, like the glowing eyes of owls.

Frell stopped periodically to ask for directions from the townspeople, who all seemed uniformly cheery, despite the perpetual fog. Kanthe understood why. Music wafted all around. Lamps glowed everywhere, glassed in every color. The air itself smelled of woodsmoke and rich loam, as if every breath held life within it.

Still, this late in the day, the avenues and winding streets were mostly thin of people, a mix of darker-skinned lowlanders and pale Kethra'kai. Most shops were shuttered, but several stands lured their passing noses with the scent of sizzling meat, bubbling stews, and frothy ale.

"Right yonder," an apple-cheeked man said to Frell from behind a fiery griddle, and pointed down the way. He looked close to burning his round belly on his stove. "Past the Oldenmast. You can't miss the Golden Bough."

Kanthe hoped the man was right, feeling already thoroughly lost. Between the mists and the meandering streets and alleys, he would have had a hard time pointing toward the waters of Heilsa, which seemed a world away. He searched around. The lamplight stretched in all directions, fading into the distance, making it hard to judge the breadth of this town.

Frell thanked the hawker for his directions and got them moving again.

Jace drew closer. "Is it me? Or are we going in circles?"

Kanthe realized he wasn't the only one confused by this jumble of a town.

Frell huffed and led the way. "It can't be far."

Jace cast a sidelong glance at Kanthe, then shrugged. "If not, I'm going to raid the next stew stand we cross."

"Or tavern," Kanthe added.

Finally, they rounded a huge bole of a tree that looked far larger than any of the others. Its bark had fallen away or been stripped, exposing a whitish-gold wood. Its surface had been polished to a sheen that reflected their passage. A pointed archway opened into it, sealed by tall doors of the same alder wood. Over it and lit from within, a huge round window glowed with brilliant shards of glass. To one side, a fiery sun cast out golden rays, lighting up a pale blue sky. Beyond those spears, the pieces of glass grew ever darker as they crossed to the other side, where stars appeared, sparkling like diamonds, all surrounding the silvery face of a full moon.

"This must be the town's kath'dral," Jace said as they passed it.

"No, this is Oldenmast. Dala told me about it." Nyx stared up at the silver moon with a haunted expression, plainly reminded of the danger that had brought them all together. "It's not our gods that are worshipped here, but those of the Kethra'kai. Here they give honor to the pantheon of the forest."

"Even so," Frell said, moving them on, "if this is Oldenmast, the inn cannot be much farther."

For the first time since entering these greenwoods, the alchymist was right.

As they cleared around the huge polished trunk, a sprawling structure hugged the next tree, whose bole was only slightly smaller than the one they had just passed. The construction climbed a dozen levels. It was timber-framed, slate-roofed, with a foundation of mossy, lichen-scribed boulders. Its entirety melded into the ancient alder behind it, which also shone with windows along its trunk. It all blended so finely that it was hard to discern where craftsmanship ended and nature took over.

Ahead, a pair of huge doors, large enough to close a barn, stood open. Merriment and music flowed out to them. Firelight danced inside. Over the threshold, a sign had been carved into the gilded shape of a tree, from tangled dark roots to the spread of a wide crown, leafed in gold.

Kanthe sighed. "If that's *not* the Golden Bough, I'm still staying here. You all can keep wandering these blasted mists."

Frell pushed him toward the open door. "Let's hope this journey has not been for naught."

NYX WAITED IN the commons of the inn, which was less a single room than a warren of interconnecting chambers. Some were small and intimate, no more than an alcove hiding a table behind a dusty embroidered drape.

Others were large dining halls, smoky taverns, tiny cookeries, and dens of games, from quiet tables bearing painted boards of Knights n' Knaves, which were earnestly labored over, to raucous spaces where Klashean tiles or rolling dice were bet upon.

As crowded as the spaces were, it was as if the entire town had come to the Golden Bough this night. Pipe smoke clouded the rafters. Spats of loud laughter burst out that made her jump. Pewter platters clanked, and stoneware clattered. Cheers and boasts and threats—some in jest, others serious—echoed all around.

After so long in the quiet of the greenwood, Nyx found the noise overwhelming. Compounding this, the overload of sights in the chaotic space challenged her returned vision and dizzied her. Seeking a respite from it all, she had found a quiet corner near a small hearth, ruddy with coals. It was as close of a reminder of home as she could find in this strange place. Kanthe stayed with her, standing at their scarred table with Jace. Frell had gone to make an inquiry with the innkeep behind a long bar.

Nyx watched the alchymist lean over, his ear cocked, then a nod. Frell slid a coin half-hidden under his palm to the thickly bearded man. Nyx caught the shine of gold. Whatever the alchymist had bought from the innkeep had come at a steep price.

Finally, Frell turned and nodded to Kanthe.

The prince nudged Jace and waved to Nyx. "Let's go. Hopefully the beds here are not piles of leaves, damp with mulch. Give me a thick dry mattress stuffed with hay, and I'll sleep like a babe in the softest cradle."

They headed over and joined Frell, who motioned to a scrawny boy with a crimson cap bearing a paper gold leaf tucked into its band. The alchymist passed him a folded slip and a brass pinch. Both vanished into a vest pocket, and the boy took off across the maze of the commons.

"Hurry now," the alchymist urged under his breath, and led them after the spry lad.

"Where are we going?" Jace asked.

"To the stables," Frell said, clearly distracted and nervous.

Kanthe scowled. "Maybe I shouldn't have said I'd be satisfied with a bed of hay."

They kept up with the boy, who dashed hither and yon, through the commons to the back, then down a series of halls. Finally, he reached a tall door and rushed forward to open it for them. As he did so, a clash of steel rang from outside, furious and savage.

Worried at the sounds of battle, Nyx slowed, but Frell hurried to the boy.

He handed him another bit of brass and waved the lad out the door ahead of him.

Frell turned and stopped them at the threshold. "Stay here," he warned, then stepped out of the door alone and crossed a few paces.

Jace kept beside Nyx, his brows pinched with the same fear as hers.

What is happening?

Past the door, a large courtyard was open to the misty skies. Lamps hung all around the square. To either side stretched a dozen archways, closed with half gates. Past the nearest, Nyx spied shadowy stalls, where a few horses stirred, likely disturbed by the commotion in the yard.

Nyx kept near Jace's shoulder.

Two men fought across the breadth of the courtyard, hacking and slashing; both bore cuts in their shirts and breeches, some spots dark with blood. One carried a silvery sword that blurred in his hands. The other wielded two blades so thin that they seemed more mirage than steel. They clashed and parried, thrust and dodged. Their boots danced across the cobblestone yard. Sweat sheened both their faces, lips grimacing or smiling savagely, changing back and forth as swiftly as their swordplay.

Nyx's pounding heart slowed as she recognized that they were merely sparring, fiercely so, but not truly trying to kill each other. The boy headed over to the pair, whistling for their attention. They finally stopped, breathing hard, gazing with irritation at the lad.

"What is it, boy?" The swarthier of the two men combed back a damp swath of blue-black hair over an ear. "It better be important, or I'll cuff you soundly for interrupting us."

The lad's shoulders rose by his ears. He fumbled with a pocket.

"Leave the boy be, Darant," the other said. He was a grizzled man with a dark scruff of beard over cheek and chin, salted with gray, which matched his lanky hair. He bore a jagged scar down one cheek. "Before the lad pisses himself."

Even in the doorway, Nyx felt the danger wafting off these two men.

"M . . . Message," the boy finally bleated out. He pulled out and handed the folded oilskin slip from Frell over to the scarred man.

With a weary sigh, the man sheathed his sword and took it. "Demand for another day's board, I imagine." He glanced sidelong at his sparring partner. "It's as if the inn doesn't trust a pirate."

Pirate?

Nyx glanced over to Frell, who waited off to the side. The alchymist's gaze remained fixed on the man who held the message. Frell's face held the same glaze of wonder as when he had observed the Kethra'kai lakeside ceremony, as if he were seeing history come to life.

The man in the yard stiffened as he spotted a crimson wax seal that secured the message. He hurriedly broke it open and scanned what was written there. He glanced to the boy, who pointed over to Frell.

"This was carried by you?" the man called over to the alchymist. "Written by the hand of Prioress Ghyle?"

Frell nodded, nearly half bowing. "Yes, but I come with much more." He turned to the doorway and whispered with a wave, "Nyx . . . it's safe to come out."

She was not sure that was true, but she stepped into the yard, drawing Jace and Kanthe with her.

Frell turned back to the man. "I come with Marayn's lost daughter."

Nyx fell back a step. She eyed the man with the same look of shock as was mirrored on the stranger's face. She barely heard Frell's next words as he motioned across the yard.

"Nyx, this is Graylin sy Moor, a man who may be your father."

They stared at one another for a frozen breath.

"No . . ." the man finally gasped out. "It cannot be."

Still, he took a tentative step toward her.

She retreated, running into Kanthe and Jace.

"I've got you," the prince whispered behind her.

"We both do," Jace added.

With their support, she stood her ground. Her shock turned to something colder. If any of this were true, here was the knight who had left her for dead in the swamps.

As he approached, he studied her, first with one eye, then another. His steps suddenly faltered. He slipped down on one knee. His voice cracked when he tried to speak.

"Y . . . You look just like her. It's unmistakable." His gaze tried to consume her. Tears welled, seeming to rise from both sadness and happiness. His lips thinned with agony. "By all the gods . . . I know you must be Marayn's daughter."

Nyx took her first step toward him, drawn by his grief and guilt, which matched her own heart. She searched his face, trying to find a similar match in his features, but she only saw a hard, broken man.

"I . . . I'm sorry," she whispered to this stranger. "But I doubt any of this is true."

Her words wounded him, but she felt no satisfaction in it, even as much as she had resented him for most of her life. There were angry words trapped in her chest, long turned to stone. She didn't know what to make of this fallen knight. She had tried to prepare for this, but she had never truly believed it would happen. She dared not even hope it.

And now that it was here . . .

She realized a hard truth.

He means nothing to me.

As if hearing her private thought, a growl echoed across the courtyard. Then another. From one of the stables to the right, a large striped shadow bounded over a half gate, followed by a twin. They looked somewhat like wolves, only each stood as high as her chest. They stalked back and forth, crisscrossing one another, heads lowered, with tufted ears held high.

Jace gasped, and Kanthe swore.

Frell tried to herd them back toward the door. "They're vargr," he warned, his voice both scared and awed.

Nyx ignored him and stood firm, captured by the dark chatter behind the beasts' growls. She listened to the underlying high whine. The pitch shivered the hairs on her neck.

Graylin, the man who could be her father, turned to the pair. "Aamon, Kalder, back to your den! Now!"

The vargr ignored him, sweeping wide to come around either side of the man. They passed him and squeezed back together in front of him, filling the space between her and the knight. The pair of vargr growled, lips rippling, baring teeth, challenging her.

She remembered Xan's warning: *There are beasts who will be drawn to your trail. They will seek to kill anyone who risks bridling them.*

Still, she faced down the pair. She picked out the thread buried in their whine. It sang of dark forests under cold stars, of the fire of the hunt, of the rip of flesh off bone, of the warmth of the pack in snowy dens. She let those wild strands inside her, to entwine through her. She accepted the vargr's feral nature, their savage lusts. She had no desire to bridle any of that, but she also refused to be cowed by them.

Instead, she gathered all the anger, grief, and guilt inside her, even her loneliness and shame, until it demanded to be loosed, to burst forth in a wild scream. She remembered unleashing that storm after her father was murdered, leaving many dead in the wake of her rage.

Not again.

She focused all that raw power onto one image. Of a small bat fighting to save her, of dying because of it. Of milk and warmth shared. Of a brother tied to her heart. She closed her eyes and keened that kinship, fueled by all that was inside her. She sang it back along the twin threads to the two wild hearts crouched before her.

As she did so, she exposed her own heart, welcoming them to it.

Slowly their two songs merged. Her keening transformed into a silent howl inside her chest. She shared their haunting cry to icy stars framed by frosted branches and brittle needles.

After a seemingly endless time, Jace gasped again behind her.

She opened her eyes.

One vargr bowed before her, then the other. Their chins lowered to the cobbles. Amber eyes glowed up at her. Tails swished in greeting. Two throats flowed with quieter mewls of reunion, welcoming a lost pack member back to the fold.

She stared at her new brothers, then lifted her gaze over their haunches to the man behind them. She offered him no kinship like she had these beasts. She faced his bewilderment, the awe in his face.

She had only one message for him.

Here is what you abandoned in the swamps.

Arkival limne of
Pyrantha
(Cloudreach)

Reach Tyger

TWELVE

BLOODBAERNE

So it is written: Magi im Rhell, First of the Klashean Dresh'ri, cut his heart out before his brothers & heald it forth as proof of his superiority. He gave it unto the Second of his ordre before finally succumbing to deth. It is claim'd, for centuries, the Imri-Ka kept the sacred talisman in a consecrat'd vault—where it still beats to this day.

—From Baskal's *History of Arcana and Thaumaturgy*

39

THE KING'S BRIGHT son stood in shadows.

Mikaen paused on the dark stairs that delved through the ramparts of Highmount. He stared out an arrow slit that afforded a view to the north, to the smoldering ruins of the city's mooring docks.

It had been three days since the craven attack on the defenseless sprawl of wyndships. Still, a pall hung over the field, like a shawl of mourning. Hundreds had burned to death, thousands more maimed. Innocents all. Past the smoke, the towering warships loomed high, waving flags of the sun and crown.

At least those ships had been spared, and thankfully so.

Mikaen settled a palm on the pommel of his sword.

War is now certain with the Klashe.

His anger stoked higher. It was not the homecoming he had hoped. He still wore the ceremonial garb from his celebratory nuptial parade. The procession of knights, nobles, and servitors had traveled from Azantiia to the Carcassa family estate in the western stretches of the Brauðlands. He had left his new wife, Lady Myella, at Hold Carcassia, a sweeping manor that spread across green hills. Its rolling low roofs were sodded in the same grasses that fed their vast herds. Rumors of war had been the pretext for securing Myella at the ranchhold, to shelter her out of harm's way. But in fact, the sojourn had already been planned, to help mask how quickly her belly grew with the prince's child, the future heir to the throne of Hálendii.

He closed his eyes against the pall outside and thought instead of holding his child in his arms. He pictured a crown of curled blond hair to match his own, and the bright emerald eyes of his beloved Myella. Already a paternal protectiveness warmed through him. He would let nothing happen to his child.

"We should not tarry," Liege General Haddan urged from a few steps below. "The king awaits. And fury has quickened his temper."

Mikaen nodded his understanding. After hearing of the Klashean attack, he had ridden hard back to Highmount, arriving with the dawn bell. His polished black boots were scuffed by stirrup and horsehair, his dark blue cloak carried half the road's mud on it, and his body stank of sweat, both his and his steed's. As soon as he had stabled his horse to be curried and cooled, he had climbed toward a cold bath and a welcome steam in the Legionary's bathiery, ready to rid the trail from his pores and cracks.

Before he could even strip off his cloak, Haddan had appeared with his father's summons. Knowing it could not be refused, nor even delayed, Mikaen had headed straight back down through the ramparts with Haddan.

And they still had much farther to go.

Mikaen followed the stone-faced Haddan around and around the stairs, past where he had stabled his horse, and deeper again, going from mortared stone to raw rock. Finally, they reached a landing and a section of wall that looked no different than the rest. A crack hid a hole that Haddan unlocked with a black key. The liege general shoved a narrow door open and stepped across the threshold.

"Hurry now," Haddan commanded gruffly.

Mikaen followed and pushed the door closed behind him. They strode down a long hall that sloped even deeper. Mikaen kept his head ducked low, sensing the weight of the ramparts over his head. No smoky torches lit their path, only softly glowing veins in the rock wall. It cast Haddan's shaved pate into a sickly pallor.

Mikaen hated coming down into the Shrivenkeep, but he understood the necessity of secrets buried deep and how some dark knowledge was best locked away from the brightness of the Father Above.

At last, an open doorway appeared, framed in firelight.

Haddan increased his pace, seemingly as happy to abandon this hall as the prince. Or maybe it was the pull of what awaited ahead. Past the ebonwood door, a cavernous domed space opened up. Its obsidian walls had been fractured into a thousand mirrored surfaces, reflecting the ring of torches flickering before other ebonwood doors, all sealed, except for the one behind Mikaen and another to the right, where two figures waited.

Haddan rushed forward and bent a knee, bowing his head. "Your Majesty."

Mikaen trailed him, but only by a breath. He dropped to the same knee. "Father, I'm sorry to have arrived so late after such a cowardly attack upon us all. I should have been here."

King Toranth waved them both up. "It gladdens me to have you back at Highmount, Mikaen."

The prince regained his feet. His father's expression did not look *gladdened*. The white marble of his skin was ashen, nearly gray. His brow lay in deep furrows, shadowing his blue eyes into a storm. He had even shed the finery of his embroidery and velvets and wore a legionnaire's boots and thin underleathers, creased at knee and elbow. It was a knight's habiliment, one put on before he donned his armor. The only adornment was a simple dark blue tunic over his leathers, emblazoned with the Massif house sigil.

Here was a highking readying for war.

Mikaen appreciated his father's garb and hard countenance. He could see the storm clouds building around the man's shoulders—and made a silent promise.

I will do all in my power to be the bright lightning to your great thunder.

The king turned to the other waiting beside him, a figure who had haunted his father's shadow for as long as Mikaen could remember. The Shrive's tattoo-banded eyes stared hard at the prince, as if irritated by his intrusion here—until the king spoke.

"Wryth, take us to the prisoner. We've given Vythaas long enough to prepare."

The Shrive bowed and turned toward the door behind him. "He should be ready when we get there, especially as we still have a ways to travel."

The king and the general followed Wryth. Mikaen took a deep breath while no one was looking before heading after them. He had never been farther than this threshold into the Shrivenkeep, and he had hoped never to do so. He was the prince who shone best under the sun, helmed in bright armor. The clash of steel and ring of shields were his music. He preferred to leave such dark places to the creatures who shunned the Father Above. Its halls were said to be shivered by screams, both from the throats of men and those of daemons.

Still, he followed the others past the door and into the bowels of the Shrivenkeep. Wryth paused beyond the threshold to unhook a glowing lamp from the wall. It was quickly needed. The torches grew scarcer as Wryth led them farther and farther. They passed down narrow stairs worn at the edges by centuries of Shrive's sandals. Every passageway was more crooked than the last.

In the upper levels, they swept past gray-robed Shriven who ducked out of their way, clutching dusty texts to their chests, likely forbidden tomes from the Black Librarie of the Anathema. One Shrive they passed had a hand wrapped in bloody bandages, being led by another, suggesting an experiment gone awry.

Eventually, as they delved deeper, the passageways emptied of Wryth's brethren.

Mikaen's ears strained for any screams, for daemonic howls, but instead there was a hushed silence, which grew to be as weighty as the stone overhead. His nose caught a faint whiff of sulfurous brimstan, which their group seemed to be following, like a thylassaur on a blood trail.

The source finally appeared down a long serpentine tunnel. Near its end, the passageway was riven by a steep-sided ravine, as if the god Nethyn had cleaved it open with his obsidian blade. A stone bridge spanned it, flanked by two black pillars.

Wryth led them toward those stone columns. As Mikaen followed, he saw a crimson asp, crowned in thorns, curled on each pillar. The two *horn'd snaken* faced each other, as if daring anyone to trespass between them, clearly marking the territory ahead as the domain of the dark god Đreyk, and thus the Iflelen.

Mikaen hurried past those dead-eyed serpents and across the stone bridge. He made the mistake of looking over its edge. The chasm stank so heavily of brimstan that it turned his stomach and watered his eyes. Still, he spotted a baleful shine far below. It was not the ruddy cheer of a fiery hearth, but the same sickly emerald of the glowing seams that ran through the black stones.

He shuddered and rushed the last of the way across the bridge, joining the others who gathered under an archway into a large tunnel. The stone of the arch was scribed with arcane symbols, all glowing that abhorrent green, as if the very veins of the rock had been bent to the will of the Iflelen to form those symbols.

Mikaen balked at that threshold.

"It is not far from here," Wryth offered, as if sensing Mikaen was near to bolting.

The Shrive headed under the archway with his lamp. His father and Haddan followed, which left Mikaen no choice but to continue after them. He certainly had no idea how to get back on his own.

Finally, Wryth reached an iron door. He hung his lamp next to it and grabbed the door's circular hasp—a ring shaped like a curled asp—in both hands. It seemed to take all of his strength to pull it open. As the heavy door swung on oiled hinges, fiery light flowed out to them—along with a scream that burst into the hall and echoed away, as if trying to escape.

Mikaen shivered, knowing that the cry had come from no daemon, but from someone being broken.

Wryth waved them inside and trailed in afterward.

Mikaen's view was blocked by the broad back of Haddan, until the liege general stumbled aside with a grunt of shock. The entire chamber looked made of hammered iron, as if they'd stepped into an oven. Only the metal riveted to all the surfaces appeared blacker than any iron. At the back, flames roared from a small barred hearth.

A chair of the same iron stood in the center. Beside it, the withered form of Shrive Vythaas greeted the king silently, then bent over a spread of silvery tools atop a nearby table. The instruments were all sharp-pointed or bladed or spiraled like an awl. Many of them were wet with blood. But it was none of this that drained the heat from Mikaen's body and left him icy with dread.

A naked woman sat in the chair, her forehead, neck, and chest secured to its back by leather straps. She hung slack in her bonds, as if she had passed out from whatever made her scream. Her head was shaven, recently from the pile of white braids left on the floor. Rivulets of blood ran down her cheeks and pooled in the hollow of her exposed neck, before spilling again down her chest.

But worst of all was the top of her head. From her skull, a half dozen copper needles stuck out. As Mikaen watched, Vythaas crossed around his table to the back of her chair. The Shrive leaned over his captive, lifted his hands, and sank another copper sliver, as long as Mikaen's outstretched fingers, through a hole freshly drilled through scalp and bone.

Mikaen pictured that needle sinking deep into the woman's brain.

What is that bastard doing?

Even the king looked aghast, turning wide eyes on Wryth. "What is the meaning of this?"

Wryth lifted a hand, asking for patience. "Prioress Ghyle has proven far more stubborn than we anticipated."

MIKAEN PACED THE room as Wryth and Vythaas finished some final preparations with the trussed-up mistress of the Cloistery. They measured the copper needles in her skull, shifted each incrementally, whispering together.

Mikaen kept his arms folded over his chest, trying to hold in his horror, to mask any sign of shock or fright in front of his father and the liege general. He smelled the blood, even the pool of piss under the chair that torture had wracked out of the woman. His tongue tasted the bitter alchymicals burning in the flames of the hearth.

He kept his gaze away from the chair. He knew Anskar vy Donn, the head of the detachment of Vyrllian Guards, had returned from the swamps, both furious and empty-handed. As best Mikaen could understand, his brother, Kanthe, had absconded with the girl who had miraculously survived the bat's poison.

Brother, what mischief have you entangled yourself in?

It was a question that needed answering. Anskar suspected there was more afoot, plots within schemes. So, he had returned with the school's prioress in hand, believing she knew more than she would admit to him. To get answers, he brought her before the king.

Mikaen swallowed and looked at the bloody woman.

And my father gave her to the Iflelen.

Wryth seemed to note all their distress. "As stubborn as Prioress Ghyle has been, I fear this is the only way to make her talk. And with our mooring docks smoking and rumors of ships massing along the coasts of the Klashe, we dare not dally with ordinary methods of inquiry."

"But what is this that you're doing?" Toranth gasped out, motioning across the breadth of the room.

"It's a technique honed by Vythaas but derived from centuries of study." Wryth turned to his fellow Shrive. "Are you ready? Can you demonstrate?"

Vythaas gave a small bow of his head and crossed back to the table. He picked up a coppery box, which had the same needles poking out of it, though each ended in a puff of feathery filaments so fine they appeared more like soft down. He thumbed a small lever on one side and a low hum rose from the box.

The noise spread around the room and grew sharper, trapped between the chamber's iron walls. In another breath, its edges grew as sharp as the finest blade, yet toothed like a saw. It scratched at his ears, stabbed into his skull. Even Haddan winced, and Mikaen had once watched the man sew a sword slice across his own thigh without a flinch, even laughing while he set needle to flesh.

The tiny tufted filaments began to glow faintly, with the very air seeming to shiver around those tips. And still the keening rose higher.

A pained gasp drew Mikaen's attention to the woman. The prioress's eyes were stretched open but appeared blind, her mouth twisted in a rictus of agony. The needles sprouting from her scalp now shone with the same glow as the filaments from the box. Their lengths looked to be shivering in her skull.

Vythaas studied her reaction until the woman's expression went slack, succumbing to whatever magick was employed here. Still, her brow remained beaded with sweat, like juice squeezed out of the flesh of a plum. Somewhere inside, she clearly labored against this assault.

Vythaas nodded to Wryth.

The Shrive turned to King Toranth, speaking louder to be heard past the screaming of the copper box. "Sire, you may now ask any questions you wish. She will not be able to refuse." He waved to the prioress. "Her will is suppressed, leaving no space for lies."

"But how . . . ?" Toranth asked, his gaze sickly but also fascinated.

Wryth sighed, clearly seeking a way to explain to those who were not steeped in Shriven knowledge. He finally settled upon an explanation. "You are familiar with bridle-song, are you not? How some have the talent to lull the simplest of beasts and sway them to do their bidding. What we do here is much like that, using sound, heat, and vibration through the air to strip others of their will and force them to bow to ours."

Haddan's voice roughened with amazement. "So, with this method, you're able to imitate or mock bridle-song?"

Mikaen felt none of the general's appreciation. *It's not a* mock *of bridle-song, but a foul* mockery *of it.*

"Indeed." Wryth turned to the king and waved toward the prioress. "Ask what you wish to know."

The king stepped forward, wincing at the noise as he drew nearer to the chair. "Prioress Ghyle, what role did you play in the disappearance of my son Kanthe?"

Those dull eyes found the strength to shift and settle on Toranth. Her cracked lips parted. "I . . . told him. A . . . A great danger comes. Moon-fall . . . it will end all."

Mikaen noted the king's shoulders rise. He knew how much store his father placed in portents of the future. Toranth kept as many soothers and bone-tossers in his palacio as he did pleasure serfs.

"Who speaks of such doom?" Toranth asked.

"Al . . . chymist Frell. He calibrated . . . stars. And another, too . . ."

"Who?"

"A girl . . . Nyx . . . heard in warnings from the cries of Mýr bats."

Haddan scoffed loudly.

The king waved him silent.

Wryth shrugged. "True or not, the prioress believes it. She cannot lie."

Haddan still was having none of it. If the general couldn't strike it with a sword, he didn't believe it existed. "Prioress Ghyle was born in the Southern Klashe, which means she has deep family roots there. Mayhap this is some plot seeded into her by our enemy, to sow discord. Spreading rumors of doom in a time of war will weaken convictions when we'll need them at their strongest. Look what it's already done to your son, sire."

Toranth scowled. "What does *any* of this have to do with Kanthe?"

The question was directed at Haddan, but the prioress heard and could not stop from answering. Her brow ran with sweat as she clearly fought this bridling. "He . . . seeks to help . . . his sister."

Mikaen stiffened, unfolding his arms. "Sister?"

"The girl who speaks for the Mýr . . . she . . . is Marayn's . . . Marayn's lost daughter."

Mikaen did not understand, but his father clearly did. He stumbled away from the woman's words.

"No . . ." the king moaned. "It cannot be."

Toranth swung to Wryth, who looked equally shocked.

"You said the babe was dead," the king accused.

"So we all believed," Wryth answered, but his expression grew shadowed.

Toranth's face darkened with fury. "A child *you* portended, Wryth. A *girl,* just as you prophesied. One who would end the Crown, and with it, the world."

Mikaen knit his father's words together, building the fabric of the tale of the Forsworn Knight. He and Kanthe had whispered such chilling rumors of their family's secret history, nestled under their bedsheets at night, when they were still boon companions, before being separated between Kepenhill and the Legionary.

Haddan's expression remained skeptical. "More likely the girl is nothing but a ploy of the Klashe, to sway a second-born prince to pair with a supposed daughter of the king, to use such stories to stir insurrection against the true heir."

The general glanced back to Mikaen, who in turn pictured the small bump in Lady Myella's belly.

"Even if she is Marayn's lost daughter," Toranth countered, "we don't even know if the girl is of my loins or the traitor Graylin's."

Their discussion was interrupted by a pained cry from the chair. The prioress struggled against her bonds, her arms yanking at the cuffs that bound her wrists to the chair. Still, she could not stop the words from escaping her throat.

"Graylin . . . Graylin goes to her even now," she gasped out. "To Havensfayre."

The king swung back to her with a bellow. "What?"

Vythaas brought the copper box closer to the chair, clearly trying to grind the woman back under his thumb.

Mikaen knew from Anskar's report that Kanthe and the others had fled up the Path of the Fallen. No one knew if they had survived such a climb, as Anskar's men had been driven back by some scourge rooted there. Still, if Kanthe had made it to Cloudreach, his most likely goal would be to reach the woodland trading post of Havensfayre. There was nothing else up there. Knowing that, the king had already ordered a warship to be readied for a flight up to Cloudreach to scout for the missing prince.

Mikaen watched his father sag, as if he were a punctured wyndship. He knew how much the king had loved Graylin, a friend from his earliest years. Toranth had punished the oathbreaker but spared his life, banishing him instead. Everyone had thought the Forsworn Knight had died in exile.

Apparently not.

And if not, Graylin was proving himself to be an oathbreaker once again. He swore never to return to Hálendii, to never set a boot upon the kingdom's soil.

Even Haddan recognized how mercy could bite you in the arse. "Can there be any doubt that insurrection is being stoked? The king's son, a suspected daughter, and now a disgraced knight of the realm returned. They must be stopped before this rancor spreads and roots deeper."

Toranth nodded, his face hardening with the general's passion.

Wryth, though, was not done with their prisoner. He crossed closer. His eyes narrowed, watching her continued thrashing. Vythaas closed on her other side with his accursed screaming box.

"What are you fighting not to tell us, Prioress Ghyle?" he asked coldly.

Her eyes rolled back, showing only white. Froth flecked her lips, which stretched to lines of agony. Still, the copper needles glowed even brighter, stabbing deeper into her will.

She screamed, returning to her native tongue. Klashean words burst from her pained throat. *Vyk dyre Rha! . . . Vyk dyre Rha se shan benya!*

Wryth rocked back a step. Vythaas shuddered, almost losing hold of the copper box. He fumbled to keep hold of it—but it was enough for the prioress to regain herself.

Her eyes snapped to center. Pain turned to fury. She yanked an arm free of its cuff, ripping skin. She lunged out and snatched a long blade from the nearby table. Before anyone could stop her, she plunged the knife into her throat.

Wryth grabbed for her hand, but she twisted the blade and yanked it back out with a great fountain of blood. She stared with such hatred that the Shrive fell back a step.

Then in a few hard breaths, life faded from those eyes.

The king grabbed Wryth by the shoulder. "What did she say at the end? What did she mean?"

"I don't know," Wryth said. "Just nonsense churned up as she fought to free her will. She clearly did not want us to know more."

Mikaen suspected the Shrive was lying. Even the king squinted hard at Wryth. But Haddan had heard enough.

"No matter. This is all further proof of a plot to spread discord and divide the kingdom," Haddan said. "A scheme fueled by the Klashe and orchestrated by one of their own. We must stamp it out immediately."

Wryth turned to them. "The general is correct. This must be ended before any war begins."

Toranth nodded. His face was as red as Mikaen had ever seen it. "Haddan, you will command the warship headed to Cloudreach. In fact, double those forces. We will end this, once and forever."

The king turned to his bright son. "And you will go, too, Mikaen. It is time for you to stake your claim against your brother's betrayal. All of Hálendii must witness it, to end all possible question of lineage."

Mikaen bowed, accepting this harsh duty. He knew, with the war to come, he would need to shine brighter than ever, to be the flag that the kingdom rallied around. Still, he also knew *why* his father risked his first son in such an endeavor.

He pictured Lady Myella's belly ripening with promise.

The Massif royal line would hold—*must hold*—no matter what.

40

AFTER ASSIGNING ANOTHER of the Iflelen to guide the royal party back to Highmount, Wryth fled farther from the sun. He descended a half league to the true heart of the dark god's domain—and the secret buried there for seven centuries.

He had left Vythaas in his scholarium, where the man intended to split the prioress's skull and pick through her brain. Vythaas intended to discern what had worked and what had failed in his procedure, all to further hone his method. The Iflelen—like all Shriven—knew knowledge was seldom gained from sudden bursts of insight, but more through painstaking failures and tiny triumphs. Few appreciated the centuries it took to gather what the ancients had abandoned and to shine such artifacts back to life.

Which was especially true for what lay ahead.

Wryth reached a set of tall ebonwood doors, inscribed with the *horn'd snaken.* As he pushed through, he split the sigil into halves and entered the inner sanctum of the Iflelen. It was not unlike the main hall far above, a dome of polished obsidian. The chamber was also lined by doors marked for various avenues of studies, all pertaining to what this chamber held.

The breadth of the room contained a convoluted web of copper tubes and blown-glass tanks, running and bubbling with arcane alchymicals. It stretched from the arch of the roof to the polished floor. The immense apparatus huffed, steamed, and beat like a living beast.

Four bloodbaernes marked the cardinal points of the Urth's magnes energies. The bound sacrifices were all children under the age of eleven, stolen from the crowded streets of the city's Nethers. Such young consecrations were the most potent for the distillation process. Each child lay limp, their chests cleaved open like little windows. Bellows filled their lungs, blowing them up and down, revealing peaks of their beating hearts.

Their blood ran through the apparatus's pipes and vessels. Their young cylls were macerated, then purified at each stage, until all that remained was a concentration of lifeforce. According to ancient tomes, those energies were held within tiny particles freed from those torn cylls, invisible motes that the ancients called mytokondrans. The recipe for this potent fuel came from those same texts. Still, it had taken centuries of Iflelen study to refine their methods, through adaptations and advancements—including the incorporation of living sacrifices.

Each child lasted five days before succumbing, giving all their life to the hungry copper-and-crystal web. Just a century ago, the same machine had once consumed a child each day, but the Iflelen had improved their methodology over the many years, such was their progress. They also learned how to use those same distilled elixirs to extend their own lives.

Wryth stepped past a small tow-headed girl, her head lolled back, a tube down her throat. He brushed fingers through her hair, silently thanking her for her gift and sacrifice.

He remembered when he had first knelt before the great machine, shortly after swearing fealty to the god Ðreyk and joining the Iflelen. That had been sixty-three years ago—but it seemed far longer.

He could barely recall his youth as an acolyte to a Gjoan mystik. He and his mother had escaped the Dominion when he was six, just before he was to be blinded in preparation for his own training to be a mystik in their mountainous stronghold. He fought down the memories of that harrowing time, being chased by Gjoan hunters, the murder of his mother by slavers, his own years of misuse, until he finally ended up at the school of Teassl, on the Islands of Tau on the other side of the Crown.

He only gained entrance to the illustrious school because a hieromonk, one who had been abusing him at a whorehouse, had noted the tattoo on the inside of Wryth's upper lip, marking him as a possession of the mystiks. Only rare children were afforded such training. Believing such a boy to be special—and maybe wanting Wryth to be closer for easy pleasuring over the next years—the monk had gained Wryth entrance to Teassl. There, he had excelled on his own, eventually gaining his first Highcryst, that of alchymy. Afterward, he had thanked the hieromonk, gutted the bastard with a dagger, and left for Kepenhill, where Wryth earned his second Highcryst, thus becoming first a Shrive, then an Iflelen.

Even now, after so long, after achieving so much, he could still awaken that old pain and humiliation of his younger years, when he was defenseless and at the mercy of so many others. It stoked the cold fire inside him, of ambition, of the drive to never again be under another's thumb. To ensure that, he sought power found in ancient knowledge, intent to let nothing and no one stop him from becoming a formidable force, one more potent than any king.

With a silent growl, Wryth cast aside such dark musings and focused back on the shining wonder before him. He had dedicated the rest of his life to divining the mysteries buried here. He searched ahead, to where one of his brothers waited.

Shrive Skerren had summoned him down here with some urgency, but Wryth could not answer that call until the king was gone.

To reach his brother, Wryth bowed and ducked and twisted his way through the maddening copper web, aiming toward its center—where a hungry spider waited, imbedded at its heart, a talisman of great significance.

Ahead, Skerren bent near the holy artifact.

Wryth caught glimpses of it as he worked his way closer. The sculpted bronze bust had been wired and tubed into the great machine. The countenance of the sculpture was that of a curly-bearded man with a crown of the same plait. His bronze skin roiled with the energies suffusing through it. The finest of his curls and strands of hair waved, as if stirred by invisible winds. Glass eyes of a violet blue glowed dully, blind to all around it.

According to the talisman's history, the bust had been discovered in Havensfayre two millennia ago. It had been found in a forgotten vault in Oldenmast, buried deep under the roots of that ancient tree. Since then, the bodiless head had passed through countless hands. No one truly knew what to make of it, but all appreciated the beauty of its design and workmanship. It traveled to the farthest reaches of the Southern Klashe and north to the sequestered Hegemony of Hapre. It had been studied, dismissed, and had come to adorn many kings' halls, until it finally made its way to Azantiia.

Over time, the revelations from ancient tomes offered some hint of its true wonder, how it could be stirred back to life if fueled in a proper manner. Still, it had taken the Iflelen centuries to wake the talisman from its slumber and glean what little they could of it. The head had spoken only four times since stirring to life. Each utterance was cryptic, whispered in a language no one understood. Those four messages were inscribed in the Iflelen's most sacred texts, waiting to be deciphered.

As centuries passed, their order had learned much. They discovered how the holy talisman produced a strange emanation, a vibration through the air. It felt like an itch on the skin when one drew near.

Even now, Wryth felt that wind blowing against him as he crossed closer.

With time, the Iflelen learned how to monitor its strength, using slivers of lodestone wrapped in copper wire. It did not take long to recognize how this strange emanation affected small animals: birds, lizards, snakes. The wild beasts would fall sway to its call, becoming docile, easily handled.

It was Vythaas who first related this to bridle-song and spent all his life trying to capture this sound and use it to control larger beasts. He eventually refined his method with copper needles inserted into key areas of the brain. After working for a time with animals, he found the dull-minded Gyn the easiest of men to manipulate, then moved onward from there.

Still, the talisman continued to radiate its strange silent song. To monitor its keening, the artifact was surrounded in concentric rings of bronze, a complicated skeletal sphere, like an orrery used to study the stars. The rings were lined by wired lodestones suspended in oil-filled crystal spheres, becoming a hundred tiny weathervanes. With those tools, the direction and strength of the talisman's invisible winds had been mapped over centuries. And so it went for the longest time, with the talisman forever calling out to the world.

Until an answer finally came.

Sixty-two years ago—a year after Wryth had sworn his blood oath to the order, which he still deemed as providential—another wind blew the vanes straight back at the sculpture's head. The wind came in from the east, and from its fierce strength, it was estimated to have risen somewhere near the coast of Guld'guhl. So, Wryth had overseen the establishment of an Iflelen outpost near the mines of Chalk and continued to watch for that sign again.

Thrice more over the past decades, those winds rose again, spinning the lodestones toward the bronze bust. This further convinced their order that something similar to their talisman must be buried out there. Then a moon ago, the mysterious winds appeared again, sporadic at first, then the gusts blew stronger. The rising storm drew Wryth and Skerren to the mines of Chalk—where the bronze woman was discovered, only to have it stolen by a shrewd thief in disguise.

Wryth reached Skerren, despairing at the full breadth of what they had lost, now likely sunk into the sea.

"About time you got here," Skerren scolded.

"What is so urgent that it required me to be pulled from the king's side?"

Skerren held a quill in one hand and a silver measuring stick in the other. He shifted aside to reveal a map on a small table. Beside it lay an open book that held an account going back centuries, charting the lodestones' movement in their crystal spheres.

"A bell ago," Skerren explained, "another signal stirred our instrument."

Wryth shoved closer. "From where? From the Bay of Promise?"

He pictured the bronze woman stalking along the seabed after the crash of the wyndship from Guld'guhl.

Skerren slid the map over, inscribed with numbers and arrows. "No, not from the sea. It was brief but appeared to rise out of the northeast. I still want to review my calculations to be sure."

"How far to the northeast?"

"I gauge no farther than the forests of Cloudreach, somewhere near The Twins."

Wryth frowned.

Cloudreach again. Where the others had fled.

It couldn't be a coincidence. Standing in the center of the bronze web, he felt the movement of unseen forces, bringing all the pieces of a grand game together.

Wryth swung around, hoping it wasn't too late.

"Where are you going?" Skerren asked.

He pointed back to the talisman. "Keep watching. Send word if anything changes."

"And what of you?"

"I'm headed to the warships. To join the prince and the legions. If that artifact is out there, I must not lose it again."

MIKAEN SEARCHED HIS rooms at the Legionary for his boots. After soaking in a hot bath and scrubbing his body to a fine polish, he felt like himself, a shining prince of the realm. His diligence with soap and brush had less to do with removing the grime of his hard ride across the Brauðlands and everything to do with ridding himself of the stench of the Shrivenkeep's brimstan.

He stood dressed in his underleathers, like his father had been, readying for the flight to Havensfayre. He would don his armor once they moored at the forest town. He had already strapped on his sword with its silver-filigreed scabbard, along with a dagger in a matching sheath. Over his leathers, he also wore a doublet of silver with a sun-and-crown crest stitched into it. He had to maintain some decorum as the prince.

But where are my sarding boots?

He didn't want to run barefooted to the war docks.

He checked under his bed, spotted them, and yanked them out. Before he could pull them on, a firm knock on the door interrupted him. From the loudness of the rap, he sensed he had best not ignore such a demanding summons. Despite being the prince, he remained an eighthyear at the Legionary, and his high standing only afforded him so much leeway here—which at most times was none at all.

He dropped his boots, swore, and crossed to the door. He pulled it open to discover a crimson mountain at his threshold. Anskar vy Donn wore light armor, as if he had been born into it and never removed it. He carried his helm under one arm.

"Prince Mikaen, I wish a word with you before we depart."

Without asking permission, Anskar pushed inside. He shoved past Mikaen and slammed the door behind him.

"What's this concerning?" Mikaen asked, trying to sound firm and princely, which was hard to pull off when bootless.

"I want you to beseech the king on your brother's behalf."

"On Kanthe's behalf?"

Anskar lifted a brow. "You have *another* brother I'm not aware of?"

Mikaen felt his cheeks warm. He glanced over to the box still resting on his desk, holding the bit of pottery of two boys locked in an embrace, the betrothal gift from his twin.

Had Kanthe been plotting against the realm even back then?

"I don't understand," Mikaen said. "You know the betrayal that Kanthe has committed. As much as I love him, treachery against the crown, conspiring with insurrectionists, it cannot go unanswered."

"But I don't think your brother's flight was an act of insurrection—it was more one of survival."

Mikaen frowned deeply, trying to mimic his father's stern demeanor. "What do you mean?"

"Just this past bell, I learned of a plot to assassinate Kanthe in the swamps. Upon the order of Highmount. To be carried out by men under my command."

Mikaen stumbled back. He found his bed with the backs of his legs and sat down heavily. "Surely you must be mistaken."

Anskar followed him and dropped to a knee to let Mikaen read his earnestness. "I believe it was that assassination attempt that sent your brother fleeing. I come to you now, to help sway your father from this bloody path."

"I don't think I can. While my father holds me in a favorable light, the same cannot be said of Kanthe."

"I understand, but during this past sojourn, I saw a worthiness in your brother. A steel long hidden behind drink and carousing. But it is there. I believe this deeply. With war threatening, two princes flanking the king will serve the realm well."

Mikaen sighed, weighing what to do.

Anskar hung his head, clearly struggling with words that would convince him to appeal to the king. The vy-knight lifted his face to try again.

Mikaen already had his dagger out and slashed the Vyrllian's throat.

The man fell back on his rear, his face stunned. Ironhard hands clutched at his neck, but they were not strong enough to stop the blood spurting between his fingers. He gurgled more of his life past his lips.

Mikaen looked down at the crimson spray across his own doublet and underleathers. He would have to change again. As he stood, Anskar looked up at him, still in shock—not at the attack but at the realization.

"Yes, I ordered my brother to be killed in the swamps. My father could never commit such an act. He has too generous a heart." He tugged his soiled doublet over his head. "In a king, such a charity of spirit might be a boon in times of peace, but it's a detriment with war now threatening."

He undid the hooks on his upper leathers. "Look at what such kindness has wrought my father. A second son who threatens chaos. Whether Kanthe does so willingly or unwittingly, it does not matter. Then there's the bastard daughter who should have been slain as soon as her mother's belly first began to swell. Even the mercy of my father's friendship with the knight Graylin now invites more broken oaths to the detriment of our kingdom."

Anskar gurgled his dissent as he slumped to the stone floor.

"From here on out, I will be the death of such mercies." Mikaen remembered his earlier promise to his father. "I will be the lightning to my father's thunder. I will strike where death needs to be dealt. I will spare the king the necessity of cold ruthlessness. That is the son I shall be to my father."

As Mikaen struggled out of his uppers, he recognized he was soliloquizing to a dead man. He stepped around the pool of blood as another hard knocking sounded from the door.

He closed his eyes with a groan and considered his options when a voice shouted from outside, "Prince Mikaen, it's Haddan. I come with Shrive Wryth, who brings urgent word from the Shrivenkeep."

Ah . . .

He crossed and opened the door. "Then it seems we all have urgent matters to attend to before we depart." He stepped aside to reveal the body on the floor. "Anskar caught wind of what we planned for my brother."

Haddan hurried inside with Wryth and rubbed his chin as he stared at the spreading pool of blood. "A shame. Anskar was a good man and a better soldier. I had hoped one day to sway him to our cause."

Mikaen did not care. The matter had been settled. Instead, he eyed Wryth. "The general said you have something urgent to address."

Wryth found his voice after the initial shock. "Yes. Word has just reached me, of a lost weapon that might yet be retrieved from Cloudreach. And Vythaas readies another set of weapons to aid us in our cause."

Mikaen frowned. "What weapons?"

Wryth told him.

Mikaen paled and stared back at Anskar's body.

And here I thought I was ruthless.

41

MIKAEN STOOD ATOP the deck of the warship *Tytan,* named after the god of storms. The massive gasbag hung overhead, swaying like an anxious horse. The balloon's draft-iron cables groaned all around. Six levels below and under the craft's thick keel, men scurried about the docks, readying the ship for departure.

Across the field, a similar skirmish was waged around a second warship, the *Pywll,* christened after the giant who held up the skies. This morning, only one such craft had been scheduled to depart for Cloudreach, but after what his father had learned in the Shrivenkeep, King Toranth had ordered the *Pywll* to join the *Tytan.* He intended to stop this insurrection before it had a chance to start.

Mikaen appreciated his father's resolve.

He watched a dozen Mongers, armored Gyn brawlers in leather and carrying axes and steel maces, file into the stern of the *Pywll.* They were followed by chained thylassaurs, even a pair of steel-helmed scythers, massive hunting cats with fangs jutting past their snarling lips.

He also knew each warship carried a full century of knights and a score of Vyrllian Guards, along with half again as many horses. The flanks of the *Tytan,* like its twin, bristled with draft-iron cannons and giant ballistas seated with iron-tipped spears. Along the ships' lower flanks, small doors hid stocks of barrels, ready to rain alchymical fires on the lands below.

Mikaen knew such power was not solely to burn out the seeds of a burgeoning insurrection—but also to salt the ground afterward. After such a blazing show of force in the highlands, none would dare raise a voice, let alone a sword, against the king. Likewise, it would rally the people around the Massif flag. Mikaen had learned how a pageantry of force could flame the hearts of the common folk to a more fervent pride in their king and kingdom.

But Mikaen also knew this spectacle was not only for their own people—but also for the armies of the Southern Klashe. The act would be a fiery flag waved at the lands to the south. Hálendii had twenty more ships like the *Tytan* and *Pywll,* moored here and at strategic locations throughout the kingdom. Word would spread from the highlands to the Klashe, showcasing the king's resolve and warning of the futility of any attack.

Mikaen rubbed a cuff of his sleeve on the breastplate of his light armor. He honed its surface to a silver sheen in the shadows of the massive gasbag, recognizing there was one final aim behind all this ferocity. It was why Mikaen had decided to follow Anskar's lead and don his armor before striding across the war docks to the *Tytan*. His father wanted his son's esteem to shine brighter. If war truly came, the people would know they had a thunderous king and a son forged of deadly silver to protect them.

Mikaen stared to the east, to the cliffs of Landfall. Maybe it was better that the assassination attempt on Kanthe had failed in the swamps. It would have been an ignoble end for his brother, the final tally of a debauched life. Now Kanthe's death would serve a greater purpose for the kingdom. The Prince in the Cupboard would be cast as the dark usurper, slain by the kingdom's shining heir.

Mikaen sighed toward those misty highlands.

Thank you, brother. Your blood will polish my armor even brighter.

The firm pound of boots drew his attention to the deck of the *Tytan*. His father approached, draped in full royal regalia, all dark blues and polished black leather. He looked like a storm cloud on the move.

Mikaen met his father, ready to drop a knee and say his good-byes.

Instead, Toranth grabbed his son and hugged him hard. "I know this is a hard task I ask of you, Mikaen." He released the prince and held him at arm's length, gripping his shoulders. "But know this. I would not be angry if you simply brought your brother home. I believe I would even welcome it."

Mikaen bowed his head, trying to hide his disappointment in his father. Even now, faced with insurrection, the king refused to harden his generous heart. Mikaen fought to keep the bitterness out of his voice, reminding himself that he would be merciless steel in his father's stead, wielding death where it was needed.

Mikaen cleared his throat to speak. "Father, I will do all in my power to return Kanthe to Highmount. This I promise."

Toranth nodded, satisfied. "I know you will. As to the girl who was prophesied to bring ruin, she must be slain with no quarter given to those who aid her."

Mikaen dropped to a knee. "It will be done," he said, again hiding yet another lie in his heart, one recently seeded there.

After the bloody events in the Shrivenkeep, he had considered if there might be a better use for the girl, a young woman of mysterious power and shadowed lineage. *I could keep her for myself.* He sensed she could become a strategic piece in a grander game of Knights n' Knaves. He even weighed bedding her, half-sister or not, and drawing her power into his own lineage.

The ship's horn sounded and was echoed in turn by the dockmaster down below. The *Tytan* was readying to disembark. Across the field, the same re-sounding notes rose around the *Pywll*.

Mikaen stood back up.

His father clasped him by the forearm, finally saying his good-bye. "I know you will do me proud, Mikaen."

"Thank you, Father." He placed a fist on his breastplate, over where the Massif house sigil had been engraved into its silvery steel. "Long may you rule."

His father offered a rare smile, like a sun through thunderclouds, then turned and headed off the warship.

Mikaen watched him depart, only to have his eyes drawn to Haddan and Wryth. The two had their heads bowed together by the other rail, looking like they were arguing. He strode across the deck. They both looked his way, straightening when he joined them.

"Is something amiss?" he asked the pair.

Haddan's hard countenance was even stonier. "Once we reach Cloud-reach, Shrive Wryth wishes to divert the *Pywll* to pursue his stolen artifact, which he believes to be somewhere northeast of Lake Eitur."

Mikaen turned to Wryth. "The bronze woman?"

The Shrive folded his hands into the wide sleeves of his gray robe. His tattoo-shadowed eyes were narrow slits of fury. "I received word shortly ago from the Shrivenkeep. A refinement of calculations that offers a more precise location of this weapon. It must be secured before it vanishes again. With war pending, we cannot risk losing it, especially to the Klashe."

Even as a prince, Mikaen could not command these ships. He was still only an eighthyear at the Legionary. His father had rightfully assigned Liege General Haddan to lead this assault. Still, both men looked to him to resolve this dispute, perhaps knowing he would be king one day, or maybe it was a measure of respect for how coldly he had dispatched Anskar. Most likely they looked to him because they needed a wind—*any* wind—to push their stalled sails in one direction or the other.

"Eitur lies to the immediate north of Havensfayre," Mikaen said. "It seems a small diversion that could promise a far larger reward. Is that not true?"

Haddan answered with a begrudging frown.

Mikaen continued, "Surely the *Tytan* can handle anything at the forest town. And with the *Pywll* still close at hand to the north, it could be sum-moned back upon the swift wings of a skrycrow or the signal blare of a horn."

Wryth withdrew his hands from his robe's sleeves. Though stoic, the Shrive was clearly pleased with the direction of these winds.

Mikaen tempered such pleasure. "What about the other weapons you promised us, Shrive Wryth? Have those been loaded?"

"They were being stored below as I boarded."

Mikaen nodded. "You will leave them here and ensure they are properly secured before you depart for the *Pywll*. Such weapons will be of little use on your quest, but they may prove vital to ours."

"Of course. I don't disagree."

Mikaen looked between the two men. The pair nodded to one another, resolved on the matter for now. As the two departed in opposite directions, Mikaen stepped to the empty rails. Behind him, men bustled with final preparations, shouting and bellowing. All around, the draft-iron cables ground a mournful wail. Overhead, gusts snapped the balloon's taut fabric.

The prince ignored everything.

He focused instead on the calming billow of clouds atop Landfall, knowing such peace would not last. Not here, not across the Crown.

A storm was coming.

And I will be its lightning.

As a final horn sounded, Wryth hurried toward the cabin buried deep within the *Tytan*. The weapons stored inside were too sensitive to the Father Above's glare to risk storing them higher. Ahead, two massive Mongers stood to either side of the cabin door. The Gyn's heavily browed eyes, further shadowed under iron helms, watched his approach, but the pair knew him and said not a word as Wryth reached the cabin and knocked on its door.

A thumping of a cane sounded from the other side, and the way was unlocked with the rasp of a key.

Wryth opened the door on his own and passed inside. The windowless room was sparsely furnished, just a narrow bed, a lamp on a hook, and a door on the far side.

"I do not have long," Wryth said as he entered. "I wrested the *Pywll* away from Haddan, but I must be swift."

Shrive Vythaas backed his gaunt body to the side and leaned on his bane-alder staff. His voice was a rub of stones. "Any further word from Skerren?"

"No, but if anything changes, he'll send a crow." He touched the heavy pouch hanging from the leather sash of his Shriven cryst. "Skerren also gave me a tool to trace those energetic winds back to our target. But it will only work once we're close."

"Then best you be on your way to the *Pywll*." Vythaas crossed to the bed and settled his withered frame atop it. His gaze swung toward the far door, one banded and latched in iron. "I will attend to the weapons here and aim them at our greatest threat."

Wryth remembered the final words ripped from Prioress Ghyle's throat. He whispered them now. *"Vyk dyre Rha . . ."*

Vythaas continued to stare at the other door. "The ancient name of the Klashean dark goddess. The Shadow Queen who is carried on wings of fire."

Wryth knew this god was not one of the thirty-three that made up the Klashean pantheon, but a creature far older. Her name was written only one time, in the most sacred text of the Dresh'ri, secured in the Abyssal Codex of their order, a vault buried far beneath the Imri-Ka's bright gardens. She was the daemon of the Dresh'ri, the god the Klashean order worshipped as devoutly as the Iflelen did Lord Đreyk. But unlike the Iflelen god, the Klashean daemon was never mentioned aloud, not even by the Dresh'ri. She had no symbols or sigils. She was worshipped in total silence and darkness.

Until now.

Ghyle's scream still echoed in his head, especially her final words: *Vyk dyre Rha se shan benya!*

Vythaas seemingly read his thoughts and translated them aloud. "'She is the Shadow Queen reborn.'"

"The Klashean prophecy . . ." Wryth muttered with an icy chill.

Vythaas's gaze turned from the door and recited the prophecy aloud. "She who would be reborn one day, in flesh and form. Burning away all that She possessed, leaving only darkness and savagery behind. A dread being who will spread fiery ruin in Her wake, until all the Urth is consumed."

Wryth remained silent for a breath, then voiced what he knew concerned them both. "Could it be true?"

He remembered fifteen years ago he had listened to the words of a soother, a witch who cast bones at the feet of a serf with a swelling belly. She predicted that a girl would be born to Marayn, which was all that Wryth had wanted to know at the time. He needed to be certain the child was not a boy who might obscure or challenge the Massif lineage. Then the soother had scooped up her bones far too quickly, her face ashen. Suspicious, he pressed the witch, who finally admitted a portent of doom and ruin shadowing the babe.

Back then, Wryth had not placed much weight upon the truth of these claims. Most witches and bone-readers were no more than charlatans. Still, her words were of great use. He used the witch's prophecy to sow fear and frighten a reluctant king into killing both mother and child. This ruse also served to rip Graylin sy Moor away from the king's ear, a knight who tempered Toranth's spirit toward a kinder aspect, which little suited a kingdom with a hostile neighbor.

But in the end, the knight's damage was done. Even after the betrayal by Graylin, Toranth waited too long to kill the mother, showed too much mercy toward an oathbreaker. Recognizing this, Wryth and Haddan had turned to the prince instead, a son under the liege general's thumb at the Legionary. They had spent the past eight years forging Mikaen into a harder leader.

Yet, now the bones of a witch have found new voice in the screams of a prioress.

Vythaas matched Wryth's concerned gaze. "It is truth or raving?" the man asked the room. "I do not know, but we cannot risk such a creature ever rising to power. When we cross to Cloudreach, you see to our lost talisman, and I will attend to this potential *Vyk dyre Rha* and make sure she is destroyed."

"And those weapons you've forged against her?"

Vythaas turned to the other door. "All is ready."

Wryth wanted reassurance before he left. He stepped to the back of the cabin and lifted the latch. He opened the door enough to let lamplight flow into the dark cell beyond. Two figures stood there, with heads bowed, their bodies wrapped in chains—but that iron was not what truly bound them.

The glow of lamps reflected off the rows of copper nodes shining across their shaved scalps, marking the site of a dozen needles, twice the number as had been used on the prioress. Vythaas wanted to ensure their wills were fully destroyed, leaving them shells who would do the Iflelen's bidding. The pair had been secured by Anskar back at the swamps and dragged here with Prioress Ghyle.

Wryth stared at the two men's slack faces and sent them a silent command.

Ablen and Bastan . . . you will be our dogs, to hunt and kill your sister.

THIRTEEN

FIRE IN THE MISTS

Fyre is a fikel ally; kindle it towardes a foe,
& often it will burn eyow more than eyowre enemi.

—Gjoan proverb

42

Nyx stared doubtfully at the moored swyftship. She gaped at the huge balloon straining overhead in the cleared fields east of Havensfayre. It seemed impossible that even such a large gasbag could lift and carry the ship beneath it.

Before now, she had never seen a wyndship up close. She had heard how they sometimes docked at Fiskur, but even that was rare. Occasionally she had caught glimpses of the larger wyndships sailing over the Mýr, little shadows skimming through wisps of clouds. Still, it was not the same as standing in the shadow of such a sight.

Jace joined her as they waited for the final preparations to be completed before departing. He hid a yawn with a fist. It was well past midmorning, but she could not fault his exhaustion. They'd all had a late night, planning deep into Eventoll for this journey across the sea.

Jace shielded his eyes against the cloudy glare to take in the breadth of the craft. "Hard to believe this is a *small* ship, meant for skilled maneuvering. The wyndship that I rode from my home in the Shield Islands had to have been five or six times as large. But I was young, only seven at the time, about to take my tests at the Cloistery, so maybe my memory of that cargo ship has grown *inflated* over time."

He grinned over at her, clearly trying to use a foolish pun to help with her unease. She offered him a weak smile. It was the best she could muster.

"Last night," he continued, "I overheard the pirate, Darant, mention the ship's name. *Sparrowhawk*. Let's hope it proves as swift as that bird. Frell said we could reach the shores of Aglerolarpok in less than two days, which seems unimaginable."

It is unimaginable.

Nyx folded her arms over her chest. She had slept little over the past night. She had tossed back and forth in her small room at the inn, plagued by dreams of the moon crashing into the Urth. Everything was happening too fast. She felt unmoored and tossed about. She had lost so much, and what she had gained left her only angry and out of sorts.

She glanced over to the knight—maybe her father—who was discussing final details with Darant and Frell. Graylin's two vargr sat grimly off to the side, the tufts of their ears high, swiveling, taking in all around them. Their two pairs of eyes swung her way at the same time, as if sensing her attention. Gazes locked on her, acknowledging the new member of their pack, clearly wondering why she kept away.

She also felt her bond with them. The whisper of a howl echoed in her skull. Still, she could not bring herself to draw nearer. She had kept away from Graylin, unsure what to make of this stranger who was so tied to her past. Her initial fury with him had tempered to discomfort and suspicion. She recognized the distance she maintained wounded him, especially when she had rebuffed any of his attempts to talk to her. Still, she could not deny that a part of her found a measure of satisfaction in his misery.

The tap of boots drew her attention around. Kanthe strode toward them along the wooden planks that coursed across the fields. He was accompanied by a pair of crewmembers, two hard-looking young women in identical gray leathers and dark cloaks. They could be sisters, except one had dark almond skin with white-blond hair, the other had the palest complexion and hair as black as a raven's wings. The pair had accompanied the prince to the markets of Havensfayre, to restock his arrows. Though from their predatory looks and secretive grins behind Kanthe's back, their escorting of the prince had a more salacious intent.

Kanthe seemed blissfully unaware, joining Nyx and Frell with a huge smile. He hefted one shoulder, then the other. Behind each, he carried a leather quiver, jutting with striped fletching, like a pair of deadly bouquets. The two women who flanked him carried bundles of the same arrows over their backs and continued toward the ship.

The prince stopped next to Nyx and nodded toward the bundles. "Kethra'kai arrows," Kanthe said, the elation bubbling from him. "Tipped in bone, shafted in black alder, and fletched in goshawk feathers. Nothing better in all the Crown."

Jace looked enviously upon the prince, who noted his attention.

Kanthe reached behind his hip and hauled around a double-headed ax mounted on a gray handle. "Found this at a smithy. Forged in Guld'guhlian steel and hafted in unbreakable stonehart, sculpted from a branch harvested out of the petrified forest of Dödwood. Such axes are prized by the foresters here. Its edge is said to never go dull."

Kanthe pushed the weapon into Jace's hands. Her friend hefted its length in a double grip, testing its weight, and smiled back at Kanthe. "Thanks."

The prince shrugged and brushed past him. "If nothing else, it'll be good for shaving that scruff you call a beard."

Jace ignored the jibe and kept grinning.

Kanthe frowned back at them. "Why aren't you two already aboard?

I thought I'd be the last one, hopping on just as the mooring lines were tossed."

The prince hurried toward the swyftship's open portside ramp with nary a care, as if riding the winds was something he did all the time.

And maybe he did.

As Nyx was dragged along in his wake, she studied the thick draft-iron cables that ran from the balloon down to the sleek wooden boat. The *Spar-rowhawk* looked like a steel-tipped arrow. A thick keel ran from its flat stern to its pointed prow, which was clad in a reinforcement of draft-iron. The bow had a pair of long, narrow windows cut into it, like the squinted eyes of its namesake. A single row of tiny round windows ran back to the stern, just below its flat deck, which rose higher at front and at back into a bow and aft deck.

She watched a crewmember fly from the forward forecastle to the stern, racing across a cable suspended under the balloon. The man hung from a wheeled grip affixed to the wire. She hid a shudder at such a carefree manner.

Back at the Cloistery, she had been taught about wyndships and learned of the alchymy of light gasses that filled their balloons. She mostly understood the dynamics driving this craft, including the special tanks of flashburn used to fire the forges of such a nimble craft.

Still, it was one thing to read about such vessels and another to actually ride one. With every step toward the open hatch, her breath grew shorter, her heart thudded harder.

Ahead, Graylin signaled his vargr, who turned and loped up the ramp. The knight followed his furry brothers. She noted how his palms had swept their flanks as they brushed past him. It was an absent gesture, a brief acknowledgment of their bond. She also saw how his shoulders relaxed for that moment, then stiffened again.

In short order, they all boarded, drawing the remaining crew in behind them. At the top of the ramp, a cavernous cargo hold stretched from bow to stern. It held stacks of crates bound in nets and barrels strapped down. A line of cages hung from the rafters, holding a stir of dark birds, maybe skrycrows.

At the back, a stern hatch was being winched closed.

She spotted a pair of shadowy domed sailrafts flanked to either side of the hatch. She prayed they would never need to use those tiny skiffs.

"This way!" Darant called from ahead. He led them over to a wooden spiral stair that led up to the living quarters. "We'll be underway as soon as the ropes are loosed."

As Graylin mounted the steps, he whistled and pointed the two vargr over to a large shadowy stall lined by fresh hay. The pair swept in that direction but diverted to pass close to Nyx. The one named Kalder stared at her sidelong, panting, tongue lolling. Aamon drew closer, his flank grazing her side as he chuffed at her, as if inviting her to join them somewhere warm and safe.

She let her fingertips comb his fur.

Another time . . .

Kanthe tried to do the same with his fingers, but Aamon snarled, baring a fang on that side. The prince pulled back his hand. Still, he gazed longingly at the pair.

"Such handsome beasts," he mumbled.

The group continued up the spiral stairs and into a long hall that divided a dozen cabins, six to a side. She spotted a door at the end of the hall to the right, guessing it led into the stern quarterdeck.

Darant headed the other direction, toward a matching door that closed off the other end. "If you want to watch this little hawk lift to the skies, you're all welcome to join us."

Frell hurried to close the distance with the pirate. "Fascinating. I've never been inside a swyftship's wheelhouse."

Kanthe continued with a shrug, but his pace quickened nevertheless.

Jace glanced back at Nyx, excitement dancing in his eyes.

She felt none of their thrill. She pictured the *Sparrowhawk* rising and never stopping, vanishing into the void. Or worse, climbing only to plunge back down into a splintering crash.

Yet, she knew if she didn't go that Jace would stay at her side. She hated for him to lose this opportunity. Still, she might have balked, except that Graylin remained in the hall, looking her way. She had no intention of remaining alone with the man, and she didn't know which cabin was hers.

So, she waved Jace ahead and fell into step behind him.

Graylin followed but kept his distance.

Darant opened the door into the forward quarterdeck and ushered them all past him. As Nyx ducked across the threshold, she realized the entire forecastle was one large chamber. Directly ahead, two long, narrow windows looked out across the fields below. Between them stood a tall wooden wheel.

The pirate crossed toward it. He waved to the two other crewmembers posted along the flanks to either side. They were the same pair who had accompanied the prince. The two women stood before a banked row of tiny screw-like wheels with little handles.

"That's Glace." Darant pointed to the white-haired beauty, then swung his arm the other direction. "And that's Brayl. My two daughters by different mothers. And let me tell you, no one knows how to tame this hawk like those two."

A horn echoed outside, signaling the ropes had been loosed.

Darant turned back to the wheel. He rubbed his palms, pressed them to his forehead, and wished for the gods' good graces. "May the winds welcome us with gentle breezes and spirit us safely to port."

He set his hands atop the wheel.

Nyx braced for some violence, expecting a sudden thrust upward. Instead, she did not even know they were moving until the fields below started dropping away. The ship sailed upward without any jolt. There was only the slightest swaying of the boat under its balloon.

Nyx took a step forward with a flicker of curiosity.

This is not so bad.

To either side, Glace and Brayl cranked various wheels, reaching to them blindly, their gazes fixed either to the forward windows or out the tiny round holes above their stations. Faint bursts of flames sounded to the right and left, likely rising from the port and starboard draft-iron rudders.

The ship continued to sweep upward, ascending ever faster. Outside, the misty fringes of the forest rolled past. Layers of gold-leafed branches seemed to wave at their departure. Then in a breath, the balloon dragged the boat into the clouds, erasing the world outside.

Nyx retreated from the ghostly view. It was as if they had been flung into a realm of spirits. Without anything to focus upon, she felt every sway, every nudge and roll. Her stomach churned queasily. She backed up into Jace and reached blindly for his arm.

A hand grabbed her shoulder. "I've got you."

It wasn't Jace.

"We'll be through it in a moment," Graylin assured her.

She jerked out of the man's grip. Anger burned away her trepidation. She turned to glare at him—when the world burst into brightness as they cleared the clouds. The sunlight revealed every line of pain etched in the knight's face: the despair in the turn of his lip, the grief in his eyes, and more than anything, the haunted look across all his features.

She had to turn from him, but it was not bitterness that drove her away. That pain was too hard to face, especially with it mirroring the same pang in her own heart.

She kept her back to him. She faced the brilliant expanse of bright clouds that extended to the horizon. Sunlight glared and ached the eye. But she did not even squint. She drew that radiance inside her, trying to use it to dispel the darkness.

They continued to climb higher, and the view stretched longer. Far off, the cloud layer spilled over an edge, like a waterfall tumbling down a cliff. Past there, a distant glint of blue shone, marking the sea.

The Bay of Promise.

Then a dark sun rose from over there, climbing from the lands below. It was massive, its blackness absorbing the sun's brightness.

"A warship," Graylin grumbled behind her.

She now recognized the shape to be a swelling balloon of incomprehensible size. Flags snapped along its top.

"Hálendiian." Kanthe stepped forward. "From my father's fleet."

The huge balloon rose higher, drawing a giant boat into view. Maneuvering flames spat along its flanks. The ship angled more to the north, toward a break in the clouds that shone green with the reflection of the poisonous waters of Eitur.

"I don't think it's spotted us," Darant called back. "Still, best we find the clouds again before we draw its attention."

His daughters heard him and set about spinning their wheels. The *Sparrowhawk* sighed and began to lower, drifting down toward the white sea. Darant turned his wheel hard, angling them southward, away from the massive craft.

"Look!" Jace said, pointing as a second black sun rose to replace the first. *Another warship . . .*

This second sun rose faster, more aggressively.

"Get us into the clouds," Darant whispered, as if fearing to be heard.

The *Sparrowhawk* dove steeply—but it was to no avail. Like a mousekin dodging a cat, their frantic movement only succeeded in catching their hunter's attention. The warship swung toward them with smoky bursts of flames. Its armored prow aimed straight at them, looming larger and larger.

Then the immensity of the sight vanished as the *Sparrowhawk* plummeted into the white sea. The world outside dissolved into swirling mists.

No one spoke.

No one breathed.

FROM THE POPPING in his ears, Kanthe sensed the swyftship continuing to descend. But he knew the craft could only drop so far. A soft scraping of treetops along the boat's keel revealed as much.

"That's as far as we can go," Darant whispered back to them.

Glace and Brayl fought their wheels, bringing the ship higher again until the scratching faded from the hull.

"No one speak." Darant turned to them. "Whisper if you must. Warships have ears, great drums that can pick up a sparrow's fart."

As if heeding this, his daughters spun other wheels until even the rush from flashburn forges fell silent. The pair stepped back from their stations, their faces grim.

The *Sparrowhawk* continued to drift through the mists.

Kanthe clenched his jaws, his ears straining, knowing what would come next. Despite being a Prince in the Cupboard, he'd had some battle strategy instilled in him, especially with the school of Kepenhill so near to the Legionary.

But he wasn't the only one with such training. Graylin shifted closer to the bow window on the starboard side. Kanthe mirrored the knight, moving to the portside. They both searched the glare of fog ahead, alert for any ominous shadow sweeping toward them.

Then a faint boom echoed through the mists, strong enough to swirl the clouds and tremor the ship. Then another and another. Flashes of fiery orange lit the distance, bursting brightly, then going dark.

Kanthe spoke, knowing the blasts would deafen the warship for now. "They're trying to cut us off from reaching Landfall. The blasts will open the mists ahead, exposing us if we try to pass through."

Proving this, more fiery blooms lit the mists, drawing a line across their path.

"That's not all." Graylin pointed lower. A deeper ruddy glow smoldered in the wake of those blasts. "They're burning a fire line across the forest. I wager they're intending to set a flaming noose around Havensfayre."

Confirming this, a new cannonade of blasts rose to the north. A peek out the round windows on the starboard side revealed flashes of fire from that direction.

"The other warship," Kanthe said. "Laying down a barrage along the shore of Eitur."

Graylin nodded. "The one ahead will soon do the same to the south, burning a fiery swath along the banks of the Heilsa." The knight glanced behind him, as if trying to peer through the breadth of the ship. "Then they'll circle to both sides and secure Havensfayre mooring fields to the east."

"Where they'll offload their forces and scour the city," Kanthe added, earning a nod from the knight.

"Then what is our course from here?" Darant asked.

"We only have a moment to decide," Graylin warned. "We can't head east as we'll run into the cliffs that front the Shrouds of Dalalæða. To climb above those heights, we'd have to rise out of the clouds and expose ourselves. The best option is to fly due south. If we hurry, we might escape that noose before it closes off that direction."

Darant frowned. "If we go that way, we'd still have to course over the Heilsa. There's no cloud cover over those waters."

"That's why we must be swift—burn every tank of flashburn if we must—and duck back into the mists on the other side."

Darant nodded, turned to his wheel, and hauled it around. He swung the prow of the *Sparrowhawk* toward the Heilsa.

Kanthe closed his eyes and rubbed his forehead, bothered by this plan. He considered his father's temperament and all that had transpired. *Toranth sent two warships.* That alone told Kanthe that the king must be hunting for more than an errant son, even one who escaped an assassination. He glanced over to Nyx, who stood beside Jace with her eyes wide and fixed open. Frell also stared at the young woman, then over to Kanthe, his expression worried. The alchymist suspected what he did.

The king knows about her, maybe even about Graylin.

He also pictured who he knew must be commanding this excursion.

Liege General Haddan.

Knowing all this, Kanthe was certain the war group would not let them escape by such an easy ploy. In fact, he imagined Haddan would already be expecting it, even encouraging it. He pictured armed hunterskiffs, maybe another swyftship, already heading to the Heilsa's far side, like a pack of wolves set loose to prowl those mists and be waiting for them.

He hurried toward Darant. "We can't go that way."

The pirate scowled at him; even Graylin's brow darkened. Both men looked little ready to consider the judgement of Highmount's Dark Trifle, a prince who had only completed his eighthyear at Kepenhill.

Kanthe pressed them anyway. "It's a trap." He quickly laid out his suspicions and finished with, "I know Haddan. That stony bastard will have that escape route covered."

Darant tightened his grip on the ship's wheel. "We'll have to take that chance. And trust me, this *Sparrowhawk* has talons. They will not take her down easily."

The pirate's confidence did not soften Graylin's frown. The knight kept his focus toward Kanthe. "What do *you* propose we do?"

Kanthe looked between the two men. "You're not going to like it."

43

NYX CLUTCHED THE edge of the draft-iron stanchion that held one of the *Sparrowhawk*'s two sailrafts. She remembered how she had hoped earlier to never have to use one of these tiny skiffs.

Now I wish I could.

Ahead of her, winds whipped into the cargo hold from the open stern. The flat hatch had been winched down and locked in place, forming a wooden tongue sticking out the back of the swyftship. Beyond that platform, mists swirled. Below them, the crowns of giant alders passed by like ominous dark shoals.

"Be ready!" Darant's muffled shout reached them through a series of metal tubing and baffles from the forecastle. "The mists brighten ahead. We're almost to the Heilsa."

That was not the only reason to be prepared.

To Nyx's left, more fiery blasts lit up the western forest as the giant warship neared the lake, as if already tracking them. Soon it would sweep along the shore toward them. She and the others would have to act fast—and swim even faster.

Graylin shifted over to their group, trailed by his two vargr, who nervously paced at his heels. "Once we reach the lake, the ship will drop fast from the treetops. So hold tight. Once we're skimming the water, you bail out the back."

She looked across at Frell, who had stripped out of his alchymist's robe and wore a borrowed set of breeches, boots, and jerkin. Kanthe had both quivers tight to his shoulders and wrapped in oilskin. Jace had his Guld'guhl ax strapped across his back.

"We won't have time to slow," Graylin warned, "so brace yourself to hit the water hard. Then make straight for shore."

Nyx knew their only hope of escape was to abandon the ship unseen and pray the continuing flight of the *Sparrowhawk* would draw all eyes and any hunters after the swyftship. With luck, the ruse would allow their group to hide within the woodland labyrinth of Havensfayre until the fires died down and the others could return.

Still . . .

She turned to the grizzled knight. She read the past agony in his face and the fear shining in his eyes, but not for himself.

He gripped her shoulder. "I abandoned you and your mother long ago. Hoping to lure the king's legions away." His fingers squeezed harder. "I won't fail you this time."

She wanted to deride him, to let him know even this sacrifice would not be enough. But she could not find any words that would hurt him more than the pain already there. She read his desire to draw her into his embrace, but also his disappointment in knowing that it would not be welcome.

Instead, his fingers released her. He turned to one of the vargr. "Aamon, go with Nyx." He pointed to her, then gripped his wrist with his other hand. "Protect her."

The vargr's amber eyes turned upon her. He shifted on his paws, a sharp whine flowing at her, bathing over and through her. The thread that bound her to this pair shone even brighter. Aamon padded to her side and nosed her hand up, letting her palm rest between his ears.

With his eyes on the beast, Graylin whispered so low the winds whipped his words away, but his lips could be read. "Thank you, my brother . . ."

Kalder took a step toward Nyx and Aamon, following those shining threads, but Graylin touched his flank. "Stay, Kalder. We still have debts that must be paid."

As the knight stared at her, she understood part of that obligation was owed to her, but from the way he kept his hand on Kalder's side, she suspected there was more to this cryptic statement, another unspoken tally yet to be settled.

Graylin stepped back and glanced at the others. "Keep her safe."

Kanthe shrugged. "We got her this far, didn't we?"

Jace grumbled, "More like she got us here."

Frell stepped forward and gripped the knight's forearm. "Well met, Graylin sy Moor. We will do all we can to protect Marayn's child until you can—"

Darant's voice bellowed from the brass tube. "We're here! Heilsa ho!"

The ship shot out of the mists and over flat waters that reflected the bright blue sky. The sudden radiance—from the lake, from the heavens—blinded Nyx. She blinked at the glare and gasped as the ship's nose dove toward the Heilsa's surface. The sudden drop lifted her to her toes, nearly threw her back into the hold, but she kept her grip on the sailraft's stanchion. Behind her, birds squawked from the hold's hanging cages.

Closer at hand, Graylin still had hold of Frell and kept the alchymist on his feet. Kanthe did the same with Jace. Then the *Sparrowhawk* righted itself, sweeping into a slight turn, running along the shoreline. The keel lowered until it skimmed the lake, casting up wings of water to either side.

"Now!" Graylin yelled, and shoved Frell toward the open hatch.

Kanthe and Jace stumbled after the alchymist.

Nyx glanced one last time at the man who could be her father—then turned before fear rooted her in place. She pounded across the dropped hatch, Aamon at her side. Ahead, the three men leaped, one after the other, out the hatch and vanished into the dark blue waters.

Nyx reached the end and nearly balked—then Aamon jumped, leading the way. Drawing on his brave heart, she followed just as the *Sparrowhawk*'s nose lifted again. Thrown off balance, she tumbled over the hatch's edge, as if being dumped out the back, and crashed into the water.

The hard impact rolled her, knocked the air out of her lungs. Then the cold grabbed her, shocked her back to the surface with a thrash of limbs. She coughed her chest back open and searched around.

Aamon popped up nearby, with a shake of wet ears. He panted, his eyes glowing at her. Past his shoulders, she saw Jace and Frell paddling for the misty shoreline. Not far, Kanthe kicked in place until he spotted her. He waved an arm toward the forest and swam after the others.

She gulped and set off for shore.

Aamon paced her, smoothly parting the water, his gaze ahead, but the bell of one ear fixed toward her splashing. She remembered Graylin's words. *Protect her.* Aamon clearly intended to honor that last command.

Her sodden boots finally struck sand. She swam, waded, and shoved out of the lake and up the bank. She spun around in time to see the *Sparrow-hawk* reach the far shore and vanish into the clouds above the trees.

A low growl warned her.

Also a shout from Kanthe. "Get into the woods!"

Nyx retreated up the shoreline and into the mists. She stumbled through low branches. The others did the same—and just in time.

Far to her right, a large shadow crested high over the canopy. It stretched its darkness over the bright waters. The prow of a ship appeared out of the clouds, along with a massive balloon.

The warship . . .

A hand grabbed her shoulder. "Keep going," Kanthe said. "We dare not be spotted by the ship's farscopes if they spy along this shoreline."

She started to turn—when distant explosions rolled out of the misty forests across the lake. Orange bursts blinked and faded, like fireflits flashing in a dark swamp.

Kanthe witnessed the same. "That bastard Haddan . . ."

Apparently, the prince had been right about an ambush.

Aamon growled next to her, echoing her own anger and worry.

She feared for the others, but also for her group.

She gazed at the spreading shadow over the water.

Would their ruse trick the enemy?

MIKAEN POINTED BEYOND the curve of the *Tytan*'s bow windows toward the wink and flash of fiery alchymicals on the far side of the lake. His heart pounded with the excitement of the hunt. His vision was a pinpoint fixed on his target.

"Get us over there!" he shouted.

Mikaen stood within the warship's forecastle, which swept the breadth of the bow. A curve of windows looked across the blinding glare of the lake below. Crewmembers, ten to a side, manned a slew of stations. Wheels were spun, levers yanked, and orders were shouted down the throats of bronze tubes. Two men on the port and starboard sides wielded farscopes, their faces pressed to their instruments' eyepieces, searching the lake, sky, and forest.

Behind Mikaen, a large map had been pinned to a circular table, depicting Cloudreach and the town below in exacting detail—or as much as was known about these misty highlands. Red and blue ink crisscrossed the chart, laying out strategies and dividing a search grid.

Mikaen had no interest in such details. He shifted over to Haddan, who stood beside a pilotman at the *Tytan*'s wheel. The liege general gazed out the tall windows with his hands clasped behind his back. His expression was its usual rigid stone.

Mikaen could hardly stand still. He searched the flashes of flame in the mists across the lake. He swore he could smell the burning alchymicals of that firestorm, but it was more likely just from the warship's own flashburn forges. He heard their roaring through the hull of the *Tytan*. Smoke billowed into view as the warship seemed to be slowing, even swinging to the east.

"Why are we turning away?" Mikaen pointed ahead. "We should be going after them. Chasing those bastards down."

"No," Haddan said.

Mikaen scowled at the general. "We have them trapped. The *Tytan* can make short work of that swyftship."

Haddan's attention was not on the distant firestorm, but on the waters below. "We can't know for sure that your brother or the others are even aboard the other craft."

"Then why did they run when they saw us?"

Haddan shrugged. "Havensfayre is a major trading city. Not all that is traded there is lawful. The ship might have been fearful of being brought low and searched."

"Still, is it not best to eliminate any chance of the others escaping?"

"You need not worry. My fleet of hunterskiffs will deal with whoever is aboard that other craft. But I do believe that you are right, Prince Mikaen. The enemy was aboard that swyftship."

"Then why don't we—"

"I said *was* aboard."

Mikaen frowned.

Haddan grabbed his shoulder and forced his nose closer to the bow window's glass. "What do you see down there?"

He shrugged in the general's grip. "Water. Lake Heilsa."

"If you hope to be a war king one day, you must learn to read signs, like a soother with a toss of bones." Haddan pushed Mikaen's nose until it was pressed against the glass. "Look at the ripples spreading across the smooth surface, parting to either side, as if a knife had been drawn across that lake."

Mikaen understood, his eyes narrowing. "Or cut by the passing keel of a swyftship."

"Before it raced off again," Haddan added, letting the prince go.

"You think they dropped something—or someone—off down there." Mikaen glared over at Haddan, but his anger was not directed at the general.

Kanthe . . .

Haddan sighed his agreement. "While those we hunt had been aboard that swyftship, I now believe they're backtracking to Havensfayre."

"What do we do?" Mikaen asked.

"We continue with the original plan. My men across the lake will bring down that swyftship and haul anyone who survives over for questioning. In the meantime, the *Tytan* will close the noose below. Once we reach the town's mooring fields, we'll offload our forces and scour Havensfayre, scorching our way from one end to the other."

Mikaen glanced back to the marked-up map and acknowledged the wisdom of this dogged strategy. He forced his hammering heart to slow. "Plainly I still have much to learn."

"You're still young." Haddan clapped him on the shoulder. "But fear not, with time I will forge you into a war king, one cunning and bold enough to challenge the gods."

Mikaen straightened under his hand, accepting this truth—and another.

Before that happens, I must first rid the Crown of my brother, a bastard sister, and that accursed knight.

CROUCHED OVER THE wheel of the sailraft, Graylin raced his small skiff along the shoreline of the Heilsa. He stayed hidden in the mists, keeping the bright waters glowing through the fog to his right, using it to guide him around the lake.

Earlier, he had shot out of the back of the *Sparrowhawk* as soon as the swyftship had entered the mists on Heilsa's far side. Darant had turned his craft sharply to the east, allowing Graylin to jettison to the west.

Darant's larger craft had fired its forges with bright spirals of flashburn and lured the wolves in the clouds along his blazing trail, affording Graylin the opportunity to escape unseen. Once free, he sped the skiff—specially designed by the pirate with larger flashburn tanks for attacking sailing ships—and circled around the western shore of Heilsa.

He finally reached the blasted path left behind by the warship. He turned to follow, intending to close upon the larger ship in its wake. Still, he felt like a minnowette hunting a rockshark.

As he flew, his boots worked the pedals, firing the port or starboard flashburn forges to wing his narrow craft back and forth, from cool mist to hot smoke and back again. He only fired his forges when the skiff sailed over the smoky trail left by the warship. The conflagration below helped mask his raft's tiny flames. Each fiery burst boosted him faster, so when he reentered the foggy mists, he could go dark and sweep silently through the cloud layer.

Burst by burst, he sped after his huge target. He was a weaving arrow, relentlessly aiming for the warship. Behind him, the hold of the sailraft was lined by two rows of wooden barrels, all on their sides and lined atop a slanted, oiled rack. The slope pointed out the open stern of the skiff. The alchymical-filled casks were held in place by ropes. His knees bumped against the levers to either side that would free those ropes and send a barrage raining out the back.

But first I have to reach that sarding gasbag.

Darant had warned him of the futility of such an attack, even offering to send one of his own crew on this attempt, a brigand who he claimed would be far more skilled at such a raid.

Graylin had refused.

I must do this.

He would not sacrifice another to settle the debt he owed Marayn's daughter. He gripped the wheel harder. He had left Kalder with the pirate, so if

Graylin failed here, he would have honored his word to the man. Darant would have the vargr promised to him.

But more than anything, his words to Marayn's daughter were etched across his mind's eye, as fiery as the path he followed. *I abandoned you and your mother long ago. Hoping to lure the king's legions away. I won't fail you this time.*

"And I will not," he swore aloud.

He continued east along the northern shore of Heilsa, winging from smoke to mists, keeping the glow of the open lake to his right. Finally, the fiery trail smothered out, marking where the warship had drifted out over the water.

Graylin did not slow. He raced ahead until the brightness to his right was eclipsed by a dark shadow.

The warship . . .

He turned toward it with a spin of his wheel. His boots hovered over the flashburn pedals, but he held off slamming them down. Not until the last moment. He could not risk exposing his presence until then.

Still, his caution was to no avail.

High and to his left, a dark shadow shredded through the clouds, spiraling the mists in its wake.

Then Graylin's sailraft shot out of the mists and over the sunny lake. The warship towered ahead. A cannon smoked from its port flank. Others fired with spats of flames. A barrage of black iron filled the sky.

Graylin realized several details at once. He had exited the clouds too low. The sailraft had come out even with the massive ship's keel. Still, it was his low height that spared him now. The cannonballs shot over his craft and into the forest behind him.

He slammed both pedals. Fire shot out the skiff's stern, shooting the sailraft forward. He hauled on the wheel, driving the nose up. He was thrown against his seatback, but he kept his legs braced to the pedals, never letting up on his burn.

The raft slipped behind the first salvo of cannon fire.

Before the legion's forces could reload and firm their aims, he blasted toward the warship. The skiff climbed the levels of the huge craft. It grew to fill the raft's windows. He passed the long row of cannons bristling from the hull. As he cleared the height of the rails, he spotted men racing across the middeck.

Graylin leaned over his wheel, craning upward. He still had to get above the balloon, a mountainous ascent that looked impossible. He held his breath, praying for the tanks of flashburn to hold out long enough until he could summit this gasbag's peak.

But the cannons were the least of the warship's armament.

Fiery spears suddenly lanced through the air all around him, shot from the line of ballista that fringed the deck rails. Smoky trails barred the skies all around.

He held his breath, never slowing.

He prayed to all the gods to grant him this one bit of salvation.

He was judged not worthy.

A spear of iron, trailing a swirl of flames, shot past his window. The raft jolted violently as the balloon was struck—then a whooshing blast of fire spun the skiff through the air.

As the raft plummeted, Graylin fought the whirl by releasing one pedal and keeping the other pressed hard. Fire died on one side and blazed on the other. The dizzying view outside slowed enough for him to catch stuttering peeks of the warship's balloon rising next to him as his skiff spiraled downward.

He ground his teeth.

Before I die, I'll do what damage I can.

He aimed the nose of his juddering raft at the open deck as it rushed up toward him. He shoved both pedals, firing all tanks. The kick of fresh flames drove his skiff toward the middeck, dragging the shredded ruins of his balloon behind him.

He watched men dash across the deck, running to either side.

The prow of his raft shattered through the portside rail and crashed between two giant ballista. The skiff's keel skidded across the deck, sending the craft spinning like a flat rock across still waters.

Graylin hugged the wheel to hold in place.

Then the careening sailraft struck broadside into a giant draft-iron cable on the starboard side with a resounding clang. The skiff slammed to a stop, splintering in half. The impact threw Graylin from his seat. His head cracked hard into the hull, dazzling his eyes. He tried to stand, only to fall woozily to a knee.

Beyond the open stern, a wall of men raced toward him.

He fought upward again. This time, he yanked out his sword, determined to fight to his last breath.

For Nyx . . .

He lifted the silvery length of Heartsthorn—only to have the world spin. His legs wove drunkenly under him. He raised his blade and swung it down. It was all he could manage in that moment. He hoped it was enough. He then crashed backward into the raft's seat. He tried to prop himself up, but the world went dark.

44

KANTHE KEPT THEIR group moving through the panicked chaos of Havensfayre. Wagons thundered down streets. Men on horseback whipped anyone in their way. Most of the crowd were simply townspeople carrying their lives on their backs. Many more cowered behind shuttered windows.

Bells clanged all around, cutting through the shouts and bellows.

Their group would have had difficulty wading against that tide, except for the large wet beast leading their way. Aamon's hackles shivered in a tall threatening ridge. His muzzle was fixed in a rippling snarl, baring white fangs. The seas parted before his menacing growl, allowing them passage through the town.

"Where do we go?" Jace asked, voicing the question plaguing them all.

Frell glanced behind them. "We should settle that before long. Especially now that we're safely into the depths of this town."

Kanthe frowned at him. "We're far from safe here."

Moments ago, they had all heard the boom of cannon fire. They did not know what that portended, but the bombardment had pushed them harder. By now, smoke choked the air, darkening the mists. All around, flames glowed off in the distance, except to the east, toward the mooring fields. That was the direction most of the townspeople were fleeing, but Kanthe knew there was no safe passage that way. One or both of the warships would soon commandeer those fields.

"Then what do we do?" Jace asked again, gripping his new ax with both hands, sticking protectively close to Nyx.

Kanthe huffed, tired of just running. "Over here."

He drew them all under the eaves of an abandoned shop, letting the crush of people sweep past them. He got them all huddled together, while Aamon guarded their privacy. All eyes were upon him.

Kanthe laid out their situation. "Knowing Haddan, once he has this place locked up, the legion will search the town, section by section, burning everything behind them to ensure nothing was missed. Afterward, if they don't find us, they'll sift those ashes."

Jace's eyes were huge platters. "Then where do we go? Where can we hide?"

Kanthe pointed ahead. "The Golden Bough."

"Back to the inn? Why there?" Frell asked. "It seems a risky choice. I paid gold for silence when we were last there, but I fear such largesse will not extend if the entire town is burning."

Kanthe laid out his points as quickly as he could. "We're not renting rooms there, Frell. We sneak in and head straight down into the wine cellars."

"The wine cellars?" Jace asked with a wrinkled brow.

"I checked the place out when you were all droning on and on about plans last night, plans that are plainly dashed. Where else would the drunken Tallywag of Highmount go to while away the night?"

Frell frowned at him, as if sensing his lie.

In fact, he had not gone down there to sample those dusty bottles. Instead, he went to canvass for a place to retreat to if the inn were attacked. After all that had happened, he saw enemies in every shadow now. Such fears had kept him sober and unable to sleep.

"The cellars are buried under the roots of the inn's giant tree. It's a maze down there. Not only does it delve deep, which could protect us from any flames that might be burning above, but there is a score of ways to slip out. A young fetcher in the red cap of the inn showed me two exits and pointed out several others. All for the cost of three brass pinches. A fee I'm now happy to have paid."

Frell studied him for a breath, then nodded. "Then that's where we'll go."

Kanthe grabbed the alchymist before the man could turn away. "Plus, there is all that *wine* down there. We can't discount the value of getting good and soused if worse comes to worst."

Frell shook loose with a roll of his eyes and pushed Kanthe back toward the clamor of the crowds. "Let's go."

They set off again, only pausing here and there to nab someone and demand directions. Aamon encouraged their cooperation amidst the panic.

Finally, the gilded sign of the Golden Bough appeared. The sprawl hardly looked all that different than before. Several of the glowing windows in the giant trunk had gone dark, but the huge doors into the commons remained open. Jolly music flowed out, along with the usual bellows and bouts of laughter.

Though to Kanthe's experienced ear, it all sounded far more drunken. Apparently, there were those who were already heeding his earlier advice.

To get good and soused as the world burned.

He led the others gallantly toward those people who shared his spirit—until a growl rose behind him.

He turned to find Nyx staring off into the smoky mists of the town. Her hand rested on Aamon's side, which vibrated with tension. The vargr's narrow eyes were fixed in the same direction. Both his ears stood stiff and tall, their bells pointing there, too.

Nyx cocked her head, as if listening to a song only she could hear.

Jace shifted closer. "What's wrong?"

She answered without looking at her friend. "Something's coming."

GRAYLIN WOKE BACK into a world of panicked shouting, accompanied by thunderous blasts that nearly sent him back into oblivion. He fought against passing out. His head ached with every heartbeat. He used each throb to steady himself. Still, his vision was like looking up from a well. The noise was muffled by a roaring in his ears.

He grabbed the neighboring seatback and pulled himself up. Somehow he had kept his grip on his sword. He hauled Heartsthorn around. He finally understood why he was still alive, still free.

Before succumbing a few breaths ago, he had committed the only act he could. He had slashed at the stanchion rope that held the row of barrels atop the nearest sloped track. The casks, full of alchymical fire, had rolled across the deck, each fuse igniting as it brushed past a wheel of flint at the track's end.

As he gained his feet, he watched a barrel with a longer fuse explode in a wash of fire, cracking the planks under it. Other pools of flaming oil already dotted the deck. Black smoke choked the ship, trapped under the expanse of the balloon. Deckhands fought the fires with pails of sand, while knights in light armor regrouped for an assault on the crippled sailraft.

Graylin knew he had only another moment before they would charge. Especially as a pair of giant Mongers joined the legionnaires, hefting huge iron hammers.

Knowing he dared not be trapped inside the broken raft, he stepped forward and slashed the rope securing the second rail of barrels. As the casks rolled away, sparking their fuses, Graylin followed after them. He stopped only long enough to lodge his dagger into the end of the track, trapping the last three barrels in place, with the foremost one's fuse sparking. With no more time, he leaped out of the raft and rushed along the wake of the bouncing, bobbling barrels.

The knights ahead fled to either side with fresh cries of alarm.

Unfortunately, the Gyn held their ground and used their hammers to knock barrels away, sending them flying over the rails. The pair then came at him with a roar of fury.

One bashed at the last rolling barrel, only to have it explode on impact. His huge body was blasted high, covered in flaming oil.

The other Gyn reached Graylin and swung at him. Expecting such an attack, he dodged under the hammer and spun away—straight toward a cluster of knights who had their swords lifted at him.

He skidded to a stop to avoid impaling himself.

Thwarted from an easy kill, they lunged at him, but he danced back while a count ran down in his head. When that number reached zero, he leaped sideways and sprawled headlong across the deck.

The knights, momentarily baffled, paused—when the last three casks inside the sailraft's hold exploded. The blast shook the entire ship, jolting the deck, sending men flying. The skiff shattered, casting out fiery spears in all directions, even into the balloon overhead.

Knowing the tough skin of a warship's balloon, he did not expect the slivers to do any true damage. Still, the barrage scattered a wide swath around him. Men screamed, some on fire, others speared clean through or peppered with shards.

Graylin felt stings in the backs of his thighs and shoulders. Still, he gained his legs, ready to bolt for one of the open doors that led down into the depths of the ship. He hoped to hide below and perhaps do more damage.

He aimed for the closest hatch, an open door in the forecastle, but a larger set of doors heaved open next to it. More knights piled out. Amidst them clambered a lone stallion, draped in black armor, saddled by a rider bearing a lance.

Graylin knew that rider, even with the man's features shadowed under a helm.

Haddan sy Marc.

The liege general had only been a commander back when Graylin had been banished. Still, he knew the cold cruelty of that man. Haddan had been the one who had broken his arm during the gauntlet of chastisement, before Graylin was exiled. Most other knights, pitying him, had only whipped, punched, or nicked him as he passed under their onslaught. Haddan had smashed his upper sword arm with a hammer, shattering the bone into pieces.

Haddan now intended to do far worse. The general spurred his steed hard, kicking the stallion into a thunderous gallop, and lowered his lance. Knights closed behind Graylin, cutting off any retreat.

So be it.

Graylin lifted Heartsthorn, bracing a leg back.

Then the entire warship bucked as a series of explosions ripped overhead. Everyone, including Graylin, was thrown flat. Only the stallion kept its footing, rearing up and dancing on its hind legs. It crashed back down with its rider still saddled and gripping his lance.

Graylin rolled to a low crouch, searching overhead, wondering if the raft's fiery splinters had actually pierced and ignited the mighty gasbag. But the underside looked intact. Farther overhead, smoke billowed, and flames trailed from the crest of the balloon.

Then a huge iron-spiked barrel came bouncing down along the flank of the balloon. It finally struck with enough force to impale itself in place—then exploded with a great gout of flame, ripping a hole in the side of the balloon. The force buffeted the entire warship, swinging the huge boat under it.

Graylin stumbled toward the rail, trying to keep his feet.

Haddan roared and charged his stallion across the teetered deck, refusing to lose his target, intending to spear him clean through.

Rather than continuing to fight the slant of the slope, Graylin turned and raced down it. He held out one hope. Overhead, a shadow glided out of the smoke above the fiery balloon. It was the underside of a sleeker craft.

The *Sparrowhawk.*

He also spotted a rope ladder unfurl from an open hatch. It draped along the side of the balloon, then swung free as the swyftship cleared the gasbag. The *Sparrowhawk* turned and dropped lower, bringing the end of the ladder closer.

Graylin ran toward the portside rail as the huge warship began to swing back the other way, canting the deck up under him. He fought the steepening slope. The clatter of hooves grew thunderous behind him. At any moment, he expected the point of a lance to pierce his back.

But he safely reached the row of abandoned ballista, lunged between two of them, and leaped to the rail. He catapulted himself off the top and dove headlong through the air. He aimed for the swaying rope ladder. He clutched Heartsthorn in one hand and stretched out his other arm.

He quickly recognized he would fall short. Luckily, Darant must have distrusted the strength of Graylin's legs and rolled the *Sparrowhawk,* swinging the ladder to meet him.

Its length struck him in the face.

He managed to hook his free arm through the lowermost rung and caught himself, but just barely. He struggled his sword back into its sheath and snatched his other arm to secure his hold. As he did, the *Sparrowhawk* heaved upward and around, running for the clouds.

The ladder swung and twisted in the air, as if trying to throw him off, but he clung tightly. He looked up at the keel of the swyftship.

How is it here?

A glance across the lake showed blooms of fire still flashing in the mists. He remembered Darant's claim about the expertise of his brigands. He pictured the *Sparrowhawk*'s second skiff racing through those clouds, haranguing the enemy. Whoever was out there must be tricking the wolves into chasing their own tails, a ruse that must have allowed Darant to escape and circle around the other side of the lake, coming upon the warship from the other direction. Once here, Darant must have decided to take advantage of Graylin's crash and make a run at the larger ship.

As Graylin spun in the air, he caught glimpses of the warship listing crookedly over the lake. He spotted the dark shape of a stallion, dancing back and forth furiously. Higher up, a good portion of the balloon puckered and smoked from the swyftship's attack. The remainder of the gasbag seemed to be holding. He knew the balloons of warships were compartmentalized with fireproof baffles. It would take more than a rain of fire from a single swyftship, even one with the talons of the *Sparrowhawk,* to bring down a warship.

Still, the damage was done.

Before Graylin was swung into the clouds, he watched the huge craft limp in the direction of Havensfayre. It continued to drift lower. To reach the town's mooring field, the boat would have to be dragged across the treetops, sustaining even more damage along the way.

But would it be enough? Would it buy Nyx and the others time to hide, maybe even limit the legion's ability to burn the town with a crippled warship grounded at its mooring field?

He could not know, but he was certain about one thing: *That wasn't the only ship prowling these white seas.*

As Graylin was pulled into the clouds, a horn echoed through the mists, rising from the foundering craft and calling to its twin.

Despite their meager victory, Graylin recognized a hard truth.

Such a ruse will not work a second time.

FOURTEEN

WHISPERS OF THE OLD GODS

As to the gods of the Kethra'kai, there are onli foure, each heralding the foure aspects of nature, the foure roots of the Oldenmast. There is the wraithlike Vyndur, of the cloudes & windes & airy hights. Then the mercuriale Vhatn, of rain, stremes, & lakes. And girthsome Jarðvegur, of loam & mulch & rok. Finally, the tempestuous Eldyr, who is both the flame of the warme hearth & the inferno of fiyri ruin. But neath those four, far deeper than even the reache of the Oldenmast's roots sleep their olden gods— whose names the Kethra'kai do not spake, lest they dare waken them.

—From Krass hy Mendl's *Under the Yoke of Gods & the Wrath of Daemons*

45

TWO DAYS OF searching through the woods of Cloudreach had left Rhaif in a foul mood. He slouched in the bed of a hired wagon. The wain was driven by a Kethra'kai guide and drawn by a pair of foul-tempered muskmules. Pratik sat across from him, staring out at the misty forests spreading forever in all directions.

With each league they traveled, Rhaif felt his purse growing lighter, along with any hope of finding Shiya. For the thousandth time, he pictured her stepping out of the sailraft's stern and vanishing through the clouds, her passage below marked by snapping branches and ringing bronze.

Afterward, Rhaif's group had landed in Havensfayre, deflated their balloon, and bought the dockmaster's silence with a gold march. It had taken nearly all of their remaining coins—even with Llyra pitching in—to hire the wagon, and two additional Kethra'kai scouts.

Rhaif glanced ahead to the pair of golden-haired tribesmen—his mother's people—who rode bareback atop sleek horses. Llyra rode alongside them on a feisty mare. Earlier, he had questioned the guildmaster's continuing allegiance to this hunt. Her answer was coldly practical: *I cast my lot with you. There is no turning back now.*

Still, they might all have to turn back soon.

If Rhaif's group didn't find Shiya in another day or so, they would run out of money. He pictured the scouts vanishing into the woods, probably their guide, too, along with those fecking muskmules.

He shook his head. "You'd think the bastards would offer a discount to someone who shares their blood."

Pratik turned to him. "The tribesmen are still our best chance of finding Shiya's trail."

"That is, if there *is* a trail. She could've been battered to ruin or broken in half by the time she struck the ground."

Pratik shrugged. "That may be true. It's why I suggested we hire this wagon. If she's damaged, we may need to cart her back to Havensfayre."

The Chaaen still wore the princely garb of an *imri* tradesman, though he had shed his outer robe, leaving him in silks that were stained by the hard days of this trek. Pratik rested a map on his knee and continued to use a wayglass to chart their progress as best he could.

With only a rough idea of where Shiya had fallen—somewhere east of the Eitur—they had hundreds of leagues to search. Along the way, the scouts who accompanied them occasionally flushed out other tribesmen. Inquiries were made about a bronze woman marching or limping through the forest. Such a sight could not be easily missed, and word would have surely spread through the region's Kethra'kai.

Still, no one had reported anything.

The silence left their group searching in an ever-widening spiral outward from the eastern shore of the Eitur's green waters. Though at this point, Rhaif would swear they were simply being led in circles, with each pass draining more of their dwindling resources.

He frowned at Pratik and reminded the Chaaen of his claim aboard the sailraft. "Do you still think Shiya might be striking for the Shrouds of Da-lalæða?"

Pratik gave him another of his damnable shrugs. "I can only presume as much. Back aboard *The Soaring Pony,* I noticed how she started her slow turn from west to east as we passed above the Shrouds. Then when our sailraft sailed over the Eitur, we turned the skiff's stern to those same cliffs in order to land at Havensfayre. It must have been too much for her, to be so close only to be dragged away again. So, she acted rashly."

"Jumping out of a perfectly good sailraft, yes, I'd call that *rash.*"

"If she landed safely enough to keep moving, I have to assume she will continue heading there. Then again, we must consider, even if she remains intact, she draws vigor from the sun." His gaze swept up to the misty canopy. "There might not be enough sunlight here to sustain her progress."

Rhaif pictured her frozen in place, a new statue decorating this forest, becoming home to nesting birds and growths of moss and lichen. Despite his frustration, worry for her iced through him. He felt foolish for such feelings. She was not a creature of flesh and blood. Still, he could not shake his apprehension for her.

What spyll has she wrought over me?

He focused on Pratik. "If you're right, why would she be intent on reaching the Shrouds? There's nothing up there but savage creatures, trackless jungles, and dark storms. Not even the Kethra'kai go up to that haunted place."

"That's not entirely true. They do ascend there, but only once. As part of a ritual. *Pethryn Tol.* Which means in the Elder tongue, *listening heart.* A journey that marks when a Kethra'kai child becomes an adult. They climb to the top of the Dalalæða and spend one day there. Afterward, they must return with a stone, which they carry in a pouch."

Pratik nodded toward the leather cord hanging from their guide's neck. "And many don't return," the Chaaen added. "Those who do come back are considered chosen by the Elder gods to be part of the tribe."

"Still, if the only things of value up there are some stray rocks, why would Shiya want to trek there?"

"Maybe it is because of those rocks."

Rhaif scoffed. "Rocks? Truly?"

Pratik turned his gaze to the east. "I can only speculate . . ."

"Speculate what? Where do you think she might be going?"

Pratik faced him, his expression worried. "Atop the Shrouds lies a dark henge, a group of standing stones that some hieromonks believe to be as ancient as the Elder gods. Not even our oldest Klashean texts offer any insight. So, if I had to guess where our bronze mystery might be headed, it seems not farfetched that one mystery might be luring another."

Rhaif sighed. "I suppose we'll have to simply ask her if we ever find her."

He turned to the forest. They were passing through a grove of silver poplars, following some path known only to their scouts. He saw no rut in the leaf litter, no stones stacked as a guidepost. He tried to imagine his mother living here as a young girl. She had been hired to work in Anvil, contracted for eight years, due to her talent in bridle-song. It was there she met Rhaif's father. They both fell in love, dying together in each other's arms during a feverish outbreak of Firepester. Rhaif had only been eleven at the time, orphaned to the streets, where he eventually found a new home, as harsh as it was, within the guild.

He tried to picture his mother with her fiery hair and skin so pale that it never tanned. He had a hard time remembering her face, the details fogged over by time. Still, what stuck with him best, as vivid as ever, was her sitting at his bedside, singing to him, brushing soft fingertips across his brow.

He closed his eyes, lulled by the rock of the wagon. He again heard the lilt of her lullaby, singing in Kethra, a lonesome pining for quiet woods set against the pound and bellows of Anvil.

As he drowsed, the old song seemed to grow brighter, as if polished by another—then he shattered back awake as a boot kicked the side of the wagon near his head.

"Up with ya!" Llyra shouted at him from atop her mare. She pointed ahead. "We got company."

He stretched up straighter as the wagon bumped to a stop. Ahead, one of the scouts had dismounted and was talking to a cluster of pale figures with bows across their backs or leaning on spears.

Another group of Kethra'kai.

"Do they know anything?" Rhaif asked.

Llyra trotted her mare ahead, while calling back, "Let's pray so! Or we may have to give up."

Rhaif hopped out of the wagon with a groan, drawing Pratik with him. They followed the trampled trail of the scout's horses. The leaf litter was already rising to fill those hoof tracks.

No wonder we've not picked up Shiya's trail. These woods seem determined to hide their secrets.

As they rounded the pair of steeds, their scout bowed his head to one of the figures, speaking quickly in Kethra, too fast for Rhaif to follow. Rhaif studied the party gathered ahead. One tawny-haired fellow with broad shoulders held a wayglass in hand, turning in a slow circle. But his motion looked more like amusement than any attempt at taking a measurement.

Their scout was nudged aside by a length of cane. A white-haired woman strode toward their group, toward Rhaif. Her eyes—one blue, the other green— stared hard at him. She thumbed forward with her staff and stopped in front of him. He started to speak, but she lifted a hand to his face, silencing him.

He leaned back, not understanding what she wanted.

She reached to his brow. Warm fingertips brushed his hair aside. With her touch, his mother's old song rose again, each note dancing brightly in his skull. Then it went silent again as her bony arm dropped. Still, he felt something drawn from him when those fingers fell away.

Her hand settled to her staff as she stared silently at him for a breath. *"Dosh van Xan,"* she said.

"Tall'yn hai." He gave a bow of his head, matching the respect of the scout. "Thank you for the gift of your name."

The elder leaned her head. *"Hai ral mai kra'mery'l whyshen."*

Rhaif blinked, sure he had heard her wrong or deciphered her words badly: *You echo with the whispers of the old gods.*

Still, Pratik stiffened at her words, glancing hard at Rhaif, proving the Chaaen was far more fluent than he pretended.

Llyra frowned from atop her steed. "What did she say?"

Rhaif waved her question away. "Nothing important."

Xan's eyes narrowed at this lie, but she stared off into the forest and switched to Hálendiian. "You and I, we seek the same song on the wind." She headed off, motioning him to follow. "We grow near to the one who calls."

Rhaif swallowed, trying not to hope. He turned to Llyra. "I think she might have found Shiya's trail."

From atop her mare, Llyra stared as the elder joined her fellow Kethra'kai. "She had better—"

A distant rumble of thunder cut her off. It echoed ominously through the forest, coming from the west. Rhaif stared off into the bright mists in that direction. He saw no darkening of storm clouds. Still, the thunder continued, rolling over and over them.

"Firebombs," Llyra explained.

Rhaif's heart pounded harder.

Pratik had his wayglass out, studying its lodestone. "From the direction of Havensfayre."

They all exchanged glances, knowing what that must mean.

Llyra voiced it aloud. "The king's forces know we're here."

Xan stared back at them and confirmed the same. "They come for the singer." As she turned away, she added something cryptic in Kethra. *"Du'a ta."*

Llyra waved to the wagon. "Get your arses back aboard."

Their guide had already nickered the two muskmules toward them. Rhaif and Pratik hopped into the wagon as it passed. The wain quickly gained speed as the Kethra'kai rushed ahead into the forests. Those on foot raced nearly as fast as the scout's horses, their pale forms growing ghostly as they ran. One of the scouts pulled the elder, Xan, onto his horseback behind him. She whispered in the tribesman's ear and pointed her cane.

They sped even faster.

The wagon bounced and rattled after the others. Rhaif gripped the seatback to hold his place. Pratik did the same, but the Chaaen ignored the forest and narrowed his eyes at Rhaif.

"What?" Rhaif snapped at him.

"The elder's words. Whispers of the old gods . . ."

He shrugged, nearly losing his hold. "I don't know what she's talking about. The old woman's probably addled by age."

"And what about her final words, about the singer being hunted?" Pratik said. *"Du'a ta."*

Rhaif frowned. "Like I said, the ravings of a madwoman."

It certainly made no sense to him. *Du'a ta* meant *both of them.* He tried to picture another like Shiya. *Impossible.*

The path grew rougher, thrashing the wagon all about, silencing any further talk. Low branches whipped at their heads. It took all their concentration not to be thrown off the back of the bucking wagon.

Rhaif's teeth rattled in his head as he clenched both hands to the seatback. Then a furious scolding rose from above. He glanced up to a swirl of small birds bursting from branches or hanging nests. They darted through the air in shades of copper and gold, flitting and diving at the noisy trespass below.

He knew those birds, even named a bronze mystery after them.

"Shiya . . ." he whispered.

The wagon suddenly slowed, throwing Rhaif and Pratik hard against the seat. The wain bounced and battered to a final stop. With the clattering wheels silenced, the thunder rose around them again, still booming, sounding even closer now.

Rhaif straightened from the wagon's bed. A knot of Kethra'kai gathered near the bole of a large Reach alder. Its roots kneed out of the leafy mulch, covered in moss. As the tribesmen shuffled with whispers of amazement, Rhaif spotted a brighter glint buried at the tree's base.

With his heart in his throat, Rhaif leaped from the wagon and rushed forward. He joined Llyra as she slipped out of her saddle. Pratik followed. They all pushed through the Kethra'kai.

Pratik grabbed Rhaif's arm as the sight opened. "I'm sorry," he whispered.

A bronze figure lay on her side, half buried in leaves. Glassy eyes stared straight back at him, dull and dead. A leg lay crooked, bent the wrong way.

No, no, no . . .

Rhaif rushed forward. "Shiya . . ."

Xan was already there, down on her knees, her palms hovering over the top of Shiya's crown of bronze hair.

Rhaif stared up, as if raising his face in supplication to the gods. Instead, he studied the fan of branches, leafed in alder gold, climbing up into the clouds. He pictured Shiya plummeting through those limbs, but it looked like not a leaf or twig had been disturbed up there.

The cold coal in his heart warmed.

She hadn't fallen here.

He turned to the forest, only now noting a path of broken bushes and bent branches. He pictured Shiya stumbling through there, grabbing at those limbs to keep moving—until finally succumbing to her injuries.

Pratik stood nearby, wayglass in hand. He wore a deep frown and caught where Rhaif was looking. The Chaaen drew nearer.

"I was wrong," Pratik said. "Her path was not toward the cliffs of the Shrouds. She was heading *away* from them."

Llyra had her arms crossed. "No wonder we couldn't find her."

"Then where was she going?" Rhaif asked.

Pratik turned to the forest. His gaze followed where she seemed to have been headed. Thunder rumbled from over there, lit by bursts of light. Each blast brightened the fog, enough to reveal a greenish cast to those mists.

"She was trying to reach the Eitur," Pratik said.

"Why?" Llyra asked.

"Maybe she was trying to rejoin us," Rhaif offered, pain lancing through him as he imagined her struggle to return to his side.

Pratik dispelled such romanticism. "Her damage may have been too se-
vere, draining her vigor too quickly. If so, she might have sought to stoke the
fires inside her with the heat of the sun before resuming her trek."

Llyra glowered at her broken form. "And now she is gone forever."

"No," Xan said, still warming her palms over the cold bronze. "She still
sings, faint though it be."

Despite Shiya's glassy eyes and broken form, Rhaif realized Xan must
be right. How else could the elder have led them here? The embers of hope
inside him warmed brighter.

Xan turned to them. "We must get her into your wagon. Quickly now."

Rhaif balked, afraid to move her.

Then a shattering boom drew their attention toward the lake. A burst of fire
bloomed, bright enough to dazzle the eyes before wafting out. The concussion
rattled leaves all around and blew the mists toward them, shredding the fog.

Rhaif caught a distant shine of emerald waters before the mists closed
again.

Xan pointed her cane at the wagon. "We have no more time."

Her words proved true as the clouds darkened to the west. A massive storm
cloud rolled off the poisonous lake and swept high over them. The forests
dimmed all around. The enormity of it felt like a great weight pressing down
on them.

But it wasn't a storm cloud that cast such a mighty shadow.

With her face craned up, Llyra identified what hung over the forest. "A
warship . . ."

WRYTH RUSHED ACROSS the forecastle toward the wheel of the *Pywll*.
"Stop!" he shouted to both the pilotman and the warship's commander, a
boulder-shouldered Vyrllian named Brask hy Laar.

The commander's crimson face turned to Wryth with a deep scowl.
"Why? We have orders to sweep to the end of the lake, then close our side of
the noose toward Havensfayre's mooring field."

"Unless instructed otherwise," Wryth reminded him firmly. "Liege General
Haddan has given me leeway to pursue an artifact stolen from the kingdom, a
weapon of great power."

Brask gave an exasperated shake of his head, but he waved to the pilotman. "Do as he says. Bring us to a stop."

With a sharp nod, the pilotman called out orders, passing the command
around the forecastle. In moments, the ship's flashburn forges roared outside, fighting their momentum forward.

Brask turned to Wryth. "How do you hope to find anything down in that misty sea?"

Wryth lifted what he held. "With this."

In his palms, he cradled a crystal orb. Skerren had fabricated this instrument back at the Shrivenkeep, designed specifically for this journey. The globe of polished crystal was filled with heavy oil. Pinned and suspended within it was a ring of tiny lodestones, each wrapped by a coil of copper threading. He pictured a larger version of a similar construction. It enshrined the bronze bust back at the Shrivenkeep. Each lodestone was sensitive to the emanations given off by such holy artifacts.

Unfortunately, Skerren's smaller design required it to be close to the source before its lodestones could respond. While en route here, Wryth had been using the tool like a wayglass, trying to discern any flow of energies in the area. It was only once they neared Eitur's eastern shores that a few of the lodestones had begun to shiver in the oil, disturbed by unseen winds. As they continued along, the slivers slowly swung and settled, pointing east of the Eitur, just as Skerren's earlier calculations had assessed.

Wryth's grip tightened on the orb, his heart pounding.

Then, just a moment ago, something had changed. All the lodestones had unsnapped from their positions and spun dizzily in place. He showed the same to Brask. Wryth held the orb with the ring of copper-wrapped stones positioned horizontally with the ground.

"I was following a trail," Wryth said, "when I lost the signal, but watch . . ."

He rolled the globe until the ring of lodestones was perpendicular to the forest. As he rotated it, the tiny slivers halted their lazy spin and snapped into position again, all the slivers pointing *down*. He stared across the orb at the dawning awareness in Brask's crimson face. Even *Pywll*'s commander understood the implication.

"The weapon is below us," Brask mumbled.

"It must be ours," Wryth added. "Even if it means burning down this entire forest."

46

RHAIF CURSED AS the shadow of the warship settled to a stop overhead. He hauled Shiya toward the waiting wagon. He gripped one of her stiff arms. The bronze was deathly cold to his touch. He could not fathom how there could be any life inside this shell.

Pratik supported her other arm, while another four tribesmen bore her legs and torso. The Chaaen's face was pinched as he stared up toward that dark cloud of the warship. "Somehow they must know Shiya is here."

"All the more reason to get her into the wagon," Llyra said, dancing her mare behind them.

Pratik looked little encouraged by this plan. "If they traced us here, they could do the same with Shiya on the move."

"We've no other choice," Rhaif grunted.

He pictured a rain of firebombs blasting this area.

Still, they made it to the wagon, and with much effort, slid and hauled her stiff form aboard. Rhaif climbed in after her. As he did, he flashed back to a corpse being dragged out of an alley in Anvil. The poor man's throat had been cut, but his limbs were rigored and held forth stiffly, as if he were still trying to ward off his attacker.

Shiya reminded him of the same, a figure frozen in death.

Xan climbed into the wagon with the help of a tribeswoman, someone named Dala. She and another three women followed Xan. Pratik was the last to clamber in. They all crowded around Shiya's bulk.

Shouts and whistles spread through the Kethra'kai, and the entire group set off through the woods. Rhaif winced at the clatter and rattle of the wagon. He knew warships had sharp ears. He prayed that the bombing had deafened the ship above.

As if the gods heard this thought, a fresh series of booms erupted to the south, in the direction they were headed. From the sharper staccato of those blasts, it was not bombs this time.

Pratik looked across Shiya's body. "That was cannon fire."

It was easy to read the worry in the Chaaen's face.

Did that bombardment herald the presence of another warship ahead?

As they fled through the woods, they tracked alongside the green glow of

the nearby Eitur. They aimed toward the only destination in that direction—
Havensfayre—that might offer a measure of shelter.

But not if another warship was already over there.

Rhaif called to Xan, waving east. "We should turn and make for the deeper
woods."

The elder ignored him, lifting her palms over Shiya's face.

Pratik argued against Rhaif's plan. "If they've tracked Shiya here, they'll
continue to do so through these woods. Our only hope is to make it to Havensfayre and seek a way to bury her somewhere safe, where they might not be
able to discern her presence. And if we hurry, maybe they won't know we've
fled there."

Rhaif looked doubtfully above. They still hadn't escaped the warship's
shadow. It looked to be drifting closer to the Eitur. He pictured it descending and offloading a hunting party. Before long, he and the others could be
pursued by air and by land.

He stared down at Shiya.

And what about her?

He knew Pratik was right. Plainly those aboard the warship had a means
of tracking her, as surely as Xan had done in leading their group to Shiya's
broken form.

He looked over to the elder, who sat back on her heels in the rocking
wagon, as if she had already given up on Shiya. Instead, Xan lifted an arm.
The other four women in the wagon did the same. The elder started singing,
which was picked up by the others. It was a wordless melody, just a lyric of
resonance and chorus, rising from throats and fashioned by lips into something even grander.

As he listened, the old lullaby sung by his mother rose again in his head,
as if stirred forth by the women's chanting. Around him, all the Kethra'kai
lowered their palms to the bronze form of Shiya. Where each hand touched,
the dark bronze melded into lighter hues of copper and gold. The magick
spread outward from their fingers, pooling across Shiya's chest.

It was as if the women carried sunlight in their touch, but Rhaif knew
the power wasn't so much in their hands as it was in their singing, raised by
voices that were strong enough to pierce bronze skin and burnish the cold
forges inside her, to warm them back to life.

Thin, strong fingers—Xan's—grabbed his wrist and drew his hand to the
center of the swirling pool. She lowered his palm between Shiya's breasts, as
if inviting him to feel a heartbeat he knew was not there.

As his skin touched bronze, the singing grew louder, heard not with his
ears, but with his own heart. His mother's old lullaby echoed there, too,

rising and falling, finding home in that greater melody. Then something new arose. It was a golden strand of warm bronze that threaded through all, joining everything together. But it wasn't entirely *new*. It was more like his mother's lullaby, there but nearly forgotten. Only this song existed within him and without. It shone brightly enough for him to follow its threads down into Shiya and back into his own heart.

He remembered wondering why he was so connected to this bronze woman. Back in Anvil, he questioned whether she had bound him up in some silent version of bridle-song. He now recognized he was right—but also wrong. What tied them was not a song of command and entrapment. It was a melody forged as much by his own loneliness and despair as it was by Shiya's solitude and displacement. They had needed each other and found each other. Here was not a song of bridling, but one of companionship, of two spirits sharing one another.

Warm fingers found his hand and pressed his palm more firmly to Shiya's chest.

While he was still lost in the song, it took him a breath to see that it was not Xan who held him.

He stared at the bronze fingers resting atop his.

"Shiya . . ."

He turned to find glassy eyes upon him. They were still cold but with the barest flicker of warmth there now.

"I'm here," he whispered.

The tribal song rose around him, but he sensed the others weren't trying to revive Shiya further. He suspected their singing did not have the fiery power of the Father Above. It only had enough strength to stir her, to sustain her for a time.

Instead, the new crescendo served another purpose. The combined voices swelled higher, slowly hiding the brightness beneath their greater song.

Soon Rhaif could barely discern those golden threads any longer. But he knew such masking was not meant to blind *his* eyes. He stared up as the wagon cleared the warship's giant shadow and rode back into sunlit mists. He squinted against the glare, watching that dark moon setting toward the glow of Eitur's green waters.

He understood.

It is those eyes that must stay blind.

STANDING ON THE shore of Eitur, Wryth shook Skerren's orb, then held it steady again. He studied the jostling spin of lodestones, waiting for them to stop, to point where he should go. But they just wobbled and twirled in the oil, some even going in opposite directions. He tried rotating the globe and turning himself in a circle.

Still nothing.

Brask watched his frustration from the end of a ramp that extended from the hovering mass of the *Pywll*. The commander's crimson features had darkened. Wryth had urged him to lower the warship over the lake and drop a ramp to shore. A trio of trackers with chained thylassaurs had already left, scouting the forest ahead. But the main hunting party, which consisted of a dozen knights on horseback, led by Brask's second in command—his brother Ransin, another Vyrllian—awaited instructions from Wryth.

"Do you have any further guidance?" Brask asked, his impatience worn thin. "I can't have my brother and the others traipsing in circles out there."

Wryth lowered the orb, ready to admit defeat. *Maybe I need to be in the air to pick up those winds again. Perhaps this close to the forest, some natural emanation masks the artifact's location.*

He faced Brask, prepared to leave the search on the ground to the trio of trackers and their thylassaurs. Until he could reestablish contact, he feared he would be wasting resources and further irritating the *Pywll*'s commander. But before he could admit as much, a commotion drew their focus back to the woods.

One of the trackers burst out, winded, clearly having run all the way back, leaving his beast with the others. "We . . . We found some encampment. An area scuffed by a great number of feet, rutted with wheels, and trampled by hooves. The mud there is fresh."

Brask looked to Wryth.

But the tracker was not done. "It appears whoever was there fled to the south."

"Toward Havensfayre," Brask mumbled.

Wryth breathed harder.

It has to be them.

If so, he realized it might explain his loss of the signal. Maybe the thieves took the artifact beyond the reach of Skerren's orb. He stared off into the mist-shrouded forest, anxious to follow that trail. He dared not lose it again. More importantly, he had to stop the others from reaching Havensfayre, where it would be much harder to root them out.

He turned to Brask and told the commander what he wanted done, what else he needed for this hunt. The man scowled but passed on his instruction. In short order, a low hissing growl rose behind him. He turned as two massive black-furred scythers stalked down the ramp. The steel-helmed cats, each the height of a Gyn, bared fangs longer than their jaws. They came with a pair of bridle-masters, the rare songsters who could control such massive beasts.

Wryth turned to the tracker. "Take the cats to the encampment you found." He then faced the bridle-masters. "Have your charges pick up the scents there, then loose them on the trail. They're to run down and slay anyone they find."

He had no fear for the bronze woman. She cast no scent of sweat and blood, and her metal body could certainly withstand the ravaging of such beasts.

With nods all around, the others took off.

Wryth turned to Brask. "I will accompany your brother and his men."

Brask looked happy to oblige, plainly ready to rid his forecastle of an overbearing Shrive. But as the man turned to his brother, the blasting of a horn cut through the mists, coming from the south. It blared three long notes of distress.

Brask frowned at the horns. "The *Tytan*. They're summoning us back. Something must be wrong."

Wryth clenched a fist. "But we can still—"

The commander turned from him, already dismissing him. He called to his brother and waved to the forest. "Ransin! Take two men and follow the trackers and the cats!"

Wryth tried to intervene. "We may need all those men and horses."

Brask swung toward the ramp. "Not until we know the fate of the *Tytan*. I've given forth enough on this matter, even lending my brother to your Iflelen cause."

He spoke the name of Wryth's order like a curse.

"I can spare a horse for you," Brask conceded, pointing back. "But that is all."

The commander headed up the ramp, drawing a majority of the hunting party with him. He bellowed orders all around, readying the ship for a fast departure.

Wryth weighed the best course: to accompany Ransin *or* try to pick up the artifact's trail from the air. He stared toward Havensfayre and the wall of fire burning along the lake's edge and made his decision.

He swung around and followed in Brask's wake.

Ransin and the others did not need his help, but if those thieves should make it to Havensfayre, Wryth intended to be there to meet them. He gripped Skerren's orb, praying to Ðreyk that he could latch on to their trail again.

Behind him, a savage leonine scream rose from the forest.

The noise firmed his resolve.

Maybe I don't need the blessing of Lord Ðreyk after all—only the ferocity of a pair of hunting cats.

RHAIF STIFFENED AS something fierce yowled through the mists behind them, loud enough to be heard above the clatter of the wagon. It was answered by another throat.

He searched back, fearful of what he knew haunted these forests. "Is that a Reach tyger?"

Xan still knelt with the other four Kethra'kai women. She nodded for them to keep their song strong and turned to him. "No. The cry is wrong. And tygers always hunt alone." She faced ahead. "We must hurry."

She leaned to the wagon's drover and spoke rapidly in Kethra. The guide nodded and whistled sharply to those ahead. The scouts on horseback continued forward, but the other Kethra'kai sped off to the east and west on foot, likely trying to lure away the hunters on their trail.

But will it buy us enough time to reach Havensfayre?

The wagon bounded fast through the forest. Shiya's bronze form rattled in the bed. The singing of the women stuttered and jostled. Rhaif cringed, fearing their masking might break. He stared toward where the warship had descended to the lake, but he could no longer discern its dark shadow.

Is it still there? Or is it already in the air, hunting us?

Another blare of horns rose from ahead, drawing Rhaif's attention forward. It blasted three times, each sounding closer than the last. Ahead, the mists glowed a fiery orange, a hopeful sign that they were approaching the outskirts of Havensfayre, but also unnerving.

How much of the town is already on fire?

He feared they were racing toward their doom, but a pair of bloodthirsty screams reminded him that death lay as surely behind them. He tried to judge if those cries were separating, maybe being drawn aside by the false trails of the others. He could not tell.

He swallowed, trying to unstick his fear-dry tongue from the roof of his mouth.

Danger lay in every direction.

He stared over at Pratik. Though the man's brow shone with sweat, he seemed to be ignoring all the threats. Instead, he focused on Shiya, as if trying to discern some last answers from her before he died.

The Chaaen lifted his eyes to Xan. "The Shrouds of Dalalæða . . ."

The name of those jungled highlands drew the elder's attention from the fiery mists ahead.

"*Dalalæða* is a word from the Elder tongue," Pratik said. "It means *deathly stones.* Does that portend some connection to the Northern Henge?"

Rhaif could not fathom why the Chaaen pressed such matters, especially now. Only then did he note the man's shaking shoulders, the way his fists knotted in his silks.

He's just as terrified as I am and likely trying to focus elsewhere.

Rhaif realized that seeking such a place of refuge in the face of terror and horror must have been ingrained into the man. It was how Pratik must have survived all those years of brutality at *Bad'i Chaa,* the House of Wisdom. He remembered the map of white scars across the man's naked skin back at Anvil's gaol. And then there was the cruel castration that had stripped him of his manhood, in all measures of that meaning. Back at that school, Pratik had likely sought solace in his studies, burying all that pain and terror under a pile of books.

Xan lifted her hand and placed her palm on Pratik's cheek. She leaned closer and whispered to him. His eyes grew wide, his mouth parting with a silent gasp. Then she dropped her hand and turned away. Pratik looked again at Shiya, only now with a measure of awe. Even his shoulders had stopped shaking.

Before Rhaif could ask what Xan had told him, Llyra appeared out of the mists. She slowed her mare to draw alongside the wagon and shouted, "We've reached the outskirts of Havensfayre!"

IT TOOK ANOTHER quarter league before Llyra's statement was proven true. Rhaif kept his gaze fixed forward, hardly breathing—both due to the tension and the choking smoke.

All around them, the white mists had been replaced with a black smolder. Fires raged all around. The heat grew to that of a furnace. Huge trees rose to either side. Some burned like torches, swirling with fiery ash. Others remained dark and shadowy.

People had begun to appear throughout the woods, fleeing the town on horseback, atop wagons, and on foot. The group forged through them, slogging onward.

Another burst of horns welcomed them to Havensfayre.

Rhaif stared to the east, searching for the dark shadow of that other warship. But the entire town was shrouded in smoke, making its presence impossible to discern.

Xan leaned forward to the drover, who nodded and whistled to the two scouts. Their path shifted to the west, away from the mooring fields. The scouts shouted ahead, stamping their horses, clearing the way for the wagon as the fleeing townspeople grew thicker.

Homes appeared to either side, built into the boles of giant alders or stacked alongside them. Bridges crisscrossed overhead, several of which burned, carrying the fire deeper into the town. As they rushed under one of those flaming spans, ash and embers rained down. Several stung the flanks of the wagon's muskmules. They brayed and swished their tails angrily. The drover sang to them, trying to calm them. Still, the mules kicked and fought their traces.

Llyra kept alongside the wagon, seated atop her mare. "Where do we go?"

Rhaif glanced to Xan.

The elder kept to the drover's shoulder, adding her voice to his. The mules slowly succumbed to the soothing bridle-song. The pair clomped along more steadily, though their cooperation might have had less to do with the singing and more to do with the wagon having cleared the fire's edge. Ahead, the center of Havensfayre lay under a layer of smoke, but so far, it had been spared the flames.

Still, the air burned the lungs with every breath.

"Where?" Llyra pressed.

The necessity of her inquiry was punctuated by a chorus of rising screams behind them, sharp enough to cut through the roar of the fires. The source of that fresh panic announced itself with savage yowls of bloodlust.

Rhaif glanced back to the flames and smoke. The Kethra'kai must have failed to draw off the cats, or at least not for long enough. The tide of people flowing out of the town around them slowly drew to a fearful stop, miring their progress forward—then slowly that current reversed, fleeing from those screams and hunting cries.

"Faster!" Rhaif hollered.

Their wagon and horses followed the receding tide around them. They sped quickly through the streets. Llyra fought to stay abreast, kicking and whipping people around her. But the press became too much. Her mare suddenly toppled under her, tripping over bodies that had been trampled.

She leaped from the saddle and sprawled headlong toward the wagon bed. Rhaif caught her and drew her around.

She panted in his arms. "I knew you'd end up killing me one day."

"I can only hope. But let's still pray that's not today."

Llyra rolled free and stared ahead. "Where is she taking us?"

The answer appeared ahead as the scouts expertly rounded their steeds near the base of an ancient alder, so old that most of its bark had been shed, leaving only age-polished wood. Its girth was as wide as one of Anvil's huge chimney stacks. So far, the tree had remained untouched by any flame, spreading a golden bower above, as if trying to hold back the smoky sky.

The wagon ground to a hard stop between the two scouts.

"Why are we stopping here?" Llyra asked.

It was a fair question.

Pratik craned at the massive tree. There appeared to be no doors in it. Still, the Chaaen seemed to recognize it. "Oldenmast," he mumbled.

Xan allowed no other inquiries and offered no explanations. "Out! Quickly!" she commanded them, then turned to the tribeswomen and spoke in a blur of Kethra.

Nods answered her. They stopped singing to Shiya and reached to her shoulders, preparing to lift her out. Rhaif went to help, but Shiya rose on her own, weakly, trembling. The tribeswomen helped guide her to the back of the wagon. It seemed the singing of the Kethra'kai must have filled a well inside of Shiya. Maybe like topping off an oil lamp, allowing her to move on her own. Still, from the shaking in her limbs, that strength would not last long.

One of the scouts came around and helped Xan out of the wagon. She then supported herself with her staff. Rhaif saw that her cane's polished white wood was the same hue as the trunk of giant alder. He also spotted a line of sculpted seashells imbedded along the cane's length, representing the faces of the moon.

He felt a chill, remembering Shiya's fixation with the same.

Xan joined the bronze woman as Shiya dropped from the wagon and teetered on one leg. The other limb, bent crooked at the knee, served as no more than a crutch. The women gathered around her, bracing Shiya's arms and back.

Rhaif clambered out with Pratik and Llyra.

Xan guided Shiya a few steps away, keeping their backs to the massive tree.

"Where do we go?" Llyra asked, searching around.

To the right, another huge alder climbed into the smoke. It rose from a sprawl of timbered structures with tiled roofs. At its base, tall doors stood open under a sign of a gold-leafed tree. Despite the chaos, firelight beckoned within. A scatter of fleeing townspeople ran for those doors, seeking shelter inside.

Even Xan hobbled with Shiya in that direction, accompanied by the four tribeswomen.

Rhaif followed. "I think we're supposed to—"

All the women stopped in the center of the square. Xan leaned on her cane and lifted her face. She began to sing. The others joined her—even Shiya. She raised her bronze features to the smoky skies, her cheeks shining with a coppery brilliance. Her eyes flashed, and a piping flowed from her throat.

The chorus grew and spread like wings through the air, wafting high and wide. It seemed impossible that so few voices could raise such a volume. The air appeared to shiver around the cluster, pushing the traces of smoke away, as if trying to open space for another.

Their call was answered by a leonine howl.

Into the square, a massive shadow stalked. A huge paw swiped at a fleeing man, sending him cartwheeling through the air in a spray of blood. The cat hissed and loosed a bollock-icing scream. Its lips curled high, slavering with drool, exposing impossibly long fangs. Its yellow eyes glowed from under a steel helm.

Rhaif knew about those alchymical-crafted caps. Each helm was attuned to its master's unique pitch and voice. They limited another from using bridle-song to ensnare their beasts.

Still, the song in the air seemed to hold the beast at bay for now.

Or maybe it was simply waiting.

A second scyther sidled around the first's haunches, assuming the same threatening posture, shoulder to shoulder with each other.

Rhaif edged away, backing into the wagon.

Those gathering around Shiya remained standing, still singing, as if oblivious to the threat.

What are they waiting for?

One of the scythers had enough. It bunched its haunches and leaped with a scream of fury. It flew with its forelimbs wide, paws outstretched, extending bloodied claws.

Before it crashed into the women, a dark shadow sped out of the inn's tall doors. It struck the cat's flank and sent it rolling to the side. The two tumbled across the packed dirt. When they finally stopped, a muscled beast with striped fur crouched atop the scyther. Its jaws were clamped to the cat's throat. It ripped back its muzzle, tearing out fur and flesh. Blood flew high as it leaped away.

The cat on the ground writhed and mewled, coughing out gouts of its life.

The attacker ignored those death throes and faced the other cat. Its entire form bristled with challenge.

Llyra gasped, "What's a vargr doing here?"

Rhaif squinted at the women around Shiya.

Had they somehow summoned this beast to their defense?

The answer to Rhaif's question arrived. A young woman, flanked by others, stepped from the firelit shadows of the inn. She sang out at the square, her melody joining the others, falling into perfect harmony.

Rhaif struggled to understand who she was.

Pratik seemed to know and mumbled with awe, *"Du'a ta."*

47

NYX SANG TO the beasts in the square. As she did, she added her voice to the chorus of women outside, while drawing their strands back into her. She cast herself out along those threads, like a spider dancing across a web. She did so delicately, unsure, still tentative about such a talent.

She recognized Xan by the silvery threads in her voice, Dala by the fire of her youth. The other Kethra'kai added their strength with every note. Somewhere she even sensed the faint chords of a lullaby.

Yet, wound through them all were thin cords of bronze, so ancient that they seemed to glow with tarnish and verdigris. From the corner of her eye, she spotted the source, a woman with painted bronze skin. She appeared to be wounded and fading. Yet, there was also something unnerving about her. With no moment to spare, Nyx shied from such strangeness for now.

Instead, she settled where she felt the most familiar, into the heart of a feral beast, tamed only by the warmth of a shared pack.

Aamon's challenge flowed across the square. His low growl, commingled with a high-pitched chittering, shivered the hairs on her arms. Still, his was a song in its own right, as beautiful in its savagery as any sweet melody.

Recognizing this, she added her song to his. In a breath, her heart became his, and his lusts were now hers. She stared through his eyes and her own.

She flashed to doing the same with Bashaliia but shoved that sorrow deep. *Not now.*

Instead, she reveled in the taste of blood on her tongue, the tremble of muscle. She studied the crouch of black fur, yellow claw, and slashing fang. She heard the hissing song of the cat, sibilant, savage, full of rage at everything and anything—but she also detected the pained misery of the harshly bridled.

She tried to draw that leonine song into her, while sending threads of the same toward it—only to run into a dissonance of steel that fought her.

Through Aamon's eyes, she saw the helm fastened to the scyther's head. *Ah . . .*

The cat crouched, preparing to leap.

Kanthe appeared at Nyx's side. He had his bow raised, an arrow already nocked.

"No," she warned him.

Frell reached to her from the other side. "We can wait no longer. We must retreat to the cellars."

Instead, Nyx stepped farther into the square. She was afraid Frell's touch would make her lose the tempo and rhythm of the entwined song. She knew she would need every note.

Earlier in the day, when she and the others approached the Golden Bough, she had caught the first faint strands of this chorus. The song had sounded distant, far off in the woods, but as she listened, it drew steadily closer. Her group had tried to drag her through the inn and down to its wine cellars, but she balked, afraid to lose those notes. She only allowed the others to draw her as far as the cellar stairs. Posted there, she could flee from any threat, yet still remain attuned to that approaching song.

As that chorus drew abreast of the inn, the song dimmed momentarily— then burst forth with an urgency that could not be ignored. She had been drawn to it as surely as any bridled beast. Still, what drew her wasn't any command in that song. It was a pleading, a melody of entreaty and hope.

She could not ignore it.

The others had tried to stop her, even Jace, but Aamon snapped them all back, leaving them no choice but to follow.

As she stepped now out into the square, the massive cat tilted its gaze toward her. She met those yellow eyes. Its haunches bunched as a yowl built in its chest.

Before it sprang, she drew the other women's songs into her—the silver, the fire, the bronze, even the strands of a lullaby—and cast a net at the beast. She did not seek to capture or bridle it. She let her threads drape over the steel helm and probe the dissonance that blocked her.

She had been taught about such alchymies. She knew how the metal of such helms was forged. A bridle-master sang to the cooling steel, infusing his or her unique pattern into it as it hardened.

Knowing this, she closed her eyes and brought forth one last song, the first one she had learned. From her throat, a soft keening rose, straining the cords of her neck. She tasted warm milk as she sent those reverberations out. She remembered when she had last sung this song, fueled by the force of a thousand bats. Back then, when she had unleashed that power, she had been able to discern the vein of every leaf, even the bones of her companions. While she didn't have that force now, its song remained inside her, etched into her, a part of her.

She gathered the strength of the others to her and sang forth with new vigor. A familiar second sight opened inside her. She could now see every facet of the helm's metal, every angle of iron patterned into its carbon. It was not unlike discerning the veins of a leaf. She read the unique lock buried in the steel and used her threads like a key. Once it opened, she sent her strands through the steel's pattern—to reach the tortured, furious creature nestled inside.

Jace called to her, nearly shattering her control. "Horses are coming."

"Knights," Kanthe corrected.

She kept her eyes closed and sang with enough force to shift the pattern in the enslaving helm, to turn the bits of iron, like lodestones in a thousand wayglasses, forever changing the lock. Freed now, the cat was no longer under anyone's thrall, not even her own. She remembered the fury of the Reach tyger from days ago, how it had attacked to keep anyone from subjugating it.

I will not be this cat's master.

Instead, she imparted a last gift.

She let it see who had subjugated and tortured it.

She opened her eyes and faced the cat's fury. But that savageness was no longer directed at her. Past its shoulders, a trio of horses thundered toward them. Knights in armor rode low on their backs. Behind them came trackers and bridle-masters, mounted double on their steeds.

The huge cat yowled one last time, spun around, and bounded toward the legion's forces. A leonine scream became a chorus of blood, ripped flesh, and screams torn from throats.

As Nyx's own song ended in the square, the threads of power wisped out of her, leaving her empty and weak. She sagged, exhausted. Her vision darkened, as if she were falling back into her formerly near-blind state. The world became pools of lights and shadows.

Kanthe caught her.

Aamon dashed over to her, too, brushing against her, holding up that side.

Her vision slowly returned but remained foggy.

As she was turned from the slaughter, she saw another was equally afflicted. The strange painted woman stumbled, having to lean heavily on the women around her. Two more men rushed to her aid.

Kanthe tried to draw Nyx toward the inn. "We must get down to the cellars."

"No!" A voice called to them from across the square. A figure separated from the cluster of women, leaning on a cane. Through Nyx's glazed eyes, her white hair looked to be shimmering around her shoulders, as if still suffused with power.

Xan . . .

The elder's voice carried easily to them. "That tree's roots are not deep enough," she warned. She pointed her cane at Oldenmast. "But those are."

Behind the elder, the others began helping the strange woman toward the ancient tree.

Frell urged them forward. "She may be right. And if there's a safe place under that ancient tree, she would know it."

Any choice in the matter was stripped from them as a huge fiery burst exploded overhead. They all ducked, while looking up. The pall of smoke was blasted apart, revealing a patch of blue sky far overhead—and the keel of a huge warship hanging there.

WRYTH KEPT HIS face pressed to the eyepiece of the farscope. The instrument's mirrors and lenses allowed his vision to extend past the hole through the layer of black smoke.

The view would not last long.

The gap was already closing.

He searched around the bower of the ancient alder, what had to be the revered Oldenmast of Havensfayre. He had been drawn to this spot from the town's mooring field.

Earlier, upon arriving here in the *Pywll*, their warship had discovered the *Tytan* tied down and grounded at that field. The ruins of its balloon still smoked. Luckily, a good portion remained intact, and repairs were underway. To aid in patching up the other warship, Brask shuttled men and supplies down. Skrycrows flew back and forth between the two ships. The *Pywll* had been warned about the shark lurking in the mists, a cunning swyftship who had ambushed the larger craft.

And it's still out there.

Even now, Wryth kept this in mind as he searched the ground through the farscope. Brask had told him who was aboard that other ship, a ghost from the past. Graylin sy Moor. Apparently, Haddan had the accursed knight momentarily trapped on the *Tytan*'s deck, only to lose the bastard at the last moment. Knowing that and suspecting whom Graylin was protecting—a girl who could be the Klashean's prophetic *Vyk dyre Rha*—Wryth had instituted his own measures to deal with this change in circumstance.

Then all that had been set aside when Skerren's orb had begun to vibrate in Wryth's palm. After leaving the shores of Eitur, he had never set the crystal globe down. His gaze seldom strayed from it. His frustration grew as the orb's tiny copper-wrapped lodestones refused to stir again to those unseen winds. He had almost given up hope—until the globe shivered with warning in his grip.

He had lifted it and saw the lodestone slivers pointing west of the mooring fields. The orb had trembled in his hand, as if it could barely withstand those forces. Still, it had taken the intervention by Haddan via skrycrow to convince Brask to drift the *Pywll* along the trail of those unseen winds to their source.

Skerren's orb had led them to a tall golden crown jutting out of the smoky pall, belonging to a tree far larger than any other. It looked like a gilded island in a black sea. To spy below those dark waters, Wryth had suggested the judicious placement of a firebomb to blast the smoke away.

Through the farscope now, Wryth studied the grounds below as the warship circled that island. He saw people scurrying to and fro, panicked by the blast. Then near an open square, he spotted a bloody slaughter of horses. Amidst the ruins were bodies bearing the livery of the legion.

He stiffened, guessing who they were.

Brask's brother and the other knights.

What had happened?

He started to pull back, ready to alert Brask, when movement in the square drew his eye. A clutch of people scrambled toward the bower of Oldenmast. He was ready to dismiss them as panicked townspeople—when a shaft of sunlight pierced the same smoky hole and glinted off a patch of bright bronze.

He grabbed the farscope with both hands and pulled the eyepiece closer. A group half carried, half dragged a bronze sculpture. His heart clenched in his chest.

At long last . . .

Without looking away, he called to Brask. "It's down there!"

This was the first time since the mines of Chalk that he had laid eyes upon the ancient talisman. He held his breath.

"What do you want me to do?" Brask strode over to him. "We're too high and the trees are too thick for us to lower the *Pywll*."

"It matters not." Wryth's fingers trembled as the smoky pall resealed the hole under him, erasing the sight. "We cannot risk that weapon ever being wielded against the realm."

"Then what should—"

Wryth turned to the commander. "Unload a firestorm below. All around that tree. Burn it down to its roots."

SUPPORTING NYX UNDER one arm, Kanthe fled across the open square. Aamon tracked her other side. A continual growl flowed from the vargr's throat. The beast's ears lay flat against his skull after the thunderous blast overhead.

Jace stumbled alongside them with Frell. They all fled toward the group of Kethra'kai. The other party hobbled more slowly, burdened by a strange woman, who appeared to be in armor, which baffled him.

But such quandaries had to wait.

More thunderous blasts erupted all around, bursting with flame and smoke. They all ducked from the concussions and ran low. Then behind them, one of the bombs struck the doors of the Golden Bough, exploding with enough force to throw them all forward.

Kanthe glanced back. The blast had torn a gaping hole into the commons, and flames were quickly spreading.

"C'mon." He helped Nyx off her knees.

By the time they overtook the others, the Kethra'kai had rounded the giant bole of Oldenmast. The tall, pointed doors in the trunk appeared ahead, along with the round window of painted glass above it.

A tribesman was already there, hauling open one side.

Another rushed to Xan and helped her move faster.

They all fled toward the open door. As they reached it, Kanthe heard a heavy cracking of branches overhead. He looked up—as a huge fiery barrel came smashing through the tree limbs, toppling straight toward them.

"Move!" he screamed, pushing Nyx ahead of him.

They piled through the door.

He urged them deeper. "Keep goin—"

The explosion tossed them all across the dark interior. Kanthe hit the floor hard and tumbled, tangled with Nyx. A fireball rolled over them, trailed by searing smoke. Shattered glass rained all around.

As soon as the worst passed, Jace scrambled to them and helped haul them up. Aamon growled, dancing a protective circle around the group. Across the dark chamber, the others gained their feet.

Kanthe glanced behind him. Both doors had been ripped off. A body remained on the floor, crushed under a shattered section of the giant door. Kanthe recognized the dead woman. With a wince, he tried to draw Nyx away.

But Nyx balked and stepped in that direction, rubbing her eyes, as if struggling to see.

Xan forced her back. "No," the elder said.

"Who . . . ?" Nyx gasped out.

Xan urged her onward.

"Who?" Nyx pressed more firmly.

Kanthe frowned, knowing Nyx would not budge. "Tell her."

Xan's eyes met hers. "Dala."

Kanthe pictured the tribeswoman, a youth who could never seem to stop smiling.

Except no longer.

Nyx wove on her feet, her face dazed and heartbroken. Jace helped get her legs moving deeper into the hollow of the ancient tree. Behind them, more blasts and explosions drove them onward.

Kanthe glanced one last time through the broken doors and shattered windows.

Fires raged past the threshold.

He swore vengeance on whoever wrought such damage.

I will make you suffer.

WRYTH SHOVED THE farscope away from his face. It took him several hard blinks for his sight to readjust back to the forecastle of the *Pywll*—but his fury could not be so easily dispelled.

"Well?" Brask asked.

He snapped at the commander, wanting to lash out at anything near at hand. "Your brother is dead."

"What?" Brask lunged at the farscope. "Why didn't you tell me—"

Wryth blocked him. "It's no use," he said, forcing a note of sympathy. "The smoke of the bombings has washed away any view below."

"Then we'll blast open a new hole."

"It'll do no good. Those new flames are pouring smoke across the ground." He faced Brask. "But I can tell you this. It was those thieves who killed your brother."

The Vyrllian's crimson features darkened into a storm.

Wryth turned to the bow windows, toward the golden crown of the ancient alder. During the bombardment, he had caught brief fragments of the view below, lit by the blast of flames. He'd had to watch impotently as the group dashed the bronze woman into that ancient woodland sanctuary, Oldenmast.

To make matters worse, through the farscope he had spotted an upraised face running across the square. Just for a breath. He couldn't be certain, but the dark features stood out among a sea of pale Kethra'kai faces.

Plus, the conspicuous bow across his back . . .

It had to be.

Kanthe.

Wryth clenched a fist.

How did the prince end up with the artifact? Was this some further plot of insurrection? Did the bastard plan on wielding the weapon against the king?

For the sake of all of Hálendii, Wryth had to put a stop to it, even if it meant destroying the treasure, or at least burying it for a time. He returned to face the fury in Brask's face and pointed to the gilded crown of Oldenmast.

"Your brother's murderers fled into that tree," he said. "They must be brought low."

Brask turned away, his voice a clenched knot. "Then I'm done casting stones."

Wryth followed, worried he might have pushed the commander too far. Brask's next words confirmed this.

"I'm going to drop a Hadyss Cauldron atop them. When I'm finished, there will be nothing below but a smoking crater."

WITH HER HEAD still ringing, Nyx stumbled through the cavernous expanse hollowed out of the alder's trunk. Jace kept to one side of her, Aamon on the other, both panting hard. She had regained most of her vision and some of her strength, enough to be able to move on her own.

Behind her, smoke rolled into the dark chamber and rose to smother a dome swathed in glowing mosses and fungi. The only other illumination came from tiny lamps that revealed tall figures at the cardinal points of the room. They appeared to be carved out of Oldenmast's trunk.

Dala had told her how they represented the Kethra'kai gods. To honor her friend, Nyx glanced all around, setting it to memory before it was lost.

As she crossed the sacred chamber, she identified each god. *Vhatn* of the waters stood with her hands cupped, from which the trickle of a hidden spring flowed into a basin near her bare feet. The heavy-browed *Jarðvegur*, of loam and rock, looked more boulder than man. *Vyndur*, of the air, held clouds over his head, inset with silver lightning bolts. Then *Eldyr*, she who was fire, stood entirely cloaked, with only her eyes glowing from under a hood, lit from within by a secret flame.

Nyx shivered as she passed the last. That fiery gaze seemed to follow her, to accuse her. Past the ringing of her ears, she heard the flames roaring outside.

Xan kept alongside Nyx, thumping with her cane near Aamon. The elder noted her attention, maybe her shiver. "Fire can also be cleansing. It is flame that clears a forest and burns cones to cast new seeds."

A resounding crash echoed from outside, marking one of the mighty Reach alders toppling somewhere in town. Nyx could not imagine how any of this ruin could serve a useful purpose.

Frell drew up to her, with Kanthe at his side. The prince's face was a dark shadow of fury. "Where do we go?" the alchymist asked.

Xan pointed her cane toward a pair of Kethra'kai scouts who had run forward and swiveled open a round door that looked like a knot in the trunk's wood. The pair also carried lamps.

"Down to Oldenmast's deepest root," Xan explained. "It's why I brought her here."

The elder glanced over a shoulder to the clutch of Kethra'kai who supported the bronze-painted woman. The shadows and smoke made it hard to discern her features. It looked like she wore a metal mask. The woman's presence still made no sense. Nyx remembered the ancient filaments, glowing a tarnished bronze, that had flowed out with the woman's song.

Nyx also noted the other strangers who helped or hovered at the woman's side. One, from the finery of his clothes and dark skin, appeared to be a Klashean tradesman. The other's shorter stance and thicker limbs marked him as Guld'guhlian, same as the hard woman with chopped blond hair and a perpetual scowl.

"Quickly now." Xan drew them all to the door that stood swiveled open, pivoting around a pin down its center.

The elder climbed over the threshold and took the lead. Even the two scouts fell back, as if knowing this was her place.

They all followed Xan down a winding stair carved out of the center of what must be a thick root—maybe the taproot of the alder. The grain of the wood was gold against a silvery white. As they continued, round and round, the veining vanished and left only a snowy wood that felt as ancient as the rock of this land.

As they continued, the roaring fires overhead faded to a solemn quiet, disturbed only by their footfalls, hard breaths, and the pad of Aamon's paws. Other doors and dark passages led off the main stairs, heading in all directions.

Xan spoke into the thickening silence, maybe to dispel their discomfort. She waved to one of the side tunnels. "The Oldenmast may seem like one tree, but in actuality, it makes up *all* the trees of this grove. The Oldenmast's roots extend outward in every direction. From this tree's ancient suckers, all the other trunks of this ancient grove sprang forth."

Nyx tried to picture that spread of roots and trunks. She stared up and around with amazement. *This entire grove is one tree.*

Kanthe took a more practical view of Xan's words, peering down a dark passageway. "Does that mean we can use those same spread of roots to go anywhere in this town? Maybe even slip past the fires above?"

"And escape those who hunt us," Jace reminded them.

Frell turned to Xan. "Is that why you had us come down here?"

"No." The elder waved her cane. "These cellars and passages grow thinner and scarcer the farther out you go. I fear you'd still end up within that trap of fire and ash above."

"Then where can we go?" Frell asked.

"To an even more ancient root, one belonging to the old gods," Xan answered cryptically. "We should—"

The world jolted all around with a crack of thunder that deafened and crushed chests. They all tumbled or fell across the wooden steps. A great ripping accompanied it, as if the very ground was being torn asunder.

Before Nyx could stand, a wall of fiery smoke, wretched with sulfurous brimstan, blasted over them. A rumbling accompanied it. Then a torrent of rocks came rattling down, bringing with it a flow of sand and dirt.

Kanthe grabbed Nyx, hauled her up, and hollered to everyone, "Go! Keep going!"

The scouts ran forward. Ignoring their earlier obeisance, they scooped Xan up and hauled her bodily down the stairs. The rest of the group raced after them, with Aamon loping and growling at Nyx's side.

Dust and grumbling rock chased after them. Then a loud splintering boom shattered above. The stairs bucked under her, nearly tossing Nyx back down. She caught herself on Aamon's flank to keep her footing and continued downward.

Still, she stared back up, picturing the great golden-boughed breadth of Oldenmast crashing across Havensfayre.

We should've never come here . . .

Finally, the rumbling and rattling settled to groans that fell farther behind them. Dust still hung in the air, but it thinned as they fled deeper. The spiral of the stairs also grew narrower, pinched as the taproot thinned around them.

Frell noted a disconcerting detail. "We've not passed any side tunnels since the blast."

Jace looked back, his eyes huge, his face streaming with sweat. "That means we're trapped down here."

"Still," Kanthe added, "that also means those hunters can't reach us. If that's any consolation?"

From Jace's aghast expression, it was not.

After several turns of the stairs, the way grew so tight that they had to continue single file. Xan freed herself from the scouts' help and stamped the last of the way down on her own. Finally, the stairs exited the giant root and entered a domed chamber. Overhead, an arching vein of burnished white wood cut across the roof. The rest of the room was polished black stone.

Nyx stared up. She recognized the vein of wood was actually the trailing end of Oldenmast's taproot, the one they'd been climbing through. It dove past this chamber, as if avoiding it, and vanished back into the rock. It was as if this room was a stone lodged in a dark river.

Nyx saw why.

Across the chamber, the obstruction around which the taproot passed stood on the chamber's far side.

Xan crossed toward it.

Nyx and the others gathered behind the elder.

Ahead of them, an oval copper door bulged into the space. Tangles of bronze and gold filaments delved outward along its edges, digging into root and stone. None of it appeared to have been crafted by any hand. It was all flowy, with no straight edges. She imagined it slithering down here and lodging in place, intent on sucking strength and sustenance from the base of the sacred tree.

To Nyx, it looked like the coppery maw of a great beast.

Or maybe a god . . .

Xan bowed her head before it, leaning on her staff with both hands. She began to sing to it. The chant rose low in her thin chest, as if she were trying to draw something from deep in her heart.

Nyx listened with an ear cocked. She sought the rhythm and melody, but it was unlike anything she had heard before. She took a step forward, but Aamon growled next to her, shifting in front of her, as if warning Nyx that this was not meant for her.

He's right . . .

From behind her, the painted woman limped forward. She shed those who had been supporting her, revealing herself fully for the first time as she stepped into the lamplight.

Nyx fell back from the sight.

Jace tried to draw her farther away, while Frell gasped and Kanthe swore.

The Guld'guhlian stretched an arm toward her. "Shiya . . ."

The Klashean grasped his arm, keeping him from following.

Nyx gulped down her initial shock and studied this strange woman sculpted of metal. Her limbs moved stiffly, as if the bronze fought the intent inside.

As the figure joined Xan, she began to sing, easily finding the rhythm that had escaped Nyx. The fragility of each note awakened the sadness and grief inside her. Still, in that moment, she knew her loss was but a drop compared to the ocean within this living statue.

As the two sang toward that coppery door, shimmering threads flowed outward from the women. The strands wafted toward the door, tangling into a complicated knot, then vanished into the metal.

Without being told, Nyx understood. She remembered her confrontation with the scyther, how she had undone the lock within the helm's steel by forging a key to open it.

It's the same here.

A deep atonal note responded to their twined song—and the copper door swiveled on a pivot down its middle, opening like the wooden door far above.

Beyond the threshold lay only darkness.

Xan sagged, exhausted from the effort. The bronze woman—Shiya—stumbled back, only to be steadied by the Guld'guhlian, who rushed forward. The Kethra'kai, along with the man's two companions, helped him.

Nyx drew closer to the door.

One of the scouts lifted his lamp higher, casting its shine past the threshold. A long tunnel, made of the same copper, extended into the darkness. She remembered Xan's description of what awaited them below.

An even more ancient root, one belonging to the old gods.

Frell joined her, possibly remembering the same. The alchymist turned to Xan. "This tunnel . . . where does it lead?"

Still tired, Xan breathed heavily but answered. "To the Shrouds of Dalalæða." She turned to the bronze figure. "To her home."

Arkival limne of
Scyther
(Havensfayre)

FIFTEEN

THE
DEATHLY STONES

Lysten with an open heart,
raper than a deaf ear.
Sing from eyowre spirit,
raper than with eyowre breath.
Sculpt each note with resolve,
raper than with a simple tunge.
Onli then will eyow see the treuth,
ferre better than any eyes can ever show.

—Chant of *Pethryn Tol,*
translation by Rys hy Layc

48

GRAYLIN CROSSED THE meadow toward the shadow cast by the *Sparrow-hawk*. The swyftship hovered in a clearing high overhead. Farther above, mists obscured the balloon. He had offloaded with a handful of the crew earlier. He had helped them anchor the ship's bow and stern lines to tree trunks along the meadow's edge.

Darant had scouted out this spot when he circled the Heilsa to ambush the warship. Now they hid and were forced to wait. The crew didn't need Graylin's help with the ropes, but he had followed them down the same ladder that had rescued him two bells ago. He could not stand being confined in the swyftship. He longed for the empty, lonely stretches of the Rimewood, just him and his two brothers. The close quarters of the boat only squeezed his anxiety to a tighter knot. He could not escape the image of Nyx and Aamon jumping out of the back of the *Sparrowhawk*. Worry about their fate ate at his gut.

So, he had joined the crew on the ground, needing to move, to breathe open air, to feel the brush of grass across his legs, to listen to birdsong and the distant howls of the wild forest. Even now, he had no compunction to return to the ship—except for the disturbing blast to the northwest of their position, off by Havensfayre.

The ground had shaken from the explosion, and branches had shivered their gold leaves. He did not know what that explosion portended, but he feared the worst. He waded through the tall grasses toward the *Sparrow-hawk*. Far above, the aft deck lay open to the sky. The lowered door formed a stout platform sticking out of the boat's stern. He spotted Darant atop there, shading his eyes, scanning the mists. The man was also worried. Then someone called to Darant, and he disappeared inside.

Graylin reached the ship's shadow and hurried to the ladder. He mounted its rungs and quickly scaled up to the open portside hatch. His arms and legs burned as he climbed. His skin had been cut and blistered by the strike of fiery splinters from the exploded sailraft. He had plucked out as many as he could with the help of Darant's daughter Brayl, but he still felt wooden slivers imbedded deep. Any further digging for them would have to wait.

At the ladder's top, he scrambled back into the ship's hold, only to be nearly bowled over by Kalder. The vargr bounded over and slammed broadside into him, a typical pack greeting. Graylin caught the door's edge with one hand and patted Kalder's side with the other. The vargr chuffed, panting hard, his ears high. He knew the beast was as anxious as him. Kalder remained nervous with his brother missing and plainly did not like Graylin being gone, too. And this lengthy confinement was not helping the vargr's unease.

To reassure his brother, Graylin let go of the hatch's frame and grabbed Kalder's jowls in both hands. He bent down and pressed his forehead atop his brother's furry crown. "I'll take you with me next time," he promised.

Kalder bumped him back, hard enough to rock him on his heels. The message was clear: *You'd better.*

A shout from the top of the spiral stairs echoed across the cargo hold. A few birds in hanging cages squawked back, but the message was for him.

"Graylin! Get up 'ere," Darant called. "You need to see this."

Graylin did not like the pirate's grim tone. He gave Kalder another pat and crossed the hold and took the stairs two at a time. In the passageway above, Darant waved for him to follow and marched toward the ship's forecastle.

"What's this about?" Graylin asked.

Darant glanced back. "You heard that blast a moment ago?"

"How could I not? Nearly put me on my arse."

"It did more than that."

Darant pushed into the forecastle, which was empty except for Brayl, who was on her back, checking something under her station. The only other crewmember was a grizzled, pock-faced old man, who stood beside a far-scope. The instrument was not standard for a swyftship, but clearly the pirate had done some modifications to turn the *Sparrowhawk* into a better raider.

Darant pulled Graylin over to the old man's side. "Hyck, show him what you showed me."

Hyck nodded, checked through the eyepiece, fiddled with some adjustments, then stepped back. "That oughta do it."

Darant waved for Graylin to look through the scope. "Hyck designed it."

"That's right, I did," the old man said. "I may've had my alchymical cloak stripped off a me, but that's their loss, I tell ya."

Graylin bent to the eyepiece, trying to fathom what of the surrounding forest could be of interest. As he fixed his face and squinted through the lenses, he had to blink a few times to make sense of what he saw. He was not peering around or under the ship, but over the vast expanse of the mist fields. The clouds spread in a white sea.

Darant explained, "Hyck used tubing, both rubber and bronze—"

"Copper," the man corrected, his breath smelling of rakeleaf and sour ale.

"And copper," Darant concurred. "Plus, a complicated slew of lenses, and mirrors. The farscope's eye can be cranked taller than the balloon, affording us a high view all around."

Graylin barely heard this explanation, too shocked by what the farscope revealed. The white sea ran off into the distance and crashed into a dark shoal of churning smoke. At the center, a thick black column rose high into the sky, roiling and writhing in a fiery tempest.

A warship hung a league away, near the town's mooring field.

But he ignored that threat, concentrating on the smoldering column. He knew it must mark the site of the earlier thunderous blast.

"Had to have been a Hadyss Cauldron," Darant said, possibly noting Graylin's shoulders drawing tighter to his ears. "I don't imagine those bastards would've dropped a Cauldron without a good reason. Like maybe spotting a certain sprite of a girl."

Graylin gripped the farscope. Fear made him lightheaded. "The others couldn't have survived such a blast."

"We don't know that," Darant said. "I've been to Havensfayre many a time. That place runs as deep as it stands tall. In some spots, even deeper than the reach of a Cauldron."

Graylin stared over at him, praying the others had found one of those places. Still, he pictured the warship hovering out there. "We have to stop them."

"Ah . . ." He clapped Graylin on the shoulder. "My little hawk has plenty of tricks, but it was never meant for long skirmishes. Attack and run, that's the *Sparrowhawk*'s strength. We have only a few firebombs left, and our flashburn tanks are nearly empty."

"Then what can we do?"

"Exactly what we're doing. We wait like we planned, rather than running off with our pricks in our hands, challenging anyone with our cocky prowess. We have to trust the others will somehow break through that noose and signal us when it's safe."

Graylin clenched his fists and crossed his arms, crushing down the bellow building in his chest.

"Until then," Darant continued, "we have to remain free and ready if that happens, to dive over, scoop them up, and get our arses out of here."

"So, we wait," he said bitterly.

"And not just for them," Darant added, his voice rising sharply.

The pirate turned and hurried to the pair of bow windows. The shadow of a small skiff glided past the *Sparrowhawk*'s prow. It marked the safe return of the ship's second sailraft. The skiff had clearly shaken loose the wolves in the mists beyond the Heilsa and had made it back to the rendezvous here.

Darant pressed both his palms against the bow glass, searching the passing sailraft. "Not a scratch on 'er," he mumbled proudly.

As the raft lowered, its small window revealed its drover, a white-haired beauty with dark skin.

With a scowl, Brayl joined Darant at the window. "How come Glace got to wreak such mischief, and I was stuck here?"

Darant scooped Brayl to his side. "It's only because I like her better."

Brayl punched her father's chest with a fist.

The pirate let his daughter go, his expression jubilant with relief. But that joy dimmed as he faced Graylin, plainly reading the misery written there.

Darant's voice firmed with a promise. "If Marayn's daughter is alive out there, we'll reach her."

Graylin stared past the man's shoulder to the mists beyond.

That's if she's still alive . . .

DRESSED IN POLISHED light armor, Mikaen rode through the smoldering outskirts of Havensfayre. Two score of knights on horseback accompanied him, along with a battle unit of hardened Vyrllian Guards. The latter kept their steeds close to his, on order of the liege general. Mikaen resented the need for such a personal detachment, but it was the only way he could convince Haddan to let him ride out into the ruins of the town.

Still, even the liege general recognized the necessity for this sojourn.

Mikaen pictured the *Tytan* listing crookedly over the mooring fields. It hung like a mark of shame for all to see. The legion's trek here had been meant in part to cast the prince of the realm, the future king of Hálendii, in a shining light. Though only an eighthyear in the Legionary, Mikaen had felt the many eyes of the knights and guards, even a few of the giant Mongers, looking upon him with far more regard, as if expecting him to pull a scepter out of his arse and wreak havoc on the kingdom's enemies.

Instead, after he could do nothing to stop the cowardly attack upon the *Tytan*—confined to the forecastle the entire time—he found those same eyes now regarding him with glints of disdain.

Or maybe it's just a reflection of my contempt for myself.

After the attack, he had done what he could to help with repairs. But hammering fresh planks over the holes blasted through the middeck did little to polish his luster.

Then the *Pywll* had crashed a Hadyss Cauldron into the center of town. The warship's commander hadn't even sent a skrycrow to Haddan asking permission to unload such a fearsome bomb. Such a dispatch was normally reserved for only the direst of circumstances. It was not to be wasted, especially as warships only had *one* Cauldron each. Mikaen had seen the one aboard the *Tytan,* strapped in the lowermost hold. The massive drum—as large as a small barn—was more iron than wood. It filled most of the space, hanging over a closed hatch that split the keel at midship.

Still, Mikaen understood why Brask, the *Pywll's* commander, had unleashed his most potent weapon. Wryth had ferried over with the explanation when the warship returned to the mooring field. The commander's brother had been killed by those below. The Shrive had also brought over word of a significant sighting—not only of the bronze weapon stolen from him, but also the possibility of a certain dark prince seen fleeing with it.

Kanthe . . .

If there was any doubt that his younger twin was fomenting an insurrection with a supposed half-sister, it was now dispelled.

Why else would Kanthe be here, meeting with those murderous thieves?

Upon hearing this, Haddan had ordered half of the *Tytan's* forces to search the town and inspect the blast site. Mikaen demanded to go along, to be seen in his armor, saddled tall, going to confront where his traitorous brother was last seen.

Still . . .

Mikaen glared at the circle of vy-knights around him, ordered to protect him.

Like that's even necessary.

Havensfayre was a dark tomb, framed by flames. A few lamps glowed through the pall of smoke, but no one was about the streets. The few townspeople spotted in the distance fled from the thunder of the knights' horses and vanished through doors to hide behind shutters or down into dank cellars, hoping to escape the worst of the flames.

The air still burned, thick with smoke. Their party rode with damp scarves about their faces. Still, the wet cloths could not keep the stench from their noses. Throughout the streets, countless bodies lay broken, trampled, or burned. The legion rode over them and continued toward the heart of Havensfayre.

Their path followed the shattered bole of a huge alder that had crashed across a large swath of the town. Toppled on its side and buried in a nest of broken branches, it rose like a white wall to his left. As they continued along its length, flames appeared amidst the branches, scorching the white wood. When they finally reached its end, they discovered only a jagged, splintered ruin. The end smoldered and smoked, blotting out any sight ahead.

The knights at the lead vanished into that darkness.

Mikaen secured his scarf more firmly as he and his guards followed. The world vanished, and the heat grew scorching. His group followed the rumps of the horses ahead until the pall thinned enough to reveal what had blasted the giant alder.

A huge crater, twice the breadth of a tourney field, stretched ahead. It was half again as deep, all the sides burning and smoking. Mikaen gaped at the enormity of it, awed by the destructive power it represented.

From *one* Hadyss Cauldron.

He found himself smiling behind his scarf.

Then a figure trotted a tall piebald horse through his guards and over to his side. Though the rider was masked as they all were, Mikaen easily recognized Wryth by the leather bandolier of his cryst and the black tattoo banded across his eyes. Wryth had left ahead of the others with a few knights. The reason was clutched in the Shrive's hand.

Wryth drew up alongside him, dancing his steed closer. He lifted the glass orb. Mikaen knew Wryth had used the tool to track the Shrive's stolen treasure.

The prince stared at the crater before them.

Wryth had set off ahead of the others to search for some evidence of the bronze artifact's presence. He announced the result. "I circled the entire hole," the Shrive panted out, breathing hard, his voice muffled by the scarf. "Nothing."

Mikaen enjoyed the bitter defeat in the other's voice. "Then you'll have to dig for your treasure."

"So it seems. But it will take many moons. And with war pending, any success may come too late."

Mikaen scoffed. "Fear not. My father will give you all the necessary resources to swiftly dig any answers out of this hole. And not just for the sake of some ancient weapon."

Wryth glanced quizzically at him.

"Also for my brother," Mikaen explained.

Wryth turned to face the sheer breadth of the blast crater. "Nothing could have survived that blast."

Mikaen had his own set of beliefs when it came to his brother. "Until I hold Kanthe's skull in my hand, I won't consider him dead."

Wryth slowly nodded. "That may be wise."

Mikaen pictured his twin and the bronze sculpture, even the shadow of a half-sister he never met. He scowled his frustration down into the smoldering crater.

If they're not dead, where could they be?

49

Rhaif trailed behind Shiya as she limped down the length of the copper-lined tunnel. Where her bronze feet stepped, the metal glowed briefly brighter, then darkened as her toes lifted away. She also grazed her fingertips along one wall, leaving a trail of brightness in their wake.

The air of the tunnel smelled with the verve of a lightning storm.

Upon Xan's insistence, Shiya led them. Still, Rhaif kept close to her back, ready to support Shiya if she should weaken or stumble. They had been trekking through the tunnel for over a bell, maybe longer, with no end in sight. But at least Shiya had not faltered so far.

Similar to the singing of the Kethra'kai woman, the alchymy of this strange metal infused some strength into her, but it appeared to be only enough to keep her moving and little else.

She still had not spoken a word.

Rhaif searched around him, ignoring the murmurs from the group of Hálendiians behind him. He examined the circular tunnel, testing the metal with his own fingers, running his tips over the seamless surface.

Not even a single rivet or nail.

He looked up. The arch of the roof rose higher than he could reach, and not even Shiya could extend her long arms to touch both sides. He squinted at the walls, recognizing when last he had seen such strange metal.

In the mines of Chalk.

He remembered where he had discovered Shiya. It had been in an egg of the same seamless copper, imbedded in the rock deep underground. He pictured her as he had found her then, standing in a glass alcove, surrounded by a web of copper piping and glass tubes bubbling with a golden elixir. She had been a perfect sculptural beauty, a sleeping goddess of bronze.

He looked at her now, with a crooked leg and the dents and scratches across her surface. *Maybe you should have never left your egg. This world is too harsh for even a woman made of metal.*

He sighed.

Pratik and Llyra followed behind him. The Chaaen looked about with wonder. Llyra simply kept her gaze fixed on Shiya's bronze form. With each flare of light from the floor, the guildmaster's eyes shone with avarice and calculation.

I'll have to watch her closely from here.

Next to her, Pratik maintained his own particular fascination—but not only with Shiya. He kept glancing back, past the clutch of Kethra'kai surrounding Xan, to the group of Hálendiians at the back, who were stalked by a large vargr.

Rhaif knew who the Chaaen focused upon back there. In truth, he was equally intrigued by the mystery of the young woman, a girl of maybe fourteen or fifteen, plainly talented with a unique bridle-song. He remembered Xan's words about *who* the king's legion was looking for in Cloudreach.

Singers.

Du'a ta.

Which meant *both of them.*

He gazed from Shiya back to the one named Nyx.

Two singers—*one of bronze, one of flesh*—yet, he sensed a connection between them. But how could that be? One was as ancient as these lands, the other only a youth.

A shout from the rear called forward. "Can we stop for a few breaths?"

Rhaif searched back and identified the oldest among the Hálendiians, with ruddy hair tied in a tail, his cheeks and chin stubbled darkly. From the formal cadence of his speech and his slight air of authority, Rhaif suspected he might be a scholar.

The man waved to the young singer. In the lamplight of the Kethra'kai scouts, her face was pale. She leaned on the arm of a robust young man with bright red cheeks and an ax on his back. The girl was close to the point of collapse. Unlike Shiya, the young woman drew no strength from the tunnel here.

Xan lifted her staff and called them all to a stop. The group settled and slid down the curved copper to rest. The scholarly Hálendiian came forward with a young man who carried a bow and two quivers on his back. They examined Shiya as she stood with her feet atop glowing pools, a palm against a shining spot on the wall.

Rhaif tried to block them from approaching too close.

Xan waved her staff as she came with them. "Let them pass, Rhaif. They have earned the right. This is Alchymist Frell hy Mhlaghifor. And Kanthe ry Massif."

Both Pratik and Llyra glanced sharply to the lad.

"The prince of Hálendii?" the Chaaen asked.

"Toranth's second son," Llyra confirmed, her eyes narrowing, plainly adding this to her calculations. "I see the resemblance now."

Further introductions were made all around. Rhaif learned the rotund guardian at Nyx's side was Jace, a journeyman from the Cloistery. The vargr was Aamon. Stories were shared. From his side, a tale of the discovery in a mine and a harried flight across the width of the Crown. From them, an account of a prophecy of doom and magick tied to Mýr bats.

Rhaif found their story preposterous, but then again, he was traipsing about with a living statue. *So, who am I to scoff?* He also learned of Nyx's connection to the story of the Forsworn Knight, who apparently still lived.

Rhaif's head spun with this avalanche of information, sensing the wheel of history turning, possibly crushing over them. As he struggled to absorb all of this, he allowed the others to examine Shiya more closely. She had returned to a statuesque stillness, sapping what strength she could from the tunnel.

Xan ended up beside Rhaif. She leaned on her staff, studying him with her head slightly turned. She reached again to his face, like she had when they'd first met. Her fingers touched his cheek, and his mother's lullaby tinkled briefly before fading as her hand lowered.

"You have Kethra'kai blood in you," she said. "You whisper with our old songs."

He shrugged. "My mother was from Cloudreach. She died when I was a boy."

"Ah, your heart sings with your love for her, stirred by a touch of bridlesong in you."

He shook his head. "I have no such talent."

Xan glanced to Shiya. "You could not be tied to her if you did not. I believe you would not have found her in the darkness without it."

"You mean back at the mines? No, it was a lodestone in a wayglass that pointed the path to her."

"Hmm, yes, those stones—sensitive to shifts of magnes energies—do stir to such songs."

Rhaif wondered if this detail might explain how the legion's forces had been tracking them.

Frell overheard this, turning from his study of Shiya. "Fascinating. There is an alchymist at Kepenhill who discovered the tiniest bits of lodestone in the brains of birds. He believed it helps guide their paths as they voyage over the turn of seasons. He even suspected we might have the same."

Pratik nodded with his arms folded. "Back at the House of Wisdom, this has been confirmed."

The two alchymists began chatting together, comparing studies and theories. Rhaif tuned them out. He pictured Shiya's song shivering and turning bits of iron in his own brain, pointing them all toward her.

Xan remained with Rhaif, studying him. "Mayhap that is what drew you through the darkness to her—a reflection of the talent inside you—far more than any wayglass."

He shrugged again.

In the end, what does it matter?

Xan cocked her head, her eyes narrowed. "May I ask the name of your mother, she who was from Cloudreach?"

Rhaif lowered his chin, reluctant to do so. His mother had told him there was power in names, a truth buried in every syllable. He remained possessive of hers, having never even told Llyra. He kept his mother's name close to his heart, an ember of his past that was his alone.

Still, Xan deserved an answer. Rhaif looked at the elder. "My mother . . . her name was Cynth . . . Cynth hy Albar, after taking my father's name."

Xan stiffened. Several of the women also stirred and stared at him, their eyes bright, reflecting the lamplight.

"What's wrong?" Rhaif asked.

Xan covered her mouth.

"I don't understand," he mumbled. "I didn't mean—"

"It cannot be," Xan said, gazing harder at him, tears welling.

The simple majesty that had always seemed to be cloaked about her fell from her shoulders, leaving only an old woman, her face pained with grief.

Rhaif sensed the depth of her distress. "Did you know her?"

Xan's voice cracked with misery. "She . . . She was my granddaughter."

Rhaif blinked in disbelief, falling back a step. He again felt the weight of history crushing over him.

"It's been so long," Xan mumbled, sounding lost. A tear rolled down her cheek. "But I see her now . . . in your face, in your memory of her song."

She turned away, clearly ashamed for not recognizing this sooner. Rhaif crossed over and hugged her, something he would never have done, but he sensed she needed his warmth to survive this moment.

Xan trembled in his arms. "She was so wild, that one. My daughter could barely keep her from running off at every new wonder around her."

Rhaif tried to picture his mother so young.

"Over time, she grew ever more willful and headstrong. When she came of age for her *Pethryn Tol,* she refused the rite, denying any desire to join the tribe. Instead, she wanted to see the world beyond the forest, not be trapped in these woods forever."

Now, that did sound like his mother.

Is that how she ended up in Guld'guhl?

Xan freed herself from his arms and placed a palm over his heart. "And now . . . now she has returned."

The old woman's cheeks ran with tears, her shoulders shook, both in happiness and sorrow. The other Kethra'kai gathered and drew her among them, leaving Rhaif feeling hollow.

Llyra joined him. "Are you all right?"

He glanced to her, reading a rare compassion in her eyes. "I . . . I don't know."

Llyra took his hand, squeezing it. "Our histories have a way of refusing to remain in the past."

He sensed there was a more personal meaning behind her statement. Curiosity helped firm his unsteadiness. He started to inquire, but she let go of his hand, clearly having drained the meager reserves of her sympathy.

"We should keep going," Llyra said. "We can't stay down here forever."

Still, it took another half-bell before the group forged on, following Shiya's glowing footsteps. All the revelations in this accursed tunnel kept everyone silent, or maybe it was simply fatigue. Likely both.

Pratik strode next to Rhaif, his gaze on the bronze mystery before him.

The Chaaen's attention reminded Rhaif of a question he had nearly forgotten. He remembered Xan whispering into Pratik's ear back on the trundling wagon. Rhaif glanced over to the elder, to a woman who might be his great-grandmother.

"What did Xan tell you back in the wagon?" Rhaif asked Pratik. "She whispered something in your ear."

Pratik sighed and nodded to the bronze woman striding ahead of them. "She said Shiya carries the spirit of an old god inside her, one who has not yet fully settled."

Rhaif frowned. He knew little about gods, cared even less. All he knew about the old gods was that they had roamed the Urth long ago, during the *Pantha re Gaas,* the Forsaken Ages. They were beings of great power and savage natures, both beauteous in their strength and merciless in their rages.

He tried to imagine such a god inside Shiya, a woman who had only shown grace and a quiet tenderness.

I don't believe it.

Still, he pictured the copper egg where he had found her, blasted and cracked open. He remembered her strength as she forged a path through *The Soaring Pony,* tossing people aside. According to legend, the end of the *Pantha re Gaas* came when the kingdom's pantheon captured and subdued the old gods, imprisoning them for their cruelties deep under the world.

He ran his fingers along the tunnel's copper, shivering at the power he sensed running through the metal, like a hidden storm.

Pratik noted his attention and quoted Xan: "'An even more ancient root, one belonging to the old gods.'"

Rhaif lowered his hand and stared past Shiya into the darkness stretching ahead. Xan claimed this tunnel led to the cliffs of the Shrouds, to Shiya's home. If that was true, then they could be marching toward the cold hearths of those hard gods.

His legs slowed.

Maybe we should not go knocking on their door.

AFTER ANOTHER TWO bells, Nyx spotted a brightness far down the tunnel. She leaned a palm on Aamon's shoulder to help hold her up and keep moving.

At last . . .

The group's pace increased, drawn to the light. Still, despite her exhaustion, she feared returning to the sky and forest. Buried in this tunnel, she had felt a moment of respite from the terrors above, but she knew they couldn't hide down here forever.

The light grew before them, becoming blinding after the dim glow of their two lamps. Still, by the time the group neared it, her eyes had grown accustomed to the misty glare. The last bit of the tunnel lost its smooth run and became crimped and twisted. The exit looked like it had been shredded open, turning its torn metal edges into coppery fangs.

When they reached the end, each member crossed through those jagged teeth with care, having to duck and twist to pass. Finally, they all stumbled out through a nest of mossy boulders, scribed with lichen. The tunnel's mouth was so hidden that it could be easily missed, like a copper viper buried in rocks.

They climbed free and faced what lay before them.

The world ended a short distance ahead, blocked by sheer black cliffs. Low clouds rolled against that dark bulwark, like waves against a rocky shore.

Nyx craned her neck, trying to pierce those mists to catch a glimpse of what lay above. *The Shrouds of Dalalæða.* Back at the Cloistery, she had learned about those storm-plagued highlands—or at least the little that was truly known about them. Only the foolhardy dared venture up there, and most never returned. Those that did came back with fantastical tales of monsters and dreadful beasts who haunted its dense jungles.

Xan led them all toward the boulder-strewn foot of those cliffs. As they drew nearer, Nyx noted steps carved up its face, climbing and vanishing into the clouds.

Frell spotted the same. "Those must be the stairs used by the Kethra'kai to ascend during the ritual of *Pethryn Tol*."

Nyx knew about that ceremony. She pictured young tribe members climbing that precarious path, intent to prove themselves worthy of their place here in the forest. Like most trespassers, many never came back.

Jace whispered, "Are we supposed to go up there?"

"Maybe not us," Nyx said.

She saw how the bronze woman, though clearly still weak, marched with intent toward the cliffs.

As they followed, a stiff wind blew and parted the roll of mists ahead. Bright sunlight pierced the cloud layer, splaying down the rock face, revealing every crevice and crack in the stone.

Nyx shaded her eyes against that brilliance. Far overhead, a fiery glint reflected the sunlight. The dark stairs led up to it and ended there. She glanced back to the fanged mouth of the tunnel, then up to the coppery shine on the cliff face.

The tunnel continues up there . . .

She pictured that long copper tube being ripped in half by whatever cataclysm had cleaved these highlands and lifted those cliffs high. Then the mists closed again, erasing the view. The world felt far darker afterward.

As they continued on, the tumble of boulders revealed themselves to be crude homes, cut with tiny windows and stacked like blocks up the cliff face. Tiny cairns of stones on the roofs looked to be little chimneys. She also noted the dark mouths of caves dotting the various levels, suggesting this small outpost dug as much into the rock wall as was piled outside it.

The place looked deserted. She imagined it must be where the Kethra'kai gathered prior to the ritual of *Pethryn Tol*. She pictured families sheltering here, praying to their gods for their loved one's safe return, huddled around the hearths inside.

The stairs climbed out from this cluster and ascended the wall.

Xan drew them toward the base of those steps, where an archway of stone blocks framed the way up. The two legs of the arch leaned against one another, perfectly balanced, forming a point at the top.

As they gathered there, Shiya tried to continue, but Rhaif stopped her with a touch on her arm. She obeyed him, or maybe she recognized that she needed to gather her strength before beginning that long climb.

Xan took up a post under the arch.

Jace leaned toward Nyx and voiced his earlier concern. "Surely we're not going up there."

Xan heard him. "No." Her gaze fixed on Jace, then swept across the group. "It's death to climb these sacred stairs. Only those with the gift of bridle-song have any hope of returning."

Jace sighed with relief. "Thank the Mother . . ."

Kanthe looked as pleased. "Then we can hole up down here while we wait. Try to signal the *Sparrowhawk*." He shifted his bow off his shoulder. "Hopefully all of the legion's eyes are still on Havensfayre and not looking this way."

Nyx touched the prince's arm, warning him to hold off for now.

Xan continued, "The Kethra'kai will assist Shiya during the last steps of her journey. But there are *three* among you who are welcome to come, who are perhaps fated to this path. Three who bear the gift of bridle-song."

Rhaif pushed forward. "If Shiya is going up there, so am I. I didn't cross half the Crown to abandon her here. And as you said, there is some whisper of bridle-song in me."

Xan bowed her head in gratitude. When the elder lifted her eyes again, her gaze fell upon Nyx. Nyx had been expecting as much and stepped forward.

Both Jace and Kanthe grabbed her arms on either side.

Jace firmed his grip. "I won't let you go."

Kanthe agreed. "If I let anything happen to you, a certain knight will have my head. And I have enough people trying to kill me."

She didn't have to fight herself free. Aamon stepped around them, perhaps sensing her desire, and bared his teeth at the two. They quickly let her go.

She silently thanked them both with a touch. "This is my path. You both know it."

She read the reluctant knowledge in their faces.

"Then we'll go, too," Jace insisted, straightening and glancing to Kanthe for support.

Nyx shook her head. She trusted Xan's knowledge and warning. "That's neither of your paths."

"Then just come back," Jace pleaded. "You have to come back."

Kanthe sighed and glanced at the stone homes. "We'll wait for you here. Maybe invite a certain knight to join us while you're away."

With the matter settled, Nyx headed to the archway. Aamon padded alongside her, glaring all around, challenging anyone to stop him.

As she joined Shiya and Rhaif, Xan nodded her approval, then stared across the group. "As to the third . . ."

Nyx studied those remaining. *Who else bears the gift of bridle-song?*

Xan's gaze settled on someone Nyx would least suspect of such a talent.

Frell stiffened. The alchymist looked shocked and dismayed, maybe even offended. "Me?"

Xan simply stared.

He scoffed loudly. "Impossible."

Xan spoke, as if to a child. "I hear faint chords rising from you. Perhaps you've grown deaf to it, putting so much stock in what's here." She touched her fingertips to her brow, then lowered her palm to her chest. "Rather than what lies here."

Frell did not look convinced.

Kanthe nudged his former mentor with an elbow. "You did tolerate me. That says you do have a heart in there somewhere."

Xan kept her gaze on the alchymist. She lifted her staff and traced a finger down the shells adorning her cane. "Consider this. What was it that first drew your interest into the mysteries of the moon, a study that led to your discovery of the doom ahead?"

Frell frowned. "Pure scholarly interest, that's all."

Still, Nyx heard doubt growing in his voice, in the crinkle between his brows. She could see him reevaluating his entire life in that moment.

"I was told you spent many years at the Cloistery," Xan said. "Like Nyx. In the shadow of The Fist, home to the bats who stir the air with their warnings. I believe, somewhere deep inside you, you heard their fears. It drove you to your later studies, to seek answers to those mysteries."

Frell's eyes grew wider, a hand drifted to his chest.

Xan turned to the stairs. "Moonfall swiftly approaches. Any hope for the future lies up there."

Frell took a step forward, then another, unable to resist.

Nyx searched the steps, remembering her dream of a fiery mountaintop, the clash of war engines, and the moon crashing toward the Urth. She had been so focused on struggling to survive these past days that she had forgotten the larger threat that had drawn them all here.

She kept a hand on Aamon's flank, feeling the silent growl vibrating in his chest. So much blood had been spilled to bring her to these steps. She had no choice but to follow this through to the end.

If there are any answers up there, I must find them.

50

KANTHE WATCHED THE departing group climb the steep stairs. He kept vigil until they disappeared, one after the other, into the clouds.

Jace stood next to him, sagging as Nyx vanished away. "What can they hope to find up there?" he muttered.

Pratik, the Klashean alchymist, offered one explanation. "It's said there is an ancient stone circle atop the Shrouds. The Northern Henge. Its presence was perhaps used to derive the name *Dalalæða,* which in the Elder tongue means *deathly stones.*"

Kanthe gave the man a sidelong glance. "That's certainly reassuring."

Jace paled. "I grew up in the Shield Islands. We have a henge down there, too."

Pratik nodded. "The Southern Henge."

"I've been to it," Jace said. "It's nothing but a ring of giant mossy slabs, a few of which had been knocked over ages ago. It sits in a sprawling heather where we graze our sheep. There's nothing special about it."

Pratik disagreed. "According to several scholars at the House of Wisdom, your henge is believed to have astronomical significance. Though in truth, no one can quite discern the meaning behind their orientation."

"Do you know who placed those stones?" Kanthe asked. He remembered Xan's assertion that the Shrouds were Shiya's home. He pictured a bronze battalion hauling huge boulders over their heads and stamping them into those heathers.

Pratik shrugged. "Those stones date to the Forsaken Ages, so no one truly knows."

Jace returned his attention to the stairs. His face was pinched with even more worry.

Ahead, Llyra crossed toward them. Her expression was dark and irritated. Earlier, Kanthe had overheard her last words to Rhaif as she pointed at the bronze statue: *Don't lose her.*

Kanthe suspected the woman's concern was not about Shiya's well-being, but about her worth. Llyra had eyed Shiya like a ranchholder judging a prized ox, calculating how much gold all that bronze might fetch if it were melted down.

She joined them, trailed by a Kethra'kai scout who had been left with them, a wiry young man named Seyrl. She glanced around the group. From the sour set to her eyes, she was not impressed with what she saw.

"Prince Kanthe." The use of his title sounded mocking. "What do you propose we do now? I heard you mention something about sending a signal."

He nodded and stared back at the alder forest. "Hopefully, with luck, we might have a means of escaping this place, if I can lure them here."

He turned from the cliff and headed to a flat rock. He laid his bow atop it and fished a pair of arrows from his quiver. He undid the ties of an oilskin satchel secured to his belt and removed two eggs of waxed leather. They were packed with alchymical powder and had threads soaked in flashburn draping from them. The pirate Darant had supplied them to Kanthe back on the *Sparrowhawk*.

He carefully tied an egg to each of his arrows, just behind their bone tips.

Jace stood next to him, staring up at the mists. "When will you launch them?"

Kanthe kept working. "As soon as I'm confident Nyx and the others are off those stairs and into the other section of copper tunnel. I don't want to risk our signal drawing the eye of the enemy this way, at least not until those cliffs are empty."

He secured another of the powder-eggs to an arrow. He planned to shoot one above the mists and another below it. Each would burst into a small cloud of blue smoke. He had to hope the legion's forces continued to focus on Havensfayre. If not, he had to pray such a signal would be dismissed as the mere billow from a campfire.

Still, more than anything, he needed this signal to catch the sharp eye of the *Sparrowhawk*.

That is, if the ship is still out there.

As he worked, he glanced back to the stairs. He had consulted with Xan before the group left. She had told him the tunnel overhead lay the same distance above the mists as below them. Knowing this, he had been keeping rough track of the passage of time.

He was as anxious as Jace to fire off his signal, but he knew he had to hold off.

It's far too soon.

He glanced back to the cliff.

Jace had already returned his attention in the same direction. Kanthe remembered the journeyman's pleading words to Nyx.

You have to come back.

Kanthe concurred. It had pained him to see her climb those stairs, far more than he would ever admit. Lately, he had to keep reminding himself that Nyx could be his half-sister. Still, he couldn't entirely quash down certain feelings that had begun to warm through him, no matter how much cold water he kept dowsing atop them.

He glanced to Jace. He remembered how he had misjudged the journeyman, believing him to be craven and soft. But now, as he watched Jace staring up, he read the full depth of the man's heart. It shone in his face for all to see, unabashed and unafraid.

Kanthe turned away.

If only I could be so bold.

NYX SQUINTED IN the bright sunshine. She shaded her eyes against the sting of radiance as they climbed free of the foggy damp mists and out onto the stretch of steps baked by the heat of the Father Above.

While she appreciated the dry stone underfoot, the air smelled of smoke and fire. A glance to her left revealed a black stain in the white sea. It swirled in a maelstrom around a smoky pillar that climbed high into the sky.

She had to look away. She studied the wall next to her as she climbed. The dark rock showed layers of gray strata, poking with bits of shell, as if marking the bed of an ancient sea. An image flashed of this same wall, from when Xan had sung to her upon their first meeting. She reached and touched one of those shells, wondering if this was the source of the decoration along the elder's staff, a row of shells sculpted to show the turning of the moon.

She dropped her hand, reminded of why they were ascending toward the Shrouds.

Moonfall . . .

She searched up the steps to where Xan led them, assisted and protected by one of the scouts. Three tribeswomen followed, with Shiya climbing behind them and Rhaif at the bronze woman's heels.

Nyx kept a few steps back, still unsure of the mystery shining ahead of her. Once in the sunlight, the sheen of the woman's bronze had quickly warmed to brighter shades of gold and copper. Shiya still limped on a damaged leg, but she moved more fluidly now, with a strength that grew with every step. Her stiff shell appeared to melt under the sun into something flowing and softer. Even the fall of her bronze hair shifted into strands that moved with the breezes washing up the cliff face.

Rhaif's tense shoulders similarly relaxed, as if he were tuned to some song only he could hear, one that reassured him of Shiya's recovery.

"She is wondrous, is she not?" Frell said behind her. He was last in line, except for Aamon, who trailed them all. "No wonder that Iflelen Wryth pursues her."

Nyx glanced off to the warship circling that smoky maelstrom. It appeared to be the same one that had rained death and fire atop them. She had no doubt the accursed Shrive was over there.

She turned away, fearful that her attention might draw the warship's eye.

She hurried after Rhaif. They dared not be on these stairs any longer than necessary, especially with the bronze figure blazing in the sunlight. Xan seemed to understand this and set a harder pace upward.

Nyx kept glancing warily at the massive wyndship, but it continued its slow swing around that black sea, showing no sign of moving this way. Finally, the group reached the mouth of the copper tunnel, torn and shredded like its counterpart below. They rushed out of the sun and into the shelter of its dark interior.

The sudden darkness blinded them all. Still, the Kethra'kai scout held off removing the shade of his lamp until they were well into the tunnel. It took until then for Nyx to realize that the copper walls no longer glowed beneath Shiya's steps.

Frell noted it, too. "This tunnel must lack the energies of the other. Mayhap the first one still draws strength from where it's rooted at the base of Oldenmast, leaching energies from the generous tree. But this tunnel, cleaved from that wellspring long ago, remains as inert as any dull metal."

Nyx believed the alchymist, but it raised a worry. What if everything up here was just as dead and lifeless?

Maybe all of this will be for naught.

Still, they had no choice but to continue. She held out one hope, one indication that something might still be atop the Shrouds.

"*Pethryn Tol,*" Nyx whispered over to Frell. "The Kethra'kai send their youths up here, to test them. Why do you think that might be?"

"I've read treatises about it, but after Xan's earlier warning, I think they're all wrong."

She glanced back, but the alchymist's face was shadowed by her body. "What do you mean?"

"*Pethryn Tol* means *listening heart*. Xan told us that only those with bridle-song could safely traverse the Shrouds. I wonder if *listening heart* is a reference to bridle-song. If so, it suggests an ancient nature to this talent, one that seems rooted in the blood of the tribes who live here."

Nyx pressed a palm atop her chest. *Pethryn Tol.* She remembered how she had felt when she sang. To her, *listening heart* sounded right.

"This ritual," Frell continued. "Each Kethra'kai must undergo it to be accepted into the tribe. I wonder if that custom keeps bridle-song rich in their blood. Those born too weak or without it would be culled by this journey. Only those with strong talent would return and add their seed to the tribe."

Nyx balked at such an explanation. It sounded unnecessarily cruel.

Frell warmed to this idea. "Perhaps the tribe uses the Shrouds as the stone upon which they sharpen their talents and keep it strong."

Nyx lowered her hand from between her breasts. "But I have no tie to the Kethra'kai."

At least, not that I know of, she had to admit to herself.

She looked back at Aamon. Did Graylin's connection to the two vargr indicate some nascent talent? She had felt nothing from him when she had sung to his brothers. Then again, she had sensed no inkling from Frell. And Graylin might not even be her father. *But what of my mother?* Had her tongueless state as a pleasure serf forever silenced her gift?

Nyx shook her head, unable to untangle such a knot.

Frell offered another possibility, one unique to her. "Perhaps your infancy spent with the Mýr bats—bathed in their cries, fed on their milk—instilled such a gift into you. Maybe you're something different, wholly new, yet connected to the tribe's ancient bridle-song."

"Jar'wren . . ." she mumbled, remembering something Xan had said when Nyx was being examined by the tribeswomen.

Frell shuffled closer. "That's the Kethra name for the Mýr bats."

Nyx nodded. "Xan claims the bats were touched by the old gods long ago. She said none of her people have ever been able to sing to the bats."

"But *you* can."

Nyx pictured Bashaliia winging through the air, whistling down at her. She could still feel him nestled in the wagon with her. He seemed too fragile to serve as a vessel for the old gods.

She gazed over at Shiya, her bronze form reflecting the lamplight like a torch. This living statue was also tied to the old gods in some manner.

That I can believe.

With no way of speculating further, the group continued in silence. A short time later, light appeared ahead, far quicker than she had expected. This tunnel must be no longer than an eighth of a league.

A distant squawking echoed to them, along with the patter of what sounded like rain on leaves. They hurried the last of the way toward the dim sunlight. Upon reaching it, the others filed out ahead of her, through an exit mangled and torn. She pictured this tunnel being ripped from the ground like the copper root of a foul weed.

After she ducked out, she straightened to face a dark jungle, a forest far mistier than Cloudreach. Every leaf and thorn dripped. The air here was so rich and fecund that she feared it would seed into her lungs, until she sprouted branches and became part of it.

From the jungle's depths, life hummed, buzzed, and sang darkly. Something screamed far in the forest, as if warning them away, but it wasn't necessary.

Nyx backed a step.

Ahead, bones were strewn across the forest floor. Skulls lay crooked or shattered, white limbs tangled and broken. Ribs formed cages for fat frogs that croaked and stared with wet eyes. Dark emerald moss grew over the deeper levels, as if the jungle were trying to swallow away what it had already digested.

Aamon slunk up next to her, his head low, his hackles high.

Nyx understood.

No one should trespass here.

51

KANTHE SAT ON the flat rock next to his line of arrows, each neatly tied to a powder-filled egg. He had prepared six, so he could shoot three volleys if necessary. He planned on spacing them out once every bell.

With his work done, anxiety had set in and grew with every breath.

Just a little longer . . .

He glanced over to Pratik, who stood a few steps away, having diligently watched over his work.

Needing a distraction, Kanthe nodded to the man. He had seldom had a chance to question a Chaaen up close, especially on a matter that always piqued his curiosity, one that concerned a unique Klashean custom. "So, Pratik, you truly have no bollocks? Do you ever miss them?"

Jace, standing nearby, looked duly aghast at this line of inquiry, but the young man also turned to Pratik for an answer.

Pratik simply glanced over at them and lifted one brow, showing not a lick of offense. "How can one miss what one mostly never had? Certainly never used."

Kanthe considered this assessment. He had to admit that he had seldom used his own.

"Still," Pratik continued, "you should know there are other ways to give and derive pleasure."

Kanthe sat straighter. "Truly? Tell me more."

Pratik started to answer, when Llyra stalked over to them from where she had been standing near Seyrl, the Kethra'kai scout.

"Enough of this feckin' banter. You can learn how to diddle yourself later." She pointed to the cliffs. "It's been long enough. What're you all waiting for?"

Kanthe scowled at her, but he didn't need any further prodding. He grabbed his bow and one of the arrows. "Jace, light a taper with the flame in Seyrl's lamp."

The journeyman was prepared for this order, already holding a length of waxed stick in his hand.

As Jace set flame to taper, Kanthe shifted in front of everyone. He nocked his arrow with the leathery egg hanging from its tip, the fuse dangling below. He angled his bow high, trying to account for the additional weight.

"Light it and step back," Kanthe warned. "Don't know if this will end up exploding in my face."

Jace squinted at the fuse, then set the taper's flame to it. As soon as the fuse started sparking, he danced away.

Kanthe pulled the bowstring a bit farther.

No reason to be judicious.

With a twanging snap, he let the arrow fly. The bolt shot high, sailing through the air and vanishing into the mists. He held his breath. All eyes stared up. They waited, but nothing happened.

Jace kept staring but called over, "Did it work?"

Kanthe shrugged. "Impossible to say. As thick as those mists are up there, the signal could have burst like a firecone at a Midsummer festival, and we'd still never know."

He turned and grabbed a second arrow. He quickly repeated his effort, only he pulled the bowstring half as taut. With the fuse snapping brightly, he fired again. The arrow sped high, slowing at the top of its arc just under the cloud layer—then exploded with a muffled pop.

A huge ball of bluish smoke burst under the mists, hung there for several breaths, then spread out under the clouds.

"That certainly worked." Kanthe looked around for praise, but he found only worried expressions.

He understood.

He glanced back at the misty forest.

Is anyone even out there to appreciate my fine efforts?

He could only hope the right eyes saw it.

And only them.

"We'll try again in another bell," he said.

"Until then," Llyra warned, pointing at the cliff home, "we should get out of sight."

It was a wise precaution.

Kanthe gathered his arrows and took his bow. The group trudged toward the shadowy abodes. He studied the slit-like windows and narrow entrances that lacked doors. It wasn't the most fortified of homes, but from the archways into the cliffs, it must dig deeper.

He didn't know how long they would have to wait here, but he intended to put the time to good use. He turned to Pratik. "So, tell me, what are those other ways to pleasure a woman?"

GRAYLIN WOKE, STARTLED by a loud pounding on his cabin door. He shoved up quickly, surprised he had fallen asleep. He'd only planned to stretch his aching body out for a bit.

Kalder growled from beside the bed, rolling to his paws, hackles shivering.

Graylin placed a calming hand on the vargr's flank. "It's all right, brother." He called out louder, "What is it?"

"If you're done napping, old man," Darant answered, "get your arse to the forecastle."

Graylin heard the excitement in the pirate's voice. He climbed from the cot with a groan and a stab of pain in his back. He limped the few steps across the cabin, stiff even after his brief drowsing. He opened the door, found the passageway empty, and headed toward the ship's bow.

Kalder followed, his hackles still up.

Graylin felt the same way. As he headed toward the forecastle, his body warmed away some of the pain, but his heart pounded. What had happened? Why had Darant roused him?

He pushed into the swyftship's small forecastle. Darant stood next to Hyck. The old man was staring through the farscope's eyepiece.

"Come see this," Darant said, and elbowed Hyck out of the way.

Graylin took the man's place. Through the eyepiece, he again found himself gazing across the tops of clouds, but the view was no longer focused on the smoky maelstrom above Havensfayre. Instead, off in the distance, a line of sunlit black cliffs divided the sky, with mists below and darker clouds masking its heights.

"What am I looking at?" he asked.

"The ramparts of the Shrouds," Darant said. "But squint dead center, at the mists under the cliffs."

Graylin concentrated there. It took him a few breaths to spot a smoky blemish, like a layer of thick dust on a white marble sill. A slight pall hung over it.

He tightened his grip and spoke without looking away. "That can't be the signal we've been waiting for, is it?"

"Could be," Hyck answered. "All day long, I've been watching that dark boil churning over Havensfayre. Looking for some puff of blue smoke. Then a bit ago, something else caught my eye in the other direction. A flash of brightness moving up those cliffs."

"What was it?" Graylin asked.

"Don't rightly know. By the time I swung my scope that way, it were gone. Still, ever since then, I kept half an eye looking that way. Lucky I did, cuz then boom, a gust of blue smoke blew from over there. Called Darant right off, I did."

Graylin straightened and glanced at the two men. "Could it just be a burst of woodsmoke from a campfire?"

Darant shook his head. "Too blue for that, I'd say."

Graylin crinkled his brow. He stared out the bow windows toward where he knew Havensfayre burned. "If it's Nyx and the others, how did they get all the way to those cliffs? Why did they even go there?"

"Don't know," Darant said. "But there's only one way to find out."

Graylin clenched a fist, his heart hammering. He wanted to burn straight over there, but . . . "What if it's a trap? Maybe one or more of the others were captured, tortured into revealing how to signal us. This could be a ruse to lure us out of hiding."

"I considered the same," Darant said. "It's why I woke your old arse before blazing up our forges."

He turned to Darant.

"Get us over there."

IN THE FORECASTLE of the *Tytan*, Mikaen stalked back and forth behind Haddan. The liege general glowered over a crewmember who manned the starboard farscope.

"What's your assessment?" Haddan demanded of the navigator.

Mikaen waited, drumming fingers on his thigh. He had just returned to the warship. He stank of smoke and horse sweat. His eyes continued to burn, and his nostrils felt packed with soot. Still, he was desperate to get back out to Havensfayre, to continue the search of the town. The legion had been rooting out homes and cellars, rousting townspeople, questioning all, trying to discern who else might be involved with an insurrection against the king. Others in Havensfayre must know of Kanthe's plot. His brother would not have come to this remote town without allies already in place, especially as Kanthe had somehow also acquired Wryth's weapon.

Mikaen was certain others were involved.

Kanthe is too dull-witted to concoct this on his own.

Mikaen was also anxious to return for a reason that had nothing to do with rooting out his brother's allies. Back in Havensfayre, he had enjoyed watching the townspeople cower before them. Their screams, protests, and prostrations stirred him hard. His own gauntlet was bloody from beating those who had balked or denied knowledge. He had watched enviously as women were dragged into shadows.

He longed to rejoin the others, to vent his frustration and enjoy every dark thrill due a conqueror. He had only returned to the *Tytan* to draw a fresh horse. His own steed had started to stumble, sick from the smoke, lungs surely caked. It didn't suit for the prince of the realm to be seen riding atop a doddering horse.

Only once back at the warship, Haddan had summoned him here.

All because of some wisp of smoke spotted off in the distance.

The navigator finally turned from his scope. "The tint is too blue. I'm sure of it. That is no trail of a campfire."

"So, a signal then," Haddan said.

Mikaen stopped pacing. His eyes narrowed.

What was this?

"Aye, General." The navigator straightened under Haddan's exacting gaze. "But I cannot offer any guidance as to *why* it was cast, or *who* it was meant for. It could simply be hunters alerting one another."

Haddan stepped toward the vast curve of bow windows and stared toward the cliffs that marked the Shrouds of Dalalæða. The general rubbed the stubble over his scarred chin.

Mikaen joined him. "Maybe it's more of my brother's plotters. They could be trying to signal others in Havensfayre. To rally those loyal to Kanthe to gather there."

Haddan huffed through his nose. He glanced sidelong at the sooty state of Mikaen's armor, lingering a moment on the blood staining his gauntlet's knuckles. Then he faced Mikaen. "You could be right."

Mikaen drew his shoulders back.

"I'll send a hunterskiff to investigate." Haddan began to turn away.

Mikaen reached to his arm, but then withdrew his hand when the general glowered at such an affront. He quickly stepped back, snapping his legs and back straight. "Let me go with the skiff."

Haddan looked ready to dismiss such a thought.

"A hunterskiff can hold a score of men, even a Monger or two. Give me your best knights, those who idle wastefully here. We'll flush out those plotters by the cliffs and put them to the question."

"They might just be hunters, like Navigator Pryce has stated."

"Still, we should know for sure." Mikaen swept a hand across his ash-stained armor. "A prince of the realm should shine brighter than this. He should be seen rooting through every shadow for those disloyal to the king."

Haddan glanced again to the blood on Mikaen's gauntlet. "And perhaps a prince of the realm shouldn't be seen beating those loyal to the crown. At least not in front of a century of knights."

Mikaen's face heated at his words, at the accusation behind them, but he knew better than to deny them, to put a lie to what they both knew to be the truth.

Haddan stared hard at him. "Do not put yourself at needless risk. I'm placing great trust in your judgement. I will assign you the captain of *Tytan*'s Vyrllian Guard. You will heed his every word. Is that understood?"

Mikaen struck his steel heels together. "Aye, General."

Fearing Haddan might reconsider, Mikaen quickly turned and headed off. He forced himself not to run. He hoped he had enough time to polish his armor before the hunterskiff sailed to the cliffs. He intended to shine his brightest.

As he left the forecastle, he smiled and rubbed at the cake of blood on a knuckle—not to clean it, but only to create room for more.

52

RHAIF CROSSED THE bone field toward the fringe of jungle. He winced at every crack and snap underfoot. Shiya led the way, an unstoppable force. Still, she had already begun to dim under the threatening clouds, her bronze darkening to a leaden sheen. As she walked, her heavy feet crushed bones to dust.

He cringed as a small skull suffered that same fate.

Shiya never looked down.

He shuddered, remembering the claim Xan had shared with Pratik, that Shiya's bronze form was possessed by the unsettled spirit of an old god, those callous and cruel beings from the Forsaken Ages.

Ahead, Xan flanked one side of Shiya, along with a scout. Another tribeswoman took up the other side. As they reached the jungle, the Kethra'kai picked out a path barely discernible in the darkness. They slipped through leaves and under a drape of thorny vine—that slithered away with a hiss as Rhaif tried to duck beneath it.

Aghast, he stumbled ahead.

Behind him, Frell and Nyx followed, stepping gingerly, their gazes sweeping warily all around. Aamon kept close to the girl's thigh, his tufted ears pricked so high they looked ready to fly off of his furry head.

After only steps into the dripping forest, the path behind them vanished. The group drew closer. Ahead, Xan began to sing. There was no brightness to her melody. It was more a dirge, which matched this jungle's dark temperament.

The other Kethra'kai found her rhythm and matched it, raising their voices with hers. As they continued, the forest seemed to scream, buzz, howl, and croak in tune with that song. Even the weeping drips added a drumlike tympani to their chorus.

Rhaif did not complain.

The wafting of their song seemed to drive creatures from their path. A bush to his right burst apart, each leaf revealing itself to be winged pests that spun menacingly through the air. More of the thorny vipers slithered away. A pack of furry damp beasts shot through the canopy overhead, using curved claws and strangling tails. They yowled down at them, baring rows of needle teeth from purplish leathery faces.

"Mandrayks," Frell whispered as they passed. "I thought them all dead from this world."

Rhaif, for one, would not mourn their passing.

A huge log, as high as his waist, blocked their path, frothy with glowing mushrooms and sprouting saplings. Once they drew nearer, its length bowed up, sprouting thick scaled legs, and sauntered off into the jungle.

Rhaif glanced back at Frell to see if he recognized the creature.

The alchymist only shrugged, his eyes wide and unblinking.

As they continued, the forest grew higher. The drips became a steady rain. The clouds darkened. The ground underfoot grew muddier. Only a thick layer of moldering leaves kept them from miring into the muck. Still, it felt like wading over a rotted corpse, one that threatened to give way under them at any moment.

The only heartening bit was that they'd left the bones behind. Though Rhaif imagined that was only because so few people had made it this far before succumbing to this place.

The Kethra'kai continued their chanting to the woods. Even Shiya had begun to add her voice, though to his ears there was a sad longing in her wordless strain.

One singer, though, remained conspicuously absent from this chorus. Fear had surely drowned any music in her heart.

"Look," Nyx whispered to Frell.

She pointed to a forest of ghostly stone pillars that appeared ahead, spreading to either side of the path, disappearing into the shadows. Rhaif imagined them continuing all around this summit in a big ring.

Rather than quarried out of the black rock of this escarpment, the pillars were made of a bone-white stone. Figures and faces had been carved into their surfaces. Men and women, all writhing in agony. Stark faces screamed at them, as if warning them away. The sight alone left Rhaif shivering. His feet dragged slower.

What are we doing here?

It was as if this entire summit had been designed by a god who sought to keep people away by any means. Flora, fauna, weather, and now rock. With every step gained, this landscape pushed harder against them.

Maybe we should heed such a warning.

"Do not slow," Xan called back, her command flowing with her song. "There is worse yet ahead."

Rhaif wanted to balk.

Worse?

"Everyone will need to use their voices," Xan intoned to them. "When I tell you, sing. Or hum, if that's all you can do."

With that dire portent and feeble instruction, she led them past the pillars and into the deeper forest. They continued for a long stretch, the jungle weeping atop them. Somewhere distant, light flashed through the darkness, briefly illuminating the underside of the dark clouds. No thunder followed, which only set his teeth further on edge.

A brittle crackling underfoot drew his attention back down. A knobbed femur poked out of the muck. Rhaif stumbled away, only to crunch through more bones.

Not again . . .

He nearly twisted an ankle as his muddy boot slid off the crown of a yellowed skull, white teeth grinning out of the bone.

The group slogged through this new graveyard and reached a narrow clearing that cut across their path in a wide arc. The dark skies glowered down at them. The ground ahead was tangled with bones.

Rhaif breathed heavily, his heart pounding, his vision narrowing in terror.

I'm not crossing that cadaverous river.

Even the Kethra'kai slowed, but Xan urged them onward. "Sing now. And do not stop moving."

Rhaif had never felt less like singing. His mouth was stuffed with the roughest cotton. He could not catch his breath. Still, he was pushed forward by Frell and Nyx. Nyx meekly added her voice to the continuing choir. Even Aamon growled louder, as if trying to do the same.

Herded forward to that bony clearing, Rhaif had no choice but to stumble onward.

Frell coughed and started humming. It was tuneless, with a pitch that could never settle. Still, the alchymist's poor effort encouraged Rhaif to try to do better. He took a deep breath, held it, and let loose a noise stuttering between a wheeze and a whistle. He sought to steady it but failed.

Still, the effort distracted him enough to keep moving.

Halfway across, a skim of mud flowed out of the jungle to either side. It flooded over the bones and coursed toward them. He tried to hurry, fearful of getting mired down. Their group fought faster across the treacherous bone field.

Frell suddenly gasped, losing his humming. But Nyx grabbed his elbow and got it going again.

Rhaif saw what had so frightened the alchymist.

It wasn't *mud* racing toward them.

Spiders . . .

Each creature was the size of his palm, their clambering legs stretching even wider. Their dark brown bodies were striped in venomous yellow. Rhaif's humming strained into a long whine of terror.

Then the horde swept through them. Spiders skittered up their legs, crunched underfoot. They fled across his chest, burrowed under his loose shirt, tickled his neck and cheek, crowned his head.

He kept humming, only to stop himself from screaming, to keep his lips pressed closed, lest they scurry inside, too.

Aamon shook a blanket of the creatures from his fur.

Still, their group all forged on—but that was not even the worst.

One of the spiders sped up his forearm, stopped there, clamping its legs in place. Then from its back, from those vile stripes, tangles of coppery filaments burst forth, writhing in the air, then diving into his skin. Scores of others did the same. There was no sting to their violation. Only the feel of maggots crawling under skin.

He shuddered, near to thrashing.

The hum died in his throat.

One spider had latched to his cheek, those coppery threads dancing before his eyes. He lifted a hand to rip it away, but fingers caught him. The firmness of bronze steadied him.

He turned to find Shiya's eyes glowing at him. She sang—but no longer to the forest—only to him. She drew him onward, step by step. Behind her tune, he heard his mother's lullaby. As it grew louder in his head, the crawl of spiders transformed into his mother's fingertips, gently calming him.

His panic ebbed.

Finally, after an interminable time, the horde fell from his body, from the others, too. The spiders retreated away, seeping back into the forest. Rhaif knew the creatures were not of natural origin. They were masks, hiding coppery constructs inside, maybe related to Shiya.

If he had any doubt, a loud crashing to his left briefly revealed something massive, stilted on tarnished green legs, moving through the trees. It stalked the edges of the clearing, seeming to draw the horde back to it. The shaking of the canopy elsewhere marked the passage of more of those huge sentinels.

Rhaif rubbed his arms, tried to stop the crawling of his flesh, the pebbling of his skin. He knew the spiders had been a test of some sort. Like how a medicum used leeches to examine what was hidden deeper in a body. He gave his shoulders a final shake of revulsion, knowing one thing for certain.

Thank all the gods that we passed that test.

Xan had stopped singing, as if knowing the jungle would let them continue from here. "It is not far ahead," the elder declared.

"What's not far?" Nyx asked.

Xan turned and started off again. "Dalalæða," she answered.

Rhaif swallowed hard, remembering Pratik's translation of that name. *The deathly stones.*

NYX MARCHED THROUGH the dark jungle behind the others. She believed the forest would never end, despite Xan's earlier assurance. Nyx could still feel the dance of bristly legs over her arms. She kept brushing away spiders that were no longer there.

The only change to this side of the forest was the increasing shatter of lightning that brightened the grim layer of clouds, casting the jungle into shades of dark emerald. Each blast carried no thunder, only a silence that felt heavier afterward.

This heft might be because the air grew thicker with both moisture and a fierce energy that could be tasted on the tongue. It smelled like the swamp after a lightning storm.

As they continued toward the source, Nyx's shoulders climbed toward her ears, her head ducked lower. Aamon felt it, too. He no longer growled, as if fearful of drawing attention this way. All of his fur bristled as he slunk alongside her.

It grew so threatening that it felt like a wind pushing against her. Frell and Rhaif shared worried glances, too.

Just before she could take it no longer, the jungle suddenly ended.

She stopped in surprise, as did all the others.

Ahead, a towering archway opened in a tall stacked-stone wall. The rampart was only visible from steps away. To either side, the forest shoved tight against the wall, with vines scrabbling up it, but the bulwark held firm.

Nyx recognized the shape of the arch. It was the same as the one framing the stairs below: two legs of stones leaning against one another, forming a point at the top. Only this one was ten times as tall as the other.

They all edged closer, the Kethra'kai with reverence, Nyx and the others warily. Only Shiya continued forward, limping on her damaged limb.

Past the gateway, the jungle stopped. Bare stone, as black as the cliffs behind them, spread outward. Another spatter of lightning lit the expanse. Its brightness stung her eyes, bringing with it a freshening wash of those strange energies.

Nyx blinked away the dazzle and headed with the others under the gateway.

The tall walls swept in a huge circle, enclosing a space as large as the first tier of the Cloistery. She remembered when she had first entered that school. She felt the same way now: lost and overwhelmed, feeling too small to enter such an intimidating landscape.

Within the walls, two circles of standing stones formed concentric rings, the outer taller than the inner, as if the stones were bowing down to the giant structure in the center. There, a double set of arches stood crossed at the middle and climbed twice the height of the walls, enclosing a cube of the same white stone as the terrifying carved pillars.

She stared around the breadth of the walls. Another three gates opened to the jungle. Each exit was marked by towering columns in the outermost henge ring. A pyramid of crystal crowned each one. Across the expanse, one of the crystals shimmered brighter in the gloom—then blasted forth with a jagged bolt of lightning. It struck the dark clouds overhead, briefly cascading smaller chains across their undersides.

The entire group ducked from the brilliant display, even the Kethra'kai.

Shiya ignored it and continued hobbling across the space. She passed the outer ring and headed toward the inner one. Rhaif hurried after her, drawing them all along.

Frell ran low with Nyx. "Keep close. If this is truly Shiya's home, we best stay in her shadow."

And in her good graces, Nyx added silently.

They caught up with the bronze woman at the inner ring and followed her toward the crossed arches at the center. Closer now, Nyx made out the shadow of a doorway inset in the cube.

As they crossed toward it, Nyx glanced to either side, to the dark jungle looming over the walls all around. She remembered the horrors out there, natural and otherwise. The threats reminded her of a hermit back home, a friend of her dah. The man had lived deep in the Mýr and eked out a living by brewing firewater, a batch said to be as hot as flashburn. He protected his brewery with a labyrinth of fencing reinforced with insidious traps. He didn't want anyone learning his secrets.

She studied where they were headed.

What needs this much protecting over centuries of time?

Finally, the door under the cube's shadowy lintel revealed itself. They had all seen its likeness before. It was a copper oval, twice as large as the one they had passed through to enter the tunnel. Here, too, tangles of copper and bronze tendrils wound into the white cube and black stone.

The group gathered a few steps away from the cube.

Nyx turned to Xan. "Have you been through there before?"

The elder leaned on her staff and shook her head. "I do not possess the strength of song to move that door."

Shiya clearly believed herself capable.

The bronze woman limped under the lintel and lifted both palms, as if testing invisible winds. Then she lowered her arms and began to sing. It was soft at first, the lightest breeze, wistful and quiet, then layers built within it. Nyx heard the firmer chords of an ancient foundation, first building, then crumbling. A rhythm overrode it, marking time, ringing the passing of centuries. An aria of hope, as light as the first notes but far brighter, tried to hold back a darker storm of bass undertones—only to be overwhelmed in the end. It was a mournful composition of time and loss, of pasts forgotten, of hopes dashed to ruins.

Nyx understood.

This was Shiya, declaring who she was, offering her truest name. The bronze woman stood at the doorstep and stated as simply as she could: *Here I am.*

As that grief swelled, a familiar reef of glowing strands—bronzed and tarnished, but still beautiful—flowed out with her song. They spread to the copper door, but unlike back at the tunnel, the strands were rebuffed, ruffling into incoherence against the stubborn metal.

Shiya drew them back, sang them brighter, and tried again.

Still, she was refused.

Shiya's shoulders slumped, marking her despair.

Nyx turned to Xan, remembering the other door. "She needs your help. Like before. She's too weak, possibly not fully herself, to open the way alone."

Xan nodded and thumped with her cane to stand with Shiya.

Frell leaned closer. "What's wrong?"

"I'm not sure," Nyx whispered.

Xan started to sing, expertly merging her melody with Shiya's. The elder didn't try to control that song, only support it, to lend her strength to the bronze figure.

Shiya drew upon that font and spun her song higher, both thickening the strands and shaping them at their ends to a fine delicacy. It was so beautiful to see. Shiya would not fail now.

Nyx was wrong.

The design of tarnished bronze reached the copper and sought to meld through it—and failed yet again. The filigree tangled to ruin and washed down the door and faded.

Xan turned to Nyx and held out her hand.

They need even more strength.

Nyx knew she must try. She walked on numb legs to join them, stepping to Shiya's other side.

The bronze woman still sang in chorus with Xan. Nyx listened, closing her eyes, her head nodding to find the rhythm. She waited until the beat of her heart found it, too. She let it build in her chest, inhaled more deeply to stoke it, then teased it out, letting it flow into their song, fueling each note with her own, building that wave higher.

Even with her eyes closed, she saw Shiya try again, weaving herself, her past, her need, into shiny bronze strands. They wove into a complexity that defied all dimensions. Shiya again cast its beauty at the door.

Nyx gasped as it collapsed into ruin once again, a wave broken on sharp rocks. Shocked and dismayed—both at the failure and at the loss of such beauty—she fell back a step.

We can't do this.

Xan hung from her staff, drained and exhausted, and admitted the same. "We are not strong enough to open this."

Shiya remained straight, but the song slowly faded from her.

Nyx shook her head and mumbled, "That's not it."

Frell pressed her. "What do you mean?"

Nyx glanced back, picturing the power in their chorus. "It's not that we're not strong enough. It's more like we're locked out."

Then she knew the answer.

She snapped straighter.

Of course . . .

Rhaif noted her reaction. "Nyx?"

"Someone changed the lock," she mumbled.

She remembered her struggle with the scyther's helm, how it had fought her as surely as this door did now with Shiya. Nyx swung her attention to the seamless copper. She knew this door's metal was no crude helm, but something far more daunting.

Xan pulled higher on her staff. "What are you saying, child? Can you mend this?"

Nyx breathed harder.

Not by myself.

She reached inside a pocket, to a paper-thin curl of white bark. Kanthe had given it to her after she buried Bashaliia. He had stripped it from the leafy sentinel over her little brother's grave, a sacred tree that the Kethra'kai called *Ellai Sha,* or *Spirit's Breath.* She remembered Kanthe's instructions to her. *If you wish to speak to those who have passed, you whisper into the curl, then burn it at a camp's fire, where the smoke will carry your message high.*

She didn't have a campfire, but she prayed that the fire in her heart would be enough. For any hope in opening this door, she would need to draw all she could from her time with Bashaliia, to commune with the gifts that he had left inside her. To do that, she needed to foster a deeper connection to him.

She closed her eyes again and lifted the curl of bark to her lips. She whispered from her heart, speaking to that past inside her, trying to stir it to life. "Little brother, hear me. I need you. More so than ever before. Please wake and add your song to mine, so I can share the sight I need."

She kissed the curl and held it to her lips, feeling a stirring of their connection. It was still there, even with him gone. She squeezed her eyelids tighter, struggling to hold those tenuous threads closer to her heart. They were so fragile and delicate. Even by opening her eyes, she might lose them. She used the crimp of bark to help maintain that bond to him. She felt the rough texture in her fingers, smelled the slight scent of tea from the tree bark.

She took a breath and sang again, not in harmony with Shiya, but with the keening of a young bat, a brother who had given his life for hers, who shared his mother's love and milk, who had never abandoned her.

Not even now.

She pined for him and used her grief as power. She cast out his song in her voice, through her throat. She sang and keened his memory, his faithfulness, his sacrifice. As she did, his unique sight opened inside her.

He allowed her to share it, as he always had.

She stared at the door with her eyes closed. As her little brother's keening reverberated off the door and returned to her, she saw the copper with perfect clarity, far more than she had with the steel of the scyther's helm. The copper was no longer seamless but riven with imperfections and blemishes. Its ancientness was as evident as the wrinkles of a wizened old man. Yet, that was only its surface. Bashaliia's song—her voice—delved deeper, showing alignments and inclusions and veins buried there.

She read a ghostly pattern and saw how it had been changed.

She lifted her free arm.

Xan and Shiya understood. Their combined chorus rose again. With her new sight, Nyx recognized their strength. It was indeed plenty. She watched from the side as Shiya built her pattern, the key to this lock. Nyx saw it was right long ago, but not any longer. She identified which threads were misplaced, which would no longer fit this door, or where a knot was twined slightly askew. She added her own song, unique to herself, while not losing her connection to Bashaliia.

She extended her strands and filled where Shiya's pattern was empty, withdrew what was wrong, and reknit what was necessary. Once done, she compared it to the lock in the door—then swept her arm down.

On this signal, Shiya cast all her force forward and struck the door with it.

A deep intonation reflected her power back outward, shivering all their threads, turning all their songs discordant, even her connection to Bashaliia.

As it all collapsed into darkness, something appeared, just for a moment. Fiery eyes stared out of the darkness at her. She read approval in them—and something else, another message. But before she could understand, they were gone.

She opened her own eyes.

Once again, she was left hollowed out and weak, her legs shaking. Still, she held her place as her vision clouded over. Such efforts clearly took more from her than mere strength. She struggled with her eyes, returned again to a near-blind state.

Then another jagged bolt of lightning flared silently behind her. The flash reflected off of the copper, brightening the surface enough for her to see it. She watched the door swivel open into darkness with an exhalation of long-dead air.

"You did it," Frell gasped out, rushing up behind her.

"Not me," she whispered, still clutching a tiny curl of bark.

SIXTEEN

THE AGONY OF SHATTERED GLASS

Histoire can foretell the future, as surely as a well-trodd'd path can lead eyow home. But stray from that track & eyow may be lost forever.

—From the introduction to *Lessons Found in Faded Ink,* by Leopayn hy Prest

53

WRYTH RUSHED HEADLONG into the forecastle of the *Tytan*. His cloak billowed ash behind him. He panted hard. His thighs still burned from his mad gallop across the breadth of Havensfayre. He had left his horse, lathered and shaky, with one of the warship's stable boys, who had looked aghast at the hard use of the steed. Wryth had tossed the leads and run through the bulk of the *Tytan* to reach Haddan.

The liege general noted the flurry of his arrival and strode from a spot where a navigator peered through a farscope. Haddan crossed to meet him.

"What's wrong?" the general asked.

Wryth drew up to him, gulping air. He held up Skerren's orb, trying to catch his breath. His vision blurred from the tears still struggling to wash the soot from his eyes. His heart pounded and pounded in his chest.

"Another . . ." he gasped. "Another signal . . ."

Dizzied by both fatigue and excitement, he fought to collect himself as the room spun. "It struck moments ago . . . when I was off by the crater." He swept a shaking arm toward the ship's stern. "Impossibly strong . . ."

Haddan stared down at the crystal orb in Wryth's hand. His brow bunched as he squinted at the lodestones. "What happened to your instrument?"

Wryth understood the general's dismay. Half of the lodestone slivers had settled through the heavy oil and were piled on the sphere's bottom. A few still remained, pinned in place and spinning lazily. Wryth pressed the meat of his thumb over a crack in the crystal, stanching a leak of oil.

"The signal hit with such power that the orb came close to flying out of my hand." He clutched the crystal harder, fearful that another signal might strike at any moment.

Back in Havensfayre, the orb had suddenly wrenched in his palm. He had grabbed it with both hands to secure it. Still, it had quaked violently, cracking along one side. As he had stared down at it, the lodestones had trembled with urgency, the copper threads glowing in the oil. Then one after the other, the slivers had ripped from their pins and were blown by those invisible winds to the back of the globe. The remaining pieces had shivered and fought to hold their place, like sails in a gale.

While watching, Wryth had spurred his horse in a circle. Once he had confirmed the direction, he had raced straight back to the *Tytan.*

Haddan frowned. "Did the signal rise from the blast site?"

"No. From beyond Havensfayre."

The signal had faded by the time he'd reached the *Tytan,* but it plainly rose from farther east.

"Show me." Haddan drew Wryth over to the circular table where a map was tacked down.

Wryth studied the schematic of the town and the surrounding area. A wayglass was fixed to the navigation chart. He used its sliver to fix his direction. He put a finger atop the town's mooring field and drew a line due east, dragging it straight off the map. He continued pointing his arm in the same direction, out the bow windows.

"It came from somewhere by the cliffs of Dalalæða," Wryth said. "Maybe even atop the Shrouds."

Haddan swore and straightened. He swung toward the starboard farscope. "Navigator Pryce! Do you still have the hunterskiff in view?"

"Aye, General, it's just approaching the cliffs now."

Wryth stiffened. "Why is a craft headed out there already?"

"To investigate a signal," Haddan spat back. "A puff of blue smoke rose from there. I thought it likely nothing, but I sent a skiff to check it."

Wryth clenched a fist, knowing this couldn't be a coincidence. "They're over there somehow. The bronze weapon, maybe the traitors, too."

"And not just them." Haddan's face had paled. "Prince Mikaen is aboard that skiff."

"What? Why?"

Haddan swiftly strode to a calling tube, while shouting angrily back, "To give Mikaen something to do. Though mostly to keep the bastard from further staining his reputation here."

Wryth followed after the general. "I must ferry up to the *Pywll.* To trace that signal."

"Do it. I'll send a crow to the warship's commander, ordering him to follow your orders."

Wryth swung away, ready to race down to a sailraft, then burn his way up to the *Pywll.*

Haddan shouted after him, "I'll unmoor this lumbering ox and follow you in the *Tytan.* But do not wait on me. Find out where those traitors are holed up."

Wryth waved an arm, acknowledging the general. He pictured the *Tytan* dragging its keels over the treetops to reach the cliffs. Half of its gasbags were still not patched. But the *Pywll* remained intact. It should make swift passage to the Shrouds.

Still, I'll not be the first one there.

MIKAEN BENT TO the left of the hunterskiff's seated drover. He gazed out a narrow window at the rising bulwark of black rock. He spotted a line of stairs cut into the cliff face. He followed them down to the mists below.

Mikaen pointed there and called across the drover's shoulder to the Vyrllian captain. "That's where the draft of smoke rose from. I'm sure of it."

As if the gods wanted to prove the wisdom of his assertion, a bolt shot out of the mists, right where he was pointing, and burst into a bluish puff.

The captain, Thoryn, grinned, splitting his crimson features. "I'd say you're right."

The Vyrllian looked to be half Gyn. He was so tall that he had to duck his head and hunch his shoulders from the skiff's roof. Behind them, a score of armored knights huddled in the cramped quarters of the attack ship. A full-blooded Gyn crowded among them, seated on his arse, a battle-ax across his raised knees.

Maybe a relative of Thoryn's.

"Hard to decline their kindly invitation." Thoryn leaned closer to the drover. "Fast-drop us through those mists. Let's not give them a chance to change their minds."

Mikaen grinned. He grabbed a leather loop hanging from the roof with one hand and settled his other palm to the pommel of his sword.

Thoryn eyed him, his brows lowering. "You stick to my side, my young prince. I dare not return you to the *Tytan* with even a dent in that pretty armor."

Mikaen gritted his teeth, resenting such attention, but he knew better than to argue.

Thoryn called back to the legion, "Clench your arses and pray to your gods! Down we go to kiss Hadyss's fiery rump!"

The captain clapped his palm on the drover's shoulder. "Reef our bag and drop us like a stone."

The drover yanked a lever. The skiff shivered—then the craft plummeted straight down. The swift drop lifted Mikaen to his toes. His blood rushed to his head as the world vanished into mists. Mikaen held his breath until the view opened up under their keel.

He searched the ground sweeping toward them. He noted a cluster of stone homes at the base of the cliffs. Another wafting of blue smoke billowed across the underside of the mists, only to be blown away by their passage. For a moment, he thought he caught sight of a figure darting into one of the cliffside homes, but it could just be a shift of shadows as the craft fell.

The drover shoved a lever, and flashburn forges fired under them, flaming the tops of the grassy hummocks below. Smoke rolled under their keel as the skiff drew to a hard stop, hovering at the height of a knee.

"Out with y'all!" Thoryn bellowed.

The stern hatch crashed open. Its end struck the ground hard enough to bounce before settling. The Gyn rolled out first, followed by the knights. A few remained inside, raising hinged crossbows to slits in the craft's hull.

Mikaen released his hold on the loop and set off after those exiting the skiff.

Thoryn stopped him with an iron gate of an arm. "Stay at my side until we gain a measure of what awaits us."

Mikaen bristled at such caution. His blood was fired. His fingers clenched to his pommel. It took all of his strength to merely nod his assent.

Thoryn judged the state outside for an extra breath, then headed to the ramp. "Stick to my shadow."

Mikaen followed, frustrated. How was the realm's bright prince to shine when confined to shadows?

Still, he obeyed.

For now.

BREATHLESS, KANTHE HID with the others in one of the stacked-stone homes nestled against the cliffs. He crouched by the slit of a window. Llyra stood posted by another on his left, past the open door. Pratik shadowed her. At the back of the small room, the Kethra'kai scout had already masked his lamp with a flap of leather. Jace stood with Seyrl, holding his ax in both hands.

"Seems like someone saw your signal," Llyra hissed across to him.

Kanthe scowled. He had gone out a moment ago to fire aloft his second round of powder flares. He had barely gotten off his last shot when a huge shadow had swept above the mists. Not knowing if it was friend or foe drawing upon them, Kanthe had sprinted for cover. He had barely gotten through the door when a whoosh rose behind him, accompanied by the roar and smoke of flashburn forges.

He watched now as knights piled out of the hunterskiff, led by a monstrous Monger in iron armor.

Kanthe eyed their ship.

The hunterskiff looked like a small shark hovering next to a stony reef. It was narrow and pointed, with a balloon sculpted for speed. Around its keel, patches of dry grass burned and smoldered, fogging the ship in a wreath of smoke. Still, Kanthe could easily spot the line of crossbow slits along its flanks, already bristling with the points of explosive bolts. Even the craft's sharp prow was actually the tip of a huge draft-iron spear, cranked by a ballista hidden in a well under its interior deck.

Jace edged across the room to peer over Kanthe's shoulder. "Maybe we should retreat to the tunnels. I searched them while we waited. They don't delve that deep, but they crisscross into a small maze."

"Not yet," Kanthe breathed out.

He wanted to better assess this threat.

Plus, I hate the dark.

He eyed the forces gathering outside. Besides the giant Monger, he counted fifteen knights. Likely a handful more inside. The legion spread out with bows and swords raised. A few men faced the forest, but the rest aimed their attention toward the stack of homes.

"We can't hold out here," Llyra said, drawing the corner of his eye. She fiddled with a steel throwing knife in her fingers. She finally pointed its tip back at the low threshold into the caves. "We need to find some narrows back there. A place where we can squeeze their numbers down, enough for us to defend ourselves."

Kanthe glanced back.

She's right.

Pratik added a cautious caveat. "That will only buy us a few breaths. They'll surely burn us out of any hole if they grow too frustrated."

Kanthe grimaced.

He's right, too.

Still, they had little other choice. He began to turn from the window, when a flash of bright silver drew his attention back. A massive Vyrllian climbed out of the hunterskiff, trailed by a smaller figure in brilliant armor. His helm reflected even the meager light under the mists.

Kanthe stiffened.

Mikaen . . .

"We should go," Llyra warned.

Kanthe squeezed his bow harder. He watched his twin brother draw toward the line of knights facing the homes. "You all go," he whispered to the others. "Find a place to hide."

Jace took a step back. "But what are you—?"

"I'm going to say hello to my brother."

He straightened and stepped toward the door.

Llyra turned back to her window and swore. "What do you hope to accomplish, Kanthe? They'll feather your body with arrows before you take three steps."

"I hope not," he said. "But either way, such a distraction might buy you those few extra breaths that Pratik has so thoughtfully counted for us."

Kanthe also had another reason.

Back in the swamps, he had dodged the blades of the assassins, but a part of him had come to believe his doom was inevitable, that he had only borrowed these extra days. Still, the reprieve had given him a chance to finally hunt the Cloudreach and meet a half-sister who was far more beautiful than she had any right being, proving the gods had a wicked sense of humor.

Plus, as much as he hated to admit it . . .

I owe it to Mikaen to at least try.

He pictured the box he had handed to his brother before he departed for the swamps, the tiny pottery of two brothers clasping arms. He remembered their youth, running wild through Highmount, laughing under blankets, playing tricks on unwitting servants, stealing sweetcakes from under the cook's nose. He stared at the shining prince on the smoky field.

He's still my brother.

Maybe Mikaen knew nothing about the assassination attempt. Perhaps his brother could be persuaded to his better graces—at least more merciful ones.

"Don't go," Jace urged.

The journeyman's plea was far less heartfelt than his good-bye to Nyx, but Kanthe appreciated Jace's concern.

Still, he stepped to the door. "Go. Hide. I'll do what I can. If nothing else, I must warn my brother about what Nyx portended. The kingdom needs to know."

Even if it means my death.

He took a big breath, lifted his bow over his head in both hands, and strode from the shadows into the misty light.

Let me shine at least this much . . .

At his appearance, archers stiffened in wary surprise. Swords were raised higher. Someone shot off a bolt that shattered against the stone wall to his right. He refused to flinch. He took slow steps toward the line of knights.

"I'm Prince Kanthe!" he called over. "I wish to speak to my brother!"

Mikaen tried to step around the tall crimson figure, only to be held back by an arm. Even under the silvery helm, his brother's sea-blue eyes shone toward him.

"Where are the other traitors?" Mikaen shouted back at him. "Send them out!"

Kanthe lowered his bow to the ground, then stepped over it. He kept his hands high. "There are no traitors here. Only those trying to stop a coming doom. You must listen to what I have to say."

By now, he had crossed half the distance toward the row of knights.

Mikaen glared across the line at him.

Kanthe's footsteps faltered. Not from the hatred shining in his brother's face—though that was there—but from Mikaen's dark measure of glee. Born from the same womb and raised together, they knew each other better than anyone else. He watched the mask fall from Mikaen's bright face, revealing the roil of shadows beneath.

"You should've died in the swamps," Mikaen called over, his voice thick with spite. "Your death from here will not be so gentle."

Kanthe finally stopped.

I should've listened to Jace.

MIKAEN SAVORED THE look of dismay on his brother's face. Knights closed off any retreat. Kanthe's allies would soon be rooted out of their holes. Mikaen planned on torturing them in front of his brother.

Thoryn shouted next to him, "Secure the traitor! Prepare to scour that rampart for any other insurrectionists!"

As the Vyrllian captain stepped forward, Mikaen rounded past his shoulder. He wanted to watch Kanthe brought to his knees. As the knights forced him down, his brother closed his eyes, as if refusing to accept his downfall.

Oh, there will be far worse to watch, dear brother, before you die.

Thoryn suddenly grabbed Mikaen's shoulder, drawing him back. With his blood fired, Mikaen shook free with a bark of frustration.

The captain lunged again. "Get dow—"

A flaming barrel fell from the sky and crashed in front of the line of knights.

The blast threw him straight back. He struck the ground hard enough to knock his breath out. Gasping, Mikaen watched the belly of a sailraft glide past. The dark shadow of another firebomb tumbled from its stern.

Mikaen curled to his side as it exploded behind him.

The world briefly became flame and smoke.

As Mikaen coughed and gasped, Thoryn dragged him up. Behind them, the hunterskiff fired bolts at the attacking craft, but it was already rolling back into the mists. On his feet, Mikaen turned. Kanthe had broken free of his captors and now raced toward the stone homes. Along the way, his brother scooped up his bow as he fled past it.

No . . .

Mikaen jerked free of Thoryn and sped after his brother through the smoke.

The captain cursed, then boomed orders as he followed. "To Prince Mikaen! Keep him guarded!"

Behind Mikaen, the hunterskiff ignited its flashburn forges. It went roaring skyward. The attack ship dared not stay grounded. It was too vulnerable with an enemy hiding above. Only in the air could such a craft prove its namesake, to become a true hunter.

In truth, Mikaen did not care what happened above.

He focused on the ground, on his brother. Ahead, Kanthe dashed through a door and vanished. Mikaen flashed to when they were boys, playing countless games of hunter and prey, often hiding in closets or pouncing over stair rails onto one another.

Mikaen smiled darkly.

And I always won.

54

NYX HEARD DISTANT thunder as she crouched under the crossed arches at the center of the dark plaza. Down on one knee with her back to the copper door, she faced Aamon's panting countenance. While she remained weak, at least her sight was returning.

Silent lightning burst in jagged lines from one of the crystal-tipped pillars and splattered across the black clouds, as if those bolts were somehow feeding the dark skies.

The vargr ducked, casting his gaze all about, tucking his ears down.

"I'm spooked, too," she whispered.

Especially with where I must go next.

Nyx lifted a palm toward the vargr's nose. Aamon stopped his panting long enough to sniff, give a small lick, then nudge her hand, as if to say: *What do you want?*

She remembered the command Graylin had given Aamon. Mimicking it, she swept her arm to encompass the immediate space outside the copper door, then gripped her wrist with her other hand. "Protect," she said firmly.

Aamon's eyes gleamed, narrowing slightly—then he padded a few paces away and turned his gaze outward, his tail to the door. He growled his challenge out to the world.

"Good boy," she whispered.

His tail wagged once in acknowledgment.

She stood up, though it took two tries with her weak legs.

Frell came forward. "Are you strong enough for those stairs?"

"I think so . . ." she muttered, then added more firmly as she stood, "Yes."

Nyx glanced over to the copper door. Past its threshold, the scout's lamp had revealed stone stairs spiraling down into the summit. They were all going down, with the exception of the Kethra'kai, who would guard their retreat if necessary, alongside Aamon.

Xan, though, would accompany them down. She stood with Rhaif and Shiya.

"Then we should get started," Frell said.

With no one objecting, they set off past the door. Shiya led the way, with Rhaif behind her. Frell followed with the scout's lamp in his hand, leaving Nyx and Xan to trail last.

The steps—carved out of the summit's black rock—were wide enough for two to walk abreast. So, Nyx kept close to Xan, who was as exhausted as she was. The Kethra'kai elder carried herself heavily on her staff.

Around and around they went. The abysmal darkness seemed to consume their lamplight. Nyx imagined themselves winding down into the fiery core of the Urth. She swore she even caught a sulfurous waft of brimstan.

Ahead, Shiya's bronze feet rang on the steps, sounding like the chiming of some mournful bell. Nyx did her best to keep up, but her legs began to tire. Xan also slowed, wheezing next to her. They soon lagged behind the others. Shiya disappeared around a turn of the stairs, so did Rhaif. Frell hung back, keeping the steps illuminated with his lamp.

How much longer?

The answer came as the ring of Shiya's feet changed timbre, from bronze on stone to the sharper clang of metal on metal.

Light flared ahead.

Drawn by that brightness, Nyx hurried. Even Xan matched her steps. They rounded the turn of the stairs into a dazzling brilliance. She blinked against a sheen that was distinctly coppery.

Rhaif stood at the edge of that light, shading his eyes with a hand.

Past him, Shiya limped across a copper floor. Again, each of her steps glowed, but rather than the light fading, her trail grew ever brighter, washing out from her heels and rebounding off the walls.

Nyx drew up to Frell and Rhaif.

The copper chamber was circular, a quarter the size of the Cloistery's ninth tier, but here there were no burning pyres. Instead, a large glass table centered the room. The walls curved up to form a rounded point overhead. Nyx noted that the lines of the roof matched the stone arches far above them.

Rhaif made his own comparison as he edged into the space. "Looks like an egg on end," he whispered. "I found Shiya somewhere like this, only hers was a tenth this size. And it looks like someone tried to crack this egg."

She saw he was right as she followed after him, careful of the chunky pieces of broken glass on the floor. All around, glowing shelves climbed the walls. Rather than holding dusty tomes, the shelves were lined with rectangular blocks of the clearest crystal. Thousands upon thousands of them. Unfortunately, half of them had been knocked from their shelves and lay shattered on the metal floor. Even the central table had a huge split across it.

Shiya slowed as she neared the table. A hand rose to her throat as she seemed to inspect the damage—then she limped past it.

As she did, the table burst forth with a column of light that shot to the arched roof. It shimmered and pulsed, as if warning them back.

Nyx shielded her eyes against the brightness.

The pillar flickered and shivered for several more breaths, before finally collapsing into a perfect globe of light shining above the cracked tabletop.

The sight reminded Nyx of the gaseous glow of a Liar's Lure, a phenomenon occasionally spotted floating through the darker bowers of the swamp.

As they watched, colors infused into the sphere: emeralds and blues of every hue, streams of milky white, streaks of richer bronzes and browns.

As they all drew nearer, Shiya continued to limp across the room. Even Rhaif let her go alone, curiosity drawing him to the table's edge. The colors swirled and spun across the sphere, then slowly began to coalesce into the globe of a world.

Lands rose, seas filled, and clouds skimmed the surface.

"What magick is this?" Frell asked, and reached a hand toward the glow.

"Don't," Rhaif warned, retreating back.

Frell ignored him and brazenly swept his arm through the world. As his fingers passed harmlessly across, they stirred the image, like wafting a hand across a fire's smoke. In a breath, though, the mirage settled back to its former shape.

Nyx stared, mesmerized. Before her, the world slowly turned, revealing every coastline, mountain range, and sea. As those lands swept past her, she searched the surface.

"I don't see anything that matches the Crown," she whispered. "This can't be our Urth."

Frell nodded. "It must be the world of the old gods, where they came from."

The image occasionally frazzled, as if the damage to the tabletop fought revealing this world. But so far, it continued to hold.

Rhaif looked across the room. "Shiya . . ."

Hearing his note of concern, Nyx circled to join him. The bronze woman had reached the room's far side. There, a tall copper shield stood against the wall, cupped around by a rim of thick glass. A web of copper tubes and glass pipes wound through the glass and into the walls.

"Looks like the cocoon where I first laid eyes upon her," Rhaif said.

Shiya reached to her shoulder and tore her shift loose. It fell and cascaded down around her ankles, baring her nakedness to all. She stepped out of it and mounted a short ramp that led up to the alcove.

"No." Rhaif hurried over, clearly fearing the worst.

He drew them all, but they arrived too late. Shiya turned her back to the shield and pressed herself against it. As contact was made, the floor shook with a resounding ring. Shiya snapped straight, throwing her head back, clanging it against the copper.

In a breath, the glass brightened around her. The copper shield glowed. A golden elixir started to flow through the crystalline tubing. Underfoot, the floor thrummed. Nyx felt it in her bones, like the pumping of a great heart that was drawing strength from below. The very air grew fraught with energies.

As they watched, all that brilliance—from crystalline glass, golden potions, and glowing copper—infused into Shiya. Her bronze began to shine as if freshly poured. Her form appeared to melt and flow. The scratches and dents warmed away. Even her crooked leg grew straighter.

Despite the miraculous healing, Shiya's mouth gasped open. Her eyes now blazed with a light that could only be described as agonizing. Her fingers curled into crabs of pain.

Rhaif moved closer, but Frell held him back.

"Shiya," Rhaif moaned.

Within a few breaths, the light began to fade. As it did, her bronze form grew stiffer. All expression faded from her features. Her hands flattened against the copper. Then her eyelids lowered, less like someone drifting into slumber and more like tiny hatches being winched closed. Shiya stood there as the surrounding brilliance dimmed to a low glow.

The heartbeat in the floor also faded.

They all stared, holding their breath.

"What happened?" Frell asked.

Nyx stared at the blankness before her. "I think . . . I think she's left us."

RHAIF PACED IN front of the glowing cocoon, his hands wringing together in consternation. He breathed heavier, but he still felt lightheaded. He heard the others whispering as he kept vigil.

He remembered finding Shiya in exactly this same posture, a glowing bronze statue in a golden web. He remembered the wonder and exquisite terror of that moment.

Now it was all gone, snuffed like a candle in the dark.

He stopped and pleaded to the bronze statue, *Please don't go.*

Still, he recognized the selfishness of this request. He stared at her body, returned again to a bronze perfection. He remembered his earlier worry, when he had watched her hobble along the copper tunnel: *Maybe you should have never left your egg. This world is too harsh for even a woman made of metal.*

Perhaps his wish had been granted.

Ignoring the risk, he climbed up the ramp and stood in the glow of her grace. He lifted a hand and reached to her chest. He settled his palm against bronze that felt as warm as any flesh.

Tears rose at his loss.

Still, he had to let her go. "Be at peace, my Shiya."

He lowered his gaze, letting his arm drop away—only to have warm fingers catch his hand.

He stared up into eyes that shone a perfect azure blue; the glass was so lifelike that he defied anyone to say otherwise. She bowed her chin in thanks. Her palm rose and cupped his cheek. His mother's lullaby echoed again in his head, only far stronger than before.

She let him go and stepped past him. She moved unabashedly in her nakedness. The others drew closer. She moved to a section of wall to the left of the cocoon. She waved a hand, dissolving open an alcove in the wall, the copper vanishing as if it were smoke.

From within, light blazed out. It rose from a crystalline cube veined in copper with a golden mass pulsing at its core.

She removed it with great care, then pressed it against her bare navel.

Rhaif flashed back to the mines of Chalk, to the Iflelen Wryth infusing his bloodbaerne elixir at that same spot. He remembered the poor girl's life pouring into Shiya, waking her to this harsh world.

Only there was no horror here.

The crystalline cube glowed brighter—then sank into her bronze flesh and vanished. It was as if Shiya were instilling a new heart, one strong enough to withstand this world.

He glanced to the others, who looked on with equal wonder.

Shiya crossed around the cocoon to the other side and repeated the gesture, dissolving open another cubby. No glow greeted her. From inside, she removed a crystal cube resting atop a pedestal. Its facets were so clear it was difficult to discern it was even there. She lifted it free and turned. She then headed over to the glass table, where the shimmering world slowly turned.

Maybe *her* world.

They all followed.

She held the cube in both palms, and a soft light infused into it. She finally spoke. It was not the whispers of before, but a voice stronger and clearer. Still, it was evident she struggled.

"Much . . . is lost," she warned. She glanced with misery across the expanse of broken glass. "I . . . am not hale . . . whole."

Rhaif swallowed, remembering what Xan had told Pratik. *Shiya carries the spirit of an old god inside her, one who has not yet fully settled.* Maybe that was still true.

"I can only hope to do enough." Her voice dropped to a whisper, but not from weakness, only confusion and fear. "I will show you what I can . . . share the little that was left to me by the missing Guardian."

She glanced back to the cocoon.

Rhaif stared over with a frown. *Had someone else once stood there and left?* If so, he sensed that abandonment had happened long ago.

Shiya again looked sadly at the ruins of the room. Rhaif now wondered if the damage here had been deliberate or was simply due to some quake, perhaps when the Shrouds were uplifted in the ancient past.

Frell shifted closer. "Shiya, what can you show us?"

She returned her attention to her crystal cube and passed a palm over it. In front of her, the shimmering world suddenly cast off a blazing sun. It shot across the room and stopped high in the air, hanging like a bright lantern. Next, a silvery moon drifted free. It circled above their heads, passing around and around the spinning world.

Rhaif grew dizzy at the pageantry of it all.

"Thus, it began . . ." Shiya intoned, and waved her hand again. "Over three hundred millennia ago . . ."

The spin of the globe gradually slowed. As it did, lands sank, oceans boiled, and winds eroded mountains. Great quakes tore the world, uplifting new coastlines, tearing apart others. Finally, the turning stopped completely, leaving one side blazing under the sun, the other dark and shadowed.

Still, time continued to pass before their eyes. Ice piled up on the dark side, while the sun blasted the other to sand. Between those extremes, a twilight band circled the world, ruddy at one edge, shadowy on the other. Lands within that band shone with forests and rivers, or were striped with tall mountains, or rolled with green hills. Blue oceans swirled throughout all, ringing this new world.

But it wasn't *new.*

Nyx leaned closer, staring wide-eyed and unblinking at a northern breadth of this twilight circlet. Her voice was pure dismay. "It's . . . It's our Crown."

NYX STUMBLED BACK from the revelation, as if it could be dismissed by distance. She refused to believe it but knew it to be true.

"The Urth once *turned*," she gasped. She tried to hold this thought in her head, but it seemed too vast.

Frell faced Shiya. "I don't understand. What stopped it from spinning?"

She stared at the frozen globe. "I cannot say. Much was lost . . ."

Nyx shifted another step back, grinding crystals under her heel. She sensed the enormity of knowledge shattered and destroyed across this space. Shiya winced at the grating noise, as if confirming this.

Shiya turned to Frell. "That is not the question you should be asking."

"What is then?"

"To understand . . ." Shiya returned her attention to the shimmering image of the Urth. She waved a hand over the cube in her palm. "The past you've now seen. But this is what's to be."

As they watched, nothing seemed to happen. The Urth remained fixed and unmoving, one side blazing, the other side frozen. Then something sped past Nyx's shoulder, a flash of silver. She ducked from it, startled, only to realize it was the glowing moon.

She cringed, knowing what was about to happen.

The moon swept around, passing ghostly through Frell and Rhaif. Xan lifted her staff against it, but it rushed through the wood, too. The moon circled the shimmering world, growing ever closer—at first slowly, then faster.

Finally, it made one final pass and slammed into the world. The impact shook the image above the table. Waves of destruction spread outward from the strike, wiping away all in its path: lands, oceans, ice, and sand. Nothing was spared. In a breath, the ruins of the Urth shone before all of their stunned faces.

"Moonfall . . ." Nyx whispered. "What I saw in my vision."

"The portent of the *jar'wren*," Xan intoned.

Shiya cast her gaze around the room. "This is what woke me. We who are the Sleepers, buried deep in the world until we are needed. But we are not the only sentinels planted here as the world slowed. Those who came before—"

Shiya stopped and frowned, clearly struggling for the words to explain, or maybe she was simply trying to knit what she knew over the gaps of knowledge shattered on the floor. She started again. "Those who came before, they instilled gifts into others, seeded into their blood, creating vessels of memory. They were *living* sentinels who watched while we slept, who could change *with* the world, while we could not. They were created to sustain an eternal memory, one shared and preserved across their many numbered."

Nyx breathed harder and closed her eyes.

I know those sentinels.

She remembered the attack in the swamps, when her mind was cast throughout the avenging horde descending on Brayk. She had shared their eyes, their lusts—but she also pictured the pair of fiery eyes gazing back at her. In those moments, she had sensed the greater mind behind that gaze, something ageless and dark, cold and unknowable. Its vastness had unnerved her.

She opened her eyes to find Shiya gazing upon her. Her bronze face shone with that same ancientness.

Nyx knew that the fiery intelligence in the swamps was equal to what lay here. That huge pair of eyes—staring out of the darkness at her—wasn't just the shared minds of the bats living now. It was *all* their minds, past and present, the memories of *every* bat that had ever lived, stretching back into the ancient past, forged into one force.

Shiya seemed to read this dawning knowledge and nodded to her. She then glanced across at the others. "The gift given to these living sentinels . . . we Sleepers also share it."

"You speak of bridle-song," Xan said. "It is our gift, too."

Shiya smiled sadly. "By mistake."

Nyx flinched, but Xan looked aghast, wounded.

"I don't malign you with these words," Shiya consoled. "This gift drifted into your lineage long ago. Maybe infused by disease, maybe by a mix of venom and blood. But once there, that seed found fertile soil, a usefulness worth passing on, and so it rooted deep among certain blessed people."

"The Kethra'kai," Xan said.

"And maybe others." Shiya's bronze brow bunched with frustration. She again struggled, perhaps brushing against another frayed place in her memory. "Not only did that seed spread inadvertently, but the gift . . . it has changed while we slept, growing branches no one imagined."

Her gaze again found Nyx.

Frell interrupted this discourse. He had been walking around the table, staring at the ruins of the Urth glowing there. "That is all fascinating, but it's not what we should be focused on." Worry lined his face. "Moonfall. When will this occur?"

Shiya's lips thinned to a frown.

Rhaif pressed his palms together. "Please don't say *much was lost* again."

Shiya's expression softened, and she reached to touch Rhaif's arm. "Not that. But the variables are many. Even for me. I can only approximate an answer."

"When will it happen?" Frell persisted.

Shiya spoke more softly. "No longer than five years. Maybe as short as three."

Frell looked down, plainly absorbing this dire prediction. No one else spoke. With a sigh, the alchymist again raised his face to Shiya. "Then how do we stop it?"

Shiya turned to the ruins of the Urth. "You cannot."

55

Wryth stood next to the maesterwheel of the *Pywll*. The warship's commander stood on its far side. Out the curve of the bow windows, a line of black cliffs divided the world ahead, with mists below and dark clouds above. Two columns of smoke rose from near the base of the cliffs.

Wryth clutched the cracked orb in his hand, his gaze fixed ahead. He cursed how long it had taken to ferry up to the *Pywll* and get the huge warship turned and moving toward the Shrouds. Apparently, some skirmish had already broken out at the base of the cliffs. As they had neared those dark ramparts, two flashes of fire had brightened the mists ahead.

Now the entire forecastle watched the skies.

What was happening under those mists?

"There!" Brask said, and pointed to the left.

The crest of a gray balloon cut through the white layer, then sank away again. It appeared to be running from the cliffs.

Brask identified the brief glimpse. "A sailraft."

Then another sharper fin of a black gasbag cut high, dragging up the hull of a narrow vessel with a pointed prow.

"The hunterskiff," Wryth said.

"It's in pursuit of the raft." Brask shifted along the bow window, watching the chase pass by their portside.

The hunterskiff dove back into the mists. Tiny flashes of fire lit the clouds as the attack craft tried to flush out its prey with explosive bolts, driving it away from the cliffs.

Wryth hoped Mikaen was safely aboard that skiff. The Iflelen had expended considerable effort to forge the prince into a useful tool. It would be a waste to lose him now.

The pilotman glanced over to Brask. "Do we turn and join the fray?"

"No, we're not as nimble as the skiff. By the time we turn the *Pywll,* it'll be over. Besides . . ." He waved farther off to port through the windows. "It looks like our help will not be needed."

Wryth crossed to that side, widening his view to port.

Behind them, the towering mass of a billowing balloon coursed in their wake. Haddan had rallied the *Tytan* and now fired all its forges to follow. It was impressive how quickly the liege general had gotten his forces moving, especially with half of the warship's gasbag ripped open to the sky. Its puckered edges flapped as it ran low over the clouds. Still, the earlier repairs had allowed the *Tytan* to rise high enough to lift the boat clear of the treetops—if not the mists. Below the balloon, the ship was dragged through the clouds, its foggy wake glowing with the fires of its forges.

Another brief glimpse of the gray balloon rose into view, then the sharper edge of the hunterskiff's gasbag. Both dove away again. Still, the trajectory of this pursuit was clear. The skiff was driving its prey straight toward the *Tytan*.

Trusting this matter to take care of itself, Wryth returned with Brask to the ship's wheel. The commander had clearly come to the same conclusion. They both faced the cliffs ahead.

"Ready for all stop!" Brask bellowed to the forecastle's crew. "Bring us to halt at the edge of those cliffs." The commander pointed to a man stationed by a calling tube. "Order all skiffs and rafts loaded below and be ready to drop."

Wryth watched the rampart rising ahead of them.

So close now . . .

He glanced down to the orb still in his hand. The handful of lodestone slivers still in place shivered on their pins. All pointing forward.

"I'm picking up a signal," Wryth warned. He stepped closer to Brask. "Coming from ahead of us."

Wryth rolled the orb, careful of the oil leaking from its crack. He sought to get a firmer bearing. He tilted it toward the base of the cliffs, only to have the lodestones lose their firm fix.

No . . .

His heart pounded harder. As he rotated the orb the other way and tilted the lodestones upward, the slivers firmed their alignment.

Trepidation set in.

Brask must have noted his stiffening. "What's wrong? Has it moved?"

"No. It's *still* due east. But it's not rising from *below*." He stared at the dark clouds churning atop the cliffs. "It's coming from the Shrouds."

"Are you sure?"

Wryth held his breath and rolled the orb back and forth again. He slowly nodded. "The artifact is definitely up above."

The commander frowned. "What about Mikaen? Were we not to look for the prince, too?"

Wryth shook his head. "We don't know if Mikaen is down at the cliffs. More likely he's already aboard that hunterskiff." He glanced over his shoulder to the far edge of the curved windows. "Either way, the *Tytan* can certainly deal with Mikaen's safe return."

"Then what do you suggest?"

Wryth lifted the orb. "We head to the Shrouds. Secure that artifact for the good of the kingdom."

And my own.

He tightened a fist. For any hope of achieving his ultimate ambition—to rise to a potency beyond that of any king or emperor—it meant supporting Hálendii, of doing his best to guide events from behind the throne. For better or worse, his fate was tied to the kingdom.

At least, for now.

GRAYLIN CRINGED BACK as another fiery blast lit up the clouds behind the sailraft. The flare was close enough to sting his eyes. He hung from a leather strap near the open stern door. In fact, Darant had the entire hatch removed to aid in rolling firebombs out the back.

The pirate shouted from the front, "That one nearly went straight up our arse! But that's the plan, right?"

At the bow, Darant leaned over his daughter. Glace manned the raft's wheel and pedals, expertly driving them through the mists.

No, this wasn't exactly the plan.

Back on the *Sparrowhawk,* they had spied through Hyck's farscope as a hunterskiff swept toward the cliffs. Clearly the legion had spotted the same puff of smoke that had drawn the *Sparrowhawk.* Unfortunately, the other craft had arrived at the cliffs ahead of them. Graylin and Darant had to quickly revise their plan to rescue whoever sent that signal.

Graylin stared at their sailraft's empty hold. Two more firebombs were strapped to the insides of the hull. It was all that the *Sparrowhawk* could spare. A moment ago, their firebombing had achieved the intended goal of luring off the hunterskiff. The hope was to open up a clear run behind them for the *Sparrowhawk* to sweep in low by the cliffs and pick up the others. At the time, Graylin had been counting on most of the legion's forces either to be in that attack ship or to be called back to it.

Not running across the ground in pursuit of a young prince.

When the sailraft had dropped out of the clouds, Graylin had spotted the legion's forces spread out before a nest of stone homes. Halfway between the cliffs and the legion's line, two knights held a figure down on his knees.

Prince Kanthe.

At that moment, Graylin had been relieved to have his suspicions confirmed that the waft of blue smoke had come from Nyx and the others. He and Darant had quickly dropped two firebombs, half their load, to free the prince and scatter the legion. Then the hunterskiff had fired back at them, sending them running.

Before they had vanished into the clouds, he had caught sight of the attack craft rising in pursuit—but he'd also watched the legion chasing after Kanthe.

Unfortunately, the sailraft couldn't head back to help, not with this shark on their tail. As a reminder, another burst of fire exploded close enough to waft smoke into the hold.

Glace called from the wheel, "I'm almost out of flashburn!"

So, definitely can't go back.

From here, it was all up to the *Sparrowhawk*. The swyftship still had a few firebombs left, hopefully enough to blast a path and chase off the legion long enough to collect the others.

Graylin knew the odds of a successful rescue were long, nearly impossible.

Have I failed Marayn's daughter yet again?

The only part of their plan that had succeeded was in drawing off the hunterskiff. There was no way for the *Sparrowhawk* to rescue the others with a shark guarding there.

Graylin took the smallest bit of consolation in this fact.

Glace suddenly hove the raft on its side, throwing the boat high—and just in time. A huge spear shot through the mists from behind, grazing a path under their keel. Boards shattered below, shaking the entire craft. The impact knocked them clear of the mists and back into the open sky.

Graylin swung on his leather loop, staring out the stern. The hunterskiff burst from the clouds behind them, far closer than he suspected. Its balloon shot high, hauling the lethal boat into view, exposing the length of its keel.

Instead of diving back down at them, the hunterskiff swung full around, firing its forges, coming close to igniting the sailraft's balloon. Then the attack ship sped away and aimed straight for the cliffs.

Graylin's legs settled to the floor as Glace evened their flight.

He frowned at the departing hunterskiff.

Why is it leaving? What could be drawing it back so swiftly?

Off by the cliffs, he saw a massive warship cresting over the edge and setting out across the Shrouds. He didn't understand where it was going, but he feared it would circle back like the hunterskiff.

"Graylin!" Darant shouted with alarm.

He turned to face the bow. Directly ahead, a huge balloon—billowing and puckering—filled the world as it swept toward them. He now understood why the hunterskiff had fled.

It was no longer needed.

KANTHE LED THE others through the dark. They had retreated into the maze of tunnels that delved into the cliffs behind the homes. Jace ran with their shaded lamp. It was slivered open enough to light their way. The journeyman's sweating face was a lamp unto itself, reflecting the meager light, shining with the man's terror.

All around, booming shouts echoed from every direction. Flickers of torchlight drove them back and forth, even up a level. All this time, they fought not to get pinned down in any blind caves. Kanthe remembered Pratik's warning about them being burned out of such a hole. Their only chance was to keep moving.

Kanthe held out one hope. He pictured the sailraft freeing him. It had to come from the *Sparrowhawk,* which meant that the swyftship had to be nearby. If that was true, his group needed to stay alive long enough for a rescue.

But doing so was becoming more and more difficult.

A scream rose behind them.

A glance back showed Llyra crouched low, her arm pointing back. A figure stumbled into their tiny pool of light and sprawled headlong with a blade through his throat.

Llyra dashed back to the body and yanked her knife out. "Keep moving," she hissed to them.

Kanthe had an arrow loosely fixed to his bowstring. Shortly after diving into these tunnels, he quickly grew to regret his choice of weaponry in such tight quarters, especially in the dark. He kept scraping the top of his bow on the low roof or striking a wall with his elbow. He had already accidentally let loose a couple of arrows, sending them skittering off into the dark.

He now followed Seyrl's example. The Kethra'kai scout shuffled sideways. He had an arrow nocked but held off pulling the string. Seyrl had demonstrated how swiftly he could snap off an arrow when a target appeared. Luckily, the knights who hunted them came with torches and lamps, making them easy to spot. The scout had dropped two men on his own. Kanthe believed he might have grazed one himself.

Still, he wasn't fooled. They could not stay ahead of this pursuit much longer.

Kanthe guided them down the curve of a narrow passage. As he rounded its bend, a wan light brightened ahead, suggesting they were nearing a section where the caves exited back into the cliffside homes. They had ascended a stairway a moment ago to reach this second level. If the *Sparrowhawk* appeared, they should be able to leap down and race toward it.

Until then, they needed to keep to the dark.

He reached a cross tunnel and aimed his group around a corner, leaving that wan light behind them. As he got them moving along the dark passageway, flames flared ahead of them, revealing a clutch of knights hiding in ambush.

Mikaen rose from near the shoulder of a Vyrllian Guard. "Dear brother."

Another two knights knelt in front of them, crouched behind a raised shield.

Seyrl snapped off an arrow, only to have it rebound off the shield. The other knight fired a crossbow. The Kethra'kai fell back, a feathered dart in his eye.

Kanthe had already raised a smoldering taper to the trimmed fuse on his arrow's egg. As Seyrl fell, Kanthe drew and fired. His shot was no more successful than the tribesman's. The knight's shield blocked the bolt—only to have the egg explode against the steel with a huge blast of blue smoke.

As the ambushers coughed and choked, a wall of smoke burst down the passageway, sweeping over Kanthe. He pushed everyone back to the curved tunnel.

But which way to go?

The answer came with a mighty roar of flashburn forges. The rumbling rose to his left, echoing from where the wan light illuminated the curved passage.

The Sparrowhawk . . .

He shoved everyone that way, but he grabbed Jace's lamp and ripped away its leather shade. The flame blazed brighter.

Jace cringed from the brightness. "What're you—?"

"Make for the *Hawk*," he said with a shove. "I'm going to lure my brother off."

Kanthe backed the opposite way. He knew Jace and the others would need every moment to make that rendezvous, which meant keeping the bulk of the legion inside the caves.

"I'll circle around," Kanthe promised. "I'll meet you there."

They hesitated—or at least Jace did. But Llyra grabbed the journeyman and dragged him away, herding Pratik ahead of her.

Once they left, Kanthe hung at the crossroads long enough for the smoke to dissipate slightly. The flames of his brother's ambush site reappeared out of the gloom.

Which means they can see my lamp.

He waited for a shout to arise from over there, then took off to the right, away from Jace and the others. As he ran, he kept his lamp glowing, bouncing against his thigh. He had to make sure to draw his brother this way. Fresh shouts rose behind him.

Good enough.

He shook the leather flap back over the lamp, reducing its illumination to a sliver.

Still, it left him blind for several steps. Failing to slow down, he slammed into a sharp corner. Wood snapped, and his bow came apart in his grip.

He tossed the ruins aside, raised his lamp, and set off again.

He ran wildly, avoiding any glows ahead, chased by shouts behind. Then a familiar roaring grew ahead of him, along with a brighter light.

Thank the gods for smiling upon me . . .

He aimed for the brighter cross tunnel and took it. Ahead, an arched frame of light marked an exit. He sprinted for it as the world roared outside. Nearing the arch, he saw the tunnel didn't dump into one of the stone homes, but atop a flat roof of the abode below. He didn't care. The homes were squat enough that it would be an easy leap to the ground.

He swept over the threshold and skidded across the sandy stone roof. To his left rose the cliff face. Directly ahead stood the featureless side of a neighboring home. He turned to the right, which faced the misty forest—and ran for the roof's edge, ready to leap below.

As he neared it, he spotted a ship wreathed in smoke out front.

He skidded again, nearly toppling over the roof's edge.

It wasn't the *Sparrowhawk*.

The hunterskiff hung out there, the rudder of its forges glowing red hot.

He glanced down. The slide of his stop had rained pebbles and sand below, alerting a huge Gyn, who craned his craggy face up at Kanthe. The iron-helmed giant hefted his ax higher, inviting him to hop down.

Another time . . .

Kanthe swung around—in time to see Mikaen stalk from the tunnel and out onto the roof. His armor shone brightly in the misty sunlight. The hulking form of a vy-knight followed close behind.

Kanthe backed a step, his heel slipping at the roof's edge.

At that moment, he recognized his mistake.

The gods were not smiling on me after all.

Instead, they were laughing their arses off.

56

WRYTH POINTED TO the dark clouds sweeping under the keel of the *Pywll*. He held Skerren's orb in his other hand. He had ordered the warship to sweep twice around the area. With the orb's lodestones, he had been testing the winds blowing from down below.

"That's definitely where the signal arises," Wryth attested. "Here at the center of the Shrouds. Down below should be the Northern Henge."

The commander scowled at the location. A storm raged under them, brightening the clouds in flashes. No thunder accompanied those crackling bolts, but the threat was plain to all. Worried glances spread across the forecastle.

Brask shook his head. "I can't lower the *Pywll* through a storm that fierce, riven through with lightning. If the gasbag were struck enough times . . ."

Wryth pictured the balloon bursting into flame and crashing into the jungles. Still, he refused to be thwarted by bad weather.

Not when I'm this close.

Wryth turned to the commander. "The *Pywll* is tall. Can you lower the bulk of the boat through the clouds but still keep the balloon above the storm?"

Brask winced at such a thought.

"What about dropping just the keel of the *Pywll* through," Wryth pressed. "Along with its lowermost levels."

Brask plainly pictured what Wryth envisioned. "You want us to drop the ship enough to breach our keel-holds through the clouds?"

"That's where the warship secures most of its rafts and skiffs. Those smaller crafts should be able to shoot out under the clouds, drop swiftly, and secure the entire area below."

Brask rubbed his chin and slowly nodded. He glanced at his crew, his eyes brightening with the challenge. "We can do that."

Wryth exhaled in relief.

Brask clapped him on the shoulder. "For a Shrive, you're not a bad tactician."

Wryth accepted the weak compliment. He turned away and headed across the forecastle.

"Where are you going?" Brask called over to him.

"Down," Wryth said. "To join the forces heading to the Shrouds."

Brask started to follow, as if to object, then simply waved Wryth off. Despite his praise a moment ago, the commander plainly wanted Wryth out of his forecastle and off his ship.

Wryth wouldn't have let the man stop him anyway.

If the ancient bronze artifact was below, he intended to secure it himself. But he also remembered seeing Kanthe fleeing with the weapon back in Havensfayre.

Knowing that, Wryth intended to be prepared.

If the prince was down there . . .

So was another.

NYX DREW WITH the others around the glass table. The ruins of the Urth shimmered before them. She stared at the blasted landscape of broken lands, boiled seas, and a sky roiling with storms. No life could survive that.

Again, she heard the rising screams from the fiery mountaintop, the clash of war machines, then a moon crashing into the Urth. But what she remembered most from her dream was the resounding silence at the end, the stillness of an ancient grave.

"And you say we cannot stop this from happening?" Frell asked again.

Shiya motioned them all closer. "To understand, you must see."

Her bronze hand swept over the cube glowing in her other palm. Before them, time started to run backward. As they watched, the world re-formed before them: seas returned, broken coastlines knit together, and the Crown forged itself anew. At the end, the moon rose from its crater and flew back into orbit, circling around them once again.

"I showed you the past. And the future sure to come." Shiya nodded to the shining world. "Here is the present you know."

"I don't understand," Nyx said. "Why are you showing us our world if we cannot save it?"

"Like I said, you cannot."

Rhaif looked ill. "Then the Urth is doomed."

Nyx clenched a fist, refusing to accept this fate.

Frell raised a palm. "If *we* cannot stop this from happening, can *you*?"

Shiya's eyes shone, clearly contemplating this, then shook her head. "Even I cannot. It will take *all* the world to do it."

"What do you mean?" Nyx asked.

"I will show you." Shiya lifted her cube and waved over it again. "This is the only hope."

The Urth looked the same for several breaths. Nyx shared a worried glance with Frell. Had something gone wrong?

Then Rhaif flinched next to her, drawing back her attention. She didn't understand what had startled him, then she saw it, too. The circlet of the Crown had shifted closer to her.

She gaped at the breadth of the world before her.

It's turning...

As they all watched, the Crown continued its spin—at first slowly, then steadily faster.

Xan pointed off to the side. "The moon . . ."

Nyx glanced over and saw the ghostly silver globe drifting farther away, swinging its orbit wider. "It's retreating," she whispered.

"Look at the Crown," Rhaif gasped out.

Nyx returned her attention. As the Urth continued to turn—now settled into a steady spin—the mountainous ice melted on one side. Seas rose and flooded across the Crown. Massive quakes shook the globe, lifting some lands, sinking others. The tops and bottoms of the world slowly frosted over with ice.

Nyx's heart pounded.

Nothing looks the same.

Frell had more dire concerns. "Millions will die if this happens."

Shiya lowered her palm atop the cube. "Yes. But not *all*."

Nyx felt little comforted by her statement.

Even Rhaif looked aghast at Shiya. "So to save the world, the Crown must be destroyed?"

Shiya didn't answer. She didn't have to.

Frell still stared at the strange new landscape. "The only way to avoid moonfall is to get the Urth spinning again." He turned to Shiya. "Is such a thing even possible?"

"Perhaps." Shiya stared down at her crystal cube. "With help."

"What help?" Rhaif asked. "From where?"

Shiya nodded in front of her, then lifted her palm off the cube.

Before them, the glowing globe shone brighter, blindingly so. Then as it faded again, their own world had returned. The Crown again shone in a twilight circlet between frozen ice and blasted sand. Only now, tiny blue and crimson dots bloomed around the map of the world, both in their lands and beyond.

Rhaif drew closer, craning around. "This red spot in the south of Guld'guhl. That's where I found you."

Shiya bowed her head. "*Red* marks sites empty or destroyed."

Nyx understood. "All these glowing spots. They mark sites where your kind were buried, who you called Sleepers."

"It is so, but few remain. Those who do are locked in landscapes too formidable for them to wake."

Nyx saw the crimson dots far outnumbered the others. The only blue one anywhere along the Crown lay far to the south, deep in the Klashe.

"But this is not what I wished to show you," Shiya said.

She tapped her cube on either side. Two larger green spots appeared on the world. One far into the ice, the other deep into the blasted sands.

Xan leaned on her cane to peer closer. "What are these new areas you show us?"

Shiya's expression grew forlorn. She glanced across the spread of broken glass on the floor. "I do not know. Such knowledge was shattered here."

Nyx heard the worry in her voice. She remembered how the door had been locked against them.

Shiya continued, "I only know—with the Guardian gone from here—I must travel to this site." She pointed to the patch within the dark ice. "I feel the drive to reach there, but I do not know the *reason* for that compunction. Something lies out there, and I must reach it if the world is to ever turn again."

Rhaif stared at the frozen expanse west of the Ice Fangs. "Shiya, such a journey is impossible. Especially alone."

Nyx knew this to be true—along with another certainty. "I must go with you."

They all stared at her.

She faced them, letting them see her determination. "Something tried to block Shiya from entering this site in the Shrouds. Even if she could reach that other spot, it could happen again there, too. She may need my help."

Nyx looked over to the bronze woman.

Before Shiya could reply, the pounding of feet drew their attention to the chamber's door. Shiya whisked a hand, and the shining globe vanished off the table, hiding what she had revealed.

One of the Kethra'kai burst into the room. She skidded on the copper floor, her gaze casting about. The shock of the sight momentarily silenced her.

"What is it?" Xan asked, thumping more fully into view.

The woman focused on Xan and answered in a fast spatter of Kethra. Xan clutched her staff more firmly.

"What's wrong?" Nyx asked.

Xan turned. "Someone comes. In a huge ship, descending through the clouds."

Nyx knew who that must be, picturing the warship that had been plaguing them at Havensfayre.

"We must go," Frell said. "Now. We can't be trapped down here. We must make for the jungle."

They all started rushing for the door.

Shiya headed the other way, moving with incredible swiftness. When she neared the cocoon back there, she raised her small cube and danced her fingers across its surface. When she finally turned around, a deep gong sounded from under the floor, shaking the entire place.

A couple of the glass tomes toppled off the shelves and shattered.

Shiya ignored the damage and rushed across the chamber. As she rejoined the group, she pushed the crystal cube into her chest. It melted through her bronze and vanished.

"What did you do over there?" Rhaif asked.

"No one else must learn what's down here." Shiya waved them onward. "Ever."

They all fled upward, with Shiya all but carrying Xan.

As Nyx ran, another gong sounded behind her, striking louder, like a bell marking the passage of time. She glanced back, sensing they needed to be far from here when that chiming reached its end.

57

KANTHE HELD HIS palms toward his brother. "Mikaen, please, you must listen."

His brother ignored him and headed across the flat stone roof. Mikaen's face showed no fear, no compassion, only malice. Each step seemed to shine his armor brighter.

Mikaen was followed by the huge Vyrllian Guard, a true crimson mountain.

Kanthe glanced back over his shoulder. Past the roof's edge, the Monger still waited below. The giant carried a battle-ax in his rocky fists. More knights gathered down there, too. Beyond them, the black dagger of a hunterskiff hovered in a pall of smoke.

Kanthe returned his full attention on his twin. "You know I am no threat to the king or to your future reign. Surely you can't believe that I aspire for the throne."

Mikaen stopped with a shrug. "Maybe not now, but there's no telling later. It's better for the kingdom that any possibility of a challenge be eliminated. Why else did I go against our father's wishes and plot your assassination?"

Kanthe went cold with his words. "What? Then the king—"

"Even now, our father wants me to bring you home. He bears an inordinate capacity of tolerance, maybe even love, for you." Another shrug. "So, I will bring you home. Or at least, your head."

Kanthe struggled to realign his world to his brother's words. He felt lightheaded, dizzy, as he fought toward the truth, agonized by his own guilt for judging his father so harshly.

The king never ordered my assassination . . .

"I tried to have you eliminated once before, back in Azantiia, when you were carousing in the Nethers. My mistake. I should never have trusted thieves and cutthroats to accomplish such a task."

Kanthe blinked in dismay, remembering being accosted in an alleyway after a night at the Point'd Blade. It seemed a lifetime ago.

"I now know better. Such a duty should have always been mine." Mikaen reached over to the vy-knight. "Thoryn, your sword, please."

The man refused with a crimson scowl.

The bright prince was not in the mood to argue. "Do so, or I'll have the king take your head. To adorn a spike next to my brother's."

The Vyrllian eyed Kanthe up and down and rightly judged him to be no threat to Mikaen. The vy-knight withdrew a broadsword and passed it over. It was so heavy that it dragged his brother's arm down. Mikaen tossed the blade toward Kanthe. It clattered over to his toes.

"Pick it up," Mikaen ordered. "Let's have one last game between brothers."

Kanthe stared down. He had seldom ever touched a sword. When he had, it was in jest, certainly not with any intent to wield it. Swordsmanship was forbidden to a Prince in the Cupboard.

From the smile fixed on Mikaen's face, his brother knew this, too. Mikaen only made this offer in malice, intending to make sport of Kanthe's death. Or maybe he would claim later that the dark prince had attacked him, and in all his bright glory, Mikaen had to dispatch the traitor. Kanthe had to admit that it would make for a good story.

But I'll not help you write it.

Kanthe lowered his arms. "No," he said firmly, realizing this might be the first time in his life that he had denied Mikaen anything.

And the bright prince clearly did not like it.

Mikaen's smile curled into a sneer. "So be it."

His brother yanked free his own blade and stalked toward him.

Kanthe backed a step, nearly tripping off the roof. Anger flared inside him, stoking a rage that had been there his entire life. At being born second to this monster. At all the slights and insults and degradations he'd had to endure in Mikaen's shadow, all so his brother could shine brighter.

And now here Kanthe was, being threatened by this same bastard.

He lunged and hauled the sword up with a bellow.

Swinging with both arms, Kanthe slashed at his brother. The shock of his attack momentarily dismayed Mikaen. Still, as his brother stumbled back, he knocked Kanthe's blade away.

The vy-knight, Thoryn, came forward, but Mikaen shouted at his approach. "No! Stand back."

Mikaen regained his stance, faced Kanthe, and lifted his sword higher in one hand. He motioned Kanthe forward with the other. "Let's do this, brother."

With his blood still on fire, Kanthe circled warily, still gripping the heavy sword in both fists. Mikaen lunged, passing easily through Kanthe's attempt at a defense. The point of Mikaen's sword plunged at his chest—only to be turned aside at the last moment and slice across Kanthe's ribs.

A line of fire burst there.

Kanthe fell back a step. Blood welled, running down his flank in a hot river. He tried to attack, but the weight of his sword was unwieldy. Mikaen casually slapped his blade aside and, with a lightning-fast riposte, opened a new stream across Kanthe's thigh.

Mikaen's smile brightened. He plainly enjoyed toying with his younger brother. Clearly, Kanthe's rage was no match against trained swordsmanship.

Kanthe tried battering wildly at his twin, hoping to force his way to the door, to perhaps make his escape back into the dark tunnels. Even this, Mikaen anticipated. He backed from Kanthe's onslaught, letting him waste his strength. By the time Mikaen reached the door, Kanthe was gasping, barely able to lift his sword.

Mikaen flourished his blade. "I think you've learned who the true prince is here. I'll make your death—"

A heavy swing of silver flashed from the doorway near Mikaen. His brother must have noted it out of the corner of an eye. He twisted and fell back—but not far enough. The edge of an ax slashed across his face, cutting deep, down to bone, from crown to chin.

Mikaen dropped his sword and clutched his face as if trying to hold it together. As he spun around, blood poured through his fingers.

Kanthe rushed toward him, reflexively concerned.

Screaming, Mikaen spun and tumbled away from the threat, knocking Kanthe aside.

Thoryn grabbed Mikaen.

Kanthe reached the doorway as Jace stepped out with his bloody ax. He was followed by Llyra, who flung an arm. A knife flashed. Thoryn twisted at the last moment and took the blade in his shoulder. Ignoring it, the Vyrllian charged with the prince and leaped over the roof's edge.

Kanthe and the others followed.

Down below, Thoryn had landed cleanly. He shoved Mikaen at the Monger. "Get the prince into the skiff!"

Thoryn glared over at them. He swung an arm in their direction, the dagger still impaled in his shoulder, plainly ready to exact revenge on them. Then the man ducked and looked at the skies to his right.

Kanthe turned there, too.

From the mists, a huge shadow dropped into view. Its keel cut through the clouds. Dark barrels fell from its stern, blasting into fire below and sweeping toward the legion on the ground.

The *Sparrowhawk*!

Thoryn bellowed as he sprinted for the hunterskiff, "Go! Now!"

The order applied both to the legion and to the hovering craft. The skiff's forges fired beneath it, spewing flames and smoke. It held off launching, letting as many men as possible reach the ship.

Thoryn hit the ramp and dove through.

A moment later, the hunterskiff blasted upward, nearly outrunning its own gasbag.

Kanthe pointed down. "Run for it!"

He feared the enemy might circle around for an attack. Then again, with a mortally wounded prince aboard, they might not risk it.

Still, Kanthe wasn't taking any chances.

He leaped with the others as the *Sparrowhawk* swept low past them. Its stern door was already open, its bottom edge dragging through the flames.

Kanthe and the others ran for the ship, racing in its wake.

The ship slowed enough for them to reach the rattling deck. They leaped, rolled, and piled inside. Gasping, Kanthe clambered farther into the hold. He glanced back as the *Sparrowhawk* climbed. He remembered leaping off that same deck. It seemed another age, another prince.

He reached the deeper shadows.

A large furry shape stalked around them, panting, its tail slashing in agitation. He searched around the vargr with a frown, noting who was missing from the beast's side.

Where's Graylin?

"HOLD TIGHT!" DARANT shouted from behind his daughter.

Graylin gripped the hanging leather loop with both hands. Through the small bow window, he watched the warship's balloon filling the world ahead. Then Glace punched both pedals and hauled on her wheel. The nose of the sailraft lifted, and flashburn flames burst from behind the open stern. The craft blasted skyward, using every last bit of fuel in its forges. The raft flew up along the rise of the balloon.

The mists below offered no refuge, especially with the bulk of the damaged warship being dragged through those clouds.

That wasn't their plan anyway.

A few stray spears were shot at them, but they fell far short. By the time the hunterskiff had chased them out of the mists, the sailraft was already high above the warship's boat.

"Get ready!" Darant called back.

The raft's forges coughed and died. The flames sputtered beyond the stern. The craft arced high, evened its flight, then glided forward on momentum alone. The massive balloon passed below them. Their keel nearly scraped the gasbag.

Darant rushed back and unhooked the cask of the small firebomb from the wall where it hung. Graylin grabbed the other.

"Nearly there!" Glace shouted from her seat.

Graylin turned to the open stern. Their plan did not involve tossing these last firebombs down at the warship's gasbag. Such an attempt would do no more damage than a couple of fiery pinpricks.

Instead, Graylin hauled the dangerous cask—already strapped in a net—over his shoulder. Darant did the same with his.

"Here we go!" Glace called to them as she rolled out of her seat. She kissed her palm and slapped the wheel, then ran toward them.

The sailraft drifted to starboard, heading toward a slide down the flank of the balloon. Glace joined them at the stern door. The air remained hot out the back. Below the open door, the draft-iron rudder glowed from its recent firing.

Graylin looked past those cooling forges to the sweep of balloon under them. As the sailraft drifted, its keel scraped through shreds of flapping fabric. A huge rip in the balloon opened up below them. It was one of the sections blasted by Darant's earlier attack. The inner skeleton of the balloon was exposed. The inside was ribbed by broken scaffolding and festooned with tangled riggings.

Darant pointed down and to the left, to where the outermost fabric of the ruptured balloon remained intact and taut. It formed a long, scooping chute into the shadowy depths. The sailraft carried them over it.

Graylin turned to Darant. "You've done this before?"

The pirate smiled, revealing the lie. "There's a first time for everything."

Darant drew the strapped cask around to his chest and hugged it with both arms—then leaped out of the stern. He dropped feetfirst through the hole in the balloon and struck the top of the fabric chute. He bounced to his rear and slid away, laughter trailing behind him.

Glace followed with a whoop, her eyes shining brightly.

They're both as mad as witches on henbane.

Still, Graylin gripped the door's edge, hauled his own cask around in a one-armed hug, and jumped. With the sailraft's keel dragging across the top of the balloon, the drop was barely higher than the roof of his cabin back in the Rimewood. Still, his boots hit the slick rubberized oilskin and took his legs out from under him. He sprawled on his back and slid down the steep chute into the depths of the balloon.

Ropes and rigging swept past him. He skated under thin bridges of walkways and spans of inner supports. The lower depths were thick with shadows. He cringed, expecting to strike some obstruction and be thrown high, but the steepness leveled out near the balloon's bottom. Sunlight from above allowed him to spot Darant helping Glace up. They stood unsteadily on the springy, taut base of the balloon.

Graylin slid up to them.

Darant smiled and pulled him to his feet. "Can't believe that worked."

Graylin agreed, slightly dizzy from it all.

They had come up with this plan back on the *Sparrowhawk*. While the hunterskiff might have believed it had chased them into the warship, the huge ship had been their intended target all along. Graylin could not risk this massive beast hauling reinforcements to the cliffs.

Muffled shouts suddenly erupted outside the balloon. Cannons fired with sharp blasts, accompanied by thrumming twangs of ballista. Graylin shared a look with Darant. They knew what was being targeted. He pictured the death spiral of the sailraft past the starboard flank of the warship. Glace had sent it purposefully down that side to draw attention and hopefully convince those aboard that the threat had been destroyed.

"Over here," Glace whispered, and drew them forward.

They reached a corner of the balloon. Through the sun-brightened fabric, a shadow loomed beyond it.

Glace glanced back to them. "That has to be one of the draft-iron cables."

"Only one way to find out." Darant pulled out a dagger. He shifted in front of his daughter and stabbed into the tough fabric. It took three strikes to pierce it.

Darant peeked through the puncture, then nodded approvingly at his daughter. He then set about carving out a squarish hole, one large enough for them to pass through.

Once done, Graylin inspected his handiwork. A draft-iron cable crossed past the opening, just out of arm's reach, but close enough. Graylin peered below. If he was properly oriented, this cable should run down to the stern quarterdeck. *Not that I can see it.* The boat under the balloon still dragged through the mists, masking what lay below.

Darant waved to Graylin. "We went first last time."

Graylin scowled, secured his small cask, and jumped across the short space. He latched his arms and legs around the cable and slid down its length. He whisked into the mists and only spotted the deck at the last moment. He hit it hard, wincing at the bang of his landing. He kept low and dashed to the side. His eyes fought to adjust to the foggy gloom.

Still, no one seemed to be back here. Hopefully attention remained focused on the starboard side, where the sailraft had been demolished. Darant and Glace quickly joined him, landing far more deftly than him—but then again, they were both raiders of many ships.

Voices echoed through the mists, rising from the middeck. Fiery pools marked lamps down below.

Graylin pointed to the quarterdeck's forward rail. They needed to climb down to the middeck and reach one of the hatches that led into the ship. With nods from the other two, Graylin led them to a narrow set of stairs and descended swiftly.

As he reached the middeck, he waved Darant and Glace toward a double set of doors into the ship. He kept low, guarding the others. Voices called through the mists. Shadows shifted out there.

Darant got the door open with a creak of hinges.

As a former knight, Graylin knew the layout of such warships and had sketched a rough map for the pirate, in case they got separated.

It was a good precaution.

A shout of alarm rose ahead of him. It spread to others. It seemed the legion here had adjusted to the fog far better than Graylin. A shape suddenly loomed before him, marking a giant Monger. Smaller shadows closed in on either side.

Graylin turned and shoved his cask at Glace. "Go. I'll lead the others away."

Darant didn't hesitate and took off into the ship with his daughter. Praying the two hadn't been spotted, Graylin dodged to the left and sprinted low across the middeck.

Boots pounded after him.

Then a thunderous clatter of hooves rose in front of him.

No . . .

Out of the mists, a huge black steed charged across his path, blocking him. Knights closed behind him, carrying torches and lamps, brightening the pool at the center of the deck. The rider dropped from his tall saddle, landed hard, and stalked forward.

Of course, the liege general had been drawn topside by the demise of the sailraft. The man had always been hands-on when it came to skirmishes.

Haddan drew closer. Not even the mists could hide the man's scowl. "Welcome back to my ship." He pulled his sword. "Now where did we leave off from your last visit?"

SEVENTEEN

A STORM ON THE SHROUDS

What be death, but the breffest of farewells. Onli in one's heart does memory transmute such partings into an eternity of payne or into the most precious of treasures. So, I wyssh you all the richest of lyfes.

—From the peroration of Sigyl the Blind,
often inscribed on gravestones

58

FROM THE THRESHOLD of the copper door, Nyx gaped at the dark spectacle that spread across the breadth of Dalalæða. They were all gathered under the tall set of crossed arches, even the Kethra'kai and Aamon.

Overhead, the skies raged against the trespass above. Lightning split the darkness in a continual storm. Bolts lanced from the crystal-tipped pillars and spattered across the underbelly of a huge ship that had breached the black clouds. The thick keel bore the brunt of the attack but appeared to resist the fire in those bolts.

From a multitude of holds in the ship, a flurry of small crafts jettisoned out, bursting forth with a billow of gasbags. Flashburn forges flamed the skies in all directions. The energetic verve in the air was laced with burning oil and smoke from all those ships, over a dozen. Hunterskiffs, sailrafts, and arrow-like ketches.

Several had already landed. The ships guarded the four gates out to the jungle, unloading legions in shining armor. Elsewhere, a few crafts burned in splintered ruins atop the stone plaza, struck by lightning during their descent.

"We're too late," Rhaif said. "There's no way we can break through that blockade."

Nyx glanced around. Their group, including the Kethra'kai and Xan, only numbered nine. Aamon brushed her flank, reminding her there was a tenth member. As she watched, more ships drew to hard stops atop the plaza, fluming fire and smoke under their small keels. One of the two-manned ketches shot low over the crossed arches, clearly scouting the ground below.

"We have to attempt it," Frell warned. "We have no choice. If we can break through to the jungle, we might have a chance of escaping."

Still, even he didn't sound convinced of his own plan.

Another did. "I will forge us a path," Shiya said.

She left the shelter of the doorway and stalked out across the plaza. She lifted an arm as if calling over to the enemy—but it wasn't the king's forces she was summoning. One of the crystal-tipped pillars blasted a bolt her way. She caught its fire in her hand and cast it at a sailraft sweeping nearby.

Its gasbag exploded with a whoosh of flame. The blast drove the raft into a steep dive and into a shattering crash, leaving a fiery trail across the rock.

The shock of her miraculous attack kept everyone frozen in place.

"Go!" Frell finally said. "Keep with her."

They all rushed out.

As they fled, Xan started singing, drawing the voices of the other Ke-thra'kai. Amidst the roaring of countless forges, Nyx still heard them clearly. The strands of their song wound outward, like the tendrils of a sprouting seed. Those threads rose higher and higher into the sky.

Nyx drew herself into their melody—if only to hold back her terror.

She didn't understand Xan's intent, but she added her strength.

Ahead, Shiya captured another bolt and flung it toward a hunterskiff that had landed. She missed the craft, proving even a living sculpture could not entirely master wild lightning. Still, the strike hit the stone near the men and sent them scattering. Her bronze form blazed in the gloom like a torch.

But that was not all that glowed.

Overhead, the silver-gold strands of Xan's chorus both rose higher and twined together, forming a shining trunk. Branches spread outward, bursting with clusters of finer filaments that wove into golden leaves.

Wonder nearly overwhelmed her terror as she gaped at the giant alder glowing and growing above them. It was as if the spirit of the Oldenmast had come to protect them under its bower.

But this shining tree offered more than shelter.

It was a flag, a rallying call.

Beyond the wall, the jungle awoke, stirred by this glorious symbol of bridle-song shining in the plaza. The forest screamed its savagery and howled at the trespass here. Through all the gates, the hostile heart of the dark jungle burst into the plaza. Poisoned fangs and ripping claws tore into the legions gathered at the thresholds. The air around them filled with painful stings and bullying bites.

Screams and cries echoed across the stone.

As the forces fled from the gates, Nyx began to hope. She should have known better.

A flurry of arrows, many flaming, streaked the skies, rising from a clutch of archers to the right. Shiya tried to sweep the threat away with a bolt of lightning, but the numbers were too many. Death rained toward them.

As Nyx stared, she was knocked down from behind. She hit the stone hard. Her skull rang with the impact, dazing her. A weight pinned her in place, a paw on her shoulder and leg.

Aamon . . .

Arrows struck all around. Steel points sparked off of the black rock. Shafts shattered into splinters. Others ricocheted away.

As the volley ended, Nyx was released. To her right, two of the Kethra'kai women rolled to their sides, both their backs feathered with bolts. Between them, Xan lay on her back. The two women had done their best to shield the elder with their bodies, but an arrow had made it through their sacrifice.

A bolt pierced Xan's throat. Blood bubbled from her lips and throat, forever silencing her song. Still, she breathed. Rhaif rushed over to her side. Shiya's bronze form had done a far superior job of sheltering Rhaif and Frell. Still, the alchymist's face bled from a glancing strike.

Nyx turned to her own shield.

Aamon panted behind her. Arrows impaled his chest, shoulders, and flank. Darkness soaked through his fur and slowly dripped under him. She despaired for him, but he stood firm and kept watch all around.

Across the plaza, a deafening series of booms drew her attention outward. She turned in a stunned circle. Bombs rained from ships overhead, blasting at each gate. The forest hordes screamed and bellowed within the firestorm below.

Nyx covered her ears, wanting to close her eyes.

She sank to her knees next to Aamon, into a pool of his blood.

Everywhere she looked was only death.

RHAIF KNELT ON the cold stone and held Xan in his arms. The last two Kethra'kai guarded over them.

"Just hold on," he whispered to Xan.

She stared up at him with eyes of emerald and azure, all of Cloudreach in her gaze. Blood seeped from her lips, which impossibly smiled at him. He saw no pain as the arrow throbbed in rhythm with her heart.

She reached a trembling arm and palmed his cheek. His mother's lullaby again rose inside him, but he knew this song was not his alone, not just a mother to a child. It was a grandmother consoling a granddaughter, a father teaching a son. It was a thousand generations of one comforting another. Even now, Xan sought to do the same for him, to offer him solace, to let him know that one end was not the end of all.

He remembered his horror at Shiya's plan. She wanted to destroy the Crown and kill untold millions, all so this spark might survive and carry on, from one generation to the next.

In this moment, he almost understood it.

Rhaif leaned down and pressed his forehead to her cheek. "Xan . . . you will never be forgotten."

She managed a whisper that reached him. "My granddaughter . . . lives in you . . . through you. As do I . . . as do all the Kethra'kai. Do not forget that."

He managed a small smile.

Even now, she still sought to teach him.

The lullaby inside him rose louder, ringing with notes both happy and sad—then it slowly faded. Her palm slipped from his cheek. He straightened to see Xan's body slump into peace.

Hands drew him away. Another shifted the body.

The last two Kethra'kai had their own good-byes to make. Rhaif let them, standing back. They took his place, kneeling, singing over her body, keeping vigil.

Rhaif stared at the legions closing upon them from all directions. Knights and Mongers, archers and pikemen. The rain of fire continued to flow down from the ships. Smoke rolled everywhere. The jungle cried out in agony.

Ahead of him, Shiya blazed before all of it, a fiery bronze torch against the darkness.

He headed toward her beacon.

Frell stood a short distance away, balanced between Shiya and a small girl on her knees next to a blood-soaked champion. The alchymist seemed lost, his face smeared with crimson.

Shiya lifted her arm, ready to summon fire to her.

Then a small arrow-shaped ship—a scout-ketch—sped past overhead. Something tumbled from its underside. Then another and another. All falling toward Shiya.

No . . .

He ran for her, a shout of warning on his lips.

Then the small casks of alchymical fire burst around Shiya, blasting her forward. Frell caught an edge of it, too, and was thrown to the side. A hot wall struck Rhaif and tossed him backward, lifting him off his feet. He hit and rolled, tumbling through smoke and air too fiery to breathe.

Finally, he stopped and stared toward where Shiya had been standing.

Only flames remained.

SPRAWLED ACROSS STONE, Nyx fought to an elbow, then a knee. She rolled around and stared all about her. The world was smoke, lit by pools of flames. Still, the fires weren't enough to pierce the thick pall. Her lungs burned. Her eyes watered. Fiery embers spun in whirls and gusts.

She searched around, partly deafened by the blasts.

Then something nudged her from behind. She startled away, only to have a cold nose touch her palm. She turned as Aamon sidled next to her, panting, nearly gasping now. He came next to her, offering his shoulder. She leaned on him. He swung his head and bumped her thighs, then faced forward, as if to say: *This way . . .*

He guided her through the smoke, skirting the fires, sticking to the thicker pall to keep them hidden for as long as possible. But it could not shelter them forever.

As they continued, the smoke cleared around them. The air felt frigid after so much heat. She shivered, so did Aamon, but not from the chill. He clearly weakened with each step, but kept on, obeying his grizzled brother's last command.

Protect.

With this thought, she sensed something sweeping through the air, coming closer, as if drawn to her. It felt like a storm building over the horizon. She hoped it was the *Sparrowhawk*—but she sensed a danger in that storm, one of grim power, trained on her.

She stared up.

What is coming?

WRYTH CIRCLED IN a sailraft above the fiery carnage across the black plaza of Dalalæða. He still clutched Skerren's orb, but he no longer needed its guidance.

He had watched a scout-ketch unload a fiery storm atop the bronze figure. She had been blasted far, torn from her allies. Smoke now covered the view. He waited for it to dissipate. Despite his desire for the artifact, he didn't fault that barrage upon her. He had watched her commanding this henge, drawing lightning to her like an iron rod, and tossing it back upon her enemies.

He had never imagined such a fearsome weapon.

His lust for her grew—along with his caution. Upon Wryth's order, the sailraft's drover kept his boat high and away. They were all fearful of one of those bolts striking the craft.

Through the raft's tiny windows, he searched the fire and smoke below.

Movement drew his eye, to a path stirring through the pall, like a finger across black water. The smoke parted enough to reveal a blazing bronze figure, looking no worse, at least from this height. From the darkness at her feet, she pulled forth two dazed figures, two men. They all looked around, lost and wrecked in those smoky seas. But they searched for something—or *someone.*

Bony fingers clasped Wryth's arm. A hand pointed in the opposite direction.

He turned and squinted. He saw two figures stumbling together, looking nearly like one. It was a large wolf or dog, accompanied by a small girl.

Vythaas drew closer, whispering in Wryth's ear, raising gooseflesh. *"Vyk dyre Rha . . ."*

Wryth stared harder. He could not imagine how that frail, staggering form could be the future vessel for the dark majesty of the Klashean god, the infamous Shadow Queen.

Still, Vythaas knew far more about this prophecy than anyone, so Wryth had to trust the withered Shrive in this matter. Moreover, despite appearances, the girl *had* fought her way all the way here to Dalalæða's dark henge, while somehow also collecting the ancient weapon along the way. If Vythaas was correct about her, she had to be stopped now, before she came into her full power.

Wryth glanced again to the blazing bronze torch. The shining woman remained dangerous and formidable. He still feared approaching too closely. For now, he would leave it to Brask's forces to grind her down, to drain and deplete her, to hopefully bring her low.

Then I'll collect her.

In the meantime . . .

Wryth touched the drover's shoulder and pointed to the two figures stumbling across the stone. "Drop us hard in front of them."

NYX AGAIN FELT the pressure in her ears as something came for her, that dark storm driving at her. She trembled in fear, sensing the menace and fury. She gave up searching the skies for it and glanced around.

Behind her, she spotted a fire far more golden shining in the smoke.

Shiya . . .

Nyx wobbled as she tried to turn. "Aamon, we're going the wrong way."

The vargr continued his path forward. Maybe it was the only way he could go. His legs quaked under him. Her palm on his shoulder lay soaked in his hot blood. He fought onward, nearly dragging himself. She didn't understand his goal, if he had one. Maybe just to draw her farther and farther from the smoke and flame.

Still, with each pained step, he seemed to be drawing her closer to that dark storm in the air. It no longer felt beyond the horizon, but sweeping toward her, coming straight at her.

Suddenly, the world roared in front of her. She ducked and gasped. Flashburn flames raged ahead of her, slowing a sailraft that dropped out of the skies like a falling boulder.

She stumbled back, tripped over her tired legs, and fell to her knees.

The sailraft blasted to the plaza, wreathed in smoke and smolder.

Aamon rounded in front of her, still ready to protect her. But he could not hold himself up anymore. His legs gave a final shake, and he dropped heavily before her, creating a wall of bloody fur between her and the fiery craft.

Ahead, the stern door of the raft crashed open. Two Mongers stalked out of the hold, unfolding their giant frames to exit. They carried hammers, but rather than approaching, the pair moved to either side.

Between them, two Shriven climbed out. One she did not recognize, but she suspected was the Iflelen Wryth. The other—all bone and sagging flesh—had to be the one Kanthe had described, the Shrive who had come to the Cloistery with the king's legion. Kanthe had said his name was Vythaas.

The pair did not approach farther than the end of the ramp. Maybe they were leery of the growling vargr. Even wounded, Aamon was dangerous.

Her hands reached to his fur, feeling the tremble of his threat.

The Shriven then parted, allowing two more figures to leadenly stalk forward. They moved stiffly, as if risen from the dead. They dragged iron pikes behind them. Each wore skullcaps of steel, like those worn by the scythers.

As they neared the Shriven, a smaller copper box—held in Vythaas's hand—glowed brighter, humming with a noise that ate at her ears, trying to worm into her skull.

She ignored it, too shocked by who had arrived.

Their features were slack and dull; ropes of drool hung from their lips. Still she knew them. They were part of a life that seemed lived by another.

She whispered their names from that other life. "Ablen . . . Bastan . . ."

Vythaas lifted his copper box. He spoke a command to it, glowing it brighter with his breath. She could nearly see his words carried through the air on threads so corrupt and inimical that she shuddered.

She also heard that command.

"Kill them . . . kill them both."

Ablen and Bastan swung their pikes up and marched forward.

RHAIF DUCKED AS Shiya cast out another bolt of lightning, scattering knights away from them. She also watched the skies, ready in case another scout-ketch should draw too near. Two ships lay in smoldering ruins, adding to the thick smoke that both choked the air and kept them hidden.

While Shiya did most of the protecting, Rhaif and Frell added to the defense. If they spotted any archers in the distance or the streak of flaming arrows in the sky, they would shout out. With such warnings, the group would hopefully have time to cloak themselves in smoke to make harder targets or shelter under Shiya's bronze form.

Still, a question remained.

Frell asked it again. "Where's Nyx?"

Their group held off making a strike for one of the gates until they found her—not that such an escape would be likely either way. As proof, Rhaif watched one of the purple-faced mandrayks go bounding by through the smoke. It raced wildly, its tail on fire. It scribed a glowing path through the pall.

On all sides, the gates burned.

As Rhaif followed the mandrayk's trail, his eye was drawn to a sailraft in the distance. It smoldered under hot forges. He nearly looked away, thinking it was yet another shipment of the legion's forces. Then he spotted a furry mound nearby—and a small girl sheltering behind it.

Nyx...

"Frell!" Rhaif shouted.

The alchymist ducked and winced, believing Rhaif was warning about another attack.

Rhaif drew abreast of the man and pointed. "That's Nyx over there."

Frell squinted and stiffened with recognition. He stepped forward. "We must get to her..."

Before the alchymist could move farther, a bronze hand grabbed his arm. "No," Shiya warned. Her lightning-hot grip smoldered on his sleeve. "I hear what is being sung over there. It is... *wrong*. No one must go there."

"But Nyx..." Frell stressed.

Shiya did not let him go. "No. She is lost to us."

NYX HID BEHIND Aamon as her two brothers stalked slowly forward with raised pikes. Though this pair looked like Ablen and Bastan, whatever approached now was not them. They might wear their faces and bodies, but those were not the brothers who had teased her mercilessly and who had loved her just as fervently.

She stared at the lengths of hard steel raised at her. Over her lifetime, she had watched them spear fish with similar weapons, able to strike at the merest flicker of silver in black water and draw out a flopping karp or a squirming eel. With stouter spears, they had hunted great armored krocs and had driven off grimwolves who harried their bullocks.

While what approached might look dull and dead-eyed, she suspected those lethal reflexes remained, all controlled by whatever sang to them from that copper box in Vythaas's hand.

The two Iflelen studied her brothers, staring with cold curiosity, as if testing what they had wrought. The pair could have sent the Gyn after Nyx and Aamon, but maybe they believed this death would pain her more. Maybe even get her to stay her hand.

She knew both to be true.

Even if I could, I have no heart left in me to kill my brothers. If they would die for me, can I do any less?

Still, she refused to simply bare her throat to the knife.

Her hands were still atop Aamon, who growled his challenge even as his life ebbed. She had tied herself to him, to his brother. She drew upon that bond.

I will be vargr.

She fought the only way she knew how. She drew a deep breath and sang to her brothers. She drew on their love, their friendship, trying to remind them who they were. Her eyelids drifted closed. She remembered them laughing, cajoling, taunting, snoring. She put all that into her lilt and rhythm.

Remember who you are.

She cast out tangles of song and reminiscences, brightening those strands with voice and heart. She tried to send them toward her brothers. But there was something foul in the air, frizzing any approach, a wind blowing against her. She shuddered from its corruption. It was a fever's heat, the stench of vomit, the boil of pus and rot. It fought the strands she cast.

Still, she did not give up. Her fingers clenched in Aamon's fur.

I am vargr.

She sang louder, pulled harder, straining all she could. Slowly her strands teased through the pestilent air until they could brush the steel. With a touch, she knew she was blocked. Still, for a breath, she caught a flash of agony, of drilling through bone, of fiery poison flowing into skulls.

She flinched from it but held strong to her song.

She tightened her throat and drew upon the strength of another brother. Though her fingers still felt the texture of Aamon's fur, she also remembered a curl of bark, the scent of tea.

A keening flowed into her song, drifting her eyes further closed. She sent those waves out with each note, testing the steel, searching for its lock. But again the corruption fought her. It wasn't only in the air, but also in the steel. She sensed there was no key she could use. It was too corrupt, too poisoned. She would never find a path through that fouled metal.

Worse, as she struggled, she caught the briefest glimpse past the steel. It was all shadows and poison. There was truly little left of her brothers in there. But for a fraction of a heartbeat, she saw the tiniest flame of them, drowned deep in the darkness.

Not all had been snuffed away.

This agonized her more than anything, knowing they were trapped.

Despairing, she let her song die, recognizing its uselessness against such vileness.

She opened her eyes.

Her two brothers reached her.

Aamon growled, struggling to stand.

She again felt that storm in the air, dark energies building in the skies. Something was nearly upon her, far more dangerous than anything here. She prayed it was just the *Sparrowhawk,* burning all its forges to reach here.

Still, she knew she was wrong.

Both her brothers stabbed their pikes at Aamon.

Nyx covered her face, knowing all was lost.

59

ATOP THE MIDDECK of the warship, Graylin stepped toward Haddan. They were surrounded by knights, trapped in mists lit by torches and lanterns. The liege general had his sword out.

Graylin slid his sword from its scabbard and raised his ancient family blade. Even in the mists, Heartsthorn shone brightly, inscribed with twining vines.

Haddan stepped away from the sweating flank of his black steed. He held a palm toward the knights gathered in the fog, making his intent clear. He wanted this kill for himself. Graylin's sword arm ached, from when Haddan had slammed a hammer against it ages ago, another lifetime ago.

Haddan eyed Graylin's blade. "I thought that was melted into slag." He shrugged. "No matter. I will see to it myself this time."

Graylin firmed his grip and his stance on the planks. He let Haddan come to him, waiting until their swords nearly touched. "Some steel can never be broken," he said in a cold, calm voice. "Not even by the hammer of a craven coward."

Haddan's lips fought against a sneer, trying not to react to Graylin's taunt. Still, the general's hand tightened on his sword. His hip shifted, giving too much away.

Graylin dodged left when Haddan came at him from the right. The general's sword plunged where Graylin no longer was. It was easy to parry that thrust and riposte back with a stab.

Still, Haddan was no firstyear. He sidestepped the blade, slid a leg back, and swept his sword low. Graylin barely twisted his sword around in time to block the blow, a strike that could've taken off his leg.

They both retreated.

Haddan cracked his neck. "You've been practicing, I see. Breaking yet another oath. To wield steel. Here on lands you swore never to set foot."

Graylin waved his free hand at the mists. "Ah, but I'm not touching land, am I?"

Haddan scowled. "You were always one to seek excuses for your actions. Like bedding a whore that was forbidden to you and claiming it was love rather than lust. Then feigning a swooning adoration when her belly swelled."

Graylin growled and lunged swiftly. Haddan easily counter-parried, nearly trapping Heartsthorn with his blade. Graylin redoubled with a twist of his wrist to free himself and his sword. He feinted quickly to the right. Haddan fell for his ploy, allowing Graylin to slice high. Still, his blade only nicked a cheek.

They disengaged. Blood ran down Haddan's face, but the general ignored it. It would be just one more scar among his many.

"It's why your men despised you," Haddan said. "Your feigned nobility and honor. Couching all your slights in pretty words. You, who had the king's ear, yet found no time to better anyone but yourself."

Graylin studied the man's fury, but also heard his words. Graylin knew Haddan was not entirely wrong. In truth, few of his fellow knights had ever counted Graylin as a friend, let alone a boon companion. It took Marayn to begin to show him his truest self, to teach him how to be a better man, someone less selfish, someone capable of being loved, of truly loving another.

He licked a lip and faced the anger in the man.

Did I create my own enemy here?

Haddan sneered. "Yet, with all the king's love, you still betrayed that friendship."

Graylin sensed *here* was the source of Haddan's loathing and scorn for him. "So, is it jealousy then? Did you wish you could bed Marayn—or was it the king's love you lusted for your own?"

Haddan bellowed at the insult, the insinuation, maybe the truth. He came hard at Graylin, chaining an attack of feints, remises, thrusts, and swipes. Graylin fought against the storm, fearing he had pushed the man too far.

A sting sliced across the meat of his shoulder, cutting deep.

He smacked the blade aside and withdrew.

Haddan's cheeks were dark, his eyes shadowed, narrowed with fury. Still, Graylin read the calculation shining there. He feared the general had only been sizing him up, testing his skill, devising an unassailable strategy.

Fortunately, Haddan took too long.

A door crashed open behind them. "Graylin! Now!"

Eyes turned to the stern quarterdeck. Darant and Glace flew out, skidding across the planks. They cranked their arms back, fuses sparking between their fingers. They threw their explosive charges high—not toward the middeck, but over the starboard rail. The blasts burst into balls of flames out in the mists.

Crewmen retreated warily.

Graylin lunged toward the flames, sheathing his sword in mid-run.

Haddan howled, clearly suspecting what was coming. Surely, by now, he realized the true feint here was not with any *sword*—but with a *sailraft*, a boat sent plunging along the starboard side, intended to draw fire and empty ballista and cannons along that flank.

All to open safe passage for another craft.

A great grinding of wood sounded from that direction. More of the crew fled from the threat. A large shadow shot upward from the mists with a roar of flashburn forges, first a balloon, then the hull of a swyftship.

The *Sparrowhawk* rose until its deck was even with this one, still scraping the flank of the warship. Darant and Glace ran toward the rail. Graylin fled in step with them.

All three swept through the emptied ballista.

A few arrows and crossbow bolts chased them. But the shuddering and shaking of the deck threw off any firm aim. Graylin leaped to the top of the rail, bounded off of it. He remembered the last time he had done this. But now there was no ladder to grab. Instead, he hit the top deck of the *Sparrow-hawk,* rolled, and slid across the planks.

Darant and Glace followed. They kept their feet as they landed in unison, proving this was not the first time they had leaped from one ship to another. Still, as the *Sparrowhawk* rolled away, banging against the side of the warship with a parting kiss, they finally sprawled to the planks, too.

Once clear, the swyftship roared away, all forges burning.

"Grab something!" Darant hollered.

Graylin crawled over to the stanchion of a cable and hugged it, knowing what was coming. He heard two sharp blasts echo across the skies. He pictured the two casks of combustibles carried over to the warship. He held even tighter, knowing where those small barrels had been planted.

Under the warship's Hadyss Cauldron.

The next explosion broke the sky, birthed a new sun, one brighter than the Father Above. The concussion struck the *Sparrowhawk* and spun it full around through the air, tipping the boat nearly vertical.

Graylin clutched his stanchion. He caught glimpses of the thick pall of smoke, the spread of flaming wreckage, the smoldering shreds of the balloon. It all hung in the sky, then began to rain down into the mists.

The *Sparrowhawk* settled into a rocking flight, eventually evening out.

Graylin gained his feet. Darant and Glace strode past him. The pirate brushed at his breeches and half-cloak, as if unfazed by any of it.

Darant glanced back to him. "Are you coming?"

Graylin followed on unsteady legs, his shoulder soaked in blood. They crossed to the door into the quarterdeck and down a steep stair in the ship's forecastle. Darant's other daughter, Brayl, stood behind the wheel.

The pirate scowled at the woman. "What was with all that scraping and grinding back there? Before I left, I told you I didn't want a scratch on the old bird when I got back."

Still, despite his scolding, he scooped his daughter high and swung her around.

"Good job, lass," Darant whispered.

Graylin turned around as more people piled into the forecastle. He recognized Prince Kanthe and the journeyman from the Cloistery. Then came two strangers, a Guld'guhlian woman and a Klashean. He searched the group, noting the bloody wraps around Kanthe's chest and thigh, but also noting who was missing.

"Where's Nyx?" he asked.

Kanthe's eyes were wild. He pointed to Brayl. "I tried to get her to listen."

Graylin's heart stuttered, fearing the worst. "Where is she?"

Kanthe swung his arm at the bow windows with a wince. He pointed toward the distant cliffs, toward where the dark balloon of another warship loomed up top.

"She's in the Shrouds."

60

Nyx cringed at the thunderous explosion to the west. It sounded like the end of the world, as if the moon had already struck the Urth.

The blast froze the entire fiery tableaux of the battle across Dalalæða. Even Ablen and Bastan had halted the plunge of their pikes at Aamon's body. The points of their spears hovered over the vargr's chest. Aamon growled and shifted back, not to escape the weapons but to better shield Nyx.

Ablen and Bastan straightened, looking confused, as if the blast had momentarily disturbed the air enough to break the connection. It did not last long. Behind them, Vythaas raised his copper box. The other Shrive—Wryth—frowned to the west, in the direction of the explosion.

Vythaas whispered into his device, glowing its filaments brighter.

Ablen and Bastan focused back on Nyx. Their pikes shifted higher, their eyes shining with the malignancy possessing them, controlling them. Again, she saw the vibration of corruption binding her brothers to Vythaas and his malevolent box. The threads coursing through the air were noxious, powered by agony and malice.

Nyx's song had died in her throat.

I cannot fight this evil.

But another rose to that challenge.

Overhead, the concussive wave of the explosion finally reached the Shrouds. The force struck the dark clouds, shredding them in places. Streaks of sunlight pierced around the flanks of the hovering warship.

Directly ahead, past the sailraft, a shadow swept down one of those bright rays. Its shape was lost in the brilliance. Nyx felt the power emanating from it. It was the dark storm she had sensed sweeping toward her.

It has come for me.

Then a savage cry broke from that storm and swept down across the plaza. Power became shape. A breadth of huge black wings. The giant bat dove toward the sailraft, toward those gathered below. It screeched its fury, a song of savagery and strength.

Like the blast a moment ago, the keening shattered the air and tore through those malignant threads. Ablen and Bastan stumbled back and swung their pikes wildly, as if searching for a threat. The copper box in Vythaas's hands grew brighter, fueled by the onslaught from above. The box became a small sun in his withered grip. The Shrive tried to drop it, but it exploded in his hand, stripping flesh and bone, leaving a stump spewing blood.

Vythaas stumbled away with a scream.

Bastan lashed out as the Shrive came too near. His pike impaled clean through the man's back. Still, Bastan seemed unaware of the strike. He thrashed his weapon, tossing the bony body about. Screams and blood flew. Arms thrashed, and legs kicked.

Wryth fled into the sailraft, yelling, "Take off!" He hollered back to the two Mongers, "Destroy them all!"

The two Gyn marched forward, hefting their hammers higher.

By now, the bat had reached them. It ignored the sailraft as the boat shot skyward. Instead, it swept down at one of the Mongers. It struck the giant's back with both claws, its talons piercing deep. With a batter of wings, it flipped high and tossed the body far.

The second Gyn bellowed and charged at Nyx and Aamon. It swung its hammer one-handed, sweeping low. Aamon lunged to protect her. The hammer struck the vargr in the hip and sent him rolling across the stone. Still, Aamon had lashed out at the last moment and snagged the Monger's ankle, toppling the huge foe as he was knocked away.

The giant crashed on his back and tried to get up, only to have a dark shadow crash atop him. Claws stabbed. The bat slashed its head down, ripping fangs across its prey's throat. Blood arced high and an iron-helmed head bounced across the stone.

The bat stayed perched. With wings wide and head low, it screeched its fury at the world.

Across the plaza, fires raged everywhere. Arrows flew. Firebombs burst into flames. Screams chased across the stone. She caught a glimpse of Shiya, blazing in the dark, casting lightning all about. Overhead, ships burst into flame and crashed.

In this relatively quiet corner, Nyx searched up and around, hoping to see more of the Mýr horde sweeping down to help with this battle. But the skies had closed up; the dark clouds sealed their cracks.

She recognized the truth.

It was only this *one* bat.

Far overhead, she spotted the sailraft fleeing upward, carrying Wryth away.

She turned to Ablen and Bastan. Unfettered, unguided, they ambled about. Drool flecked their lips. Bastan had already dropped his pike. Vythaas's body was still impaled but no longer moving. Ablen settled to his seat, staring down at his own spear, as if surprised to be holding it.

Bastan followed his example, dropping next to Ablen.

Their eyes remained dull. She remembered the tortured flames deep in the darkness. She knew how much of their brains had been burned out, leaving only these husks. Those flames of her brothers could never rise again to fill what had been taken from them. All they could do was scream in the dark, forever locked in pain and torture.

She gained her feet and tried to step toward them.

Ablen's fingers tightened on his pike in reflexive threat.

She stopped, unsure what to do, knowing she could not help them.

Then the bat lashed out a wing, sweeping its tip around. The razor-tipped edge sliced through their necks and sent them toppling backward. Their limbs stirred dully for a breath—then went slack. Blood spread damply around them, reflecting the fires and lightning.

Nyx fell back, horrified. The bat clambered around on its perch atop the Gyn to face her. Huge dark eyes glowed. Velvet ears stood tall. For a moment, her vision doubled: seeing both the bat and herself standing there. An image flared, too, of a borrowed knife slicing a tender throat, a mercy granted as much as it pained.

She glanced over to her brothers.

Here was the same . . .

Before she could make sense of it all, a scraping of claws on rock drew her attention around. Aamon struggled against the stone, his neck stretched, trying to return to her, but his hip had been shattered.

She ran to his side, both to stop his struggle and to be with him.

She fell to her knees next to him. She hovered her palms over his body, fearful to add to his agony. Aamon panted deeply, but he managed to shift enough to rest his head across her thighs. He settled heavily against her.

She placed a palm on his cheek.

He thumped a tail.

She stared past him at the fires of the plaza, the rolling smoke. The bat left its perch and stalked over to her and Aamon, knuckling on its wings. When it reached them, it folded and tucked its wings. She saw the bat was not as huge as she had thought. If she stood next to it, the crown of its head would not even reach her shoulder.

It sidled closer and lowered its nose to sniff at Aamon. The vargr lifted a lip, snarling, stating firmly: *She is mine.*

The bat did not argue. It crouched on its hindlegs, staring at her. The softest keening flowed from it, a mournful and sad melody, tinged with a note of regret, as if it were sorry it hadn't come sooner to save Aamon.

She found herself looking into those eyes, feeling something more there.

Her throat tightened, and unbidden her voice flowed into its song. It took no effort. The rhythm drew her with its familiarity, rising from her heart. She felt a curl of bark in her fingertips, the scent of tea in her nose. Then the taste of warm milk on her tongue.

She stared into those eyes and knew who stood there, who had returned to her.

"Bashaliia . . ."

The bat leaned closer. His soft nose lifted her chin and nestled its warmth near her throat. She flashed to the little bat cuddled in the sledge, the swamp humming and buzzing around them. Gramblebuck softly lowing as he waded in front of them.

She left her palm on Aamon's cheek, but she lifted her other hand and found an ear, the tender spot her little brother loved to have scratched. Her fingers easily found it as they sang together, both bowed over a champion with the stoutest heart.

She knew this was Bashaliia. She didn't know how. She remembered Shiya describing the gift given to the denizens of The Fist, a commonality that spanned flesh and time. All their minds and memories preserved for eternity.

She recalled her last moments with Bashaliia, crouched over her little brother's frail form in the forest. She had sung to him then, too, lifting him away before the sting of the cut.

She pictured those fiery eyes staring back at her during that moment.

She sensed the truth.

You took him, she thought. *You gave him a new body, gifted from another who was willing to step aside and let him return to me.*

She leaned back to search across the battlefield.

Flaming arrows arced across the dark skies.

Legions closed in from all sides.

Bashaliia had returned to her.

All so he could die at my side.

WRYTH LEANED OVER the drover of the sailraft. The screams of the bat still ached his ears. He had never felt such power. He pictured Vythaas's box flaring so brightly it stung—then the explosion, the blast of copper, flesh, and bone.

He searched below and caught a glimpse of the huge bat, now crouched next to the girl. Vythaas's words rasped in his skull.

Vyk dyre Rha . . .

He remembered the Klashean prophecy about the return of their dark god.

She who would be carried on wings of fire and destroy the world.

Wryth pictured that bat sweeping out of a sky fraught with lightning and fire. He had witnessed the bat tearing through the Gyn, even killing the girl's brothers. No doubt, here was a creature of merciless power.

He remembered his earlier doubts about Vythaas's claim. He cursed himself for his narrow-sightedness.

For the sake of the kingdom, I will not underestimate either beast or child again.

Still, such a fear might not ever be a problem. Knights closed upon her position, along with archers. Mongers stalked from the other side. At present, the girl was not possessed by the *Vyk dyre Rha.* One arrow could end that threat.

He searched across the breadth of the plaza and the battle ending below. Even the bronze weapon was fading, faltering, depleting. She cast her bolts with less strength, less control. She staggered in the smoke, trying to protect the two men with her. They appeared to be trying to reach the girl now, drawn by the arrival of the fearsome bat.

He doubted they had the strength to do so.

More ships dropped down from the warship, preparing to expand the legions below. It would soon be over.

The drover spoke next to him. "Our flashburn tanks are nearly emptied," he warned. "We should refresh them at the *Pywll* before heading back down."

Wryth craned up at the underbelly of the warship. It was an impregnable fortress, perhaps the best place to weather the last of this storm.

"Take us there."

The drover leaned over his wheel, and the flashburn forges roared louder. The raft sailed upward. Wryth started to turn away, when a blinding flash of light drew his gaze back out. He shielded his eyes against it.

A massive column of light blazed before them. It rose from the center of the henge and struck the keel of the *Pywll* at midship. There was no blast or thunder. The radiant column just shone there for a long breath—then winked out.

Wryth frowned, mystified by such strangeness. He peered down at its source, remembering a pair of crossed arches sheltering a block of white stone. They were gone. He squinted, his eyes still dazzled by the blinding flash. He blinked to try to make sense of what he saw. A hole delved deep into the plaza, perfectly circular and smooth-walled, as if a god had taken an awl and drilled into the henge, leaving not a speck of debris.

The drover cried out and rolled the raft sharply. Wryth grabbed his seatback and saw the man was staring up, not down. Wryth followed his horrified gaze.

The same hole had drilled through the clouds, through the center of *Pywll*. The warship was gutted in the middle. Bright sunlight shone through that hole, revealing the blue skies far above. Again, there was no debris. The hole had cut clean through the center of the ship.

Slowly, the stern and bow halves of the warship cracked away from the middle, shattering what little still connected them. The two halves ripped apart and plummeted together toward the dark plaza.

The drover fought his craft wildly, trying to get clear of their path.

"Go!" Wryth demanded. "Get us out of here."

"Where?" the man gasped, struggling with his controls.

"Havensfayre. Away from the Shrouds. Anywhere."

As they fled away, the world grumbled under them. The ground began to buck and quake, spreading outward from that infernal hole. Cracks skittered away from the pit, pouring with smoke.

The sailraft raced across the plaza. Directly behind them, the stern of the *Pywll* plummeted past, dragging cables and shreds of balloon. Clear of the wreckage, the raft angled upward and into the clouds.

Once it shot back into bright sunshine, Wryth finally exhaled and loosened his white-knuckled grip on the drover's seat.

Other ships popped through the clouds as more of the legion fled. Then something swept past their portside, heading the other way.

A swyftship with a scraped, raw hull.

It dove into the clouds.

Wryth narrowed his eyes. The drover saw it, too, and glanced back to him. Wryth pointed ahead, to where a heavy pall hung over the mists in the distance.

"Keep going," he ordered.

If anything survived that devastation, he would find a way to deal with it. Events here had taught him much. He would use that knowledge.

And turn it against them.

61

GRAYLIN HELD HIS breath as the *Sparrowhawk* plunged through the dark clouds over Dalalæða. He did not know what to expect, or what he'd find. He heard an ominous rumbling coming from below.

After learning that Nyx had climbed up into the Shrouds, Graylin had challenged Darant to prove how swiftly his hawk could fly. While racing toward the cliffs, Graylin had kept his eyes fixed to the tall balloon of the second warship. Then a spear of blinding light had torn through the ship, splitting it down the middle and sending the wreckage plummeting below. Once at the summit, smaller boats had shot into view and sped away. Ignoring them, Darant had fired his ship's forges and dove into the clouds.

As they descended through that dark pall, Graylin stood to the left of Darant. Kanthe had taken up a post on the pirate's other side, with Jace at his shoulder. All eyes stared below as the swyftship dropped out of the clouds into a landscape from Hadyss's worst nightmare.

No wonder everyone fled from here.

A dark expanse of stone spread below. Smoke masked much of it, lit by burning shipwrecks. The two halves of the warship had crashed, forming mountains of fiery ruin.

Graylin saw a large hole directly under them. The ground quaked steadily, breaking into jagged cracks that seemed to spread from that pit. More smoke churned from those fissures.

"Nothing could survive that . . ." Jace whispered.

"Take us lower," Darant ordered his daughters.

Graylin placed a palm on the pirate's shoulder, thanking him, knowing all he was risking.

Darant glanced over. There was none of his flippancy, only fear shining there.

Then Kanthe jerked straighter. He gasped and pointed off the starboard bow. "There! See that torch moving through the smoke and rubble."

Graylin crossed to the prince's side to see better. He followed where he pointed and made out what looked to be a suit of molten armor, striding across the landscape.

"Shiya . . ." Jace said.

Kanthe nodded.

The two had given Graylin a sketchy account of events after Nyx and the others had leaped from the *Sparrowhawk*. He hadn't placed much credence on a story of a living statue, but plainly he should have.

"Get lower," Kanthe pleaded breathlessly. "Follow her."

Darant nodded and spun his wheel to glide them in that direction, while his daughters deftly dropped the ship.

"Look." Jace pointed toward the bronze woman. The torch of her body now revealed four figures trailing her fiery path. "That's Frell and Rhaif. I think two of the Kethra'kai."

"Nyx?" Graylin asked, trusting their younger, sharper eyes.

Jace turned to him, his expression grim.

No.

Kanthe leaned until his nose was touching a window. "Shiya is taking them somewhere, rather than toward the nearest gate in those walls."

Graylin clenched a fist, praying and hoping.

BURIED IN SMOKE and heat, Nyx still knelt on the trembling stone with Aamon's head resting on her lap. He no longer panted, just breathed hard and heavy. She rubbed the base of his tufted ears.

She saw no reason to move, not after a blast of brilliant light broke the skies. She remembered the gonging bell from Shiya's chamber. Here was the ruin it foretold. The world was now fire, smoke, and shattering rock. She heard the screams of the dying. The ground continued to quake. But where she had come to rest, the immediate expanse of stone held for now.

So, she stayed.

She would not leave Aamon.

Bashaliia kept vigil with her. He crouched on his haunches, occasionally flapping one wing to clear the worst of the smoke. He settled closer and leaned against her, still surprisingly light for his size. He brushed her with his cheek.

His chest vibrated gently against her. Though he wasn't keening aloud, she felt the purr inside him. She closed her eyes and listened. *I remember this.* She had been warm under wings, a belly full of milk, nestled against velvet. He had purred then, too. She fell back to that time, enveloped in love both maternal and brotherly.

She heard the song in that purr and added her own, a hum of contentment and happiness. Golden tendrils, so fragile a gust could break them, flowed between them. But they were not the only ones listening. Aamon whined softly, asking to be drawn in. She stretched her strands to him, brushing against his wildness, his feral heart, but she also found the suckle of a nipple, the sweetness of a mother's milk, the batter of brothers and sisters, still blind to the world with tiny sealed eyes.

She drew them all together and felt no fear. They sang together, entwined deeper than bone and blood. There was no fire, no breaking stones, no suffocating smoke. Time passed, or didn't, she couldn't say.

Finally, Bashaliia stirred, the fragility of their song wisping away. Aamon growled faintly, but he was too weak to raise his head.

She searched for what had alarmed them.

Then to her left, the smoke brightened with approaching fire, heralded by thunder and shattering stone. She tightened, expecting the worst. Only the flame that approached grew golden, shimmering with hues of bronze.

She shifted, keeping a palm on Aamon's cheek.

Bashaliia sidled to guard her. His wings shouldered higher, spreading outward. She calmed him with a palm, with a whisper from her heart.

"It's all right," she said.

From the smoke, Shiya strode forth, blazing like a sculpted sun. She stared down at her, at the others, lingering on Bashaliia. "I heard you," Shiya simply said, "and came."

Behind her, Frell and Rhaif stumbled into view, covered in soot, bleeding from multiple cuts. Two Kethra'kai followed, their eyes haunted and lost. They all kept their distance from the dark sentinel shadowing Nyx.

Shiya craned her neck to the dark skies, which were beginning to tatter.

Nyx then heard what had drawn the bronze woman's attention.

The roar of forges.

She stared up as a ship rounded into view, wafting smoke. She feared it was the last of the legion, drawn here as inevitably as Shiya. Instead, as the ship's descent billowed away the smoke, she recognized the craft. She struggled for the reason behind this miracle.

The *Sparrowhawk* lowered to a hover. The stern door was already open. Shadowy figures bailed out and rushed forward. She spotted Kanthe and Jace. Graylin and Darant. Even Pratik and Llyra. A large furry shape bounded out and rounded past Graylin with hackles raised, growling menacingly.

Aamon chuffed a greeting to his brother.

The others skidded and stiffened as the full view of the site opened. Several swore. Weapons were drawn. All attention focused on one spot.

Nyx gently slipped Aamon's head from her lap. She stood, needing to ensure there were no mistakes. She stepped in front of the tall bat and lifted her arms, like protective wings.

"This is Bashaliia," she said.

Only a few expressions softened with her explanation.

Kanthe was the first to move closer. He raised an eyebrow and inspected her companion. Then he simply shrugged. "I have to say he's grown a bit."

Graylin edged closer as the ground shook. "Everyone aboard quickly."

Nyx stopped them. "Wait. Aamon. He's . . ." She stared at Graylin, not sure she had the words or the strength to tell him. "I won't leave him here."

Graylin circled the bat enough to see Aamon's sprawl, the blood soaking his fur, the twist of his legs. Still on his side, Aamon saw him, too. He pawed his front legs, as if trying to run to him.

Graylin rushed forward to stop his struggle. Anguish strangled his voice. "Aamon . . ."

Darant came up behind him. "We'll get him aboard. Don't you worry."

A blanket was used as a makeshift travois. As they hauled Aamon up and carried him toward the ship, Nyx kept close to one side, Graylin on the other.

Bashaliia followed, crabbing on his wings and hindlegs.

Darant looked skeptically back at the bat, but Nyx waved him onward. In moments, they all retreated into the dark hold. Bashaliia balked at the confinement and burst upward, clearly preferring his own wings.

Once everyone was aboard, the forges flared under the *Sparrowhawk*. The ship shot upward, leaving the final destruction of Dalalæða below. As if it had been waiting for them to depart, the ground shook violently, tearing apart the rest of the stone plaza. Walls broke and tumbled. Gates collapsed. Standing stones sank into the rock like foundering ships in a stormy sea.

Then the *Sparrowhawk* crested into the clouds, and a moment later, into bright sunshine. Nyx kept near the open stern door. She searched the skies, then saw a familiar black crescent glide into their wake and follow behind.

Satisfied, she turned to the two forms bent over the travois.

Graylin knelt next to his dying brother. Kalder sniffed, nosed, then slumped beside Aamon, pressing close against him. Nyx hung back, not sure if this was her place to intrude.

Graylin spotted her and lifted an arm, then dropped it, plainly not trusting himself to speak. Nyx edged over. She settled to her knees. They flanked Aamon's head. The vargr's tired eyes were closed. His breathing slowed.

"He . . . He was so . . . stupid," Graylin said.

She glanced over, shocked, but he was smiling sadly, tears shining.

"Trying to train him." He shook his head. "Kalder caught on quick. Aamon . . . he preferred to splash at trout in a stream, nose any crotch, chase after anything that bleated or squawked. He had an ongoing war with cricka'burrs in my cabin, searching nonstop for their chirping."

She tried to imagine this stout-hearted champion being so carefree. She closed her eyes, seeking that happy heart. She placed her hand on his furry crown. She started with a hum, soft, just a summer's warm glow. She layered in breezes through the woods, the rattle of leaves. She sang of dewy grasses, dappled streams. She let those strands sink through his bloody fur, past a pain nearly faded.

She lured him with birdsong and chirping cricka'burrs.

She felt him rise to her, casting out threads of winter woods and ice that broke branches. *That's your home, isn't it.* He answered with the warmth of a hearth, the absentminded scratch, the pride in a voice, even the scold. She saw a bed too small for all three. She tasted offal tossed from a kill, shared by all.

She understood his heart, what he was saying in the end.

This is my home, always my home.

She reached a hand and found hard fingers and a calloused palm.

Yes, here is your home.

As she held that hand, she sang deeper, drawing in one brother, then the other. Kalder whined, weaving in the raucous trail of the hunt, the wild run across sunlit meadows, the tussle of brothers. It came with the scent of frost in the morning, the call of a mate, the warmth of a den. Graylin softened next to her, maybe not hearing that song as clearly, but still sensing it. She twined them all together, letting them all share one another, to say farewell as best they could.

She knew this was why Aamon had held out through all the smoke and misery. To rejoin his pack, to savor its warmth one last time. Now that he was here . . .

She withdrew herself, letting these three brothers sing this most private of songs together. She waited and listened from afar. She heard Aamon's song slowly fade, drifting farther and farther away. It passed her briefly, nudging her gently. For a moment, she saw a tall forest, full of endless trails and misty distances.

Aamon glanced back once at that threshold—then turned and raced off into that last wilderness.

She sighed her farewell, knowing he was gone.

Graylin shook next to her.

Kalder moaned softly, mournfully.

Graylin draped over Aamon, gripping Kalder, too, as if trying to hold the pack together by sheer will. But no one had that much strength.

She touched Graylin's back. He reached an arm over to her. She drew nearer, to a man who might be her father. She let him pull her even closer.

62

THREE WEEKS AFTER arriving back in the Rimewood, Graylin trotted his pony across sunbaked sands toward the thundering waterfall that hid the pirate's lair. Kalder trotted alongside him, his tail flagging. The vargr growled at the nearby bustle of the ramshackle town nestled under the high cliffs.

The two of them had just returned from a three-day journey to the western heartwoods to bury Aamon. Graylin had picked the spot where he had first found a pair of scared, savage pups. He had thanked those cold, dark woods for lending him such a stalwart brother. After Aamon was buried, the forest had howled with the songs of the vargr. Kalder had answered it, even vanishing for a night.

Graylin stared down from his saddle at his brother. He had feared Kalder wouldn't return, but by morning, the vargr had slunk back to his campfire, his tongue lolling, his eyes gleaming with a shine of the wild forest. Graylin would've understood if Kalder had kept to his forest, but when his brother returned, Graylin had shaken with relief.

Thank you, brother. I could not lose you, too.

Graylin straightened in his saddle and cantered his pony toward the gap between the waterfall and the cliff. Behind him, he had passed Kanthe and Jace. The two had been sparring with one another in the sand, one with a sword, the other with an ax. Those two made for an odd pairing, an unlikely friendship, especially as there was clearly an ongoing competition for Nyx's attention, not that she gave either of them much satisfaction in that regard.

He glanced back.

Nyx stood at the edge of the river pool, staring up at a dark crescent circling high in the sky. The bat—Bashaliia—consumed most of her time, and he suspected a good chunk of her heart. The two young men would have a hard time competing with that.

Not that I've had much more success with her.

While an impasse had broken with Nyx, their relationship remained tentative and wary. He still caught flashes of anger toward him, some brittleness that had not yet softened, if it ever would.

Sighing, Graylin left such matters for now. He edged his pony behind the tumult of cascading water and into the warren of river tunnels and dry caves that spread far into these barbarous lands. Immediately behind the waterfall, a towering grotto climbed in ferny walls to a high black roof. He craned up at the scaffolding surrounding the bulk of the *Sparrowhawk* as it floated within the grotto. The cavernous space echoed with hammering, shouts, complaints, and the ring of smithies and the low grumble of forges and bellows.

Graylin edged around the chaos. He gaped at how much had changed, even during his short absence. The *Sparrowhawk* was undergoing repairs after its rough treatment in Hálendii, but it was also being overhauled and reconstructed for the journey ahead.

A loud bark drew his attention to the underside of the swyftship. "Graylin! You're back!"

Darant climbed out from where he was ducked under the ship's keel. The pirate wore boots, breeches, and a loose shirt with the sleeves ripped off. Soot and grease streaked the man's face and clothes; his hands were stained black with oil. Darant patted the *Sparrowhawk*'s prow and crossed over to him.

Graylin slid from his pony's saddle to greet him. "I see you've made progress."

"Aye." Darant glanced back, wiping a brow, leaving it more grimed. "We've been riveting rails along both sides of the hull, to support the new draft-iron tanks. We'll need all the flashburn reserves that my little hawk can carry. Both for her forges, and of course, to keep us from freezing our bollocks off."

Graylin nodded. The journey across the ice would be a treacherous one, but they all knew the necessity. Shiya had shown them the doom that lay ahead, using a crystal cube that trapped a glowing version of the world inside. He pictured that ruin even now.

Moonfall.

Darant stared over at Kalder. "So, things went well with my vargr?" he asked.

Graylin sighed. Despite all that had happened, the pirate had insisted on sticking to the deal struck with Symon. It felt like ages ago, but Darant had not forgotten. The pirate had kept his word, ferrying Graylin to Hálendii as planned. Though, in the end, Darant had done so much more.

Still, upon returning here, the pirate had demanded his original payment. *One of the vargr.*

Graylin glanced over to Kalder, who glared all around, his lips fixed in a threatening snarl at all the banging and commotion. Back when that deal had been struck, Graylin had insisted that he would decide *which* of his brothers he would forsake to the pirate. Then that choice had been stripped from him back at Dalalæða.

After landing and securing the *Sparrowhawk,* Darant had stood at this spot, hands on his hips, and pointed to the vargr he wanted.

"Yes," Graylin answered. "Everything went well. Your vargr is safely buried up in the heartwoods."

Darant had picked Aamon.

"Good." Darant stepped closer, hooked a grimed arm around Graylin's shoulder, and drew him toward the *Sparrowhawk*. "Let me show you the new talons I've added to this fine bird."

SWORD IN HAND, Kanthe backpedaled across the sand. Jace pursued him, deftly flipping his ax from one palm to the other.

They both sweated profusely, stripped to just breeches. The sand burned his feet, the sun blinded him, and his chest still ached from the healed sword cut. He wanted to blame all those reasons for why a journeyman from the Shields was besting a prince of the realm.

Kanthe finally conceded, throwing down his sword. "Enough! You've already disfigured one prince. Best you not make a matching pair of us." He placed a palm on his cheek. "This face is too darkly handsome to ruin."

Jace grinned, puffing hard. "Yes, you do love yourself so."

Kanthe crossed over and clasped Jace's forearm. "Well done." He squinted sourly across the bright sands. "Though at some point, we probably do need to find someone who knows how to wield an ax or sword to teach us what we should be doing."

"That's true." Jace rubbed his shoulder and nodded to the sword in the sand. "*You* can definitely use more training."

A shout drew their attention around, coming from the bustle of the town climbing the cliffs behind them. Two figures approached. Frell carried a sheaf of pages and a quill. Pratik hauled a stack of books in both arms.

Kanthe groaned. "Speaking of training . . ."

Frell nodded his head toward the waterfall, alerting Kanthe that it was time for his lessons. The two alchymists had set up a makeshift classroom behind the falls.

Kanthe picked up his sword, shook off the sand, and with a grumble followed his teachers.

Jace accompanied him. "Klashean is not that hard to learn. The grammar can be tricky, but it's not dissimilar to Gjoan."

Kanthe frowned at the journeyman. "You read too many books."

Jace shrugged. His face and manner grew more pensive. Both knew their time together was running short. Jace was headed to the ice with the others, but not Kanthe. He had his own path from here, one that led far into the Southern Klashe.

"Do you think you can find it?" Jace asked.

"Apparently, that's why I need to learn Klashean."

Jace gave him a sidelong grin. "Then we're certainly doomed."

Kanthe batted at his shoulder.

Still, his own mood darkened.

He pictured the blue dot on the map Shiya had revealed, marking the possible site of another Sleeper like her. She believed they might need such an ally in the time to come. Frell and Pratik had accepted that challenge, especially as the Chaaen also wanted to pursue an angle of research involving Klashean prophecies tied to an apocalypse, stories found in their most ancient books, written shortly after the end of the Forsaken Ages. Those tomes were secured at the Abyssal Codex, the librarie of the Dresh'ri, said to be buried under the gardens of the Imri-Ka.

To gain the emperor's cooperation to enter—and hopefully enlist an ally— another needed to accompany the two alchymists. Pratik could not return to the Klashean capital empty-handed. And he certainly could not bring Shiya. Which left only one other choice.

Kanthe sighed.

They needed someone who could intrigue an emperor, maybe sway him to their cause, someone who might serve as a pawn in a war between kingdom and empire.

In other words, they needed . . .

The Prince in the Cupboard.

RHAIF PACED AROUND the circular table in the center of the cavern. The blackoak surface was scarred and stained, clearly the site of many heated discussions among brigands, pirates, and rogues. Shortly, it would become the stout platform upon which the fate of the world would be balanced.

He stared at the platter of ripe cheeses, bowls of dewy berries, and steaming loaves as big as his head. There were also flagons of wine and a stack of small casks of ale.

At least we'll be well fed and can toast the doom to come.

He crossed around again to reach Shiya, who was already seated. She wore a hooded cloak, which helped hide her bronze. Though in this private space, she had the cowl thrown back. Her hair remained soft, stranding in hues of gold and copper. Her lips were perfect pillowed arches. The azure of her glassy eyes tracked his passage around and around the table.

"Rhaif . . ." Shiya whispered softly.

The rare use of his name flushed him warmly. He glanced away, embarrassed by his reaction. He remembered that moment when Xan had shown him how intimately he was tied to this bronze woman. But Rhaif knew it was more than bridle-song that bound him to her.

"Are . . . Are you ready for the gathering?" Rhaif stammered, glancing across the spread on the table. "They'll be here soon."

She acknowledged this by parting the front of her cloak, exposing her nakedness beneath. She placed her palm on the center of her chest. The bronze glowed brighter around her hand as she inhaled. As she exhaled, she lowered her palm, withdrawing a perfect cube of crystal from between her breasts.

Once done, she closed her cloak demurely and set the glass atop the table.

Rhaif pictured the other cube she had pushed into her body, near her navel, back at Dalalæða. It had been the same size as this one, only riven with copper and containing a globule of churning gold at its core. After that, she no longer seemed to suffer her earlier weaknesses, whether under clouds or in these caves. It was as if that cube continued to sustain her—which was a good thing. Considering where they were headed next—to lands frozen in perpetual darkness—she would need that tireless force.

Shiya still stared at him and perhaps sensed his consternation, though she mistook the reason. "You do not need to come with us."

Rhaif winced. She may have thought she was offering him a kindness, but instead she wounded him. He dropped to a knee and touched the back of her hand. "You know I must."

Does she feel nothing of the same? Is her heart forged of the same bronze?

Shiya rolled her hand under his. Warm fingers enclosed his hand. She turned the glow of her eyes upon him. Her lips parted with a whisper. "I know."

The door banged open behind them. Startled, he let go of Shiya's hand and jerked to his feet. Llyra marched in without invitation. Out in the tunnel, shadowy figures stirred.

"I'm leaving," she said sharply to him.

He stumbled around to her. "Already? You'll not be coming for the . . ." He waved at the spread atop the table.

Over the past weeks, their motley group—gathered from across the northern Crown—had slowly and somewhat warily grown into a makeshift alliance, united by blood, grief, and purpose, all centered on one word.

Moonfall.

Llyra eyed the table, as if reconsidering his offer to attend the meeting. Instead, she studied the spread and took what she wanted—like she always did. She grabbed one of the small casks of ale and tucked it under her arm. She scowled at the rest. "I have no interest in chattering and arguing. I know what I must do."

She glanced over to Shiya. Llyra's eyes shone with no avarice, not even for the block of crystal sitting on the table. The guildmaster of thieves had also witnessed the doom to come. In that moment, Rhaif had watched the greed fade out of her. Llyra was nothing if not practical. If he had any doubt, he just had to remember how she had sold him off to the mines in order to firm the guild's footing in Anvil. So, she certainly recognized that all the wealth in the world would not matter if the world was not here.

"Do you think they'll listen to you?" Rhaif asked.

Llyra frowned. "I wasn't planning on giving them any choice."

The guildmaster was headed out with a clutch of Darant's men, to rouse as many of her ilk to their cause, to forge a secret army spread through whorehouses, thieveries, low taverns, and dark dens. With the drums of war echoing across the Crown, their group might need an army of their own before long—along with a certain cropped-hair Guld'guhlian to command them.

Rhaif nodded. "I have no doubt you'll earn their—"

She crossed over, scooped the back of his head with her free hand, and pulled his mouth to hers. She kissed him hard, then maybe a bit tenderly in the end. She had never let him kiss her before—then again, she was the one doing all the kissing here. It was a heated reminder. If there was something she wanted, she took it.

She let him go, wiped her lips. Her eyes glinted with dark amusement. "Just wanted to prove to you, flesh can be tastier than bronze."

He swallowed, his cheeks red hot.

She swung toward the door. "Don't get yourself killed," she called back.

He appreciated her rare concern, but mistook it, forgetting who he was talking to.

"You have a magnificent cock," she finished. "I may want to use it again."

Rhaif blinked as she slammed the door behind her.

Well, for last words . . . those weren't bad.

NYX FELT THE press of time, not just for this meeting, but also for the world at large.

Still, she stood in the small cave far from the others. The floor was sand. A tiny spring-fed pool brightened a corner. Far overhead, an old collapse had opened the roof to the forest and sky above. The sunlight fueled a bounty of curl-leafed ferns and chains of climbing roses in blushes of pink. A few blooms had darker red petals, like sprays of blood.

She tried not to look at those.

Instead, she focused on the bright open skies, waiting. Then a shadow swept high and vanished. She held her breath. A moment later, the hole darkened with the passage of a large form. Black wings snapped wide once the bat was inside.

The wind buffeted her, carrying with it the scent of a gingery musk, laced with a touch of carrion. Bashaliia was long past feasting on gnats and meskers of the swamp. His larger body needed more sustenance. Gnawed bones were piled to one side of the cave—but no more than one might find in a vargr's den.

She could not fault him for his new hungers.

Bashaliia landed in the sand, beating his wings high, then tucked them.

She crossed to him.

He shifted on his legs, prancing a bit, as he would do when he was small. It was a reminder that despite his large size, he was still her little brother at heart. He keened to her in greeting, enveloping her in his song. As her sight flickered between their two sets of eyes, she sang back to him. She sensed his unease with this new place, maybe even with his new body.

We both have much to get used to.

Still, she knew what troubled him the most.

As it did her.

She reached him and opened her arms as much as her heart. Even song could not replace the reassurance of soft touches and shared warmth. He tucked his ears, snuffling her face, taking in her scent. A warm tongue tasted her salt. He settled against her, framing her and balancing on the knuckles of his wings.

She lifted both hands and scratched his ears, rubbing the tender velvet in her fingers. She sang to him, entwining their strands, sharing his finer senses. Again—as she had noted upon arriving here—she could barely sense that greater mind any longer. It was still out there, like a storm on the horizon, just a whisper of distant thunder, but those winds could no longer reach her. The storm was too far off.

Understanding pounded her heart.

Bashaliia was losing his connection to his tribe across the sea. Their reach—as mighty as it was—had limits, distances they could not stretch.

She felt Bashaliia's sense of loss.

Still, she had a greater fear. She considered where they would soon be headed. To icefields even farther away, on the other side of the world.

She knew what that meant. There would be no resurrecting him; his memories would not be preserved with his brethren.

If Bashaliia dies out there, he will be gone forever.

It was why she had come down here. She lifted his chin and stared into his eyes. *You must not follow.* While her heart quailed at the thought of being away from him, the possibility of losing him forever was too much to bear.

His eyes glowed back. He keened with sorrow, experiencing her fear and agony as much as she did his senses. Still, his strands wound tighter to her. He refused to leave her side, to abandon her again. She sought a way to convince him, to argue against his coming.

But another had had enough.

Up from within the dark well inside Bashaliia, a black wave struck out at them. Fiery eyes flashed from that shadowy darkness, clearly taking significant effort to reach this far. Still, the command was cold and resolute, veiled in threat.

No.

Then that enormity vanished from them both, leaving a hollowness that chilled. Bashaliia pressed closer. She knew she could not ask this of him again. Instead, she leaned over, touching and singing him calmer, until her heart settled, too.

Finally, the press of time squeezed them apart.

"I must go," she whispered.

After a final few touches of reassurance, she left and headed back through the series of tunnels. She moved leadenly, weighted down by her worries and fears. Still, before long, she reached the proper door and heard voices behind it. She was clearly very late. She took another breath, then opened the door and pushed into the warm chamber.

A stone hearth glowed in a corner. Atop a table in the center, a jumble of platters and mugs separated stacks of books and a spread of charts and maps. Everyone seemed to be talking at once.

Graylin was bent between Frell and Pratik. "When you reach the Klashe, seek out the Razen Rose. Something tells me that secretive order knows far more than they let on."

Graylin straightened as she entered and waved to an open chair, then returned to his conversation with the group due to depart to the south. Kanthe caught her eye and shrugged with a shake of his head.

From the neighboring seat, Jace shifted her chair back.

She crossed to it and sank down.

Her friend leaned closer. "You missed most of it," he said. "I think everyone's questions have been answered as best they could be."

She stared around the table, ignoring the cacophony. Shiya sat quietly across from her, with Rhaif on one side and Darant on the other. The two men leaned forward and spoke across Shiya's nose as if she weren't even there.

Nyx knew what that felt like.

Shiya's eyes glowed at her, unblinking. Nyx sensed there was a question the bronze woman was waiting for someone to ask. As Nyx stared back, she heard a faint song, of distant drums.

Shiya's crystal cube sat on the table, framed by her fingers. It glowed softly, while above it shimmered a tiny globe of the Urth. Small crimson and azure blips shone more brightly across its surface. Nyx knew the blue dot deep in the Southern Klashe was where Kanthe and the alchymists were due to head. Angst at the prince leaving spiked through her.

Their group had only recently been forged, but already it must break again. Still, she read the determination in each face. It united them all. While they might be separating in different directions, they all knew their ultimate goal, to stop what seemed unstoppable, to keep the moon from crashing out of the sky—which first required discovering a way to fire up the Urth's forges and set the world to turning once again.

Jace tried to say something more, but Nyx lifted a palm and waited. Slowly the room quieted. One by one, they noted her sitting silently, a hand raised.

"I have a question," Nyx finally said, and nodded to the cube, to the glowing globe of the Urth. She focused on the green marker shining deep in the ice on the dark side of the world. "Where exactly are we headed? Was there ever a name for this place?"

Shiya's eyes glowed brighter. She shifted higher and gave the smallest nod to Nyx. "Yes, it has an ancient name."

All eyes turned toward the bronze sculpture poised at the table.

Shiya continued, "From a language older than the Elder tongue. The name is meaningless, perhaps, but it roughly means *where the winged protectors gather.*"

Nyx pictured Bashaliia and the rest of the Mýr horde. Those winged guardians had looked upon the world for ages on end. Did that mean there were others out there like them?

Ever the scholar, Frell drew a sheet closer and lifted a quill in hand. "I'm curious. What is that name in this ancient tongue?" he asked.

Shiya looked across at Nyx, her eyes aglow.

"The City of Angels."

63

IN THE BOWELS of the Shrivenkeep, Wryth leaned over the shoulder of his fellow Iflelen brother. Skerren sat at a narrow table, its surface covered with rusted bits of arcana, twined copper, vials of caustic compounds, crucibles of both metal and stone, and items that defied Wryth's own considerable knowledge.

Skerren had summoned him here to reveal a discovery, something his brother believed was significant enough to interfere with Wryth's own schedule this morning.

Wryth glanced back into the depths of Skerren's personal scholarium. It stretched off into a maze of chambers, closets, and sealed rooms. Wryth recognized a tall stack of curved copper sheets leaning high against a back wall. They were part of the copper shell that had preserved the bronze artifact deep in Chalk's sunless tunnels. Skerren had spent the past two moons carefully dismantling and shipping it from the mines.

The laborers had been killed afterward. None could know what the Iflelen had discovered, what they hoped to learn from it. Wryth suspected Skerren's discovery came from that same collection.

"Show me," Wryth said.

Skerren reached to a leather cloth that hid something beneath. He slid the covering away, revealing a wonder that drew a gasp from Wryth. It was a perfect cube of crystal, veined through with copper threads. But what squeezed Wryth's breath was the mass of golden fluid at its core, pulsing and undulating.

"I found it in a hidden chamber behind the copper shell," Skerren explained.

"What is it?" Wryth came around for a closer look.

Skerren leaned possessively over it, his eyes narrowed. "I think it serves like a tiny flashburn forge. A source of unknown power. I've performed some tests with intriguing results."

"What tests?"

Skerren waved absently at the two halves of a glass sphere resting atop his table. It was all that was left of the instrument that Wryth had used to track the bronze artifact. The cracked orb had been drained of the clear oil, and its tiny copper-wrapped lodestones were meticulously lined up in a row.

Skerren explained, "I believe, with this tiny forge, I can build a more powerful version of the instrument that I gave you before. The new device should be capable of detecting emanations from the bronze artifact over a far greater distance."

Wryth breathed heavier, desire burning through him. He could barely speak. He did not know if anyone had escaped the ruins of Dalalæða, but he was plagued by the sight of a swyftship diving into the clouds as he fled.

With such a new tool, I might learn the truth.

"Do it," Wryth ordered. "Set aside all other inquiries except for this."

Skerren nodded and glanced back. "How goes your own labors?"

Wryth straightened, reminded of his schedule. "We are close," he answered. That was all he would admit. "I must be off. There is another who wishes to confirm my progress, and his temper is foul at best, even when he's not left waiting."

Wryth rushed off. He swept out of Skerren's scholarium and headed toward another, one belonging to a dead brother. Once he was close enough, torchlight revealed two figures waiting in the hallway by the door. Wryth's guest was accompanied by a tall Vyrllian Guard named Thoryn. The visitor stood stiff-backed. Torchlight reflected off his silvery armor. It was said he rarely removed it anymore, fearful of another attack.

Wryth closed the distance and lifted an arm. "Prince Mikaen, thank you for coming all the way down here."

The prince turned, revealing the silver mask covering half of his face. Its surface was inscribed with a sun and crown, the Massif family sigil. When the light struck it just right, that sun would blaze like the Father Above. Right now, it reflected the angry flame of the torch.

Wryth also knew what lay hidden behind the silver. He had seen it once, shortly after Mikaen's face had been stitched together. Or at least the little of his face that was still salvageable.

Mikaen grumbled, his voice still hoarse from all his pained screaming, "Show me why I came down here, so I can be gone from this wretched place."

Wryth slipped past the prince and keyed open the door to Vythaas's scholarium. "Do not draw too close," he warned, and entered first.

The iron-walled chamber was as hot as a furnace. Chains jangled and snapped. Mikaen and his guard came behind him. Both gasped at the sight ahead. With his back to them, Wryth simply smiled.

"How . . . ?" Thoryn asked, speaking out of turn.

Still, Wryth answered him, "Poison. It took more than you would imagine."

Mikaen stepped nearer. "Can you control it?"

"Soon," Wryth whispered longingly, unable to hide his raw desire.

Skerren's discovery might hold the promise to track any bronze artifacts, but Wryth now followed in the footsteps of Vythaas, the brother who rightly feared the Klashean *Vyk dyre Rha*. Wryth's labors were intended to purge that threat, to forge a weapon against her, to plant a seed of corruption in her very garden.

The chains thrashed and clanged in front of them.

He stared across at the large bat, with its wings wrapped in leather, its body subdued with steel—but what truly bound it was *copper*.

From its shaved skull, a score of bright needles stuck out, suffused with the alchymies extracted from Vythaas's journals.

Wryth stared silently at the creature. *Soon you will be mine.*

Dark eyes glared at him, challenging him. It opened its jaws and screamed savagely, madly, at the world.

Wryth smiled at that song, one of pure hatred.

Yes, that's a good place to start.

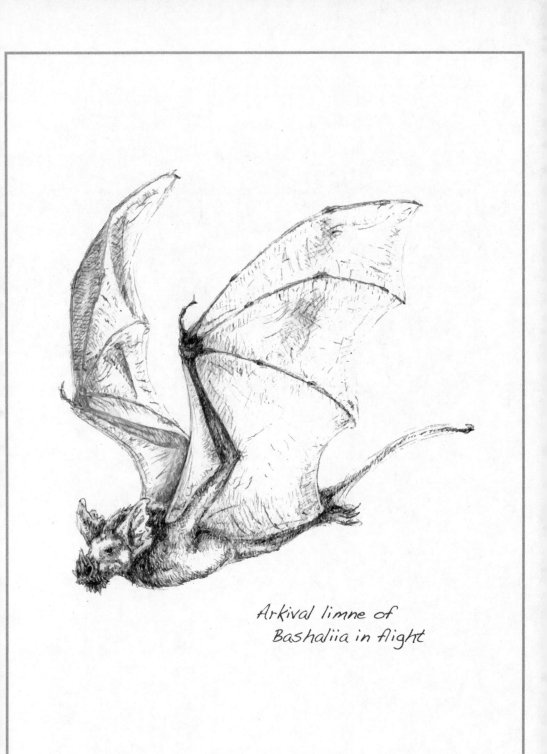

Arkival limne of
Bashaliia in flight

ACKNOWLEDGMENTS

It has been well over a decade since I last forged a path across a fantasy land-scape, so each step along this new journey has been tentative. Before starting this adventure, I looked for trail markers left behind by writers I had admired while growing up: Anne McCaffrey, Terry Brooks, Stephen R. Donaldson, Robert Jordan, Roger Zelazny, Gene Wolfe, Robin Hobb, Edgar Rice Burroughs, J. R. R. Tolkien, George R. R. Martin, and countless others. I also took note of the impressive new paths being created by authors today: Naomi Novik, Patrick Rothfuss, Brandon Sanderson, Brent Weeks, and N. K. Jemisin. I also leaned on the shoulders of a bevy of writers who have stood at my side for decades, who have traveled with me in the past to the lands of Alasea and Myrillia, and who helped me to polish this first entry into a new world: Chris Crowe, Lee Garrett, Matt Bishop, Matt Orr, Leonard Little, Judy Prey, Steve Prey, Caroline Williams, Sadie Davenport, Sally Ann Barnes, Denny Grayson, and Lisa Goldkuhl.

Of special acknowledgment, I must cast a sweeping bow of thanks to the cartographer who crafted this world's first map, Soraya Corcoran. Her work can be found at sorayacorcoran.com. And, of course, I can't sing the praises loud or long enough to encompass my appreciation for Danea Fidler, the artist who sketched the handsome creatures found throughout the pages of this book. To view more of her skill, do visit her site: daneafidler.com.

On the production side of this creation, I wanted to thank David Sylvian for all his hard work and dedication in the digital sphere.

Lastly and most importantly, none of this would have happened without an astounding team of industry professionals. To everyone at Tor Books—especially Fritz Foy and publisher extraordinaire, Devi Pillai, thank you for taking a chance at opening this new chapter in my career. Additionally, no book would shine as well without a skilled team behind its marketing and publicity, so I was blessed by the talents of Lucille Rettino, Eileen Lawrence, Stephanie Sarabian, Caroline Perny, Sarah Reidy, Renata Sweeney, and Michelle Foytek. And a big thanks to the team who made this book look its very best: Greg Collins, Peter Lutjen, Steven Bucsok, and Rafal Gibek. Of course, a special acknowledgment must go to the editor who held my feet to the fire and pushed me to bring this story into its best and fullest light—a HUGE thanks to William Hinton. Plus, to those who furthered his efforts—editorial assistant Oliver Dougherty, copy editor Sona Vogel, and two astute authenticity readers, Dominic Bradley and Elsa Sjunneson—a big thanks for all your painstaking work and expertise.

And as always, a big shout-out to my agents, Russ Galen and Danny Baror (along with his daughter Heather Baror). I wouldn't be the author I am today without such an enthusiastic set of cheerleaders and friends at my back.

Finally, I must stress that any and all errors of fact or detail in this book fall squarely on my own shoulders.

Turn the page for a sneak peek at
the next novel in James Rollins's Moon Fall series

THE
CRADLE
OF ICE

Available Winter 2023

1

NYX HELD HER HAND UP AGAINST THE BRILLIANT SWATH OF STARS. THE warmth of her breath misted the icy darkness, obscuring the view enough to make it look like some spellcast illusion. Alone atop the middeck of the *Sparrowhawk*, she gazed at the wonder above. She had never imagined such a radiant glittering existed beyond the sun's glare.

Then again, how could I have known?

As the wyndship continued its westward flight under the arch of the night's sky, she recognized how small her existence had been until recently. All her life had been spent within the Crown, where night was but a dimmer gloaming of the day. She pictured the bronze orrery in her old school's astronicum, where the sun was represented by a spherical kettle of hot coals around which tiny planets spun on wires and gears. She pictured the third orb—the Urth—driven by the orrery's complicated dance. As her world circled the sun, it never turned its face away. One side forever burned under the merciless blaze of the Father Above, while the other was forever forbidden His warmth, locked in eternal frozen darkness. The Crown lay between those extremes, the circlet of lands trapped between ice and fire, where the life-giving love of the Father Above nurtured those below.

And now we've left it all far behind.

She shifted her hand toward the reason for this perilous flight. With the cold numbing her bare fingers, she measured the full face of the moon, as bright as a lantern in these dark lands. She tried to judge if its countenance had swollen any larger, searching for evidence that her prophecy of moonfall could be true. She again heard the screams from her vision, felt the thunderous quake of the land—followed by the deafening silence of a world destroyed as the moon crashed into the Urth.

She could not tell if the moon's face had grown any bigger, but she did not doubt her poison-induced prophecy from half a year ago. Alchymist Frell had confirmed the same with his own measurements, in scopes far more precise than Nyx's fingers. According to him, the full moon had been growing incrementally larger, more so over the past decade. The bronze woman, Shiya, had even assigned a rough date to the world's end: *No longer than five years, maybe as short as three.*

Nyx felt the pressure of that narrowing timeline. It weighed like a cartload of stones sitting atop her chest. Even when resting, she often found it hard to breathe. Their group had spent the tail of summer and most of autumn in preparation for this journey into the dark frozen wastes. They dared not rush their efforts, especially when so little was known about these icy lands. And now with the winter solstice rapidly approaching, they still had hundreds of leagues to travel, with time ticking rapidly away.

Despairing, she lowered her arm and slipped her fingers back into her fur-lined gloves. Since crossing over the mountainous Ice Fangs—that jagged barrier of snowy peaks that marked the boundary between the Crown and the frozen wastes—the moon had waxed and waned three times over. Thrice, Nyx had watched the dark Huntress chase the bright Son around and around. Each time the Son showed his full face again, Nyx had snuck away, like now, and climbed to the open deck of the *Sparrowhawk* to judge the moon's cold countenance.

Still, that was not the only reason she had abandoned the warmth of the ship for the frigid ice of the open middeck.

She shifted along the starboard rail, craning past the girth of the ponderous gasbag that obscured most of the sky. She searched for the telltale sickle of her brother's silhouette against the stars. Her ears strained for his call through the darkness. She heard the ice cracking loose from the huge draft-iron cables that linked ship to balloon, but all else lay quiet. Even the flashburn forges that propelled the vessel through the air remained silent, their baffles sealed against the cold, trying to keep the warmth locked inside the wyndship.

For most of the journey, the crew had relied on the current of the westward-flowing sky-river to carry them ever onward. The ship's forges certainly could have hastened their flight, but their supplies of flashburn had to be conserved, even with the extra tanks welded along the *Sparrowhawk*'s hull. They needed enough fuel not only for the trip out across the wastes, but also for their return if they were successful in their quest.

She leaned farther over the rail, scanning the sky, her heart pounding slightly harder.

"Where are you?" she whispered through her scarf.

As she searched, the wind brushed the loose strands of her dark hair about her cheeks. The breeze no longer carried any hint of its former warmth. She pictured the twin rivers that flowed across the skies. The higher of the two—through which the ship traveled—carried the scathing heat of the sunblasted side of the Urth in a continual westward flow before returning in a colder stream that hugged land and sea. It was those two streams—forever flowing in two different directions—that blessed the lands of the Crown with a livable clime. Hieromonks believed it was due to the twin gods, the fiery Hadyss and the icy giant Madyss, who blew those rivers across the skies, while alchymists insisted it was due to some natural bellows created between the two extremes of the Urth.

She didn't know which to believe. All she knew for sure was that this far out into the wastes, that hot river carried little of its life-giving warmth. And from here, their way would only grow colder. It was said that, if one traveled far enough out into the wastes, the very air turned to ice.

Knowing this, she searched the stars for her bonded brother. He needed these brief flights to stretch his wings and escape the tight confines of the *Sparrowhawk*'s lower hold. But he had been gone far longer than usual. Concern constricted her throat. Her limbs shivered from more than just the cold.

Come back to me.

As Nyx kept her vigil, the chime of the second bell of Eventoll echoed up to her from the ship's interior. She shivered in her coat, drawing its hood tighter to her cheeks. Her teeth had begun to chatter.

He's been gone a full bell.

Both frustrated and worried, she stared down at the spread of broken ice far below, reflecting the silvery sheen of the full moon. Finding no answers in the unending landscape of the Ice Shield, she stared upward again. She hummed under her breath, casting out a few strands of bridle-song.

"Where are you?" she sang to the stars.

Then she felt him: a tingle at the top of her spine that spread a warmth across the inside of her skull.

Relief escaped her in a misty exhalation.

"Bashaliia . . ."

A massive shadow swept low over the balloon and out in the sky before her. As the Mýr bat's wings cleaved across the starscape, he angled over on a tip and spun back around. With that turn, the tingling warmth grew into a soft keening, less heard than felt, a slight vibration of the bones in her ears.

She danced back from his approach. As he dove, his wings spread and cupped the air, slowing him. She retreated farther to make room. Luckily, she did. When he ducked under the gasbag, his claws released a massive haunch of some large beast. The chunk of carcass—easily a hundred stone in weight—bounced and slid across the deck, leaving behind a steaming trail of blood.

Bashaliia then landed himself. His claws skittered across the planks, digging for purchase, before finally coming to a stop.

Nyx sidestepped the gore and rushed up to her friend.

His wings folded around her, enveloping her. Velvety nostrils found her cheek. His warm breath panted over her. His body was a flaming hearth in the cold. She nestled into that warmth. Her fingers rubbed the dense fur behind one of his tall ears. Her other palm rested on his chest, feeling the thump of his heart. The beat was already slowing from the exertion of his hunt.

"Bashaliia, you mustn't be gone so long," she scolded softly. "You had me worried."

He hummed back his reassurance.

As he did, her fingers dug into his pelt. She appreciated how thick it had grown. His body had quickly adjusted to the cold—amazingly so. She was not the only one to notice. Krysh—the alchymist assigned by Frell to accompany them—had noted the changes: the extra layer of fat, his shaggier fur, even the thickening of Bashaliia's nasal flaps. It was as if the bat were mimicking the baffles of the ship's forges, narrowing all openings to keep heat inside. The young alchymist had also leeched blood from her friend and reported changes there: *an increasing volume of red cyllilar matter, accompanied by an ever-protracted time for his blood to freeze.* Krysh attributed the latter to the appearance of ice-resistant chymicals, agents that still stymied identification. His conclusion: *It's as if the creature's entire form is rapidly changing to fit his new circumstance.*

Nyx wished the same were true for her.

Even encased in Bashaliia's warmth, she shivered. They needed to retreat below. She lifted her chin and softly sang, letting threads of bridle-song slip from her to him, sharing her desire to return to the warmth of the ship.

He briefly drew her tighter, using his long tail to reach around and scoop her closer. His heavy musk enveloped her. Despite his bodily changes, his scent remained a constant. She drew that musk into her lungs, letting it become part of her. It smelled of briny salt and damp fur, underlaid by a sulfurous hint of brimstan. Despite the passage of time, he still carried the scent of the swamplands with him. It reminded Nyx of her own home in those drowned lands, and all she had lost.

Her dah, her brothers, Bastan and Ablen . . .

All dead.

She drew in a deep draught of Bashaliia's musk, using that scent to stoke her memory. And not just that past shared with her family, but to one that lay further back, nearly forgotten. She could picture little of it. It was a time made up of smells, tastes, touches. As a babe, she had been abandoned in the swamps after the death of her mother. She would not have survived that harsh landscape, but a she-bat discovered her and took her in. Nyx was nursed and sustained by the massive creature.

And not just me.

Nestled under those same wings, a small furry brother had shared those milky teats.

Her fingers dug deeper.

Bashaliia . . .

His scent, the warmth of his body, served as a reminder that she had not lost *all* of her family during that horrible summer. She wanted to keep him close, to stay here longer, but she knew they both needed to retreat below.

She placed her palms against his chest and pushed out of the blanket of his wings. The cold struck her immediately. Frost already crusted the outer edges of Bashaliia's tall ears.

"Let's find us a warm stove and hope its coals have been freshly stoked."

She turned toward the raised aft deck and the doors that led down into the lower hold. Before she could step in that direction, the doors to the forecastle banged open behind her. She spun around, startled. The flare of lamplight momentarily blinded her.

Bashaliia's wings snapped wider, defensively, as he responded to her distress.

She lifted a calming hand to him, recognizing the intruder through the glare.

"Jace?" She struggled to understand his arrival. "What are you doing here?"

She knew her friend and former tutor despised the cold. Still, he headed toward her, huddled under a thick blanket, his breath huffing streams of white. He kept a wary eye on his footing as he crossed the frosty planks of the deck.

"There's something I wanted to talk to you about in private," he said. "Something curious, maybe important. Then Graylin caught me as I headed up here. He's ordering everyone to the wheelhouse. Darant spotted something ahead. Something worrisome, from Graylin's grim tones."

"He always sounds grim," she reminded him.

"Mayhap, but we'd better hurry. Especially since he doesn't know you're up here alone."

"I'm hardly alone." She patted Bashaliia, who had tucked his wings in again.

"I don't think Graylin would take any solace in that detail."

Nyx knew Jace was correct. Despite their confinement in the swyftship, she and Graylin had grown no closer. The man might be her father, but then again, he might not be. Still, he continually sought to assert some manner of control over her. She rankled at his ever-present shadow and searched for any moments to escape it.

Like now . . .

She recognized that it was not only Bashaliia who needed a respite from the ship's close quarters.

Jace frowned at her, his lips set in a familiar firm line whenever he was confronted by her obstinance. "If Graylin ever learns that I knew about your little sojourns onto the open deck, he'd yank the beard right off my cheeks."

She reached over and tugged at the drape of red curls under his jawline. "It seems secure enough to me."

He pushed her hand down, a blush rising to his cheeks despite the cold. "Let's keep it that way."

She smiled. "The heavier beard does look good on you. It seems both you and Bashaliia are growing furrier with each passing league."

His cheeks flushed a deeper crimson. "Like him, it's not for *looks,* but to keep me warm."

She shrugged, casting him a doubtful glance. "Help me get Bashaliia below, and we'll head over to the wheelhouse."

He gruffed under his breath, but she saw him comb his curls back into place after her ruffling. As the wind caught and parted his sheltering blanket, she also noted how else her friend had changed. Where Bashaliia had added a layer of warming fat, Jace had trimmed down. During the voyage, he had been sparring regularly with Darant and Graylin, honing his skills with both fist and ax. Additionally, as the ship's larder was tightly rationed, he had shed a fair amount of his bulk.

Still, there was no removing the scholar from this novice warrior.

Despite his plain desire to escape the cold, Jace crossed toward the bloody haunch left on the deck. "Where did this come from?"

"Bashaliia's been hunting," she explained.

He squinted at the hoofed end of the carcass. "Three-toed and white-furred. He must've taken down one of the martoks. Though from the leg's small size, one of their yearling calves." He reached to the pelt and pinched up a bit of moss, which glowed faintly in the dark. "Fascinating. We should bring this leg to Krysh and see what else we can learn about those giants that roam the Ice Shield."

Nyx disagreed. "It's Bashaliia's kill. He clearly needs more sustenance than can be found in our thinning stores. In fact, he should probably hunt more often before it gets any colder."

"True." Jace straightened and rubbed his belly. "The more he can sustain himself, the slower our larder will wane. I'll have a couple of the crew drag the leg below and salt it down."

"Thank you."

As they headed to the aft deck, he stared longingly at the haunch, but with a hunger born of curiosity. "Who imagined such massive creatures foraged these frozen lands?"

Nyx understood his interest. Through the ship's farscopes, she had spied the massive herds of martoks ranging the broken ice fields. The shaggy, curl-horned bulls looked to stand as high as the third tier of her old school. The cows were only slightly smaller. The herds appeared to feed on tussocks of phosphorescent moss that grew across the ice, ripping up sections with their tusks. Krysh—whose decades of alchymical interest focused on the wastes—had studied dried samples of the same plant, collected during rare excursions by foolhardy explorers. He said it was called *is'veppir* and claimed the cold foliage was more related to mushrooms than mosses.

"Who knew such life could exist out here?" Nyx said and stared to the west. "We'll soon be beyond where anyone has ever set foot."

"Not necessarily." Jace's voice lowered with a studious distraction that was as familiar as Bashaliia's musk. "I've been reading accounts of those who dared venture beyond the Fangs. *The Kronicles of Rega sy Noor. The Illumination of the Sunless Clime.* Even a book that Krysh claimed was stolen from the Gjoan Arkives, a tome that dates back seven centuries. It's what I found in those pages that I wanted to discuss with you, to talk it over before I brought it up with the others."

By now they'd reached the double doors that led off the deck and down into the ship's hold. She tugged the way open and turned to him. "What did you find?"

"If what's written is true, we may not be alone in the wastes. There could be other people."

She scowled in disbelief.

That's impossible. Who could live out here?

Jace held up a palm. "Hear me out, and I'll—"

The entire ship jolted under them. Thunder boomed across the clear skies. On the starboard side, a plume of flame shot from the lower hull and across the sky. Chunks of draft-iron and shattered wood exploded high above the rail. A few pieces came close to ripping through the balloon. The blast shoved the *Sparrowhawk* into a hard spin. Strained cables screamed and twanged under the sudden assault. The deck canted steeply.

Nyx lost her footing, but she kept a grip on the door.

Untethered, Jace slammed hard to the planks, hitting his chest. He slid across the icy deck away from her. Half tangled in his blanket, he gasped and clawed and scrabbled to halt his plunge.

"Jace!" she hollered and dropped to her backside. Maintaining her hold on the door, she shoved out a leg for him to grab, but he was already out of reach.

Bashaliia lunged past her, flying low. He dove at Jace, falling upon him like a hawk on a rabbit. Claws stabbed through the blanket. Jace cried out in pain as those sharp nails found flesh, too. Then with a single beat of wings, Bashaliia wrenched back to Nyx with his captured prize.

"Get inside!" Nyx yelled and led the way.

With alarm bells echoing throughout the ship, she fell through the door and crawled down into the short passageway. Bashaliia tossed Jace after her, then clambered in behind them, ducking low and squeezing through.

Jace groaned, sat up, and leaned his back against the wall. "What happened?"

Nyx stared past the open door. By now, the *Sparrowhawk*'s spin had already slowed, the deck leveling again. The flames had sputtered out, but a smoldering glow persisted on the ship's starboard side.

She faced Jace, swallowing hard before speaking, fearful of even voicing the possibility, knowing the disaster it portended. "One of the ship's forges must've exploded."

2

It didn't take long for Nyx's fears to be confirmed.

She stood beside Jace in the crowded wheelhouse of the *Sparrowhawk*. Everyone gathered around a pock-faced crewman named Hyck. Time had weathered the old man down to tendon and gristle, but his eyes still shone with a sharp fervor. He was a former alchymist who had been defrocked ages ago and now served as the ship's engineer.

He rubbed a rag between his hands, trying to erase a residue of greasy flashburn from his palms but only smearing it around instead. "Lucky it were only the starboard maneuvering forge that blew. If it were the stern engine, we'd never be able to limp our way back to the Crown."

Nyx shared a concerned look with Jace. She knew the swyftship had three forges, a pair to either side and a huge one at the stern end of the keel.

"Have the fires been put out?" Darant asked.

"Aye," Hyck answered. "First thing we did. Flames be the greater danger here than any blast. Your two daughters be surveying the rest of the damage, seeing if there's anything to be salvaged."

Darant paced the breadth of the wheelhouse. This was the brigand's ship, and any damage it took was as if it were to his own body. His face remained a dark thundercloud. He kept a fist clenched on the hilt of one of his whip-swords. A dark blue half-cloak flagged behind him, a match to his breeches and shirt, as he pounded across the planks.

Graylin lifted a hand. "Does this mean we'll have to turn back, return to the Crown?"

Hyck opened his mouth, only to be cut off by Darant. "Sard we will!" the pirate exclaimed, half withdrawing the slim blade as if ready to attack anyone who challenged him. "This li'l hawk might have a damaged wing, but she can still fly true enough. We can compensate for the loss of the starboard forge. Like Hyck said, our stern engine is what matters most. We continue onward."

Graylin turned to Nyx. Concern narrowed his eyes, allowing only a hint of silvery blue to show, like a vein of ice in his rocky features. There was little other color to be found in the man. It was as if the legend of the Forsworn Knight—a tale that wove Nyx and Graylin together in tragedy—had turned him into a book's etching, a figure drawn in shades of black and gray. His dark hair and scruff of beard were salted with white. Some strands were weathered by age; others marked the sites of buried scars. Yet not all of his old wounds were hidden, like the crook in his nose and a jagged weal under his left eye. They were all testaments to his punishment for falling in love and breaking an oath to the King of Hálendii.

A growl rose. While it didn't flow from Graylin, it might as well have. It expressed a mix of frustration and anger. The knight's shadow shifted farther into view. The vargr's amber-gold eyes glowed out of coal-black fur. Muscular haunches bunched, ruffling the tawny stripes buried there, like sunlight dappling through a dark canopy. The vargr's tufted ears stood tall, swiveling back and forth, seeking the source of the danger that had set everyone on edge.

Nyx hummed under her breath and wove over a calming thread of bridlesong. It wound into the rumble of that growl, tamping down the vargr's guardedness.

Graylin tried his own method, resting a callused palm on the beast's shoulder. "Settle, Kalder."

The vargr swished his tail twice more, then sank to a sit, but his ears remained tall and stiff.

During her brief connection with Kalder, Nyx had sensed the wildness constrained in that strong heart. Some mistook Kalder to be a mere hunting dog, one obedient to Graylin. Nyx knew their attachment ran deeper, a bond born not only of trust and respect, but also shared pain and loss. The memory of Kalder's brother, lost half a year ago, still echoed inside that stalwart chest. She heard whispers of chases through cold forests, of a warmth that only a brother curled at one's side could bring.

Kalder's edginess was also likely due to the months of confinement aboard the *Sparrowhawk*. Such magnificent beasts were never meant to be caged.

Graylin turned from the group and stared out the row of forward windows. "Darant, I trust your faith in your ship, but perhaps caution should outweigh conviction in this regard. If we lose the *Sparrowhawk*, then all is lost. Rather than rush headlong—"

"No!" Nyx blurted out.

As everyone turned her way, she refused to shrink under the combined weight of their gazes. She remembered the three turns of the moon it had taken them to get this far. To return to the Crown would take just as long. And they'd still have to make the crossing again to return to this spot.

"We'd lose half a year," she said. "We can't afford that. We must reach the site Shiya showed us on her globe."

"We understand," Graylin said. "But Shiya also told us we had at least three years, maybe five, before moonfall became inevitable. We have some latitude for cautiousness."

"No. No we don't."

"Nyx . . ."

She shook her head, knowing a good portion of Graylin's restraint was born of concern for her. Pain shone in his eyes. While she might not be his daughter, she was still the child of the woman he had once loved. Graylin had long believed Nyx had died in the Mýr swamps, only to have her miraculously resurrected and returned to him. He clearly did not intend to lose her again.

But she dismissed his concerns. They did not matter.

Instead, Nyx pictured the shimmering mirage of their world cast forth by Shiya's crystal cube. An emerald marker had glowed deep in the frozen wastes. That was their destination, though little was known about it. Not even Shiya could guess what lay out there, only that the site was important. For any hope of stopping the moon from crashing into the Urth, they had to set their world to turning again, as it had countless millennia ago. Somehow that glowing marker was vital to accomplishing that seemingly impossible task.

"We don't know what we'll find out there," Nyx warned. "Or how long it will take to pry answers from that mystery. We can't risk any further delays. For as much as we know, we may already be too late."

She kept her face fixed, both to show her determination and to hide the deeper part of her that hoped they *were* too late. If they set the Urth to spinning again—something that still seemed incomprehensible to her—it would herald its own catastrophe. The world would be ravaged in that turning tide. Shiya had shown them this, too. The massive floods, the quakes, the storms that would rip around the planet. Millions upon millions would die.

Nyx understood this fate was far better than the eradication of *all* life should moonfall occur. Yet, in her heart, she could not dismiss the untold suffering that would result if they were successful. She knew it was necessary, but she kept a secret hope guarded close to her heart.

Let those deaths not be by my own hand.

"The lass is right," Darant said. "If we turn around, we may never make it back out here again. War is brewing across the Crown. Back when we left, the skirmishes between Hálendii and the Southern Klashe had been worsening. Coastal villages raided and burned. Sabotage and assassinations. On both sides of the Breath. Who knows what we'll discover if we return? We could become trapped and embroiled by the fighting. And don't forget your old friend, King Toranth, and his Iflelen dogs. They're still hunting us. Best not we give them another chance to close that noose."

"Still, those arguments don't take into account what lies *ahead* of us." Graylin pointed at Darant. "Even before the explosion, you had me summon everyone to the wheelhouse because you were already worried about the path of our flight from here."

Nyx glanced at Jace. She had forgotten how Graylin had ordered everyone to gather here. The explosion and mayhem had diverted all attention.

"What's wrong?" Nyx asked. "What lies ahead?"

"See for yourself." Graylin led them toward the arc of windows fronting the wheelhouse. The view looked out across the moonlit fields of broken ice. "The navigator, Fenn, spotted the danger earlier through the ship's farscopes. But you can see it plainly enough now that we've sailed closer."

The group spread out across the bay of windows. Nyx searched below the ship, but the view looked the same as it had for months. The full moon's brightness reflected off the ice, casting the world in shades of silver and blue. Huge swaths of *is'veppir* moss, aglow in hues of crimson and emerald, etched the frozen landscape. As she squinted, she made out swaths of darker dots. *Martoks,* she realized. They gathered into vast herds, sharing warmth, moving slowly.

Nyx frowned. "I don't see what—"

Jace gasped next to her. "Look to the horizon."

She shifted her gaze out farther. The ice spread all the way to the night sky, dappled in bright stars. She shook her head, still not seeing anything. Then she realized that the stars did not reach the ice. They vanished high above the horizon line. Her vision shifted, or maybe a drift of cloud cleared the moon. Then she saw it, too. The world ended at a line of jagged peaks, blocking the stars and their path ahead. The range of mountains, all black and sharp-edged, thrust high out of the ice, forming a shattered rampart.

"That must be Dragoncryst," Jace said. "The peaks were named by Rega sy Noor in his *Kronicles.* During his first overland expedition two centuries ago, the explorer sighted them from a distance but couldn't reach them. He named the range because the mountains looked like the crested back of a great sea creature bursting through the ice."

"He's not wrong about that," Darant grumbled. "But this beast may prove more troublesome."

"Why?" Nyx asked.

Graylin answered, not turning from the window, "The peaks don't just breach the ice, but also block both sky rivers."

Nyx pictured the high warm winds driving them westward and the colder flow running eastward, hugging closer to the ice.

Darant turned to the ship's navigator, who was bent over the eyepiece of the *Sparrowhawk*'s farscope. "How's it look, Fenn?"

The navigator straightened and turned to face them. He was young, likely only seven or eight years older than Nyx. He was lithe of limb, with white-blond locks and green eyes that suggested he might have some Bhestyan blood, a people who dwelled on the far side of the Crown—though he refused to talk about his past. Still, he was also the least dire of the crew. He always had a ready smile and a boundless well of jokes.

That smile was gone now. "It's worse than I thought," Fenn said. "The skies are roiled into a huge storm that sits atop those peaks. I wager that tempest never subsides, forever powered by the war of those contrary winds."

"Can we cross through it?" Graylin asked. "Especially with one of our maneuvering forges gone?"

Fenn glanced at Darant, who nodded for the navigator to speak his mind. Fenn sighed and shrugged. "Only one way to find out. No one's ever sailed over those peaks. We'll be the first."

"That's not necessarily true," Jace corrected.

Everybody turned to him.

Jace explained, "Rega—the explorer knight who named those mountains—set off on a second expedition, intent to cross the Dragoncryst, only this time he traveled by air, in a ship called the *Fyredragon,* named after those peaks."

Fenn's eyes twinkled, showing a gleam of his usual amusement. "Aye, but as I understand it, he never *returned* from that second trek."

"True," Jace admitted dourly.

Nyx nudged him. "You should tell them what you told me outside on the middeck."

Graylin stiffened with shock. "The middeck? Nyx, what were you doing outside?"

She ignored him. "Tell them, Jace."

Her friend nodded and faced the others. "I've had plenty of time to read through most of the historicals that relate to the wastes, recorded by those rare few who dared travel into the ice. One claims that there are clans of people who live beyond the Dragoncryst."

Darant grunted sourly. "Who? Who could live out here?"

Jace's brows pinched with concern. "According to *The Annals of Skree,* a book secured from the Gjoan Arkives, they're *a chary tribe of daungrous peple who abide amidst dedly beasts and gret monsters.*"

"They sound delightful," Fenn mumbled.

Jace turned toward the storm-riven horizon. "It is said Rega read the same tome and set off to search for those tribes during his second expedition."

"From which he never returned," Fenn reminded them again.

Before anyone could respond, a clatter of boots and raised voices erupted from the other side of the wheelhouse. The door to the main passageway burst open, and a flurry of figures rushed inside. They were led by the bronze figure of Shiya. Though sculpted of hard metal, she moved with grace. The shining glass of her eyes took in those gathered in the wheelhouse. From the look of the dark stains marring her modest shift, she had accompanied the others to survey the ruins of the flashburn forge. They had likely leaned upon her considerable strength to help search the wreckage. As she entered, the lamplight reflected off the contours of her face, but her expression remained unreadable.

Those who came with her were far less stoic. The stocky form of Rhaif hy Albar—the Guld'guhlian thief who had rescued the bronze woman from the depths of the mines of Chalk—came around Shiya's left side. A litany of curses flowed from his lips.

"What's wrong?" Darant asked, stepping closer.

Rhaif stemmed his tide of profanities and waved to Shiya's other side. "Best your daughter tell you."

Glace crossed around the bronze woman to meet her father. Her almond complexion was flushed darker. She shoved a braided blond tail behind her shoulder with one hand and held forth her other palm.

"We found this buried amidst the ruins of the forge's fuel assembly."

They all gathered closer. A knot of dark iron lay twisted in Glace's white-knuckled grip. It looked like a black egg that had burst open. A bitter smell of burnt alchymicals accompanied it.

"What is it?" Nyx asked.

Graylin scowled. "A stykler."

Nyx gave a small shake of her head.

Jace explained. "A shell packed full of iron filings and glass that turns molten."

Glace kept her eyes upon her father. "Brayl and Krysh are already examining the other two forges, to make sure there are no more bombs hidden there, too."

Nyx stared down at the blasted object. "A bomb?"

"Not just a bomb," Darant growled and glared around the room. "It's sabotage."

ABOUT THE AUTHOR

David Sylvian

JAMES ROLLINS is the #1 *New York Times* bestselling author of international thrillers sold in more than forty countries. His Sigma series has earned national accolades and has topped charts around the world. He is also a practicing veterinarian who still spends time underground or underwater as an avid spelunker and diver. Rollins recently debuted *The Starless Crown,* the first book in a major new fantasy series, revealing a riven world trapped between fire and ice. The second in series, *The Cradle of Ice,* continues his journey, merging his fascination with the natural world, his love of adventure, and his knowledge of the wonders found at the evolutionary fringes of scientific exploration. It is a fantasy series unlike any attempted before.